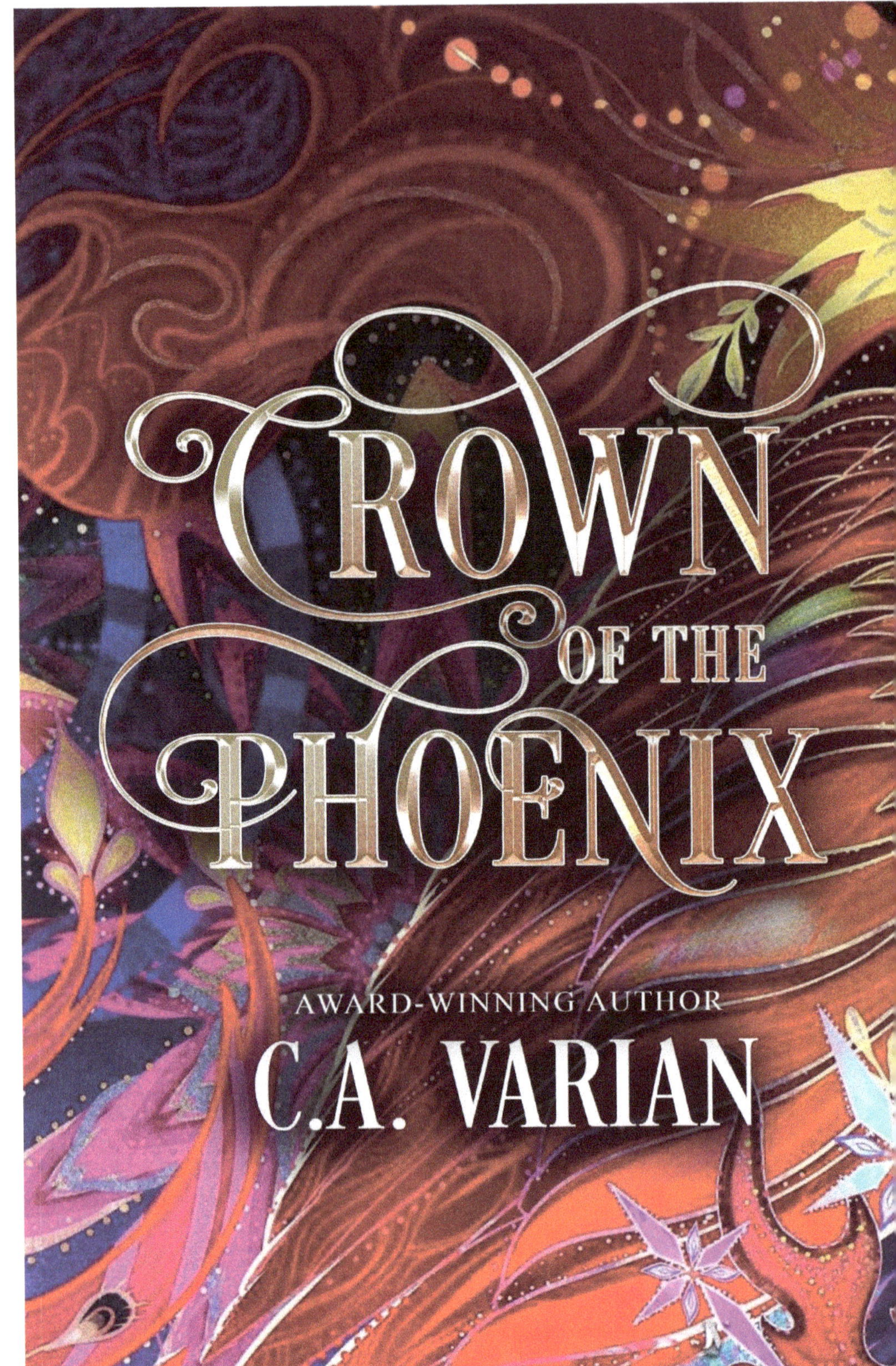
CROWN
OF THE
PHOENIX
AWARD-WINNING AUTHOR
C.A. VARIAN

C. A. VARIAN, AUTHOR
ROMANCE SPANNING REALMS

Contents

CROWN OF THE PHOENIX SERIES PREQUEL

MATE OF THE PHOENIX

C.A. VARIAN

Aegrician Mountains
Aegricia
Flamecliff
Norithae
Windreach
THE WORLD OF EKOTORIA
Marella Arch
Spectre Forest
Claywind
Elder Sea
Undying Desert
Diapolis
Embershell
Warbotach
N

THE WORLD OF INAS
EL-WAHBA
BREQAN
KOTOL
MONEN
ILLEVER
HARMUE SEA
HOWLING FOREST
N
MARELLA ARCH
VAEKROS

The Scorched Realm
Voiceless Mountains
Cineris
The Emerald Enclave
The Inferno Territories
Irribola Sea
N

CONTENT WARNINGS

There are mature themes throughout this book,

and it is not intended for readers under 17 years of age.

The following themes are explored in Mate of the Phoenix:

Graphic (consensual) sexual content,

captivity, slavery, abduction, vulgar language, and murder.

Chapter One

Holera

"What are you doing tonight?"

Holera Glowbrook pulled her bowstring taut and took aim, hitting the bullseye on a target that was more than one thousand yards away while waiting for her friend to answer. She barely allowed herself a nod. Anything less than perfection wasn't worth noting, and she'd sooner scowl than gloat. Even in the ranks of hundreds of Aegrician warriors, she was one of the best with a bow.

Her best friend, Exie Cinderdraft, whistled as she eyed the target. Her whistle was so loud a pair of rookies two rings over startled and dropped their arrows. Exie only grinned, unbothered as always. "Heading to the Singing Lantern. You?"

"No plans yet." Holera lifted a brow, her tone dry. "Hot date?" She was not at all surprised that Exie planned to go to the tavern. Unlike her, Exie liked to go out and be sociable. Holera, on the other hand, had been spending too many nights in silence—the kind where even her mother's steady stitching by the hearth couldn't drown out the ache of loneliness.

Exie barked a laugh, her long, blond mane flailing forward as it always did when she was being overly dramatic. "No. I don't have a date. Do you want to come with me? You rarely go out anymore."

Of course her friend was correct. Their military training had been rigorous so, although Exie still had energy when they were done for the day, Holera didn't. Exie could spar all day and still find the strength to drink and flirt. Holera, meanwhile, felt every bruise settling into her muscles. It may have been all in her head. She realized that. Ever since her father had died, she'd had less desire to socialize with anyone aside from Exie, and even her patience for that had been limited. Grief had made her quieter, sharper around the edges. Some days she feared she'd carved herself into stone, with only Exie loud enough to chip at the surface.

Both she and Exie were phoenix shifters. All the Aegrician female warriors were. But unlike the others, who were serious more often than not, Exie spent most of her time with a lighthearted exuberance about her that was infectious, or completely annoying. Yet when trouble came, Exie was the first to throw herself into it, wild grin and blade flashing. Loyalty burned hotter in her than whiskey. Still, staying home every night with her mother who spent her own time making clothing, had become more than lonely for Holera. She was still young, and she longed for a steady hand at her back, a voice that spoke her name like it mattered. But all she had was empty nights and the rasp of thread through cloth.

She nodded, but with a sardonic smile. Her tone was flat as steel, though the corner of her mouth betrayed her amusement. "I'll go with you, but the minute you start building your harem, I'm out of there."

It only took Exie a second to laugh again, smacking Holera hard on the back, nearly knocking the bow out of her hand. Holera grunted and barely kept from snarling — Exie's affection always came with bruises. "Deal, but my harem does need building."

Holera had no response to that but an eye roll.

The friends left the training ring after their discussion, fire erupting from their skin as they shifted into phoenix form. Heat rippled the air before their wings caught the sky, carrying them in opposite directions. Exie shot off toward the heart of Flamecliff, reckless arcs of rainbow fire lighting her path, while Holera angled north, her silver wings steady and sharp.

Although they both lived near the capital, their homes couldn't have been more different. Exie kept a cramped apartment above the main square, close to the taverns and the pulse of the city. Holera preferred the quiet edge of the world, sharing a small cottage with her mother on the outskirts. Quiet didn't always mean peace. Sometimes it felt like exile. Still, after a day of sweat and dust, she would rather face silence than walk into a tavern stinking of training leathers and send the entire crowd running from her stench.

Aegricia—the kingdom Holera called home—was the northernmost realm of Ekotoria. It was the cradle of phoenix shifters, though not every Aegrician carried fire in their veins. Only women chosen for the warrior class could shift into flame and wing; the rest of Aegricia's people, men and non-warrior women alike, kept their fae forms. Holera still remembered the first time her skin had ignited and feathers had replaced flesh. Terrifying. Exhilarating. The mark that she was destined to fight.

The warriors of Aegricia guarded the Marella portal, a jagged arch of sea glass where the cliffs met the Elder Sea. It connected their world to the human one, though neither side had crossed in generations. Treaties held. Laws held. But the portal still pulsed with magic, whether mortals respected it or not. The only way across was on the wings of a phoenix—or clinging to the back of one—and so the burden of protection rested squarely on Holera's kind. She doubted she'd ever see a human brave the crossing, yet still she knew: guarding the portal was the greatest honor their kingdom could give.

South of Aegricia lay Norithae. Its people were all born with leathery wings, every man, woman, and child. Holera thought it unfairly convenient. Aegricians had to earn their fire.

Most of the continent's center was swallowed by Spectre Forest. Plenty of fae had crossed it, though few bothered to linger. The farther in one went, the stranger and darker the beasts became—reason enough, in Holera's mind, to steer clear.

On Ekotoria's southeastern edge lay Diapolis. Holera had never flown so far, though she often dreamed of the warmth there. It was said that dragons still curled in its volcanic peaks, and that its people could slip into the sea, trading legs for shimmering tails. Even in Aegricia's cold taverns, travelers spoke of Diapolis with awe, their voices painting it bright as a jewel in her imagination. One day, she promised herself.

The opposite corner of the continent held only ruin. The Undying Valley crept outward year by year, its sands devouring farmland and rivers until little remained of the once-fertile southwest. Warbotach clung to what scraps were left, a kingdom of barbarians penned into a shrinking corner by desert and sea. Their king was said to be cruel. Their warriors, vicious. Holera had no wish to test the rumors. She prayed she never would.

By the time she reached the outskirts of Flamecliff, the sky had turned into a sweep of orange, pink, and purple. She landed in front of her mother's cottage in a flare of silver flame, boots crunching on packed snow as her wings folded into nothing. The mountains rose behind the city, jagged and white, their crowns eternal in snow, their distance untouchable to all but the gods. Holera lingered, watching the younger phoenix warriors wheel in perfect formation above a lower ridge. Show-offs, she thought with a smirk, though pride still swelled in her chest. Training drills or not, they made the sky beautiful.

Chapter Two

Holera

Thanks to the fae magic within their city, most dwellings had heated water that came from the tap. In Flamecliff proper, pipes hissed with enchanted steam. Out here, on the edge of the wilds, Holera and her mother relied on firewood and patience.

Kissing her mother on the forehead, Holera added water to the pot hanging from the mantle and heated it for her bath. Her mother smelled faintly of lavender and smoke, a comfort Holera had never outgrown. Her fighting leathers reeked of sweat and dirt, as did her long, silver locks. Tossing the soiled clothing to the floor, she lowered herself into the copper tub. Sweat, leather, and ash clung to her until the bathwater steamed around her skin, carrying the day's grime away. She ducked beneath the surface and soaped her hair, groaning at the way the hot water loosened every knot in her muscles.

For a moment, she debated staying home. Why bother going out to watch Exie sing off-key and drink herself stupid? Exie had plenty of friends to keep her company. But Exie wanted *her* company, and that was reason enough. Holera might complain, but she would never leave her friend to drink alone.

So, pushing her hesitation aside, she climbed from the bath, dried her body with a cloth, and pulled on a tunic over damp skin and a pair of trousers. No gowns, no frills—just the armor of a warrior who couldn't quite pretend to be anything else.

After flying into the city proper, Holera's silver hair was still wet when she shifted back into her fae form, so she pulled it into a braid as she approached the log entrance of the Singing Lantern Tavern. Sounds of the tavern's revelry assaulted her before she even had a chance to open the heavy wooden door. Fiddle strings screeched over the roar of laughter, and the sour-sweet smell of spilled ale hit her nose. Her hand hesitated on the handle. Why she ever let Exie drag her into places like this, she'd never know. But then a familiar voice rose above the din, sharp with fury. Exie sounded like she was about to get into a fight.

Darting into the building, the door slamming behind her, Holera spotted her best friend near the bar, hair disheveled and a scowl on her face, squared off against a large male with an eye patch. Exie's wild blond mane clung to the sweat on her brow, her scowl promising violence. Holera's long legs carried her across the room in a few strides, and she wedged herself between them, face set in an exasperated scowl. At times she felt less like Exie's equal and more like the keeper of her chaos.

"What's going on, Ex? I can hear you screaming like a hellhound from outside!"

The man grumbled behind her before slinking away. Holera barely spared him a glance before turning back to her friend. Exie was taller and more muscular than she was, and Holera never found her intimidating—until she was angry.

"That Warbotach scum was insulting our queen!" Leaning around Holera's form, Exie shouted to the room at large. "He needs to grab the rest of his bandit crew, get back on his ship, and go back to his own damn kingdom."

The crowd bristled. Tankards stilled. A few muttered curses hissed through teeth. As if Exie's words had carried weight—or maybe it was the harsh stares of the Aegrician locals—but the group of stout, scarred Warbotach men filed out. Exie smirked in triumph.

Holera tipped her chin at the barmaid, silent but firm. A drink in each hand was the fastest way to keep Exie from storming after them. Forcing her friend into a chair, she slid a mug of Aegrician whiskey across the bar. Thankfully, the busy woman dropped two steaming mugs of the liquid fire before them a moment later.

"Were you just going to take on them all, Exie? You may be tough, but every one of those men were beasts."

Exie grinned, taking a deep draw of her whiskey, her eyes already glassy with drink. "The rest of the bar would've joined in the fight. I wasn't scared of them." Her grin widened, sharp as a blade. She'd fight the whole world if it meant defending Otera's name.

Holera caught her wrist before she could raise the mug again, exhaling through clenched teeth. "I would've stayed home if I'd known you were going to be in here starting fights." Bathing was wasted effort if she was just going to end up mopping up after Exie.

Exie's eyes widened at her tone. She lowered her hand, her features softening. "You're right, you're right. I'll calm down. I promise."

After an hour of watching her best friend sing along with the band, it was clear Exie hadn't calmed down, but at least she was happy. Holera leaned against the bar, watching as the intoxicated warrior sang song after song, adding lyrics wherever she saw necessary, but the band didn't seem to mind. Patrons roared with laughter, tankards pounding the tables in rhythm. Exie soaked in the attention like fire taking to dry kindling.

"Your friend is...um...lively."

Unbeknownst to Holera, a male had taken the stool next to her, ordering a whiskey from the barmaid. Holera stiffened, ready to elbow whoever dared invade her space—until she caught the green of his eyes. His long, black hair was pulled back with a leather cord at his nape. Rolled up to the elbows, his heavy white tunic strained against his muscled arms and chest, dark tattoos peeking through where the fabric failed to cover. The mischievous sparkle in his green eyes was a stark contrast to his fierce appearance.

Holera smirked. "That is certainly an understatement." Although she hadn't necessarily gone to the tavern to find a male, she couldn't deny how sexy this one was, so she didn't move away. Trust her luck to meet someone like him on a night she smelled of sweat, ale, and Exie's bad decisions. If anything, she could soak in the view of him and think about him when she slipped her hand between her thighs that night. It had been such a long time since she'd found pleasure.

"Warrior?" His question caught her by surprise, her head tilting.

"Hrmm?"

Taking a sip of his drink, he set it back down on the bar. "I asked if you and your friend were warriors. Sorry to pry. If you were, I just wanted to thank you for your bravery."

"Oh." She grinned, a flush coloring her cheeks. "We are, but you don't have to thank us." She pointed behind herself where the shadow of a silver wing flared out of her back. Silver fire shimmered faintly in the darkness, a reminder of what she was born to be. "I was born this way, after all."

Grunting his acknowledgement, he took another sip of his whiskey and smiled. "Well, I still admire the warriors of this land. I've been all over the continent, but none are as fierce as Aegricia's."

Pride tugged at her, though she tried to smother it beneath a scowl. She couldn't help but smile at his compliment before dropping her face into something more neutral when she realized she was starting to behave like a flirty young maiden, which she certainly was not.

Just as she was about to thank him again, Exie grabbed her by the arm and pulled her toward the exit. All she could do was glance back at him as the door closed behind her, blocking him from view. She hadn't even gotten his name.

"What's going on, Ex?" Before her friend could respond, Exie pulled Holera around the side of the building where the blond warrior retched, the whiskey finally taking its revenge on her stomach. Holera held back Exie's wild mane, careful to keep it out of her friend's face. Exie could pick fights with a whole ship of Warbotach, yet lose to a bottle of whiskey. If she hadn't regretted going to the tavern before, she was beginning to as Exie stood, only to wobble on shaky legs.

"Come on, let's get you home."

Thanks to Exie's inebriated state, Holera didn't dare leave her to fly back to her cottage. She hoped her mother wouldn't worry, but her mother was probably already asleep. Holera was more concerned her friend would get herself into trouble if she left her alone. In the morning, she would need to have a conversation with Exie about her behavior. Her best friend, already unconscious on her bed, was not in the right frame of mind for a lecture. So, only slightly grumbling under her breath, Holera grabbed an extra blanket from a wooden chest and settled down on the sofa, still thinking about the sexy male from the bar. She wondered if she'd ever see him again and hoped she would. Not that she'd admit it to Exie—or even herself.

CHAPTER THREE

HOLERA

"Get up, Ex. We're going to be late." Holera shook her friend's shoulders, but all she got was a whine and a groan. Exie's hangovers were infamous. Holera had survived enough of them to know they came with whining, swearing, and at least one dramatic declaration of impending death.

"Go without me." Exie's voice was muffled by the pillow, but her tone was beyond dramatic. Holera pulled the pillow out of her friend's grasp, swatting her on the back with it. If she didn't drag Exie to training, she'd end up cleaning blood out of the woman's tunics when Blaedia punished her.

"Blaedia would kill you if you didn't show up to training. Going without you isn't an option, and you know it."

Tossing off her blankets, Exie climbed out of bed, but not without a string of swear words as she did. "Just for the record, I'm only getting up so Blaedia doesn't kill me." Her voice carried the same theatrical weight she used when singing with the tavern band—as though the gods themselves needed to hear her suffering.

"Noted. Oh, I'm going to need some fighting leathers, since I was forced to stay at your place last night."

Exie shot Holera a sideways glance. "First of all, you didn't have to stay. I would've been just fine. Second of all, my clothes would swallow you whole. But, if you still want to wear them, they're in the first drawer on the right."

Holera didn't even bother reminding her friend that she had no choice but to stay because someone had to watch over her in her drunken stupor. Instead of responding, she let it go and grabbed a set of leathers from Exie's dresser, pulling them on although they were absolutely too large. The sleeves nearly swallowed her hands, and she scowled at how ridiculous she must look. Exie would find it hilarious. Holera found it humiliating.

"You look like a fledgling drowning in her mother's cloak," Exie croaked with a grin.

Holera grunted and tugged the belt tighter. "Laugh it up. If I faint from embarrassment in front of Blaedia, it's your fault."

The two phoenix warriors arrived at the training camp fifteen minutes later than they were expected, earning an icy blue glare from their general, Blaedia. Even from across the yard, that glare could strip flesh from bone. With her chin-length, razor-straight black hair shaved on one side, she looked every inch the blade she wielded, her posture sharp and her movements disciplined, danger coiled in every line of her body. She was Queen Otera's lover, but that wasn't how she'd earned such a high-ranking position. Blaedia had traveled throughout the continent, learning military strategy and techniques from the best generals in Ekotoria, and she had returned to lead Aegricia's military. Her warriors knew tardiness was not something she tolerated, so Holera clenched her teeth as they shifted, hoping they wouldn't get into trouble.

The clang of steel rang through the valley, sweat and dust hanging thick in the air as rookies stumbled through drills under the unforgiving sun. To Holera's relief, their general was fully involved in a training exercise with the younger warriors and didn't approach them to give them a piece of her mind. The look on her face said enough.

Hoping to lessen the blow, Holera drew her sword and pointed it at Exie. If Blaedia was going to skin them alive for tardiness, Holera could at least pretend they'd been training all along.

At the first slash of her sword, Exie jumped back with a screech. Her voice cracked so loudly it startled a pair of rookies in the next ring. "You could at least warn me first!" She drew her own weapon, her movements slow and awkward from the late night of drinking as she held it out in front of her. "Some friend you are."

Huffing a breath, Holera circled her. Exie followed her movements and waited for the next strike. "I was a good enough friend to stay with you last night." She lunged, her weapon swinging toward Exie's vulnerable left side, only to be met midair by her friend's blade.

Chuckling, the hungover warrior feigned to the right but slashed to the left. Holera didn't fall for her bluff. Unlike Exie, her senses weren't dulled by the overabundance of whiskey the night before. "I don't think this is about you having to deal with me last night at all." Exie swung again, Holera's blade meeting hers with a clang. "This is because I pulled you out of the tavern before you could take that sexy male you were talking to back to your bed."

Holera tried to deny it with her face, rolling her eyes as she dodged another blow, but there was no way to hide anything from her best friend. Exie knew her too well. She hadn't planned to bring him back to her bed, at least not last night, but she hadn't gotten his face out of her mind since she'd left the tavern. There was something about him she couldn't forget, even if she knew little about him.

"I wasn't going to take him to my bed." Her words were less than convincing, but she still decided to go all in anyway as she pivoted out of the way of Exie's sword. "Besides, my mom would murder me if I brought some strange male home while she was sleeping. The cabin is way too small."

Throwing her head back in her usual dramatic fashion, Exie laughed, her sword limp in her hand. Holera took the opening and swung, knocking her friend's weapon to the ground. Too wrapped up in her laughter, Exie didn't even notice. "So you did want to take him to your bed, but you didn't want your mother to hear?"

Unable to deny it, Holera shrugged and plopped down on the ground, lack of sleep catching up with her in the heat of the midday sun. Aegricia was colder than most of the continent, but the valley in which they trained lacked the tree cover of the southern side of the mountain range.

When her friend sat beside her, their weapons on the ground instead of in their hands, Holera knew they were going to be in trouble with their general but didn't care enough to stand and keep sparring. Loosening a breath, she wrapped her arms tightly around her bent knees and watched a group of young phoenixes fly into the mountain pass.

For once, Exie's grin faltered. "Theoni would've laughed at all this, you know. Called me reckless and kissed me anyway." Her voice dropped, softer than Holera was used to. "Sometimes I wonder if I'll ever stop hearing her."

Holera turned, her chest tightening at the rare glimpse beneath her friend's bravado, but before she could respond, Exie gave a sharp toss of her blond mane. The grin snapped back into place, armor as quick as any blade. "But since I can't, you're stuck with me."

"It doesn't matter. I'll probably never see him again." Saying it aloud made Holera's chest twist, as if she'd confessed a weakness she hadn't meant to share. Her need for a true companion was clearly deeper than she wanted to admit.

Exie leaned forward and rested her elbows on her knees, her playful laughter gone. "Did you at least find out where he was from? Maybe you could track him down." Her tone was light, but the gleam in her eye said she'd gladly help, if Holera only asked.

"I didn't even get his name. I was a little too preoccupied with you." She arched an eyebrow in Exie's direction, but her friend had turned away, watching as Blaedia approached from the direction of the training rings.

"Oh," Holera groaned under her breath as she stood, dusting off her leathers before reaching out a hand to Exie.

Blaedia may have been their general, but she was also their friend, so Holera was hoping she wouldn't be too harsh. It was Exie's fault, after all, and Holera fully intended to throw her friend onto the coals if she needed to.

CHAPTER FOUR

HOLERA

Holera cringed inwardly but tried to keep a neutral face as her general stepped in front of her, knowing she and Exie's tardiness hadn't gone unnoticed. Two young warriors trailing behind her, the females no older than their teens, Blaedia's glare could have ended wars. Holera's stomach twisted. She'd rather face a Warbotach warband than that look.

"Glad you found time to come to training today, although—" She paused for impact, pulling a small dagger out of its sheath and using it to clean her nails. "You haven't done much training since you got here."

Tilting her head toward Exie, Holera cleared her throat, shoving her friend over the coals indeed. Blaedia didn't miss the gesture and arched an eyebrow at her as well.

"Do I need to ask why one of my best warriors tried to start a fight in the tavern last night?"

The two young warriors flanking Blaedia failed to hide their snickers, but the general didn't turn her attention away from Exie.

"They insulted Otera."

Blaedia lifted an eyebrow, incredulity clear on her face. "What did they say to insult Otera?"

Kicking at the pebbles at her feet, Exie looked like a child who was being scolded by its mother. Which, in a way, she was. Blaedia had raised half the army by glare alone.

"They praised Joneira, called her the rightful queen."

Blaedia stiffened. Joneira, the usurper queen, was a sensitive topic for all Aegricians. She'd killed the previous queen, Otera's grandmother, and had stolen the throne for a short period of time before she was forced out of the kingdom. The name Joneira still echoed through Aegricia like a curse. Holera hated even hearing it spoken aloud.

"Did they?" Although her face showed no emotion, Holera could tell Blaedia was still frazzled. "Well, let's hope they don't return to this kingdom then."

When Blaedia tipped her head toward the young phoenixes, giving them a nonverbal direction, Holera knew their punishment was coming. She swallowed, waiting for it.

"These young warriors need some practice with the bow. The two of you," she said, leveling her eyes at Holera and Exie, "will collect their arrows."

Holera let out a breath, relief washing over her. Collecting stray arrows wasn't as bad of a punishment as they could've been given. Tedious, but not difficult. If all they had to do was chase after fledglings' missed shots, she could endure the humiliation. At least it wasn't latrine duty.

Exie nodded, no argument on her tongue. As Blaedia began walking away, she turned to look over her shoulder. "Otera's having a party tonight. There are some emissaries here for a meeting. The two of you are coming."

There it was. The punishment. None of them liked going to court, hated it actually. Blaedia didn't want to go, but she had no choice. She and Otera were lovers, mates even. Since she had to suffer through it, she wanted them to as well. Exie may have been quiet about chasing arrows, but she groaned at this. Holera couldn't blame her. A night at court was worse than chasing a hundred stray arrows. Not that it would make any difference. They weren't going to get out of it.

As Blaedia walked away, with a noticeable strut in her step, Holera could have sworn she heard the general chuckle. Holera blinked. Blaedia never chuckled. Which meant their misery was entertaining her more than it should have.

The archery practice for the two young warriors lasted for two hours, and they hadn't taken it easy on Holera and Exie. Instead of aiming at set targets, where the arrows would all land on relatively flat soil nearby, they darted around, shooting at everything under the sun. Holera was half-convinced the fledglings aimed for the muddiest ground they could find just to watch her scramble. Trees, boulders, a scurrying critter—the young warriors found joy in making them chase every last shaft.

By the time they'd tired out and most of their arrows had been broken, Holera was drenched in sweat and covered in filth. Sweat plastered her tunic to her back, and twigs clung to her braids as though the forest itself had joined in mocking her. Shooting her friend a few thoughtful glares, she shifted into her phoenix form and left the training field for her mother's cottage. If she was going to attend court, she needed a bath and a clean set of clothes.

Having not returned home the night before, she'd expected her mother to be a little more worried than she was, but she found her mother where she'd always been—sitting in her chair by the fire, contentment on her face.

"Glad you found your way home, wildfire. Late night?" The wooden chair creaked as her mother rocked, the threaded needle moving swiftly in her hand as she sewed a piece of fabric. Her mother's voice was smoke and softness, worn but steady, and it made something in Holera's chest unclench.

Walking past her mother, Holera hung the pot of water on the fire. "Where Exie is concerned, it's always a late night, momma."

Her mother chuckled, the sound warming her heart. With her father being gone, her mother was all she had left. "You never know what to expect with that one. How is she? I know she's had a hard time in the past years..."

Holera lowered herself onto the arm of the settee, the topic of Exie's fallen lover an unexpected one. Her mother hadn't said it explicitly, but it was implied. Exie's former lover, Theoni, the female she thought would be hers forever, had been killed in an explosion at the docks five years earlier. It had nearly broken Exie, leaving her a shell of who she once was. Even now, Exie's laughter carried a sharp edge, as if she had to fight for every scrap of joy.

Holera loosened a breath. "She's Exie. She's strong."

Her mother nodded, the movement seeming to flow with the rocking of her chair. "Stones are strong, wildfire, but they still erode away in the storm. If she doesn't take time to properly grieve, it'll just eat away at her."

Holera swallowed hard. Her mother wasn't just speaking about Exie. The same could be said of her father, of herself.

If anyone knew about grief, it was her mother. Holera touched her mother's hand as she stood, taking the pot from the hearth. "I know that, momma. I'm looking out for her."

It felt like a promise spoken aloud—one Holera already carried like armor.

CHAPTER FIVE

HOLERA

All Holera could do when she shifted back into her fae form in the palace courtyard and smoothed out her crisp white tunic was exhale. The marble courtyard gleamed under torchlight, polished too bright for her taste. Everything in the palace smelled faintly of beeswax and formality. She refused to wear a gown, no matter the occasion, but she knew she'd earn at least one raised eyebrow from Otera. If anyone wanted her in silk, they could pry her into it after death. It may have been court, a party in the palace, but she was who she was.

Staring at the enormous wooden doors for a moment, and at the two uniformed males standing on either side, she counted to ten to build her patience. If Exie acted up tonight... Well, she didn't want to think about that. She needed to stay out of trouble, at least for a little while. Tightening the buckle of her sword belt because she was a warrior first, Holera took a step forward, opening the door and entering the foyer.

With the arrival of emissaries, the palace was in full swing, servants bustling around, holding trays and shuffling people to where they needed to go. The air smelled of roasted meats and polished silver. Everywhere she looked, strangers glittered in velvet and gems, their voices a chorus she wanted no part of. Holera ignored all of them, walking briskly toward the eastern wing, the location of the ballroom. She knew the drill. It hadn't been her first time at such an event, although she'd always hoped one would be her last.

Unlike queens in the past, Queen Otera didn't usually bother with such finery, with constant balls and royal events. Otera was a queen who focused on the kingdom's people and running its military and economy. She didn't have time for such distractions, but when visitors from other kingdoms came by—that was when the silver had to be shined and appearances had to be kept up. There were expectations of royalty in Ekotoria, and Otera wasn't one to break that mold, at least not in the face of allies.

Music met Holera's ears before she could even see the golden embossed ballroom doors, and she gritted her teeth. It was not the style of music she preferred, the unrefined quartets of the taverns her preferred style. Instead, stringed instruments fluttered in the air, all plucks and flourishes, so precise it set her teeth on edge. Give her a tavern fiddle out of tune over this any day. The double doors of the ballroom opened, and she had no choice but to enter. It was her punishment, after all.

Although there were dozens of people already in the ballroom when Holera entered, Exie stood out among the crowd. With as tall as she was, as wild as her blond mane was, it would have been nearly impossible for her not to. Exie stood out like a bonfire in a room of candles, mane wild, grin reckless. She turned toward the entrance as soon as Holera walked in, a mischievous smirk on her face, and Holera realized they were already in trouble again. They hadn't done anything yet, but she could feel it. When her friend shot back a glass of whiskey and turned on her heel, making a beeline for her, there was no doubt in her mind. Exie was up to something.

Holera groaned, snatching a glass of the liquid fire from a passing servant's tray and drinking it quickly as Exie swaggered toward her, full of more bravado than one person should ever have. When she finally stopped walking, flicking a nonexistent piece of lint from the collar of her solid black tunic, Holera rolled her eyes. The gesture was so exaggerated it made her want to groan louder than she already had. "What? What are you so uppity about, Ex? I'm not in the mood for any of your shenanigans tonight. I—"

One very long finger pressed against Holera's lips mid sentence, stopping her monologue. "Can you just hush for a second, Holera? I promise to show you what I'm smiling about."

When Exie's finger moved, Holera sighed loudly. "Well? Then spill."

Exie's honey-tinted eyes nearly glowed in the candlelight of the space as she looked over her shoulder, still not sharing the secret she seemed to be keeping. "Have you seen Otera yet?"

Holera followed her line of sight but didn't see the crimson hair of the queen anywhere. People dressed in finery moved about the room, some Aegrician, others with the leathery wings of Norithae, even a few from kingdoms Holera did not recognize, but she didn't see the queen. "No. Exie, I just got here. Obviously I didn't see Otera." Stomping her boot on the ground, the patience she'd been counting on already running out, Holera loosened another breath. "Stop playing games, Ex. Why are you asking if I've seen Otera?"

One of their friends sauntered up, interrupting the conversation. Calista, one of the healers from the Aegrician capital's main infirmary, looked stunning in an emerald ball gown. Roughly the same age as the two warriors, they'd learned how to read from the same tutors when they'd been merely children. "I didn't expect to see the two of you here." She smirked, taking a deep sip of her wine. "Let me guess...punishment?"

Impatience building inside her, Holera reached for another glass of whiskey just as a servant passed them by. There wouldn't be enough alcohol in all of Flamecliff if Calista didn't scurry on and let Exie get on with her story. She wandered away for a moment, allowing the two females to talk amongst themselves.

By the time the burning had settled in Holera's throat from her second glass, and she'd thoroughly scanned the ballroom a second time over, Exie had finished telling of her harrowing ordeal in the tavern the night before, and Calista had walked off. "Well?"

She knew there had been a clip in her voice, but Exie didn't seem to notice. The whiskey seemed to be dulling her senses already, which was always the way her shenanigans started. It seemed to be a common theme in any event in which she got into trouble, and she always seemed to pull Holera down with her.

Exie leaned forward, speaking just into Holera's ear. "The sexy male you met last night...he's meeting with the queen."

Holera nearly choked on her drink. Of course Exie would drop that bomb here, in the middle of the queen's ballroom.

CHAPTER SIX

KASON

Kason's meeting with Queen Otera had been planned for weeks; it was why he'd traveled by ship from the southern part of the continent to be in the city of Flamecliff in time. What he hadn't intended when he'd gone to the Singing Lantern Tavern the night before—a place he'd frequented often before becoming a diplomat for the crown—was that he'd have to deal with two Warbotach mercenaries shadowing his mate and her friend.

He'd only just met the silver-haired warrior, but one glance into her violet eyes had been enough to tell him she was his bonded. The female he would make his in all ways... if she didn't kick his ass first. It wouldn't have surprised him; he had that effect on women. Still, he already wanted to give her everything.

His knuckles still ached pleasantly from the tavern brawl, a reminder of how satisfying it had been to put the Warbotach dogs in the dirt before the guards dragged them into the dungeon below the palace. Kason wasn't sure what the mercenaries had planned for Holera and her friend, but he hadn't minded bloodying them for daring to follow her. What came next would be Otera's decision, though Kason had plenty of ideas himself.

Queen Otera was the perfect ruler for Aegricia, strong but fair, fierce, and with a mind for governing and commerce. Kason had seen rulers all across Ekotoria, and none of them measured up.

The crown had not passed through bloodlines but by choice, and Otera had been fortunate to grow under the guidance of her grandmother, Queen Faenia Lumino. Faenia had reigned for nearly a century before her life was cut short. Her death came not by age but by Joneira Eternus, a young noblewoman twisted by ambition who sought to seize the throne by force. In her bloody rise, Joneira had claimed the lives of Faenia, Otera's mother, and even her sister Messalina, who should have worn the crown next.

After losing her entire family, no one would have blamed Otera if she'd crumbled, if she'd turned away from the palace forever. But she hadn't. When the crown chose, it had chosen her, and she had stood tall, carrying its weight with unrelenting pride. It was no wonder her people found her inspiring. Kason did too.

The queen's eyes lit up as Kason approached and set a fresh glass of whiskey in her hand, raising his own for a toast. "To prosperous trade," he said, draining the liquid fire in one swallow and setting the empty glass down.

"With you handling our trade agreements, Kason, I think we will have nothing but prosperous trade." Otera was not one to flatter idly, so he knew she meant every word. He was damn good at his job, and it was satisfying to hear his queen acknowledge it.

Blaedia caught his eye. He smiled at her, though she rarely returned the gesture, at least not when she was in uniform. Come to think of it, he wasn't sure he had ever seen the silver-eyed general without her uniform. When Otera turned to her lover, however, and held out a hand, Blaedia's lips tipped upward in the faintest of smiles—a rare sight, like catching steel soften.

"Shall we return to the party?" Otera asked, turning her attention back to Kason. He nodded, snagging another glass of whiskey from a servant's tray before following them.

Holding his drink in one hand and smoothing back his long dark hair with the other, Kason trailed the queen and her mate out of the private offices and into the ballroom.

The whiskey was strong, and he was glad for it. It would take several glasses to endure the frilly music echoing from the quartet. If it had been up to him, he would have left the party entirely and gone back to the tavern—maybe even crossed paths with the gorgeous warrior again. He needed to see her. Needed to make her his mate. Maybe he could slip away once Otera was occupied.

That thought vanished the moment he saw her across the ballroom. Her violet eyes locked on his, wide with recognition, and it hit him harder than any punch ever had. She took one step forward before halting, snatching a glass of whiskey from a nearby table instead.

When she threw the liquid fire back in one swallow, Kason chuckled under his breath. He'd never wanted a dainty female who hid behind dresses and needlework. What caught him was the cut of muscle in her arms and the fire in her gaze, the promise of strength and defiance. Just imagining her drawing a bowstring, her body taut with focus, made heat surge through him. She was the sexiest thing he'd ever seen, even in simple trousers and tunic—but gods, he wanted to see her in her fighting leathers. Maybe he could even get her to wear them to his bed.

Tired of waiting for her to come to him, Kason finished his glass and sauntered across the room, a mischievous smirk tugging at his mouth. Her expression mirrored his.

"If I had to guess, beautiful warrior," he said, his voice pitched low for her alone, "I would say you're following me."

Chapter Seven

Holera

It was unlike Holera to find herself without words, but when the sexy male from the tavern stepped in front of her, all swagger and confidence, asking if she'd been following him, she couldn't find her tongue. Her mouth opened, but all that came out was silence. Holera hated silence—it made her feel exposed.

Unfortunately, the borderline inebriated Exie had no such reservations, slamming her whiskey glass into his in an overly dramatic cheers. "And I would guess you may be following Holera." She winked at Holera like a mischievous older sister before sauntering away, parting the crowd as she went, leaving chaos in her wake.

The male's face turned to the blond warrior, one eyebrow arched to a point, and grinned. The pure cockiness in his expression only made him sexier. Dipping his chin in Exie's direction, he turned his sights back on Holera, who'd yet to utter a word. "Holera, is it? I'm Kason. Nice to officially meet you."

"I...um...nice to meet you too." Exie's playful hum still lingered in Holera's ears, but when she turned back to Kason, he was watching her. "Sorry about Exie. She's not exactly shy."

Chuckling, he handed her another glass of whiskey. With her nerves where they were, she needed it. "We all have a friend like her. They keep things interesting."

She may have known little about Kason, but he certainly spoke the truth. Taking a deep drink of her whiskey, she willed the liquid fire to calm her nerves. She hated how her hands trembled. Battle she could handle. This? This was worse. Something about this male made her forget how to use her voice.

He seemed to understand this and lifted his arm for her to take. "Shall we find a place to sit and talk, preferably far away from the band?" When he turned to glance over his shoulder, she stifled a giggle and then silently berated herself for acting like a lovesick fledgling. "The music at this party is awful."

Sliding her arm into his, Holera took another sip of her whiskey, the liquid warming her from the inside out. "We can sit in the gardens. The fountains may adequately drown out the music."

The suggestion only broadened the smile on Kason's handsome face, and he dipped his chin, holding out his hand before him, signaling for her to show him the way.

They walked arm-in-arm at a leisurely pace, Holera paying little mind to everyone else at the party. She saw Otera in her peripheral vision, the queen in deep conversation with her mate, but she didn't see Exie again before they'd crossed through the open doorway and out into the back gardens. All she could hope was that her friend stayed out of trouble so she could actually learn a little bit more about the powerful male on her arm, a privilege she had not been afforded the night before.

The night air was brisk, the breeze from the sea leaving the scent of brine on the air. The sharp cold bit her cheeks, carrying salt from the sea. After the heavy perfume of the ballroom, it was a relief. Holera breathed in deeply, the masculine aroma of the male on her arm filling her senses as he led her to one of the several benches facing the sea. With the moon full, its light reflected off the surface of the water, along with the sparkles of a thousand stars. The large fountain at their backs drowned out the sound of the band, as well as the voices of the other partygoers, leaving them in an intimate silence. Kason's arm remained hooked in hers as they sat on the bench, his long legs stretched out before him. They remained quiet for a long moment, the tranquility of the garden too perfect to interrupt.

"I have a confession to make," he said as he turned to face her, his green eyes brilliant in the moonlight.

"You do?" She'd been almost afraid to ask, but she knew he would say whatever he had on his mind anyway. "What is it that you have to confess, Kason?"

Grinning, he drained the rest of his drink and set the empty glass on the ground at his feet. "After last night, I'd hoped to see you again."

It wasn't what Holera had expected him to say, but she wasn't disappointed. Gods help her, she liked the way he said it. After so long without a lover, her heart had chilled with the temperature of her bed, and she yearned to warm it once again. "Is that so?"

Sliding his arm out of hers, Kason took her hand, bringing it to his lips and kissing it. He did it so easily, like she was already precious to him. No one had ever treated her that way before. Her breath caught in her throat as she held his eyes in hers. "It is."

Interlacing his fingers with hers, Kason laid their joined hands on his lap as he gazed out over the water. She couldn't help but to smile to herself as she watched him. It was such a simple gesture but it meant more to her than he realized. She wasn't naive, however. There was no guarantee she'd ever see him again after this night, but just to be touched for that moment was enough. It would have to be.

"I hoped to see you again too."

She'd never admit it aloud—not to him, not even to Exie—but her chest ached with how much she wanted more.

CHAPTER EIGHT

KASON

Holera. Her name sounded powerful, yet alluring, which was exactly what the female sitting next to Kason was. It fit her—every syllable steady, unbending, like the warrior she was. He'd meant to tell her about the Warbotach mercenaries, but what good would that do? Better to let her believe the night had been untouched by danger. Better she slept soundly.

Holera stretched her long legs out in front of her, and Kason found it impossible to avoid admiring her figure, her long limbs, muscles finely cut from her life as an Aegrician warrior. She was incredible, but he had a feeling she didn't realize how incredible she truly was. He wanted her to see herself the way he saw her, someone fierce enough to face the world and extraordinary enough to change it.

"You are stunning, Holera." Even among the fae, silver hair and violet eyes were rare. Sitting below the night sky, her hair had the appearance of liquid moonlight as she turned to look at him, her hair sliding over her shoulder.

He expected her to speak, to say something, but she only gazed at him, her free hand twisting into the hem of her cloak. She was nervous, he realized, and he wanted to ease that in her too. Even though he knew little about her, something in her nearness, in her scent, made him want to give her the world, to lay it out at her feet if it would make her his. The porcelain skin of her cheek begged for him to touch it and he didn't want to fight it. Instead, Kason lifted a hesitant hand to her face, searching her eyes for resistance as he cupped her cheek.

Her breath hitched, and the sound faltered in a way that made his chest ache. A tremor moved through her beneath his palm, and he knew his touch had set her alight. She didn't look away. That silence was all the permission he needed.

He leaned in slowly, giving her every chance to turn aside. When his lips finally touched hers, the world dropped away. For a moment she went still, her jaw tight as though she meant to push him away. Kason braced for rejection, but then her shoulders eased, her lips softened against his, and the heat of her answer surged into him. Whatever protest she had died unspoken, and he knew then she wanted this as much as he did. The first kiss was fleeting, a spark testing dry tinder. The second burned deeper, certainty replacing caution, and the warmth of her mouth consumed him.

The fire inside him roared, rising higher with every beat of his heart. Her mouth moved against his with an urgency that caught him off guard, and the sound of it—the soft catch of her breath between kisses—nearly undid him. He tasted whiskey and salt, but beneath it was something wholly her own, something that already felt like addiction.

What had begun tentative became hungry. His control slipped with every stroke of her lips, every answering push of her tongue. She wasn't simply returning the kiss; she was claiming him as surely as he longed to claim her, and the thought sent heat flooding his body until nothing mattered but holding her closer, kissing her harder, and never letting her go.

Although her conversations had been reserved, shy even, ever since they'd met, her kisses were not. When Kason wrapped his arms around her body, pulling her in close, she climbed onto his lap, straddling him as they sat on the bench by the sea. The wind whipped at her hair, sliding under her cloak and making her shiver, giving Kason permission to hold her tighter, to wrap her up in his cloak and against his body while their mouths explored one another, while their tongues tasted. Caressed.

With as hard as she'd made it, he knew Holera could feel his cock pressing against the fabric of his trousers. It didn't give her pause. If anything, it fueled her as she wrapped her legs around the sides of him and ground against his hardness, the friction pulling a breathy moan from her mouth. The sound threatened to make him come undone, but he didn't want to rush things with her. She wasn't just some female at a brothel, or a night of release with a stranger at a tavern. Holera would be his forever, so he wanted to take his time with her. He wanted to do things right.

When she pulled her lips away from Kason's, he was left panting but wanting more, and she knew it. With a seductive smile, she leaned forward and ran her tongue up the curve of his neck, licking and sucking her way up to his ear. He groaned, his hips bucking up against her in spite of himself. "Are you trying to make me lose control, Holera?"

Huffing a laugh, she returned to his mouth, kissing him hungrily as his arms slid around her waist and gripped her backside.

"Maybe you need to lose control." After being as shy as she'd been the entire night, those were the last words he'd expected to hear from her, and he felt the sultry tone in which she said them all the way down his shaft. If she wanted him to lose control, she wouldn't have to try very hard.

Holera's fingers slid into his hair, removing the leather strap, allowing his long locks to fall free against his back, before returning her attention to his neck. A growl rose from deep in his belly, and resisting taking her right there on that bench was taking more willpower than he'd even thought he had. She ground against him again, the warm friction from between her thighs nearly making him release in his trousers.

"Is there somewhere we can go?" she asked, her voice no more than breath against his ear. A surge of excitement filled him, even if he didn't intend to claim her that night. He still wanted to wait, but he wasn't opposed to finding somewhere they could be alone together.

Nodding, he stood, lifting her with him before gently setting her back onto her own feet. If they were going to walk around where there were others, he didn't think it would've been appropriate for her to still be straddling his waist. Placing his hand on the small of her back, Kason led Holera through the gardens and toward the gate. "I have a room nearby."

Chapter Nine

Holera

Holera had never considered herself to be one to succumb to passions over having good sense, but there was something about Kason that made all her methodical planning flee from her mind like it was running from an enemy. Her head told her this was reckless, but her body didn't care. For once, she let it win. Just the scent of him, and the feeling of his fingers interlaced with hers, had her straddling his lap and sucking on his neck. She didn't know what had come over her, but she wasn't strong enough to fight it. She wasn't even sure if she wanted to. If only for a moment, she wanted to let her heart lead her and not her head. Fate, it seemed, had other plans.

Just as they were making their way toward the back gates of the palace, intent on finding somewhere more private to spend time together, a clean cut Aegrician male with golden hair and deep umber eyes stepped out into their path.
"Kason. Sorry to interrupt your evening, but there's a situation the queen needs you to attend to."

Kason stiffened at her side, and she fought back a disappointed groan. The words slammed into her like cold water, and she wanted to bare her teeth at him for daring to steal the moment. She didn't even know what he did for the kingdom, or what kind of situation the male was talking about, but she knew her fling, at least for the night, was over. When he turned to face her, the fire in his eyes dimming with an exhale, she knew it was over.
"Wait for me," he said, the words crushing her somewhere deep inside her chest. She hated the way her chest ached, as though she'd let herself hope for more.

All she could do was nod as he gave her one more kiss and his hand slipped out of hers before he disappeared through the open doorway and into the crowd. She stood there for a moment, watching the space where he'd passed refill with revelers, before taking a step inside. Something was going on, and she knew he'd told her to wait for him, but she wasn't the sit-and-wait type. If she was going to get herself in trouble, however, she would need a partner in crime, so instead of going after him, she headed for the bar. First, she needed to find Exie. Thankfully, her friend was right where she'd expected her to be.

Seeming to have sensed Holera approaching, Exie spun around to face her. "There you are! I thought you'd gone home."

The queen catching Holera's eye, she watched as Otera spoke discreetly to one of her guards before leaving the room, Blaedia at her heel. "There's no time to talk about where I've been, Ex. Something's going on and I need to figure out what."

The mischievous sparkle in Exie's eyes nearly made Holera regret going for her friend instead of following Kason. Trouble lit her faster than whiskey ever could. After only a moment, it passed. "Something with Kason?" Draining a glass of water, Exie turned toward the direction in which Otera had gone. "I saw him go that way just before Otera left with Blaedia."

It wasn't their place to get involved in emissary business. Holera knew that, but it didn't sway her. Blowing out a breath, she headed toward the door that would lead them back into the palace corridor, Exie following her lead. If her queen was involved, then she would make it her business.

Walking past the guards posted at the doors, Holera merely nodded once in their direction, hoping her brisk pace would convince them she had urgent business that was not to be interrupted. She hadn't expected them to let her pass, but they did. With no indication of what direction Kason and the queen had gone, aside from the faintest imprint of his scent, she turned left toward the lower levels of the palace. There wasn't much down there aside from the dungeons, but she hadn't mistaken Kason's scent, or Otera's, so she knew that was the way they'd gone.

"What happened between the two of you?" Exie asked as they walked briskly down the corridor leading to the back stairwell. Aside from the guards at the doors, they hadn't passed anyone else.

"We can talk about that later." Stopping at the end of the hall, Holera peered around the corner and down the darkened stairway. With only a few sconces on the wall, most of the space was in shadow. The torches hissed, shadows leaping across stone walls, the air damp and cold enough to raise gooseflesh. "Someone came to get him from the courtyard. Said there was a situation he needed to take care of." Taking one more look over her shoulder, she stepped into the stairwell. "They came this way, Kason and Otera, with a few others."

Lifting her finger to her mouth, Exie silenced any further questions as they began to move down the stone stairs into the subterranean level of the palace. The silence stretched too long, broken only by the echo of their boots. Each step felt heavier than the last. When they arrived at the bottom of the stairs, where a heavy wooden door separated them from the dungeon, the sound of a scream nearly brought Holera to her knees.

Chapter Ten

Kason

Kason knew why he'd been summoned before he even walked into the ballroom. There had been trouble with the Warbotach prisoners, and since he'd brought them in, he knew they were his problem. Although there had been about a dozen Warbotach traders at the tavern the night before, only two of them had been stupid enough to follow Holera and Exie when they'd left the bar, therefore there were only two of them in the dungeon below the palace. At least, that's how many there had been when he'd last seen them. The problem was, once he arrived back in the dungeon after the queen summoned him, there had been only one prisoner remaining. Somehow, one of the bastards had escaped.

Kason growled under his breath. He'd found the female he'd been dreaming about, one he'd surely settle down for, but he had been forced to leave her standing in the courtyard with no explanation. Once he finished interrogating the remaining prisoner, he would have to find Holera and beg for her forgiveness. If he could even find her. Panos' interruption as they were making their way off the palace grounds had drowned their fire like a bucket of cold water.

Otera, Blaedia, and two guards entered the dungeon behind Kason, the prisoner already tied to a chair. Torchlight guttered along damp stone, the air thick with mildew and the iron tang of blood.

"How'd this happen?" he asked no one in particular. The prisoner struggled against his bindings, spewing curses in his own language. Kason understood every word but refused to dignify the filth with a translation.

"Seems the other prisoner overpowered our guard, left through the servant's entrance." Taking a cursory glance at the unconscious guard leaning against the stone wall, Kason cracked his knuckles. It appeared as though he wouldn't be returning to his female anytime soon. The thought made his jaw tighten. Every wasted moment here was one stolen from her.

Otera moved further into the room, Blaedia at her side. "Has anyone gone after the prisoner? We need him captured before he gets on a ship. Needless to say, Warbotach would see his imprisonment as an act of war."

The male guard nodded, his body language showing signs of his frayed nerves. "I sent out six guards, Your Majesty. Four on foot and two in the sky."

"How long ago?" Kason demanded, still not understanding why there had only been one guard watching the prisoners to begin with. It was an oversight that wouldn't happen again.

"An hour, maybe less."

With the unsure tone of the guard's voice, Kason was betting it was less. He gritted his teeth. "Send out more." With a swift nod, the guard left the room and headed back into the palace proper.

Otera turned to her lover, squeezing Blaedia's hand. "Go. Send your own trusted warriors after him. We have to get that prisoner back."

Blaedia nodded, but just as she turned toward the heavy wooden door leading out of the dungeon, there were two figures standing in the doorway. "Holera. Exie. What are you two doing here?" Her voice cracked like a whip in the stale air, and the weight of her glare could have crushed stone. The general sounded less than pleased, but both females had the appearance of someone caught in a trap. They knew they had been found somewhere they shouldn't have been.

Holera's mouth opened and shut a few times like a fish out of water before she finally spoke. "I—I heard a scream. I thought someone was hurt."

Mouth twisting in a smirk, Kason knew Holera was lying. She'd heard a scream, but not until she was already in the dungeon, exactly where she shouldn't have been. Eyes like slits, Blaedia glared at her two warriors for a few awkward moments before seeming to realize they were not in the right frame of mind to go after a barbarian, Exie being slightly intoxicated and Holera too distracted by the male across the room to be given orders. With one more glance over her shoulder, Blaedia left the dungeon.

Once her general was out of the way, Holera stepped further into the room, confusion clear on her face as she took in the space. "What is this, Kason? What's going on?"

Kason hadn't intended to disclose the truth about how he'd followed them home the night before because they were being trailed by barbarians who'd intended on doing them harm. He'd hoped to leave that storyline out of their night together, but he no longer had the choice as the beautiful warrior glanced from the Warbotach prisoner tied to the chair, and back to the male she'd just been kissing in the gardens.

With nothing else for her to do, the queen left the room, leaving two guards behind to watch over the remaining prisoner. Still, Kason didn't feel comfortable walking away just yet. Instead, he dragged the bound male back into his cell, double checking the lock once he closed the door. He needed the prisoner secured before he could even think of touching her again. Only then did he allow himself the indulgence of reaching for her hand. Taking Holera by the hand, he pulled her to him and kissed her deeply, relieved when she fell into him instead of pulling away.

"Come, let's take a seat just outside and I'll explain everything."

Chapter Eleven

Holera

Holera's mind whirled as she'd glanced from Kason, to the queen, to the prisoner tied to a metal chair in the dungeon. She was relieved the scream hadn't come from her newly found lover, but she recognized the Warbotach brute in the chair. He'd been the same male Exie had had an altercation with the night before, and she didn't know why he'd been captured. As she walked hand in hand with Kason through the servant's exit and out into the crisp night air, Exie remained behind to give them privacy. Kason walked her to one of the stone benches, dropping to sit beside her.

"I haven't been completely forthcoming with you tonight," he said, the words sending Holera's heart into her gut. "After you left the tavern with Exie last night, two of the Warbotach merchants followed you."

The words struck her harder than any blade, leaving her stomach hollow. Knowing she'd been followed by two males didn't ease the sinking in her stomach. Holera shook her head, disappointed in herself for having been so distracted by Exie that she hadn't even realized they'd been in danger. "I can't believe I didn't know. I was so caught up with—"

"Don't." Kason cut her off, sliding his hand to the nape of her neck and rubbing the flesh between her shoulders. His voice was steady, a warmth meant to anchor her even in the cold night air. "Don't blame yourself for what they did, or what they tried to do. I have no doubt that, if they had attacked, you would have been able to defend yourself. What matters is that you didn't have to. I saw them through the windows of the tavern, and I cut them off before they could do whatever it was they intended to do."

Just thinking about what those merchants had planned for her and her friend made bile rise in Holera's throat. "Thank you for protecting us." In all her life, she had never seen herself as needing anyone's protection, but in that moment, she felt helpless, and she hated it.

Kason pulled her closer, wrapping his arm around her waist. "But one of those bastards got away—about an hour ago. They've sent out more guards to look for him, but I need to look for him as well. We can't let him get on a ship. I just didn't want to leave without seeing you. I didn't want you to think I'd run away from you."

"I want to go with you."

Although she expected Kason to deny her request, he didn't. Instead, he rose from the bench, reaching a hand down to help her up before pulling her into a kiss. For just a moment, the world around them disappeared as Kason's scent filled her senses, and his tongue caressed her own. The kiss was brief but consuming, a promise more than a surrender, and it left her aching when he broke away.

When they parted, it took every bit of her restraint not to drag him back to her lips again, but they had to find the missing prisoner. She didn't need Kason to explain what would be the fallout if the Warbotach merchant got on a ship and returned to his own kingdom with claims of being imprisoned by the Aegrician monarch. Lesser grievances had started wars in their world.

Returning to the dungeon, Holera filled Exie in on what had happened the night before, how her near bar brawl had gotten them followed, had nearly gotten them into more trouble than they could have even imagined. Kason saw to the remaining prisoner while Exie and Holera talked, ensuring he was not only secure in his cell, but that there were enough guards watching him to prevent him from escaping. If Exie's argument in the tavern had started a war... That was something Holera couldn't even think about at the moment, but she could tell by the look on her friend's face that Exie felt some moniker of regret for her temper, even if she'd been defending their queen. Her shoulders slumped in a way Holera rarely saw, her bravado cracked by the weight of what might have been.

They left the dungeon a moment later. Kason held onto Holera, with Exie on their heels, as they climbed the stairs out of the lower levels and back into the palace proper. There were many warriors now guarding the lower levels of the palace, including the doors into the ballroom. Bypassing the party area altogether, the trio left through the front doors and stepped out into the cool night air.

"We should fly," Exie said, coming to a stop in front of them. "With Kason on your back, we'll have more eyes in the sky. We'll find him."

Kason nodded, securing his weapons on his back. Holera hadn't had many people on her back, but she knew it could give them a better chance. In a flash of fire, she shifted, a brilliant silver phoenix standing where she had been. Her feathers shimmered under the moonlight, heat rippling the air as sparks skittered across the stones. Wasting no time, Kason climbed onto her back and shifted his weight until he was nestled and out of the way of her wings.

Pulling reins out of her satchel, Exie secured them onto her friend, passing the handholds to Kason before shifting into her own phoenix form. Where Holera's phoenix form was silver with a flare of violet feathers on her tail and wings, Exie was a brilliant fire red, with tail feathers of every color of the rainbow, and a tuft of blond feathers on her head. Even in that shape, Exie radiated chaos, her wings slicing the air with reckless power.

The two phoenixes nodded to each other and then spread their wings, their tails fluttering in the wind as they lifted into the sky, eyes searching for their prey.

Chapter Twelve

Kason

In all his decades of life, Kason had never ridden on the back of a phoenix warrior, so he was hesitant to climb onto Holera. The birds were massive, but so was he, and he didn't want to hurt her. Her feathers radiated heat, the air around her shimmering faintly with phoenix fire. Ultimately, however, Exie's words made sense, and he knew Holera was more than capable of carrying his weight, even if he always saw himself as carrying his female, and not the other way around. Thinking of her as his brought warmth to his chest, even in the cold night. A mate was something he'd never imagined for himself. Truly bonding to a mate, having fate know exactly who was meant for a person, was rare.

Soaring through the air, firmly positioned behind the phoenix's neck, Kason pulled his bow from over his shoulder, notching an arrow and peering into the darkness. With Exie in the lead, they flew low over the city streets and toward the harbor. Below them, lanterns glimmered in crooked rows, the alleys alive with faint shouts and torchlight.

In the darkness, even with his advanced fae eyesight and the even more impressive eyesight of the phoenixes, it would still be difficult to find the escaped prisoner. The number of merchants and ships in the harbor would only make the search that much harder. He could have hidden in plain sight from them among the crowds and gotten on a ship before he'd ever been found.

Blowing out a breath, Kason leaned forward, stroking Holera's silky feathers as he leaned into the wind. Her avian face was severe, every line marked with danger, yet to him she was still beautiful, extraordinary. He knew what she could do, what all the phoenix warriors could do. Her talons were the size of his fingers, and her razor-sharp beak was a weapon. She could rip a man apart in her phoenix form, but she was no less fierce in her fae form. When they were back on the ground and had time to spend together, he wanted to spar with her, wanted to see her slick with sweat and wielding a sword. He couldn't imagine anything sexier than Holera in fighting leathers, swinging a weapon, and kicking his ass. The thought alone had his blood surging with more force than the wind on his face.

The memory of her straddling his lap, grinding against his hardness, pulsed through him with every wingbeat. Her scent in his nose and the taste of her skin against his lips had nearly driven him over the edge, and his body yearned to have her on top of him again. If they found the missing prisoner, Kason hoped he and Holera could return to the night they were heading toward. A night of passion and getting to know each other better so he could convince her that he was meant to be her mate. The more time he spent with her, the more he needed her.

His cock already firming in his trousers, Kason shook the thoughts from his mind and returned his eyes to scan the harbor below. The Warbotach ship still bobbed against the docks, merchants loading cargo on and off the craft while others completed the last of their tasks in the city. The masts rocked like skeletal fingers against the night sky, ropes creaking under the weight of crates. Just as he scanned the barbarians who were loading crates across the ramp, he laid eyes on the male who'd gotten away.

"There!"

Both birds' eyes darted in the direction of Kason's outstretched hand, their eyes locking on their target. Exie dove first, her vibrant wings whipping out at her sides to aim her decline as her brilliant tail ribbons fluttered behind her, coloring the sky like a rainbow in the darkness. Following her friend, Holera's strong body shot like an arrow at the Warbotach vessel, her massive silver wings tilting to control their descent. Kason held onto her back with his thighs, his bow held high with the arrow pulled taut as he pinned his eyes on the escaped prisoner. If the male got away, war would return to Aegricia's shores, and that was something they needed to prevent.

The other guards and warriors approached from multiple directions, some flying in over the sea, and others through the forest, or from the road. They were all closing in on the Warbotach ship. The entire situation was precarious. If Aegricia forced their way onto a Warbotach vessel and took one of their people, even that could be seen as an act of war, so there were no perfect options on how to deal with the situation.

Exie swooped past them, a keening call erupting from her beak as she signaled the other winged warriors to follow her into the forest and out of sight of the Warbotach ship. Holera followed as Kason gestured to the soldiers on the ground to watch but wait. They knew where the prisoner was. Now they needed to figure out the best way to apprehend him without drawing too much attention.

Chapter Thirteen

Holera

Following Exie into the forest, Holera landed in a clearing next to her friend and allowed Kason to climb off her back before shifting back into her fae body. The clearing smelled of damp earth and pine, the forest pressing in close as though listening. Although she could communicate with the other phoenixes in her phoenix form, she could not speak that way, and they needed to discuss what to do next.

"His men know he's back on board," Kason said, sliding his bow over his shoulder. "There won't be any way for us to detain him without alerting his friends."

Exie kicked at the dirt, her boot striking hard enough to scatter pebbles, her restless energy a storm barely contained. "So, either we let him go or get into a fight with the entire ship of Warbotach merchants? Is that what you're telling me?"

It was a scenario Holera had been afraid of. Their kingdom didn't want to go to war, no matter what the Warbotach soldiers had been intending. "So, what do we do? Do we just let him go? The risk of there being a battle if we enter their ship is too high."

"Unless…" The tone of Exie's voice was enough to make Holera clench her teeth because it was one that usually came before an idea that would get them both into trouble.

"I want no part in your schemes, Exie. I already got into enough trouble with Blaedia today. My legs are still sore from chasing arrows all over the mountain and one of those fledglings nearly took my ear off. You can shove whatever mad plan you're brewing right back into that reckless skull."

Kason chuckled, but didn't disrupt Holera's diatribe until it was over. "I hope this doesn't make you angry with me, my fierce warrior, but I'd like to hear her ideas, even if they're crazy enough to get us into trouble." His grin made it impossible for Holera to stay angry, though she tried.

The smirk that grew on Exie's face only made Holera cringe more, but she didn't object again as her friend laid out her plan.

The plan was foolish to say the least, but Holera went along with it against her better judgment, mostly because she had been overruled. Although infiltrating the Warbotach ship would be asking for a fight, that was exactly what they planned to do.

Under the cover of darkness and swooping in from the water, Kason and Exie intended to sneak onto the Warbotach ship and recapture the prisoner. There were about a million things that could have gone wrong with the plan, including getting themselves captured or killed, but Otera had made it clear they needed to prevent the prisoner from leaving Aegricia, so they didn't see any other options.

Kason kissed her before he left on her friend's back, and it had taken nearly everything in Holera to let them go. She was a warrior, so she knew the risks associated with her station in life, but it didn't make it any easier when doing something that put herself or those she cared about in danger.

While Exie and Kason took to the skies and out over the water, Holera snuck through the dense forest toward the harbor. Exie intended to drop Kason on the stern and then return once he had the prisoner in hand. While Exie circled overhead and Kason snuck onto the ship to find their target, Holera was to be the lookout.

She waited near the bank, the brush of the forest's edge and bustle of the port keeping her well hidden, and watched as her friends disappeared into the darkened sky. Salt wind stung her nose, carrying the creak of rigging and the muffled shouts of sailors. Every sound set her on edge. Time seemed to stand still as she listened for the sounds of yelling, or the clanging of swords, but for many long moments, there was only the sound of merchants and travelers moving around the city. Her grip tightened on her sword hilt, her pulse thudding in her ears as the quiet stretched too long. Just when she was warring with herself over whether she should go after them, the first sign of trouble erupted from the water's edge.

Chapter Fourteen

Kason

Kason had known Exie's plan was a long shot from the beginning, but they'd had no other choice if they wanted to take the escaped prisoner back into custody before he fled Aegricia. When Exie had first swooped low over the water, allowing Kason to leap onto the poop deck, he'd done so without being seen. With his dagger in hand, he crept across onto the quarterdeck, his dark hooded cloak disguising his face, and slipped into the galley. The ship creaked around him, the stink of stale ale and sweat hanging thick in the air.

He'd found his target quicker than he'd expected. Seeming to feel confident he was as good as free, the male they'd been looking for was lounging just below deck, a tankard of ale dripping down his wrist, his grin smug with false freedom. Holding his dagger at the Warbotach male's side, Kason had escorted the prisoner back to where Exie had left him only a few minutes before. The problem was, although he'd snuck onto the ship without being seen, his dagger hadn't been enough of a deterrent, and the male in his hold put up a fight once Exie had appeared in the distance.

Kason tried to neutralize the issue, slamming his fist into the male's jaw as his dagger clattered to the planks, the sound sharp as a bell in the chaos. But Warbotach males were raised to fight, and the strike hadn't so much as phased the prisoner. Before he knew it, Exie had landed on the deck, shifting into her fae form, and three more Warbotach males had joined them for a full-on brawl.

Ducking a swinging sword, Kason drew his own from its scabbard and pivoted to face two of their attackers. Exie, wielding a blade of her own, slashed at one of the males, hitting him in the arm. Blood sprayed across the deck, slicking the boards beneath their boots.

"Cunt!" he barked out, the wound gushing as he swung his other arm out, his machete narrowly missing the side of her face.

Exie barked a laugh even as she swung her blade. "You wish you got some!"

From what he'd seen of her, Exie had no fear—not in a tavern, and not here—and somehow that reckless spark made Kason grin even as steel whistled around him.

He pulled his other sword from over his back, slicing both through the air. Although he missed one of his opponents, the male jumping back to avoid the blow, one of his blades caught the escaped prisoner across the chest. Without the magic of a healer, the wound had the potential to kill him, and he seemed to realize that. Stumbling to the railing of the deck, the prisoner dropped, his arm wrapping across his chest as the male who'd been fighting Kason ran for help.

Taking advantage of the distraction, Kason reached for Exie, yanking her by the top of her leathers toward the railing. "We need to get out of here. Now!"

Nodding, she shifted in a burst of brilliant flame. Tossing the injured prisoner over his shoulder, Kason jumped onto the phoenix's back right before her wings launched them into the air and over the water.

Just as Exie soared closer to the land, an enormous silver figure surged toward them. Holera approached, her massive phoenix wings carrying her alongside them as they flew against the chilly wind. Although he'd asked her to remain in the forest as a lookout, mostly because he'd wanted to keep her safe, she'd completely ignored him when she'd heard the fight break out, and it only sharpened his hunger for her. She was reckless, yes, but gods, she was glorious. She would be just as fierce of a mate, loving when she needed to love, and fighting when she needed to fight. Even though he couldn't communicate with her in that form, Kason winked at the beautiful warrior, her severe violet eyes flaring before both birds turned, aiming toward the palace just as the sun began to rise.

Chapter Fifteen

Holera

By the time they'd landed back on the palace grounds with the escaped Warbotach prisoner, Holera was exhausted and more than a little frustrated with what had come to pass. She hadn't slept, and the night's chaos pressed down on her like lead. They'd retrieved the Warbotach male, but nothing else had gone as planned. She hadn't been on the ship when Exie and Kason had grabbed him, but she'd heard the commotion from the forest. Whatever happened on that ship, the rest of the Warbotach merchants probably knew about it. She didn't even want to imagine what the fallout would be once they returned to their home country and reported the attack. Even though two of their merchants started the whole mess by following her and Exie, that didn't mean the barbarian king would see it in the same way, nor did that mean he would see the attack on their ship as having been warranted. She was grateful Kason and Exie were unharmed, but that was about all she was grateful for at that moment.

Shifting back into her fae form next to Exie and Kason, Holera reached to help Kason with the prisoner, who was bleeding profusely from a chest wound, as her friend shifted. Blood slicked her fingers as she steadied him with Kason, the stench of iron sharp in her nose.

"He needs a healer quickly or he's not going to make it," Kason said, the prisoner's head lolling to the side as he fought for consciousness. Exie nodded, darting toward the palace and disappearing through the doors.

"What happened?" Each taking on some of the injured male's weight, Kason and Holera staggered toward the infirmary inside the palace after Exie.

"Everything went to shit when I tried to get him off the ship. The bastard started fighting and his friends joined in. Exie and I had to fight off a few before we were able to leave."

Holera's jaw tightened, her teeth grinding as she wrestled her frustration down. "I knew it was a bad idea from the start. Now the entire ship of merchants is going to go back to Warbotach and their king will wage an attack."

Just as they were about to attempt to open the palace doors with limited free hands, several guards came out with a board and they were able to set the injured male on it to relieve themselves of the burden. The guards disappeared into the corridor with the prisoner, leaving Kason and Holera on the foyer, both of them drenched in blood.

"I still have a place nearby, if you want to get cleaned up. I have a room at the inn above the Singing Lantern."

Holera watched his face for a minute, the male incredibly rugged and sexy, and debated if she wanted to pick up where they'd left off in the courtyard. There were many bathing rooms in the palace they could use if they wanted to, but after everything they'd gone through in just over twenty-four hours, she didn't know if she was ready for everyone in the palace to know about their budding romance just yet. She also couldn't get their encounter in the gardens out of her mind, even with the events that had occurred since.

Looking down at her hands again, sticky with the blood of her enemy, she made her decision. The gore on her skin was jarring against the thought of his kiss in the gardens, both fresh in her mind, both impossible to ignore. "Yeah. Let's get out of here. As long as the queen knows where to find you if we're needed. Exie can just assume I went home to clean up and rest. I can do without her getting me into trouble for a while. I may need to borrow clothes though...even if they're way too large for me."

Kason chuckled, touching a bloody hand to the small of her back and leading her toward the palace gates. His chuckle was low, the touch at her back both steadying and possessive. "I'm sure we can manage to find you something."

Chapter Sixteen

Kason

With his hand against Holera's back, Kason led her toward the palace gates and onto the street. He realized the fallout of their fight on the Warbotach ship could end up causing a bigger conflict, but he and Holera needed to step away from the situation for a while, at least long enough to eat, bathe, and sleep. Many guards and warriors would be sent to monitor the activity in the city and harbor, and others would be used to watch over the injured prisoner, but what the Warbotach male really needed at that moment was a healer, and neither him nor Holera were healers.

Even with the smell of blood and sweat on her skin, the beautiful warrior's scent filled his senses, reminding Kason of the moments they'd shared in the gardens. Although he wanted her more than he'd ever wanted anyone, he had no expectations of moving any farther with her than what she was comfortable with. If she chose him as her mate, they had forever to be together. Holera was worth waiting for.

The sky threatened snow as they made their way down one of the alleys behind the buildings on the main street, not wanting to cause a scene with their gory appearances. Their boots left faint red smears on the cobblestones, reminders of a night that was far from finished. They slipped into the back door of the tavern where they'd first met.

"I'll talk to the barkeep before we go to the room and ask for food and drinks to be brought to us."

Holera nodded, remaining near the stairs as Kason crossed the room and approached the bar. Butterflies filled her belly for the first time in a long time, the feeling unsettling her more than battle ever had. Since she'd been younger and had a male who'd meant something to her, she hadn't felt this way. He hadn't turned out to be the male she wanted to spend her life with, and she'd moved on.

Watching the way the barkeep, an elderly male with graying hair, smiled as he spoke to Kason squeezed her heart. The old man's easy trust in him only deepened the warmth Holera felt watching Kason in his element. Even with his rugged exterior, Kason was kind, personable, someone people naturally liked, except when he had a blade to their throats. He may have been skilled with diplomacy, but he was a trained warrior.

After a brief conversation at the bar, Kason walked back toward her with a grin on his face and a decanter in his hand. "My good friend, Spyro, will be sending up two breakfast plates in a bit, and his mate has plenty of clothing to spare. Actually, he seemed glad to get rid of some of it. He said her things take up the entire cabinet."

Smirking and shaking her head, Holera followed Kason as he led her up the darkened stairway and onto the second level of the building. They walked past several guest rooms down the long corridor, the boards creaking under their weight, lanterns flickering shadows along the narrow hall, before he used a key to unlock the door of the last room on the right, opening it so she could enter first.

"I never did ask you where you live," she said, hesitating for only a moment. Having only known each other for a day, she didn't want to pry. "Since you're staying at the inn, I assume you don't live in the capital?"

Kason closed the door behind him, setting the key and decanter on the table before dropping his weapons to the floor. Holera did the same. "I travel a lot as an emissary for the kingdom, so I don't see my home much, but I do have a cabin in the mountains north of the capital."

Dropping to his knees, he started to unlace her boots. The simple act made her chest tighten; a warrior of his stature humbling himself at her feet was something she'd never imagined. "Can I run a bath for you, my beautiful warrior? We both could use one before we touch any of the furniture in here. I don't want Spyro to demand my head if we destroy anything."

Holera lowered herself into a chair, kicking her boots off as he finished loosening them for her. "That's the best idea I've heard all day."

Chapter Seventeen

Holera

Steam circled in tendrils through the air above the tub as Kason ran Holera's bath. The warmth fogged the glass panes and wrapped the room in a cocoon, shutting out the world beyond the door. She watched him for a moment as he leaned over the tub, in awe of how such a rugged male would get on his knees for her, especially when they'd only just met. Although she'd had lovers before, she'd never felt the pull of a mating bond, but she couldn't deny the attraction her body had to Kason. Her body wanted him on a level she would have had a hard time fighting, not that she wanted to fight it at all.

Pulling on the laces of her tunic, Holera loosened the bloody garment enough for it to slide to the floor. As soon as her chest was bare, the chilled air of the room perked her nipples, and Kason turned to look at her, a mischievous look on his face. The heat of the bath beckoned, but the way Kason's gaze swept over her was hotter still. He licked his lips, rising onto his muscular legs and closing the distance between them.

"You are stunning, my fierce warrior." The depth of his voice sent shivers racing across her body. It wasn't just desire in his voice—it was reverence, and that undid her more than lust could have.

Reaching toward him, Holera untied the laces on Kason's tunic and tossed it to the floor, the filthy garment landing just beside hers. The sight of his bare tattooed chest and the rippled muscles of his stomach turned her mouth to sandpaper. She licked her lips, sliding her hands up his chest and around his neck. "You aren't so bad yourself."

Chuckling, he leaned forward and nuzzled into her neck, his mouth against her skin turning her molten. "When this is settled with the Warbotach prisoner, I'd like to take you back to my cabin for a visit—if you'd like to join me."

Nodding, she pulled away to look into his enchanting green eyes. "I'd like that a lot."

Holera reached to unfasten his trousers, but he placed his hand on top of hers, stopping her. "Let's get you a bath first. I'll clean up after."

He watched her eyes as he traced strong fingers from her collarbone, down to her stomach, resting them on the buckle to her trousers. Hesitating for a moment, there was a question in his eyes, a need for permission before going any further. Slipping her hand between them, she unclasped her buckle and pulled him into a kiss as her trousers hit the ground at her feet. Before she'd had a chance to react, Kason scooped her up in his arms and set her down in the deliciously warm water.

Instead of getting in the tub behind her, since it wouldn't have been big enough for the two of them anyway, Kason pulled a stool behind her head and sat down. "Do you want me to wash your hair?"

Although she'd never had another person bathe her, aside from her mother when she was a child, she nodded, closing her eyes as she leaned back. Scooping up water with a cup, Kason poured it slowly over her hair and shoulders, the sensation of the warm water cascading down her body relaxing her nearly to the point of putting her to sleep. She groaned as the scent of lavender hit her nose, the fragrance clinging to the steam, blending with the warmth of his touch until she melted beneath his hands. His deft fingers massaged it into her scalp.

"You shouldn't spoil me like this. I'm going to have a hard time settling for washing my own hair after this."

Kason chuckled and leaned over to kiss her on the shoulder. "I'll spoil you as long as you let me."

Cracking her eyes open, she turned around to face him. "That's quite a commitment."

The look in his eyes was genuine, cherishing even. "It is a commitment, but it's a commitment I want to make to you if you'll have me as your mate." The words, spoken so simply, carried more weight than any vow she had ever heard.

Chapter Eighteen

Kason

Sliding her damp hand around his neck, Holera pulled his lips to hers, kissing him deeper than she ever had before. When she pulled away, Kason was halfway in the bathtub with her, the arms of his tunic soaked. He chuckled, straightening as he peeled off the damp garment and tossed it to the floor. Standing in the tub, Holera's damp silver hair rested over her full breasts as water cascaded over her curves. Droplets tracked down the slope of her stomach, glinting in the candlelight. Just looking at her turned Kason's mouth to sandpaper, stiffening his cock until it pressed uncomfortably against the seam of his trousers. He stepped forward, grabbing the towel from the side of the tub and wrapping it around her body before lifting her and carrying her into the bedchamber. The towel clung to her damp skin, heat radiating through the fabric and straight into his hands.

"Do you want me to set you on the floor or the bed?"

Leaning forward, Holera nuzzled into his neck. "The bed."

Her voice was nothing more than a purr against his skin and he took no more convincing, taking the last few steps to the bed and setting her down, hesitating only a moment before climbing onto the bed next to her.

"Are you sure you want to be my mate, Kason? Even with how little we know each other?" Her voice carried both steel and hesitation, the kind of question only someone who had lost too much before would ask.

Cupping her cheek with his hand, he kissed her, lingering as her scent filled his nose. "I've never been surer about anything. I knew the moment we first touched when we were in the courtyard. I knew I would give you anything."

Her violet eyes watched him for a moment before she spoke and he waited, not wanting to rush her decision. No matter what she decided, he would respect it. "What about your travels? Will I ever see you?"

He chuckled. If that was her biggest concern, it would be an easy fix. "After decades as an Aegrician emissary, I'm tired of always being on the road or on a ship. If I could trade that life for one with you as my companion and my lover, I would make that trade without thought. It's not even a question."

Sliding her hand up his chest and around his back, she pulled him on top of her, Kason settling his hips between her thighs. He'd thought they would take things slower, but if she was ready for more, he had no intention of denying her or himself. She was perfect, and she was under him. He would have been a fool to turn her away.

"We definitely need time to learn more about each other," she said, pulling him into another kiss.

When she licked the seam of his lips, the groan that left him was full of need. The taste of her was intoxicating. Opening for her, his mind got lost in the slide of her tongue against his, of the warmth of the apex of her thighs against the bulge in his trousers. The garment was maddening, but he didn't dare remove that final barrier between their bodies, not until she asked him to. Every muscle in his body screamed to tear the fabric away, but her choice mattered more than his need.

When they came up for air, they were both panting. "I look forward to learning everything I can about you until the day I die."

He stifled a chuckle as a smirk spread across her face. "Which could have happened tonight, and I would have been very upset, so no more listening to Exie's wild ideas." Wrapping her legs around his waist, she ground herself against him, nearly making him lose himself completely. "I didn't wait this long for a mate for him to be taken away before I even got to feel him inside me." Her bluntness set his blood on fire, her need stripping away every wall he might have built.

At that moment, he no longer cared about the Warbotach prisoner, or anything beside the female beneath him. In a short amount of time, she'd become the only thing that mattered in his life, and he was okay with that. "Otera can do what she pleases with those prisoners, and I will take your advice on any wild schemes in the future."

"Good," was all she said as she pulled him into another kiss, her hands sliding between them to unbuckle his trousers, the moment a desperate relief when the clasp came loose and her fingers wrapped around his aching cock. "Can you help take these off for me?" She didn't have to ask him twice. His trousers hit the ground next to the bed before she'd even had a chance to move her hand. The cool air barely touched him before her warmth drew him back under.

CHAPTER NINETEEN

HOLERA

No matter how long they'd known each other, having Kason's skin against hers just felt right, like it was how it should have always been. Every line of his body against hers felt fated, as if the bond had been written into her skin long before they touched. The fact that his body was delicious, well-endowed and with the bulk of a seasoned warrior, only tempted Holera more, making it impossible for her to slow the progression of their night.

Tossing his trousers to the floor, Kason lowered himself over her, his hardened length sliding against her center as he nuzzled into her neck, kissing and licking, the tenderness of the touches setting her aflame. She writhed beneath him, seeking out the friction of his body where she was the most sensitive, the desperate need to be filled consuming her.

Running her fingers up the corded muscles of his back, she luxuriated in the tenderness of his lips on her as he trailed kisses down the column of her neck. His hands explored her curves, cupping her breasts and feeding the taut peak into his mouth. Breath burst out of her when the warmth of his mouth wrapped around her nipple, a surge of pleasure shooting through her body. The sound that tore from her lips was raw, unrestrained, too primal to be contained.

There was no question Kason knew his way around the female form, but she couldn't even spare a moment for jealousy when the culmination of his experience was being used to pleasure her, and would be until he took his last breath. No matter where they'd been before, they'd committed themselves to each other. A mating bond wasn't something their kind took lightly. It was for life. The certainty of that truth wrapped around her as surely as his arms did, steadying her even as her body burned.

"I need you inside of me." Her breath came out as a breathy plea, the rub of his cock against her folds driving her near the edge. "Now."

They had the rest of their lives to take their time, but in that moment, she could no longer wait. Sliding her hand between them, she gripped his cock, fitting it at her entrance. He kissed her as he worked himself inside. The tightness of the fit was exquisite. Her body stretched around him, pleasure and pressure mingling until the line between the two blurred. Relief flooded through her body as Kason's hardness filled her completely. She moaned, every thrust driving her to the edge of ecstasy.

Hooking her leg around his waist, he pulled her against his chest, falling back on his heels as she straddled him. He lifted her, driving his hips up as he pulled her down, the thickness of him forcing the coil low in her belly to twist tighter, threatening to snap.

Slipping her hand in his shoulder-length hair, Holera freed it from the tie binding it and twisted her hand in the thick locks before pulling him to her lips. Kason kissed her deeply, slowing his movements as his tongue caressed hers, the tenderness of it making her moan into his mouth.

Never leaving her body, he laid her back onto her back, his hips rolling into her as her climax built with every thrust. "I want to watch you cum for me," he said as he pulled out of their kiss, the green of his eyes deepening as they locked on hers. "You're so beautiful like this."

His strong hands slid beneath her hips, lifting them slightly, the new angle shattering the coil inside her as her climax hit her with the force of a tidal wave. Her vision blurred, stars sparking behind her eyes as the world narrowed to the heat of his body and the sound of his voice. Sweat dripped from his brow as their eyes remained locked on each other, the intensity of the moment only strengthening her orgasm. The sounds coming from her were loud enough to have been heard from down the hall, but she didn't care.

Burying his face in her neck, Kason's movements became erratic as he reached his own climax, her name on his lips as he collapsed over her. For a few moments, the only sound in the room was heavy breathing as they remained wrapped in each other's arms, trying to catch their breaths. The release drained all of Holera's remaining energy from her and she allowed her eyes to close, falling asleep in her mate's arms for the first time. Safe, claimed, and cherished, she drifted into sleep with his heartbeat steady against her ear.

Chapter Twenty

Kason

Waking up with his mate in his arms and tucked against his chest was how Kason hoped to wake up every morning for the rest of his life. Even with everything that had unfolded at the party, their night together had been perfect. She was everything he could have ever wanted in a female. For the first time in centuries, he felt content, as though fate had finally stopped testing him.

He watched as Holera slept, her chest rising and falling with gentle breaths. Although he knew they needed to get back to the palace, the darkness outside telling him they'd slept through the day, he didn't want to wake her. After only a short time, however, she sighed as she woke, stretching her long limbs and smiling up at him.

Tucking her silver hair behind her ear, Kason leaned forward and kissed her on the cheek. "Good morning, beautiful. How did you sleep?" Holera grinned, pulling him to her and kissing him, her soft lips lingering on his for a long moment, until his cock hardened against her thigh. "After the night we had, I slept like a baby."

At the thought that it was his lovemaking that had made her satisfied enough to sleep well, Kason smirked, the expression purely wicked as he leaned in to kiss her again, this time with unbridled passion.

He groaned against her mouth, the feeling of her tongue against his lips, her tongue, caressing his, only reminding him of how badly he wanted to kiss her in other places. His mate had not been patient the night before and had insisted he sheath himself inside her before he'd been ready. If he'd had it his way, he would have worshiped all of her. He would have kissed every inch of her, worshiped her with his tongue until she cried his name to the rafters, but she had not been patient, therefore he had not been able to taste her yet.

Deciding he couldn't go another moment without having the taste of his mate on his tongue, Kason pulled away from her lips and trailed kisses down her neck, and then moved lower, stopping to kiss and lick her perfect breasts. He settled there for a moment, sliding his body down hers until he could put his face against the pillow softness of her chest and give each of her nipples the attention they deserved. Caressing one with his hand, he fed the other into his mouth and sucked on it gently, twirling his tongue around the tight peak as she moaned and writhed beneath him.

"I was thinking we needed to get back to the palace when we woke," he said, his words no more than a breathy growl. "But then I looked at you and was taken aback by your beauty, and then I remembered that I hadn't gotten to taste you everywhere, so I need to do that before we go anywhere or I may not be able to survive the day."

Holera giggled, bucking her hips as he slid down her body further, settling his shoulders at her thighs. "Are you telling me you would truly die if you didn't taste me this morning, my mate?"

Instead of responding, he decided to show her how badly he wanted to taste her and lifted her leg, putting it over his shoulder and giving himself better access for when he leaned forward, licking her folds, groaning at how perfect the taste of her was. She arched into him, the sound of her pleasure filling the chamber like music meant only for him.

Breath burst out of Holera's beautiful mouth as he licked her a second time, going all the way up to the bundle of nerves and sucking gently on them, knowing that was the spot that would drive her to the edge. "I'm glad to be able to kee-eep you alive then, my ma-te."

Holera's words stuttered out as he devoured her cunt, and the taste of her on his tongue, the smell of her arousal, had him grinding against the bed, desperate to be inside her again. Slipping two fingers into her channel, he licked and sucked on her in steady strokes, knowing exactly what he needed to do to bring her over the edge. "I want you to cum for me, my fierce warrior."

Breathy moans leaving her lips, Holera's hips bucked and writhed as she tried to increase the friction against his face. She fucked his fingers and his tongue until her body stiffened, her legs squeezing around his head as a flood of intoxicating wetness hit his tongue, and she fell limp and panting. The intensity of her release had him gripping her thighs, holding her to his mouth as if he could drink her in forever.

He thought she would need a moment to recover from her orgasm, but as he tried to crawl over her, Holera pulled him to her, flipping him onto his back and straddling him. Her movements were so desperate, so determined, as she reached between them, gripping his cock in her hand, and sliding down onto it, their bodies fitting together as though they were made for each other. Her silver hair tumbled forward around them like a curtain, her violet eyes blazing with hunger and something deeper—claiming.

Chapter Twenty-One

Holera

Still in an orgasm-induced high, Kason and Holera dressed and made their way back to the palace. Although they would have preferred to remain in bed as a newly-mated couple, they had obligations to their kingdom that couldn't be ignored. The weight of duty pressed heavier than any sleepless night, though Holera couldn't help wishing she was still tangled in Kason's arms. Holera just hoped they were allowed more time alone once the situation with Warbotach was settled.

Arriving back at the palace gates, not only had more guards been posted around the perimeter, but phoenix warriors soared through the sky between the palace and the harbor. The air itself felt tense, thick with the threat of war.

"I was hoping this conflict would be resolved by the time we returned," Holera said, drawing a chuckle out of Kason.

"I was hoping the same, but hopefully a resolution is at least in the works."

Holera nodded as they crossed the lawns of the palace and entered through the front doors as a guard held them open. Although a resolution may have been in the works, which she did not doubt, she also realized any solution would end up being short lived. Warbotach always leaned toward being aggressive in their relations with other kingdoms, and Otera wasn't one to show weakness. Aegricia had to uphold their reputation of being a strong kingdom. Being the only kingdom on their continent ruled by a female, there was always a risk of their land being taken over again.

Traveling down the corridor toward the queen's meeting room, Holera reached for the door handle just as Exie was walking out, nearly knocking her over.

"Oh! Sorry!" Exie said, holding the door open for them to enter. "Where have you two been?"

There had been more than a little mischief in Exie's smirk. Holera scowled at her, not wanting the queen, or anyone else in the room, questioning her personal life. Exie's mischief always came at the worst times, and Holera could feel her cheeks heating under the queen's gaze. Even before she'd had a mate, she'd never been someone who discussed her sex life, aside from with her closest friends.

"I have to deliver a message. I'll be back soon."

Exie darted off before they'd had a chance to respond.

Looking up from the long table that took up much of the room as they entered, the side of Otera's mouth lifted in a strained smile. Her crimson hair caught the lamplight like fire, but the weariness in her eyes betrayed how much the crown cost her. A gentle hand grazed the small of Holera's back as Kason circled behind her and approached the queen's side, peering over the table where a number of parchments and other various items were strewn about.

"Has Warbotach made a move yet?" he asked.

Otera shook her head.
"I just sent a letter to King Uldon, notifying him of the events of the past few days. Their merchant ship has been causing a scene at the harbor, but there has been no more violence."

Loosening a breath, the queen lowered herself onto a chair. "We will let their ship go soon and hope they don't cause any more trouble. The prisoners will be detained for now, although the injured male is in critical condition. He won't be able to travel anytime soon. If it wasn't for their metalworks and glassware, I would cut off trade with Warbotach altogether. Sometimes I wonder if it's worth the stress."

Kason pulled out a chair for Holera to sit just as a servant entered with a decanter, filling their empty glasses. They sat beside each other, leaving little question about their blooming relationship, although Otera paid little mind.

Taking a deep sip of his whiskey, Kason cleared his throat. "If we need to, we could try to establish a trade agreement with one of the other kingdoms to the south, perhaps pay a tax to exchange goods there. I wouldn't recommend going through Diapolis due to the distance and the king's isolationist policies, but Norithae would be willing."

Tapping her fingers on the table, it was clear Otera was debating his suggestion by the way her eyebrows furrowed.

"If we did trade through Norithae, it would benefit Warbotach as well. They wouldn't need to travel as far when making their routes."

Setting her glass back down on the table, Holera watched as Exie walked back into the room and whispered in the queen's ear. Otera listened closely, returning her eyes to Kason as Exie moved aside.

"Blaedia and others are near the harbor. Please inform them to allow the ship to leave—if they're even willing to leave without the others."

Holera's stomach knotted. Letting the Warbotach ship sail away felt too much like loosing a beast back into the wild.

Chapter Twenty-Two

Kason

Sparing not a moment longer, Kason and Holera left the meeting room and headed for the palace courtyard. They made it outside quickly and Holera shifted in a flash of fire, allowing Kason to climb onto her back before launching them into the sky. The wind tore at his hair as they rose, the palace shrinking beneath them, the city bristling with unease. The sun was bright, warming the air and giving Holera's silver wings an ethereal glow.

Soaring through the air, Kason watched as several phoenixes patrolled the city, both on foot and by air. The highest concentration of warriors and guards were in the harbor, at least a dozen surrounding the Warbotach ship as its sailors stormed about the deck, preparing to sail as soon as they were able. The shouts of sailors carried even to their height, sharp and angry, the clatter of crates and chains echoing off the water.

Just as Kason caught sight of Blaedia standing guard near the tree line, Holera leveled her great wings, slowing them as they lowered to the ground.

As soon as Holera's talons met the dirt, Kason slid off her back, waiting at his mate's side as she shifted back into a beautiful, silver-haired female. He watched her as she adjusted her clothes, amazed at how seamlessly she was able to transform from one fierce creature to another. Her silver hair shimmered in the sunlight, every strand gleaming as if dusted with frost. Smoothing out her cloak, she grinned at him, sliding her hand into his as they gave their attention to her general.

Turning toward them, Blaedia sheathed her sword. Another warrior stood by her side. Kason had not yet met the female, but the pin she wore on her cloak's collar told him she was a commander. Her near-silver eyes were sharp and assessing, cool as steel as though she weighed every word before it was spoken.

"Do you bring words from Otera?" Blaedia asked, tension clear on her face. Her jaw was clenched, her hand never straying far from the hilt of her blade. Being the queen's mate could not have been an easy position, especially in times of possible war.

"We just left the palace. The injured prisoner survived surgery, but he is still in critical condition," Holera said, taking her weapons from Kason and securing her bow and quiver over her shoulder, before sheathing her sword. "Otera has sent word to the Warbotach king, letting him know why his two merchants were arrested and detained. The letter also explained that we do not want war. However, we'll be keeping the two prisoners until Otera is satisfied that they were not planning to harm Exie and me when they were caught following us after we'd left the tavern. We have still not been able to discover what their intent was that night. She also said that if the ship is willing to leave without the two prisoners, then they can go back to Warbotach."

"And if they return?" the commander asked, her near-silver eyes scanning them before turning toward the harbor.

"If they return, then we fight."

Pulling her blade back out as though she couldn't decide her next course of action, the general let her arm fall at her side, the tip of her sword digging into the ground.

"Then we should get this over with and go instruct the barbarians of the queen's plans so they can get out of our harbor. I know we would all like to move on with our lives. Kason," she said, turning to look at him. "You'll need to stay behind since you sliced up a few of their men last time you boarded their ship."

Although he hadn't missed the way his mate rolled her eyes, Kason couldn't help but smirk, not because he enjoyed killing, but because the general had said it as though he'd been a naughty child. "It would definitely be best for Exie and I to stay far away from that ship."

When the general turned back to the commander, there was no longer indecision on her face. "You, Holera, and I will go to the ship. With any luck, they'll leave and never come back."

Luck had been in short supply, Holera thought grimly, but she squared her shoulders and followed.

CHAPTER TWENTY-THREE

HOLERA

Kissing Kason goodbye, Holera left her new mate in the forest as she, Taryn, and Blaedia headed toward the harbor on foot. She hadn't wanted to leave him behind, the new bond between them making it nearly impossible for them to be apart. The thread of the mating bond tugged at her chest with every step away from him, a constant reminder of what she was leaving behind. Still, she had a duty to her kingdom as a born warrior, so when Blaedia asked her to provide backup as the Warbotach sailors were notified of the queen's decision, she had no choice but to follow.

Queen Otera's decision was fair, at least from Holera's perspective. Warbotach could leave Aegricia and sail back to their kingdom at the southwestern tip of the continent, but the two prisoners would not be able to join them, not until Otera was satisfied with their explanations of why they'd followed two of her warriors. If the queen believed the merchants had planned to harm her warriors, they would pay with their lives.

Although the harbor had quieted down, the Warbotach merchants now readying their ship instead of antagonizing the Aegrician guards, the area was still filled with a noticeable tension. The air tasted metallic, like the bite of a blade just before it was drawn. It was a difficult situation to manage, and Holera didn't envy her queen in having to navigate it. No matter what decision she made, there would be backlash.

Leading them toward the docks, Blaedia made her way around the guards and warriors stationed there, each with their hands on the hilts of their swords. Their eyes never left the ship, and their bodies were taut as bowstrings.

"I'll go up alone but remain close. I'm hoping the fewer people involved in the resolution, the less likely we'll have pushback."

Taryn and Holera nodded but did not follow their general as she walked up the ramp and toward the deck of the Warbotach ship. If Blaedia felt any unease, it didn't show on her face as she stood only a few feet away from the Warbotach captain.

Noticing the grimace on her commander's face, Holera stifled a grin. Glancing ahead at the barbarian speaking with their general, she knew exactly why Taryn was making such a face, although she hid it well.

Blaedia was so put together, her hair shiny and sharp as a blade, her clothing immaculate. The Warbotach captain, on the other hand, looked as though he'd clawed his way out of a trash heap, hair matted and armor stained with sweat and grime. The barbarian race may have been fae, just like the rest of Ekotoria, but their people couldn't have been more different.

They stood there for several long moments, Holera and Taryn watching over their general as she relayed the queen's message. From the look on the Warbotach male's scarred face, Holera couldn't tell whether he was angry or content. She strained her ears, trying to hear what the two leaders were saying, but their voices did not carry on the breeze. She may have had strong hearing, but they were talking much too low for her to make out any of it.

The longer Blaedia stood in front of the Warbotach ship as the sailors readied the craft to sail in the background, the tighter Holera's chest became. Her hand drifted to the hilt of her sword, though she knew steel would be too slow if the captain chose violence. They may have been surrounded by armed guards, but it would only take a second for the Warbotach captain to strike against their general, and they were too far away to stop it.

In the corner of her eye, Holera watched as Taryn shifted on her feet, the commander clearly growing restless as well. When she turned her eyes back to the ship, Holera's blood turned to ice as her fear was realized. Blaedia no longer stood face-to-face with the ship's captain. Instead, he had her back flush against his chest, a blade held to her throat. Holera's stomach dropped. Every muscle in her body screamed to act, but the distance between them might as well have been a canyon. The barbarians were going to try to hold her hostage.

CHAPTER TWENTY-FOUR

KASON

Kason clenched his teeth as his mate walked away and into the danger brewing in the harbor. Although he'd wanted to follow her, he knew it would have only put her at more risk. Every instinct in his body screamed to follow her, but instinct had to bow to reason. After he and Exie had created chaos on the Warbotach ship, killing two of their people and capturing another, he knew his presence would only anger them more.

Straining his eyes to see into the distance, he watched the entire scene unfold. He saw how the Warbotach captain had flipped Blaedia's back against him and pressed a dagger against her throat. With the general's extensive fighting and negotiation skills, he trusted Blaedia enough to know surrender was part of her strategy, not weakness. He didn't know what had been discussed in their conversation, but he believed she had a plan.

Hands clenched into fists at his side, Kason fought the urge to sprint toward the harbor and protect his mate, but before he'd had the chance to take that first step, Holera turned, her long legs sprinting forward and racing back in his direction. Her braid streamed behind her like a silver banner, her face carved with resolve.

"What the fuck happened?" The words left his lips as soon as his mate's eyes met his, the violet blazing to a near silver in the sun. There was so much tension in her face that he regretted his demanding words.

"There's no time for explanations," she responded, checking that her weapons were secure at her back before placing a kiss on his lips. "Taryn wants us to follow the ship. Shoot to kill, but don't endanger Blaedia."

Although Kason knew the general would have never wanted them to endanger more warriors at her expense, he nodded.

Without another word, his mate shifted into her phoenix form, dipping her head low for him to climb onto her back. Only a moment later, she launched them into the air.

Notching an arrow in his bow, Kason spotted the Warbotach ship in the distance, the wind and current having already taken it miles offshore. Other phoenixes already soared in the sky around the craft, but Blaedia was no longer visible.

"They must have taken her below deck," he said. Holera couldn't respond in her phoenix form, but she could hear him.

Her wings flared, taking them higher into the clouds. Circling the ship from a safe distance, away from the arrows sailing into the sky from below, Kason scanned the upper decks, looking for the general and counting the ship's crew.

No less than thirty armed sailors moved around the craft. The deck bristled with blades and bows, a wall of bodies ready to kill rather than yield. All thoughts of peace were over as they launched their arrows at the Aegricians. The phoenix warriors were well-trained, agile as they dove and circled, the arrows missing their targets every time. Each beast held a rider, someone on their back, using their weapons to dispatch the enemy below.

An arrow narrowly missed Holera's wing and Kason screamed, alerting her just in time to fly out of the way. The shaft grazed so close he swore he felt the wind of it across his cheek. His arrow shot toward the male who had tried to harm his mate, hitting him in the eye before he'd even had a chance to know he had become a target.

Caressing the feathers on Holera's neck, Kason leaned forward to kiss her. "There's no one on the eastern side of the deck. Swoop low and I'll jump onto the ship to look for Blaedia."

Fierce eyes met his as his mate's beautiful phoenix head looked back at him, a look telling him he was crazy and she didn't approve. The bond between them thrummed with her resistance, a silent roar of her disapproval.

Kason chuckled, amusement filling his eyes at the stubbornness of his new mate. "I'll be fine. In and out. You can swoop down and pick me up in a few minutes and then we can go back to my room so I can worship you."

CHAPTER TWENTY-FIVE

HOLERA

Although Holera hated the idea of her mate going back on the Warbotach ship, she had to admit that finding a way on the craft was the best way to get Blaedia back. With all the phoenixes circling over the ship, the Warbotach merchants had their eyes on the sky, shooting arrows at the massive birds. There were very few of the enemy paying attention to the deck itself, especially the rear. Still, Holera's chest tightened. Every instinct screamed to shield her mate, not deliver him back into the viper's den.

Letting out a call the other phoenix warriors would understand, Holera flared her wings, taking them into the sky and away from the chaotic scene. Before she could land on the back of the ship, she had to make sure all eyes were off her. Lowering them into the trees, she did just that.

Holera landed on the ground, needing to shift back into her fae form quickly so she and Kason could talk about their plan. As soon as she landed on the leaf-littered ground, the scent of damp earth and pine clung to the clearing, grounding her for a heartbeat before the storm ahead. Her mate jumped off her back. She shifted a moment later.

Slinging his bow over his back, Kason grinned at her as he closed the distance between them and pulled her into a kiss. She submitted fully to him, knowing it could be the last time he held her if their rescue attempt went wrong. The thought sliced through her resolve, making her cling harder, memorizing the heat of his mouth.

When they parted, Holera was breathless.
"We need to come up with a plan. I don't like the idea of sending you onto that ship again, not after what happened last time."

Kason grinned, the gesture filled with confidence.
"I'll be fine. I have too much to live for now." The conviction in his tone steadied her even as it infuriated her, because she knew he meant her.

Wrapping his muscular arm around her waist, he pulled her in close again, kissing her on the neck. The intimate touch made her want to pull down his pants and ride him right where they stood, but her obligation to Blaedia urged her to pull away.

"We'll try to sneak up on the ship, but I'm going with you."

Before she'd even finished her statement, Kason was already shaking his head.
"Let me go in alone while you circle to the south. I won't be long. There's no reason to put you in danger, my fierce warrior."

Just the thought of sending him in alone turned her stomach.
"I'll stay on the back deck and keep watch, but I'm not leaving that ship without you." Her voice was iron. No amount of persuasion would move her from his side.

Before he could argue, Holera shifted back into her phoenix form, nuzzling her beak into his leg. He stroked her feathers, smirking as he climbed onto her back.
"Although I've only known you for a short time, I feel like I'll never win an argument with you."

She couldn't laugh in her phoenix form, but she let out a chitter as she spread her great silver wings and launched them into the air.

Soaring above the tree canopy, Holera cut further to the south, her silver wings nearly invisible in the gray sky as she aimed like a dart for the back of the ship. As had been the case before, all the Warbotach sailors were near the front of the ship. The phoenixes continued to fly in an unpredictable pattern while their riders fired arrows at the enemy. She watched as one of her friends, Andrianna, dove toward the bow of the ship, plucking up one of the Warbotach males and dropping him into the sea.

Swooping low over the water, Holera lifted them just as they neared the rear of the ship, landing on the deck with a near silent thump. Kason slid off her back, drawing his sword from its sheath and scanning their surroundings. The planks groaned beneath their boots, the smell of salt and tar thick in the air. Every shadow felt like an enemy waiting to strike. Holera shifted, standing on the tips of her toes and kissing her mate on the lips.

"If you make it back to me safely, I'll suck your cock when we get back to the room."

Giving her one more heated look, a growl rumbled out of Kason's chest as he crept toward the stairs that would lead him to the lower deck.

Chapter Twenty-Six

Kason

Leaving his mate on the back deck and hoping no Warbotach scum found her there, Kason moved on silent feet toward the stairs that would lead him below deck. The bond thrummed faintly at his chest, Holera's presence tugging like a lifeline even as he forced himself away from her. With the total chaos on the front of the ship, no one seemed to notice him as he disappeared into the darkened stairwell. Well, he hoped no one noticed.

Although Kason had been on a merchant ship before, the shadowed space was difficult to map out. Peeking inside each door on the first level as he passed, Kason quickly realized that Blaedia was probably locked up on a lower level. He also realized the more levels below deck he went, the more likely he would get caught.

Scanning the corridor around him and not seeing anyone, Kason turned the doorknob for the stairs that would lead him to the lower levels. The door let out a low squeal as he shut it behind himself and headed down the narrow staircase.

With as broad as his shoulders were, claustrophobia hit him quickly, tightening his breaths, but he continued to descend. They always made his lungs fail to pull in enough oxygen. Sweat broke across his brow, not from heat but from the walls pressing too close.

The smell of musk and urine hit him hard as he rounded the last turn into the bowels of the ship. The reek clawed down his throat, making his stomach lurch as bile threatened to rise. Fighting the urge, Kason took the candle closest to the stairs and stepped further into the dank, dark space. With no light from windows, the lowest level of the craft was heavily shadowed, making it difficult to see. He passed each crate and barrel, remaining vigilant just in case an enemy was waiting to ambush him.

As he approached the back of the space, the hold appeared, the figure of a female standing inside.

"Blaedia?" Keeping his voice at a whisper, he took the last remaining steps forward toward the cage the Aegrician general was being held in. "Are you okay?"

She jolted at the sound of his voice, her silver eyes wide as she met his. Aside from blood dripping from a gash on her arm and a busted lip, Blaedia appeared to be unharmed. Her stance was still proud, her gaze unbroken — the look of a warrior who would die on her feet before she begged. With her fae blood, the wounds she had would heal quickly.

"Kason? What are you doing here?" Although he would have expected the general to be relieved to see him, she seemed agitated. "Please don't tell me my military is putting lives at risk for me. They know better." Her tone cracked like a whip, even weakened, as though discipline itself kept her upright.

Kason chuckled as he fumbled with the lock on her cell. "They may know better, but even if they refused to go after you, the queen wouldn't have let Warbotach take you."

Just thinking about Holera being in that cage, Kason knew he would've made the same decision. The thought made his blood boil; he would have burned the ship to ash to keep her safe.

The cell was locked, but he had become a master at picking locks, so it only took him a minute and a small tool from his pocket before the door swung open. Not hesitating for a moment, Blaedia stepped out of the cage.

"They've got my weapons," she said, reaching for a sword that wasn't there.

Pulling a short sword from the scabbard at his waist, Kason handed it to her. "I can't guarantee we'll find yours, but you can use this one for now."

Blaedia took the weapon, holding it at the ready as they began walking toward the stairway, but before they took more than a few steps, muffled voices met Kason's ears.

Grabbing Blaedia by the arm, he pulled her behind a stack of crates, quieting his breaths as they watched the bottom of the stairway, waiting to see who came inside. Every second stretched, the shadows heavy with the promise of violence.

CHAPTER TWENTY-SEVEN

Holera

While Kason crept below deck, Holera remained on the back of the ship, crouching behind crates to observe the chaos on the bow. She'd believed that all the Warbotach merchants were entangled with the phoenixes pursuing them from the air. So, when an arm grabbed her from behind, and a dagger's blade pressed into her neck, she was completely caught off guard.

"Well, well. Aren't you a pretty thing?" he snarled, forcing her to step forward. "Walk, cunt. Let's go get reunited with your general."

Despite her desire to fight back, Holera knew better. In such a vulnerable position, she would die if she lashed out. She had too much to live for to be reckless.

With the Warbotach beast's blade at her throat, she took small steps toward the stairway leading to the lower levels. As she took each step down, she held her back straight to prevent her flesh from being cut by his knife.

Throughout the lower decks, they passed several doors, but the man behind Holera kept leading her forward into the ship's deepest interior.

In the dark, her attention was fixed on the level below them as they neared the opening to the bottom. Assuming the hold was on this level, she hoped Kason had managed to free their general by the time she and her captor entered. As she took those last few steps and the floor of the dungeon came into view, her ears almost missed the hushed conversation between her general and her mate.

When Holera realized Kason and Blaedia were still there, her heart sank into her stomach. They had not escaped.

In a last desperate attempt to stall, she shoved her backside back into the male behind her, nearly sending him to the ground. Blood trickled down her throat where the blade had dug in just enough to cut her.

"Stand up straight and walk, you dumb cunt," he growled, the beast's hot breath smelling of stale whiskey and tooth decay as it flickered across her cheek, nearly making her vomit.

As she walked into the dungeon with the male behind her, Holera peered into the darkness. She scanned the darkened space for her mate and her general, but they weren't there, or at least they weren't visible. Her relief lasted only for a moment as the male behind her leapt forward, cursing and pushing her to the ground. As the guard approached the empty cage where she assumed Blaedia had been kept, he growled and swung his fist at the metal. The crack of his fist against the metal reverberated against the cavernous space, making her flinch.

Setting his angry stare on Holera, the guard moved toward her as though he intended to kill her. With no hesitation, she pulled her dagger from its sheath at her thigh. She skittered back, trying to get back to her feet. Before he reached her, however, an arrow flew through the air from the other side of the room and struck the beast in the temple. As soon as the arrow penetrated his brain, Holera's attacker fell to the ground in a heap, his eyes staring at her vacantly.

As soon as her attacker fell, Kason's broad shoulders moved out from behind a stack of crates. He closed the space between them in an instant and pulled her into his arms.

"We have to get out of here," he said. "Fast. Blaedia has a plan, but we need to get off the ship as soon as possible."

Holera's heart beat like a war drum, the relief of seeing them gone at the mention of leaving Blaedia again. On the ground behind Kason, Blaedia lined up the whiskey bottles she'd pulled out of a crate.

Ignoring Kason's hand on her arm, Holera moved forward to assist her general with whatever task she was trying to accomplish. "What's the plan?" All three of them needed to get off the ship as soon as possible, and she didn't understand why they were stalling, but if Blaedia had a plan, she wanted to help.

Blaedia's silver eyes were filled with pure determination and annoyance when she lifted her eyes. "You and Kason need to get off the ship. That's an order," Her tone was demanding, expecting no arguments. Blaedia's attention returned to the task at her feet, but when her warrior didn't leave as commanded, the general lifted her gaze again, her features softening. "There's no need to worry, Holera. Yes, I'll get off too, but not before I light the ship on fire. There is no way these bastards are leaving Aegricia. When I leave this ship, they will burn to ash and sink into the sea."

Without further explanation, Kason grabbed Holera's hand and pulled her to the stairs. Within a few seconds, they were back on the top deck.

Putting aside her trepidation, Holera morphed into a phoenix and launched into the air with her mate on her back. As she flew, her massive silver wings worked hard to maneuver around the arrows flying overhead and to the rest of the phoenixes.

She gave a loud cry, ordering them to abandon the attack. As Holera moved out of the reach of the arrows, they followed without argument.

Working her wings as hard as she could, they soared through the sky, her mate leaning nearly flush against her back to remove any resistance against the wind. An explosion echoed through the air, the force of it throwing them forward. Leveling her wings to regain their balance, Holera turned to look behind them, hoping her general had made it out safely.

As she watched the horrific scene unfold, holding them steady as Kason smoothed his hand along her neck, a massive crimson and black phoenix pierced the cloud of smoke, Blaedia's wingspan creating a majestic silhouette against the bright orange flames of the burning ship.

Chapter Twenty-Eight

Kason

Once there was nothing left of the Warbotach ship but smoke trails in the air, nearly everyone had been swept up in damage control. After an extensive meeting with her top officials, Queen Otera agreed with the idea of fabricating an alternative story. She wanted to keep the truth from the enemy, so she announced that the ship had been lost at sea. Trusting their queen, the citizens accepted her story, though some may have been skeptical. The truth of what had happened remained a secret between the Queen and her advisors. Secrets this heavy had a way of surfacing eventually, but for now the lie gave Aegricia the illusion of safety.

The plan could only work if they were able to prevent her earlier message from reaching the Warbotach king, so Blaedia sent the fastest phoenix to intercept it, while the rest of their plan was put into place. Since the harbor had been blocked off by a perimeter of Aegrician guards and warriors, most of the people in the capital city, locals and travelers alike, had not seen what had happened over the water. With that hope in mind, an Aegrician ship was sent south with meticulous instructions on how to lay a false trail, to make it look as though the Warbotach craft had sunk on the high seas. With any luck, it would work. Still, Kason couldn't shake the feeling of unease whenever he looked east, toward the sea, as if the waves themselves carried whispers of vengeance.

He hoped Otera's plan would hold, but he knew better than to trust fragile peace. Conflict was always a tide—it came back eventually. When it did, Aegricia would need to be ready. For now, though, he and Holera needed time to themselves.

On the fourth day after the sinking of the enemy ship, Kason and Holera left Flamecliff behind, intending to take some time away. They headed to Holera's family home so he could meet her mother. Becoming mated was one of the most pivotal moments in a fae's life, and forging ties with her family was important. The thought made him more anxious than any battle—winning a mother's approval was a war of its own.

As they arrived in front of the wooden cottage, the sky was colored in an array of pastel shades accented by fluffy white clouds. The snow on the mountains had started to melt, but there were still white caps on the tallest peaks. A small stream cascaded down the side of the mountain, the sound of its running waters reminding him of a lullaby. For the first time in a long time, there was peace in the air.

Holera shifted back into her fae form, and Kason immediately moved to her side, taking her weapons and holding them for her as she led the way to the front door. The door swung open before they could touch the knob, and a tall silver-haired female stood in the doorway. Her violet eyes glistened with tears, and even before she spoke, Kason knew this was Holera's mother.

"Oh! I was so worried!" she cried as she closed the distance and pulled Holera into her arms. Watching them, Kason felt something stir in his chest. His mate was his everything, and seeing her loved so fiercely by her mother filled him with warmth. It also carved an ache in him, a reminder that he had no family left.

They stayed like that for a few moments until the matriarch finally let go. Wiping her eyes, she turned her attention to him. A grin spread across her face, and as if to say she approved, she gave him a knowing nod. Kason straightened unconsciously, pride stirring in his chest.

"I thought I'd smelled a mate bond on my daughter," she said as she squeezed Holera's hands and smiled at them both, unconditional love in her eyes. "Should congratulations be in order, my beloved daughter? Who is this handsome male you've brought home to meet me?"

Holera stepped aside, raising one of her hands to take his. "Kason, this is my mother, Aura. Mother, I would like you to meet Kason, my mate."

Beaming with a brilliant smile, Aura stepped forward. Her irises were a darker violet than Holera's but no less enchanting. She reached out and wrapped her arms around Kason. He stiffened for the briefest moment, unaccustomed to such maternal warmth, then let himself sink into it. For a male who had spent decades with no family, her embrace nearly undid him. When Aura stepped back, her eyes were bright with joy.

"I am so glad to meet you, Kason. I've been hoping for Holera to find a suitable male for a long time. If the bond has clicked into place, then you surely must be the finest of males."

Her words, spoken without hesitation, sank deep into him—a blessing more powerful than any oath.

Epilogue

Kason

Having spent two days with Holera's mother, Kason and Holera set off for Holera's cabin in the mountains for the first time. In the short time since they met, he'd told her about his cabin, but now he was looking forward to showing it to her. He was excited for them to finally spend some time alone.

The excitement in his heart was palpable as they crested the last cliff, and he captured his first glimpse of his property while they soared through the clouds on her magnificent silver wings.

"We're home, my fierce warrior," he said as he stroked the feathers on her neck, then leaned forward to kiss her. The words felt heavier than he intended, but true—this place was no longer just his, it was theirs. Making the cooing sound that was her approval, she bent her head back to rub it on his knee.

Minutes later, they landed near the creek on the edge of his land, and he dismounted, standing aside as she transformed into her stunning fae form. Closing the distance between them, he lifted her into his arms and pressed his lips to hers. A spark of electricity coursed through his veins the moment she melted in his arms. A fire ignited in his heart every time she touched him, one he knew would never go out. He pulled away reluctantly, her kiss leaving him breathless as he hurried to the front door.

Holera giggled, stroking his hair that had broken loose from its tie. "Are you excited about something, my mate?"

With a grunt, he turned the knob and stormed inside, kicking the door shut behind him. "You told me you would suck my cock once the battle was over," he said with no shame. The memory of her promise had burned through his mind during every clash of steel, every arrow fired—survival itself had hinged on it. Although she laughed harder, he was not deterred. Passing through the rooms, he did not stop to give her a tour before entering his bedroom.

"So that's what all the rush is about? You think I'm going to suck your cock? Well…" She paused just long enough to make his stomach clench. "That's what I said, isn't it?"

Upon entering the room, he kicked off his boots and set her down on the bed. As she pulled her tunic over her head and tossed it to the ground, her face was pure feline mischief. "What would you be willing to do for me?"

Chuckling, he tossed his weapons on the floor, not paying attention to where they landed before dropping his tunic beside them. "My beautiful mate, I will do anything and everything to make you happy."

To his surprise, she scooted forward on the bed, unclasping his trousers' buckle before pulling them down his hips. Already pulsing with need, his cock sprung free. A flare of excitement filled her eyes as she dipped her head closer and rubbed her tongue over the length of his shaft.

"Is this what you want?" she purred as she leaned forward and wrapped her mouth around its swollen tip, the feeling of it forcing a gasp from deep in his chest.

Unable to form words, he nodded and slipped his fingers into her hair, pulling the band out so that her silver locks flowed freely across her back.

His hands fisted in her hair as her lips encased him, squeezing and licking and drawing out a guttural moan of pleasure. The glint in her violet eyes nearly undid him more than her mouth did. His hips bucked, pushing against her eager mouth as he felt himself nearing his peak.

Although he'd always prided himself on having good stamina, he knew if she didn't stop immediately, he was going to spill his seed into her mouth. Although he tried to pull away so he could get his head between her legs and devour her until she climaxed first, she wouldn't let him.

With her arms around him, she clung to his backside and pulled him closer, sucking and caressing him with her exquisite mouth until he was on the verge of exploding. He clenched his teeth, trying to delay the inevitable, but he couldn't.

"Stop. I'm about to," he huffed out, but she shook her head, eyes flicking up to look at him as her lips stretched around his cock.

As she massaged his balls, she sucked him in deeper, his cock hitting the back of her throat. It was too much for him to bear. His orgasm hit him like an explosion, the release ripping through him like lightning, stealing the air from his lungs. His eyes rolled back in his head as he rode the waves of it. As he emptied himself into her mouth, she licked up every last drop, seeming to savor the taste of him. When he was completely spent and panting, he collapsed back onto the bed and she crawled up beside him, a satisfied smirk on her face. He kissed her passionately, their tongues intertwining as he pulled her closer, still trembling from his pleasure.

Although they would face hardships in their lives and in their kingdom, in that moment, he vowed that every touch, every kiss, would remind her that she was cherished beyond measure. After that, the future was still uncertain, but he knew that whatever lay ahead, they would get through it together.

"Are you sure we need all this stuff?" Kason asked as he shoveled another load of dirt into the rows Holera had dug for her new garden project. "You know I can hunt, right?"

His fiery mate looked at him like he'd said the most idiotic thing she'd heard all day. "I'm aware you can hunt, my oh-so helpful and very sexy mate, but I eat more than just meat. If you want me to live here part of the year, I need something other than things that bleed to eat." The word *home* lingered in her voice, and it struck him with a warmth that had nothing to do with the sun beating down.

Chuckling, he pulled the already sweaty rag from his pocket and wiped his forehead as he watched her bend over the dirt to smooth it out.

"You know, if you want to take a break..." Moving in close behind her, he tried to slide his arms around her waist to spin her around, but she tossed a handful of dirt back at him, hitting him in the face. Her shoulders shook as she stifled her laughter, but the dirt to the face hadn't been a deterrent.

Wiping his face again, he wrapped his arms around her and pulled her to the ground. The soil was cool beneath them, the scent of earth clinging to their skin as he held her close.

"Kason! No! I'm trying to finish this before dinner."

Ignoring her protests, he slid his dirty fingers into her hair and pulled her lips to his. "You'll have the rest of our lives to make our home perfect, and I'll always help to ease your burden."

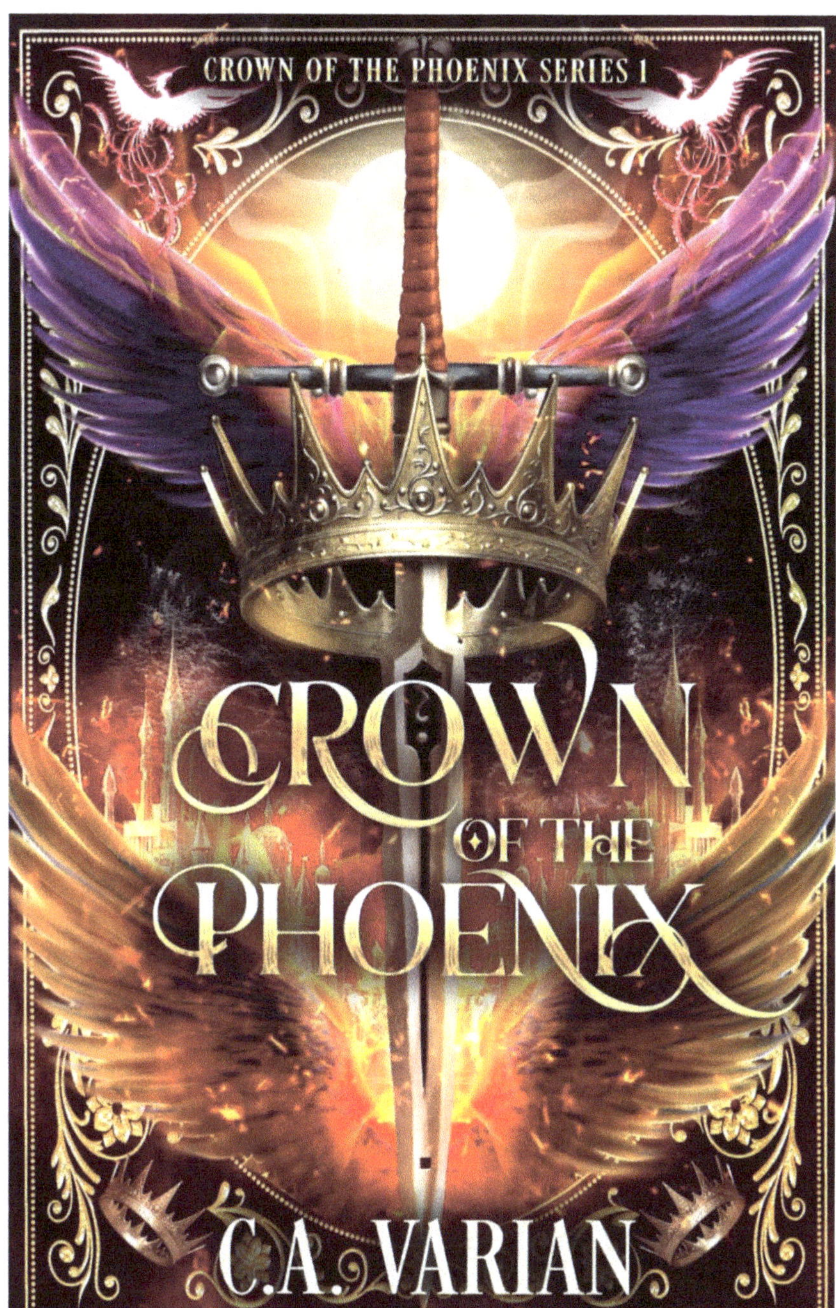

CROWN OF THE PHOENIX SERIES 1
CROWN
OF THE
PHOENIX
C.A. VARIAN

PROLOGUE

Two decades later, the flames of the phoenix burned quietly in Aegricia, but destiny stirred beyond the arch. In the human realm, Aurelia Vesta would soon step into a fate she could never have imagined.

Aurelia staggered to her knees at the edge of the cliffs, the roar of the Elder Sea crashing below. Salt spray stung her lips, but it was nothing compared to the fire tearing through her body. Blood thrashed her veins like it wished to erode her very being, much like the sea upon the rocky shoreline. Pain unlike anything she'd ever known raged within her as she felt the call. She wanted—*needed*—to go to the arch. The irresistible longing was an unbearable weight on her chest, sharpening each breath, and telling her to fly.

Chapter One

Vaekros

Aurelia

"Aurelia, you'll never defend yourself swinging like that. Are you even trying?"

Aurelia wiped the sweat from her brow and tightened her grip on her sword, swinging at Amadeus's larger blade, only for him to slap hers to the ground. She grunted.

"It's not a fair fight, you know. Your blade is bigger, and I am a girl!"

Her brother snorted, bracing his feet in a defensive stance.

"Blade size shouldn't matter. If anything, a smaller blade should be lighter—easier to maneuver."

"Room for me?" Septima called as she strolled across the training grounds. Just as Amadeus turned to look at their sister, Aurelia slammed her sword into his, forcing it from his hands. It clattered loudly as it hit the grass.

"Hey!" His outraged shriek held little threat with Aurelia's blade now leveled with his gut. "I wasn't ready."

Waiting until she thought he just may urinate on himself, she smirked and lowered her weapon to her side. "Horse's backside, Amadeus."

Dropping her sword, Aurelia ran to Septima, wrapping her arm around her sister's shoulder. "We have room for you, but I doubt you want to fight against that old nag's tail." She flipped her thumb over her shoulder, pointing at their brother, who rolled his eyes.

"I'll fight you then," Septima said as she darted for Amadeus' sword, swiping it from the ground, and wielding it in her sister's direction.

Aurelia retrieved her blade and swung it at Septima, only for her strike to be blocked. Her jaw dropped as Septima sneered at her. When her look morphed into a mischievous one, Aurelia braced herself for retaliation.

Amadeus began walking toward the house. "I'm going to head home. I'll grab my sword later. Have fun and try not to cut off each other's ears."

The sisters barely paid attention to him as their eyes remained on one another, waiting for the next move to be taken. Septima circled left, waving her weapon in arcs. Taking a step back, Aurelia dropped her weapon on the ground and took off running toward the gardens. She was tired of sparring, and leading a chase was far more fun. Glancing over her shoulder, she noticed Septima in pursuit, her lips spread into a bright smile.

Once they entered the gardens, the pair fell to the ground and began giggling uncontrollably. They lay among the flowers, admiring the cloudless sky and the breeze rolling off the Harmuz Sea. The sea, ever crashing against the weather-beaten white cliffs, carved dramatic rock faces. Though the cliffs were too high to climb down for a swim, the view was magnificent. Lying in the gardens, overlooking the water below, was one of their favorite pastimes.

"It must be such a thrill," Septima said, rolling onto her side to face Aurelia. Her dark eyes shone in the sunlight and her long ebony braids shimmered like black silk.

Aurelia turned to face her sister, twirling a yellow wildflower between her fingers. "What would be a thrill?"

The longing for adventure played across Septima's features. "To fight... to be a fearless warrior. I'm sick of being expected to be a proper lady who spends her time doing tedious things."

Sighing, Aurelia flicked the flower toward her sister. It landed near her hand. "Father would never allow it. You know we are to be wed. It's what is expected of us. I'm surprised he hasn't married me off yet. My twenty-first birthday will be here soon." The number felt heavy on her tongue. Twenty-one, and still waiting for her father to decide her fate. She knew why her sister wanted to seek adventure instead of marriage, but she did not know how to help make that happen for her. It was something she thought about often, knowing Septima did not fancy men at all. She was only attracted to women, but marrying the same sex was not allowed in Vaekros. Neither were women warriors. The options to bring her sister happiness were slim, and that was heartbreaking.

Rolling her eyes, Septima turned onto her back to gaze at the sky. "I'm not getting married to a man, expectations or not."

Aurelia's chest tightened at her sister's plight. "Marrying a woman isn't an option in Vaekros. You know that."

Septima's voice sharpened to steel. "That may be true, but I will not be forced to marry a man. I'd sooner die, Lia. I swear it."

Aurelia's chest ached at her sister's words, not just for the danger of defying their father, but for the quiet truth between them: she wanted to love freely, and their world had no place for that. Aurelia wanted to promise she'd find a way. Still, she had no answers, only the ache of knowing Septima's cage was tighter than her own.

Instead of responding, Aurelia bit her lip and turned to stare at the sky as well. They lay in silence for a while, neither knowing how to continue the conversation. They did not know how to solve a problem that had no solution in their society.

After a moment, Aurelia stood and dusted off her clothes. "I'm going to go check on Kano. He needs to get out of the house before he shreds up everything in it. I'll catch up with you a bit later." She leaned over to give her sister a kiss on the cheek before heading toward the house. Septima waved as she walked away.

Reluctantly rising from the flowers, Aurelia brushed the dirt from her clothes. The carefree afternoon had ended; the villa loomed ahead, full of its shadows and rules.

While Septima was not Aurelia's sister by blood, she was the single most important person in her life. Aurelia's father had found Septima when she was only a baby, while his army lay siege to El-Wahba. Septima's father had been killed in the attack, and her mother had been enslaved. Aurelia's parents became Septima's, although they could not have been more different in appearance.

While on campaign to foreign lands, Septima was not the only baby their father saved and brought back to their home in Vaekros. He had also given Aurelia a tiger cub. Her beautiful Kano, who, aside from Septima, was her best friend. She remembered it like it was yesterday. She was less than two years old when she met her baby sister, but was ten years old when the tiny cub was placed in her arms. She named him for the Sun God, for his striped fur shimmered gold like sunlight on water. He'd been a runt, a fragile cub no one believed would live, but under her care, he had grown into strength. To others, he was a beast to be shunned; to Aurelia, he was everything—guardian, confidant, and the only warmth in a house that too often felt like a prison.

As Aurelia moved across the grounds, she approached the villa through the back door. She adored the home, which was dramatically situated along the rocky cliffs near the Howling Mountains and Forest. The seaside estate, adorned with mosaics and frescoes, was designed around a sunlit atrium. Servants lived in a separate stone building at the edge of the property. A small wooden cottage, also located on the outskirts of the estate, belonged to Amadeus, who was still unmarried.

The stone atrium was filled with a variety of potted trees, vines, and flowers. A large pool sparkled in its center—a pool the girls frequented in the warmer months since reaching the sea was impossible from the height of the house.

Inside, polished marble gleamed across endless rooms—reception halls, bathing chambers, even a grand library, each space immaculate under Proteus's exacting rule. To others, it might seem like a palace. To Aurelia, it often felt like a barracks, patrolled by a commander instead of a father. Discipline lived in every stone of the house, but warmth had long since died with her mother.

When Aurelia entered her bedchamber, Kano stretched his massive body and slinked up to her to nuzzle her legs. She dropped into the vanity seat and untangled her braid while she gazed at herself in the bronze mirror. Her large blue eyes and crimson hair were such a contrast to Septima's long midnight braids and her deep tawny skin.

Some said her red hair was a gift from Veena, the Goddess of Life and Death. Not unlike the goddess, Aurelia loved to spar. She loved learning to wield weapons, even if it was all but forbidden in her society. She had to be a respectable Vaekrosan lady, and that meant never making a man feel weak in her presence. Even so, she sparred with her brother and with Septima to practice her swordsmanship. With as many fights as Vaekros picked, she never knew when such skills would be helpful.

Aurelia turned to admire her bedchamber. The aqua walls mirrored the sea, catching sunlight in the tall windows so the room glowed like water. A huge four-poster bed took up a large part of the suite, large enough for Kano to sleep alongside her and keep her warm.

Beyond her window rose her favorite sight, the Marella Arch, carved by the sea into a jagged portal of stone. Some in Vaekros called it cursed, others blessed, but Aurelia clung to the version from her dreams: a doorway to freedom, a world beyond her father's reach. Yet whenever the waves struck its base, foaming like teeth in a dark maw, she wondered if it promised escape... or demanded sacrifice.

Curled up like a mountain at her feet, Kano let out a mighty snore. She reached over and caressed his sleek fur, rousing him from his slumber. He yawned wide, fangs flashing in the light, his amber eyes heavy with sleepy yet watchful, as if he alone sensed what the house concealed. Rising to his feet, he rubbed against the cloth of her pants as she rubbed his head.

"You're being lazy today, Kano. I think it's time for us to play outside."

He bobbed his head like he understood her. Leaving her chambers with the great cat trailing behind her, Aurelia took the stairs quickly to look for Septima and sunshine.

After searching the villa twice over, she found both at the same time. Septima sat on a stone bench in the rose garden, soaking in the sun and reading a book. Kano sprinted at the sight of her, nuzzling his enormous head against Septima's legs. She giggled, ruffling his fur.

"Hey there, big guy," she said, placing a kiss on his head before gleaming a toothy grin at Aurelia. "What are you two up to?"

Aurelia shrugged, dropping to sit beside her. "Kano has been too lazy today. I thought a game of hide and seek would be good for him. Do you want to play?"

Septima chuckled. "Aren't we a little old for such games?"

Rising from the bench, Aurelia straightened her tunic. "I'm older, and I still play." She shrugged. "Let's go, Kano, the last one in the forest is a horse's backside."

Running as fast as she could, Aurelia darted into the tree line. The sound of Kano's enormous paws thudded close behind her.

The forest was vast, dense, and rich. Its canopy comprised pine, Buxus, and holly. Enough light shimmered through their crowns for a medley of shrubs to take advantage of the fertile grounds below. Silent vines suspended from many trees, and a range of flowers, which grew in a sprinkled, disorderly fashion, brightened up the otherwise homogeneous scenery. A mishmash of noises, predominantly those of critters, echoed throughout and were backed by the occasional sounds of birds of prey gliding in the air.

Aurelia laughed as she ran, climbing into an abandoned hollow just big enough for her to fit. Holding her breath, she knew he could smell her, but he seemed to pretend he couldn't, like he knew the rules of the game.

Quick footsteps paced in the distance. She pulled herself as far into the tree as she could, hoping there weren't any rodents nesting in there that would bite her like last time.

"Got you!" Septima's braids fell into the hollow, nearly slapping her in the face. They both began giggling as Kano bounded up to them as they kneeled, licking their faces.

Aurelia wiped the slobber off her cheek with the back of her hand. "I thought you were too old for this game?"

Septima shrugged as she wiped her own face. "You know I'll be playing in the forest with you even when my hair turns gray, especially with this big guy." She reached out and scratched Kano behind his ear. He leaned into her.

They played for hours. Each taking great care in where they hid, only for Kano to find them each time.

Dirt clung to their clothes as the sisters and Kano trudged back toward the villa, the sinking sun setting the Howling Mountains aflame. Before the threshold emerged from the shadows, Kano stiffened, ears pressed flat, a rumble rising from his chest. Aurelia's hand skimmed his fur in a futile attempt to calm him, even as unease coiled in her stomach. Then she looked up. Her father waited in the foyer with two strangers at his side, and her heart dropped like a stone.

CHAPTER TWO

AEGRICIA

OTERA

Otera dragged her feet as the cloaked brute hauled her through the depths of the dungeon, iron fingers digging into her arm. The air was bone-chilling, her thin nightdress clinging uselessly to her damp skin. Every step scraped her bare feet against the rough stone.

"You don't have to drag me," she snapped, though the tremor in her voice betrayed her. "I can walk on my own."

He grunted in response and yanked harder, bruising her flesh.

The dungeons beneath her castle had rarely been used. Only the most dangerous criminals ever rotted here, and even they did not linger long. The cells were damp, foul, and unfit for beasts, let alone a queen. Never had Otera imagined she would be the one cast behind these bars.

The Warbotach cavalry had come swiftly, their siege forcing her hand: open the gates or see innocents slaughtered. Her military had not abandoned her; they had retreated to build strength, gather allies, and return when the time was right. That had been the plan when word of Norithae's invasion first reached them weeks ago. But knowing the plan did little to soothe the gnawing weight of uncertainty.

And so, she endured, captive in her own fortress. Uldon, the Warbotach leader, wanted her crown and power, but he could not spill her blood to gain them. Her life was guaranteed; her dignity, however, was not.

Shoved into the stone-walled dark, Otera stumbled to the straw pallet in the corner as the iron door clanged shut. The echo rattled down the corridor until only silence remained.

She pressed her hands against the damp wall, as if she might still feel the heartbeat of her kingdom through its bones. But there was nothing, only the stench of mildew and the faint drip of water echoing like a slow clock.

Uldon fancied himself clever, demanding her crown without spilling her blood. He thought stripping her of comfort would make her weak. Yet Otera knew that crowns could be stolen, but loyalty could not. Her people's faith in her would outlast his tyranny.

The silence pressed harder than any shout, filling the void with memories of voices she would give anything to hear again—the laughter of her warriors, the songs sung in Flamecliff's halls. Now there was only stone, straw, and the slow rot of time.

She hated that the Warbotach could cage her body, but they could not cage her will. Her crown was not made of iron or gold; it was the fire that still burned inside her.

And so, she sat in the gloom with nothing but a slit of light high in the wall and her thoughts, sharp as chains.

CHAPTER THREE

VAEKROS

AURELIA

Proteus's eyes swept over the dirt on his daughters' clothes, his lip curling with disdain. He cleared his throat, lifted his glass in a gesture of dismissal, and pointed toward the stairs. His expression was unyielding, leaving no room for argument.

"Aurelia... Septima... go make yourselves presentable and come introduce yourselves to the men you will marry."

Aurelia's lungs lost their ability to expand, and she saw the same expression of dread twist her sister's face. Their eyes locking for only a moment, Septima wrapped her arms around her chest, and the sisters forced their feet upon the steps. They climbed the steps as though ascending a scaffold, each creak beneath their feet tightening the noose around their throats. Instead of heading to her own chambers, Septima followed Aurelia.

"I can't do this, Lia," Septima said as she pulled her filthy clothes over her head. Not waiting for a response, she scurried through the bathing room that separated their chambers to grab a suitable dress. "I will not marry that man."

Heart hammering against her ribcage, Aurelia stepped out of her trousers, tripping over the fabric as her chaotic thoughts whirled. "I know. We'll figure this out. I promise. But we have to go back downstairs. We can't just disobey him."

Septima grimaced as she tied her dress into place, ignoring her disheveled hair, and walked toward the door. With no other choice, Aurelia followed.

Stumbling down the stairs to the strangers whom her father had promised them to, Aurelia held her sister's hand, silently begging for a way out, but Aurelia knew prayers to the gods could not help her. If their father wanted them married, then there was no way for them to get out of that arrangement.

Already at the dining room table, Proteus and the two men chatted amongst themselves, glasses of brown liquor reflecting the firelight in their hands. Both men looked to be in their late twenties, nearly a decade older than their potential brides, but that wasn't uncommon in Vaekros. The sisters took seats opposite their suitors, with Proteus at the head of the table—a king in his castle. His face was carved from stone, void of humor or patience. The warning in his eyes told them clearly: objections would not be tolerated.

Aurelia glanced at the vacant chair opposite their father—her mother's chair. Fifteen years had passed, yet the emptiness at that place still hollowed her chest. She had dreamed of her mother at her wedding, of learning from her how to cradle children and keep a family whole. Instead, servants had raised her, and cold marble halls had become her cradle.

Their mother, Messalina, had succumbed to the plague. Their father, having been away on campaign in a foreign land, was not infected. Aurelia and Septima, only children then, were also spared, kept away at the first sign of illness. Aurelia wasn't allowed to watch her mother waste away, a fact that comforted her. She'd loved her mother dearly and was glad to keep the memories of her mother's beautiful face in her mind, not her deathly visage. Still, it left Aurelia without closure. She'd never been given the chance to say goodbye.

"Aurelia," Proteus said, interrupting her thoughts. "I'd like you to meet Philo."

The man directly across from her dipped his head in acknowledgement as a half-smile spread across his face. "Nice to meet you," he said.

"And you," she responded, forcing a smile of her own, although she knew it did not reach her eyes.

Philo was handsome, but he was at least five years her senior. Sandy blond hair swept across his forehead but was pulled back into a tie at his nape. His eyes, the color of summer grass, eased her nerves ever so slightly. She didn't want to marry him. She didn't even know him, but she was relieved that he at least appeared to be kind.

"Septima," her father said, motioning to the other man. "I'd like you to meet Caius."

Septima's face drained of color, her lips pressing into a thin line as her eyes flicked toward Caius. It wasn't rudeness, Aurelia knew it was revulsion she could not hide. He greeted her kindly, but Septima wore her rejection on her face. It was something their father would not miss. After breathing what appeared to be a hello, Septima reached for Aurelia's hand below the table. Lacing their fingers together, Aurelia ran her thumb over Septima's trembling hand, hoping to soothe her nerves. The air in the room was suddenly too thin as she struggled to inhale.

Dinner was brought out as Aurelia and Septima sat in silence, the meal seeming to go on without them. Roasted duck and vegetables were placed in front of them, as well as a tomato and cream bisque. The soup was Septima's favorite, but she didn't accept the bowl when Aurelia pushed it toward her. Aurelia ate a small amount of each dish. Still, she had lost her appetite after being accosted at the door by their father with unwanted engagements.

Not taking a moment to acknowledge his daughters, or even ask about their day, Proteus rambled on with the men, discussing business and political matters. Aurelia sat quietly, more out of place in her own home than she'd ever been, jaw tense as she waited for her father to dismiss them from the table. It wasn't as though they were needed in the conversation anyway, not even when it involved their own lives.

Septima's hand continued to grip Aurelia's, although the tremble had subsided. Aurelia couldn't help but dwell on what her sister was going through at that moment. What would she do if forced to marry a man? Aurelia didn't want to marry a stranger either, but marrying for love in Vaekros was unheard of. Still, it was a dream she had always held in her heart, a hope for their society to change.

Most marriages in their world were arranged for purely political reasons. The potential to gain power and connections was the only thing that mattered. Fathers arranged their daughters' unions, usually as soon as they reached eighteen years of age, to someone who could advance the families' political futures. If the bride's family was of a lower class than the groom's, a dowry would be paid to entice the prospective suitor.

Aurelia didn't know what arrangement Proteus had made with the two men, but she knew he did not need money or political power. She assumed the arrangement was, at the very least, mutually beneficial to the two families. Although she couldn't imagine it would be beneficial to her or her sister. Philo caught her eye several times, smiling kindly at her. Maybe she could grow to love him, but her sister could not do the same with her own betrothed. Even if she could come to care for him as a person, she would never be able to love him as a wife should.

Their father cleared his throat loudly as they finished dinner. Aurelia frowned. Septima's dish remained untouched. Proteus noticed the full plate but allowed the servant to take it away. The scraps would undoubtedly go to Kano, who was sleeping in the bedroom upstairs.

Rising from the table, her father lowered his eyebrows and leveled them with a stern look that left no room for argument.

"Well." He reached over to shake the suitors' hands. "I have some work to do in my study. Lydia will bring out dessert. Girls," he said, looking at his daughters. Aurelia's stomach tied in a knot as she hung on to Proteus's following words. She didn't want to entertain the men, although it didn't appear she had a choice. She held Proteus' gaze as Septima dropped her head and rubbed her eyes. "Get to know these fine young men. I'll be in my study if anyone needs me."

Dipping his chin to the men he'd selected for his daughters, their father strolled out of the dining room, heading toward the stairs.

Once he was gone, and although it would infuriate him, Septima rose from the table without warning and dashed out of the room, leaving her betrothed at the table, his mouth falling open as he watched the empty doorway. Having already ascended the stairs, Aurelia knew there was no way he wouldn't see Septima with his study being so near their chambers, and she knew he wouldn't be so forgiving.

Murmuring an apology to the men, Aurelia left them in the dining room alone, leaving the room to look for her sister.

A loud clap echoed around her as she took the stairs two at a time. The slam of Proteus' study door echoed behind her like the crack of a whip. Aurelia's pulse still thudded with the fear that he had seen Septima flee, and that punishment would come swiftly.

When she opened the door to her bedchamber, she found Septima curled up on her bed, sobbing into Kano's fur. The massive feline looked up as Aurelia entered the room, but Septima's eyes never lifted as sobs wracked her frame, her fingers curling into his striped fur.

Crawling onto the bed, Aurelia folded her body around her sister's, wrapping her in an embrace.

"Are you okay?" Although Aurelia knew Septima wasn't okay, she didn't know what else to say. Proteus didn't have to hit her, but he did a lot of things he didn't need to do. Without their mother's light, his heart had grown dark. He'd never remarried, never dated. His wife had been his everything, and without her, he'd become a shadow of who he once was.

"I can't do this, Lia." Septima's voice hitched as she spoke into Kano's fur, her throat bobbing. Unsure of what to say or do to ease her pain, Aurelia squeezed Septima's arm.

"I know, sissy. I just don't know how to fix it."

Rolling onto her back, Septima stared at nothing, tears trailing down her beautiful face as the mark from Proteus' hand began to turn purple on her cheek. She continued to pet Kano, the motion seeming to be more to soothe herself than him.

"I can't stay here. I can't let him do this to me. I don't know where I'll go, but it won't be here."

Aurelia swallowed around the lump of emotion in her throat. "What do you mean? You can't... but..." Although her mouth continued to move, Aurelia fell silent. Septima turned to face her with unspeakable sadness reflected in her eyes.

"I can't stay here. I won't. I'll run to the forest, a town beyond, I don't care where. Anywhere but here. Anywhere but at his mercy."

Aurelia stewed on her sister's words, trying to make sense of the situation. She couldn't lose her. It wasn't an option. They remained in silence as the sun fell behind the mountains, throwing the room into darkness. When Aurelia finally rose from the bed to light a candle, dangerous thoughts flooded her mind—thoughts she was willing to entertain for Septima.

"I'm coming with you."

Lifting herself onto her elbow, Septima's eyebrows rose. "You don't have to sacrifice your own marriage for me."

Aurelia snorted, returning to bed. "I have always wanted to marry for love, and he's just a stranger. I want to make my own way. I can't do that under Father's thumb."

A mischievous smile crawled across her sister's face. "I said I wanted adventure, but this may be more than we bargained for. Where will we stay? There are creatures in those woods. How will we protect ourselves?"

Aurelia glanced sidelong at Septima before reaching out to scratch Kano under the chin. "As long as we have this big boy, we'll be safe. As far as food, we can pack our satchels with as much as we can carry." Pulling two leather bags out of her armoire, she tossed one to her sister. "We can figure the rest out as we go."

Septima sat up, grabbing the bag and pulling it against her body. "When do we leave?"

Looking at the clear night outside the window, Aurelia turned to face her sister. "Tonight."

Neither sister had ever stepped beyond their father's shadow, let alone into a world that could devour them whole. But that no longer mattered. It was better to face the unknown than to remain shackled in Vaekros. They would escape—into the forest, into danger, into freedom. If only they could avoid being caught.

CHAPTER FOUR

Vaekros

Aurelia

Sneaking into the kitchen once the servants had turned in for the night, the sisters stuffed their bags with fruits, vegetables, dried meats, and bread. The smell of roasted fowl and hearth smoke clung to their cloaks as they worked in silence. They knew there were wild berries in the forest, and they could learn to hunt if necessary, but they grabbed what they could to get themselves started.

Both sisters strapped their swords to their backs and secured daggers around their thighs. They dressed warmly in tunics and trousers, wrapping hooded cloaks over their shoulders.

After taking a final look at the bedroom they cherished, Aurelia and Septima left the house unnoticed and entered the cool night air of the back gardens. They took a fortifying breath and braced themselves for what the forest and the future had in store for them.

Exchanging a silent nod, they pulled up their hoods and headed toward the forest, with their brother, Kano, following stealthily behind. The sisters crept to the tree line in silence, careful not to wake their brother, who lived in a cottage at the edge of the property.

They didn't have a plan beyond traveling west through the forest. They knew there were small towns bordering the woods, as well as larger cities, including El-Wahba, the place of Septima's birth. All they knew of the world beyond the forest was the existence of war-torn cities, none of which seemed like a suitable home. Initially, they intended to settle in one of the smaller towns to learn more about their surroundings.

Both women carried gold and silver coins in their bags, money they had saved over the years—funds that their father would not miss. They hoped to support themselves for a time with what they had gathered.

The dense brush of the Howling Forest took on a more ominous appearance at night. It had been named the Howling Forest for a reason. A menacing howl echoed in the distance as an owl hooted from above. Aurelia gripped Kano's leash so tightly that her hand ached; she flinched at every sound. Septima held a torch that illuminated their path as they navigated through the dense branches and vines. After several miles, the underbrush finally gave way to a clearer trail.

Knowing they couldn't stop for long, but too exhausted to go any further, they paused in a thicket to rest. Exhaustion weighed more heavily than fear. Curling into the thicket, they leaned against a hollowed-out tree, the forest looming around them with shadows and unblinking eyes. Their father would undoubtedly begin searching for them soon, sending servants to scour the extensive property. They had little time to rest, but they could afford to sleep until at least first light.

They built a small fire and settled against the trunk of the hollowed-out tree. Septima took the first watch while Aurelia tried to sleep. Kano remained alert, his instincts heightened as they sat in the darkened forest. Aurelia leaned back against the great cat, closing her eyes and allowing unconsciousness to consume her.

Tendrils of mist recoiled in front of her, beckoning her forward like the inward curl of a finger. Its invitation was seductive and alluring, but the path ahead was dark. Where was it leading her? She did not know. Her feet moved of their own accord, even though her mind screamed to stop. The mist coiled tighter, and with it came a chill, as though the world itself were holding its breath.

"What are you doing here?" the woman demanded, sitting upright in the corner. Her trembling hands straightened the hem of her filthy, tattered dress. Dirt was caked under her nails as if she had tried to claw her way to freedom. "I cannot give you what you want! You're wasting your time."

The man, his face hidden in shadows, huffed angrily and stomped away. "Maybe some more time in the cell will change your mind."

The sparkle of a glittering crown faded into the darkness as the iron door slammed shut. It no longer sat atop the head of the crimson-haired woman, imprisoned in filth. Instead, it floated away in the calloused hand of the stocky man who had stolen her freedom.

Aurelia jolted awake to rough hands on her shoulders and Kano's low growl vibrating through the ground beneath her.

"Lia, someone's coming. Wake up." Septima crouched beside her, whispering in her ear. Rubbing her eyes and shaking off the strange dream, she sat upright and peered into the distance.

"What's going on?"

"The branches cracked, and I heard voices. I put the fire out, but I think it's too late. They'll see the smoke."

Aurelia nodded as she pulled her legs closer to her body, trying to make herself as small as possible. The faint rustling of trees could be heard in the distance, almost like an animal. But the voices... the muffled voices made it clear that people were nearby.

The forest was still black. There was no telling the time, only that it was sometime past midnight and before sunrise. It was too late to run. Their footfalls and the inevitable stumbling through the forest would be too noisy for them to escape unnoticed. Their only option was to sit quietly and hope the others would pass them by. Aurelia's hands were slick with nervous sweat as her heartbeat thundered in her ears. They sat still, afraid to breathe, hoping to remain invisible.

The voices grew closer as the sisters huddled together. Aurelia cringed, clutching at her throat, realizing the people would walk right by their hiding place, and there was nothing they could do about it. Kano's snarling lowered in volume as if he understood they were supposed to be hiding and not drawing attention to themselves.

"Do you smell that?" a woman whispered. "Hang on, someone is out here."

The sound of dragging metal slithered through the air, setting Aurelia's teeth on edge. Someone had drawn a weapon.

"Who would be out here?" another female voice asked. The voice spoke louder, more demanding. "We know someone is out here… no sudden movements… just come out nice and slow."

Eyes wide and seeing no other option, the sisters looked at each other. Aurelia grabbed Kano by his leash, and they slowly stood from their place behind the trees.

Two women stood on the trail, only feet from them. They were tall, and although the darkness hid most of their features, the glint of moonlight revealed the sword in the hands of the blonde woman. Aurelia's stomach did a nervous flip, causing the meager food she had consumed to rise in her throat.

"We don't mean any harm," Aurelia said quickly, her voice tight as she stepped back and clutched Septima's hand. "We are just hiding from our father. By morning, we will be on our way."

The woman who wasn't holding a weapon, tall with long black hair draping over her shoulders, tilted her head, eyeing the large tiger at Aurelia's side. "And the beast?" she asked, fingers brushing the hilt of a dagger, moonlight glinting off the steel.

Aurelia gulped, glancing down at Kano before returning her gaze to the woman. "He's not a beast. He's my friend… my pet. His name is Kano. I've raised him since he was a cub. He protects me."

The women exchanged glances, lingering for a few agonizing moments, as though communicating silently. The same woman spoke again. "And when we walk away, will you have him tear us to shreds?"

Pursing her lips, Aurelia shook her head vehemently. "No, of course not. He's only here to protect me. He won't harm you if you don't harm us."

The other woman, the one with the sword in hand and hair that appeared white in the moonlight, spoke next. "You said you were hiding from your father. Why?"

Septima squeezed Aurelia's hand gently before responding. "Our father intends to marry us off to strange men. We refuse. We are trying to find somewhere else to create a home—a place where we can decide our own futures."

The woman snickered. "It's a foolish endeavor. In a world like this, in Vaekros, there is no escaping such a plan. Your father will find you. Women do not have the rights you seek. Not here."

The black-haired woman shot a warning look at her companion, causing the one with the sword to look down submissively. There was somewhere else; Aurelia felt it in her bones. The way the woman had said "not here" suggested there was another place, one where women had more rights. Aurelia decided to ask.

"My name is Aurelia. This is my sister, Septima." Aurelia lifted their intertwined hands. "If you know of a place where we could be free, please tell us." She thought about explaining why Septima could not—*would not*—marry a man, but she hesitated, unsure of their prejudices.

The woman without a weapon, clearly of a higher rank, responded first. "My name is Taryn. This is Exie." The woman with the sword nodded. "We knew of a place like that, a place where women had more rights, but it's no longer safe, so it doesn't warrant discussion."

Aurelia frowned. "Where are you from? Are you from Vaekros?" Although it seemed apparent they were not from Vaekros, she felt it polite to ask rather than assume.

"We are from a long way away," Exie responded, showing no intention of explaining further.

"But you're in Vaekros," Aurelia pressed. "I don't mean to pry. Do you know of anywhere safe that my sister and I can go? Somewhere we could survive away from our father?"

Taryn arched an eyebrow, examining them both. "Can you fight?"

Aurelia started, eyes widening as she glanced at her sister. "Fight?"

"Yes. Can you fight? With a weapon? If you can, then I can use you. Maybe." Taryn waited for their response, shifting her weight and taking a sip of water from her canteen.

Meeting her gaze, Aurelia nodded, and Septima did too. However, Septima spoke, "We train with our older brother. Aurelia trains more, but we both know the basics. We can learn. We don't want charity—just a chance to live free."

"There are towns through this forest, but I doubt you would ever reach them, even with a tiger. If your father didn't find you first, there are enough beasts in these woods that are the stuff of nightmares. I do not want your deaths on my conscience. We will take you to our camp, but I will tell you this once..." Taryn paused, scanning both sisters. "Once you enter our camp, there is no turning back. If you come with us, you sever your ties to Vaekros forever. Decide now if you can bear that."

Catching her sister's gaze, Aurelia bit her lip as she weighed their options. She tried to steady her voice and fill it with resolve as she responded, "We will not miss our lives in Vaekros. A part of us will surely miss our brother, but staying here isn't worth losing control of our futures."

Nodding, Taryn held out her hand to Aurelia, and they shook to seal the promise. "Very well. Gather your things. Our patrol is ending, and we must return to camp before first light. We need to move before your father's search parties scour this forest looking for you."

The sisters had little to gather. They had brought barely more than the clothes on their backs and the food they had stuffed into their satchels, but they collected what they could. Aurelia wrapped Kano's leash around her hand, gently petting him for reassurance, before stepping onto the path to follow the two mysterious women deeper into Howling Forest.

They walked for what felt like hours. Aurelia's legs grew weak, threatening to buckle beneath her. The brisk chill in the air was not enough to stop the sweat from beading on her skin. They continued walking until night began to fade into day. Sunlight peeked through the gaps in the trees, but Exie still held her sword at the ready, bracing for an attack, and Aurelia had no idea what to expect.

As they approached a clearing, the previously buzzing forest fell eerily silent. After a moment, Exie sheathed her sword and reached for Septima's hand. Septima stared at her as if the gesture would bite her, taking a hesitant step back. Before Aurelia could ask what was happening, Taryn reached for her hand as well.

"If you want to follow us," Taryn said impatiently, "you'll have to take my hand and trust me. You can't cross the barrier on your own."

"Barrier?" Aurelia asked, her confusion evident. Fear of the unknown weighed heavily on her, making her exhausted limbs feel even heavier.

Exie smirked, waiting for Taryn to explain.

"There's more to this world than just stone and trees," Taryn said. "If you want to see ours, you must trust me. Take my hand—or remain blind forever."

In an unspoken agreement, the sisters released each other's hands and grasped the hands of the mysterious women, allowing themselves to be led through an invisible barrier into a place un- known.

CHAPTER FIVE

HOWLING FOREST

AURELIA

The air rippled as the sisters stepped into what appeared to be a clearing in the forest. It felt like entering a vacuum, and the sudden change in pressure made Aurelia's ears pop. She swayed slightly, trying to regain her equilibrium. The air felt torn, as if a veil had been ripped aside, and for a heartbeat, the world seemed to hold its breath.

The clearing, previously quiet and empty, suddenly teemed with life as the sisters crossed the invisible barrier. This sight left them both in awe.

Hundreds of women warriors were scattered throughout the clearing. Some sparred, while others ate and chatted around various bonfires that flickered across the area. The clang of steel echoed amidst bursts of laughter, and the smoke from roasted meat perfumed the air. Their escorts had released the sisters' hands after they crossed over, but the sisters moved closer to each other, staring at the vibrant scene unfolding before them.

The women looked nothing like those from Vaekros. They were tall and muscular, their bodies honed like living armor, and none of them wore gowns. Instead, they were dressed in trousers, tunics, or fighting leathers embellished with fur-trimmed cloaks of animal skin draped over their shoulders. Leather belts cinched their waists, adorned with a variety of weapons, including short swords, daggers, and arrows for the bows slung across their backs.

Aurelia reached over and touched her sister's cheek. Exie noticed their shock and chuckled. She waved her hand in front of her and said, "Welcome to the Aegrician war camp."

Septima tilted her head, confused. "War camp? In the Howling Forest?"

"It's in the Vaekrosan woods, but it's not. The space is shielded. The humans won't be able to see us."

Aurelia's mind was a whirlwind of questions. These women were not human? Who were they? What were they? Exie's words seemed like a jest, but the seriousness in her eyes told a different story.

"What do you mean by 'the humans won't see you'? And what kind of shield?" Aurelia's voice trembled as her questions spilled out in a rush, tumbling over each other and making her sound incoherent. She did not—could not—understand. Exie smiled mischievously as Taryn returned, and Aurelia hadn't even noticed she had left.

Just before Taryn came within hearing distance, Exie turned to the sisters. "There's a lot you don't know, but you'll learn in time. Until then, just trust us. You are safe."

Aurelia nodded as Taryn joined them. Now that there was some light, she took in the warrior's appearance. Taryn's attire resembled that of the other women in the clearing, but she wore an intricate gold and jeweled pendant of a phoenix that glimmered near her collarbone. Both women stood a head taller than Aurelia and Septima, who were not exactly short among Vaekrosan women. Taryn had black hair that flowed like night and was braided down her back, ending just above her waist. Aurelia had encountered Taryn with her hair in a wild mane, so the sleek braid was unexpected. As she wondered how Taryn had tamed her hair so quickly, she noticed something that made her breath catch in her throat: the tips of Taryn's ears were slightly pointed, a startling contrast to the rounded ears of humans. A prickling sensation crawled down Aurelia's spine. Not human, then. Not even close.

Turning to Exie, she noticed her ears were the same. Aurelia wanted to ask them why, but didn't want to seem rude or critical. So, instead of seeking an explanation, she swallowed her comments as Taryn spoke.

"Blaedia will see them now," she told Exie, who nodded in response.

Aurelia felt her chest constrict as she squeezed Septima's hand. Septima grimaced at the strength of her grip and loosened her grasp slightly.

Their new companions led them forward toward a cluster of large tents, but Aurelia hesitated. She couldn't control the trembling in her body. Fear of what she had gotten herself and her younger sister into consumed her. The anxiety of the unknown was overwhelming. What if I made a mistake?

Septima gave her a reassuring smile and took the lead, addressing Taryn. "Who is Blaedia? What's going to happen to us?" Septima hesitated, but the women did not interrupt her. "I'm sorry if I sound ungrateful or if it seems like we don't trust you..."

Taryn stepped closer, her voice gentle and reassuring. "You don't need to apologize. We understand your confusion. Everything will be explained to you soon, I promise. Blaedia is our general. I can't tell you more without her approval. Just know that you are safe. Blaedia will tell you everything. She's agreed to offer you protection in our camp. Follow me, and we will get your tiger set up in an enclosure before you meet her. Then we will find a tent for the two of you so you can rest. You must be exhausted."

Without another word, Taryn turned and walked toward the cluster of tents once more.

Aurelia and Septima looked around, their heads swiveling as they scanned the extensive camp concealed within the Vaekrosan forest. Hundreds of tents of various sizes were erected around the perimeter of the clearing, extending back into the trees. Near the back of the camp, in the direction they were heading, was a larger tent that Aurelia assumed was where Blaedia was waiting for them. However, they passed the large tent and cut between it and the structure adjacent. They approached an ample fenced-in space within the trees, clearly meant for Kano. A chunk of bloody meat and a water trough came into view as they drew closer. Kano licked his lips at the scent of the meal wafting toward him, pulling on his leash, eager to get inside.

"Will he be safe here?" Aurelia asked, nervous about letting him out of her sight.

Taryn nodded as she placed her hand upon the gate, causing the latch to click and the door to swing open. Kano darted inside, yanking his leash from Aurelia's grasp and tearing into the meat. Aurelia snickered. "Well, I love you too." The great cat looked up at her, gore dripping from his face, before dipping his head back down into his meal.

"Here," said Taryn as she handed a bronze medallion hanging from a leather cord to Aurelia. "There are wards around his enclosure. This will open it. Just place the emblem against the gate, and it will open for you. Only a few individuals have access, which is as much for his protection as for everyone else's."

Clutching the medallion in her hand, Aurelia placed the cord around her neck before tucking it beneath her shirt for safekeeping. She'd been given many necklaces in her life, but never a magical one, never one so important. She prayed she would not lose it.

"Ready?" Taryn asked as she strode toward the largest of the tents. She didn't wait for a response, her pace increasing as they rounded the corner. The flaps of the door were already slightly ajar, but a heavily armed woman stood guard in front of the opening. She moved to the side as they approached, allowing them entry without a word.

Aurelia's mouth fell open as the tent revealed itself to be impossibly vast. The space seemed to stretch wider than canvas should allow, every corner humming with restrained power. It was only a single room, but furniture and screens separated it into sections. Aurelia could just make out the view of an enormous bed behind one screen and a kitchen area in one corner. A modest throne sat before them, but it was empty. Instead, a woman with jet black hair stood at a table in the center of the room, leaning over a large map. The woman straightened as they walked in, nodding to their guide.

"Taryn," she said.

"Blaedia," Taryn responded, ushering them further into the room. She introduced the sisters to the general, gesturing to each in turn. "This is Aurelia and her sister, Septima."

The general smiled at them, although it didn't quite meet her eyes, and returned her gaze to the map. Aurelia shrank into herself, feeling dismissed, until Blaedia covered the map with a cloth and indicated for them to follow her to a table near the kitchen. They were glad when Exie's friendly face entered the tent and joined them at the table.

"I'm sure everyone is hungry," Blaedia said. Her voice was sharp but not unkind. "Exie, ask Manara to bring in some stew. Please, sit. Let's talk."

"Any fresh developments?" Taryn asked, lowering herself into one of the chairs. Blaedia rubbed her eyes with her palms, shaking her head. Her responding voice was tense.

"None. From the messages I've received from the ravens, she is still holding onto her strength. He has the crown, but that is it. However, we will need to move in closer soon. The arrival of the ravens has slowed. I suspect they are being captured as they try to bring news."

Taryn slumped at the general's response. Aurelia knew nothing about these people or the plight that had driven them to set up camp in the Howling Forest, but whatever they were discussing felt important. It was like a switch flipped within her, and suddenly she knew this was where she was meant to be. Although she had no idea why.

Blaedia shifted her eyes to the sisters as a woman entered the tent with a large steaming pot and set it on the table. Aurelia met Blaedia's stare. Every instinct within her told her to lower her eyes, but she held firm.

Blaedia's beauty was arresting, her eyes so bright they seemed forged from molten silver. Just like Taryn and Exie, she was impressively tall, even as she sat at the head of the table. Unlike Taryn's long locks, Blaedia's hair was cut shoulder-length and shaved on one side. She also wore a phoenix pendant on her cloak. Aurelia suspected it was a symbol of authority among their people. They all waited for the general to dip her spoon into her stew before digging into their own.

"Why are you running?" she asked, catching Aurelia by surprise. Taryn nudged her under the table when she didn't respond. Dropping her spoon back into the meaty stew, Aurelia glanced at Septima before returning her gaze to Blaedia.

"Our father is trying to arrange our marriages to strangers, and we cannot go through with it. We ran away to stop those marriages from happening."

Blaedia's eyebrows lifted as she took another bite. "I imagine these types of arrangements are common in your family."

Aurelia nodded. "Yes. It's a common practice in Vaekros for all women."

The general grimaced and turned her attention to Septima. "Is there any particular reason why you won't marry the man chosen for you by your father? Were they evil men?"

Aurelia started to respond, but Septima interrupted. "I doubt they were evil men, but I have no interest in men. My sister ran away with me because we swore to stay together—no matter what."

Nearly choking at her sister's admission, Aurelia took a sip of water. She stared at Blaedia, anxiously waiting for a response. What if desiring the same sex wasn't acceptable in their society, either? She braced herself for the worst, but Septima seemed resigned to her fate, no longer hiding who she was. No matter how the general responded, Aurelia felt proud of her sister.

Aurelia's heart pounded as though the words had been spoken in a temple. She had feared this confession would doom them, but Septima's eyes shone with a fierce kind of freedom, unashamed at last.

Blaedia's lips curved into a smirk as she raised her glass. "I, too, would sooner die than be bound to a man. Thank you for your honesty, Septima. Here, you will find no shame in it—only freedom."

"Probably because our society is not run by a bunch of horny men," Exie chimed in. Blaedia lifted her glass toward Exie as well, in a silent toast.

The tension in Aurelia's heart began to ease. From the way Septima's body visibly relaxed, she could tell her sister felt the same relief. A society led by women sounded like a myth. Aurelia couldn't imagine what that was like, but it certainly seemed better than her own.

"What brings your camp to Vaekros?" Aurelia knew it might be too bold to ask, but the uncertainty filled her with unease. Blaedia's grin faded, and Taryn cleared her throat as the general met Aurelia's gaze.

"It's a long story, so I'll shorten it for you. Aegricia, our kingdom, was invaded. Our queen, Otera, has been captured. We are here while we plan to reclaim our lands."

"I've never heard of Aegricia," Aurelia said, glancing at Septima, who shrugged. "Is it far from here?"

The general pushed her empty bowl away and wiped her face with a cloth. "Yes and no." Blaedia's gaze hardened, and for the first time, Aurelia understood—this was not just a camp, but an exiled army coiled like a spring in the shadows of Vaekros.

CHAPTER SIX

HOWLING FOREST

AURELIA

The sisters slept through the afternoon, waking only when the resounding clang of the dinner bell reverberated through the camp like a war drum. Aurelia stirred with a start, relieved that this time her sleep had been mercifully blank—no strange dreams, no crowns or cages. Usually, her dreams were unpleasant and confusing, so this respite was welcome.

Groggy from their nap but famished, the sisters climbed out of bed and staggered out of their tent. Kano trotted to the fence as they approached, giving a happy flick of his tail. Aurelia cooed at him as she passed, promising to visit soon.

As they rounded the bend toward the sparring ring, they saw a gathering of women at the entrance of a massive tent. They approached hesitantly, unsure of how the strangers would receive them. Exie spotted their uncertain approach and jogged over to them.

"I thought I was going to have to wake you two up!" she said, leading them to the dining tent. Aurelia began to realize that behind Exie's sharp blade and wild laugh lay a rare ease. The night before, she had been focused, her sword at the ready as she escorted them back to camp. But within the safety of the barrier, she seemed to be a free spirit. She floated on her feet, almost skipping her way into the dinner tent. Her golden hair was just as wild as when they met, but her brown eyes were a smooth caramel in the setting sun and held a softness that hadn't been there before.

Food lined the back wall of the tent buffet-style. Aurelia's eyes grew wide at the sight, her rumbling stomach reminding her that she had long since burned off the stew they had when they first arrived. After taking their fill, the three of them sat down with bowls of stew, rice, and a variety of roasted vegetables. Chatter filled the space, overflowing with what must have been hundreds of women. Aurelia scanned the area for men but saw very few.

"Exie," Aurelia began cautiously, her eyes scanning the sea of women. "Where are the men? You said your society is led by women, but I expected to see more of them here—at least among the warriors."

Exie swallowed a mouthful of stew and smiled before responding. "They're around, but most of our military is made up of women. Men can't fly. It's a gift born solely to females in our society, although not all are blessed with it. If a woman is born with the ability to transform, she is usually trained to be a warrior and gatekeeper. That is the expectation. Many of our men remained in Aegricia. Since they cannot fly, they work in various other professions and continue to support our territory in their own ways." She gestured to the room. "Many of the women here are bonded, or married, as you would say, but their husbands are back home."

"Your people are under the control of Warbotach?" Septima asked. Exie nodded grimly.

"Yes. But just because the men cannot transform does not mean they are not strong or useful in a fight. For now, our people at home are biding their time. When we return to fight, they will be ready to help us win. We left solely to protect our forces because our army would have been the first target of their stealth attacks. Warbotach has no interest in murdering our innocents because they do not want to live in our territory. They want the human lands. That is the big prize. Their lands are no longer suitable for grazing animals or the way they were accustomed to living before their land became inhospitable. So, for now, our civilians are safe. We will return—with any luck, accompanied by allies. Norithae is currently weak, but we know there are still those who want to fight. We also plan to send emissaries to the kingdom of Diapolis. They are not involved in the conflict, but we hope they will help us."

Exie waved at a red-haired woman at another table before returning to the conversation.

"Do people from the other kingdoms have abilities like yours?" Septima asked. "I know your general said the Warbotach people could not fly, but what about the others? Do they have powers?"

"The land of Ekotoria contains magic, so all its peoples have powers that humans do not. Those powers are usually based on their environment, as though they developed to survive within it, but not always. The people of Diapolis live on the coast. Their powers come from the water, and many of them can even live below the surface if they choose. The Norithae people are fae, like us, and have wings, but they maintain their human appearance even with them. They do not shift as we do."

Aurelia was so engrossed in the latest information being revealed that she had forgotten about her dinner. She took a mouthful of her stew before asking the questions that had been burning in her mind. "What about your queen? Her crown? I don't understand how Warbotach can take her powers." Septima's gaze turned distant as she ran her fingers through her long braids, appearing just as confused as her sister.

Exie let out a sigh and pushed her plate away, the lively sparkle in her eyes dimming. "They believe they can steal the power of her crown. The crown's wearer can control the gateway between realms. Without it, Warbotach's warriors cannot cross through the portal. The Aegrician crown is not passed down by blood; fate decides who becomes our queen and wields its power. Right now, the Warbotach king, Uldon, scours the realms using every dark art he can find to twist the crown's allegiance. He has sought the help of witches, consulted oracles, and is now searching for the Elemental of Spectre Forest. So far, nothing has succeeded in bending the crown to him, but Uldon is not a man who yields. He would tear the world apart before accepting defeat. A man has never worn our crown, but he is not one to give up easily."

Rubbing the back of her neck, Aurelia glanced around the nearly empty dining area. The need for answers consumed her, but she had so many questions that she didn't know where to start. Almost everyone else had eaten and left by the time she asked her most pressing question. "What do you think the outcome will be?"

Exie shrugged casually, but her voice grew stern. "We will seek alliances, bolster our strength, and fight until we drive every single Warbotach warrior from our cliffs. That is our plan, and it's how I prefer to think. We cannot stay here for much longer, so I expect we will learn of our fate soon."

"What will happen to us?" Septima asked. "When all of you leave Vaekros, what will become of us?"

Aurelia remained still, awaiting Exie's response. Exie looked at them both with unwavering conviction. "We will take you with us. Both of you. Kano, too." She reached across the table, taking each of their hands. "Taryn and I wouldn't have brought you here if we planned to abandon you. We asked if you were willing to give up your old life to come with us because we intended to take you back to Ekotoria if you agreed. Have you changed your mind?"

She arched an eyebrow and studied the sisters cautiously. They both shook their heads, but Septima spoke up. "No. We want to come with you. We just didn't know if we'd be able to. You said only your kind could cross through the portal."

"You can cross as long as you're holding on to one of us. I'll carry you on my back to ensure you make it across."

"On your back?" Aurelia's question made Exie chuckle.

"Yes, Aurelia. On my back. The only way through the portal is to fly, remember? I can't fly in this form. I'll go through it as a phoenix, so I hope you're not afraid of heights."

Aurelia gulped, trying to swallow her nerves. She felt as if the entire story was a trick. It seemed too fantastical to be real. Just as she was about to question the tale's legitimacy, she caught a glimpse of shimmering light—brilliant wings flared from Exie's shoulders, feathers gleaming like molten jewels, radiant and otherworldly. They spread wide, brushing the lamplight with sparks before folding back into nothing.

Both sisters sat slack-jawed, their eyes wide with wonder, as Exie threw her head back and roared with laughter.

"I think you two have had enough adventure for one day," she said. "Blaedia told me your training starts tomorrow. I'll walk you to the showers and then off to bed with you. Come now." She stood from the table, stretching her long arms above her head. Aurelia couldn't help but stare at her extended limbs, recalling the vibrant wings that had been visible only moments before.

Septima and Aurelia showered in adjacent stalls, enjoying the warmth of the water amidst the cold forest. For Aurelia, the water symbolized more than just warmth; it was the last connection to the life she had known in Vaekros. As each rivulet trickled down her back, it felt as though it washed away a layer of her old self, leaving her feeling both lighter and more apprehensive about who she was becoming.

They dressed quickly, having to hold up the hems of their nightclothes, which were tailored for women much taller than they were.

Aurelia used the medallion still hanging from her neck to enter Kano's enclosure and say goodnight before bed. She hated the thought of leaving him outside overnight, though she recognized how silly that sounded. He was a wild animal, after all, but he had been raised in the comfort of her family villa. He was used to sleeping in Aurelia's bed, not on the cold forest floor. Despite her heart aching at the thought of leaving him behind, when she saw him looking quite happy and even comfortable outside, she placed a gentle kiss on top of his head and closed the gate behind her.

After visiting Kano, they returned to their tent and crawled into bed immediately. However, falling asleep proved to be a challenge for Aurelia. Her mind raced as she replayed the information Exie had shared with them. The image of the wings flaring out from the female's back was etched in her memory, and she found herself wondering what the true form of a phoenix was like. She contemplated the other abilities they might possess in that form and, more than anything, she pondered what it would be like to fly: to burn, to rise, and to soar above every chain her father had fastened around her.

Chapter Seven

Howling Forest

Aurelia

Sniffles filled the dimly lit room, making her listen harder as she searched for the source. Someone was crying, and they needed help. She tripped as she fumbled around the room, trailing her fingers along the rough stone wall to guide her progression. She strained her eyes but could hardly make out more than the mouse that skittered past. The rodent startled a gasp from her, but she continued on and called out.

"Who's there?"

The only response was another sniffle and a breathy sigh. She drew closer to the sound as a single stream of moonlight shone through a narrow window set high on the wall. But the spot it illuminated was empty.

The ancient metal door clanged as it opened, its hinges squealing in protest as it moved. A burly man, dressed in leathers and a fur cape, loomed in the doorway, torchlight carving his scarred face into something monstrous. His head was too large for his body, its lopsided shape more grotesque than human. Everything about him radiated menace, as if cruelty itself had been given flesh. The flame of a single torch flickered, highlighting the rage that painted his sharp features. She could make out tan skin and eyes so dark they were void of color. A vicious scar ran down his cheek, adding to the sinister aura that surrounded him.

The muffled cries ceased the moment he entered, replaced by a frantic scrambling in the far corner.

"Reconsider yet, Otera?" His rough voice sliced through the silence. It was deep and unyielding. Though his words held the lilt of a question, it sounded like an expectation—a demand.

"No." Otera's tone was just as inflexible. Whatever the decision she was expected to change, she had no intention of doing so.

His responding chuckle was smug, a mixture between a snort and a grunt. "You will. Either you will give me what I want, or the crown will, but I will get it either way. The only question is how much you will suffer before then."

The resounding slam of the cell door punctuated his statement, and the soft cries of a fallen queen filled the room once more.

Aurelia's fantasies of soaring through the sky—the wind whipping through her hair and wings lifting her toward freedom—had eventually lulled her into the fitful sleep she longed for. But sleep betrayed her, twisting into visions of chains and dungeons. Everything she had been told about the Aegrician queen infiltrated her mind and invaded her dreams. The thought of Otera locked away in a dungeon made her blood run cold. Still, she wondered which was worse: the reality of the queen's situation or her own imagination.

No light filtered through the canvas tent. As Aurelia jolted awake from her dismal dream, she pondered whether it was still night or if the sun had already risen above the horizon. The breakfast bell hadn't rung yet, so she knew it must be early. Her heart continued to race. The face of Otera's captor was burned into her mind's eye, but Septima's even breathing provided an anchor to reality that comforted her.

Their training was set to begin after breakfast, and the prospect was terrifying. Although they trained with Amadeus often, Aurelia sensed that the phoenix-shifting warrior women would be more demanding than anything their big brother had ever put them through. The thought of Amadeus felt like a knife pressed into her ribs. It was a constant ache, sharp and unyielding. She knew they had made the right choice, but the knowledge that she would never see her brother again left a wound that would never fully heal. The agreement they made with Exie and Taryn had been explicit, but sometimes the right decision was painful.

Dwelling on what they had left behind would do no good. She turned her thoughts away from the open sore that was Amadeus and began to wonder about the enchanted lands of Ekotoria. She was curious about the appearance of the different territories and whether leaving the human world would prevent her from getting married when she was older. In a land devoid of humans, would she be able to find someone she loved? She was running from an arranged marriage, but that didn't mean she wanted to give up on her desire to marry for love. Even so, the thought of someday marrying a non-human man was inconceivable. There was much to consider about the future—far more than she had contemplated when she agreed to leave Vaekros behind forever.

Climbing out of bed, Aurelia lit a candle before quietly digging through the wooden trunk at the foot of her bed. She pulled out a pair of trousers and a tunic resembling the ones the warriors wore around the camp. The deep brown pants were made of buttery leather and secured around her waist with laces. They hugged her body as if they had been tailored for her. The green tunic was composed of heavy cloth to keep her warm in the chilly temperatures. After she dressed, she checked Septima's face to ensure she hadn't awakened before slipping out of the tent and into the brisk morning air.

The sun's rays barely penetrated the dense trees as Aurelia made her way to Kano's enclosure. Already awake, he prowled around his space as though he were stalking prey in the wild. She admired the fluidity of his movements for a moment before crossing the threshold where the magic of the medallion met its mark.

Kano's head shot up at her approach, and he abandoned his hunt to greet her. He nuzzled his massive muzzle into her legs. Aurelia bent down to rub him behind the ears. "I know. I missed you, too, Kano."

She sat cross-legged beside him, her fingers never leaving his fur. After the distance that had separated them since arriving at the camp, she couldn't bear to part from him a moment sooner than necessary. He flopped onto his back, his tongue lolling happily from his mouth, and his massive paws curled up like an oversized kitten. Aurelia laughed softly and obliged with a belly rub, her fingers sinking into his warm fur. For a brief moment, the weight of kingdoms and crowns lifted, replaced by the simple comfort of home.

A few women passed by the enclosure, eying the massive tiger warily. Aurelia flashed them a friendly grin, hoping to ease their worries. She wondered if the camp knew about her and Septima's arrival. Would they embrace them with open arms like Exie had, or had they simply traded one tragic situation for another? She didn't know how the people of Ekotoria viewed humans. All she could do was pray they would be accepted in their new land and not face discrimination over something they could not control, just as her sister had in Vaekros.

Suddenly, the bell rang throughout the clearing, signaling the start of breakfast. Aurelia tried to ignore the pit of anxiety forming in her stomach as she placed a kiss on Kano's head. Mealtime meant training was that much closer, and as she stood and dusted off her clothes, her hands trembled with nerves. She left the enclosure, forcing herself to put one foot in front of the other, and went to wake Septima.

To her surprise, not only was her sister awake, but she was eager to start her day. Septima collided with Aurelia as she rushed from the tent. All the fears that Aurelia battled didn't seem to affect Septima. Her sister appeared lighter and happier than she had ever seen her. Perhaps that was the power of being able to truly be herself. Freedom had already changed her. The shadows that once clung to her in Vaekros seemed to have burned away in the glow of this new life.

As she had the night before, Exie waited outside the dining tent. Aurelia hoped to make friends with more women in the camp, but Exie taking them under her wing meant the world to her. She huffed a laugh at her unintentional pun under her breath and waved at Exie, who flashed a brilliant smile as they approached.

"Morning, ladies! How did you sleep?" Exie asked.

"Like a rock," said Septima.

"Same," Aurelia lied. Images of the dingy cell and the barbarous man from her dreams flashed through her mind. Her rest had left her feeling more exhausted than she had been the night before.

Exie motioned for them to lead the way into the dining tent.

They grabbed bowls of porridge and eggs before sitting at one of the few unoccupied tables. Most of the camp's occupants had arrived before the bell had even rung. Aurelia wasn't sure if she'd ever be that punctual.

"Are the two of you ready to start your training?"

Aurelia gave a noncommittal shrug while Septima nodded. "I'm definitely ready to train, but I hope the trainer is forgiving. We have a long way to go before we can be considered warriors."

Exie smirked. "I'll try to go easy on you."

Aurelia sputtered, nearly choking on her water. "Wait, so you'll be the one training us?"

"Yep! Very few of the warriors in this camp need a beginner's course, so I'll oversee your training." Exie puffed out her chest a little, sitting up straighter, clearly proud of her new position. Aurelia nearly giggled.

Relief flooded through Aurelia, and she was sure Septima felt the same. She watched as the tension in her sister's shoulders disappeared.

"So, Exie..." Aurelia hesitated as Exie exchanged a high-five with a red-haired woman passing by. Turning back to the sisters, she shoved a huge bite of porridge into her mouth and raised her eyebrows in response. Taking this as a signal to continue, Aurelia asked, "How will we be received in Ekotoria? How do the people there, and those in this camp, view humans? I don't know what to expect, and it's been weighing on me."

Exie lifted her eyebrows and nodded as she chewed her food. "That's understandable, but don't worry." However, her shoulders tensed, belying the positivity in her tone, which Aurelia noticed. "I mean... Some will never forget old wounds. To them, humans are careless, greedy, and dangerous. Prejudices linger, as they always do. It's the main reason the ability to traverse the portal is limited to Aegricians now, not the rest of Ekotoria or the human lands."

Aurelia's eyes widened. "You mean others used to be able to cross? Do more humans know of your existence? I've never heard of you, at least not in any way that wasn't a fairy tale."

Exie nodded. "Yes. A treaty was established long ago between our crown and the rulers of Vaekros. The portal was reforged in secrecy, bound with the same fire as our crown. Only those chosen by its will can pass safely. The crown chooses its bearer not by blood, but by destiny—by who can best guard the veil. That's why the Warbotach leader needs our crown to favor him. If the crown were to bow to him, he would tear open the portal and unleash his armies upon your world."

Aurelia swallowed, a mix of fear and the meager breakfast she'd eaten rising in her stomach. "Can he do it, though?"

"Do what?"

"All of it. Changing the allegiance of the crown, crossing the portal, conquering the human world... Can he really do it?"

Exie shrugged. "I'm not sure, but he seems to think so. He will certainly exhaust all possibilities before ever giving up. I don't think even our queen could surrender what he seeks. But magic is vast, and Uldon is relentless. He will scour every crypt and cursed forest until he finds a way. He is not a man who stops. He is only a man who conquers."

CHAPTER EIGHT

HOWLING FOREST

AURELIA

"Show me how your brother taught you to fight." Exie stood on the outskirts of the practice ring with her arms folded across her chest and a smirk on her face.

She seemed to expect the sisters to fight like court jesters putting on a show, and not like actual fighters. Just the thought of it made Aurelia's stomach churn. Lifting their swords, the sisters went through some of the movements Amadeus taught them. Aurelia disarmed Septima. Her sword fell from her hand as Aurelia halted her blade inches away from slicing her sister's gut open. Exie clapped slowly, although Aurelia was not sure if she was being facetious or if she was impressed.

"Not bad, Aurelia. If it had been an actual fight, Septima would be dead. I'm surprised you have so much power in that tiny body of yours." She looked at Aurelia as though she were some strange creature glimpsed in a traveling menagerie—curious, fascinating, and not quite real.

"I spent more time with Amadeus. Otherwise, Septima would kick my backside." Septima looked discouraged as she retrieved her sword. Aurelia gave her an encouraging smile and squeezed her shoulder.

Exie shrugged. "We all have to start somewhere. One thing I noticed, Septima, is that your defensive stance and footwork need a bit of help."

Approaching her from the side of the ring, Exie slid in close, one arm bracing Septima's waist, the other guiding her grip. Her voice was all business, steady and instructive, but her nearness sent a crimson flush flooding Septima's cheeks. Unable to help herself, Aurelia lifted her hand to her mouth, stifling a giggle.

As they lingered in the training ring, the air around them shifted. Aurelia's heart sank as her eyes fixed on a group sprinting from the trees, one woman sagging between the others, blood streaking down her leg. Three females hurried through the clearing, one of them leaning against the others as she limped heavily on one leg. Aurelia held her breath as they approached, stepping out of their way as the group moved right past her and toward Blaedia's tent.

"What was that all about?" she asked Exie, who remained silent for a moment, jaw tensing.

"I'm not sure. I'll be right back."

Before either sister could respond, Exie jogged toward Blaedia's tent, Taryn following closely behind. Septima and Aurelia exited the training ring, watching Blaedia's tent in silence, unsure of what to do.

"What do you think is going on?" Septima asked, barely concealing the nerves in her voice.

"I don't know, but I don't think it's good."

Aurelia wasn't sure how much time had passed before Exie exited the tent and hurried back to where they sat, her face no longer holding the same lighthearted humor it had before. Without halting her steps, she motioned for them to follow her. The sisters exchanged apprehensive glances as they followed, barely containing their questions.

"What's going on?" Aurelia asked as soon as the tent flap fell shut, her voice coming out higher-pitched than she intended.

"It's your father." Exie paced, her voice low and controlled, her tone even. "He's hunting you. We didn't expect him to draw so near so quickly, He cannot see our clearing, yet his hounds must be gifted with a predator's nose. Already, his men have found our patrols. One of our warriors was injured trying to escape them."

Septima gasped, and Aurelia reached out to take her hand.

"Is she okay?" Septima asked, her voice hitching as she choked out her question, her fear obvious. "Do we have to go back?" Aurelia knew the idea of returning to their seaside villa was no longer an option. Life with their father had never been easy, not since they'd lost their mother, but after running from him and their intended husbands, there was no telling what their life would become.

Exie's eyes softened as she moved forward to embrace Septima, but hesitated, her arm hovering awkwardly in the air before she lowered it to her side. "No. Don't worry. Some wards prevent humans from seeing our camp. He's found the clearing, but he hasn't found us. And she'll be okay. Our bodies heal quickly. More than anything, Blaedia is concerned because your father's people have set up camp near the clearing, so our scouts barely made it past without being noticed. We have groups who go out throughout the day to hunt and check our perimeter. They cannot do that with your father's men so close by."

"So, what are we going to do?" Aurelia asked. Her sister's hand was still trembling in hers.

"We're going to leave. Blaedia is coming up with a plan for where we'll go next."

"Our father will keep searching," said Septima. "I don't think we will get away from him if we stay in the Howling Forest."

Exie nodded. "Blaedia is considering that in her decision. I don't think we will stay in these woods much longer because of that. We will have to cut training short today, but stand by for Blaedia's decision."

Aurelia nodded, her heart pounding in her chest. Just the thought of Proteus finding them, of what he would do to them for running away, chilled her to the bone.

"Should we pack?" she asked, unsure how to pack their tent and all its contents. She had no idea how they had gotten all the tents and furniture into the encampment to begin with.

Exie shook her head. "Don't worry about any of that. It'll be moved for you."

Septima's eyebrows drew together as she glanced around the space. "How?"

A mischievous grin spread across their companion's face as she wiggled her fingers playfully. "Magic."

For the next several hours, the sisters remained in their tent awaiting the general's orders. With hunting dogs as skilled as their father's, they would be tracked down no matter where they were in Vaekros. If there was even a trace of their scents, Proteus would find them. A lump formed in the back of Aurelia's throat as tears of fear and guilt for endangering the camp threatened to spill.

There was no escape as long as they remained on the continent. Blaedia must have come to the same conclusion because when Exie returned a few hours later, they were informed that the entire camp would leave the Howling Forest in seven days.

Although there were dangers to doing so, Blaedia planned to lead the entire camp back through the veil, into Ekotoria—the realm of the fae. The word alone made Aurelia's chest tighten. Until now, it had been myth, whispered in tents and fireside tales. Now it was their destination. Once there, the warriors would regroup in the Spectre Forest and continue plotting to dismantle Warbotach's hold over their territory. All they waited for was to receive confirmation from their allies on the other side of the portal, and then they would leave Vaekros behind for good.

Knowing their father was near made Aurelia uncomfortable, but Blaedia was confident in the wards that obscured the camp. The general did, however, restrict her forces from leaving the safety of the protective enchantments to patrol the forest. Everyone was ordered to stay inside the protected space, and the magical wards were reinforced regularly.

Now that the camp was mobilizing, everything felt more concrete than before. Traveling to another world was no longer a fantasy, but an impending reality. Aurelia was admittedly terrified of journeying to Ekotoria. She was frightened of flying through the enchanted portal on the back of a fairytale creature. Once they arrived, they would encounter countless magical beings she'd never imagined truly existed. Everything frightened her. Even the idea of increasing the distance between them and their home was a scary concept, but she would follow through with her choice for her sister. While Aurelia's inner turmoil ceaselessly rampaged inside her mind, Septima appeared unbothered. It was as if anywhere was better than the life their father had planned for her.

With nothing else to do and nowhere else to go, Blaedia announced a meeting would take place after dinner, where she would share her plans with the camp. Aurelia didn't know what kinds of shenanigans went on in a primarily female warrior camp, but Exie promised that a night of foolishness and revelry would follow the meeting. After all they'd been through over the past few days, Aurelia was simply looking forward to meeting more of the people she would live with for the foreseeable future.

While Septima took a nap that afternoon, Aurelia went to spend time with Kano. Someone had delivered a deer just before she'd arrived, so Kano was buried headfirst in the carcass when she approached, not even lifting his head to acknowledge her. She stifled a gag at the sight of the gore and found a tree stump to sit on, as far away from the carnage as possible. Even with the grotesque view of Kano's mealtime, however, she opted to enjoy the outdoors rather than remain in the dark tent with her grim thoughts.

After he finished eating, Kano perched next to her seat and enthusiastically groomed himself. With the sun's rays warming her, Aurelia dozed off in the forest beside him.

The dinner bell woke her from her slumber. She kissed Kano on top of his head, careful to avoid any bits of deer he'd missed while cleaning himself, and returned to wake Septima. Her sister was already awake and sprawled across her bed, her blank stare fixated on the ceiling.

"What's wrong?" Aurelia climbed onto the bed.

Shrugging, Septima rolled to face her. "I can't stop thinking about him. What if Father finds us? What if he drags us back in chains? I don't know what I would do."

Aurelia wrapped her arm around Septima's shoulders. "Don't worry about that. Blaedia promised we would be safe. They can't be caught here by the humans either. Seven more days. After that, we will be where he can't find us, no matter how many hounds he has."

"Aurelia... Septima..." Exie called from outside their tent.

Climbing out of the bed, they wrapped their cloaks around their shoulders and left the tent. They found the blond warrior leaning casually against a tree, cleaning her nails with a dagger.

"I was just hoping the two of you hadn't changed your minds and left the camp."

"That's not happening." Septima patted Exie on the back. "Sorry to say that you are stuck with us."

With a smile from ear to ear, Exie wrapped her arms around both sisters' shoulders, pulling them into her and leading them to the dining tent. "Good."

On this night, unlike others, there was music playing in the camp as they approached the crowd of warriors near where dinner was served. Instead of everyone lining up inside the dining tent, many were standing outside and moving to the music.

As they grew closer, Aurelia could see and hear why. Three females played a festive blend of fiddles and drums. The attending warriors, most with glasses of brown liquid in their hands, watched the musicians instead of securing their meal. Tables of roasted meats and vegetables were set up outside, as well as containers of that mysterious brown liquid, which Aurelia assumed was some sort of alcohol.

Instead of leading them to the food, Exie tugged them straight toward a long trestle table laden with bottles and kegs. The sharp, sweet tang of spirits filled the air, mingling with roasted meat and smoke. She poured three glasses, shoved the drinks into their hands, and clinked both of theirs with her own.

"Cheers!" Exie shouted enthusiastically. She finished the alcohol in one gulp and slammed her glass down on the table. Aurelia and Septima followed suit, but not with the ease their friend had. Both sisters gagged as the liquid fire hit their throats.

"What is this?" Aurelia choked out, still feeling the residual burn in her chest.

Chuckling, Exie refilled her empty glass. "It's Aegrician whiskey. Don't tell me it's too much for the two of you?"

Septima forced back the rest of the liquid in her glass and failed to completely stifle a gasp as the liquor hit her throat. "It's different from the berry wine we are used to, but I can handle it."

Raising an eyebrow, Exie clanged her glass against theirs once again, nearly toppling the glass from Aurelia's hand. "To a night of fun," she said as she tossed back another glass of liquid fire. She grabbed a roasted turkey leg and tore into it greedily. Aurelia couldn't help but laugh. Exie may have been a warrior, but she sometimes seemed like anything but.

"So," Aurelia started as she reached for her own piece of roasted meat. "You mentioned other warriors had husbands at home. Do you have one waiting for you to return?"

Exie snorted and almost choked on her food. "Definitely not! Binding myself to a man is at the bottom of my list. Like your sister, I've no interest in husbands."

Septima smiled down at her glass before scanning the perimeter.

"Come on," Exie said, moving toward the crowd. "Let me introduce the two of you to some of my friends."

CHAPTER NINE

Howling Forest

Aurelia

By the time they stumbled back to their tent, the world spun violently as the trees danced. The trek seemed far more perilous and salacious than it should have been. Exie led the way, but she was not much help since she, too, was heavily intoxicated. She led them into three different tents, all belonging to other warriors, before they found the path that led to theirs. All but the last was vacant, thankfully. After witnessing the nude acrobatics in the occupied tent, movements that had the trio backing out with their hands over their eyes, they were afraid to enter the wrong tent again. Blushes colored their cheeks as they made their way home, hoping the occupants would forget their faces by morning.

Their giggling grew more obnoxious, and Septima's stumbling got progressively worse as they soldiered on. Exie and Aurelia had to carry Septima the latter half of the way, because she had consumed a few too many glasses of the Aegrician whiskey.

Aurelia was a little more conservative with the quantity she drank, wanting to focus more on socializing than getting wasted and not remembering anything the next day. It was a decision she would be proud of by morning while teasing her hungover sister.

The night had been fun. Exie introduced them to several of the female warriors and a few of the males who traveled with the camp in other capacities. Everyone had been incredibly friendly. Still, Aurelia couldn't help but wonder if that was because of the free-flowing alcohol or if they genuinely accepted the human sisters who entered their camp and put them at risk.

From what she could tell, Exie's best friend was a silver-haired woman named Holera. They had a snarky friendship where banter laced nearly every line spoken between them. Watching them pick on each other nearly brought Aurelia to tears of laughter.

Exie explained that she and Holera met when they attended warrior training. They were in the same group because they were close in age. Aurelia did not know how old the warriors were. She thought it rude to ask, but she knew they were far older than she was. From the snippets of conversation she'd overheard around the encampment, she surmised Ekotorians had longer lifespans than humans, and Aegricians were nearly immortal. Their abilities as phoenix shifters allowed them to regenerate life in their fire. So, although they could be killed, they didn't die of natural causes as humans did, nor did they age quite as fast. While she didn't fully understand how it all worked, she assumed Exie was ancient compared to her.

At first, Aurelia thought Exie and Holera may have been lovers. They were so comfortable with one another that it was a fair assumption. The speculation was erased, however, when Holera stuck her tongue down a man named Kason's throat. There weren't many men at their camp—not one had piqued Aurelia's interest—but clearly Holera found one worthy of kissing and seized the opportunity. He had not seemed shocked by her unprovoked advances, so it must not have been the first time. They ran off together as Exie broke out into song and dance, drawing Aurelia's attention away from the fleeing lovers.

Blaedia and Taryn did not attend the party. They showed their faces long enough for Blaedia to make a few announcements to the crowd about their plans to return to Ekotoria by week's end. There was a bit of rumbling through the crowd, mostly concerns about their collective safety, but the general did her best to put those insecurities to rest before she and Taryn returned to their tents for the night.

After what felt like a never-ending journey to their tent, Aurelia and Exie deposited Septima on her bed and tucked her in for the night. Septima did not say a word when she collided with her bed. She rolled over and fell asleep instantly. Exie patted Aurelia on the back hard—her movements rough and clumsy in her inebriated state—and reminded her of their early morning training session. She turned to leave, walking into the canvas wall before stumbling out of their tent in search of her own.

Aurelia almost followed her, to ensure she actually made it back. In the end, she decided Exie could take care of herself. Still, she peeked through the tent flap to watch Exie until she turned toward her tent. She wasn't totally a rotten friend, after all.

Unlike Septima, who still wore her fighting leathers that reeked of sweat and dirt, Aurelia changed into her nightdress. They had missed their nightly shower, which left her feeling disgusting. She promised herself she'd shower immediately after their morning training as she crawled into bed. For the first time since she'd joined the Aegrician camp, her thoughts were quiet, and she fell into a dreamless sleep quickly.

Exie did not wake the sisters at dawn, nor did the toll of the breakfast bell disturb their rest. By the time they had awoken, still groggy from their drunken stupor, the cooks were already preparing lunch. Even their trainer had slept in after the long night of drinking, singing, and dancing, and did not look for them.

After peeking into the dining tent to see when the next meal would be served, they made their way to Exie's quarters, lamenting the breakfast they missed.

When they reached Exie's tent, they heard emphatic grumbling and moaning from outside. They didn't dare barge in, but Septima called out to her, just to ensure their friend was okay.

"Come back tomorrow," Exie whined. "I'm too busy dying today. I'll never drink again." The sisters laughed, twinging at the pain that lanced through their battered brains, before they poked their heads inside. They were greeted by the sight of Exie, clothes askew with hair that resembled a rat's nest, sprawled across her bed with one shoe still on.

"Are you going to make it?" Aurelia teased. She pulled off Exie's shoe and worked to twist her until she was lying on the bed the right way. The only response she received was somewhere between a grunt and a whine. "We'll bring you food when they serve lunch."

Septima grabbed a pitcher of water from the bedside table, poured a glass, and offered it to Exie. "Here. Drink this. You need to rehydrate if you want your head to feel better."

The hungover warrior rolled just enough to take a sip before she buried her face into the bed. "How are you not suffering right now, Septima?" The mattress muffled Exie's words. "You were drunker than me last night."

Septima's cheeks flushed. She sat on the foot of the bed, slouching forward to hide her embarrassment. "Because I woke up before dawn and drank nearly an entire pitcher of water before going back to sleep. I felt just as awful as you this morning."

Before Septima uttered the last word, Exie let out a booming snore. The sisters left as silently as they could, letting their friend sleep off the alcohol.

Knowing they still had time until lunch, Aurelia and Septima took a stroll around the camp. They had yet to get a proper look at their temporary new home, nor did they get to meet many of its occupants.

It was the perfect day to explore. The breeze blew gently through the trees surrounding them. The temperature was tolerable thanks to the layers of leather, cloth, and fur they wore.

The camp was larger than they realized. Hundreds of tents spread throughout the tree line surrounding the clearing. Most appeared to be sleeping quarters for the warriors who filled the dinner tent every night. There were surprisingly only a few people out and about as they wandered. Aurelia figured the long night of debauchery had claimed many victims who needed to sleep the Aegrician whiskey off.

Although Blaedia decided they would no longer leave the protection of their wards to patrol the beyond, warriors remained stationed along the perimeter. Aurelia wondered, as she and Septima approached the outermost path on the eastern border, if her father's men were still searching nearby with the hounds. The thought sent a foreboding chill through her. She hoped he had moved on by now, though a part of her knew her father would never stop searching. Their escape was a slap to his pride and damaging to his reputation. He would hunt them to the ends of the world. It was enough of a reason to be thankful they would be traveling to another world soon.

Septima spoke, slicing through Aurelia's inner musings. "So, what do you think about all of this? Truthfully."

"About what, specifically?" Aurelia realized what information her sister was probing for, and her stomach tightened into an uneasy knot. Septima was clearly concerned about how much Aurelia was giving up, worried there would be resentment between them in the future if Aurelia sacrificed her own life solely for Septima's happiness.

Aurelia watched Septima from the corner of her eye as she shrugged, her head hanging mournfully. She reached out and grasped her sister's hand. "I don't know. I suppose I just want to know what you think about us leaving Vaekros behind. It's a big change."

Aurelia gave her sister's hand a reassuring squeeze. "I know it is, and I'm happy to do it. Don't worry about me. I didn't have much of a life or a future back home, either. I go where you go. It's always been that way. You and Kano are my home, not the home that awaited me after entering a loveless marriage and definitely not the villa. That place stopped being home when Mother died."

"What about Amadeus?" The question was a physical blow to the gut. Aurelia swallowed thickly, trying to keep her voice from cracking.

"I'll miss him, of course, but he has his own life. He's an adult who will be married and create a family of his own soon. I'm surprised he isn't married yet."

Septima chuckled fondly as they spoke of their brother. "That's because someone would have to put up with him." Aurelia joined in on the joke. Their brother's pride was the size of a continent, but it didn't translate to cleanliness. He could dominate in a sword fight, but he couldn't seem to keep his dirty underwear and socks off the floor.

"Yes. She will need to be great at apologizing for things that were not her fault and picking up behind him. Poor woman."

"I'll miss him, too." Septima sighed loudly, catching the attention of the guards who stood along the boundary of the path they traversed.

The sisters waved sheepishly before they turned in another direction. "I'm starving. Do you think they've laid out lunch yet?" Aurelia glanced toward the clearing, barely able to see through the trees. "Only one way to find out."

Arm in arm, they dropped the conversation about their family, and any hesitation about leaving the human lands, and ventured into the trees toward the dining tent.

CHAPTER TEN

HOWLING FOREST

AURELIA

Septima and Aurelia approached the dinner tent and saw a long line of people waiting to be fed. The hungover warriors trudged through the open flap, lacking their usual chatter and energy as they grabbed their food. The sisters quickened their pace when they spotted Exie. Although she still seemed to be feeling the effects of the night before, her hair was at least brushed now. Slumped against a tree trunk, she shyly avoided the sun's rays as she waited for them. Aurelia couldn't help but notice the smile that crept onto her sister's face as they approached the blond.

"Before you say anything," Exie quipped, "you didn't see me like that. I'm a terrifying, fully in-control warrior. Got it?"

They snickered and nodded in unison.

"Got it," Aurelia replied. "Well, let's get this beast of a warrior some food, shall we?"

Exie raised an eyebrow skeptically, but then gestured with her hand for them to lead the way.

The tent was still crowded, but there were a few more empty tables than usual, a sure sign that some were still sleeping off their hangovers. After grabbing bowls of stew for themselves, the trio joined Holera at her table. She leaned over her bowl, greeting them with a grunt through half-lidded eyes. Kason, the man she had left the mixer with, was shoveling food into his mouth faster than he could chew. He looked up, nodded at them, and then returned to his lunch.

Aurelia studied him for a moment. She had been told that Aegrician males held various jobs, but he certainly looked like a warrior. Aegrician women were taller than average humans, and so were the men. Kason was exceptionally tall compared to human men, with muscles that seemed endless. His thick, black hair, which he had pulled back into a leather strap at the nape of his neck, contrasted starkly with Holera's long, silver hair and accentuated his sharp jawline.

With his size, muscles, and the intricate tattoos covering his arms, Kason made Aurelia's mouth water. Although he was clearly taken, she briefly wondered if her future might include a man like him. If all the Ekotorian men resembled Kason, and she hoped they did, maybe mating with someone from a foreign magical land wouldn't be so bad.

She was so lost in thought that she didn't realize she was still staring. He caught her appreciative gaze and flashed her a wry smile, even winking at her before turning back to Holera. Aurelia's cheeks flushed a deep crimson as her eyes darted downward. If she kept her gaze fixed on her bowl, perhaps she could avoid embarrassing herself any further.

The venison and root vegetable stew smelled rich and earthy. It was a version of the same meal they had been given nearly every day since arriving at the camp. She couldn't complain, however, since all they had fled the villa with was a bit of dried meat and fruit. At least they were getting hot food with more than one ingredient.

Exie, who had been gagging since the moment the aroma hit her nostrils, forced down her first bite. For a moment, Aurelia was sure the stew would come back up, but Exie's determination seemed to win the internal battle with her stomach. She continued to make herself eat. "Next time I try to drink that much," she said, slumping her shoulders over the table, "knock me unconscious."

Septima laughed, nodding as she patted the warrior on the back. "I'll make it my personal mission. But I really enjoyed that performance last night and was hoping for an encore. How did that song go? Was it something about wine and a stone wall?"

Aurelia snorted, covering her mouth with her hand to avoid spewing food at Kason.

Exie scowled and buried her face in her palms. "Oh, gods. Did I really sing that damned song again? Forget you ever heard it." She glared at them through her fingers. "How large was my audience? Please say it was only the two of you."

Aurelia grinned and shook her head. "Sorry, friend. You basically performed in front of the entire camp. You even danced. Did you choreograph those moves, or were they all spur of the moment?"

Exie flew forward, her hair flailing wildly as she repeatedly banged her head on the table. "This is so embarrassing."

Septima chuckled. "Just own it, Exie. Everyone else was just as drunk as you were. I doubt anyone remembers."

Lifting her head from the table, Exie shot her an incredulous scowl. "That's highly unlikely."

"So," Aurelia interjected to give her friend a break, "are we going to train tomorrow?"

"Absolutely." Exie's tone turned serious; any thoughts of her performance were forgotten. "Blaedia would probably skin me alive if she knew we skipped today."

"What would she expect after a party like that?" Septima asked as she pushed her empty bowl away. "I doubt anyone trained today."

"You're right," Exie sighed. "And that's unfortunate. The likelihood of us being drawn into battle soon is high. We can't afford distractions like last night. So, although it was fun, I doubt we will have another celebration until we take our territory back."

Even though the impending war made a pit form in her stomach, Aurelia nodded. She didn't fully understand the conflict in Aegricia. Still, she knew enough to recognize how crucial it was to reclaim the crown before the Warbotach leader found a way to manipulate it to his advantage. Their success was vital not just for the Aegricians but also for the humans on her side of the portal. If Uldon and the Warbotach army crossed into their realm, they would face certain destruction, utterly unaware of the danger.

Later that night, Aurelia was jolted awake by the sound of barking. She knew there were dogs in the camp, but there weren't nearly enough to create the cacophony echoing around her tent. Grabbing the fur cape from beside her bed, she and Septima rushed out into the still-dark forest, their heads whipping around for any clue as to what was happening.

Aurelia didn't know what time it was, but the full moon hung high in the sky, and the sun showed no signs of rising. Kano's ears were pulled back against his head, and his teeth were bared. Though the sisters were still confused, the tiger's reaction indicated that there was a threat nearby.

The sisters scurried between the row of tents, holding hands for fear of being separated, and dashed toward the sparring rings, where they spotted a large group of wide-eyed warriors, all circling the space, trying to determine the source of the incessant barking. Blaedia and a pajama-clad Taryn rushed from tents on opposite sides of the clearing and joined the group.

No one dared to speak as they fixated on their general. The silence kept the dogs from hearing them, but it also prevented any information from being shared. Several warriors, including the general and commander, ran toward the southern end of the camp, communicating only with hand signals.

No one followed them. The vicious barks and snarls shattered the otherwise peaceful night. The air was still, not even a slight breeze blowing, as if it were aiding in hiding the sisters and their scent. Aurelia sensed that the aggressive hounds belonged to her father. She could feel it in her gut, but it only added to her fear of what that meant.

Pushing her way through the mass of warrior women, Exie grabbed each sister by the forearm, yanking them toward Blaedia's tent without offering any explanation.

"What's going on?" Aurelia whispered, but Exie shook her head roughly, her eyes wide in a silent warning as she continued to pull them along.

As soon as they entered Blaedia's tent, Exie lit a candle and sat at the table, her face pinched in distress, aging her youthful features by at least a decade. She dragged her hands down her face in a slow, measured movement, as if trying to avoid answering Aurelia's question. After a long moment, she heaved a sigh and met the eldest sister's gaze.

"Your father's hounds have scented you through our wards. They are going wild just outside our barrier. We thought the wards would block your scent from escaping, but we were wrong. Blaedia and the others are reinforcing the boundary now, but it will not hold for long. The animals will break through, even if the humans cannot, and when they do, the enchantments will fail. We will not last five more days here. The time to leave Vaekros is upon us. I wouldn't be surprised if we cross through the portal before sunset, maybe even before sunrise."

Aurelia's heart gave a pitiful squeeze before racing wildly. Its erratic thumping overwhelmed her ears and made her head throb painfully. Exie said something else, but Aurelia couldn't make it out. Her panic was too intense, too consuming. Everything was happening so fast that her world spun.

Taking slow, deep breaths, she tried to steady herself so she could rejoin the conversation. She attempted to lick her lips, but her mouth felt like a desert. "Will it be safe to go to Ekotoria right now? Where will we go? What will we do?" The words came out rough and garbled as she forced them out.

Septima wrapped her arm around Aurelia's shoulders, giving her a comforting squeeze. Exie was visibly struggling to keep a neutral expression, but worry broke through her mask.

"We'll set up camp in Spectre Forest," she said. "Is it safe? Well, nowhere is truly safe right now. But this isn't your fault—us having to leave, I mean. We weren't supposed to be here anyway. It was only a matter of time before we returned to Ekotoria to prepare for our attack. We came here first because Warbotach could not follow. There are also more dangers in Spectre Forest than the one we're facing now, but our warriors are strong. We will be fine."

Septima swallowed loudly and moved closer to her sister. Exie attempted a weak smile of reassurance.

"What do you mean by more dangers?" Septima asked, her voice barely above a whisper. It was a question echoed in Aurelia's mind as well.

"Magical beings. Some are monstrous brutes, while others are devious and use their wits rather than sheer strength. We will shield our camp, just as we have done here, but we'll need to be on higher alert there. It doesn't really matter, though. We must get back to Ekotoria, regardless. Training is just a minor part of the plan to reclaim our territory. We need to form alliances, and we can't do that from here. We would have returned whether you two had crashed the party or not. Now, go back to your tent and dress in warm layers. Spectre Forest is frigid this time of year. Kano will soon be caged and ready for transport. I suspect it won't be long before we leave this forest for good."

Aurelia's eyes widened in shock as she let out a gasp. Her mind started to process the implications of everything they had been told, leading her to a horrifying conclusion. "Exie... won't my fath—I mean, Proteus, and his men see us? You said we would have to fly to Ekotoria. Can the wards shield us in the sky? Vaekrosan soldiers are renowned marksmen."

Exie shook her head grimly, and Aurelia felt a wave of regret wash over her for the first time. The Aegricians had taken them in, expecting nothing in return, and now they had brought an enemy to their door. If their father harmed even one phoenix, it would be their fault.

Not privy to Aurelia's inner turmoil, Exie continued, "Once we fly above the treetops, we will be visible. That's why we need to be prepared to leave at a moment's notice. If we can't leave before sunrise, we'll have to struggle to maintain our wards until sunset. The darkness will help to obscure us. If they see us, well, I hope we're far enough away to dodge their arrows."

With that frightening reminder, the sisters followed Exie's advice and returned to their tent to pack their belongings. They dressed in the warmest layers they could find and filled their wooden trunks with the clothes and blankets the Aegricians had given them. Clad in leather pants, tunics, and fur-lined capes, they returned to the clearing and joined the gathering of warriors. Aurelia was unsure how the large camp, overflowing with tents and other belongings, would be relocated, but Exie had mentioned that magic was involved. With her limited understanding of the mystical world, she could hardly imagine how such a feat could be accomplished.

The barking that penetrated their invisible barrier had decreased in volume but not in intensity, as if they had moved further away. The aggression of the sound indicated that the threat had not left their borders; rather, the placement of new wards had been successful. Hopefully, this would provide them with enough of an opportunity to flee the clearing without being spotted. Blaedia and her commander approached the cluster of women, appearing more determined and fierce than Aurelia had ever seen them.

"Our plans have changed. The threat outside our wards has increased. We will evacuate this camp before sunrise." No one made a sound as Blaedia addressed them, not even the creatures of the forest. Her voice carried authority, confident and resonant. It was clear she was an experienced general who expected everyone to follow her orders without hesitation. "Prepare yourselves. We'll reconvene at the rendezvous point in one hour. Lanistas, the tiger comes with us. You know what to do."

"Who is Lanistas?" Aurelia whispered, startled by Exie's presence, having been so focused on Blaedia that she missed her friend's arrival.

"Lanista is a job title, not a person. They are our animal trainers. Don't worry. Kano will be in capable hands. They'll sedate and cage him. It will be best if he isn't conscious during the flight."

Aurelia wasn't convinced. It wasn't that she didn't trust the lanistas, but Kano had been agitated by the barking and was on high alert. She was worried about him but nodded in acknowledgment before returning her attention to Blaedia, who was busy assigning specific tasks to the warriors.

A group of approximately twenty females and a few males left the meeting, breaking off into smaller groups as they approached the tents surrounding the clearing. Aurelia watched as the canvas structures began to disappear before her very eyes, and her mind struggled to comprehend the sight.

Septima's eyes widened in surprise as she focused on the vanishing act, but no one else seemed to notice.

Once the general finished issuing orders, the remaining warriors splintered off to complete their assigned tasks. Aurelia and Septima stayed in the clearing, unsure of what to do next. Exie seemed to take pity on them and hooked her arms through theirs, pulling them toward Kano's enclosure.

"Let's go get that beast of yours into a cage," Exie quipped, attempting a cheerful tone.

When they approached Kano's enclosure, Exie released their arms and opened the gate with a medallion identical to Aurelia's. Kano prowled the area, his tail twitching in agitation. He straightened from his defensive stance when he spotted the sisters and dashed over, nuzzling his face into Aurelia's legs as she rubbed his head. He let out a low purr at her touch. As Aurelia petted him, Exie placed her hands on his back. His eyes grew heavy, and he lay at their feet. He was unconscious in seconds. Aurelia's heart ached at the sight. She knew he would be okay; she trusted Exie. Still, seeing her constant companion bend to her magic, watching his joyful greeting turn into an unnatural slumber, was almost too much to bear. She fell to her knees and wrapped her arms around him, tears streaming down her cheeks.

"It's okay, it's okay." Exie crouched beside her, affectionately petting the enormous cat. "He's only been sedated, so he isn't stressed during travel. This is a better alternative for him. He will wake up feeling like he had the best nap of his life." Sniffing, Aurelia lifted her head to meet Exie's gaze. She nodded, setting her jaw in determination as she fought back tears, but her heart struggled to keep pace with what her mind knew.

He's not dead. It's just magic. He'll be okay. She mentally repeated this mantra to soothe her frazzled nerves as she stood, gazing down at her beloved pet. Exie waved her hand slightly, and a large metal cage formed around him. The enclosure vanished, replaced by trees and foliage that blended in with the surrounding forest. Aside from the three women and the great cat, it was as if the enclosed area had never existed.

The forest appeared natural, as if the encampment had been a figment of Aurelia's imagination. The only evidence of their presence was the hundreds of warriors fumbling with various-sized packs and containers as they prepared for departure. None of the luggage seemed large enough to hold the camp's contents. This made Aurelia wonder if they had magically shrunk everything to a portable size or if they had somehow teleported the larger items. The concept of magic still felt foreign to her; she couldn't help but contemplate both its possibilities and limitations.

Her thoughts did nothing to calm her nervous stomach, which churned uneasily as they waited to leave the clearing. The moment was nearing. Soon, she would be leaving her home—her realm—to venture into a world she had never known existed. She reached for Septima's hand, expecting it to be trembling, but it was steady, showing no hint of fear or unease that Aurelia felt. She recognized that familiar spark in her sister's eyes. Her longing for adventure had returned. Septima's unwavering gaze and steadfast presence gave Aurelia the strength to confront her fears.

A short while later, Taryn joined them, patting Aurelia on the shoulder and flashing her a reassuring smile before approaching Kano's cage to check its security. Two others moved closer and connected large cables to the metal crate that would carry him as they flew.

"What if they drop him?" The thought made bile rise in Aurelia's throat, and she forced it down, unable to bear the images her imagination conjured.

While she watched Kano being prepared for their journey, Blaedia stepped forward, facing the group of warriors. The muffled whispers of the crowd fell silent as she raised her arm above her head. She communicated a few silent hand signals, and the clearing erupted into bright, colored flames, the heat washing over Aurelia as the warriors transformed before her eyes.

Chapter Eleven

Howling Forest

Aurelia

The scene was both magical and horrifying. Aurelia took a step back at the sight, unsure of how to react. Just moments earlier, she had been surrounded by hundreds of warriors. Although they were much taller than she, they still appeared human. But now, she and Septima were the only women left. Apart from a few dozen men, they were engulfed in a storm of wings and firelight—enormous, iridescent birds with feathers that shimmered like living jewels. The clearing exploded with color: scarlet, gold, sapphire, emerald—each feather catching the moonlight as if the stars themselves had descended.

When Exie explained their ability to shift forms, Aurelia tried to picture it. She imagined they would be the size of an eagle or perhaps a small dog, but they were far larger than she could have ever imagined. Most of them were the size of small horses.

Exie remained beside them in her stunning phoenix form. Feathers of nearly every hue shimmered across her avian body, creating a living rainbow. However, the crest atop her head still bore streaks of blonde, a reminder of her fae self. Her warm brown eyes anchored Aurelia—familiar amid the nightmare of beak and talons curved to rend flesh. Her long tail feathers fluttered in the stiff breeze, resembling the colorful ribbons Aurelia had played with as a child.

Exie's familiar golden eyes were set in an eagle-like head that looked fierce. Her sharp beak and pointed features were the stuff of nightmares. With talons longer than Aurelia's fingers, there was no doubt that her friend could tear flesh from bone as easily as slicing through butter. Her wings, primarily red and gold, spanned wider than their tent as she stretched and shook them out.

Exie dipped her head slowly, as if afraid to startle them. Her eyes held a reassuring gaze. She couldn't speak in this form, but it was clear she was trying to communicate that she was still herself and not to be feared.

They were in the presence of a friend, a friend they trusted with their lives. Yet, Aurelia and Septima could only stare at Exie in stunned silence, unsure of how to react.

Harsh winds whipped around them, causing their cloaks to snap against their bodies. Dust clouds formed mini tornadoes as the phoenixes took to the air in small groups. Aurelia watched her beloved Kano being lifted up, held firmly in the talons of a bird the color of fire. He was pulled into the sky, still asleep from Exie's magic.

Forced to look away from her feline friend, Aurelia noticed another phoenix, crimson-feathered with accents of black, approaching them from the direction Taryn had just stood. Stepping in front of the sisters, Exie and Taryn bowed their heads, giving an encouraging nod when the sisters did not move.

Despite her uncertainty, Aurelia trusted the warriors who had taken them in and promised a future. The Vesta sisters exchanged a glance, their resolve evident, and climbed onto the backs of the impossibly large birds.

Aurelia settled into the groove at the nape of Taryn's neck, mounting the phoenix as she would a bareback horse. Reins adorned her friend's neck, and Aurelia gripped the handhold firmly before ensuring Septima had done the same. The warriors waited until their passengers were secure before stretching their wings.

The moon had long since begun its descent, but the sun had yet to make an appearance as the flock of phoenixes flapped their enormous wings and rose into the treetops with a few swift beats.

Terror and exhilaration intertwined in Aurelia's chest. Every rise and plunge made her stomach lurch, yet the sheer power of the wings beating beneath her thrilled her to her bones. Part of Aurelia wanted to vomit, but the other part wanted to laugh. The feeling was overwhelming, a paradox of fear and wonder that she couldn't shake off.

Relief flooded her as they moved away from the camp, placing them beyond the range of arrows. If her father's party had aimed at them, no arrows had found their mark.

Taryn and Exie flew alongside each other, leaving just enough space to avoid crashing their massive wings into one another. Septima's face was filled with joy as she leaned forward on Exie's back, periodically closing her eyes against the wind that lashed at them.

The sun peeked over the crest of the Howling Mountains as they gained speed, soaring low over the Harmuz Sea toward the Marella Arch. Aurelia had spent her entire life marveling at the arch, dreaming of traversing the rough sea to reach it, but she had never expected to make that journey on the back of a phoenix. She closed her eyes in fear as they drew nearer, bracing for a crash and the threat of drowning.

Taryn folded her wings against her massive body and shot toward the target. Aurelia gripped the reins so tightly that her fingers went numb, but her terror proved unfounded. She forced herself to look as Taryn glided through the center of the arch without so much as a feather brushing its weathered surface.

Stealing a glance back to ensure that Exie and Septima were still following, Aurelia slammed her eyes shut once more. She felt the environment shifting around her as they traversed worlds. The air thickened, rippling like water across her skin. Every breath tasted strange, heavy with metal and smoke, as if she were inhaling another reality. Her ears rang, her stomach dropped, and then it was gone.

When she dared to peek again, her eyes widened in shock. They were so high, flying just above the clouds, and Aurelia felt an urge to reach out and touch them. Shock was the only reason she had refrained from doing so. A line of colorful phoenixes flew in front of them, capturing her attention away from the white tufts they soared over.

The clouds thinned as they pressed forward, and Aurelia cast another glance down. The view was both terrifying and stunning. They soared over water that shimmered a deep sapphire, far darker and more brilliant than the Harmuz Sea that their villa overlooked. The sight and the violent gusts that buffeted her took her breath away.

Although the experience was unforgettable, Aurelia soon found herself ready to reach their destination. Her hands, which had once gone numb from her fearful grip, now felt numb for a different reason. She had dressed as warmly as possible, but the temperatures were harsh as they raced across the sky. She'd lost feeling in nearly every limb, her eyes stinging and dry from the relentless wind, and she wasn't sure how much more she could endure.

Just as she was about to tell Taryn that she couldn't handle flying any longer, shades of dark green appeared on the horizon, growing closer with every flap of their wings.

Aurelia focused on a solitary black feather at the back of Taryn's head as they began their descent. The rapid elevation change made her ears pop and her stomach flip violently. Suddenly, she was grateful they hadn't eaten breakfast before leaving. Taryn's wings stretched wide as they glided toward the forest floor, fluttering slightly just before they landed with a soft thud. Aurelia slid from Taryn's back and took a moment to absorb her new surroundings.

At first glance, the Spectre Forest could be mistaken for ordinary woodlands, but the longer she stared, the more it revealed its true nature. Shadows clung to the trees in unnatural ways, stretching beyond what the light could explain. The ferns shimmered faintly as if dusted with starlight, and tiny spheres of pale fire drifted between the trunks. Coiling vines wrapped around certain trees, while a variety of flowers—desperately trying to claim the last remnants of light from their taller neighbors—adorned the muted forest floor. A symphony of sounds, dominated by songbirds and descending phoenixes, echoed through the air, creating a chaotic orchestra in harmony with the wind whistling through the swaying treetops.

Exie had warned them about the magical creatures dwelling in the forest. Still, Aurelia noticed nothing unusual until she looked more closely. Tiny balls of light twinkled as they flitted among the trees. She didn't know what they were, but she was mesmerized until a gust of wind swept her hair across her face, redirecting her attention.

Phoenixes shifted back into women all around her. Taryn joined them, transforming back into her tall, beautiful fae form.

Aurelia spotted Exie and Septima a few yards away and ran to her sister, wrapping her in an embrace. Tears blurred her vision until the entire forest swam before her eyes. Relief, grief, and terror mingled within her. She couldn't untangle the emotions. All she knew was that something inside her had cracked open, spilling out years of fear and longing.

Their reunion was cut short by Blaedia's command. Her voice sliced through the clearing—brisk and unyielding—reminding them that even moments of wonder demanded vigilance. Despite the long flight, they still had to walk a few hours inland to find a secure location.

Kano, now awake and freed from his confines, strolled between Aurelia and Septima on a long leash, which he periodically tangled by darting into the tree line to snatch small animals to eat.

By the time they found a suitable clearing to set up camp, Aurelia was exhausted. If they had given her more than a moment of rest during their relentless trek, she would have fallen asleep in the dirt. She forced herself to stay awake as Blaedia, Taryn, and several other warriors erected wards around the perimeter of their camp. Aurelia didn't know much about the magic they wielded, but she watched, transfixed, as the environment seemed to bend to their will with each sweep of the warriors' hands.

The clearing was not as large as the one in Vaekros, but the phoenixes were making it work. Everyone had a job to do except for Aurelia and Septima, which made Aurelia feel out of place. Tents were being set up around them, and the smell of food being prepared filled the air.

"So, how was your flight?" Aurelia asked as she and Septima approached the dinner tent. After getting Kano settled in his new enclosure and visiting their tent, the sisters had nearly sprinted at the sound of the lunch bell. After leaving Vaekros before dawn and flying for hours, they were famished.

Septima turned to her, grabbing her hands, her eyes sparkling with excitement. "Oh, my gods, Lia! It was so thrilling! The wind in my face... I felt so free. I've never felt more alive. What about you?"

Septima's enthusiasm was so infectious that Aurelia forgot her earlier complaints about the journey. They chatted about their flying experiences as they stood in line, giggling as they grabbed their stew and found a place to sit. Exie plopped down beside them and dug into her meal without a word. They all ate in ravenous silence. Aurelia was so hungry that she didn't even ask what kind of meat surrounded the chunks of potatoes and carrots.

"How sick did you get?" Exie asked with a wide grin.

Aurelia rolled her eyes. "I didn't get sick, but thanks for your concern."

Exie chuckled. "I'm just kidding. I'm glad you didn't get sick. Taryn wouldn't give you another ride if you lost your stomach on her, and we'll likely have to fly again. Septima did great. She giggled almost the entire time."

Aurelia glanced at her sister, whose cheeks were flushed. "I heard all about it," she said before changing the subject. "What are we going to do now?"

Exie looked around the camp before returning her gaze to Aurelia. Her grin faded, and she hesitated before answering. The warrior's usual swagger seemed to falter as she spoke barely above a whisper. "Blaedia, Taryn, and the other officers will convene to make a solid plan. For now, we will train as we did before. Emissary groups will be sent to Diapolis and Norithae for negotiations, but I'm not sure when that will happen. We need to form alliances, but Norithae was attacked by Warbotach before we were. Their government is in disarray right now; at least, that's what we've heard through received communications. Their king, Orpheus, was killed, and his heir is missing while a Warbotach general oversees their territory. The remaining inhabitants of Aegricia and the Norithae people are biding their time, unwilling to lose more lives until they are strong enough to reclaim their kingdoms. Our most likely allies will be them. They have more to lose than Diapolis, which is on the opposite end of the continent and not currently in danger of invasion. Diapolis might very well choose to stay out of the conflict. I wouldn't blame them if they did."

"So, we will start back with training?" Aurelia asked, focusing on the one thing they had control over in this situation. Septima stared at Exie, her longing for adventure still shining in her eyes despite everything they had been told.

"Yes. Training begins at first light. For today, eat, sleep, and prepare yourselves. Tomorrow, the real work begins."

Chapter Twelve

Aegricia

Otera

The iron door to Otera's cell groaned open on rusted hinges, the shriek of metal against metal echoing through the stone chamber like a scream.

A small, hunched figure shuffled into the darkness, the tray rattling faintly in her trembling hands. Her cloak dragged along the filthy floor, gathering straw and dust. The slender window allowed just enough sunlight into the shadowy prison for Otera to make out the frail woman's features: *Bremusa*.

From the shadows beyond the door came the guttural rumble of a guard clearing his throat—a reminder that danger lingered just steps away. From under Bremusa's hooded cloak, Otera caught a glimpse of her darting eyes as they flicked to her right hand and then back to the open door behind her.

Otera's hands trembled as she lunged at the hunched woman, her heart pounding with the weight of their risky defiance. She discreetly pulled out a folded sheet of paper as she took the tray of food into her own hands. Her fear was not just for herself, but for Bremusa—frail, loyal Bremusa—who risked a horrific death for this one chance at defiance. If Uldon found out the elderly woman had slipped her a note, he would carry out his threat to punish anyone who defied his rule. Bremusa would be strung up between two of his fire-breathing horses and torn apart.

"Hurry up, you old crone," snapped the gruff voice from the poorly illuminated hall.

Bremusa squeezed Otera's hand with gentle affection before scurrying back out and closing the door behind her.

Otera rushed to the window and held the note under the solitary ray of sunlight that fought its way into her bleak accommodations.

The birds have landed.

That was all it said, but those four words blazed brighter than a hundred torches. Otera pressed the paper to her chest, closing her eyes and absorbing the fragile hope she had thought extinguished. The relief was palpable, a beacon of light in the darkness of her imprisonment.

Raising her palm, she summoned a single flame. Without her crown and trapped within Uldon's wards, it was the only power she could wield, but it was enough. Otera cupped her palm, and a small, weak flame flickered to life. She fed the note to it, watching as the fire consumed the paper, curling it into black ash. She lifted her hand to the barred window, allowing the ashes to scatter into the wind like a whispered prayer. She hoped her people and her land could feel the promise of help that those ashes carried. Her connection to them was unbreakable, her hope for their freedom unwavering.

CHAPTER THIRTEEN

HOWLING FOREST

AURELIA

"Remember how I told you there was more to this world than what your eyes can see?" Taryn's gaze locked onto Aurelia with such intensity that it felt like she was being weighed on unseen scales. Aurelia shifted uncomfortably in her seat. The way they stared made her feel like she was being evaluated, as if they had something crucial to share but wanted to ensure the sisters could handle it. Aurelia nodded, reaching for her sister's hand under the table.

"Our land is not of the same realm as yours. It is close, but not everyone can cross over the threshold. That is why we are at war."

"Your realm? What threshold?" Aurelia's mind spun. Who were these women?

Taryn tilted her head toward Blaedia, who continued the explanation.

"We are not of your world, Aurelia. We are not of the human world. You may know us as *ignis avis*—phoenixes. Fire-born. Eternal. We wear this form, the shape of women, because it suits us. Beneath the skin, our true selves blaze with wings and flame. Humanity is a mask, not our essence. We take this form unless our powers are needed. But we are not human; we are fae. We enjoy the advantages of a human-like body, such as the ease of having opposable thumbs, but this form is not our only one."

Aurelia went utterly still, her thoughts churning too quickly to focus on any one thing.

"Who invaded your territory?" asked Septima, her voice surprising Aurelia because she had been so quiet. Blaedia turned to her.

"There are many kingdoms within our world," Blaedia began.

Aurelia interrupted, finally grasping onto one question she needed answered. "What world? Is it not part of this planet?"

Allowing her interruption, Blaedia turned to Aurelia. "Our world is called Ekotoria. It lies alongside yours, a realm hidden by veils and barriers, so close that you breathe its air without knowing. It is not of your world, and yet not wholly apart." Although still confused, Aurelia nodded. Blaedia returned her gaze to Septima. "As I was saying, there are other kingdoms within Ekotoria and beyond. The territory of Warbotach invaded Aegricia, our home. We, along with the territory of Norithae, are the last barrier between our realm and yours. Norithae fell quickly; the Warbotach attack on them was unexpected. Their scribes managed to send a raven to us before their king fell, barely allowing our warriors to retreat here before our queen was captured." Blaedia began to twirl the hilt of a jewel-encrusted dagger in her hand, digging the blade into the table. "Our queen is safe for now. Warbotach will not kill her until they manage to take her power. They want to enter the human realm to conquer it."

Aurelia swallowed thickly, going rigid in her seat. "Can they get into our realm? Why did they attack your lands? What do you mean, 'they want to take your queen's power'?" Her words spilled out in rapid succession, full of desperation as she struggled to understand, but Blaedia remained patient.

"The lands of Warbotach are dying, starving both animals and people. They want the human lands to survive because they are vast, but they are an evil people. Our queen still lives, though in chains. Warbotach will not kill her until they have stolen her fire—the crown's gift of crossing. With it, they will rip open the veil and pour into the human world, not to share it, but to conquer and devour it. If they find their way through the portal, the humans won't stand a chance."

Gasping, Septima squeezed Aurelia's hand. "What's stopping them from coming here?" she asked, her voice trembling. "Can they get through the portal like your people did?"

Taryn shook her head, but the general spoke up. "No... Well, not for now. That's why they are trying to take our queen's power. Our people are the gatekeepers. We can cross, but only in flight and only with the crown's favor. The people of Warbotach cannot fly and can't cross the portal, thankfully. But that doesn't mean they aren't trying to steal that gift from our crown."

Blaedia rose from her chair and placed her dagger back in its holster. The sound of the blade sliding into the leather marked the end of their conversation.

Aurelia's mind swirled with words she barely understood—portals, realms, phoenixes. Her world had shattered, and she wasn't sure how to piece it back together.

"Exie, please show Aurelia and Septima to their sleeping quarters so they can clean up and rest. Their training will start tomorrow."

Exie nodded and stood, motioning them toward the door. Without hesitation, the sisters followed out into the action of the clearing. They passed Kano's enclosure, ensuring he was safe, and stopped at a newly erected tent right beside it. Exie opened the flap and led them inside. "Showers are in the tent beside Blaedia's. There should be clothes in the trunks beside the beds and water on the shelf against the wall. You'll hear a bell when it's time for meals to be served. If you overlooked the eating area when we came in, it's the large tent just beside the sparring rings. You won't miss it if you walk back the way we came. If you need anything, my tent is just to the right of yours, on the other side of Kano's enclosure. Rest and get to know the camp later. I'll see you at dinner."

Tipping her head in farewell, Exie left as the sisters shared an overwhelmed look and took in the space that would serve as their new home. Just as with Blaedia's tent, their tent was also larger than it appeared from the outside, although it was not as big as the general's. There were two double beds against one wall, with a large screen near another wall for privacy when changing. Wooden trunks sat at the foot of each bed.

Throwing herself onto one of the beds, Septima sighed loudly. "So, what is going through your mind right now?"

Aurelia, still dazed, lowered herself onto the remaining bed. "I don't know. We've always lived in a world where magic was nothing more than legend and definitely didn't exist, according to our father. I'm not sure what to think. Did we make the right choice?"

Septima faced her, tucking her arm under her head. "It's hard to say so far, but I have a good feeling. I feel safe with them—even if the things they've told us are overwhelming. Can you believe their society is ruled by women? Who would have thought a place like that existed? I feel so empowered with them, or at least more excited about our futures." Her face was filled with wonder as she spoke of their saviors.

"I know. What did you think of Blaedia? I've never met a general quite like her."

Septima drew idle circles on the blanket as she took a deep breath and exhaled slowly. "I think she's fascinating. She's in a position of power, and she's like me. I think she's more amazing than I can vocalize."

Aurelia's mouth spread into a slow grin. She could almost see the moon-sized admiration growing in her sister's eyes. "Oh, you'd better make sure she isn't taken before you start making moves on her."

Septima shot a playful glare her way before throwing a pillow at her sister's face as she explained it wasn't like that. Aurelia laughed and ignored the denial. Teasing Septima gave her a sense of normalcy that had been absent since the moment her father had announced their pending betrothals. "I bet you want to see her fire, don't you, dear sister? Her true fire."

Before Aurelia could brace herself, Septima launched herself across the beds and smacked her with another pillow. They fell into a fit of laughter. As their joy faded into soft, sporadic chuckles, they realized how exhausted they were. Their journey through the Howling Forest and the discovery of a whole new world took a toll on them. Without bathing, they drifted into slumber in Aurelia's bed, laughter fading into silence. Only the absence of Kano kept their little family from feeling whole.

Chapter Fourteen

Spectre Forest

Aurelia

After lunch, Aurelia led the way to Kano's new enclosure on the far side of the camp. She couldn't help but fixate on the little sparkling lights that floated through the trees, as though they were following her and watching her.

"Exie," Aurelia hesitated as one of those buzzing lights floated right in front of her before zooming away. For a brief moment, she thought she glimpsed a tiny humanoid face peering out from within the glow—sharp, mischievous features blurred by the light. It moved too quickly for her to see any specific details, but the vague outline was enough to send a shiver down her spine. They were beautiful yet unsettling all at once. "What are those?"

"Sprites. They're curious and mischievous little creatures. I'd suggest avoiding interaction with them if you can," Exie replied.

Septima shrieked and swatted at one that nearly collided with her face.

"Well, don't smack it," Exie laughed. "Just ignore it if it talks to you. Their voices are both sweet and dangerous. Tricksters to the core. And if any of your belongings go missing, they are definitely to blame."

Aurelia eyed the tiny creatures warily as they passed by. The little figures filled the area, clinging to tree trunks, sitting on branches, and hovering in the air as the trio walked. A few daring sprites continued to dart around them, flying between their feet as if trying to trip them. She wondered how such small creatures, no larger than a hummingbird, could cause so much trouble.

"Do they always light up?" Aurelia asked.

"No, only when they're excited or trying to defend themselves. They can control their glow like fireflies, except their entire bodies light up, not just their rears. You'll find that a lot of things glow in Spectre Forest."

By the time Exie pressed a medallion to the gate, Kano had already made himself at home in a fenced-in enclosure. He was devouring a hunk of meat with reckless abandon, his muzzle slick with blood. He raised his head slightly in acknowledgment as the women approached before returning to his macabre feast. Aurelia guessed he was just as starved as she had been.

"Your medallion will still work on this enclosure," Exie said, gesturing to the necklace hanging from Aurelia's neck with a lazy flick of her wrist. "I placed your tent next door because I thought you'd be more comfortable in close proximity to him."

"Thank you, Exie," Aurelia said, placing a hand on her friend's back. "Thank you for taking care of Kano for me."

"Of course," Exie replied with a nod and a smile before exiting the enclosure. She called over her shoulder, "I'll see you two at dinner later. Take some time to rest and explore the camp. And remember to stay away from the sprites!"

Aurelia and Septima played with Kano, running around his new home in an intense game of tag until they were sweaty and exhausted. The forest air was brisk, reminiscent of Vaekros, but it carried a humidity to which they were not accustomed.

The sprites continued to flutter around, watching from a distance. Since they had no trouble flying near the sisters, Aurelia figured they were afraid of the tiger, and with good reason. Kano would not hesitate to snap them up in his maw for a quick snack.

As the sun began its descent beyond the horizon, the great cat let out a yawn, stretched, and then curled up to take a nap. The sisters left in silence, not wanting to disturb him, and made their way to the bathhouse. They were too tired to linger. After a quick shower, they stumbled bleary-eyed to their tent and fell into a deep slumber as soon as their heads hit their pillows.

It wasn't until the dinner bell rang that Aurelia finally rose from her nap. The past twelve hours had felt like a dream. When she walked outside and was greeted by a horde of flickering sprites, she realized they were no longer in Vaekros. The realization of being in a new world filled her with a mix of excitement and apprehension.

"Are you ready to eat?" Septima asked through a yawn. Aurelia looked back through the open tent flap as her sister threw her legs over the side of her bed and tied her dark braids into a ponytail at the nape of her neck.

"Beyond ready. Hurry, and put your shoes on. I'm starving."

Septima chuckled as she slipped on her boots and flung a cloak around her shoulders. "Good to see traveling to a new world hasn't dampened your dramatics, Lia."

Aurelia, ever the mature adult, stuck her tongue out at her younger sister and let the tent flap fall in her face. This action incited a playful war of antics between the two. They bickered and joked the entire way to the dining tent, which took much longer than it should have.

They took the long route, mainly because they did not know where they were going, but they didn't mind the chance to explore the encampment. The layout was similar to what they had in the Howling Forest, but it was by no means identical due to their surroundings. They marveled at the differences, from the unique flora to the unfamiliar sounds of the forest.

The trees in Spectre Forest were thicker and taller than those in their homeland, and the colors were more vibrant than they were used to. Everything felt heightened here—colors were too vivid, shadows too deep, and the air hummed faintly as though magic breathed from every surface. Even the moonlight appeared altered, its silver glow so bright it burned, bathing everything it touched in an ethereal light. The sprites accompanied them the entire way. Aurelia couldn't be sure, but she thought one of the sprites had tried to trip Septima as they played around.

The tiny glowing creatures became less frequent as they approached their destination. Still, a few curious ones fluttered around the warriors gathered outside the dining tent. To Aurelia's dismay, she had yet to get a closer look at any of them. She knew that once the novelty wore off, they would become the nuisances that Exie claimed they were. However, her curiosity about their appearance remained.

Exie waited for them, as always. Her hair was wet and slicked back, a far cry from her usual wild blond mane.

"Looks like we weren't the only ones to hit the showers early," Septima quipped as they approached the smiling warrior. Exie wore a layer of fur over her usual leather pants and tunic. The fur of the cloak was like a silken night wrapped around her shoulders. Exie arched an eyebrow as Septima mindlessly caressed the fur on her shoulder. Septima chuckled, flushing in embarrassment, as she quickly pulled her hand away.

"You like my cloak, Septima?" Exie's tone was teasing, but her eyes lingered just a fraction too long, as if gauging her reaction. Septima's cheeks turned a shade darker.

"I... It's a beautiful cloak," she stammered before spinning on her heel and rushing into the dinner tent. Aurelia and Exie followed her inside.

The trio joined Holera, Kason, and a few unfamiliar faces at their table. One of the warriors, Thaestris, was the fiery red phoenix that had carried Kano through the portal. Her shoulder-length hair was as brilliant crimson as her feathers. Her eyes were a bright emerald, and her complexion was more bronze than that of most of the other warriors. She was soft-spoken and kind, her subdued nature a stark contrast to her intense features.

The other woman at their table, Marpesia—better known as Rockie—was introduced as an expert archer. Unlike Thaestris, Rockie was loud and lively enough to rival Exie. Her jet-black mohawk was laced with blue highlights that complemented the blue of her eyes. She was shorter and slimmer than the other warriors at the table, but she made up for it with her bravado. Her laugh was sharp enough to cut through the entire tent. Together, they embodied the camp's dual nature: discipline and chaos, steel and flame.

Their stew and tea had a distinct flavor, different from the stew in Vaekros, and Aurelia wondered what plants and animals were used to create it. She had a feeling they were not ingredients that could be found in her native land. Although it differed from what she was used to, she enjoyed the rich, earthy flavors and finished it quickly, just as her sister did beside her.

"Card game?" Exie asked after most of the table had pushed their empty bowls away. "We can play in my tent."

Rockie and Thaestris eagerly agreed, but Holera leaned over to consult with her partner. After a brief whispered conversation, they declined, claiming to be tired, and promised to join another night. The pair were the first to leave, and Aurelia could only imagine what they would do instead. She secretly wished she had the same excuse.

It had been over six months since she had been with a man. Although she could still remember the warmth of Savvas's hands and the sweetness of their stolen nights together, those memories were now laced with bitterness. Her father had sent him away like tossing scraps to the wind. Pushing aside thoughts of both him and how much she missed a man's touch, she placed her dishes in the dirty bin and followed the others back to Exie's tent.

Aurelia quickly realized that by "card game," Exie meant getting too drunk to see the cards and ultimately forgetting about the game altogether. The cards Exie had laid out on the table were neglected entirely as the Aegrician whiskey began to flow. Laughter, jokes, and singing took precedence as they drank.

The sisters returned to their tent a few hours later, stumbling less than they had after their introduction to Aegrician liquor. Feeling her first sense of true joy since leaving Vaekros, Aurelia couldn't help. Training began the following morning, and although she feared what this new world held for her future, she was excited to finally have a purpose in life. She was no longer expected to be a doting housewife with no rights. She was going to be a warrior. For the first time, her future felt like her own, and though fear coiled in her stomach, it was braided with something new, something fierce. She was ready.

CHAPTER FIFTEEN

SPECTRE FOREST

AURELIA

The following week passed without incident. Septima and Aurelia trained every morning and shared meals with Exie, occasionally enjoying after-dinner visits in one of the warriors' tents. They felt safe within the protective bubble of the camp, lulled into a routine that almost felt like a new life. Yet, every clang of steel in the sparring rings and every whispered strategy they weren't privy to reminded Aurelia that this fragile peace teetered on the edge of war. They had adapted to life in Ekotoria with relative ease. Still, there was always an undercurrent of anticipation, a sense of something looming.

Although they were left out of the strategic planning led by Blaedia, Taryn, and the other inner workings of the camp, Aurelia didn't mind being excluded.

"How do you feel about your training? Are you confident in your abilities?" Exie asked at the end of their seventh session. She wiped sweat from her face with a rag hanging from her belt and took a sip of water from her canteen.

Aurelia's answer was complex. She had always been a better fighter than her sister. While she trained with Amadeus more often, Septima had shown herself to be a natural under Exie's guidance. They had definitely improved over the past week, and their growing confidence was a beacon of hope. They were still nowhere near the level of the other warriors, but they were making strides. If that extent referred to staying inside their isolated camp with no real enemies to confront, then she felt pretty confident in her skills.

Aurelia shrugged noncommittally, but Septima responded to their instructor. "I feel more confident every day, but I'm still not confident enough to face an enemy. However, I'm not sure anyone is ever truly ready for potential death." Her voice wavered slightly, betraying the fear she tried to conceal. Aurelia watched her sister drag her sword across the dirt, drawing lines while avoiding Exie's gaze.

"It's hard to walk into a battle you may not survive," Exie said, her tone measured. "Every warrior carries fear in her gut like a stone. But when you're fighting for something worth dying for, fear becomes a companion, not an enemy. It sharpens you. This war that is coming is worth dying for. But I understand that it isn't your fight, and I recognize that you aren't ready. We will keep training until time runs out. I would never throw either of you to the wolves."

Aurelia frowned at her friend's words. It was their fight. Warbotach wanted to invade the human lands. Sure, it wasn't their queen who was captured, but they had a stake in the war just the same. However, she didn't correct Exie. Asserting ownership over the war wasn't something she was mentally or emotionally prepared to do just yet. Their emotional journey was a turbulent one, filled with uncertainty and fear.

The sisters remained silent as she continued to address them. "Anyway, Blaedia wants me to take both of you with me on my hunts. It's not the same as killing an enemy, but it'll give you more real-life experience with the weapons. It will help familiarize you with the land as well."

Although she had never hunted in her life, Aurelia was flooded with relief. She'd much rather stalk a beast through the forest than be sent on a dangerous mission for the cause. She simply wasn't ready for that yet.

They were set to head out at dusk. They had just enough time to eat lunch, check on Kano, and rest the muscles they'd overexerted during training. It was unclear how long they would remain outside the protective barrier, but being exposed to the elements made her nervous.

The weather was vastly different from Vaekros. From what Aurelia could tell, it followed different rules from the non-magic world. The air was cool and crisp but still filled with enough humidity to make her crimson hair frizz and nearly double in volume. They had yet to see rain or snow, yet the forest remained vibrant.

Exie advised that they add a warm cloak over their usual leathers. It didn't seem cold enough to do so at the time, but they followed her instructions, nonetheless. Aurelia did not realize how much the wards controlled the weather until Exie led them through the invisible wall into the wilderness.

As soon as they stepped through the shimmering veil, the air punched her lungs with ice. The sudden change in temperature took her breath away, and she struggled to adjust to the biting cold. Snow lashed her cheeks, stinging like tiny needles, and the forest beyond looked utterly transformed—a silver world of frost and shadow. A blast of snow smacked against her as soon as they passed through the warbling air of the barrier. She understood and was thankful for the added layers.

"Damn, Exie." Aurelia's voice was unsteady as she shivered and secured her cloak around her neck. "You could have warned us about the weather."

Exie shrugged. "I told you to bring a cloak."

Aurelia grumbled but didn't talk back as Exie continued.

"We are hunting for anything edible, really, but deer are our most likely targets. There are more threats to contend with here than in the forests you are used to. Keep your weapons ready and keep your wits about you."

The snow coated the land, glistening on tree branches, and gave the forest an ethereal feel. Aurelia tried not to let the beautiful scenery distract her as she pulled her bow from her back and locked an arrow into place. She practiced archery with Rockie a few times, but she was nowhere near confident in her ability to hit a moving target.

The moon and the bobbing lights of the tiny sprites illuminated their path. They navigated the trees and brush gingerly, afraid to slip on the slick snow, as they made their way to the natural blind that the Aegrician hunters reinforced beside a nearby stream. The silence was suffocating. Every crunch of snow, every creak of a branch sounded thunderous in her ears. Her muscles ached from holding still, fingers stiff on the bowstring, when at last a shape ghosted between the trees—a deer, pale as the snow itself, stepping with dreamlike grace to the stream.

Enthused by the break in monotony, Aurelia took aim and fired. She missed the first few shots but was able to strike the snowy white deer.

It took all their strength, and a good bit of Exie's magic, to carry the fallen animal. Exie congratulated Aurelia for her kill as they made the trek back to camp, but Aurelia could not share the triumph. As she gazed at the deer's lifeless body, her stomach twisted. Its glassy eyes reflected the moonlight, and she felt as if they accused her. She knew survival demanded such acts, yet grief pooled in her chest, heavy and unexpected.

The snow cleared as they reentered the boundary of the encampment. They passed the deer off to the cooks, and Aurelia headed directly for the showers without another word. She shed her bloody clothes and stood beneath the scalding water until her skin flushed raw, as though she could scour away the guilt itself. But no matter how long she stayed, the memory of the deer's fall clung to her like blood she could not scrub away.

By the time she returned to their tent, Aurelia was utterly drained. Even walking had become difficult. Without so much as a word to Septima, who stood freshly showered at the foot of her bed, Aurelia lay down and closed her eyes. She fell asleep almost immediately to the crackling of the small wooden stove that heated their room.

CHAPTER SIXTEEN

SPECTRE FOREST

AURELIA

The snow fell lazily, settling on the forest's surfaces like a fine layer of sparkling dust in the moonlight. A rabbit with cloud-like fur nibbled on a patch of grass, keeping a watchful eye on its surroundings as it chewed. When it heard the rustling of the trees, its ears perked up, and it scanned the forest once more, fluffing its already thick fur to appear larger. Before the snowy rabbit could react to the danger, a snarl pierced the silence, and a legendary black-coated beast burst from the shadows. Its jaws snapped shut with a crunch that silenced the rabbit forever. It glared back over its shoulder with burning eyes before vanishing into the dark.

Aurelia awoke with a new appreciation for the forest. She didn't know if the creature in her dreams truly prowled these woods, but the thought of it set her blood ice-cold. Dreams had been cruelly prophetic before. She couldn't shake the fear that this was no mere nightmare. Light could not infiltrate the thick walls of the tent, so she stared into the blackness, hoping the snarling beast wasn't watching her from one of the dark corners.

They were far away from home, in a world that felt completely different from their own. Aurelia took a deep breath, hoping it would settle her nerves, and exhaled slowly. Septima was still asleep, and the sound of her peaceful breathing was reassuring.

Aurelia kicked off her blankets and climbed to her feet to add another log to the wood burner. She rubbed her hands against her chilly arms. The camp was quiet, and she wondered if the protective wards also kept out the sounds of the forest. From the lack of light filtering through the small slit in the tent flap, she could tell that day had not yet broken. Aside from the flickering sprite lights floating throughout the camp, the only illumination came from the sliver of moonlight that cut through the thick canopy of trees.

Her heart tugged at her to visit Kano in his enclosure. They had spent so much time together before she and Septima ran away, and it made her feel guilty to leave him alone, even though it was a perfect space for a tiger.

Pulling on her cloak and boots, Aurelia slipped out into the night to see her loyal companion. The chilly night air carried the scents of pine, moss, and a faint cloying sweetness—like a floral perfume wafting from unseen sources. It unsettled her, but knowing she would spend time with Kano was grounding. She breathed deeply as she made her way to his enclosure, relishing the crisp air.

The medallion against his fence worked quickly, creating an opening large enough for her to walk through.

When she entered, Kano, having locked onto her approaching scent and the crunch of her footsteps, came to meet her. He nuzzled her leg as he always did. Aurelia sat down on the forest floor with her legs tucked under herself, and Kano curled up beside her. The more she caressed the great cat's fur, the heavier her eyelids grew until she drifted back to sleep with her head resting on him. It was a familiar sleeping arrangement, reminiscent of their time back in Vaekros.

Holera joined their hunting party the following night, and this time they were prepared for the snow, dressing appropriately for the weather that awaited them outside their bubble. Wearing their thickest wool and leather, the sisters felt ready for the journey, even if Aurelia wasn't entirely sure she was mentally prepared to take another life.

The sun had just begun to dip behind the trees when they met up with the armed phoenixes, still in human form. Holera and Aurelia were tasked with hunting using bows. At the same time, Exie and Septima carried swords for protection against any outside threats. Aurelia chose not to dwell on what kind of threats they might encounter.

The sisters took their weapons from the warriors and secured them before being led through the barrier.

As soon as they entered the forest, snow flurried around them in spirals, settling on the ground beneath them. Aurelia tucked her sleeves into her gloves, her feet sinking ankle-deep into the cold slush as they stepped into the tree line. The forest was quiet, except for the crunch of their boots trampling the hidden brush—a perfect warning system for their prey and an enticing beacon for any predators.

Aurelia notched an arrow and scanned her surroundings, hoping to find their next meal before they became hypothermic. Nothing stirred, and she hated the relief that flooded her. She wanted to assist the camp, but to say she was eager to kill again would be a lie.

They moved as quietly as possible, weapons raised toward the blind they had used the night before. Their progress was abruptly halted by the sound of wings flapping in the air. Boots impacted the forest floor, surrounding them. Fear surged through Aurelia, rooting her to the ground. The cold had made her shiver before, but this terror hollowed her bones and left her lungs straining for air.

Septima remained stationary as well, but their experienced companions moved without hesitation. Great, colorful wings exploded in a burst of fire from both of their shoulders, but they didn't entirely shift as they fell into defensive stances, weapons at the ready. Holera quickly grabbed Aurelia, shoving her behind her, while Exie did the same for Septima. The warrior women stood back-to-back with the sisters between them.

Humanoid men with leathery wings, rivaling the size of phoenixes, were accompanied by a handful of others sitting atop crimson horses. They completely encircled the four women, cutting off any path of retreat. A fight seemed imminent, and survival was their only hope, but they were outnumbered five to one.

"What is this?" Exie demanded. Her impressive wingspan blocked most of Aurelia's view as she peeked over. Still, she could tell by Exie's stance that the warrior was prepared to strike if provoked.

One of the men on horseback urged his mount a few steps closer. Aurelia struggled to suppress a shocked gasp as his grotesque face came into view. Nearly every inch of his tawny skin was marked by jagged scars, as if his very flesh had rebelled against him. Dark veins stood out like cords beneath the surface, and his features were twisted into something neither fully man nor beast. His grotesque form served as a living warning of what awaited those under Warbotach's dominion. He had a stocky stature, in stark contrast to the tall and fit Aegricians.

Exie didn't so much as twitch as he advanced, but the tension in her shoulders was palpable.

The shuffle of feet broke the silence of the stand-off. Two men, one winged and one not, restrained a struggling woman. Her long black braid was disheveled, but even as she thrashed wildly in an attempt to get free, she was recognizable. Aurelia's breath caught in her throat as she locked eyes with their commander.

Taryn's gaze wasn't pleading. It was determined. She could not speak with the gag in her mouth, but the message was clear: Do not bargain. Do not break. If it cost her life, so be it—better her blood than their freedom.

Exie didn't react to the sight of her captured commander, but Aurelia was sure that she would not abandon one of their own.

"What do you want?" Exie demanded. The monster on horseback grinned, his feral expression further disfiguring his face.

"We knew it was only a matter of time before the infamous fire birds returned," he taunted, as Taryn continued to struggle against her restraints. Aurelia wished she could reach for her sister's hand, but she didn't dare lower the bow she aimed beneath Exie's wings

"You don't belong in this forest, Warbotach scum," Exie spat fiercely, but the monster's grin only grew wider.

"This land is ours. Norithae is ours. Aegricia is ours. What did you expect after fleeing like cowards?"

Aurelia thought she saw the winged captor on Taryn's right grimace at his words, but the expression vanished so quickly that she couldn't be sure.

"Spectre Forest belongs to no one, least of all you! And Aegricia is not yours. Our crown will never bow to your worthless king."

He snarled when she insulted their ruler before composing himself. Then he chuckled, the sound rough and menacing, and nodded to the stout man on Taryn's left. The man reacted to the unspoken command and pulled a dagger out of its sheath, pressing it to their commander's neck. Aurelia held her breath as the blade pierced Taryn's flesh, a tiny drop of blood pooling at its tip.

"You are trespassing, fire bird. Unless you want to see this bitch bleed out, you will come with us."

Aurelia couldn't tear her eyes away from the restrained phoenix. Taryn stopped thrashing and went stock-still as soon as the steel bit into her.

"Where?" Exie shifted her weight, sword at the ready. The tiny bead of blood grew, leaving a thin trail down the column of Taryn's throat, punctuating his threat.

"You are not in a position to ask questions."

Several men moved to the front of their ranks with iron chains in hand. *Chains.* The sound alone—iron clinking against iron—curdled Aurelia's stomach. Her lips trembled as she stifled a sob, the wordless knowledge sinking in: they weren't captives to be bargained with. They were spoils.

Before Aurelia could lower her weapon and reach for her sister, Exie threw her sword down at her feet and whispered to them over her shoulder. "We will get out of this. For now, for Taryn, we will go. Don't fight. Everything will be okay."

She held her hands above her head, palms out, as she retracted her wings and stepped forward in surrender.

Aurelia dropped her own weapon to the ground, reaching back to squeeze her sister's hand before following Exie's lead. The women stood shoulder to shoulder as they waited for the inevitable. The men approached in pairs, each flanking a side, and wrapped the irons around their wrists.

Aurelia stumbled as the men on either side of her yanked her forward. Her heart raced, her breathing frantic, as her vision blurred. Her eyes darted around, looking for a way, any way out, but there was no escape.

They were thrown in a cage pulled by the same fire-red horses the deformed men rode. Aurelia, Septima, and the three phoenixes were taken deeper into the forest. The longer they traveled, the greater the distance between them, and the safety of the encampment grew. They could not fight or run. They could only lie bound like animals as they were led into darkness like beasts to the slaughter, each jolt of the cage dragging them further from freedom and deeper into enemy hands.

CHAPTER SEVENTEEN

SPECTRE FOREST

AURELIA

Aurelia did her best to study the faces of their captors while she remained trapped in the rolling cage for what felt like an endless amount of time. The men on horseback shared similar features to the monstrous creature that had ordered their capture. They were all stocky men with tawny, scarred flesh, and slightly deformed heads. She assumed they all hailed from Warbotach.

While she didn't know much about Ekotorians, she'd been told that those from Warbotach could not fly, and that Diapolis had control over water. That led her to believe that the winged men were from Norithae. She studied the guard that marched beside the mobile prison.

His leathery wings were folded at his back as he stared straight-ahead, not sparing so much as a glimpse at those he imprisoned. With jet-black hair that made his ocean eyes shine brighter, he was by far the most beautiful man she had ever seen. She tried not to stare, but she could not help it.

He'd deigned to glance at her once and caught her watching him, but she looked away immediately. He was her captor, whether by choice or force, and did not deserve her attention. Still, she wondered if he was just as powerless as they were. Her mind kept going back to the grimace she thought she saw as he restrained Taryn. Norithae had been conquered before Aegricia, after all. Maybe he was just as much a prisoner as she was.

She shook herself in an attempt to dislodge the growing empathy and looked at her companions. Septima had stopped sobbing after a few miles and now sat in silence, her eyes puffy and bloodshot. Taryn slumped against the back of the cage, the fight draining out of her the moment the others were bound. Exie and Holera sat beside each other, eyes scanning their surroundings. Aurelia could almost see their brains working overtime. She wondered what the trio of warriors were thinking as they were hauled further and further away from their people.

Their jailers did not speak as they marched forward with weapons drawn. No matter what evils existed in Spectre Forest, she had a hard time believing they were worse than the men who had kidnapped them. They remained vigilant, nonetheless. With nothing but the monotonous, snow-covered landscape and fear to occupy her, the rhythmic trotting of the horse eventually lulled Aurelia to sleep.

A guttural growl, deeper than any Aurelia had heard before, startled her awake. A beast, black as night with saliva dripping from its maw, crouched just inside a thicket of trees they were passing by. Their captors continued to push forward through the forest, ignoring the threat. Their group was large enough that she was surprised the animal approached at all.

The beast, which appeared to be the mixture of a wolf and something eerily human-like, was not deterred. It stalked after them the same way Kano did when he'd locked onto his prey. Its growl intensified as they pressed on. One of the captors, a burly male with an eyepatch that boasted more scars than the other Warbotach soldiers, notched an arrow and shot at the beast. The creature dove behind the bushes, and the arrow did not meet its mark. Aurelia did not see the animal again, but she still felt its gaze as they traveled.

The horses slowed and pulled to a stop. Aurelia didn't know where they were, but it was at least several hours away from their encampment. The leader spoke in a language she did not recognize. The door to their cage was ripped open immediately after, and she was dragged out by her chains. She was thrown face first onto the wet ground, barely able to stop her head from smashing into the forest floor. Four thuds echoed beside her as her companions were dumped on the ground as well.

Most of their captors busied themselves with setting up camp for the night. Only one guard remained to watch over them—the beautiful, winged man she'd watched from inside the cage. From her spot on the ground, she noticed his ears had a slight point. He was obviously fae, like the Aegricians, but that was one of the few similarities between him and the phoenixes. Unlike the fire birds, his wings were featherless and a solid inky black. Except for being exceptionally handsome, the rest of him looked no different from the human men of her world.

"Are you okay?" Exie whispered under her breath.

His eyes shot to them at the sound of her voice, but he said nothing. They all nodded in answer as they watched the men intently.

"What's the plan?" asked Holera, her eyes never drifting from the men laying out bedrolls nearby.

Taryn's head drooped as they sat, her slumped posture full of defeat. Her guilt over getting captured was clear. It made Aurelia's heart ache. It was not her fault, and she wished Taryn knew that.

"We can't get away right now," Exie murmured. "Our people will find us. Play along and, most importantly, stay alive. Don't be more trouble than you are worth."

The winged male shushed Exie, his eyes wide almost in warning, before his face hardened once more. She scowled but did not respond.

Although the snow had stopped, Aurelia still shivered as the frigid air made its way under her cloak. The frozen slush they sat in only made it worse, but she didn't dare stand for fear of drawing attention.

Another russet-complexed, winged male took pity on them and gave them blankets made of animal fur. The sisters cuddled together, using their body heat to keep warm. The chains and shackles made getting comfortable impossible, but Septima's proximity helped to calm Aurelia's frayed nerves ever so slightly.

They did not remain stationary for long. Some men stood guard while others slept. They switched after a few hours. Once they'd all had a chance to rest, they began breaking down their camp.

The women were escorted into the tree line to relieve themselves behind the shrubbery. It was humiliating and demoralizing to use the bathroom behind the bushes in front of a guard, but—with the only option being to soil themselves—they complied. As their jailers broke their fast, the women were given a pitiful amount of water, bread, and dried meat. As soon as the men finished eating, Aurelia and her friends were stuffed back into their cage to continue the journey.

The forest's terrain became increasingly rugged as they traveled. The monstrous leader that ordered their imprisonment refused to tell them where they were headed, so Aurelia had no way of knowing how much longer they'd be trapped in their tight confines. But as the sun continued to move across the tree-covered sky, Spectre Forest gave way to mountains and plateaus. Evidence of a city emerged, the building outlines filling Aurelia with a sense of dread. As uncomfortable as the ride had been, the idea of reaching their destination filled her with fear. How would Blaedia and the others save them once they were in a Warbotach stronghold? As they traversed out of the forest and descended toward the city, all of her hopes of being rescued died.

"Norithae," Holera whispered, confirming Aurelia's fears.

ODETTE.A.BACH

Chapter Eighteen

Norithae

Aurelia

The city of Norithae stood proudly along the coast of the Elder Sea, the same sea they had flown over after crossing the portal. Aurelia felt a tightness in her chest, filled with dread, yet she couldn't help but marvel at the city. Norithae appeared vibrant and bustling, but to Aurelia, its pride felt grotesque—a place thriving under the weight of conquest, hiding decay beneath its colorful market stalls.

Tented shops lined the dirt street as their captors led them through, selling everything from fresh food to beautiful tapestries. Patrons browsed the stalls, filling their wicker shopping baskets, wholly absorbed in their routines. Hardly anyone paid attention to the captives as they were carted by, and most even went out of their way to avoid contact with the men marching down the center of the bustling street.

Their passage through the town center went unhindered, and soon Aurelia's gaze was drawn to an overcrowded harbor. Dozens of ships were moored at the docks, and thick storm clouds darkened the sky. The sea had begun to toss violently. She doubted anyone would dare brave the waters in such conditions. Still, she would gladly take her chances with the rough waves if it meant escaping their Warbotach jailers.

All thoughts of fleeing by boat vanished as her attention was stolen by a majestic palace in the distance. At any other time, she would have been in awe of the hulking structure. Now, it only served as a reminder of her impending doom. Each tick of her pulse echoed in her mind—a drumbeat toward catastrophe. *Tick.* Her lungs constricted. *Tick.* Her body urged her to flee. *Tick.* The palace walls loomed larger, like the jaws of a trap waiting to snap shut. *Tick.* She needed to get free. *Tick.* Before it was too late.

Unable to bear it any longer, she whispered frantically, "Help us. *Please.*" She directed her plea toward the handsome winged man walking alongside them. Maybe she hadn't imagined his grimace the night before. If he honestly reacted to the Warbotach leader's words, perhaps he would help them.

Throughout the journey, he remained just a foot away, issuing commands only. It was a foolish hope, but she had to try. His expression tightened, the only sign he acknowledged her words, but he didn't respond or even glance her way. In anger and frustration, she yanked at her manacles, nearly drawing blood in the process. To her surprise, he reached out and grasped her wrist. His gentle touch contradicted his hardened features, yet he still refused to meet her gaze.

"Help me. *Please,*" she pleaded again. The fury she had felt faded quickly, leaving only sorrow and fear behind. Her eyes burned as tears fell. Half-heartedly, she pulled on her manacles once more.

His ocean-blue eyes softened for a brief moment, like sunlight breaking through storm clouds. Hope pierced her chest so sharply that it almost hurt. But the moment passed—his jaw tightened, the storm returned, and her fragile hope was crushed beneath it.

"Stop doing that. You're going to hurt yourself," he whispered, earning a grunt from the Warbotach beast who steered the cart. Her escort's face hardened again. The sharp lines of his features closed her out, and her paper-thin optimism was torn to shreds.

Aurelia turned her attention back to the palace that marked the end of their journey. It was enormous, with twelve round towers linked by small bridges and connected by thick walls of dark granite. Rough windows dotted the walls in a seemingly random pattern, alongside symmetric crenellations for archers. A vast gate with giant metal doors and a drawbridge was guarded by armed men. Remnants of catapults, swords, and shields littered the fields surrounding it—a painful reminder of the recent siege that had resulted in the Norithaean king's murder and subsequent replacement by a Warbotach war leader.

Fighting was useless while they were bound and caged, so Aurelia gave up her struggle as they approached the palace. Each of the women was pulled from their temporary prison by a pair of guards and forced into a line before being led toward the palace door. Aurelia expected to be brought inside the palace to meet whoever ruled over the battle-torn castle, but they were escorted around the side of the courtyard and into a narrow alleyway. The passage was tight, the stone walls forcing her captors to trail closely behind her as she walked. Her chains were secure, keeping her hands restrained behind her. The other women were ordered to follow suit, dashing any opportunity for escape.

They were led through an iron door on the side of the palace, down a dimly lit hall, and thrown into an even darker chamber. Candles burned low in hills of melted wax, their flames trembling as if afraid of the darkness. The scent of their overused wicks mingled with mildew and damp stone, creating a thick atmosphere that felt suffocating. Shadows pooled in the corners like living things. Aurelia followed Exie's lead and remained quiet until the iron doors clanged shut behind them. The sound of heavy bolts sliding into place echoed around the musty walls of their new confinement as they were locked inside.

"What are we going to do?" Septima asked as she sank down onto one of the wooden benches that lined the perimeter of the square room. Aurelia sat beside her, interlacing their fingers while Septima rested her head on her sister's shoulder.

"For now, we rest," Exie replied. "There isn't much we can do in this box while we're exhausted and starved. Blaedia will find us. Our people will track us down. It's only a matter of time. Have faith."

Holera and Taryn each claimed a bench of their own, following Exie's advice. Taryn lay down with her back to the others and tucked her arm beneath her head like a pillow. Aurelia worried about the commander. She wasn't acting like herself, but it was clear she didn't want to talk. Setting aside her concerns about the somber phoenix, Aurelia rested her hand on Septima's and closed her eyes. Silence filled the room as they each drifted off to sleep, one by one.

The metal door creaked open, pulling Aurelia from her restless sleep. The handsome man who had escorted them to Norithae, the one she had begged for help, entered with a tray of bread and water. His wings were tucked behind him, and his chiseled face revealed nothing as he handed her the tray.

"Can you help us?" Aurelia whispered, her eyes locking onto his.

Her fingers trembled as she gripped the tray, but she kept her gaze steady. He didn't respond with words. The answer was clear when he turned and left. She slumped in defeat, staring at the reinforced iron door. The sound of the heavy bolts sliding back into place, locking them in, was like a nail being hammered into her impending coffin.

Taryn gently placed a hand on her shoulder and guided her back to the benches where their companions sat, waiting for the meager food she held. It wasn't nearly enough to help them regain their strength, but it would prevent death by starvation, at least for now.

While they ate, they searched the damp stone room for anything that could be used as a weapon or a means of escape, but found nothing. There was no way out. They had no way to defend themselves, except for their quickly dwindling physical strength. Aurelia hesitated to ask the phoenixes if they could still shift or use their magic, fearing what their answer might be.

They remained in the dungeon for what felt like days. They had no way of knowing if it was day or night, so they could only guess at the passage of time. Aurelia wondered what would become of them and whether they would make it out alive. The only person who visited their prison was the handsome winged man who delivered their meager sustenance.

Just when she thought Warbotach had forgotten them, the door squealed open and the beastly man with the patch over his eye barreled in.

"Which one of you is the leader?" he growled. His voice low and guttural. Taryn went to stand, but Exie beat her to it.

"I am," Exie said, pointedly avoiding Taryn's stare. Her message was obvious to Aurelia. She wanted the commander to stand down and trust her. Taryn's jaw tightened, fists clenched at her sides, as she read Exie's face. She gave an almost imperceptible nod, face grim, and leaned back against the wall.

The one-eyed man kept his eyes on the warrior who claimed to lead them, not seeming to notice their silent interaction. He advanced on her, a sadistic smile fixed on his grotesque face, and his fist sank into Exie's abdomen with the sound of breaking breath. She folded forward, the air knocked from her lungs in a strangled gasp, her arms clutching her stomach as though to hold herself together.

Septima leaped to her feet and started forward as the woman doubled over in pain. Aurelia gripped her arm and yanked her back down roughly. The sisters glared at each other. Aurelia tried to communicate with her eyes. *Don't. Just trust Exie. She knows what she's doing. We have to bide our time.* From the way the fight drained from Septima, sorrow etching her face, she knew the message had been received.

The one-eyed man signaled to someone in the hall. The handsome man came in, approached Exie from the back, and placed manacles on her wrists. He led her out of the room. The door slammed behind them. That was the moment Aurelia gave up on the fantasy of him helping her. Whether or not he was voluntarily working with Warbotach, he was the enemy.

Septima dropped to her knees and sobbed into her hands as they heard Exie's grunts of pain through the door, the agonizing sound growing more distant. Aurelia dropped beside Septima, pulling her sister's head into her lap, and caressed her braids softly. Taryn kneeled beside them and placed a tentative hand on Septima's arm. Holera remained on a bench, watching them in silence. Her expression contained the same worry as the others, but there was nothing they could do. They simply had to wait and have faith that Exie would return.

"She'll be okay," Taryn murmured. "Exie is a well-trained warrior. She knows what she's doing."

That was the last time anyone spoke for what felt like hours. The iron door swung open later, startling them. Exie was unceremoniously dumped back into the room. She collapsed into a heap on the floor as the door banged shut behind her.

Septima rushed to her side, cradling Exie's battered face with trembling hands. Blood smeared her palms, and her sobs filled the chamber like a hymn of grief. The warrior's lip was split and bleeding. One eye was swollen shut and had turned a sickly shade of purple. Her clothes were crumpled, splattered with blood and dirt. Had they been properly fed, Aurelia would have lost her stomach at the sight of what was done to her friend.

Exie's one uninjured eye fluttered shut as she lost consciousness, while Septima held her and wept.

AEGRICIA

OTERA

The birds have landed. That was the last message Otera received. Since then, she had received no further communications. She didn't know where her warriors were or when they would come for her. For the time being, she remained in the dungeon, counting the passing days by a sliver of light that filtered through the window.

The small flame she could summon remained steady, her only companion in the desolate prison. Sometimes, she whispered to it as if it were a friend, its glow trembling against the damp walls like a heartbeat refusing to die. The flame was fragile, just a flicker compared to the blazing inferno of her power that she had once wielded, but it was still hers. As long as she could call forth fire, she knew she was not broken.

The Warbotach leader had been making fewer and fewer visits to her dungeon, and she was not complaining. It seemed he had given up on demanding that she relinquish her power and had moved on to trying to sway her crown's allegiance. She knew it wouldn't work. The Crown of the Phoenix was older than kingdoms, older than Uldon's cruelty, and it would never bow to such barbaric scum. Let him rage. Let him drain his oracles dry and carve the flesh of his witches with failed rituals. The crown answered only to destiny, and destiny would ultimately reject him.

Several days had passed since Bremusa's visit. Otera could not shake the fear that Uldon had discovered the elderly woman's act of rebellion. Every echoing footstep in the corridor made her tense, expecting the shuffle of Bremusa's frail body dragged in chains. She prayed silently to every god she knew that the old woman's courage had not cost her life. The queen had no way of knowing for sure, but, given the level of Uldon's sadism, she thought it likely Bremusa still lived. If the old woman had been caught, the cruel king would have ensured Otera watched helplessly as he tore her apart.

Two levels above the dungeons, while Otera tormented herself over Bremusa's fate, Uldon prowled through the royal chambers he had stolen. His boots struck the marble with such force that the sound echoed through the hollow palace. He hated the gilded walls, despising their reminder of a long line of monarchs who had ruled here before him—particularly the women whose power far exceeded his own. Soon, he vowed, the stones would remember no name but his.

His patience had just about reached its end with his confidant, Ezio. The man fed him an endless stream of excuses as to why the crown had not yet bent to his will. Petty justifications. Hollow delays. Uldon wanted results.

The Marella Arch glimmered on the horizon like a phantom doorway, taunting him with promise. He could almost hear the surf beating against it, as though the sea itself mocked his inability to pass. He wanted it—no, *needed* it—more than breath itself. If he could master the crown, if he could seize the gateway, his people would swarm the human world like a flood. His horses needed pasture. His soldiers needed conquest. His land was dying, and he would bleed the living world to feed it.

"We searched, Sovereign," Ezio muttered. "The Elemental of Spectre Forest cannot be found. We received word from the legion in Norithae. No trace of her was located, but they captured some of Otera's warriors in Spectre Forest."

Uldon grunted, turning on his heel to face the man. Ezio shuddered, his fear clear. The king grinned, reveling in his subordinate's terror. "How many fighters did they capture?"

"Five. They believe one is a commander."

His vicious smile grew wider, teeth flashing like a predator's. "Excellent. I want confirmation that it's a commander. Tell the legion to do whatever it takes to get my answers." His voice dropped into a hiss, savoring the words. "Break their bones. Peel their skin. Burn their wings. I want a commander broken at my feet, and I want the crown's secrets bled out of her veins."

CHAPTER TWENTY

NORITHAE

AURELIA

Exie violently heaved from the corner of the room, sending vomit splattering onto the floor. She sat up from her place on the bench and saw Septima holding back the warrior's matted blond hair.

The beating Exie had taken the day before left her in terrible condition, and the lack of food did not help. Everyone gave the injured warrior a portion of the bread they had been given for dinner, hoping the increased calories would help her heal.

Holera remained stone-faced. She did not speak or move about much. It was almost as if she'd dis-associated entirely from their reality and retreated into the deep recesses of her mind. Taryn hovered around Aurelia when she wasn't checking on the others, which she did periodically. Septima had not left Exie's side since she was returned to the cell.

"We have to do something," Septima said from the corner as she rubbed a soothing hand over Exie's back. The warrior's face had gone an unsettling shade of gray as she slumped against Septima's lap.

"Our only option is to fight when they open the door, but we don't know how many guards are out there. We don't know how many guards are surrounding this city." Holera spoke for the first time in days as she pressed her palms against her eyes. "We may break out of this room only to be struck down in the hallway."

"We have to try." The pain in Septima's voice was audible as she stroked Exie's hair away from her pallid face. The warrior had drifted off to sleep, her body positioned in an awkward manner.

"She can't even walk!" Holera snapped, gesturing violently at the unconscious warrior.

Septima opened her mouth to respond, but Taryn cut her off. "Enough." The commander, who had been a shell of her former self, was back in all her glory. Authority filled her voice as she stood and motioned for them to gather round.

They spent the next few hours planning their next move. They decided to set a trap for the guard when he brought their food. If they were lucky, they might be able to steal a weapon or two from him. Whether they could escape the city was uncertain, but they knew they had to try. They agreed to postpone their plan until the following day to allow Exie time to recover from the beating she had received. Phoenixes healed relatively quickly, but the lack of nutrients was slowing her recovery. They hoped this extra time would be enough for her. Their escape would be doomed if Exie were immobilized. They needed to be swift and silent if they were to have any chance of success. They could be neither if one of them could not walk on her own.

When the metal bolts that locked them inside the dungeon slid open later that night, Aurelia stiffened. She expected them to retake Exie. The warrior had not, and would not, give them any information. If they took her and beat her again, their hopes of escape would be dashed once more.

To their collective relief, it was not the beast with the scarred face that entered, but the winged man. His eyes darted around the room as he entered, scanning their faces, while Aurelia approached to take the dinner tray.

Her heart sat in her throat as she neared him, just as it had every other time he entered the prison. Someone cleared their throat in the hall, the sound echoing off the damp walls. Glancing over his shoulder, his jaw clenched.

When he faced Aurelia, his eyes locked onto hers with an intensity he had never displayed before. Aurelia reached out for the tray, but he caught her by surprise, gripping her hand and forcing a small piece of paper into her palm. She froze for a moment, then pressed the note between her hand and the tray. Their gazes remained locked for what felt like an eternity, her heart thundering in her chest, until he turned and walked away. As if under a spell, she stood there, watching his retreating form until the lock clicked shut.

The only one not staring at her in confusion was Exie, fast asleep in the corner. The tray quivered in Aurelia's trembling hands. He had slipped the note to her so deftly that she was certain none of her companions had seen it. They could not know why she was frozen, too afraid even to unfold the scrap of paper. If an enemy spotted it, their only lifeline might be lost. The winged man had spoken scarcely a handful of words since her capture—what could he possibly have to say now? Part of her, foolishly, hoped it was a promise of escape. After he had ignored her tearful pleas for help, that seemed unlikely. And yet, if he meant her harm, why take such a risk? She didn't know his name, his allegiance, or his purpose. All her questions waited in that folded note, but her courage faltered at the thought of opening it.

"What's wrong?" Septima asked. Her eyebrows furrowed as she approached her sister and reached for the tray. Aurelia hesitated, afraid of dropping the paper, but she relented and pulled the note further into her palm when the tray slid out of her grip. Septima's eyes widened when she caught sight of what Aurelia was holding, but she quickly schooled her expression.

"Come," she said. "Let's sit down and eat."

Aurelia squeezed the note so tightly that her nails dug into her palms. They huddled around the sleeping Exie, sharing the stale bread and water while making sure to leave enough food for the wounded warrior.

Leaning over the meager scraps that made up her portion of dinner, Aurelia allowed her long red hair to fall forward, concealing her face. She held the sheet of paper in front of her eyes, ensuring that her curtain of hair hid her hands, and unfolded it carefully.

Help is coming.

That simple, brief message lifted the enormous weight that had crushed her chest since they were imprisoned. She didn't know what the note meant, nor did she know the man's name, but the thought of help on the way brought her a glimmer of hope. She wasn't sure if it meant he was getting assistance or if Blaedia had somehow tracked them down, but the promise of help did wonders to lift her spirits. They didn't need to attempt a dangerous escape, nor did they need to attack him when he brought the next food tray. As hard as it was, they knew they needed to wait.

Unsure of what to do with the paper but unwilling to risk getting caught, Aurelia placed the note in her mouth and chewed, swallowing it quickly. She shared the contents with her companions in the quietest whisper she could muster.

The night was eerily silent as the women sat in their cold cell, huddled together for warmth. Exie had stopped vomiting but could still hardly stand. Aurelia was uncertain of what had been done to her. None of the women wanted to ask and force Exie to relive her trauma, but it was evident that her injuries extended beyond just a black eye and busted lip. Septima held Exie close, never straying out of the wounded woman's reach since her return, and comforted her as best as she could.

Later that night, a loud thump echoed outside their door, startling them. They remained silent, eyes wide, as the metal door creaked open. Their winged guard stepped into the cell and peered into the darkness. A flickering torch in the hallway behind him illuminated his figure, casting an ethereal glow. Aurelia still wasn't sure whether he was good or evil, but she hoped with all her might that he was good. Her heart raced as she watched him approach.

He moved cautiously and squatted down in front of them, speaking just above a whisper. "Follow me quietly. I'm going to get you out of here."

"Who are you?" Holera asked, matching his hushed tone but clearly skeptical. She stared at him, disbelief etched on her face.

"Cristos. Save the introductions for later. We have to go now."

They looked at each other before Taryn nodded. As carefully as they could, the group worked to heft Exie onto shaky legs, but the warrior was too weak to walk on her own. Holera and Taryn braced their friend on their shoulders and led their friend out into the shadowed hallway. The guard that stood watch outside their cell lay in a gigantic heap and partially blocked their path. His dark-skinned, scarred face stared lifelessly at the ceiling. A puddle of blood formed around him, still seeping from his slit throat. Cristos had killed him. Aurelia didn't see any blood on their savior, but she knew it was true.

Cristos slowed his brisk pace as they reached the end of the hallway. He turned to them, shadows obscuring his handsome face, and thrust a dagger into Taryn's hand.

"In case we have to fight," he said.

Taryn accepted the weapon, nodding as she stared at the door that separated them from the outside—and from freedom. Slowly nudging it open, Cristos peered outside.

A horse-drawn cart, typically used to carry fruits and vegetables to the market, was parked a few yards away from the building. He lifted the back cover and motioned for them to climb in. Silently, they obeyed his command and approached the makeshift caravan in silence.

Exie turned a sickly green as Taryn and Holera helped her up, her teeth clenched against the pain she endured. Yet, she made no sound.

Once the women were hidden among the crates, Cristos climbed in after them and pulled the heavy canvas down, tucking it snugly around the cargo. A sharp smack on the cart's wall, the answering crack of a whip, and they jolted into motion.

Silence held as the wheels rattled over the uneven road. Six bodies crammed into the narrow space left Aurelia pressed against their unlikely rescuer—so close that one shift more and she would have been in his lap. His scent, warm and spiced like sandalwood, surrounded her, drawing an involuntary heat to her cheeks. She could only imagine how foul she smelled after days without bathing, but if he noticed, he gave no sign. His arm rested near her thigh, close enough that the nearness alone made her pulse quicken.

Fixating on Cristos was perilous—her racing pulse and heated cheeks already betrayed too much—so Aurelia willed herself to look elsewhere. The cart's interior pressed in around them, cloaked in shadows and heavy with the smell of soil and potatoes. The stacked crates hemmed them in, narrowing the air until every breath felt borrowed. From the outside, it would seem no more than a farmer's haul, but inside she could not forget what it truly was: a fragile disguise, hiding fugitives from the wrath of a kingdom.

After hours of jostling over uneven roads, the cart shuddered to a halt. Cristos threw back the canvas and hopped down with an easy motion, then turned to offer Aurelia his hand. Her breath hitched as their palms met, his steady grip grounding her even as his piercing blue eyes set her heart racing. Heat crept up her neck, and she tore her gaze away before it betrayed her, stepping aside to make room for the others. One by one, they clambered out of their cramped hiding place, blinking against the light as though surfacing from a long, suffocating dream.

Cristos retrieved a few sacks from the cart and tossed them onto the ground, then lingered beside the driver. She caught only the faintest glint of coin—or perhaps some other Ekotrian token—before the man gave a curt nod and flicked the reins. In moments, the cart rattled down the road, leaving nothing but the fading creak of its wheels and the heavy silence of the forest.

Now it was only them and Cristos, the trees crowding close as if to listen. He returned with a tense expression on his face, slinging one of the packs across his broad shoulders before offering the rest. Aurelia accepted hers with Septima at her side, while Holera and Taryn braced Exie between them. The fragile relief of being free warred with the sharp knowledge that, in truth, they were anything but safe.

"Why are you helping us?" Holera asked, her voice sharp with suspicion. The edge in her tone mirrored the frustration building in Aurelia's chest. Cristos had risked everything to get them out, yet he offered nothing in the way of explanation. Who was he? What did he stand to gain? Did he plan to leave them stranded the moment it suited him? A thousand questions pressed at her tongue, but he answered none.

Instead, he caught Aurelia lightly by the arm and drew them off the road, guiding the group into the shelter of a copse of trees.

"I'm helping you because my kingdom needs Aegricia's strength," he said at last. His voice was steady, but beneath it Aurelia thought she caught a flicker of weariness. "Warbotach killed our king. My people have no freedom. We cannot reclaim Norithae alone."

Taryn's clipped reply cut through the hush of the forest. "Our own queen is a prisoner. Surely you know that. How much help can Aegricia spare another kingdom when we are drowning ourselves?"

Cristos nodded grimly, scanning the tree line as if expecting enemies to lunge from the shadows. His gaze returned to them. "I know about your queen. That is why I mean to travel to Diapolis. Perhaps together we can sway their king. Alone, none of us can stand against Uldon. Together, we may yet have a chance."

Holera's arms tightened around Exie, adjusting the weight of the half-conscious warrior. Her voice was practical, but laced with strain. "We can't do much until she heals enough to walk or shift. Taryn and I can't carry two passengers. We need a place to stop. How far are we from our camp?"

Aurelia's throat closed as she looked at Exie's limp form, her head hanging low against Holera's shoulder. Fear pressed against her chest until even breathing felt like work. They had escaped, but freedom still felt thin and breakable. All she wanted was the safety of wards, the comfort of Kano's playful weight against her legs.

Cristos lowered the packs to the ground. "I know a place to hide," he said. "It's a few hours from here. I'll carry her." He bent, sliding one arm behind Exie's back, the other beneath her knees, and lifted her with disarming ease. "Take the packs. We move quickly, before anyone finds us."

They set off in the same direction the cart had taken, keeping to the shadowed tree line. Each step farther from Norithae loosened the knot in Aurelia's chest, though not by much. The silence pressed heavy on them, too risky to break, but Aurelia welcomed it. Words could not chase away the memory of stone walls and barred doors, nor the dread of being dragged back to them.

Chapter Twenty-One

Spectre Forest

Aurelia

A snarl shattered the silence of the forest. A large obsidian wolf stood several yards ahead, blocking their path. Its massive shoulders rolled forward as it prowled, every muscle straining with coiled menace. With unblinking eyes, it watched as most of their group approached. Aurelia halted, frozen in fear, staring back at the creature. Her throat tightened, dry as bone, and every nerve screamed at her to flee. The air was thick with the scent of wet fur and soil, and its low growl reverberated through her ribcage like a warning drumbeat. Although it did not advance toward them, its wary gaze tracked their every move, as if deciding which of them to devour first.

Cristos, however, did not stop, appearing unfazed by the ferocious-looking wolf. Instead, he carried Exie closer to the beast and called out in a steady, almost friendly tone, "Calm down, Variel. It's me, Cristos."

The snarling maw of the massive wolf snapped shut the instant Cristos spoke her name. Recognition flickered in its dark eyes, and with a ripple of grotesque elegance, fur melted away into skin, limbs reshaping with audible cracks until an elderly woman stood in its place. Her long black hair tumbled nearly to her waist, untouched by gray despite her evident age. The same darkness lingered in her eyes—irises and pupils blended into a bottomless void. She radiated danger, but also the weight of ancient wisdom.

"What trouble did you bring to me today, Cristos?" the old woman asked as she turned and headed deeper into the forest.

He flashed a smile in response. The first time Aurelia had seen him do so. He trailed behind the old woman, still carrying Exie with ease. Confused and uncertain, they followed Cristos and Variel to a clearing that opened within the dense forest. They came to a halt just outside of the vast expanse, and Variel muttered a few words under her breath. A door appeared. Before Variel muttered to herself, there had been nothing but a forest clearing, but when Aurelia went through the door, a cottage appeared. The woman obviously used wards to camouflage her home from unwanted visitors, but they were unlike the ones the Aegricians used. The air did not warble as they entered. Had it not been for the home appearing out of thin air, she would not have even realized they passed through a magical barrier.

"Let's get her inside," Variel said as she opened the door to her cottage. "What happened to her?" The last question was directed at Cristos, and all of Exie's companions listened intently. They wondered the same for days now.

"She took a beating." Cristos set Exie down on a plush brown sofa against the far wall. "I think the Warbotach general used his abilities on her and choked her aura, or something like it. I don't know much about their powers, but that's what I gleaned from their conversations."

Variel nodded curtly and leaned over to examine the injured woman. "Get these ladies some food and show them where to clean up. Give them clothes from my chambers." Cristos nodded and faced them.

"This way," he said, pointing to a door at the back of the room. Aurelia could not take her eyes off the male as she walked beside him. His face, which was so severe back in Norithae, softened and filled with kindness as soon as they entered Variel's sanctuary. She didn't think he could become any more appealing to her, but he did somehow. Her heart fluttered dangerously as his gentle expression made something blossom inside of her.

She mentally shook herself, focusing on more pressing matters—like getting clean. The door led to a bedroom with a large soaking tub in the corner.

"I'll heat some water." Cristos grabbed the two buckets next to the tub. "There are clothes in the chest at the foot of the bed. I'll be right back." He left the bedroom, and the four women stared at each other, still not quite believing the events that had led them there.

Part of Aurelia still wasn't sure their escape was real. If not for the gnawing hunger and muscle fatigue, she would have easily believed it was all a dream.

"So, what do the three of you think about Cristos?" Aurelia asked as she opened the wooden trunk and carefully riffled through its contents. She found a tunic and trousers, holding them against her body to make sure they would fit. They were a bit large, but they would have to do. She tucked them under her arm and turned to face her friends. Holera didn't answer as she approached the basin, using the cold water within to splash her face.

"It is so obvious that you have a crush on him, Lia." Septima's mischievous smile made Aurelia blush. She gave a dramatic gasp, trying to pretend her sister's observation was inaccurate. She was not wholly convinced he was their friend yet. He had been a part of the group who captured them, after all. She could not deny how she felt when she looked at him, but she was not quite ready to admit it out loud.

A light tap sounded before Cristos walked in, carrying a steaming bucket of water in each hand. Aurelia tried to force back her flush as her companions' bore holes into him with their intense stares. He crossed the room, muscles flexing under the weight of the buckets, and poured the hot water into the tub.

She could tell he was trying to pretend he didn't feel their eyes on him, but his wings tucked tighter against his back like he was trying to make himself small. When his back was to them, Septima made kissing faces in the air, providing much needed comic relief. Aurelia covered her mouth to muffle her giggle.

"I'll check with Variel for more blankets and bedrolls, and light a fire in the grate," he said as he set the buckets down. "It's best for you all to get some sleep tonight. One of you should return to your camp tomorrow to update your people. The rest of us will remain here until your friend is able to travel."

"Will she be okay?" Septima asked. Her concern for Exie was clear in her tone.

His voice softened in response to her emotion. "Variel is a powerful healer and oracle. She is more than capable of nursing her back to health, and your friend's firebird abilities will help her heal faster than a mortal would. She just needs time. Don't worry."

Septima nodded and went to wash her face in the basin.

"I'll check on that bedding and grab wood for the fire." He left the bedroom, closing the door behind him.

"I'll go back tomorrow," Holera said as she stripped off her grimy clothing. Her utter lack of concern at being stark naked in front of them caught Aurelia by surprise. She tried not to stare as the silver-haired beauty snagged a cloth from a nearby pile of towels and washed herself. It was times like this that reminded Aurelia she truly was in another world. The proper, snooty women of Vaekros would never disrobe in front of others.

Holera continued speaking as she scrubbed at her skin. "If I fly back to the sea and head there from the arch, it should be easy to find our camp. I'll let Blaedia know what's happened and hopefully prepare a diplomatic envoy to send to Diapolis."

"It's a good plan, Holera, but be careful. We don't know if Warbotach has men searching Spectre Forest or the skies. They have to know we've escaped by now," Taryn said as she used the fresh water to wash up. Septima and Holera dug through the wooden chest for clothes, pulling out matching tunics and trousers for themselves. Aurelia doubted the clothes would fit, but anything was better than the disgusting rags they were imprisoned in. Variel could burn those clothes as far as Aurelia was concerned. She never wanted to lay eyes on them—and the memories they held—ever again.

Once they'd all washed up and changed, the four women climbed onto Variel's large bed and waited for Cristos to return to light their fire. Aurelia and Septima grew impatient after a while and went to the living room to check on Exie. Variel sat on a wooden stool and spoon-fed the injured warrior who reclined on the sofa. Her eyes were barely open as she swallowed bits of soup.

"There is root vegetable soup in the kitchen, dears," Variel said, not bothering to look over her shoulder. "Cristos is chopping wood out back. He should be back soon."

Septima approached the sofa and lowered to her knees beside Exie, offering to take over spoon-feeding duties. Variel obliged and rose onto her long legs. The shifter prowled into the kitchen, her human body as lithe and graceful as her animal form. Aurelia could hear the woman readying bowls of food, but she headed for the back door instead of offering her help. She walked out into the night in search of their savior. While part of her wondered what was keeping Cristos, she honestly just wanted an opportunity to learn more about him.

A loud chop echoed through the clearing, as Aurelia closed the door behind her. The candlelight from the cottage subtly illuminated the shirtless, winged male. Cristos' tunic was tucked into the waistband of his leather trousers. He pulled it out and wiped his brow as he stood next to a pile of wood he had just finished chopping.

An ax hung loose in his grip as he wiped beads of sweat from the back of his neck. His muscles gleamed with moisture despite the chill in the air. Between the perspiration and the soft moonlight, his tanned skin glistened, causing the black swirling tattoo that extended from his chiseled pectorals all the way down his left arm to stand out.

Aurelia's mouth went dry at the view. She knew she should look away, but his body held her transfixed. Cristos turned and noticed her gaze, his ocean eyes holding her captive. A tense silence passed between them. How could she explain why she sought him out? What if she told him she had come outside just to speak to him and ended up gawking instead? His intense stare drifted down the length of her, returning the favor. Her entire body heated at his gaze, although she knew the borrowed clothes did nothing for her figure. Suddenly, she felt far too hot for such a frosty night.

Aurelia cleared her throat to break the charged tension between them. "I, uh, was just checking to see if you would like some soup," she said as she flipped her thumb back toward the door. "Variel is serving some for everyone."

The tilt of his head, the sly smile teasing at his lips, told her he did not buy her reason, at least not completely. She could feel the blush that colored her cheeks and was glad for the darkness.

"Why are you nervous?" he asked. The forest seemed to go too quiet.

"What? Why would you say that?" Her face grew hotter.

He shrugged, finally looking away as he set another log onto the stump to chop. "I can sense emotions. Smell them." He ruffled his wings as he swung the ax. The split logs hit the ground. "And you are nervous."

She hadn't been able to tear her eyes from his rippling muscles, so the sound startled her. Her mind had been so wrapped up in him, in his words, that she hadn't even noticed the wood.

"Sorry, I didn't mean to rattle you. I'm starving. I'd love something to eat."

He flashed a disarming smile and pulled his tunic back on. She watched panels on the back of his tunic fold around his wings, and she had the urge to caress the leathery appendages. Now that his enticing muscled body was covered, Aurelia could think straight again. She stifled that thought and opened the door, holding it ajar as he brought the wood inside with ease. Before they entered the cottage, she worked to calm the redness on her face. Her sister would read into the smallest expression.

Exie remained laying on the sofa, and Septima sat at her feet, eating a bowl of soup. Holera and Taryn had left the comfort of the bedroom and sat at a small table as they all but inhaled the dinner Variel had laid out for them. Variel shoved a bowl into Cristos' hand as soon as he dropped the wood in front of the fireplace.

Aurelia wondered how the winged-fae knew the shifter oracle, but she didn't feel like it was her business, so she did not ask. Instead, she grabbed her serving and slumped onto a settee by the window in the corner. She gazed out of the pane, looking at the shadowy forest, and smiled softly at the muted flicker of sprites. A rustle of wings was the only warning she received as Cristos stealthily approached from the kitchen and sat next to her.

"You seem to have calmed," he said as he swallowed his first spoonful. He was so at ease in the cottage, so much more than she had ever seen him, and the change enthralled her. "I'm glad to sense it."

She grimaced. "It's kind of creepy that you can get into my head like that."

He chuckled. "I'm sorry. It's not intentional. I can try to stop, or at least stop telling you. Besides, I'm not in your head, per se. It's more like I'm in your heart."

She giggled at his words, trying desperately to prevent her blush from returning. *In her heart.* The words should have made her cringe, but nervous butterflies fluttered in her stomach instead. "Great. Then I'll just be wondering what you're thinking about me and my emotions."

"It's not anything bad, I assure you."

His smile was sheepish, and Aurelia did not know how to respond. She did not know what he meant by his admission, and she was afraid to read too far into it. *Is he flirting with me?*

Before she had a chance to respond, Septima approached her from behind. "Holera said she's leaving tomorrow. Any idea how long we will be here?"

Aurelia's frazzled mind took a moment to realize her sister was speaking to Cristos and not her. He shrugged.

"It's hard to say. It depends on Exie's recovery time. We will leave as soon as she can travel, either on foot or in her phoenix form. Traveling by air would be the fastest, but it takes a great deal of physical strength and energy for her to shift. I doubt she will be able to do that for a few days, at least."

Septima nodded and squeezed her butt into the small amount of space between the two. Cristos excused himself, giving her more room to sit. He returned to the kitchen, where Variel and the others were cleaning up. Aurelia glanced over her shoulder at the sleeping warrior on the sofa.

"How's Exie feeling?" Aurelia asked. Septima's eyes had glazed over, and she did not know if it was because of exhaustion or sadness.

"She's weak, but not in much pain anymore. She needs to rest. I'm going to make a bed on the floor next to her for tonight. I don't want her to be left alone."

"Won't Variel be watching over her?"

"She will, but Exie doesn't know her. I don't want to leave her without a familiar face. Where is everyone else going to sleep?"

Aurelia shrugged. She had not even thought about where they or Cristos would sleep in the two-bedroom cottage. "That's a good question. The property seems heavily warded, but I assume someone will still stand watch while the others sleep. I guess whoever sleeps first will lie down in bedrolls and blankets wherever they can."

Septima patted Aurelia on the shoulder and stood up. "Well, I'm exhausted. I'm going to get ready for bed. Get some rest, Lia. I have a feeling we won't have time to sleep soon enough. We should get it while we can."

Aurelia nodded. "You too."

Chapter Twenty-Two

Aegricia

Otera

A glass vase crashed against the stone wall, shattering into a thousand glittering fragments. The sound echoed through the chamber like a death knell. Ink pots rattled, quills toppled, and Ezio flinched as he stood on the other side of the table.

"How did they lose them?" Uldon roared, his voice thick with rage, spittle flying from his lips. His face flushed a violent crimson, and the web of scars across his skin stood out like fissures in cracked stone. He paced like a caged beast, the heavy thud of his boots echoing in the vaulted chamber, his breath coming in ragged snarls.

Ezio dared not move more than an inch. He kept his eyes lowered, trembling, every line of his posture screaming submission. Uldon's fury was a storm he had weathered many times, but today it felt more volatile than ever, like standing in the path of an avalanche.

"Someone helped them escape, sire," Ezio stammered, his voice quaking as if he might choke on the words. "Humbert is not sure who aided them or how they managed it yet, but we believe it was a Norithaean."

Another crash echoed through the chamber as an inkwell flew across the room, striking the stone wall. Dark red ink splattered like spilled blood, dripping down the white stone in thick rivulets. Papers burst into a rain of parchment, fluttering to the floor like defeated birds, while heavy tomes fell with dull, broken spines.

A delirious part of Ezio noted how much effort it would take to reorganize all of this later. His stomach twisted at the thought. He bit his tongue to stifle the absurd urge to sigh. The slightest sound could set the king's wrath upon him.

"Bring me the queen," Uldon hissed, his voice suddenly level, quiet as death. He eased himself onto the ornate wooden throne, leaning back with a predator's languid grace. The calm after his storm was always worse, always more dangerous. The rapid switch in temperament made him seem unhinged, his sanity dangling by the thinnest thread.

Ezio bowed low, his gaze fixed firmly on his boots, his heart hammering as he backed away from the chamber. He did not dare breathe until the door closed behind him.

Uldon sat in silence, his scarred fingers drumming against the carved armrest of the throne. His eyes fixed on the distant horizon, where the Marella arch loomed like a taunt, like a promise. His blood boiled. Time was running out. He could almost hear *her* whispering—could practically feel her presence pressing against him. Soon she would demand results. If he failed to find a way across the portal—if he failed to seize the human world—his own fate would be far worse than death.

Frustration tightening his chest, he let out a ragged breath, the sound closer to a growl.

The heavy door creaked open. Guards shoved the crimson-haired queen inside. Her gown was ripped, her bare feet blackened and calloused from her captivity. Chains clinked as she stumbled forward, but even in ruin, she carried herself with the unmistakable bearing of a monarch.

Otera's nostrils flared when she saw him seated on her throne. The fire in her blue eyes blazed brighter than ever, a defiance that filth and hunger could not smother.

"Get out of my throne," she snarled. Her voice cut through the chamber like steel drawn from its sheath—sharp, imperious, and utterly fearless.

Uldon chuckled, the sound low and taunting, as he dragged one scarred hand across the polished wood of the throne. She tracked the motion as though her sheer will could scorch his hand away. He leaned back, enjoying the blaze of hatred in her stare.

"I rather like this chair," he said, his voice thick with mockery. "I was thinking of taking it with me when I crossed the Marella portal."

Heat radiated from Otera, the flame in her blood answering the insult. Standing, she took a defiant step forward, but the guard yanked her chain with brutal force. She fell hard to her knees, the iron shackles biting into her skin. Still, she hissed like a wild creature, her teeth bared.

"You will never cross that portal."

Uldon gave a careless flick of his wrist, though his eyes gleamed with fury. "It's only a matter of time. We captured your commander in the Spectre Forest, as well as several of her companions."

Otera's freckled face blanched for the briefest heartbeat, but she schooled her expression with queenly composure. Her eyes, sharp as blades, flicked around the room as though assessing every possible advantage before she threw her head back and laughed.

"You lie. If you captured my commander, then why did you throw a tantrum and destroy my chambers?"

The insult struck like an arrow. Uldon's snarl split the silence, feral and animalistic, as he shot to his feet. His heavy boots hammered across the chamber until he towered over her, shadow blotting out the light. Before she could take a breath, his hand shot out and clamped around her face, his fingers digging viciously into her cheeks.

"You forget yourself, prisoner," he growled, his scarred visage inches from hers, his breath acrid with fury. "You no longer rule Aegricia. I do. These are my chambers. Your little bitch and her band of misfit warriors may have escaped, but it won't be for long. We will find them again—and when we do, my men will bring them here so I can kill them in front of you."

Without flinching, and even as his grip bruised her skin, Otera met his glare. The fire in her eyes only burned hotter, a silent promise that his triumph was temporary, that Aegricia's spirit was far from broken.

SPECTRE FOREST

AURELIA

A single flame blinked in and out of existence, calling to her and beckoning her forward. However, it disappeared every time she stepped closer. With each vanishing moment, the darkness pressed in around her, as if the world itself were intent on swallowing her whole before she could reach the light. She paused, took a deep breath, and exhaled slowly, rubbing her palms across her eyes. How was she supposed to get the flame if it kept vanishing? The light flickered again, but before she could attempt to approach it once more, a face appeared behind it. A face that looked hauntingly like hers.

Aurelia's sleep was restless, though everyone managed to catch a few hours of much-needed rest. From the roof of the cottage, Cristos kept the first watch. Part of her longed to join him, eager to learn more about him, yet the only way up was to ask him to carry her, and she didn't have the nerve.

When Taryn took the second watch, she also chose the roof. From the back door, Aurelia watched as the commander transformed into her phoenix form in the forest. A burst of fire spilled from her, providing a brief reprieve from the cold.

Holera had already left the protective wards of the cottage, returning to their camp well before dawn. With all her heart, Aurelia hoped the warrior would find it. The wards would make it difficult after such a long absence, but she knew Holera wouldn't give up until she succeeded.

By morning, Exie was sitting upright on the sofa when Aurelia stepped from the bedroom. Septima was beside her, both eating a bowl of what looked like porridge. They glanced up as Aurelia trudged into the living room. Taryn, exhausted from her long watch, still slept soundly in the bedroom. The oracle had risen with the sun and busied herself in the kitchen, while Cristos and Variel sat at the table, their hushed conversation weaving between them. Aurelia wasn't sure where the fae male had slept; she only ever saw him enter the bedroom to feed the fire.

"Good morning," Cristos called as she approached. "Would you like some tea?"

Regret pricked her as Variel's gaze flicked to her hair. She hadn't checked the mirror before leaving the darkened room. Running her hands through her crimson locks, Aurelia nodded. "Tea sounds great. Thank you."

She headed for the kettle, but Cristos beat her to it, filling a steaming mug and placing it on the seat beside him.

"How did you sleep?" he asked. Her heart fluttered at the sight of how much his face had softened since leaving Norithae. Worries once etched deep into his features had melted away. The peace would be temporary, she knew, but distance from the palace by the sea, and the scar-faced men who controlled it, had done wonders for his mood.

"Good, and you?" She lowered herself into the chair beside him, unable to resist his sparkling blue eyes. He smiled back.

"I got a few hours," he said, gesturing toward the space near the fireplace. His leathery black wings were tucked tight against his back, restrained as though he caged a storm within his body. Aurelia wondered at the strength it must take to fold something so powerful so neatly. Desire burned to touch them, but she didn't dare. Still, curiosity gnawed at her—*what did they look like in flight?* She had never seen anyone like him.

Variel placed a bowl of porridge before Aurelia, then went to check on Exie, leaving them alone. The moment she walked away, Aurelia's chest tightened.

"Why are you nervous again?" Cristos asked, half-mischief, half-concern in his expression.

"I am not," she replied, far too defensively. He studied her knowingly, unconvinced.

"If you say so. I'm just here to help." Rising from the table, he washed his dish before glancing back. "I'm going to hunt. Variel will need help feeding all of us."

Aurelia shot to her feet, enthusiasm bubbling despite herself. "Can I come? Exie taught me how to hunt, and I'll go crazy if I stay inside all day."

He raised an amused brow. "All right, as long as you stay out of trouble."

Clutching her chest dramatically, she gasped. "I never get into trouble."

"Did I not just break you out of prison?" His incredulous smile made her roll her eyes.

"Captivity aside, I never get into trouble."

"You should bundle up before we leave. It's cold beyond the wards."

Draining her tea, Aurelia rinsed the mug and slipped into the bedroom. Taryn was still asleep when she pulled a cloak from the chest and laced up her boots. Careful not to wake the warrior, she closed the door softly behind her.

Cristos leaned against the frame, bow and quiver already strapped to his shoulder, a sword peeking from between his wings. "Here you go," he said, handing her another bow. "Let's make it a compe-tition. Winner brings home dinner." His grin was cheeky, and when she reached for the weapon, her heart flipped. He was flirting.

"Be careful," Septima said as they headed toward the back door. Aurelia promised she would, waving to her sister before stepping into the cold.

Snow had ceased, but the world remained frigid. She tugged her leather gloves higher, tucking them into her tunic sleeves. Cristos' sandalwood-and-spice scent drifted on the wind, making her skin prickle. The faint shift of his wings against leather carried danger and beauty both. Breathing him in, she admitted silently: she was in trouble.

"You're quiet today," he murmured, so low she had to strain to catch it.

"Shouldn't we be quiet, so we don't scare the game?"

"In theory, yes. But I haven't spoken to many people since Warbotach took my kingdom. I guess I'm desperate for conversation."

"So you're only talking to me out of desperation?" Her teasing tone hid a sting.

He stopped abruptly, forcing her to catch herself before running into his back—or worse, his wings. "That's not what I meant. You aren't the only one who's nervous."

Swallowing hard, she dared to ask, "Why would you be nervous?"

Color crept into the tips of his pointed ears. "It's not every day a beautiful woman falls into my life and I have to risk everything to save her."

Her heart hammered. The war, the cold, even the bow in her hand—all faded at the weight of his words.

"You didn't have to save us." The moment the words left her mouth, she wanted to smack her forehead. Smooth, Aurelia. What a way to ruin a compliment.

He turned to face her. "You have no idea how untrue that is. I absolutely had to save you."

"Thank you." It was all she could manage, but the softness in his smile made it enough.

They continued in silence after that, Aurelia trailing close behind him. To her surprise, she could keep pace despite her time being imprisoned. His movements through the trees were fluid, mesmerizing—the flex of muscle under leather, the shift of wings, the scent of spice and smoke clinging to him. She should have been searching for prey, but her focus was drawn only to him.

Dense forest closed around them as they left the main path, the trees pressing in until they reached a narrow stream. The woods opened into a glade, where Cristos quickly set protective wards. Shielded from Warbotach's gaze, they hunkered behind a cluster of shrubs and trees, the makeshift blind offering cover as they waited for prey.

Biting her nails, Aurelia risked a glance at him. "What you said back there... did you mean it?"

"Of course I did. Why do you ask?"

Her pulse quickened. "You called me beautiful."

His smile was slow, flirtatious, and his oceanic gaze locked onto hers. "I meant that."

The thumping in her chest grew erratic. She glanced at his lips, licking her own. His eyes hooded as he leaned closer, lowering his head. The space between them evaporated. She knew he was about to kiss her, and she would absolutely kiss him back.

Then a rustle sounded behind them. Cristos pulled away, finger pressed to his lips in a silent command. Her mouth should have been there, not his hand. The ache of the missed kiss lingered, sharp and hollow.

He turned to peek through the brush. Even unseen, they had to remain silent.

From the treeline, a snow-white stag emerged, lowering its head to drink. Aurelia reached for her bow, but Cristos lifted his arm to stop her. Instead, he motioned for her to look closer. Leaning forward, her cheek brushed his. When the deer turned its head, antlers erupted in flame—yet the animal remained unharmed.

Wide-eyed, Aurelia lowered her bow.

"It's a Ceryneian deer," he whispered, warm breath curling over her ear. Shivers chased through her as the desire he'd almost unleashed returned. "Sacred creatures. Their antlers flame when threatened."

She nodded quickly, ducking back into the brush, grateful for the distraction. The deer lingered a moment longer before bounding away, leaving her breathless.

"It was beautiful," she murmured.

Cristos inclined his head. "Not many see one in their lifetime. Consider it a good omen."

"We could use some luck," she said with a smirk.

"I agree. Hopefully, fortune favors us with dinner instead of omens."

The hours crept by in silence. Aurelia forced herself to focus on the forest instead of the broad span of Cristos' shoulders or the way his wings twitched faintly, restrained storms at rest. Just as hope began to wane, a branch snapped to their left.

Peeking through the brush, she spotted a wild pig rooting among leaves. Cristos gave a small nod—confirmation enough. Aurelia notched her arrow, lined up the shot, and let fly.

The boar collapsed instantly.

Her breath caught. Though not her first kill, the familiar wave of grief rose all the same. At least its end was quick, and for that she was grateful. Father would have called her soft; Exie would have said it was training. But Aurelia knew better. It was her heart refusing to harden.

"Excellent shot!" Cristos' cheer startled her, though his grin softened the sting. Crawling from the blind, he turned back, wings fluttering as he reached for her hand. His thumb traced soothing circles across her skin. "It's natural to feel sadness after a kill. Don't punish yourself. Life feeds life—it's the circle we all live by."

His words steadied her more than she expected. She managed a quiet agreement, then watched as he secured the pig with rope and a pole so they could carry it together. The animal was heavy, but Cristos slowed his stride so she could keep pace.

Snow crunched beneath their boots on the trek back. Aurelia stumbled more than once under the weight, though never enough for him to comment. When the cottage came into view, Taryn's phoenix form perched on the roof, wings tucked close as she scanned the forest. Variel hung laundry on the line, her motions calm and domestic in the cold air.

Cristos dropped the carcass on the outdoor table, and Variel stepped forward without hesitation. "I'll take it from here," she said, rolling up her sleeves. The elderly healer showed no qualms about butchering the boar, and Aurelia was relieved to let her.

She and Cristos slipped inside, mud and blood clinging to their clothes. Septima sat with Exie in the living room, both asleep in awkward positions that made Aurelia's neck ache just to look at them. Neither stirred when the pair crept past and retreated into the bedroom, closing the door softly behind them.

The intimacy of being near a bed was not lost on her. Even if all they meant to do was wash and rest, her heart still raced. Cristos had called her beautiful—*twice*. He seemed drawn to her, and she to him. Yet doubt gnawed at her: she was human, he was not. He lived in Norithae, and she was a fugitive in the middle of a war. What future could they possibly share?

At the basin, Cristos poured cold water over his face, scrubbing away the hunt. He filled the bowl again, then stepped aside.

"Thank you," Aurelia murmured, squeezing past him. Their shoulders brushed. Her hand accidentally grazed the edge of his wing.

He stiffened. The quick retreat that followed stung far more than she wanted to admit. *Was touching his wings forbidden? Or was it simply too intimate?*

"You won the competition," he said at last, voice rough and husky. "Think about your prize." Crossing the room in long, sure strides, he unrolled a bedroll near the hearth and stretched out with his back to her.

She washed quickly, changed behind the screen, and slipped into bed. Part of her hoped he might follow her, close the distance, press his body against hers. But when his steady breathing reached her, she couldn't tell if he was asleep or simply feigning it. Questions piled up in her mind, unspoken and unanswered, until exhaustion finally pulled her under.

Aurelia's heart still raced as they settled into the room. Proximity to the bed made everything feel more intimate, even if all they intended was rest. Cristos' earlier words echoed—*beautiful, twice*, and she couldn't shake the dangerous pull between them.

She reminded herself of the obstacles: he was fae, she was human. He had a kingdom waiting for him, while she had nothing but uncertainty and the fragile safety of her companions. Once, in Vaekros, her father's plans had mapped her future out clearly, even if she hadn't wanted it. Now, freedom felt both exhilarating and terrifying—an open road she had no idea how to walk.

Cristos crouched over the basin first, splashing cold water over his face. Droplets glistened along his sharp jaw as he stepped aside for her, filling the bowl once more.

"Thank you," she murmured, easing past him. Their shoulders brushed, and her sleeve skimmed the edge of his wing.

The reaction was instant. He stiffened, shifting out of her way so quickly the sting of rejection pierced deeper than she wanted to admit. Had she crossed some unspoken boundary? Or was touching a wing something far more intimate for his kind?

"You won the competition," he said after a pause, his voice gravelly, husky in a way that sent a shiver down her spine. "Decide on your prize and tell me when you're ready."

In long, measured strides, he crossed the room, rolled out a bedroll before the fire, and lowered himself onto it, back turned.

Confusion burned in her chest. His retreat seemed at odds with the huskiness in his tone, with the warmth in his eyes earlier. *What had he felt when her shoulder brushed his wing? Did he flee because of rejection—or because of desire?*

Pushing away the questions, Aurelia returned to the basin, splashing water over her face and arms as he had. Behind the dressing screen, she pulled on fresh trousers and a tunic. A reckless, irrational part of her wished Cristos would follow, step into the shadowed space and close the distance between them. But he did not.

By the time she crawled into bed, his steady breathing suggested either sleep or a convincing imitation. She didn't disturb him. Curling beneath the covers, she let exhaustion finally claim her, though her mind still wrestled with unspoken fears and unspoken wants.

For tonight, the questions could wait.

SPECTRE FOREST

AURELIA

Aurelia had no idea how long she slept, but she was not surprised by the faces that greeted them when she and Cristos walked out of the bedroom that evening. The sun had already set, and the smell of roasted pork filled the cottage. She was not looking forward to explaining that nothing happened, and that they only stayed in the bedroom to avoid waking Septima and Exie. Both of whom were now awake and staring at her and the winged fae. She was tempted to return their accusatory looks, but refrained. She got the impression her sister was trying to hide her growing feelings for Exie, but they were obvious to Aurelia, all the same. If Septima and Exie were falling in love, she would support her younger sister and be happy for her. That did not mean, however, that she would not tease Septima mercilessly if she made so much as one taunt about her and Cristos.

Without a word, Cristos went out the back door to relieve Taryn's watch. Only the flush at the tips of his ears betrayed that he had noticed her sister's intense stare. Mustering the most unamused face she could manage, Aurelia approached Septima and Exie and dropped onto the sofa beside them.

"Nothing happened," she whispered before they even had a chance to comment, but her sister did not look convinced.

Septima smirked. "Sure, Lia. Whatever you say."

Aurelia bumped Septima with her shoulder. "I'm serious. I haven't even kissed him. You and Exie were asleep when we returned, so we went into the bedroom, so we didn't disturb you. He slept on the floor, and I slept on the bed. Nothing happened."

"I believe you," countered Exie. "Not that you have to explain it to us."

Septima shot Exie an indignant glare and called the warrior a traitor under her breath before addressing Aurelia again. "Don't listen to Exie. Of course, you must tell me everything. I'm your sister."

"And what about you two?" Not ready to talk about the almost-kiss on the hunting trip, Aurelia turned the tables on them. She would not lie to her sister, but she had no qualms about distracting her. Her lips curled into a sly half-smile as Septima's eyes widened. "Did you truly think I hadn't noticed?"

Septima's mouth fluttered open and shut repeatedly, too shocked to respond. Exie smiled wryly.

Rising from the sofa as her sister continued her nonsensical sputtering, Aurelia left the cottage. Better to let Septima stew on her probe, and to flee before she came to her senses enough to throttle Aurelia for asking such a question in front of Exie.

The cool night air wrapped around her while she took a moment to appreciate the view. Moonlight streamed through the canopy of the trees, creating a magical glow upon the foliage of Spectre Forest. Sprite lights flickered between majestic pines and dense shrubbery, like the fireflies Aurelia loved as a child. The only time Howling Forest held true magic was when the phoenixes inhabited it, but at night, the fireflies gave it a whimsical appearance. Drawing parallels between the world she'd always known and the one she currently occupied gave her a sense of calm. While Ekotoria differed vastly from the human world, at least she had some familiarities to enjoy.

The swish of wings cutting through the air, and the brush of wind that stirred her red locks around her shoulders, announced Cristos' arrival. When she turned to face him, a shy smile graced her lips.

"I wanted to go on watch with you," she offered in explanation after a long, silent moment. "I want to be helpful."

The corner of his mouth quirked up, his eyes brightening with a playful gleam. "You brought home dinner. That was quite helpful, Aurelia."

The way he said her name was like a verbal caress, making her ordinary name sound exotic and sexy. Her pulse quickened, but she maintained her composure as she smiled at him. "You're right. We still need to discuss my prize."

"What do you have in mind?"

Her heart continued to increase its erratic pace. She was not an experienced flirt, but Cristos tempted her enough to try. Every time she laid eyes on him, her desire grew, and she new she was in trouble.

"I don't know yet. Take me to the roof, and I'll think about it."

Cristos looked her up and down, and she forgot how to breathe. "How will you defend us without a weapon? You will need one for watch."

That's what he was looking for. A weapon. She felt silly for assuming he was admiring her physique. Trying to hide her embarrassment, Aurelia grinned as she replied. "That's a fair point. I will be right back."

Aurelia hurried inside, snatched up her bow and quiver, and darted back out. Cristos' low chuckle followed her as he opened his arms in invitation. Calm on the surface—though giddy laughter threatened to bubble out of her—she stepped toward him.

His embrace closed around her, firm enough that her cheek pressed against his chest. Heat radiated from his body, seeping through her cloak, and the sandalwood-spice scent of him filled her lungs. Beneath her ear, the steady thrum of his heartbeat grounded her even as the world seemed to tilt.

With a powerful kick, he launched them skyward. Leathery wings snapped open, beating twice with effortless strength before the cottage roof rose to meet them.

After she steadied her footing on the wooden shingles, he released her gently. The roof creaked softly beneath their weight, and Aurelia's stomach dipped at the sudden awareness of how high they were. "Don't get too close to the edge. I wouldn't want you to fall."

She smirked as she sat. It wasn't as if she wanted to fall off the roof, either. He settled beside her, a hair's breadth of distance between them, his wings stretching behind him like a dark shield against the wind.

"At least it's not freezing tonight." One wing stretched around her back, blocking her body from the breeze. She tried not to make it obvious, but she noticed.

"So," she hesitated. "What are we looking for?"

Cristos' gaze swept over the moonlit forest, searching the tree line for threats. Aurelia, however, remained fixated on him. His black hair was still tousled from sleep, and she clenched her fists at her sides to resist the urge to brush away the stray locks falling across his forehead.

"Honestly, I do not expect to see much. Variel's wards are quite secure."

"How do you know her?" Aurelia had been dying to ask, but had never found the right opportunity before now.

"She knew my mother," he said, nostalgia in his tone. Without him having to say it, Aurelia realized he had also lost his mother too.

"I'm sorry." She chanced to grasp his hand, but he did not pull away. Instead, he interlaced his fingers with hers. Nerves made her mouth go dry, but she tried to ignore it as she comforted him.

"Thank you. It's been a long time since she passed on, but it's not something one gets over easily." She knew that feeling all too well.

"I understand. My mother is gone as well." Cristos met her gaze. Silver lined his brilliant blue eyes as he waited for her to continue. "I was five years old. She got sick, and it all happened so fast. They secluded us—Septima, our brother and I—to keep us from catching it. I never even got to say g-goodbye."

Her voice, thick with emotion, cracked. He squeezed her hand gently, his face softening even more. "I lost my mother many years ago as well. She was killed by a rebel sympathizer. A Warbotach general killed my father during the invasion, too, so it's now only me."

Aurelia's heart twisted. He carried loss like armor, where hers still felt like an open wound. She covered their entwined fingers with her other hand and drew soothing circles on the back of his. He had lost both of his parents in such violent ways. A tinge of guilt hit her when she thought about how she'd left her own father by choice. It didn't matter if he tried to control every aspect of their lives. He was still her father, and she still had love for him. She didn't regret her decision, but there were moments when she missed the rest of her family.

"Cristos, I'm so sorry. I don't know what else to say."

He gave her a small smile before looking out upon the forest once more. "Thank you. Variel was one of my mother's advisors. She fled the capital after my mother's murder and has secluded herself in this forest ever since. I dislike her being alone, though I know she enjoys the solitude, so I visit whenever I can. She's always remained an important person in my life."

Aurelia thought about the elderly female in the house. She spoke so warmly to Cristos and treated him like family. Aurelia smiled. "I think it's amazing that you still have a relationship with her. She seems like a great person."

He nodded. "She is."

Silence settled easily then, both of them watching the tree line. The fluttering sprites created patterns in the darkness with their glowing bodies, almost like they were trying to spell out words.

The conversation gave way to silence as they both watched the tree line. The fluttering sprites created patterns in the darkness with their glowing bodies, almost like they were trying to spell out words.

"They are so energetic," Aurelia giggled. A group of sprites had gathered only yards from them, dancing through the air. Their tiny lights pulsed like sparks shaken from a fire.

He chuckled as he let go of her hand. "That they are. They are very mischievous. I think they like the attention. Watch this."

She missed the warmth of his hold but watched as Cristos held out his arm and four sprites broke away from their group.

Aurelia stiffened in surprise but watched in awe as the tiny creatures with wings like starlight landed on Cristos' arm. Their glow illuminated the strong planes of his forearm, turning the faint swirls of his tattoos to molten shadows. They looked like miniature humans with slightly pointed ears, ears just like her other Ekotorian companions. Aurelia leaned in closer as the sprites, all female, twirled their little legs, their feet tracing patterns along his arm. They stared up at him with bashful admiration.

"What are you all doing out there, Dewdrop?" He spoke to the sprite closest to his elbow. He knew them. Her tiny teeth gleamed as she smiled at him, batting her eyelashes flirtatiously. Aurelia could almost hear the sprites swooning.

Jealousy surged, making her chest tighten. Cristos did not belong to her, and the sprites were far too small to even dream of being with him, but the emotion reared its ugly head within her and left her feeling utterly ridiculous.

The sprite, Dewdrop, responded in the tiniest voice Aurelia had ever heard. "Dancing for you, your..." The sprite trailed off. "Dancing for you, Cristos. Who is your friend?" The sprite turned to eye her. Cristos followed the sprite's gaze, his smile joyful.

"This is my new friend Aurelia. She will be traveling with me for a while."

The little sprite crossed her tiny arms over her chest. Cristos noticed, and his smile widened. "She will be traveling with me, along with her friends. Don't you worry, Dewdrop. You will always be my number one female."

The sprite beamed and cupped her flushed cheek with her hands. The three sprites next to Dewdrop crossed their own tiny arms over their chests. Apparently, they all thought they were his number one female.

"You are quite the ladies' man, Cristos," Aurelia teased, the sprites' reactions too adorable for her envy to last. She watched the angry faces of the other sprites. He just continued to smile at them. "Are you going to introduce me to your girlfriends?"

All four sprites giggled at her, but Dewdrop spoke. "Cristos, you said I am your female, but Dragonfly said she was your female yesterday. And Ash," she pointed to the golden-haired sprite to her right, "Ash said she was your female last week. Flora even had the nerve to say she was going to be your female next week! Tell them it isn't so, Cristos! Tell them I'm your one and only female. I'm your true mate, Cristos."

He watched Dewdrop in pure amusement while Aurelia stifled a chuckle at the amount of times she said his name. He used his fingertip to smooth back her auburn hair, which had become ruffled in her monologue. "I could not fit in your tiny house, Dewdrop, so we cannot be mates. But you are all my special girls. Can you ever forgive me?"

Aurelia nearly lost the tenuous hold she had over her giggles. The sprites stared at him as he forced a sad but contemplative look on his face. They huddled together in a heated, whispered discussion before turning their angry eyes back on him, their tiny arms crossed over their chests in solidarity.

"We will think about it," huffed Dewdrop before they flew off and darted back into the forest. Aurelia's giggles escaped as soon as they disappeared into the darkness.

"They are so mad at me." There was little more than amusement in his tone. "I guess I will have to find a new female."

He stared at Aurelia, a flirtatious grin in place, but she leaned back and grimaced at him.

"Don't look at me. You have too many females for me to join your harem. I do not share well with others."

He looked offended, but he let out a roar of laughter after only a few seconds. It was a belly laugh Aurelia had not heard from him yet, and it warmed her inside.

"Will you be okay if I fly down and grab dinner for us? I'm starving, and it's probably ready now." Aurelia nodded, and seconds later, he spread his wings and hopped off the side of the cottage.

She waited in silence while he was gone, watching the remaining sprites dance across the darkened tree line. She wondered if Dewdrop and her friends were still angry, but hoped they weren't. They were by far the cutest things she'd seen since Kano was a cub. Just thinking about her feline friend was enough to dampen her spirits, but Cristos returned before she could wallow too much.

He landed with two bowls in his hands, and a fur blanket draped over his shoulder. He wrapped the blanket around her and set a steaming bowl of pork, vegetables, and rice into her hands.

"Thank you, especially for the blanket. It's colder than I realized."

He reached his wing around her back again to block her from the wind. "I thought you may have been colder than you were letting on."

"I think Dewdrop and her friends abandoned the party." She pointed toward the trees, where only a few sprites remained.

"Yep. I think I lost her love for good."

Aurelia snickered, taking a bite of her food. "That's too bad. She was pretty cute."

"That she is, but not quite as beautiful as you."

Aurelia lightly rammed him with her shoulder. He chuckled.

"What? It's true."

"If you keep flirting with me, you're going to make my sister think something is going on between us."

"Good," he said. "Or is that a bad thing?"

She glanced side-long at him but did not respond. He smiled, disarming her slightly. Any part of her that previously believed he was not flirting had been converted. He was without a doubt flirting with her shamelessly, and she didn't know how to feel about it. She wasn't sure if she should be flattered, scared, or tempted. Maybe she was a combination of all three.

"A bad thing for your miniature girlfriends, because I don't share. But I haven't decided what it is for me yet."

He fixed her with a curious stare and arched an eyebrow. "Is that so?"

She shrugged, trying but failing to look away.

He reached up and cupped her cheek. She unconsciously leaned into his touch. The warmth of his palm sank into her skin, chasing the chill from her bones.

"What would it take to convince you it's a good thing?"

Her eyes flicked up to meet his gaze as he leaned in closer. She could feel his warm breath on her face.

"I don't know. I guess I would like to know more about you and for you to know more about me. I want to know about what my future holds."

"No one knows what will come to pass, but we all make choices to shape fate the way we desire." He stroked the cheek he held gently with his thumb, his brilliant eyes so close as they bore into hers.

Her eyelids fluttered shut as she nodded. His touch was a subtle hum of lightning against her skin. It vibrated throughout her body, striking and igniting the deepest places within her.

When she opened her eyes again, his gorgeous face was only an inch from hers. Breath caught in her lungs as she scanned his piercing blue gaze. Before she could turn away or second guess herself, his lips brushed against hers.

His hand slid up to cup her other cheek, and he cradled her face ever so gently as he gave her another soft kiss. Liquid fire flowed through her veins at the first touch. His simple kiss was electrifying, but it wasn't enough. She wanted—*needed*—more.

He pulled away, and every part of Aurelia wanted to scream in frustrated protest. He scanned her face, looking for any objection, for any reason for him to stop, but found none. His eyes darkened, heating with a desire that rivaled her own. She smiled, feeling unexpectedly shy in the moment, and his responding look was sensual.

He kissed her again, tangling one hand in her hair while the other wrapped around her waist to pull her closer.

A moan escaped Aurelia as his tongue traced her bottom lip. Her future was uncertain and there was a chance he'd have no part in it, but he was there now. They were together, and they liked each other. Maybe it was the tantalizing feel of his touch, or maybe it was his intoxicating scent, but that moment was all that mattered to her.

She placed her hands on his shoulders and slid them up, wrapping her arms around his neck as her chest smashed against his. Her fingers wandered, stroking the dark wings she'd so longed to caress.

He groaned deep in his throat, his fingers biting into her hips as their kiss grew more frantic.

The click and low squeal of the back-door opening forced their lips apart. Aurelia jerked back, immediately blushing, though no one could see them on the roof. Cristos placed a gentle kiss on her cheek before he scooped up their dirty dishes and jumped down. His wings flapped once in what was more of a graceful fall than actual flying.

"Thought you and Aurelia may want this," Variel said.

Aurelia could not see what the oracle handed to Cristos, but she heard the woman retreat into the cottage before Cristos returned with a flap of his wings. He held two steaming mugs in hand and passed her one before returning to his seat beside her.

"What can I say?" he said, blowing into the hot tea. "She's the best."

Aurelia smiled. It wasn't lost on her that Variel treated Cristos as a son. She was grateful for the wolf shifter taking them in and caring for them. They may very well be dead by now, if not for her.

SPECTRE FOREST

AURELIA

For hours, Aurelia and Cristos scanned the darkened trees, though no threat ever emerged. He slipped an arm around her shoulder, shielding her from the cold breeze with the steady shelter of his wing. Between that warmth and the blanket draped across her lap, she felt cocooned in comfort. Words seemed unnecessary. They passed most of the watch in silence, content in each other's arms. She didn't want to dwell on what their kiss meant, nor on the day when he might no longer be in her life. The war made any plans for the future impossible, so she resolved to savor what happiness she could.

When Taryn arrived to relieve them, Aurelia crept quietly into the cottage. Expecting teasing stares from Septima and Exie, she instead found both asleep on the sofa. Septima had curled protectively around the injured phoenix, her arm resting across Exie's stomach. Aurelia's smile grew as she took in the sight, carefully stepping over the discarded bedroll. The firelight cast the pair in amber hues, as though the forest itself approved of their closeness. Their hasty escape from Vaekros had spared Septima from being forced into a life she didn't want—and offered her the chance to find love. That alone made every hardship worth enduring.

Variel slept soundly in a reclining chair near the fireplace, not stirring even when Aurelia and Cristos passed by. With a quiet gesture, Cristos beckoned her toward the bedroom. She followed, knowing they were only seeking privacy so as not to wake the others. Still, she was well aware of the looks they would earn in the morning when they emerged together. She found she didn't care. Let them believe she and Cristos had something between them, because they did.

Cristos placed new logs on the fire and slipped out with the buckets in silence. A few minutes later, he returned carrying fresh water. While he heated it over the fire, Aurelia rummaged for clothes, hoping to find something that would fit. Every Ekotorian female she had met so far stood taller than her—taller even than most women in the human realm—so she wasn't surprised when the trousers she found needed to be rolled several times to keep from dragging the floor. They would have to do.

"I thought you would want a bath," he said at last, pouring the hot water into the tub.

Heat bloomed in her cheeks the moment his eyes found hers from across the room. "And what about you? Don't you want one?"

His grin made her heart flip. "I do, but I'm more interested in why you're so... I don't know... excited? Maybe my senses are off, but I'm trying to figure you out."

Her eyes widened in embarrassment, the scarlet flush deepening. Rolling her eyes in a desperate attempt to mask her initial thought, Aurelia muttered, "I'm excited to take a bath. So, thank you for the water. Make yourself scarce for a little while."

Pouting playfully, he leaned down to press a lingering kiss on her lips before quietly leaving to give her the privacy she'd requested. For several long moments, Aurelia simply stood in the center of the room, the ghost of his kiss still tingling on her lips. She debated calling him back to join her, precisely what she had initially wanted to suggest, but restraint won out. Regretfully, she removed her clothes and lowered herself into the deliciously hot bath alone.

Steam curled around her as she sank deeper. The water could not cool the warmth pulsing through her blood. Desire, first awakened during their hunt and magnified during their watch, now threatened to spill over. She was headed into uncharted territory with Cristos, but she would no longer try to stop it. The vow to move slowly with him remained, though it grew harder to keep whenever he lingered so near. Still, she would move forward.

Sliding back until she was completely submerged, Aurelia closed her eyes and let memories replay. Each kiss relived became a danger to her self-control—the way his fingers slid through her hair, the grip on her hip as he devoured her, the arm wrapped firmly around her waist. A sigh escaped her lips, louder and more frustrated than she intended. She reached for the soap and scrubbed quickly, telling herself she wasn't rushing. The longer Cristos lingered in the living room, the more chance he had of waking the others. That was the excuse she clung to as she dried off in haste, dressed, and cracked the door open to wave him back inside.

Cristos slipped into the bedroom just as she sat at the vanity to brush her hair. "I'll leave so you can bathe in a moment. I just need to braid my hair."

"You don't have to leave."

The brush slipped from Aurelia's fingers and clattered against the vanity. She jumped, whirling to face him. Cristos sat casually on the wooden chest at the foot of the bed, unlacing his boots. That mischievous smile tugged at only one corner of his lips, and she nearly melted into a puddle of lust.

"It doesn't bother me if you stay, Aurelia. I wouldn't want you to wake your sister, after all. Whatever you are comfortable with is fine with me."

His eyes glimmered with playful mischief, the smirk tugging at his lips even more flirtatious than his tone.

Speechless, Aurelia simply stared. He unlaced his boots, peeled off his socks, and then crossed the space to kneel before her. The closeness made her breath hitch.

"There are no expectations," he said gently. She nodded, unable to summon words. "I just wanted to make that clear. You can stay while I bathe, or you can go, but either way, I don't expect anything more than what you're willing to give. I would like more of your kisses, of course, but that is up to you as well."

Her lips parted, but only a smile and another nod emerged, betraying her like a love-struck fool. Somehow, he seemed to sense her deeper thoughts anyway. His smile softened as he rubbed his thumb over her palm, sending little sparks racing through her nerves.

"Can I have more of your kisses?"

All she managed was yet another nod. He leaned in and brushed his lips against hers. The kiss deepened slowly, heatedly, yet still he touched nothing beyond her hand. Kneeling before her vanity stool, holding only her hand, Cristos kissed her as though they had forever.

His arm slid around her shoulders, fingers tangling in her damp hair, and he kissed her so deeply she felt herself falling. She was ready to beg for more when he pulled away and began to unbutton his tunic.

She sat breathless, eyes tracing every deliberate movement as he bared his chest. The tattoo scrolled across his torso enhanced rather than distracted from his strength. "I'm going to take a bath, so we can lie down and I can kiss you for the rest of the night—if you want me to. You can leave or stay. It's completely up to you."

The tunic slid from his shoulders, leaving her swallowing hard with the urge to touch him. He set the garment aside and poured another bucket of hot water into the tub. Candlelight painted golden shadows over his sculpted stomach, making her turn back to the mirror before temptation won. *If I turned, just once, there would be no going back.* Her fingers trembled as she braided her hair. Behind her, trousers hit the floor. He chuckled, then the splash of water signaled he had slipped into the bath.

"It's safe to turn around, Aurelia. I am fully covered by water."

Her face flamed hotter, but she turned anyway. Pretending indifference was pointless; he could sense every ripple of her emotions.

Cristos reclined in the tub, wings draped along the rim, steam curling around his face. In that moment, he looked like a god, and she struggled not to gape. Forcing herself upright on shaky legs, she crossed to the bed and lay down with her back to him, blanket pulled up to her chin to keep from sneaking glances. She listened to the water splash as he washed, fighting the urge to roll over. Even without seeing what was beneath the water, the very thought made her resolve to "move slowly" with him feel laughably fragile.

"How's your bath?"

"Fantastic." His voice held an edge of sensuality—whether natural or imagined by her own desire, she couldn't tell. "I'm going to get out now."

Biting her lip at his warning, Aurelia kept her eyes fixed on the wall. "Do you have other clothes?"

"I brought a few things in my bag. No stolen glances, Aurelia."

Suppressing a giggle, she burrowed deeper into the blanket. She waited for his call that it was safe to look, but no such invitation came. Instead, the mattress dipped as he crawled in beside her. His warmth spread instantly as he slid an arm over her stomach and pressed a delicate kiss to her forehead.

"What are you doing, Cristos?"

"Going to sleep. What are you doing, Aurelia?"

She rolled to face him, half-smiling. "Apparently, I'm going to sleep. And trying not to think about how impossible you make it."

"Can I kiss you goodnight? I don't think I could fall asleep without it."

She smirked. "If you can't sleep without it, then I guess I have no other choice. You'll need your rest if you're going to protect us."

"Please." He snorted. "None of you needs my protection."

His lips claimed hers before she could even protest the compliment. Soft as silk, the kiss lingered, deepening just enough before he drew her closer, her cheek pillowed against his chest.

A final kiss pressed to the top of her head came with a whisper. "Sleep well, my beautiful Aurelia."

She smiled into his skin. "You too, my handsome Cristos."

And as slumber claimed her, the last thing she heard was the steady rhythm of his heartbeat beneath her ear, carrying her into dreams.

CHAPTER TWENTY-SIX

SPECTRE FOREST

AURELIA

Aurelia feared she'd be unable to fall asleep with Cristos in bed beside her, but it was the most peaceful she had slept in weeks. When she woke up, however, she was alone. She knew Cristos needed to relieve Taryn from watch in the early hours of the morning, but had not noticed him leave. When she exited the bedroom, she found Septima and Exie were where they'd been the night before, but they sat up eating instead of snuggled up on the sofa. There was no one else in the cottage—not even Variel, who was usually bustling around the kitchen.

"Where is everyone?" she asked.

Septima pointed at the back door. "They saw something on the watch last night. They are all outside talking."

Aurelia froze for a moment, her breath snagging in her chest. For a fleeting instant, she remembered the frantic barking of her father's hounds back in Vaekros, the way their snarls had seemed to claw right through her skin. She had woken safe and warm, but the mention of scouts twisted that safety into smoke. She shook herself and headed out to get the details of the sighting firsthand.

Cristos, Variel, and Taryn stood in the backyard, whispering amongst themselves in a tight circle. Cristos pointed into the tree line and spotted Aurelia's approach. Their conversation ceased as she neared.

"Good morning, Aurelia." Cristos' smile was genuine as he reached for her hand. She didn't stop to consider her actions as she reached for him, letting him pull her in for a quick hug. Neither Variel nor Taryn seemed surprised by their show of affection.

"What happened?" She searched his eyes for any sign that they were in imminent danger.

"Everything is fine, don't worry. A few Warbotach scouts were out that way." He gestured at the same spot he'd been indicating to the others when she joined them. "They couldn't get through the wards, probably didn't even sense them, but I think it would be best to leave as soon as we're certain they're no longer in the vicinity and Exie is fit for travel."

"Are we in danger?" The comfort and security Aurelia felt when she woke up were shattered. She no longer felt safe. She felt hunted.

"Those beasts won't get through my wards," Variel said. "The three of us will reinforce them, but you all are safe. There is no need to rush off, Cristos."

Cristos pulled her closer, his hand trailing up and down her back in comfort, as he kissed her softly. "Get some breakfast. I'm going to help Variel reinforce the wards, and then I'll come back inside."

Aurelia scanned their faces once more before she nodded and went inside. Exie and Septima were no longer occupying the sofa, but she could still hear them talking in the bedroom. She did not dare enter uninvited, fearing she might walk in on them in a compromising situation. She knew her sister would give her the same courtesy if the roles were reversed. Before Aurelia could knock on the door, Septima opened it with empty buckets in hand and bumped into her.

"Oh, hey, Lia. I'm just grabbing some water so Exie can bathe. She is feeling funky. She smells it, too."

"Tell everyone, why don't you?" Exie groused from inside the room.

Septima giggled and squeezed by Aurelia to go fetch water. Aurelia peeked through the doorway and saw Exie sitting on the stool next to the tub. She looked so much better than she had when they first arrived. Her swollen eye and the bruises that mottled her skin, visible to Aurelia, were gone. Aesthetically, she appeared perfectly healed, but her slow, careful movements were unlike the energetic warrior. Her wounds clearly went far deeper than the flesh wounds that no longer marked her. Whatever Variel was doing, it was helping, but Exie still had a way to go before she was in perfect health once more.

"How are you feeling?"

The warrior smiled, but the dark circles under her eyes spoke to her exhaustion. "Better, but your sister is right. I do need a bath."

"I would have to agree. You reek, my friend." Aurelia pinched her nose, making a disgusted face before bursting into a fit of laughter.

Exie swatted her arm. "Hush, you. Enough about my odor. What's going on with you and that fine winged male you keep sleeping with?"

Aurelia blushed at the phrasing and covered her face with her hands. "I told you two that nothing happened. Well, we've kissed since then, but that's it. What's going on with you and my sister?"

Exie shrugged. "She's been taking care of me. She's a good female."

Aurelia could not argue with that. Septima was the best woman in her very biased opinion.

"I kissed her."

Aurelia choked on her own saliva at the unexpected confession. She coughed uncontrollably, struggling to breathe as she gaped at the blond warrior. "I figured I should tell you, since you and Septima don't keep secrets from each other."

Aurelia knew her sister had a mountain-sized crush on Exie, but she was unsure of the Aegrician female's feelings. If Septima had kissed Exie first, she wouldn't have batted an eye, but the reverse had shocked her. She wanted to question the woman's intentions—like any protective older sister worth her salt—but she knew Septima would return soon. She decided to put the inquisition on the back burner and joked instead.

"You kissed her while smelling like that?"

Exie slapped her arm again, with a bit more force this time, as Septima reentered the room and hung the buckets over the fire.

"I'll ready her bath if you want to help her undress," Septima called over her shoulder.

"I can take off my own clothes." Exie's tone was firm as she pulled her shirt off and tossed it on the floor. The independent warrior was clearly not used to being babied. "Your sister is such a worrier," Exie complained to Aurelia as she stood and pulled off her pants, kicking them to the side. "Help me into the tub and then I'll take care of it from there."

Septima poured the water in and set a towel next to the tub before wrapping her arm around Exie's bare waist and motioning for Aurelia to do the same. Exie was pretty steady on her feet, though still weak. They lowered their friend into the water and handed her a cloth. Septima added another log to the fire and then headed for the door, with Aurelia trailing behind her.

"Call me when you're finished. Do not try to climb out on your own." Septima lectured, giving Exie a firm glare before closing the door behind them.

Aurelia went into the kitchen and filled the teakettle, hanging it over the fire to boil while she prepared their mugs. Septima sat at the table in the chair closest to the bedroom, ears peeled for Exie's summons. Aurelia studied her sister for a moment, searching for signs that she had fallen in love. She didn't know what she was looking for—some change in Septima's eyes, some softness in her voice—but what she saw was contentment wrapped in worry.

"Are you happy?" The question caught the younger Vesta sister by surprise. Her head tilted as she stared at Aurelia as if she was waiting for her question to make sense. Aurelia did not elaborate.

"Happy about what?"

Aurelia shrugged. "Exie said the two of you kissed. I was curious if it made you happy?"

Aurelia watched her sister's deep complexion flush. "I care about Exie, so I guess I am. I haven't had a chance to really process everything we've been through and encountered. Our lives have changed so drastically, and I haven't had the time to make sense of it. What about you? And don't you dare tell me nothing is going on with you and Cristos."

Septima knew her better than she knew herself, and Aurelia could no longer deny there was something between her and Cristos. She just did not know how to define what that was yet.

"He kissed me, but that's it. We are getting to know each other, but it's kind of hard to do when we don't even know where life will take us in a fortnight, much less after the war. If we survive, he will probably go back to his kingdom, but where will we go? I can't answer that question right now."

Septima nodded and considered everything she said. Before she could reply, Exie called out.

"Do you need some help?" Aurelia asked.

Septima's side-long glance was the only response she needed. If Septima and Exie wanted privacy, she had no intention of standing in their way.

Feeling dismissed, Aurelia washed her mug and decided to head to the backyard to see if she could help those who remained outside. She pulled on her cloak as she opened the door. The air was warm compared to days past, but it still had a chill to it.

Cristos and Variel approached the cottage from the tree line as she exited, and Taryn was perched on the roof in her phoenix form. The sun reflected off the crimson feathers, making them look as if they were aflame. Aurelia took a moment to admire her as the warrior tipped her head in greeting before she looked back out into the distance.

Cristos' smile broadened when he caught sight of Aurelia hovering near the home.

"Were you and Variel able to reinforce the wards?" she asked. Variel smiled as she walked past and went inside.

Cristos nodded. "Yes, they are secure." He reached for her cheek, and she leaned into his hand. "Don't worry."

"How much longer until we leave?"

"That will be up to Exie. We will leave once she can shift. Hopefully, that will be sooner rather than later. We need to start building alliances before more people die."

"Do you think the other territories will help us?"

Cristos shrugged. "I don't know what to expect from Diapolis, since they have no vested interest in the war. Warbotach has no interest in them—at least not yet. They can be invaluable if they choose to be. We can only hope that they decide to fight for both Ekotoria's future and the future of the human world. But their king is an isolationist. So, I really don't know what to expect."

"What are you going to do today?"

Cristos pulled Aurelia into a hug as he glanced around the clearing. She tucked her head under his chin and breathed in his sandalwood and spice scent. "I would like to spar a bit. I need some exercise and to blow off some steam. I was going to ask Taryn when I got back."

Aurelia pulled away just enough to meet his eyes. "I'll spar with you. I need practice anyway."

He arched an eyebrow. "As long as you go easy on me."

She snorted out a laugh as she eyed his much larger frame. "I can't make any promises."

Cristos' long sword was already strapped to the center of his back, framed by his glorious black wings. A second sheath hung at his hip, encasing a shorter sword. He pulled out the polished titanium blade and offered it to her hilt-first.

Aurelia took the weapon, weighing it in her hand as she examined it. It was heavier than her sword, but it would have to do since her blade was back at the war encampment. Kano prowled in her mind's eye as she thought of the camp. She knew he was probably wondering where she had gone and why she had not yet returned. She hoped the lanistas were taking good care of him while she was gone. Aurelia's heart ached for her loyal companion, but she forced the thoughts of him away as she turned her attention back to the sword she held.

Aurelia admired the intricate blade as she tried to steady her emotions before Cristos commented on them. The entire length of it was engraved with symbols and glyphs she did not understand. For a brief moment, she wondered if the symbols were simply ornamental—or if the glyphs hummed with some kind of hidden power. She passed her fingers over the engraving, careful not to touch the razor-sharp edge. She didn't know how sharp it was, but she figured Cristos would not carry around a weapon unless it could slice through skin and bone.

Cristos pulled the gleaming long sword from his back. The muscles of his arm flexed, straining against his fighting leathers. Aurelia did her best not to stare, but she could not help it. *Pull it together, Lia,* she scolded herself. *He's going to disarm you twice as fast if you keep gawking at his arms.*

The pair sparred as Taryn watched from the roof. Cristos taught her new maneuvers, focusing on how to best block against an opponent on horseback. However, she hoped not to come face-to-face with one during the war. Hopefully, the people of Diapolis would join them in arms once the battle against Warbotach ensued. Still, it didn't hurt to be prepared, anyway.

Cristos refused to end their sparring match until she managed to disarm him. Aurelia, always one for a challenge, spun and kicked out to throw him off balance. When his focus was on her leg, anticipating another kick, she swung her blade. It collided with the center of his longer sword, and the impact wrenched the hilt from his hand. His blade landed with a thud in the grass, and she let her own weapon fall as she leaned over with her hands on her knees, panting. He chuckled as he bent over to retrieve his sword.

"Well, that was unexpected." Cristos lifted the bottom hem of his tunic and wiped the sweat from his face. Aurelia swallowed hard as she traced his defined abdominals. He dropped the fabric before he spoke again. "Who taught you to fight?"

She took a beat to answer, trying to forget the sight of his bare torso, to no avail. "My brother, Amadeus."

Aurelia snatched up her weapon without warning and took aim at the hard stomach that was burned into her brain. He expected the attack and blocked the strike with ease. The sound of their blades clashing rang throughout the clearing. They remained clinched; their eyes locked as she further explained. "We used to spar almost every day."

"Beautiful, strong, and a skilled fighter. You really are intriguing."

Her heart skipped despite the offended glare she gave him, and she hated that he could probably sense it. She rolled her eyes, trying to look unimpressed, but inside her pulse was a frantic drumbeat. Cristos took advantage of the momentary distraction. He swung his sword at hers, knocking it from her hands with ease. Her mouth fell open, and she narrowed her eyes in an offended glare.

"Hey! I wasn't ready."

He chuckled again and grabbed her blade. He handed it back as he lectured her. "You must always be ready. You never know when an enemy will strike, especially if they are running their mouth. It buys them time to find an opening."

Aurelia rolled her eyes and fell back into her defensive stance. "There are plenty of beautiful women who can fight. I've lived in an entire camp full of them." Aurelia swung her sword high, but Cristos parried.

"Oh, there are, sure. But you are a Vaekrosan human. From what I've heard, women are not taught or even allowed to fight in your homeland. Unless what I've been told isn't true?" His voice lilted questioningly, but he swung low. She jumped out of the way, dodging the strike, and he raised his eyebrows in surprise.

"No, you're right. Where I come from, women do not fight. We are expected to get married and have children. Maintaining a home and raising a family is indoctrinated into us at a young age. Still, my brother believed Septima and I should be able to defend ourselves."

"Sounds like a good man. Is he still in Vaekros?"

Aurelia handed her sword back to Cristos, her face falling as she thought of Amadeus. Her brother was probably beside himself with worry at their disappearance, but he would not have wanted them to be forced into a life they did not want to live. Still, she wished she could at least tell him they were alive and well. She settled on a bench near the tree line in silence. Cristos sheathed the swords before he followed and sat next to her.

"He is in Vaekros with my father." Aurelia avoided thinking about her family on the other side of the portal since they had run away. Once they arrived in Ekotoria, there was too much going on to ponder what she'd left behind, and—when she did have the time—it hurt too much. Now that Amadeus was on her mind, she couldn't bury the pain that missing him caused. The backs of her eyes began to burn as she clenched her jaw in an attempt to fight back the tears that threatened to fall. Cristos reached out and held her hand, no doubt sensing her internal anguish.

"I never did ask... Why did you and your sister come here? How did you even cross the portal?"

Aurelia swallowed around the lump rapidly forming in her throat. She stared at their interlaced fingers that rested on her leg. "Septima and I ran away. Taryn and Exie found us in the forest and took us in. Without their sanctuary... well, I don't want to think what would have happened to us."

"Ran away? What made you leave your home? Your world?" Her entire body tensed at his words, making it harder to breathe. How was she supposed to explain why she abandoned half of her family to a man who had been brutally taken from him?

"My father promised our hands to two men we didn't even know. They seemed nice enough when we were introduced, but Septima...," she hesitated, licking her lips with a bone-dry tongue. "Septima didn't fancy the man she was to marry. She doesn't fancy men at all, but same sex couplings are not allowed in Vaekros. I couldn't let her be miserable for the rest of her life just because my father had laid out our futures for us. I'm the eldest sister. It's my job to protect her, and she is more important to me than anything in the human world."

Cristos nodded and squeezed her fingers gently. "You are so brave. Both of you. I'm sure Septima would have done the same thing for you."

The corner of Aurelia's mouth ticked up as she lost the battle, and the first tear fell. "She absolutely would have. Having to choose between Septima and my father, I chose her. I will always choose her. I miss my brother so much it hurts, but I can handle never seeing him again to save my sister. He is a man, and he has rights in Vaekros. He will be okay."

Cristos let go of her hand and wrapped his arm around her waist, pulling her in against his side. His embrace was so tight, Aurelia felt like he was the only thing holding her together at that point. "You made the right choice. After the war, you can both build happy lives in Ekotoria. I won't let anything happen to you."

His promise burned in her chest like an ember, small but steady. It was becoming increasingly difficult to picture a happy future unless he was part of it.

"And your sister and Exie... they seem pretty close."

Aurelia nodded. "I just found out this morning that they kissed. I'm happy for her."

"Sounds like they are getting closer, just like me and you." Aurelia closed her eyes as he kissed her temple. The ember in her chest turned into a small fire, begging to be stoked into a blazing inferno.

"My father would be furious." Aurelia joked, but she knew the statement was true. Proteus would be furious, but luckily, he was too far away for her to be on the receiving end of his wrath.

"I do not doubt that. But you would have stayed in Vaekros if you were concerned about his opinion, so don't fret over it." He stood from the bench, their hands still clasped together as he gave a gentle tug. "I'm starving. Are you ready to eat?"

CHAPTER TWENTY-SEVEN

SPECTRE FOREST

AURELIA

Variel was already in the kitchen making sandwiches when Cristos and Aurelia entered the cottage. She gestured for them to sit at the table and placed a plate of food and a mug of tea in front of each of them. Septima and Exie were eating on the sofa. Septima flashed a wry smile at her sister, raising her eyebrows suggestively as she looked from Aurelia to Cristos. Aurelia didn't want to dwell on what Septima might be thinking, especially as she observed the post-sparring sweat still covering them.

The wolf shifter sat across from them with her own food and drink, setting her gaze on Aurelia.

"You look so much like your mother did as a child," Variel said.

Aurelia set her mug down with a thud, her fingers clenching tightly around the handle, barely registering the hot tea sloshing over the rim. The words hollowed her out. Her mouth went dry as she stared at the elderly woman. How could Variel know what her mother looked like?

"My mother?" Aurelia's voice came out sounding distant and brittle. She felt absurd for even considering Variel's words. There was no way the shifter had known her mother. She must be mistaken. "My mother is from the human realm. You couldn't have known her."

Variel's lip curved into a knowing smile. "Your mother lived in the human realm when you were born, yes. But, my child, your mother was not human."

The look on Cristos' face mirrored Aurelia's disbelief. Her heart pounded loudly in her ears, so fiercely that she could hardly hear. Septima walked up behind her and joined them at the table.

"What do you mean our mother wasn't human?" Septima asked, interrupting Aurelia before she could find her voice.

Variel arched an eyebrow as she looked from one sister to the other. "Your mother, Messalina, was from Aegricia. She left this realm when the disgraced queen, Joneira, took the throne. Did she not tell you?"

Time seemed to slow as Aurelia froze in place, her muscles feeling weak and numb as if they had atrophied over years instead of mere seconds. She stared blankly into the distance, her breath shallow, her pulse a wild hammer in her throat. For a fleeting moment, she thought she could smell lavender and parchment—the faint memory of her mother brushing her hair at bedtime and humming a lullaby. That cherished memory now felt stolen, altered, and foreign.

She could sense Cristos watching her, likely awaiting a reaction beyond her shock, but she couldn't summon one.

Septima's expression turned to disbelief as she continued her conversation with the oracle. "We never heard of Ekotoria before meeting Exie and Taryn. This makes little sense. She died when we were young, but she always appeared to be human... not that we knew what to look for to know she wasn't."

Variel nodded, her expression serious. "The queen before Otera killed anyone who challenged her for the throne. Your mother was selected by the crown as the next queen of Aegricia, but Joneira seized the throne anyway. The false queen clung to power until the rightful family, the Lumino family, rallied allies across the continent and forced Joneira out. The current queen, Otera, is your aunt—your mother's sister."

Bile rose in Aurelia's throat, coating her mouth with a bitter taste as she swallowed. "Could my mother shift?" She wasn't certain if she believed Variel or if she even wanted to, but the oracle had no reason to lie.

Variel shook her head and took a sip of her tea. "Your mother did not come from a warrior bloodline, so she could not shift into a phoenix. However, she would have gained that ability the moment the crown was placed on her head."

Aurelia rubbed the base of her neck. "I thought the Aegrician people were nearly immortal. Our mother died from the plague. How could that happen if she were an Aegrician? Wouldn't she have survived?"

Variel's eyebrows furrowed at Aurelia's question. For a moment, Aurelia thought the shifter realized she had the wrong person, but nothing could have prepared her for what came next. "Messalina Lumino did not die from a human disease. She was murdered."

Aurelia didn't blink as a painful sensation seized her chest. Her ears rang; the crackling fire and even her own breathing faded beneath the roar of her pulse. Surely, the oracle had misspoken.

"Who would kill her? Why would anyone kill her? She was just a Vaekrosan stay-at-home parent. Why would my father tell us otherwise?"

Cristos wrapped his arm around Aurelia's shoulders, pulling her close as her entire frame trembled at the revelation.

"Before Joneira was overthrown, she planted rebels within the Aegrician military to kill your mother. With the favor and protection of the Aegrician crown, they could cross between realms to reach her." Variel hesitated, scratching her chin. "I'd imagine your father told you differently because he thought you were too young to learn the truth."

Aurelia's thoughts shattered: He lied. He lied about everything.

"What happened to her?" Aurelia pursed her lips, forcing the words out through a throat that felt strangled. The backs of her eyes burned. Had her father truly tried to protect them from the truth? Everything she knew about Proteus seemed to contradict that theory. Did he truly care for his daughters? No, she had to stop thinking like that before she regretted her choice to leave.

"Who?" asked Variel, scooting closer in her chair.

"The other queen. Joneira. What happened to her?"

Several moments passed in silence. Aurelia bit her bottom lip in a vain attempt to lessen her anxiety. Variel peered deeply into Aurelia's eyes as she responded, making Aurelia feel as if the woman could see her very soul. "No one knows. Most say she fled, but to where? There is no telling. I cannot even confirm if she is still alive, but the Elemental of Spectre Forest has foretold her return."

Cristos' eyebrows furrowed in a worried frown as he leaned forward. "Are you talking about a prophecy?"

Turning to him, Variel nodded. Her voice softened, carrying the weight of ritual. "Raging fires will fade to gentle embers, and a new day will bring a new dawn. When the throneless queen falls, the phoenix will be reborn from the ashes and rise again, bringing unity and peace once more."

The cottage seemed to still as she spoke. Even the fire in the hearth dimmed as if it were listening. Aurelia's stomach roiled; the words struck her like iron. Reborn from the ashes... Her mind twisted back to her earlier dreams, flames chasing her through the dark, fire threatening to consume her.

"Could the throneless queen not be Otera?" she asked.

The shifter considered this but shook her head. "I don't think so. The throne will always be Otera's, at least until she dies. She will never be throneless."

"So, if our mother was not human..." Septima interrupted, reaching out to take Aurelia's hand. "Does that mean Aurelia isn't either? I mean, is Aurelia immortal?"

"Not necessarily," responded Cristos, looking to Variel for confirmation. The shifter nodded. He continued, "If a human mates with a fae, there is a chance their offspring will inherit part of their fae parent's lifespan, but it isn't guaranteed. If Aurelia stops aging within the next few years, we will know. Unless Aurelia begins to exhibit powers before then." He traced the rounded tip of Aurelia's ear gently. "Your ears are human-like, but that could change if you develop any powers."

Aurelia reached up to touch her ear as she looked around the room, taking in the slightly pointed tips of everyone else's ears except her own and her sister's. Variel stood from the table.

"I know this is a lot to take in, Aurelia, and I'm here if you want to talk more. I'm going to bring food to Taryn and work in the garden. There are some beans I need to harvest today. I'll be nearby if you need me." With a single nod, the wolf shifter grabbed an extra sandwich and a cup of tea from the counter and left the cottage.

Cristos rubbed his palm along Aurelia's arm, pulling her momentarily out of the downward spiral of her thoughts. She glanced at him, feeling completely numb inside.

"I'm going to speak to Exie."

She heard his words but couldn't quite grasp their meaning in her frazzled state. With parted lips and wide eyes, Aurelia watched him approach the warrior on the sofa. She was unsure what to do with the bombshells Variel had dropped on her. Septima held her hand as they sat together in silence. The weight of the quiet pressed down on her like a heavy burden, making her aware of every tiny sound—the scrape of Cristos' boots, the ticking of the firewood as it cracked. Time lost its meaning. Even when Exie and Cristos went out the back door together, her silence remained unbroken.

"Do you want to get some air?" Septima asked after what felt like an eternity or perhaps just five minutes. She squeezed Aurelia's hand and gently pulled her. "Come on. Let's go outside."

Aurelia glanced vacantly at the door and then back at her sister before reluctantly rising to let Septima lead her out. She was so young when their mother died that there was much she couldn't remember. She couldn't bring herself to doubt Variel's story, no matter how much she wished to. It was too overwhelming to comprehend all at once. It would take time—time she wasn't sure she had—to dissect and absorb everything she'd just learned.

They found Cristos beside the cottage, standing next to a rainbow-colored phoenix that stretched its wings.

"I guess we will be leaving soon," Aurelia sighed as they approached the unlikely pair. Exie had recovered enough to shift, which was exciting. She pushed aside the earlier revelations and focused on the thought of being reunited with Kano. While she wasn't looking forward to the inevitable war that would follow their return, at least she'd see her feline friend again soon.

Cristos grabbed her hand and pulled her close, her head resting beneath his chin. She watched the blond plumage atop Exie's head shine in the light of the setting sun as she dipped her head to Septima. "I'm going to take over watch soon, if you want to join me."

Cristos' smile was innocent, but there was a mischievous glint in his eye when he glanced down at Aurelia again. She knew exactly why he wanted her to join him on the roof, and after the day she'd had, she looked forward to the distraction. His kisses might not cure her melancholy, but she was more than willing to try.

"Possibly." Her voice came out sultrier than she intended. His eyebrows shot up at her tone, and he tightened his muscular arms around her. Aurelia momentarily lost herself in the warmth of Cristos' embrace, forgetting that her life had just irreparably changed. She even failed to remember that her sister and Exie were only a few feet away.

Returning her focus to Cristos, she noticed his ocean eyes deepening to an impossible blue before he leaned in and whispered in her ear, "What must I do to convince you?"

Heat rose in Aurelia's cheeks as his breath brushed against her neck. His usually smooth voice had an alluring growl that made her shiver.

"I'll join you if you promise to keep me warm."

Cristos chuckled and gave her a slow kiss. "I promise to make you as hot as you'd like."

Each whispered word made his lips brush against hers, and the flush in her cheeks ignited into a fire at his words, but it was her eyes where the heat truly shone. She held his gaze, allowing him to see her desire. Although her inexperience made her uneasy, it felt pointless to hide her feelings when he could sense her emotions.

"Do the two of you need some privacy?"

Aurelia jumped at Septima's voice, her sister effectively shattering the moment. She buried her face in Cristos' chest, ducking her head to hide behind her curtain of crimson locks. Peeking at Septima through the veil of hair, she felt absolutely mortified. Her mind hadn't yet found balance after Variel's story, and that was the only reason she had forgotten about their audience. It was definitely not because Cristos had captivated her attention—at least, that was what she told herself.

Aurelia steeled her nerves, preparing for the merciless teasing she knew her sister would unleash. Before she could pull away from Cristos, his strong hold remained unyielding.

"Yes."

She frowned up at him for a moment, confused by what he was affirming. Then it dawned on her. Her face flushed harder than ever before. Was he really asking Septima to grant them privacy? There was no way her sister would ever let her live that down.

Septima threw her head back and laughed before mentioning something about a test flight. Feeling embarrassed, Aurelia couldn't focus on the conversation. Her face was still buried in Cristos' chest as she caught a glimpse of her sister and Exie flying off in her peripheral vision.

Chapter Twenty-Eight

Aegricia

Otera

Otera's agitated footsteps echoed as she paced in her cell. She couldn't get Uldon's words out of her mind. The fact that his men had been able to capture her warriors concerned her. She was enthused over their escape, but they should have never been caught in the first place. Not being in the loop was slowly driving her mad. What were her people doing that led to their imprisonment? And how had they escaped?

 The scabbed cut below her eye cracked open as she squinted in thought and sent blood dripping down her face. Uldon took his fury out on her after her commander had slipped through his clutches. It had only been a few days since, but she began to fear the deranged king. He was becoming more unhinged in his desperation, and it showed. If he discovered the crown in his possession was a fake... The very thought turned her blood to ice. He would kill her. He would kill her and all of her people.

When her warriors fled Aegricia, swapping the crown was an easy decision to make. She did not think he would find a way to bend it to his will, but it was not worth the risk. For now, her crown, the most powerful one in Ekotoria, was hidden away and safe. But she could not ensure it would remain that way from her place in the dungeon. It was only a matter of time before he discovered the truth. She just hoped to have it back on her head when that time came.

She changed her train of thought, afraid that even thinking of her deception would bring it to light. She brought the age-lined face of Bremusa to the forefront of her mind's eye. The elderly woman still lived and was tasked with cleaning Otera's wounds after Uldon beat her. They were unable to speak much. The guard hovered close, but her friend was still alive and that was enough to ease at least part of her worries. Seeing Bremusa was the glimmer of hope needed after her last encounter with the king.

The woman was sent to her cell as a common servant. She'd managed to tell the imprisoned queen that while Uldon knew her warriors had returned, he did not know Bremusa's true identity. While Uldon's men scoured the forests for the Elemental of Spectre Forest to help him take over the power of the crown, she was right under his nose, cleaning wounds and delivering meals, as a hunchbacked elderly female. When Bremusa finally unleashed her power, she would not be using it to help Warbotach, but to destroy them.

Chapter Twenty-Nine

Spectre Forest

Aurelia

By the time Aurelia finished eating, bundled up, and joined Cristos on the roof of the cottage, Septima and Exie had already completed their low-hanging flight and retired inside to bathe. Exie's ability to shift and carry Septima meant they would return to the Aegrician camp come morning—if they could find it.

Aurelia glanced at the bow lying on the roof beside her. She hoped she wouldn't have to use it on their journey, but she knew a time would come when she would need to wield the weapon without hesitation. She realized she needed more practice. Training would be grueling but necessary when they returned to the safety and routine of the war camp. Although the likelihood of fighting in a war was slim, she was determined to improve as much as she could.

Nevertheless, as she stared at the bow, unease lingered. She recalled the deer she had killed, the pig she had felled, and the blood that stained her hands. She remembered how her stomach had clenched with guilt afterward. She wondered if she would be strong enough when the ones charging at her weren't animals but soldiers. The forest groaned faintly in the wind, and she couldn't shake the feeling that the trees were listening.

"What are you thinking about?" Cristos stretched his wing around her back, wrapping her in a firm embrace. The chilly night air completely eclipsed the earlier warmth. Tiny bumps dotted Aurelia's skin, and she fought back shivers as she leaned into his warmth. "You seem worried. Is it because of what Variel shared today?"

Admittedly, she had avoided thinking about the onslaught of familial information since she and Septima had stepped outside hours earlier. Instead, she focused on returning to the Aegrician camp and Kano, as well as her watch with Cristos on the roof, to distract herself. She shrugged.

"I'm just thinking about the war and how unprepared I am to fight in it. I wish I had more time to train. I don't have the mental capacity right now to delve into thoughts about my mother. Realizing that I never truly knew her is... hard."

Cristos frowned and gently squeezed her shoulder. "I will teach you all that I can until our time runs out. But don't worry, Aurelia. I won't let anything happen to you."

She nodded, relieved he had dropped the topic of her heritage, but his words did not comfort her. A part of her warmed at his vow, but another part recoiled because no promise could stop the chaos of war. Exie had once said that no one could ever be fully prepared for war, and that statement resonated with her more now than before.

Pulling away just enough to look into her eyes, Cristos took her cheek in his hand and kissed her. The kiss was brief, but the sensation of his lips lingered, creating a ripple of warmth throughout her body. When he pulled away again, his eyes were soft. "I promise you, Aurelia. I won't let any harm come to you. Even if I have to set you on a perch until the war is over."

The thought of being perched in a tree to wait out the war was oddly funny. She chuckled and leaned against him for warmth. "I know what Variel told us will hit me eventually."

"That's completely understandable. I still haven't accepted that I'm in the presence of a princess. How should I address you? Your Highness, perhaps?"

She swatted at him playfully, but he only held her tighter as he chuckled softly. "Okay, I'll stick with calling you princess."

"Please don't," she drawled. "Aurelia is fine. I'm not a princess. I don't know what I am, but I'm not that."

"Aurelia, it is. I'm quite fond of that name, anyway."

They spent the next few hours cuddled together on the roof of the cottage, watching a few sprites dance along the treeline. Their bodies fluttered about, their glow shining through the darkness like a promise of brighter days to come. Every now and then, Aurelia thought she heard something deeper in the forest—twigs snapping, a distant growl—but each time, silence enveloped it again like a suffocating blanket. With their bodies pressed close, she tried to convince herself it was only her nerves.

Taryn took over the watch, and the couple returned to the house. After quickly washing up, they crawled into bed and slept in each other's arms once more. Nothing happened aside from a few innocent kisses. Still, Aurelia did not want to imagine what her sister would say when they exited the bedroom together come morning. They were returning to the Aegrician war camp, and that took precedence over entertaining her sister's curiosities—a fact she would be eternally grateful for.

The next morning, everyone ate breakfast and gathered their belongings. They met on the front lawn, where the five took turns saying their goodbyes to Variel. Taryn and Exie stepped away and shifted into their phoenix forms. The temporary flames that engulfed them shone so brightly that Aurelia had to squint. Septima climbed onto Exie's back, and Taryn lowered her head for Aurelia to mount her. Cristos reached for her as she approached the phoenix.

"I was hoping you would fly with me," he said, hesitating as a flush colored his tan cheeks. "If you want to, of course."

Aurelia grinned. "I figured you wouldn't want to carry me. It's a long flight. Your arms might get tired."

The corner of his mouth quirked up, and he pulled her into a kiss. Time seemed to stand still until he pulled away. "I can handle it. I would consider myself lucky to have my arms around you, uninterrupted, for the entire flight. The longer, the better."

Warmth spread in Aurelia's chest, a feeling that had become common since Cristos joined their group. Taryn launched into the sky before Aurelia had a chance to respond, flapping her large crimson wings until she reached the treetops. She perched there, waiting for the others to join her.

Cristos scooped Aurelia up in his arms and kicked off the ground, followed by Exie. They rose in tandem through the canopy of trees and into the open sky as the first rays of sunlight broke beyond the horizon.

The air was crisp, and Aurelia felt grateful for Cristos' warm body against her. The scent of sandalwood and spice was intoxicating, overwhelming her senses. She could feel his smile pressed against her forehead as each beat of his leathery wings carried them farther from the safety of Variel's cottage. The wind tore at her cloak, mixing the saltiness of the sea air with the fading scent of the forest. Below them, the world shrank into ribbons of blue water and green canopy.

"Are you warm enough?" Cristos asked, tucking her cloak snugly around her as they flew, trailing behind the phoenixes. Taryn led the group, with Exie and Septima close behind. Aurelia watched her sister lean her head back, holding Exie's reins and clearly enjoying the breeze on her face.

"I'm warm enough. You're like an oven," she replied, and he chuckled.

"I'll take that as a compliment."

"Until it gets hot outside, it is a compliment."

As they flew over the Elder Sea, the thick trees gave way to sapphire water. Aurelia wondered how they would locate the heavily warded camp, but Taryn seemed confident in her path, likely capable of tracking the camp that remained invisible to most. When they landed back in the forest, Aurelia sensed they were close. She could feel it.

Taryn shifted back into her human form and stretched her limbs. She sipped water from her canteen before speaking. "The camp is only a few miles inland. We should eat and use the restroom quickly. I don't want to be exposed for long; there could be Warbotach scouts around."

Aurelia followed Septima into the tree line, doing as instructed. When they returned, bread and cheese, along with berries from Variel's garden, were already being passed around. The group quickly inhaled the food while watching their surroundings cautiously. After they finished eating, they started hiking deeper into Spectre Forest.

The forest's wildlife created an orchestra of sounds as they moved through the area. The incessant noise was unnerving, and Aurelia imagined what kind of creatures might have been stalking them through the dense brush. The thought frightened her, but she was even more afraid of what sounds could be concealed by the cacophony. What if Warbotach soldiers were nearby? She moved closer to Cristos, clasping his hand in an attempt to calm her nerves. He sensed her anxiety and pulled her closer, wrapping a muscular arm around her shoulders.

As they ventured deeper into the forest, the sounds of life gradually faded away, leaving an eerie silence that terrified Aurelia even more than the noise had. The air felt heavy, as if the trees were holding their breath. It became so silent that the rustling of leaves sliced through the stillness like an arrow aimed directly at them. The hair on the back of Aurelia's neck stood on end, and she knew they were in trouble.

Cristos halted and scanned the forest as both Aegrician warriors unsheathed their swords. Cristos drew his own weapon, shifting his stance to protect Aurelia from an incoming threat. Exie thrust a dagger into Septima's hand, and Aurelia pulled her own blade from its sheath on her thigh.

She broke into a cold sweat as they huddled together, eyes darting around the trees for signs of movement. Each member of the group held their weapons at the ready, waiting for danger to reveal itself. Aurelia held her breath and listened intently.

A wet, guttural snarl pierced the uneasy calm and rumbled through Aurelia's bones. The forest darkened, as if even the sun feared the creature stalking them. Her hand trembled as she tightened her grip on the dagger. A foul stench, reminiscent of sulfur and rot, filled her nostrils—she knew the creature was close even before she saw it.

Red eyes peered through the bushes. The creature tracked their every movement down to the terrified tremors that wracked her body. The creature's fur-covered body was a black void that swallowed up the surrounding forest. Its vicious, fire-filled stare was the only source of light.

"What is that?" Septima's voice shook. Aurelia wished she could reach out for her, but was too afraid to look away.

"Hellhound." Cristos' response sent a wave of dread crashing over her. Her knuckles went white as she gripped her weapon even harder.

The black creature was like an enormous, macabre version of a dog from the human realm. Its elongated canines gleamed as it snarled, the promise of a meal making it salivate profusely. The fluidity of its movements as it slowly prowled from the brush was startling. No creature that large should be able to move as silently and easily as it did.

The beast did not hesitate as it stalked closer, unfazed by the size of their party. Her companions huddled close with their backs pressed together, creating an unbreakable center. They did not move as they waited for the hellhound to attack, but it did not strike. A second snarl filled the air and made Aurelia jump. Another hellhound crept out of the brush on the side opposite the original creature, hovering a few feet from them.

"They're herding us," Exie said. "There are probably more hiding."

Cristos pulled his wings tighter to his back as he cursed.

The hellhounds sprang forward in unison, snarling and barking as they snapped their massive jaws at them. Cristos swung his sword at the first dog's neck. The beast was too quick. It jumped back, Cristos' blade barely making its fur flutter. The second hound charged at Exie and Septima. They stood back-to-back with Cristos and Aurelia, and she dared a glance back at them. She could not tell if the creatures were trying to separate their group or force them closer to their companion. Exie struck out with such speed her weapon blurred. The animal crumpled to the ground; its maw opened in a yelp that never had the chance to escape.

Three more hellhounds darted from the brush and surrounded the group as they scrambled to regain their formation. Taryn pulled out a bow and let loose an arrow, hitting one of the creatures in the eye. It dropped where it stood, but its demise did nothing to slow the remaining hounds. They passed the carcass, one pausing to bite a chunk from its fallen friend. Aurelia could not look away from the blood that dripped from the cannibalistic beast as it neared. Cristos shoved his bow and quiver into her hands, forcing her to focus on fighting once more. He raised his sword and charged forward. He swung his blade, severing the head of the nearest hellhound from its shoulders.

The body hit the ground with a sickening thud, its head rolling a few feet away. Exie followed Cristos' lead and slashed at the beast in front of her. Her blade arced gracefully as she attacked, but she was too slow. The hellhound dodged her blow and wrapped its jaws around her arm. Exie screamed as a loud crunch echoed around them.

Aurelia's stomach roiled as she notched an arrow and waited for a clear shot. She watched in horror as Septima sprang forward. She hefted her arms above her head and brought her dagger down forcefully, burying it deep into the skull of the creature gnawing on Exie. The hellhound's jaw remained latched on the warrior's arm. Aurelia stared transfixed as she watched Septima grab the beast's maw and wrench it open to free her lover.

They fell back into formation as they eyed the final hellhound. Aurelia was sure it was going to attack, but it did not. The lone beast turned tail and ran so fast that in a matter of seconds, she could no longer see it. And that was worse than its presence, because now it could be fetching more.

Chapter Thirty

Spectre Forest

Aurelia

It took several painstaking hours of hiking through Spectre Forest before a clearing opened before them, and Aurelia recognized their location. Her legs ached, and her nerves still hummed with the memory of snarls in the dark. A slow smile spread across her lips, though unease lingered. They had made it back to the camp, but would the wards truly keep them safe this time?

She and Cristos took Taryn's hand while Exie held onto Septima, and the five of them entered through the ward that concealed the Aegrician war camp. The air rippled around them like a welcoming embrace as the barrier let them in.

The moment they stepped foot on protected ground, Exie's knees buckled beneath her, and she hit the ground hard. The sound jarred Aurelia—a cruel reminder that survival came at a cost. Septima's cry tore through the air, sharper than any blade, as she kneeled beside the warrior and cradled her in her arms.

"I'll fetch the healer," said Taryn before she ran deeper into the camp.

Cristos and Aurelia watched over Septima and Exie as they waited for help to arrive. Moments later, a rush of Aegrician warriors charged toward them, with Blaedia, Taryn, Kason, and Holera among them. The healer, a woman Aurelia did not recognize, took charge of the situation. She pointed at the medical tent, her leather bag clutched firmly in her hand, and instructed Kason to carry Exie there. He obliged, lifting her gingerly before setting off at a brisk pace. Holera and Septima followed, the latter barking her own commands to ensure the man did not jostle the wounded phoenix during the transport.

Cristos and Aurelia remained with the others who had joined them, unsure of what to do next. Blaedia approached them, looking fiercer than Aurelia had ever seen her.

"Get cleaned up," Blaedia said, eyeing Cristos warily. Then she turned to Aurelia. "Bring him to my tent afterward. We need to talk, and I'll have food waiting."

The general walked away, her commander trailing behind her.

"Please tell me there are hot showers here," Cristos grimaced as he looked down at himself. Aurelia was covered in grime, too, but Cristos had traded blows with the hellhounds. Dirt, blood, and an oddly gooey substance she refused to identify coated his clothing.

She giggled at his tone. "You are in luck. Come. I could use one as well."

Aurelia led them to her tent to grab a change of clothes and then showed Cristos to the showers. They cleaned up quickly before making their way to Kano's enclosure. She knew Blaedia should be a priority, but she could not bear to wait any longer. She had not been separated from her feline friend for more than a few hours since her father brought him home. The need to be reunited with him was unbearable.

Tears stung the backs of her eyes as she neared the fence and caught sight of the great cat lounging near the trunk of a tree. His head perked up when he saw her approach. He sprinted to the fence and jumped onto his hind legs in an enthusiastic greeting.

"I'll go in first," she said. "He doesn't know you, and I don't want to take any chances."

Cristos grabbed her hand and pulled her back, catching her by surprise. "You're going to go in with the beast? You could get hurt."

Aurelia snickered, realizing she had never mentioned Kano to him. "Kano is my pet. He would never hurt me. I've had him since he was a cub."

His eyes were still unsure, but he nodded and released his hold. He stood back while she used her medallion to enter the enclosure and closed the gate behind her.

Kano rubbed against her legs so hard that Aurelia lost her balance and fell to her knees. Grabbing the tiger by the sides of his face, Aurelia kissed him on the top of his head, and Kano immediately rolled onto his back, demanding belly rubs. Aurelia obliged, tears wetting her cheeks. She laughed as Kano batted at her arm when she stopped, acting like an average house cat. After days of snarls and blood, seeing Kano's golden eyes alight with joy nearly undid her. He was safety, memory, home—all the things the hellhounds had threatened to take from her. She wished to spend all night with him, but the general was waiting for them, and so was her bed. Aurelia stood and kissed her friend's furry head, reassuring him that she would return in the morning.

She exited the enclosure, smirking at the nervous expression on Cristos' face as she led the way to Blaedia's tent. She found his unease amusing. The man had no hesitation when fighting hellhounds, but her friendly tiger unnerved him. She refrained from teasing him as they made their way to the general's quarters.

Aurelia could smell the rich stew awaiting them as the guard opened the canvas flap and allowed them inside. Blaedia sat at the table, sipping from a mug when they entered. She stood up as soon as she saw them and waved them over.

Taryn slipped inside just as they each took a seat across from the general. Her long black hair dripped water onto her fresh tunic as she hurried to join them. "I just checked on Exie," Taryn said. "She's stable and sleeping. Septima entered the shower tent just as I left. She asked me to tell you that she will stay with Exie in the medical tent tonight."

Aurelia nodded in acknowledgment.

The pot of stew steamed in the middle of the table, its rich herbal scent mouthwatering. Aurelia's stomach growled so loudly that she flushed with embarrassment. They waited for Blaedia to fix her bowl before serving themselves, and thankfully, the general did not keep them waiting long.

"So," Blaedia said as she took her first bite of stew, "tell me about the state of your kingdom."

Cristos set his spoon down and took a sip of his tea before responding. "What do you want to know?"

"Is your king dead?"

Although Aurelia noticed a shadow of emotion cross Cristos's face, he simply nodded. "Yes. War-botach installed one of their generals to control the kingdom, but my people are ready. They are waiting to fight back."

"And your prince—is he dead?"

Cristos hesitated for a moment before shaking his head. "No."

Blaedia resumed eating while Cristos watched her, undoubtedly waiting for her next question. She turned to Taryn. "Meet with Kason and assemble an envoy to travel to Diapolis. Their assistance is imperative if we are going to take back our kingdoms." The commander bowed her head and rose from the table, leaving the tent without another word.

Blaedia shifted her attention back to Cristos. "Get some rest. We have set up a tent for you. We will meet again tomorrow to plan your trip to Diapolis. I'm sure you understand how crucial their warriors and dragons are if we are to defeat Uldon and his band of barbarians."

"Dragons?" Aurelia blurted out before she could stop herself. The word hung between them like thunder. She had encountered all manner of magical creatures since running away from her cliffside home, but the idea of dragons was something she could scarcely comprehend. Blaedia nodded in affirmation.

Pushing away his plate, Cristos turned his attention to Aurelia, smiling briefly before returning his focus to the general. "Thank you. I can't express how much it means to me, and to my people, that Aegricia will fight alongside us."

Blaedia gave him one last nod before he and Aurelia exited the tent.

Aurelia shivered in the chilly air, and Cristos pulled her in close. "I suppose I need to find out where my tent is, but I can walk you back to yours first." The thought of being alone weighed heavily on Aurelia's chest. The vicious snarls of the hellhounds haunted her, and she didn't want to be by herself. She nuzzled into his chest as he held her close.

"Cristos..." Her voice was low, but he heard her. He pulled away just enough to look into her eyes.

"What's wrong?"

She swallowed hard. "Do you think you could stay in my tent? There are two beds."

He smiled. "I'd rather sleep with you, but I'm happy to stay in your tent either way. I don't want to be by myself either." One of his shoulders lifted in a shrug.

Aurelia's heart pounded hard enough to make her lightheaded as they arrived back at her tent. She had shared a bed with him before, but there was always someone else in the same cottage. The tent didn't have solid walls or locks like the room at Variel's, but she knew no one would enter her tent and disturb them. Not that there would be anything to disturb, or at least that was what she told herself.

Grabbing a nightdress, Aurelia changed behind the divider while Cristos changed into his nightclothes on the other side. After she finished, she joined him and froze. Cristos had removed his tunic and changed into looser trousers that hung dangerously low on his hips. She tried not to stare, but her eyes had other plans. As he looked at her, she swallowed hard. Forcing herself to blink, she busied herself with the oven, setting new logs inside and lighting the fire with a candle that illuminated the tent.

She didn't rise from the oven until she heard water splash in the basin. Cristos was cleaning his teeth, seemingly unaware of how nervous she was. Considering he could smell her emotions, she figured he was just being courteous, which she appreciated. Aurelia waited until he finished at the basin to close the distance between them. The corners of his mouth lifted as he turned to see her behind him. He moved aside so she could clean her teeth as well.

"What bed should I sleep in?" The question caught Aurelia by surprise. She hadn't yet decided whether he would sleep in her bed. Honestly, she wanted him to be beside her. The more time they spent together, the more she wanted everything he was willing to give her. Yet the practical side of her worried about their future, or lack thereof. With the looming war, there was no way to know what lay ahead.

"That one." She pointed toward her bed without thinking. Cristos climbed into the bed, unaware it was hers. She could always sleep in Septima's bed, and he would not know the difference. That was how she justified her choice as she repeated her options in her mind. Aurelia swallowed hard as she settled on her decision and climbed into the bed where Cristos lay. His grin was wicked, and she knew she was in trouble.

Her heart fluttered as she slid under the covers. She could feel his body heat radiating, warming her insides at the sensation.

"I thought you wanted me to sleep in your sister's bed." Cristos rolled onto his side, his wings tucked tight, and rested his head on his fist as he stared down at her. Aurelia shrugged, trying to appear casual.

"I changed my mind. It's cold, so I figured your body heat would keep me warm. You are like an oven, after all."

Cristos grinned at her excuses, but played along as he pulled her against his chest and wrapped an arm around her waist. "How's this?"

Aurelia's cheeks grew so hot she thought she was going to burst into flames. She tried to calm herself, but his gaze seemed to see everything she was trying to hide. "This is good. I mean... I'm warm. Thank you."

He leaned in so close his breath skittered across her face. She bit her lip, but her entire body felt too sensitive. One minute they were looking at each other, and the next minute his lips were on hers, sending the fire in her cheeks exploding throughout her body. Cristos was everywhere at once. One hand was tangled in her hair, while the other gripped her waist. She opened her mouth for him, and his tongue delved inside, sliding against hers in luxurious sweeps. Her hands roved over his body, sliding up his arms and into his thick hair. Cristos dragged his mouth from hers and trailed his tongue up the side of her neck, eliciting a breathy whine from her. When he pulled away from her, they were both panting.

"Can I touch you?" His voice was full of desire as he gazed down at her. She nodded, digging her fingers into the muscle of his arm. "Is that a yes?"

Aurelia's breath caught in her throat. She licked her lips. "Yes."

Cristos' lips claimed hers again before returning to her neck. Her fingers threaded into his hair, tugging as he trailed his lips lower. He kissed every part of her neck as the hand in her hair slid down to cup her breast. She arched into his touch as she gasped.

Aurelia writhed beneath him, her body begging to be touched. The spreading heat that engulfed her pooled at the most intimate part of her. Cristos untied her tunic and pulled it over her head before he lowered his mouth to her breast, taking the taut peak into his mouth and sucking gently. She squeezed her thighs together, trying to soothe the ache that had developed there.

It was not her first time with a male, but she knew nothing she had experienced before could compare to him. Her stable boy had kissed her with clumsy eagerness. Cristos kissed her like he was carving her into memory. Pleasure filled her, coursing through her like lightning, with every caress of his tongue on her breast. No human man could do that.

His hands gripped her thighs, spreading them open as he settled between them. He rolled his hips, and the feel of his excitement against her core made her moan as she raked a hand down his back. He bit down on her nipple gently, and the lightning surged stronger inside her. Aurelia opened her mouth to beg him for more, to beg him for everything, when a flash of light illuminated the tent. A throat clearing yanked Aurelia out of her lust-filled haze as Cristos rolled off her and yanked the blanket to her chin.

"Don't mind me," Septima murmured. She stared at the ground, her cheeks flush with embarrassment, as she shuffled over to the foot of her bed. Aurelia did not—could not—speak.

Her sister pawed through her wooden chest, grabbed something, and scurried from the tent without looking at them. Aurelia's heart thumped erratically as the tent flap closed, and they were left in the candlelit darkness once more.

Cristos' laughter shocked her senses and pulled her back into the present.

"Why are you laughing?" she demanded. The deep rumble of his laughter continued as she pulled the blanket over her face and let out a mortified groan. Cristos' laugh was infectious. Aurelia removed the blanket from her head and met his gaze before joining in.

CHAPTER THIRTY-ONE

SPECTRE FOREST

AURELIA

Septima's interruption extinguished the passionate heat that enveloped the couple. After the extensive giggles subsided, Aurelia rested her head on Cristos' chest and fell asleep. After her fitful bouts of unconsciousness in the Norithae dungeon and in Variel's crowded cottage, deep slumber was a friend she missed dearly and welcomed with open arms.

Aurelia and Cristos slept through breakfast. Exhaustion muffled the bell that signaled mealtime, and no one came to wake them.

When Aurelia finally began to stir, she felt disoriented. She couldn't remember where she was, but the warmth of Cristos' body eased her panic before it had a chance to escalate. Waking beside him was a comfort she found she could get used to. She rolled over and looked into his ocean-blue eyes, which were alert and full of the clarity her sleep-addled mind wasn't yet capable of grasping.

Aurelia yawned and stretched, her body arching against the arm that wrapped around her bare stomach. Cristos' gaze darkened with a hunger that she sensed had little to do with food. Heat prickled across her skin, and she bit her lip, feeling a wave of embarrassment. During the night, she had felt desirable under his caresses. Still, with the morning light came uncertainties. Part of her longed to roll back into his arms, while another part whispered warnings about losing herself too quickly.

She rolled away and slid from the bed, her back to him as she tugged on her tunic. She felt his gaze burning into her, but she kept her eyes forward as she flitted around the tent to get ready for the day.

Aurelia sat lost in thought at a small vanity, wrestling with the last of her sleep-tousled hair to braid it, when his hands landed on her shoulders. Startled by the contact, she jumped. Her inner turmoil had distracted her so much that she hadn't noticed his approach in the mirror she was vacantly staring into. Cristos leaned forward, pressing his cheek against hers while meeting her eyes in the reflection as he murmured in her ear.

"No pressure, Aurelia. Remember, we will only do what you're comfortable with."

Her face flushed at his proximity, and she realized he had misinterpreted her unease. She didn't correct him—it was embarrassing to admit that she had limited sexual experience, especially when it was clear he was pretty knowledgeable about a woman's body. The stable boy she had been with had been just as much a bumbling virgin as she had been. How many females, especially magical ones, had he disrobed? She had never felt the need to compare herself to others before, but insecurity crept in now.

Of course, she'd rather die than admit any of that aloud, so she nodded and kissed his cheek before standing.

"We should go. It should be lunchtime soon, and we shouldn't skip a second meal."

He dressed quickly, and she followed him out of the tent. The aching need that Cristos had ignited within her still lingered, and she couldn't help but admire his form from her peripheral vision as they walked hand in hand toward the dining tent. In a way, Septima had done her a favor by preventing her from moving forward more than she was ready for. Her body and mind responded to him at different paces, with the former moving much faster than the latter. Rational thought became elusive whenever he touched her.

The moment they stepped out into camp, Aurelia felt the shift. The clang of sparring blades, the shouts of warriors giving orders, and the scent of roasted meat greeted her like a slap of reality. It was jarring after the private cocoon of their tent. She was pulled from her inner turmoil by the sound of her name being called. Exie and Septima sat on a bench near the training ring, waving. Cristos changed their direction and headed toward them with a calmness she hadn't expected him to have among the Aegricians. She had not forgotten the shadows that passed over his face when he spoke with Blaedia, but he seemed confident in their camp now. He knew his people would receive their help, which visibly lifted some of the burden he carried on his shoulders, and in turn, it eased some of her own worries.

Although Exie's wrist was wrapped in bandages, she looked well. After everything the warrior had gone through over the past weeks, Aurelia was surprised she appeared so healthy and happy. Septima smirked as they approached, and the look on her sister's face sent a wave of heat across Aurelia's that she could not hide, no matter how hard she tried. Her tight braid prevented her from hiding behind her hair, and suddenly she regretted not leaving it loose. She rolled her eyes, attempting to appear nonchalant, but Septima's expression did not waver.

"Well, good morning! Did you get plenty of rest last night?" Exie's tone was neutral, but her grin confirmed that she had not kept to herself what Septima had walked in on. Aurelia's face matched the crimson of her hair as she fidgeted awkwardly and murmured a yes.

"We have a while until lunch, but they saved breakfast plates for us in the dining tent, if the two of you worked up an appetite."

Aurelia tried to walk away to save herself from further embarrassment, but Cristos held her in place. "How are you feeling, Exie?" he asked, changing the topic. Aurelia sagged in relief, grateful for the reprieve. She was so mortified that she had not even considered inquiring about her friend.

Exie flourished her bandaged arm but smiled. "Sore, but good. I hope to avoid injuries for a while."

Cristos chuckled. "That would be good. Will you be joining us in Diapolis?"

Exie shook her head. "Aello, the healer, forbade it. She insisted I take time to heal." Septima nodded in agreement, but Aurelia's heart dropped into her stomach. If Septima stayed with Exie and Cristos left for Diapolis... The thought of being separated from either of them made her chest ache.

Cristos gave her hand a reassuring squeeze, and she knew he felt the shift in her emotions. He turned his attention to her. "Are you ready to grab breakfast?" She nodded, still lost in thought over the idea of separating from either of the two people who mattered most to her. Neither option appealed to her, but there wasn't much she could do about it.

They said their goodbyes and left Exie and Septima on the bench as they went for their food. Aurelia and Cristos grabbed the covered trays waiting for them when they entered the dining tent and sat at a table in the corner to avoid getting in the way of people dashing about the space as they prepared for lunch.

Lifting the lid, she saw a bowl of porridge, eggs, and a strip of what looked like ham. It was no longer hot, but Aurelia did not care—she was starving.

The pair ate in silence, but their gazes repeatedly found their way back to each other. The awkward tension that had separated them since they woke lingered. Neither could deny how much they wanted each other. There was something unstoppable blossoming between them, but she wasn't sure if or when she'd be ready to take the next step.

The trip to Diapolis hung over them like a guillotine, and Aurelia wasn't sure what to do. She had a decision to make: stay with Septima within the safety of their encampment, or join Cristos and the diplomatic envoy on their quest to the seaside kingdom? If she were completely honest with herself, she wanted to go to Diapolis.

Septima no longer seemed to need her company, and Aurelia did not want to be a third wheel. Her sister had someone else now, someone she may even be in love with. Swallowing hard, Aurelia took a sip of her tea. If it were just a trip, free from the dangers of war, there would be no question. She would travel to Diapolis and explore as many unknown places as possible. She would experience new things and learn more about the realm she would call home for the rest of her life. Adventure seeking was one reason they left home in the first place. But their reality was far grimmer than she had imagined when they ran away. There was a chance she would never see Septima again if she went beyond the wards, and that prospect terrified her.

Cristos reached for her hand, pulling her from her thoughts. "What's wrong?"

Aurelia shrugged and smirked slightly. "It's going to take some getting used to... You being able to sense my emotions. I can't seem to keep anything to myself."

Cristos chuckled as he gently squeezed her hand. "I don't need to rely on my senses to read you. You make faces when you're thinking—adorable faces."

Aurelia blushed, wondering how her face hadn't permanently stained red yet. "What kinds of faces?"

He reached out and touched her nose. "Well, for one, you scrunch your nose." She swatted at his hand, and he laughed again. "What's on your mind?"

"I was just thinking about Diapolis."

Cristos' expression softened as he reached for her other hand, holding it across the table. "Are you trying to decide whether you will come?"

She nodded, focusing on their clasped hands to avoid his gaze. His sun-kissed hands were much larger than hers. "I want to be with you." She hesitated, intertwining their fingers. "But I've never been away from my sister."

Cupping her cheek, Cristos ran his thumb gently across it. She closed her eyes. "I'll understand if you stay."

Aurelia shook her head, trying to push away the burning sensation of unshed tears. "Septima has Exie now." She opened her eyes to meet his gaze. "I want to go with you. I'm just afraid I'll never find my way back to her."

Her voice quivered at her admission, and she clenched her jaw to fight back her emotions. Cristos held her face carefully, his expression determined. "I promised I would protect you. If it's the last thing I do, I will ensure you return to your sister. I give you my word."

Promises were fragile things in war, and Aurelia knew that. But the way he spoke—steady and unflinching—made her want to believe.

They stared at each other for a long moment as his words sank in. She swallowed, pushing down her hesitation and fear. "I want to join you on the trip to Diapolis. I'm the only one, besides my sister, from the human lands. Regardless of my mother's true heritage, they are my people, and the outcome of this war affects them as much as it does Norithae and Aegricia. It affects my family. Because of that, I believe I should be part of the discussion."

Cristos tilted his head slightly, still holding her hand across the table. "I agree with you."

"Thank you." Aurelia took the last sip of her tea and pushed her tray away. A woman swooped in to take their trays before disappearing into the food preparation area. "We should probably find Blaedia and ask about their plans. I imagine we will need to leave soon."

Cristos stood and walked around the table, pulling her into a tight hug. Aurelia didn't object. The feel of his strong body against hers brought memories of the previous night to the forefront of her mind, and heat swept through her. She shoved her impure thoughts aside and accepted the comfort he was offering. He didn't speak, but the embrace conveyed everything: everything is going to be okay.

They found the general in front of her tent, speaking with three other phoenixes in their human forms as she looked toward the sky. They stood back, not wanting to interrupt, but Blaedia noticed them and waved them over. The warriors departed as they approached, and Blaedia passed through the tent flap, followed by Aurelia and Cristos.

"We sent a raven to Diapolis this morning to notify King Ailani of your group's arrival," Blaedia said as she let the canvas fall shut. She led them to a large table at the center of the room and pulled the cloth that covered it off to reveal a map. Cristos leaned over for a closer look while Aurelia shifted her weight, unsure of what to do. "If you fly at least eighty percent of the way, it should take about three days to reach the capital city of Embershell."

Cristos scratched his chin, clearly deep in thought, as he traced his finger along the path outlined in blood-red ink. "Any particular reason why you suggest only flying eighty percent of the way?"

Aurelia moved in to inspect the map, though nearly everything was unfamiliar to her. Dense forests separated them from Diapolis. The thought of what lived within those trees made her stomach knot, and she felt her breakfast threatening to resurface. Images of the hellhound crushing Exie's arm flashed in her mind, nearly enough to make her reconsider leaving the encampment.

"It's a safety precaution to ensure the messenger ravens make it there before you," Blaedia said, rolling her shoulders and leaning forward, bracing her hands on the table. "Dragons patrol their borders. Trust me when I say that you do not want to come across one if they are not expecting you. The odds of surviving the encounter... Well, let's just say it's improbable."

Cristos made a noise in the back of his throat, halfway between a grunt and a gasp. "Point taken. I would rather not become a dragon's meal."

He flashed a smile at Aurelia, but she couldn't manage one in return. Blaedia's warning had left her mouth dry, and her heart raced in response. She had grown up hearing tales of dragons around hearth fires—stories meant to frighten children into obedience. The realization that they were real, and that she might encounter one, sent chills down her spine.

Blaedia chuckled as she covered the map again. "Take the day to rest. I'll prepare a map for you, and my people will have packs ready for your journey. It's best to leave at first light."

Cristos thanked the general, and they set out to find Septima. Aurelia was determined to travel to Diapolis and wanted to spend the day with her sister and Kano before they were separated. She hated leaving her tiger again so soon, but knowing that Septima would be able to spend time with him eased some of her guilt.

Septima and Exie were still sitting on a bench, watching two warriors spar in the training ring. When Septima saw them, she stood and slung her arm around Aurelia's shoulder, her sheepish grin indicating she was done teasing for now. "What are the two of you up to?" she asked, sounding happier than she had in days, which softened the dread building in Aurelia's chest.

Cristos responded before Aurelia could. "We just received instructions from the general about the diplomatic envoy setting out tomorrow." He sat on the bench beside Exie and pulled Aurelia onto his lap. She yelped but did not resist.

"Are you going too, Lia?" Septima asked as she sat on Aurelia's other side, her tone resigned as if she already knew the answer.

Aurelia nodded. "Since you and I are the only two people here from the human world, I think one of us should be there. Since Exie can't go..." She hesitated for a moment before continuing. "Can you watch over Kano while I'm gone?"

Aurelia began to bite her nails, a habit she only slipped into during her most troubling moments.

"Of course," Septima replied without hesitation.

"The lanistas looked after him while we were gone, as they do with all our animals," Exie added. "I'll return to that job tomorrow and help Septima look after him. Don't worry. He's in excellent hands."

Cristos gently squeezed Aurelia's shoulder, and she smiled through the tears welling in her eyes. "I hate being away from him, but I'm glad he will have you both. I look forward to the day when he can live with me again, like he has since he was a cub. I can't imagine what he's thinking now that he is stuck outside."

"Trust me, Aurelia. Kano is spoiled rotten by the lanistas. He may be used to being indoors with you, but he's meant to be in the wild. He's had the chance to hunt and run around. I don't doubt he misses you, but he's not suffering." Exie smiled as she held onto Septima's hand.

The sight of their interlaced fingers warmed Aurelia's heart, easing the pain of leaving her sister behind. She voiced her concerns about Kano but couldn't bring herself to speak of her worries about Septima. Uttering those words would surely break her heart, but seeing the joy on her sister's face as she looked at her warrior strengthened Aurelia's resolve. All she ever wanted for her sister was love and acceptance, and it was clear that she had found that among the Aegricians.

Aurelia hadn't expected either of them to find a partner so quickly, but she was happy they had. Now her only wish was that their hearts remained intact as they fought for a place to call home. The transient camp was not a true home. Thoughts of where they would live after the war and which kingdom they would settle in weighed heavily on her. Living a nomadic life was not for her; she just hoped they would survive long enough to put down roots.

The lunch bell tolled, breaking the silence that had fallen between them. The two females they had been watching spar shook hands and exited the ring. People poured out from all over the camp, converging in front of the dining tent. Aurelia had no appetite yet, but she and Cristos joined Exie and her sister anyway. The only thing that mattered was spending time with Septima while she still could.

CHAPTER THIRTY-TWO

SPECTRE FOREST

AURELIA

Cristos and Aurelia visited Kano after lunch, while Exie and Septima went to the medical tent for Exie's bandage change. Upon arrival, Aurelia encouraged Cristos to enter the enclosure and introduced him to her tiger. To her surprise, the majestic cat immediately approached Cristos, nuzzling against his legs before rolling onto his back for a belly rub. They spent hours lounging around, showering Kano with attention as they enjoyed the lovely weather.

Aurelia wondered about the temperature outside the camp. She knew from experience that the wards made the conditions within much more pleasant than they truly were. She removed her cloak and turned her face to the sky, basking in the sunlight. Not knowing what awaited them in the morning, she savored the warmth while she could. Beyond the barrier, it was undoubtedly colder, and she could only speculate about the weather they would encounter on their journey to Diapolis.

The enclosure's gate creaked open, causing Aurelia to turn her head in curiosity. Her tension eased when she spotted Septima and the freshly bandaged Exie. Kano leaped from his perch at her feet and raced over to greet them, clearly missing Exie just as much as he had missed Aurelia. This reaction filled her with relief, assuring her that he would be fine with the two women while she was away.

They greeted Kano, returning the affection he craved, before joining Aurelia and Cristos on the ground. The tiger yawned, his prominent teeth shimmering in the daylight, and then curled up in front of Aurelia, his heavy frame resting on her feet. She didn't mind; she ran her fingers through his fur, cherishing their time together.

The four of them sat in a comfortable silence for a while before Aurelia's curiosity got the better of her.

"What do you expect will happen in Diapolis?" she asked Cristos, who was scratching behind Kano's ears. Septima and Exie turned to him as well, their curiosity evident.

"Are you referring to the alliance or the situation in general?" Cristos asked.

"The alliance. Do you think King Ailani will side with us?" Aurelia clarified.

Cristos paused, stopping his petting of Kano to meet each of their intense gazes. "Honestly, I'm not sure. The king of Diapolis tends to avoid any conflict that doesn't directly impact his territory. He may be inclined to let Warbotach pass through the portal, assuming they don't head south toward his kingdom," he replied, then resumed stroking Kano's fur. "But I could be wrong. This world has never faced a threat of this magnitude before. He may well decide to aid us in our efforts to send Uldon and his people back across the Undying Valley."

"If he doesn't," Exie interjected, "we may need to reach out to the Queen of Karinia."

Cristos nodded and looked into Exie's eyes. "Yes, but she's even less likely to assist us. Her territories are so far removed from the conflict, and the chances of Warbotach heading that way are slim."

"Karinia?" Septima asked. "I thought the only territories here were Aegricia, Norithae, Diapolis, and Warbotach."

Cristos responded, "In Ekotoria, yes. However, it is just one of the continents on this side of the portal. There are others."

Aurelia blinked, realizing for the first time how vast the magical realm was and that there was more to it than just Ekotoria. The sheer size of this world both intrigued and unsettled her; there was still so much she didn't know about the place she intended to call home one day. "Are there many other continents on this side of the portal?" she asked.

Exie nodded. "Yes, there is Karinia, ruled by Queen Thalia. Then there are the Inferno Territories, but I'm not sure who leads them. They are so far away that I've never been there."

"Nor have I," Cristos added.

The four of them spent the rest of the day in Kano's enclosure. As the sun began to set, the dinner bell rang, but no one rushed to move from their sprawled positions on the forest floor. Aurelia lay on the ground with her head in Cristos' lap, watching as sprites danced their nightly ritual within the tree line. She giggled to herself, wondering if Dewdrop was nearby with her group of lovesick friends. Cristos gave her a questioning look, but she waved him off as she climbed to her feet.

Exie stood next, dusting off her fighting leathers before offering a hand to Septima. A bright smile lit up her sister's face as she accepted Exie's help.

"Will you be sleeping in our tent tonight?" Aurelia asked, nervous about Septima's response. She wasn't sure what she wanted the answer to be.

Septima shrugged and glanced sidelong at Cristos as she murmured under her breath, "I doubt I'm the one you want to have a slumber party with, Lia. I'll leave that decision up to you. Either way, I'm fine."

Aurelia nodded, trying to hide her embarrassment, but she failed miserably. The blush on her cheeks was a dead giveaway. Thankfully, the two women headed toward the gate and did not notice her rosy face. Unfortunately, Cristos did. His grin was filled with playful mischief, deepening her flush. He grasped her bicep as she made for the exit, dragging his palm down her arm in a slow, practiced motion until he reached her hand. He intertwined their fingers, gently pulling her toward the gate.

"Should I move my things to the tent Blaedia set aside for me?" he asked.

She could still feel the warmth of his touch radiating from her arm, which made it hard to think. Aurelia bit her lip as she pondered her answer. "What would you prefer? I'm unsure. It's hard knowing I'll be leaving my sister in the morning. We haven't been apart since the day my father brought her home."

"That's completely understandable. I'm truly fine either way, Aurelia. We have a lifetime to be together..." He trailed off, his face darkening in an unexpected blush. He stumbled over his words as he rushed on. "I—I mean, if that's what you want. Anyway, it won't hurt my feelings if you decide to spend the night with your sister." The mention of a future together caught her by surprise. Though she often pondered the possibility, they had never discussed it. Planning didn't seem to fit amidst the backdrop of war.

Ignoring his comment about the future, Aurelia felt unsure of how to respond. She simply nodded and focused on the matter at hand. "I'm leaning toward spending the night with Septima since I won't see her for a while. We'll figure it out after dinner. If she stays in our tent, we'll find out where yours is."

Cristos squeezed her hand in acknowledgement, his shoulders tense as they walked through the camp in silence.

As soon as they reached their destination, they lined up for dinner. Aurelia scanned the tent for her sister and spotted her sitting with Exie, Holera, and Kason. Exie waved them over as soon as they grabbed their meal trays, motioning toward the empty seats at the end of the table. The group was engrossed in conversation when Aurelia and Cristos joined. Holera and Kason were leaning back casually in their seats, their bowls already empty. Kason had his muscular arm draped over the back of Holera's chair, his fingers absentmindedly playing with the ends of her hair as he spoke.

Exie, ever the extrovert, eagerly interrupted and introduced Cristos to him. The two men hit it off immediately, chatting about weapons and their upcoming journey to Diapolis. Aurelia tuned them out as she dug into her dinner. Kason was apparently part of the diplomatic envoy and would set off with them in the morning. If their conversations remained as dry as their talk about swords, she was in for a boring trek. However, the way their eyes lit up while they exchanged stories indicated they were thoroughly enjoying themselves. Aurelia didn't understand their fascination; as long as her arrows flew true, her bow was taut, and her sword was sharp, she was satisfied.

As the men continued discussing their preferred type of hilt, she turned her attention to Holera. The warrior shared details about their mission and travel companions. Their party would consist of five people, including herself and Kason, along with a healer named Calista.

Dinner was filled with further discussions about the impending war. Aurelia mostly kept to herself, aside from a brief conversation with Septima to plan their evening. The sisters decided to spend some time together before bed, but Septima would sleep in Exie's tent. Since Aurelia and Cristos were set to leave at first light, her sister thought it made sense for them to share a tent, making preparations easier.

Once everyone finished eating and cleared their table, they headed to the sparring ring. After their extensive discussion, Kason and Cristos decided they needed to test their weapons against each other.

Exie sat on a nearby bench, her eyes gleaming with excitement as she watched the men fight. She bounced her leg and rotated her injured wrist, clearly itching to join in. Holera handed a sword to both Septima and Aurelia, insisting that they brush up on their skills. After the time away from the camp and the minimal training she managed at Variel's, Aurelia felt more than a little rusty.

She would much rather watch the two handsome men trade blows, but she knew Holera was right. They were about to embark on a dangerous journey, and she couldn't waste valuable training time. So, with the sounds of clanging swords and grunts in the background, the sisters practiced blocking, slashing, and footwork until the sun disappeared behind the trees. The full moon shone through the treetops, accompanied by glowing sprites that gathered to watch the sparring match, illuminating the clearing like little floating candles as they gawked at the now shirtless men. Aurelia chuckled to herself as she realized all the sprites were female.

Shortly after, they headed for the showers, with Cristos and Kason calling the match a draw. Her muscles felt like jelly from the exertion, and she hardly had the energy to walk across the camp.

After washing up, Septima hugged her tightly and told her to stay safe. Aurelia fought back tears as they held each other and bid farewell for the night. It was by far the hardest thing she had ever done, and a part of her hoped Septima wouldn't see her off in the morning. Aurelia already found it difficult to end the embrace, and she wasn't sure if she'd be able to leave if she saw her sister in the morning.

Cristos had promised to protect her, but a nagging voice in her mind insisted they were saying goodbye forever. The thought of being apart longer than they ever had before formed a knot in her stomach. Every step she took toward her tent and away from her sister felt like a knife to her gut. She knew she was being dramatic, but the sense of doom wouldn't ease.

Worries about leaving Septima and Kason behind and venturing into the unknown plagued her. She remained silent as she and Cristos entered her tent and packed for the trip. Even as they prepared for bed, doubt and fear continued to consume her.

That night, Aurelia crawled into bed beside Cristos, all thoughts of the burning desire he had previously awakened within her forgotten. They lay in silence, but her mind had never been so loud.

Letting out a loud huff, she flopped onto her back to stare at the darkened ceiling. "Tell me I'm making a bigger deal out of leaving than I should."

Cristos wrapped an arm around her waist, a small gesture that comforted her. "I'm not here to tell you that your feelings aren't real or warranted. You've never been away from your sister, and that's scary. You left your world behind for her, and now your paths are diverging for the first time. It's a perfectly reasonable response."

"Thank you for being so patient with me," she murmured, his words easing a bit of her anxiety. He propped himself up on his elbow and gazed down at her for a moment before pressing a kiss to her cheek. Her heart fluttered at both the action and the tender look in his eye.

"You don't have to thank me. I'm happy to support you in any way I can." His tone was casual, but his expression was intense as he kissed her forehead. "Thank you for letting me be here with you tonight. I would have missed you if I had to sleep alone."

Her initial trepidation faded as she smiled at his words. In that moment, she couldn't deny how much he meant to her. His fingers traced a lazy pattern on her hip, and he stared at her with such affection that the butterflies he sparked took flight. "What would you miss the most? Tell me more."

His chuckle had a throaty quality as he rolled to hover over her. He braced himself with his hands and leaned down to softly kiss her. It was a gentle peck, but it left Aurelia longing for more. "I would miss seeing your face as soon as I wake up the most."

Next, he kissed her jawline. "I would miss feeling your smooth skin against mine."

Her heart raced as she squirmed beneath him, trying to ease the pressure his seductive tone was building between her legs. He trailed his lips from her jaw to her neck and gently bit the sensitive flesh. She moaned at the sensation, instinctively arching into him. "I would absolutely miss hearing those delicious gasps and moans from you."

Aurelia struggled to breathe as he continued to press kisses over her neck. Every word, every touch, held her captive. When he finally pulled away, she was about to complain when his mouth descended on hers. The kiss was intense and passionate, yet he stayed hovering above her. His lips and tongue were the only parts of him that touched her, and it was maddening. She refused to let any doubt ruin the moment, wrapping her legs around his hips to pull him closer. She ran her hands over the taut muscles of his back, moving them up to stroke the base of his wings. They felt as soft as leather, but she didn't have the chance to appreciate them for long. He groaned low in his throat and pulled away.

"My wings are... sensitive."

Aurelia smirked up at him, her expression filled with lust and mischief. "Is that so?"

Before he could respond, she caressed them again, and they fluttered at her touch, eliciting another moan from him. He pressed his forehead against hers, his expression strained. "If you do that again, we won't get much rest before our journey."

"Good." Her response was breathy as she leaned up to reclaim his lips. She ran a hand along the space between his wings before dragging it over the base of one.

Their kiss grew more frantic as he ground himself against her. His hard length rubbed against her center, and she moaned at the friction. He pulled away and rose up on his knees between her legs.

Cristos slid his hands to her thighs, eliciting a tremor of anticipation from her. "I want to touch you." His voice dropped an octave, his tone so husky and seductive, she almost moaned again.

"Then touch me."

Her words were all the reassurance he needed, apparently. His mouth descended on hers, their tongues warring for dominance as his hands moved higher. He slid her nightdress up slowly, breaking their kiss to pull it off and toss it aside.

He stared at her naked body like a starving man ready to devour her. The heat in his gaze set her aflame, and she pulled him down on top of her. Only he could douse the burning need that consumed her. They became a tangle of limbs as they rolled over.

Aurelia straddled his lap, rotating her hips as his hard length rubbed against her again. Bolts of pleasure shot through her entire frame as she pulled his tunic off. Being with Cristos empowered her in a way she'd never felt before. He worshiped her with every kiss. Every touch killed her reservations about moving too fast. She'd forgotten about how experienced he'd seemed compared to her. The only thing that mattered was the two of them. They didn't know what perilous road they'd head down tomorrow, but at least she had these stolen moments now.

He rolled them again and pulled his trousers off. The candlelight flicked softly in the tent, illuminating him as he hovered above her.

"Are you sure you want this?"

She met his stare, reaching out to wrap her hand around his cock as she answered. "I want you."

She stroked him; her grip uncertain as she took in the sheer size of him. Cristos was much larger than the man she'd been with before. A part of her was unsure if he'd fit, but she was more than ready to try.

He groaned when she grasped him tighter, and it nearly undid her. The sound of his pleasure was all the encouragement she needed to guide him toward her entrance, tensing in preparation for the pain that was sure to come.

Cristos pulled his hips back, chuckling against her neck. "What is the rush?"

Aurelia frowned at him, but before she could speak, his hand was between her thighs. His fingers were deft as he teased her heated flesh. Her back arched as she moaned, her body trembling from the overload of sensations. Her desire built with every stroke, and she cried out as he pinched her sensitive bud. Before her scream of ecstasy had quieted, he shoved a finger inside her.

She writhed under his touch as he added another. Her climax built with his relentless movements. She opened her mouth to say something—anything—but all that came out was a breathy moan. She tried again, finally succeeding. "Cristos. More."

Whole sentences were beyond her, but he understood. He kneeled between her thighs and grabbed her hips, yanking her down on the bed until their pelvises aligned. He reached between their bodies and rubbed circles on her most intimate part as he began to ease inside her.

Aurelia wiggled closer, trying to take more of him, but Cristos grasped her hips and held her still.

"I don't want to hurt you." He leaned forward and dotted kisses along her face and neck as he continued to enter her inch by inch. He returned his mouth to hers in a sensual kiss as he filled her, but once his entire length was buried inside her, he stilled. She could feel her body stretching around him. The pain was there, but bearable. After a moment, she lifted her hips beneath him.

Needing no further encouragement, Cristos lifted her from the bed and sat back on his heels, their bodies never parting as she straddled him.

Aurelia wasn't sure what to do in that position. She'd spent her time with the stable boy on her back. Embarrassment started to bloom, but before it could take hold and ruin the mood, he moved. He hoisted her up until he'd almost slid out of her and then pulled her back down. He threw his hips up to meet hers, and stars exploded in her eyes. He repeated the motion, increasing his speed with each thrust.

She threw her head back as she moaned, forgetting the uncertainty that had just plagued her. She rolled her hips as she matched his motions, using her knees for leverage.

Her hands roamed his body, and she could feel his back muscles ripple beneath her palms. She touched the base of his wings, and this time she felt him twitch inside her. She continued to stroke them as their bodies slammed against each other. Her release came hard, and she clenched her fists as she screamed his name. She hardly noticed her nail biting into the leathery appendages as euphoria filled her, fogging her mind. Her body quaked as she rode the waves of her climax. Cristos groaned and buried his face in her neck as he thrust into her a final time. His wings flared out majestically behind him as he reached his own release, and Aurelia knew she'd never forget that moment for as long as she lived.

Cristos collapsed beside her, his chest still heaving, his skin damp with the sheen of exertion. Aurelia curled into him instinctively, her ear pressed to the steady thunder of his heartbeat. His wings, still trembling faintly from release, folded around her like a living blanket, cocooning them both in warmth.

The world outside the tent—war, kingdoms, even her sister—felt impossibly far away. All that existed was his arm draped across her waist, the steady rise and fall of his chest, and the comforting weight of his body beside hers. For the first time in weeks, her mind was quiet. No dread. No doubt. Just him.

"Sleep, Aurelia," he whispered, voice hoarse but tender. He brushed a kiss across her temple, and she smiled against his skin.

And so she did—falling into a deep, dreamless slumber, tangled safely in Cristos' arms, with the memory of his wings unfurled in the candlelight burned forever into her heart.

CHAPTER THIRTY-THREE

SPECTRE FOREST

AURELIA

Waking up in Cristos' arms, with his naked body curled around her, made getting out of bed even more difficult. Aurelia wished they could stay there all day, repeating the wonderful night before, but war waited for no one, and allies were important. For a fleeting moment, she imagined what it would be like to remain wrapped up in him, free from the fear of pursuit or battle. The thought brought a deep ache that had nothing to do with lust.

Aurelia groaned as she sat up and stretched, hoping her movements would motivate her. Instead, the delicious soreness between her legs reminded her of their passionate night together. She never realized how vivid her imagination was until Cristos crawled out of bed, his arousal evident as he pulled on a pair of trousers. Oh, how she longed for just one more round.

"Stop staring at me like that, or the envoy will leave without us," he teased.

She giggled at his words but forced her gaze away as he adjusted himself. As tempting as he was, they had a mission. The two hurriedly prepared to leave, already running late.

The camp appeared deserted as they made their way to the dining tent, their weapons strapped to them. After a quick breakfast, they would set off immediately. Their group needed to complete the flying portion of their journey before camping for the night, leaving them little time to spare.

Still rubbing the sleep from her eyes, Aurelia took a seat at the table with the rest of their party. Their packs, prepared by the Aegricians, were already stacked in the corner when they entered the dining tent. Aurelia packed the knapsack she'd brought from Vaekros, filling it with a few changes of clothes and some essentials. She hoped the other bags contained the rest of their basic necessities.

They ate in hurried silence before grabbing their gear and making their way to the edge of the wards near the sparring rings. Blaedia and Holera had finalized their travel plans with the group the night before, so after those responsible for flying reviewed the map one more time, they felt ready to embark on the first leg of their journey.

Sliding one arm under Aurelia's knees and the other around her waist, Cristos lifted her as if she weighed no more than a feather. Kason, the only other member of their group who could not fly, climbed onto Holera's back once the flames that ignited during her transformation faded.

In her humanoid form, the silver-haired woman was gorgeous, but as a phoenix, Holera was stunning. Unlike the crimson plumage of many other warriors, Holera's feathers were mainly silver, with delicate streaks of violet highlighting her wings and tail. Calista rounded out their party; her phoenix form displayed the signature fire-colored feathers of her kin, but flecks of blue and green distinguished her from the rest.

Cristos, dressed in dark fighting leathers with leathery wings, was the least colorful in the group. Still, as Aurelia gazed at his bronzed face, she felt that he shone the brightest in her eyes. She tucked her tightly plaited hair into the hood of her cloak, which matched her fighting leathers, and wrapped her arms around Cristos' neck as he prepared to take off.

Kason took one last look at the map before securing it in his pocket. He nodded to the rest and pulled on Holera's reins. The enormous silver bird flapped her great wings at his signal, lifting through the tree canopy and into the open sky. Calista followed closely, with Cristos and Aurelia right behind.

As they ascended, Aurelia stared down at the camp, her eyes fixated on the tent where her sister slept. She was relieved that Septima hadn't come to bid them farewell, but it still hurt to leave without seeing her sister's face one last time. Leaving without Septima felt like tearing away a piece of herself, and the ache was as sharp as it was familiar. She closed her eyes, willing the tears that were rapidly forming to stay at bay, and buried her face in the crook of Cristos' neck for comfort. The protective barrier rippled around them as they passed through, a feeling as unsettling as plunging into cold water and surfacing gasping for air. She swallowed hard, realizing this was it—she had officially embarked on her first journey without Septima.

"How long do you think we'll be in the sky today?" Aurelia asked, attempting to distract herself. She pulled back just enough to gaze at the sapphire waters of the Elder Sea, which glimmered in the distance as the sun began to rise. The scene, where rolling blue waves met the dark green of the lush forest, was a breathtaking masterpiece.

"Probably about six hours. Are you already tired of me?" Cristos quipped, eyeing her with an arched brow. She grinned back.

"Not at all. I'm just worried I'll make your back ache."

He chuckled and gave her a playful bounce in his arms as they soared through the skies. "You are not heavy. Besides, I've told you before that it's an honor to carry you." He placed a kiss on her forehead, and the warmth of his affection washed over her. "I'm strong. I can handle it."

They fell silent after that, and Aurelia savored the heat radiating from him, which countered the chill of the wind whipping around them as they cut through the air. She tried to memorize the sensation—the feel of him, the sky, the world unfurling beneath her—because there was no telling if she'd ever experience this again.

As they traveled further south, the landscape underwent a transformation. Palm trees began to mingle with the evergreens and deciduous trees of Spectre Forest. The further they traveled, the more common tropical greenery became. Time passed quickly as Aurelia marveled at the beauty of Ekotoria.

As daylight waned, the mountainous coast gave way to sandy shores. She watched as the Elder Sea took on a turquoise hue, its rising tide lapping at the shoreline. The rapidly fading sunlight reflected off the water, making the surface glow. Their party began to descend into the trees below as she admired the serene view, painting a mental picture to share with Septima upon their return. The dying rays of light cast dark shadows over the clearing where they landed. Although they could have easily exited the forest, they unanimously decided to set up camp within the tree line, using the dense woodlands as an added layer of camouflage. The men pitched the small tents they had packed while Holera and Calista erected wards to shield their temporary base. Aurelia, unable to assist with either task, gathered firewood.

Once the setup was complete, they all gathered around the now roaring fire and shared a simple dinner of dried meat, cheese, and bread. Aurelia nestled into Cristos' side; his wing extended behind her, blocking the wind. Although the temperature had lost its frigid edge as they traveled south, the air had turned brisk without the sun. Still, between his warmth and the heat from the flames flickering at her face, she felt perfectly content. She inhaled the scent of smoke and leather, grounding herself in the ordinary while her mind danced with thoughts of hellhounds and dragons.

After dinner, Aurelia and Cristos retired to their tent, both exhausted. She longed for a bath, already missing the comforts of the phoenix encampment. Feeling dirty after their hours-long flight, she noticed that Cristos seemed unfazed. He joined their bedrolls and snuggled against her, her back pressed firmly against his chest as his arm wrapped around her.

His warmth permeated her thin nightdress, and the feel of his powerful body against hers ignited her desire for his intimate touch. The image of his wings spread behind him during their previous climax was still fresh in her mind. Though the location lacked romance and privacy was nonexistent, she couldn't help but crave him. After experiencing the bliss he brought her, it was nearly impossible to suppress that longing.

"Are you nervous to meet the king of Diapolis?" Aurelia rolled over, pressing her cheek against his chest as she sparked the conversation to redirect her lustful thoughts. He shrugged.

"I'm not nervous about meeting him, but I am concerned that he won't help us. I've heard enough to know how little he involves himself in the affairs of other kingdoms. He may decline to align with us, but we won't know unless we try."

Cristos rolled forward, pinning her back against the bedroll with his body. "Let's not dwell on uncertainties. We will have our answers soon enough, and I can think of far better ways to occupy ourselves."

His hand slid between her thighs, effectively ending any further discussion about Diapolis.

Cristos was already gone when Aurelia woke the next morning. She could hear him chatting with the others outside, but she did not rush out of bed. It was going to be a long day, and she wasn't looking forward to it. The only light at the end of the dreary tunnel was the prospect of a bath when they rested in Diapolis before their audience with the king.

While she was trying to convince herself to get up, a head of shaggy black hair and bright blue eyes peeked through the tent flap. She covered her face with a blanket and grumbled, "I'm still sleeping."

Cristos chuckled as he crawled inside and pulled the pillow just enough to slide his head beneath it. "No, you are not."

She stuck her tongue out at him. Instead of being offended, he leaned in and caught her tongue in his mouth. As he sucked on it, Aurelia found that while she had no interest in getting ready for the day, she had plenty of energy to kiss Cristos. Their lip lock grew increasingly heated, but when she tried to untie his trousers, he pulled away. "I would love to stay here with you all day, but we really need to get going. We'd like to arrive at Starcrest by lunchtime. We should be able to find horses somewhere in town."

Aurelia rose from the bed begrudgingly and pulled on her boots. If she couldn't stay in bed with him, she might as well get a move on. The sooner they left, the sooner she could bathe and sleep in a proper bed. That was her motivation for the day.

Holera and the others were fastening the last of their gear as she stepped into the blazing sun. They began taking down her tent before she was more than a few feet away. Cristos handed her a sandwich while he fastened his weapons to his body. When he caught her watching him, he grinned, and she didn't look away. The fighting leathers left little to the imagination, and she enjoyed the view as she hurried to finish her breakfast.

A few moments later, they left, quickly passing through the rest of Spectre Forest. Even after exiting the woods, trees still dotted the rolling hills. The group traveled in silence to avoid drawing any unwanted attention to themselves. The second leg of their journey was uneventful. The only other person they encountered was a lone man pulling a cart. Aurelia was bored but relieved that the weather was tolerable. Unlike the forest surrounding the war encampment, the sky was clear, and there was no possibility of snow. A cool breeze blew from the sea and ruffled her loose crimson hair, although it wasn't cold enough to warrant a cloak.

By the time the sun reached its zenith, empty fields had given way to fenced pastureland, and the grass was bisected by a rough, cleared road.

"Looks like a few more miles until we reach Starcrest," Kason said as he examined the map. "From there, we should have time to pass through a few more towns, especially if we can purchase some horses. If we stop in Claywind, we won't make it to the capital today. Still, I'd rather stay at an inn than sleep in a tent again. Plus, it wouldn't hurt to wash up and look presentable for our meeting with the king. I'm uncertain they'll allow us time to do so when we arrive at the palace."

Cristos agreed with Kason, and the women nodded their assent as well. Everyone was tired of walking and being covered in dirt and sweat. Where there was an inn, there would be a tub, and that thought put a spring in Aurelia's step as they pressed on.

CHAPTER THIRTY-FOUR

DIAPOLIS

AURELIA

Starcrest was a small frontier town bustling with activity. From what Aurelia could see, there were no divided neighborhoods; just a plethora of ranch-style homes spread across the plains. The hastily cleared road they traveled smoothed out as they passed through the town's main strip, which seemed to be the heart of the community. It contained everything the residents needed: a small corner store, a tavern and restaurant, and an infirmary, all of which were open for business. Townspeople came and went, hardly giving Aurelia and her group a second glance. The scents of hay, roasted grain, and smoke from the forge drifted through the air, while the rhythmic clang of a blacksmith's hammer mixed with chatter in lilting fae dialects. Even the laughter had a cadence that sounded unfamiliar and strange, reminding her that this was no human town.

Going unnoticed was a welcome experience for Aurelia, one she hadn't had often since arriving in Ekotoria. In Norithae, she had felt like a sideshow attraction, with citizens sneaking fearful glances when they thought the guards weren't watching. Here, anonymity felt like slipping into shadow, a rare moment of invisibility.

As they made their way to the tavern, she took note of a few other establishments, but their signage was in a language she didn't understand. They entered the restaurant and chose a corner table near the door, as Cristos and Holera's warrior training dictated they avoid vulnerable positions. After walking for hours, Aurelia didn't care where they sat; she just needed to rest her legs, which felt like they might give out at any moment. Cristos offered to carry her, but her stubbornness prevented her from appearing weak to the rest of the group. This was a decision she regretted with every throb of her muscles as she collapsed onto a wooden chair.

Kason didn't join them immediately. Instead, he approached the bar to ask where they could purchase horses and send a messenger raven back to camp. Once his inquiries were finished, he rejoined the group. They ordered their meals as Kason filled them in on what the barkeep had said. According to the man, Claywind was five hours south by horseback, and if they continued down the main road for another mile, they would find a ranch that sold horses. The barkeep had also helped Kason send a message back to Blaedia. With the next step of their plan solidifying, they waited for their lunch to arrive, chatting amongst themselves.

Unlike the stews Aurelia had grown accustomed to since joining the Aegricians, their meal consisted of grilled fish served over rice with a side of steamed vegetables. She didn't typically enjoy fish, but whoever had prepared it had done an excellent job. The flesh flaked apart with the press of her fork and was infused with lemony herbs she didn't recognize, filling her mouth with brightness. Even the rice tasted different, faintly spiced with a hint of something sweet and floral. It was unlike any dish from Vaekros, reminding her again that she truly lived in another world. The white fish was mild and perfectly flavored; in fact, she thought it might be the best meal she'd ever eaten.

After they finished their meal, they wasted no time heading south, as instructed. The rancher was already outside, talking to a woman as they approached. At least a dozen horses of various colors grazed in a long grass corral. The man smiled and met them halfway up the long lane that led to the only house on the property. He extended his hand to Kason, who shook it firmly.

"I take it you are looking for horses?" the rancher said.

Kason nodded. "We need three horses to take us to the capital. Lokela sent you our way when I inquired at the tavern. Your name is Bane, right?"

The man smiled and glanced over his shoulder. "Yes, I am Bane, and that is my wife, Kai, over there. I can certainly get you set up with three horses. Follow me."

They trailed behind Bane as he led them to the stables, and Kason paid him for the animals. Aurelia wasn't sure how much money Blaedia had sent them with, but she hoped Kason had enough for the inn and whatever they would need on their way back to camp.

When they left the ranch, they mounted some of the most beautiful horses Aurelia had ever seen. The healer, Calista, rode a black mare named Scoudra, the smallest of the three. Holera and Kason shared the largest horse, a black and white stallion named Tasu. The mighty beast seemed unfazed even under the weight they carried. Aurelia and Cristos rode a large red stallion called Teoron. He was so big that Cristos had to help Aurelia climb into the saddle. Even after she was seated, she couldn't reach the stirrups. Holding onto the saddle horn felt like a life-or-death situation, which it probably was. She imagined Cristos smirking at her unsteady seat and envisioned Kano looking smug if he could see her now. "Some warrior," she thought wryly, "brought low by a horse."

As they headed for Claywind, Aurelia grew more comfortable on the enormous animal. She leaned back against Cristos, nestled between his thighs. She hadn't expected how intimate riding together would feel, especially when he slid his hand under her cloak and rested it on her thigh. His fingers drew small circles on her pants, moving higher with every rotation, making it hard for her to concentrate on the path ahead. It took all her willpower to refrain from grabbing his hand and placing it where she truly wanted him to touch. The others seemed oblivious to his hand's position, and if they noticed, they didn't care—it was no secret that they were lovers.

"I sensed your excitement when Kason mentioned staying at an inn tonight. Don't tell me you're already tired of camping. I have fond memories of tents lately," Cristos said, his breath brushing against her ear, sending a shiver down her spine. His voice resonated through her bones in a way no other had, a low vibration that felt almost elemental, like something ancient in his fae bloodline.

"If I never spent another night in a tent, I wouldn't complain. We can create memories under a real roof, too," Aurelia smiled, leaning her head back against his chest. "But I suppose you're right; it's not that bad. You really should stop what you're doing to my leg, though. It's quite distracting."

Cristos moved his hand, brushing against the part of her that ached for his touch, and her hips bucked. "Distracting you from what?"

She threw her elbow back, hitting him in the stomach, and he chuckled. "You're distracting me from maintaining my seat. You're going to make me fall."

He cupped her womanhood and pulled her flush against him, his hard length pressing against her backside. She gasped and bit her lip to stifle a moan as he teased her through her trousers. "Don't worry. I won't let you fall."

Calista glanced at them, and Aurelia felt her cheeks redden. The healer was not talkative, but Aurelia was sure she was perceptive enough to sense what was happening beneath her cloak. She swatted Cristos' forearm, and he removed his hand, flattening his palm atop her thigh. However, he did not behave for long, and the more he secretly touched her, the more desperate she became to find an inn. Her self-control was already weak when it came to the handsome winged man, and it was rapidly deteriorating.

They passed through two small towns, stopping only to relieve themselves and stretch their legs. They wanted to reach their destination by nightfall, so they continued southward at a brisk pace.

Aurelia attempted to admire the landscape as it became increasingly tropical, but focusing was difficult due to Cristos' relentless teasing. The rolling hills evolved into a more chaparral landscape as clay and sand replaced the lush grass and dirt.

The temperature rose as they covered more ground, prompting Aurelia to shed her cloak. She draped it over her lap, which only encouraged Cristos to stroke her thigh more. He brought her to the edge of release, retreating just before she climaxed again and again as they journeyed. By the time they arrived in Claywind, Aurelia felt molten, sure that she would combust at any moment. Her entire body felt aflame, as if she had swallowed phoenix fire that now burned in her veins.

Her legs were numb and tingly, and she wasn't sure she would be able to stand when they dismounted.

Upon reaching Claywind, their party headed straight for the clearly marked inn. A white-haired young man met them outside the stables. He approached Scoudra first, helping Calista off the mare before grabbing the reins.

"What brings you all to Claywind?" he asked. "Will you be staying with us long?"

"We will be leaving tomorrow," Kason replied as he climbed down and headed inside to secure their rooms. Holera guided Tasu as she followed the stable hand. At the same time, Cristos wrapped his arms around Aurelia and hopped off Teoron, his wings fluttering as he slowed their descent. They made sure the horses were secure before joining Kason indoors. By the time they entered, he had already rented three rooms and secured a table for dinner.

From the outside, the inn appeared well-maintained, enchanting, and cheerful. Plaster walls and stone pillars formed the outer structure. It was tough to see much through the small curtained windows, but a pleasant atmosphere filled the air. As they stepped through the thick metal door, they were welcomed by the aromas of roasted food and cheerful singing.

A tavern occupied the first floor, filled with an enthusiastic assortment of patrons. The bartender greeted them with a short wave as he filled glasses with ale. The establishment was just as enchanting inside. Aurelia could see the stairs leading up to the inn, with tables scattered throughout the space.

They were served plates of grilled fish and vegetables, similar to their meal in Starcrest, but with a side of flavored rice. Cristos left for the bar and returned with five glasses of whiskey. The alcohol burned Aurelia's throat as it went down. They unwound from their journey while indulging themselves. By the time they settled their tab and retired upstairs, Aurelia was one glass away from stumbling.

The rooms above the tavern were small but cozy. Aurelia was unsure if she and Cristos would fit on the little bed because of his wings. Even with them tucked to his back, they would have no choice but to sleep close together—not that she was complaining.

Aurelia opened a small door in the corner of the room, assuming it was a closet, and nearly cried when she discovered a tiny bathing room with an actual tub. It was small, but she didn't care. As long as she could soak in the hot water and clean herself, she was happy.

Cristos warmed the water over the fire and poured it into the small tub.

"Would you like me to wash your hair?" he asked, standing behind her and brushing his fingers through her loose waves. The combination of whiskey and his teasing her made her crave more of his touch. She unbuttoned her tunic while he ran his fingers through her hair, carefully untangling the knots. She closed her eyes as every nerve ending came alive under his fingers.

"I would love that. I'm so tired."

Cristos turned her around and took over, unfastening her tunic. His eyes were heavy-lidded, his exhaustion clear after the long day in the sun, but he quickly unbuttoned the rest. When the last button came undone, he slid the fabric off her shoulders, letting it fall to the floor as he cupped her cheeks and kissed her. She leaned into him on weakened knees, wrapping her arms around his back as she undid the cloth panels of his tunic that surrounded the base of his wings. His lips left hers just long enough to pull off his tunic, and then he pulled her to him once again.

The kiss was ravenous, their pent-up desire bubbling over. Cristos pulled away first, and their bare chests heaved as they both struggled to catch their breath. Sliding her trousers off, Cristos led her to the tub. He helped her climb in, and her eyes nearly rolled when the hot water touched the most sensitive parts of her. Cristos used an empty glass to pour the water over her exposed chest and shoulders until her entire body was dripping.

"Lean back," he murmured as he kneeled behind her. They could not fit in the tub together, but she wished they could. The only thing that would make that bath better would be having a naked Cristos pressed against her. "He kissed the back of her neck, and she moaned but did as he asked. Warm water flowed down her head as he brushed the hair away from her face. She realized with a jolt that this felt more intimate than even their wildest kisses. To bare her throat, to let his fingers lather and untangle—it was more vulnerable than sex, and somehow, more tender.

Cristos massaged lavender-scented shampoo into her hair, and it was one of the most sensual moments of her life. By the time he rinsed her hair and helped her to dry off, she thought she would explode if he didn't take her soon. Aurelia did not bother with clothes. There was no need for modesty with him. She sat on the edge of the bed and watched as he shed his trousers and bathed, her desire ever increasing as she admired his muscular form.

As soon as Cristos finished drying off, he came over and eased her down on the bed. He pulled her forward until her hips reached the edge and spread her thighs, falling to his knees between them. He buried his handsome face between her legs, and she bit a pillow to stop from screaming as he finally drove her over the edge. By the time he sheathed himself inside her, the pillow hit the floor. When they came together, she couldn't care less if anyone heard their pleasure.

CHAPTER THIRTY-FIVE

Diapolis

Aurelia

Cristos' face was the first thing Aurelia saw when she opened her eyes, and it put a smile on her face. He lay sleeping on his back, one wing unfurled and the other tucked beneath him. Aurelia couldn't imagine trying to lie comfortably with wings, but he had clearly perfected the skill. One of his arms draped across her stomach while the other hung limply off the bed. His warmth enveloped her like a blanket, and the faint scent of spice and smoke that always surrounded him still lingered from the night before.

She watched him for several moments, admiring the view and hesitant to wake him. His long lashes rested like dark crescents against his cheek, and his lips parted slightly with each steady breath. When she finally attempted to slip out from under his arm, one brilliant oceanic eye popped open. Before she could fully slide off the bed, he tightened his arm and pulled her close again.

"Where are you sneaking off to?" His voice was raspy from sleep.

She grinned and brushed his black hair from his eyes. "I was just going into the bathing room. I'll be right back."

He released her, playfully smacking her bare backside as she scurried from the bed. She gasped and shot him a playful glare, though her stomach flipped at the sudden sting, before grabbing her clothes and heading into the bathing room.

They joined their companions in the tavern an hour later. The five of them were a sorry sight; one glance was all it took to know they had stayed up too late the night before. Aurelia hoped the bags under her eyes would fade before their audience with the king. She pinched her cheeks, trying to bring some color back to her lifeless complexion as she assessed the others.

The tavern itself was lively despite their sluggishness—low lanterns glowed in the rafters, smoke curled faintly from the hearth, and the sounds of mugs and cutlery clattered amid the murmur of voices. Holera's silver hair was disheveled, but she attempted to wrestle it into a rough braid as they sat down at the table. Kason, having consumed more whiskey than the rest, didn't even bother to button his shirt before coming down for breakfast, exposing his broad chest. Even Calista looked like she had stayed up late. However, her silky red hair and bright green eyes still exuded an enviable polish. Aurelia wondered what Calista had been up to and with whom. She knew Calista was beautiful—any of the unattached patrons in the tavern would have happily entertained the healer for the night. However, Aurelia didn't know her well enough to ask, but couldn't stifle her curiosity.

After a quick breakfast, the group set out. They didn't look much better after the meal, but at least Holera's hair was somewhat contained, and Kason was now fully dressed. The stable hand who greeted them immediately retrieved their horses. After reviewing the map and exchanging a few words with the barmaid, Kason informed them that they had a four-hour ride ahead before reaching the capital city.

According to Cristos, Embershell was situated on the southernmost coast and was said to be the most beautiful city in Ekotoria. A high wall separated Diapolis from the Undying Valley, a vast desert that consumed everything in its path. The king of Diapolis, Ailani, and his male consort, Makoa, ruled the kingdom. Although he didn't involve himself much in the affairs of other kingdoms, Aurelia had learned that he was equally indifferent about the inner workings of his border towns. Still, from what she'd heard around the tavern, the king was well-loved by his people.

They began the final leg of their journey under the palest blue sky Aurelia had ever seen. The temperature was warm enough to ride without cloaks, and she pushed her sleeves up to expose more skin to the brilliant sunlight. Wispy clouds drifted across the sky as they pressed on, bringing a refreshing breeze from the sea. Though they couldn't see the coast from the road, Aurelia could smell the salt in the air, indicating that it wasn't far away.

There had been no time for Aurelia to enjoy the sea since they crossed the portal. It was always too cold, too dangerous, or too far away. The villa where she was raised was set too far above the sea, and it was much too treacherous to reach, even if she could. She spent plenty of time in Vaekros longingly watching the waves crash against the rocky cliffs she'd called home. She hoped they would be able to visit the water while they were in Diapolis, even if just once, so she could feel the sand between her toes.

Cristos leaned forward, resting his chin on Aurelia's shoulder, effectively distracting her from her inner musings. She studied his face out of the corner of her eye. If Cristos was nervous about their visit, he didn't show it. His blue eyes glistened in the morning light as they rode, a smile playing at his lips. His fingers caressed her thigh—protective yet teasing—and she found herself wondering if he was recalling their night together. She blushed at the thought of how many times he had made her scream his name while—

"Have you ever been to Diapolis?" Aurelia blurted out, desperate to steer her thoughts in another direction.

He shook his head and sat up straight. "I haven't, but my father has... had. He used to tell me stories about it."

Aurelia noticed his smile falter as he spoke. "I'm sorry," she said, feeling guilty for bringing up his loss.

He leaned forward again and kissed her on the cheek. "For what?" His hand left her thigh and wrapped around her waist, squeezing gently. "What happened to him was not your fault, so there's nothing to apologize for." She leaned back against him, savoring the warmth of his presence. "Plus, I don't mind thinking of the good memories."

She felt his smile return as he pressed his cheek against hers and tightened his hold around her. Unsure of how to continue the conversation, Aurelia said the first thing that came to her mind. "I hope we get to go to the beach."

Cristos returned his hand to her thigh and chuckled. "Do you now? I think we can work that out."

A flutter of excitement filled her at the thought. Just her and her bare-chested fae enjoying the sea and sun sounded like the perfect day. For a moment, she felt as if there were no looming war overhead and that they were not on their way to Diapolis to beg the king for an alliance. They were simply a new couple planning an outing.

As they continued south, Aurelia envisioned their date. The dense evergreen forests of the north had disappeared, giving way to a mixture of oak and massive flowering shrubs. As they neared the coast, the plant life became even more distinct. The flowers grew larger and more vibrant than any she had ever seen, complementing the surrounding trees rather than overshadowing them. Sugarcane fields and fruit trees replaced the plains they had crossed upon entering Diapolis.

They took their last rest in the town of Armaday, where Aurelia had the chance to try a mango for the first time. It quickly became her new favorite fruit. She was sure she could eat mangoes every day without growing tired of them, though peeling them was a bit of a challenge.

However, the general mood among their party shifted as soon as they departed Armaday. A cloud of wary hesitance descended upon them, and the unease of her companions intensified her own sense of dread. No one knew what to expect from King Ailani, and that uncertainty weighed heavily on them. He could choose to align with them, or he could abandon them, making it nearly impossible to defeat Warbotach and protect both realms. The possibilities raced through her mind, varying from the mundane to the perilous—he could lock them in a dungeon as soon as they arrived or feed them to his dragons. Lost in a swirl of what-ifs, she finally caught sight of the colossal wall that enclosed the city of Embershell. Although she had known the protective barrier surrounded the town and extended along the western border of Diapolis, the sheer size of it astounded her. She craned her neck to gaze up at it as they approached, certain it nearly reached the clouds.

Aurelia hadn't expected a wall to keep nature at bay, yet she could see no signs of the expanding dead lands from where she sat.

As they reached the city's entrance, she nearly forgot the wall. Statues stood sentinel on either side of the road leading into the city, towering higher than the Norithaean palace, and she couldn't help but marvel at them.

On the left stood a beautiful female statue holding a large fish in her hands, but she had no legs; instead, the lower half of her body was a jewel-encrusted tail, like the fish she held. Her deep violet hair flowed elegantly, and her eyes sparkled like pure amethyst. Iridescent patches of color speckled her skin like scales, resulting in an enchanting effect.

On the right stood the statue of a male. He had legs, but that was the only ordinary aspect of the sculpture. A massive dragon perched atop his shoulders, its mouth open in a fierce snarl. The dragon, covered in emerald scales, glistened in the midday sun. The male's muscular arms extended dramatically into the distance, pointing toward the direction from which they had come. His hair was a vibrant bronze that rivaled the beauty of his sun-kissed skin.

Aurelia felt overwhelmed, unsure of where to look. Everything around her was bright and elaborate, as if the very stones radiated wealth and power. She closed her eyes and took a deep breath. "Wow," she whispered.

Cristos held her close and murmured in her ear, "The sight is almost as beautiful as you are." Her cheeks flushed, and it was only partly due to the sun.

Kason and Holera led the way, walking a dozen steps ahead of them. Suddenly, six men on horseback approached, blocking their path as they neared the gate. The thud of hooves on stone echoed like the drumbeats of a warning, and the bridles jingled with each shift of the riders' hands. Cristos stiffened behind her, his hand instinctively brushing the hilt of his weapon.

"What's happening?" she whispered.

Cristos leaned closer to her ear, his voice barely audible. "I think they're the welcoming committee."

Chapter Thirty-Six

Diapolis

Aurelia

The Diapolis welcoming committee, as Cristos called them, was like no males Aurelia had ever seen. Their tanned bodies were so sculpted they looked like they were carved from stone, muscles gleaming in the sunlight as if polished by the sea air. Just like the statues nearby, their skin bore scattered iridescent patches. The way the sunlight glanced off them sent a shimmer across their bronzed flesh, and Aurelia couldn't tell if the markings were tattoos, natural pigments, or something altogether otherworldly. Her curiosity burned, but she dared not ask.

They were all dressed in matching sleeveless tunics and loose-fitting trousers that reached their knees, with leather sandals wrapping up their muscled calves. Between the identical clothing, their synchronized posture, and the swords swinging at their belts, Aurelia assumed they were guards. Their stillness carried the weight of discipline, like predators waiting for the signal to strike.

Cristos guided their horse forward, pulling him to a stop as they reached Holera and Kason's side. Calista flanked the other side, and they stood as a united front before the blocked path. A guard with shoulder-length golden hair broke from the rank and approached them at a trot.

"King Ailani is expecting you." His accent was unlike any Aurelia had heard before. The words rolled off his tongue with a lyrical lilt, as if the sea itself had taught him how to speak. "I am Kimo, Captain of His Highness' Guard. I've been sent to escort you to the palace."

Kason nodded, slipping into the role of their leader, and followed as Kimo turned his horse and led them through the gate and into Embershell.

Cristos' hold on her remained firm as they silently trailed behind. The Elder Sea bordered two sides of the city, and its bright turquoise water sparkled in the sun to their right. That side of the road was nothing but sand, dotted with umbrellas and laughter. Beachgoers lay sprawled in the golden light, or else splashed in the surf, their carefree voices carried on the breeze. Aurelia envied them—their freedom, their laughter, their ability to bask without thought of war.

She tore her gaze away from the waves, stifling the ache of longing, and forced herself to study the left side of the road. It was lined with tidy storefronts, eateries with open shutters, and colorful stalls overflowing with fruit and woven fabrics. Patrons bustled in and out, their laughter and chatter blending with the clang of blacksmith hammers and the jingle of bells above shop doors. Aurelia had never seen such prosperity; the air itself seemed rich, humming with life.

As they continued on, the palace came into view. Its eight slender, round towers pierced the skyline like spears of light, each one banded with silver stone that glittered in the sun. Narrow walls, also of silver stone, connected the towers. Countless floor-length windows blazed with sunlight, reflecting the sea back in fragments of dazzling turquoise. Aurelia could only imagine how breathtaking the view must be from within. Effigies of past kings, carved with exquisite precision, stood vigil at the castle gates, their expressions solemn and timeless.

"This city is amazing," she whispered, trying to keep her voice low.

Cristos nodded and squeezed her waist in silent agreement.

Kimo slowed to a stop as they reached the castle's gates, his men halting a few paces behind him. An archer saluted from atop the wall before vanishing, and moments later, the enormous wooden gates creaked open, revealing the courtyard within.

A sudden, violent wind whipped Aurelia's hair across her face as a piercing squeal split the air. She resisted the instinct to cover her ears and tilted her head back.

Her breath left her in one sharp exhale.

A dragon.

Fierce jade eyes burned into her from above as massive wings churned the air. Its scales were the deep green of an ancient forest after rain, glistening as sunlight spilled across its body. It let out another shriek that rattled through her bones before banking toward the water, wings carving through the sky with terrifying grace.

Her companions craned their necks skyward, awe etched into every line of their faces. But the Diapolis guards barely reacted. Even the horses barely twitched. To them, this was routine, just another day in a kingdom where dragons soared overhead. To Aurelia, it was staggering, humbling—proof of how small and mortal she truly was.

The group passed into the courtyard, which curved toward a cluster of buildings within the palace grounds. Guards lined the walls, posted at every angle, their eyes sharp and watchful. Aurelia could feel the weight of their stares pressing down on her, cold and unrelenting, until her stomach twisted itself into knots.

When they finally reached the cluster of buildings, Kimo and the other guards dismounted, signaling for them to do the same. A boy no older than sixteen sprinted from a doorway and grabbed Kimo's reins. Cristos dismounted slowly, then looped an arm around Aurelia's waist to lift her down as though she weighed nothing.

Her boots touched the ground, but her nerves kept her unsteady. Kason dismounted next, scanning the courtyard warily. Aurelia could see the same unease reflected in his features that gripped her own chest. The Aegrician females climbed down on their own, every movement brimming with the confidence of warriors who knew their strength. Aurelia envied them deeply. Variel had told her she bore Aegrician blood, but standing among phoenixes and fae, she felt painfully human—pitifully frail. A little mackerel in a shark tank.

The memory of chains, of Norithae's cold dungeons and jeering guards, gnawed at her mind as they were ushered into the castle proper. She wasn't bound this time. She wasn't a prisoner. Yet her legs felt just as heavy as they carried her down a long marble corridor.

Cristos' hand closed around hers, their fingers entwined, his warmth steadying her trembling resolve. He knew. Of course, he knew. He could sense every shred of her fear.

They passed through a golden set of double doors and into a throne hall lit like fire. Great braziers ringed six marble columns, their flames casting waves of heat that licked against her skin. The light glimmered off mosaics of beasts—griffins, hydras, leviathans—etched in vivid color across the walls. Stained glass windows blazed with sunlight, scattering ruby and sapphire shards across the ivory floor.

A plush ivory rug stretched the length of the hall, leading them toward a throne that all but blazed in the sunlight. Its gold surface glinted so brightly that she had to squint; the engravings on its frame caught the light like molten metal. Yet the throne itself was not what stole her breath.

It was the man who occupied it.

King Ailani was the sun made flesh. Not rugged like Kason, nor sharp-edged like Cristos. No, he was beautiful in a way that was almost inhuman—gentle, radiant, effortless. Loose golden curls spilled down to his chest, shimmering with every shift of light. His turquoise eyes rivaled the sea itself, warm and endless. His silk jacket, dyed the deepest shade of eggplant, shimmered with dragons embroidered in threads of gold along each arm, paired with fitted black trousers that moved like liquid shadow. When he smiled, it was like the hall itself exhaled.

Beside him stood another man—dark-haired, raven strands sleek as ink, emerald eyes glittering like jewels set against sun-burnished skin. His tunic and trousers were darker still, hugging his lean figure. Where Ailani was sunlight, this man was nightfall, balanced and compelling in his own right.

Kimo bowed and retreated, leaving them exposed under the kings' twin gazes.

King Ailani's brow furrowed briefly, confusion clouding his features before his radiant smile returned. "When I received a raven from the Aegrician general, it said nothing about the king of Norithae visiting as well."

Aurelia's chest tightened. King? The word struck her wrong. The king of Norithae had been slaughtered when Warbotach seized the throne.

She felt Cristos stiffen at her side. His hand clamped tighter on hers, as if bracing for a blow.

"I am no king, Your Highness," Cristos said, bowing his head. His voice was steady, but she heard the faint strain at the edges.

King Ailani chuckled softly, shaking his head. "A king without a throne is still a king. You look just like your father. He was a great ruler, and an even better man."

Aurelia froze, her breath catching as her eyes snapped to Cristos.

He wouldn't look at her. His gaze stayed locked on the floor.

The dots connected like sparks catching flame. There was unease in his eyes whenever his past was brought up. The way he deflected questions. The weight of his grief. He hadn't told her.

Anger surged hot and sharp, mingling with a sick twist of betrayal. Her hand ripped itself free of his grasp before she even realized she'd moved.

She turned from him, fury and hurt clashing like storm tides in her veins, and crossed the aisle to stand beside Calista. Putting space between them was the only way she could breathe.

CHAPTER THIRTY-SEVEN

DIAPOLIS

AURELIA

King Ailani studied their group with a sharp eye that belied the carefree exuberance he projected. His gaze followed Aurelia as she stormed away from Cristos.

"Oh my. It appears you did not share your identity with the Aegricians after all."

Aurelia heard Cristos grinding his teeth before he spoke. "My lineage holds no importance in this war. All that matters is freeing Norithae and Aegricia from Warbotach's hold." His tone was amiable, but she could hear a tinge of bitterness in his words, the rasp of pain that cracked through his polished demeanor.

King Ailani rose from his throne, waving his hand dismissively, his golden curls glinting in the shafts of sunlight streaming through the tall stained-glass windows.

"Enough about war for now. Did you witness the statues that line the palace wall?"

Aurelia watched Cristos nod in her peripheral vision. Just a glimpse of his face reignited the anger burning in her chest. He knew everything about her—her heritage, her fears, her dreams—and she hadn't even known who he truly was. She could understand him not revealing his identity immediately, but there had been plenty of opportunities over the last few weeks: moments whispered in the firelight, in the quiet of bedrolls, when trust was laid bare.

They had grown so close, and now that felt fake to her. He was no longer her handsome winged lover; he was the king of Norithae.

Her eyes watered as she fixed her gaze on the Diapolis ruler. She wasn't sure if sadness or fury caused the tears, but she refused to let them fall. A small part of her wished she'd remained in the encampment with Septima and Kano, continuing to live in ignorant bliss, but it was far too late for that. It was better to know the truth, even if that truth shattered her heart. She had fallen for him, and all the while, he had lied and concealed things from her. She had no interest in being with a liar and knew it was better to cut ties now rather than risk having him destroy her heart later. That realization didn't lessen the pain.

"Those effigies are my family. Those statues—those men—were beloved rulers and symbols of hope for our people for centuries. Lineage holds far more importance than you can imagine, especially in times of unrest. You are not just the king of Norithae; you are the promise of a better future for your nation."

King Ailani's jovial tone turned passionate, and his eyes bore into Cristos as if he were trying to drill the words into the depths of Cristos's soul. The man standing beside the throne stepped forward and placed his hand on the king's shoulder as he addressed Aurelia and the others.

"It is growing late. You have all traveled far. Kimo will escort you to the guest chambers. Get cleaned up and rest. Servants will bring dinner for you. We can discuss the purpose of your visit tomorrow."

The king placed his hand atop the other man's, his intense gaze softening with affection as he looked at him. Aurelia's stomach pinched at the sight. She hoped Cristos would look at her with that kind of love in his eyes one day, and now that prospect felt dead. She envied the men and their happiness, the type of unwavering and unapologetic devotion they shared.

When the king turned back to them, the fire that burned in him as he lectured Cristos was gone. He smiled and nodded in agreement. "This is my consort, Makoa. He is a far more gracious host than I. Please rest, and we will continue our discussion tomorrow evening."

Kimo approached from the entrance and bowed to his rulers before gesturing for the group to follow. They trailed behind him in silence, and Aurelia stayed as far from Cristos as possible. She couldn't even enjoy the intricate décor of the palace they walked through—the marble mosaics that glittered like jewels, the painted domes overhead, or the lingering scent of incense. Her mind was still roiling from the revelation about Cristos's royal status. Kason and Holera marched on either side of her, helping her maintain the distance. She assumed they were also upset by his secrecy. Still, at that moment, she couldn't bring herself to care about anyone else's feelings. Her own emotions were far too overwhelming.

The captain of the guard came to a halt in the center of a long hall. Polished oak doors lined the walls, and torches illuminated the space. She could feel the warmth of their flames licking at her skin, but her heart remained too frigid to thaw.

"How many rooms do you require?" Kimo asked.

"Three," Cristos replied before anyone else had a chance to speak.

"Four," Aurelia snapped, venom filling her tone as she pointedly ignored the look her former lover gave her.

"Aure—"

Kason interrupted him, confirming that they needed four rooms.

Kimo shifted uncomfortably as he showed them to their chambers. Based on his size and physique, Aurelia was sure he was an excellent warrior, but he seemed at a loss when it came to dealing with the tension in her traveling party. He nodded awkwardly and informed them that servants would bring dinner within the hour before leaving immediately.

As soon as they were alone, Kason whirled on Cristos. "You had no right to hide this from us. Your title changes everything. We could have requested more aid, knowing the whole of Norithae would back you as their king. Instead, our general planned our negotiations around the belief that you were just a warrior who could gather an average number of soldiers to fight."

Cristos' eyes hardened as he stepped forward. "I told you my people were ready to fight and were only waiting for an opportunity. Never did I say it was only a fraction of my people. It is not my fault you drew your own conclusions."

Kason growled low in his throat, but Holera placed a hand on his arm. "This isn't the time nor the place. We need to write to Blaedia."

He nodded and shot Cristos another glare before claiming the chamber nearest him. Holera followed him as Calista entered a room across the hall.

Aurelia hesitated at the rapidly emptying passage, unprepared to be left alone with Cristos. She darted to the nearest door, trying to escape, but he grabbed her forearm before she could retreat.

"Please, talk to me."

His pleading tone felt like a knife in her chest. She felt torn in two directions. Half of her wanted to listen to him, to understand why he'd concealed his identity; the other half wanted to rage at him for lying. Regardless of which side won out, she knew she would have to hear him out. She yanked her arm out of his grasp and gave a single nod before entering the room. She left the door open—this was the only invitation he would receive from her.

The guest chambers were massive. Floor-to-ceiling windows lined the far wall, allowing the sun's dying rays to bathe the room. A four-poster bed occupied a large portion of the space, its size rivaling the one she had in Vaekros, which comfortably fit her, Kano, and Septima. An ivory down comforter and pillows covered the mattress, and she admired the hand-carved frame. Intricate swirls decorated the posts, and the footboard depicted a fish-tailed female with a serene expression. Aurelia longed to feel the same tranquility the woman expressed, but her emotions continued to swirl violently within her.

She turned her attention to the left and spotted an unlit fireplace. Two armchairs faced it, with a small table between them. She took a seat in one of the ivory chairs, absentmindedly noting that the color seemed quite popular in Diapolis. Glaring at Cristos, who sat opposite her, she observed his dejected demeanor as he leaned forward, his head hung low, his arms resting on his knees.

His melancholy angered her. How dare he act as if he were the one who had been wronged?

"How can I help you, Your Highness?" she asked.

He flinched. She wasn't sure if it was due to the ire in her tone or the title, but she was glad it affected him either way. Lashing out at him helped to bury some of the hurt that threatened to overwhelm her.

"Please, Aurelia, don't be angry. I didn't tell you at first because I wasn't sure if I could trust you. Once I knew you were truly on my side, there never seemed to be a good time to tell you," he replied, his ocean-blue eyes dull as they gazed up at her.

"Never a good time? What about when we talked about your father visiting Diapolis before?"

"What was I supposed to say? 'Oh, well, I've never been, but my father visited frequently to negotiate trades. The work of a king is never done'?"

His sarcasm grated on her nerves. Her nostrils flared as she exhaled angrily and jumped to her feet.

"That would have been better than lying to me. I shared my bed with you. I shared my body with you. All you offered were half-truths. There is nothing about me that you don't know. I kept nothing from you, yet you hid something so significant from me."

His expression shifted as he responded to her harsh tone, shooting up from his seat. He shoved the small table aside with his foot, his wings twitching behind him as he stepped into her space. Both their chests heaved as they glared at each other.

"I did not lie to you. I told you about my parents and how I feel about you. Yes, I hid the fact that I am the new king, but I never lied. My father was just murdered. I still don't feel worthy of the title."

His superior height fueled her already fiery temper. She refused to back down as he crowded her.

"Concealing the truth is just a polished way to disguise a lie. Even if you're not ready to claim the title, you were still the prince, and you said nothing about that either. Even when asked if the prince still lived! You dared to talk about our future together while knowing you'd return to rule Norithae after the war. We have no future anymore."

Pain filled his features as he took a step back, as if she had struck him. Regret tinged her anger, but she stood by her words; they were true. He would return to Norithae, and she would travel across Ekotoria with Septima until they found a place to call home.

"Aurelia," his voice was small, his morose eyes staring at her. "Is that truly how you feel? That we have no future together?"

His question stole the wind from her sails. She slumped back into the armchair and buried her face in her hands. "I do not know anymore. You have a responsibility to your people."

He kneeled in front of her, gently wrapping his fingers around her wrists as he pulled them away to gaze into her eyes. "I have a responsibility to you, too. Why can you not join me in Norithae?"

She snorted derisively. "Ah, yes. That sounds lovely. The king's human lover is not an appealing title."

"You're not solely human, Aurelia, and even if you were, I would not care. Your lineage means nothing to me. Only you do, and I care for you far more than just as a simple lover. Why is my title so important to you?"

Her anger flared again. She pulled her hands from his grasp and stood, pacing around the room. "Because you lied, Cristos. You lied, and you let me foolishly fall for you. It's not as if we can live happily ever after together. You are the king."

"Then be my queen."

"You are being ridiculous."

"I do not know how else to get through to you. We have not known each other for long, but you are the most important person in my life. If you cannot forgive me, then I will live with that regret for the rest of my life, but I will not beg for forgiveness. I kept my position a secret to protect the interests of my people. What if the Aegricians sacrificed me to Warbotach to form a treaty?"

"They would never do that."

"And how was I supposed to know that at first? There are so many lives that depend on me. I have to be cautious."

Aurelia stared at him, betrayal clear in her eyes. "Fine. Let us say I understand why you did not confide in Blaedia, but why did you not trust me?"

He sighed and stood, walking over to her. "I do trust you. There was never a good time, and I did not want to burden you with the knowledge. How would you have felt if you had to hide the truth from Blaedia? From Exie? From Septima?"

His words made her recoil as if he had slapped her. "Was it never a good time? Or are you going to insist you lied for my own good? Make up your mind."

He groaned, throwing his hands in the air. "You are the most frustrating creature I've ever met. Both. The answer is both. I couldn't find the right time to tell you, and I didn't want to cause you unnecessary stress. I just want to make you happy."

"Well, Your Highness, that is not how reality works."

"Stop calling me that."

"Would you prefer King Cristos?"

"Aurelia." He growled her name, and even in her angry state, the sound sent a shiver down her spine.

"Yes, King Cristos?" They both leaned in, fire in their eyes.

"What will it take for you to believe me? I must take care of my people, but I want a future with you. I am sorry that I did not confide in you of my own accord, but the truth is out there now, and I cannot change the past."

"If you ever lie or hide things from me, I will not forgive you again."

His eyes brightened, a cautious optimism filling his features. "Does that mean you forgive me now?"

"No. I have not forgiven you yet."

His face fell at her words, but she grabbed his tunic and yanked his face to hers before the sad look could color his expression. The kiss was hard and passionate as they poured everything into it. Their tongues wrestled for dominance. Aurelia channeled her hurt and anger into the kiss, amplifying her desire. She hoped he could taste her bitterness.

She tangled her fingers in his hair and pulled at the strands as she leaped up. He caught her, his fingers digging into her backside as she wrapped her legs around his waist. A moment later, her back slammed into the wall beside the bed, and he rubbed his hard length against the junction between her legs. She threw her head back and moaned at the sensations that zipped through her entire body.

Cristos' mouth descended on her exposed neck, his teeth biting into the sensitive flesh before he sucked roughly. Her pulse quickened as she rolled her hips against him. The clothing that separated them was a frustrating barrier, and she pulled at his tunic while he ripped the fabric of her trousers, tearing them from her body.

Aurelia slid her hands between them and pulled at his trousers' fastening before she shoved them down to his thighs. They were both feverish in their movements, and as soon as Cristos' stiff cock sprang free from its leather confines, he slammed into her. She arched her back as she screamed in pleasure. His thrusts were punishing, but she met each powerful stroke as she braced her hands on his shoulders. The anger that consumed her from the moment she'd found out about his secret fed into the force of her movements. He pulled out of her and set her on her feet.

"Wha—"

Before she could finish a word, Cristos spun her around and placed his palm between her shoulder blades. He pushed gently and bent her over the bed, her chest flat against the mattress. She looked back at him, watching as he widened her stance. He held her gaze as he slammed into her once more from behind, and Aurelia's legs buckled beneath her.

Aurelia soaked in an oversized clawfoot tub with Cristos behind her, his arms wrapped around her. They had spent the better part of the night and most of the morning releasing their pent-up emotions, leaving a delightful ache between her legs. They hadn't talked much, but Aurelia had made a conscious decision to forgive him. Until the war was over, she would savor her time with him. She knew her heart would shatter into a million pieces when he ascended the throne and left her behind in Aegricia, but she realized it was too late to turn back now. Although she hadn't said it aloud, she knew she loved him. Whether she rejected him now or lost him after the war, she would still feel pain. At least they could create more memories together before then.

"Why are you so sad?" Cristos asked, sniffing the air.

"Stop doing that."

"I can't control what I smell."

"Then stop breathing."

Cristos snorted and leaned forward, kissing her shoulder. He trailed his nose along her skin until he reached her ear and whispered, "But your scent is intoxicating."

His fingers slipped beneath the water, trailing over her legs as he reached between her thighs. He brushed against her, but a knock on the bathing chamber door interrupted them. Aurelia slouched down in the water, hiding her breasts below the surface as she called out. The heavy oak door cracked open, and Leinani, the servant charged with delivering their meals since last night, peeked inside.

"His Highness was unsure if you two had appropriate clothes for a royal party, so he sent some just in case. I'll hang them in the armoire." She glanced down at the couple awkwardly, then quickly looked up. "They should fit."

Cristos caught Aurelia's eye and raised an eyebrow before turning to the servant. "Please pass along our thanks."

Leinani flushed under Cristos's gaze, bowed, and then closed the door.

Aurelia chuckled and rolled her eyes as she leaned back against her lover.

"What?" he asked, twirling the ends of her hair.

"It's like Dewdrop all over again. Females are weak when it comes to you."

He chuckled and pressed a kiss to her cheek as he poured soap onto a cloth. "It doesn't matter. You're the only one for me."

"How quickly you forget your sprite harem."

His deep laughter made her back vibrate as he pulled her arm from the water and began to wash her skin. "Well, you said you do not share, so I had to disband the harem."

They finished their bath and continued to banter back and forth with each other. His title still weighed heavily on Aurelia, but they both carefully avoided broaching the subject. She exited the bathing chamber first and headed for the armoire as soon as she entered the bedroom.

Throwing the heavy wooden doors open, Aurelia gasped the moment she laid eyes on the dress King Ailani had provided. A stunning emerald gown spilled out before her. The silken bodice sparkled as the room's light fell across it. It was sleeveless, with a flowing chiffon skirt.

Aurelia ran her hands over the fabric and smiled. The shimmering masterpiece was unlike any party dress she had worn in Vaekros, and she was excited to wear it. The upcoming gathering made her nervous, but as she caressed her luxurious attire, she felt certain she could handle Diapolis' high society. A small, anxious voice in her mind whispered that she was just an average human playing dress-up, but she pushed that thought away. Ekotoria would fracture, and the human world would crumble beneath the weight of Warbotach if they failed in their mission. Doubt had no place within her—not when the stakes were this high.

"Do you like it?" Cristos' voice interrupted her thoughts. She lifted the trim that had escaped the armoire back inside and closed it before turning to him. His wet hair dripped, leaving trails of water over his defined torso. Her eyes fixed on the deep V of his waist, interrupted only by the plush ivory towel hanging low on his hips. She swallowed hard and averted her gaze, wondering when the effect he had on her would lessen in intensity.

"I like it very much," she replied, sitting at the vanity in the corner to dry her hair. The emerald gown would be her chainmail for the evening, and the cosmetics laid out in front of her would serve as her war paint. Convincing King Ailani to come to their aid was a different kind of battle, one that required intellectual weapons to win. The better she looked, the more confident she would feel, and that could make all the difference.

"I look forward to seeing you wear it."

"I'm sure you will steal all the attention. I can hear hearts breaking already."

Cristos snorted. "We shall see, won't we? I hope the tailor took my wings into account, or I'll be going in trousers." Aurelia was sure no one would mind too much, but it was probably best if the king of Norithae did not show up half-naked.

Her stomach flipped uncomfortably at the thought of his title. She was trying to accept it, but it bothered her far more than learning about her own royal status had. Yes, she was technically a princess, but she did not feel like one. Besides, outside of a few Aegricians, Variel, and Cristos, none of the fae knew her true lineage, so it was easier to ignore. However, her lover had a throne waiting for him to claim, and that concept was something she struggled with.

Aurelia watched Cristos's reflection in the looking glass and noticed his smile falter as her emotions fluctuated. She often wished he did not have the ability to sense her unsteady feelings.

He pasted a forced smile on his face as he held her gaze. "We still have some time before we need to get ready. Would you like to visit the beach?"

Aurelia beamed at the suggestion and agreed instantly. She quickly plaited her wet hair and pulled on a simple tunic and trousers. Cristos was ready before her, and as soon as she slipped on her boots, they left the guest chambers.

The palace corridors were bustling with servants rushing about, no doubt preparing for the night's events. With people darting in and out, it didn't take Aurelia and Cristos long to find the courtyard. The sun hung high above them, and a cool breeze blew in from the sea. The smell of saltwater filled her senses as the wind ruffled the little hairs that had escaped her braid.

The guards patrolling the area didn't stare as they approached the palace gates, which was a welcome change from their arrival. The gate guard gave a quick nod in greeting and let them pass. As they headed down the main road toward the sea, Aurelia hoped they would be allowed re-entry upon their return.

The brilliant turquoise water crashed in stunning waves against the pale, golden sand. The contrast was intense yet complementary. Cristos slipped off his shoes, and Aurelia quickly followed suit before they crossed the road, hand in hand. The warm sand between her toes mixed with the scent of saltwater, creating the perfect combination of tranquility.

Aurelia closed her eyes and tilted her head back to bask in the warmth of the sun's rays. She was reminded of the summer trips her family took to the eastern coast of Vaekros. Lowering her gaze to the water, she pushed aside the happy memories, realizing how much she missed her siblings. Nothing good would come from dwelling on experiences she could never repeat.

She watched the waves crest and crash over a shipwreck just off the shoreline, admiring the rippling effect that danced across the surface. Cristos rubbed the back of Aurelia's hand with his thumb, tightening his hold when she nearly lost her footing as they neared the water. They sat in the sand, just out of reach of the tide, and everything felt perfect in that moment.

"It's beautiful," he said, wrapping his arm around her waist and pulling her close. She nodded and leaned her head against him.

"I could get used to this view. It almost makes me forget the war."

She smiled as she watched a mother, father, and their two young sons splashing about in the sea. What she wouldn't give to have a happy family like that one day. The youngest child splashed his feet once, then twice, and then Aurelia gasped.

"Cristos, look! He has a tail!"

Cristos chuckled at her enthusiastic surprise and kissed her cheek. "Most Diapolisians can shift forms to live in the water."

Her grin was so broad that her cheeks ached as she continued to watch the child. His expression was pure joy as he used his tiny tail to splash his family, who laughed good-naturedly at his antics. It was a beautiful moment, and she felt fortunate to have witnessed it.

With the lovely Diapolisian family playing before them and the massive dragons flying overhead, Aurelia snuggled into Cristos's side and enjoyed a slight reprieve from the horrors their future held.

CHAPTER THIRTY-EIGHT

DIAPOLIS

AURELIA

They returned to the palace after two hours. Aurelia would have loved to remain on the beach until sunset, to watch the golden fire sink into the sea while Cristos' hand remained twined with hers, but duty tugged at them like an anchor. They needed to prepare for their evening with the king.

The cool hush of the marble corridor enveloped them as they climbed the sweeping staircase. The scent of salt still clung to her hair, but the air here was perfumed with lilies and smoke from oil lamps. Her sandals whispered against the polished stone, and she might have let herself be lulled by the rhythm—if not for the shadow leaning in the doorway ahead.

Kason stood there.

He looked as if he were carved from the same stone as the pillars flanking him, with broad shoulders rigid and arms crossed. Aurelia stopped short, her fingers tightening nervously around Cristos'. The Aegrician had been as furious about Cristos' secret as she was, and she feared a confrontation was brewing. They had to be on their best behavior while trying to secure the alliance, but her worries turned out to be unnecessary.

"Holera and Calista are waiting for you inside," Kason said, jerking his chin toward his chambers. His voice was steady, no longer brimming with the anger that had crackled last night. "Holera brought your dress over. They want to get ready for the party together."

Aurelia smiled with relief, though her eyes darted to Cristos and then back to Kason. "Where will you get ready if we're taking over your room?"

"We'll dress in your chambers. Holera put my dress clothes in there already." Kason scratched the back of his neck, an awkwardness softening his usually hard features. "Besides, I believe Cristos and I need to talk."

His tone was now devoid of hostility, almost sheepish. Aurelia's lips twitched as a laugh bubbled in her throat at Holera's clever machinations. It would be best for the men to make amends, but the way the phoenix orchestrated it—leaving them little choice—was almost comical.

Cristos kissed Aurelia's forehead before watching her slip into the women's company, then he followed Kason into their chambers.

Holera's lips curled into a mischievous grin as she peered over Aurelia's head, watching the two men disappear behind the heavy oak door. "Perfect," she murmured, satisfaction gleaming in her silver eyes.

Moments later, a polite knock sounded. Calista let Leinani and Akela into the chambers. The two palace servants carried armfuls of supplies, their dark hair bound up in jeweled combs, their hands deft and assured. King Ailani had sent them to arrange hair and cosmetics before the women donned their dresses.

The air quickly filled with the scents of crushed flowers and fragrant oils. Aurelia was painted, poked, and prodded into perfection. The easy atmosphere reminded her of the evenings she had once prepared for elaborate Vaekrosan balls, when she and Septima giggled and stole each other's rouge and hairpins. The memory struck her heart with a bittersweet pang—how she wished her sister were here.

Hours later, when they finally stood before the massive looking glass, the transformation was complete. Diapolis' tropical culture seemed woven into their very beings. Holera's long silver braid was laced with fresh white hibiscus blossoms, Calista's fiery hair gleamed with pearl pins, and a delicate dolphin-shaped pendant glittered against the healer's collarbone.

The Aegrician women were stunning, but Aurelia's gaze kept drifting back to her own reflection, hardly able to reconcile the painted stranger with herself. Her heavily lined eyelids smoldered darkly, making her blue eyes blaze like a clear midnight sky. Her lips, stained with the juice of native berries, looked lush and ripe. Her crimson hair had been tamed into shining curls that spilled down her bare back.

And then—the gown.

The emerald dress King Ailani had gifted her fit as if it had been conjured for her alone. One shoulder was bare, the other fastened by a jeweled brooch shaped like a dragon; the bodice clung to her like green fire. The skirt spilled into an airy chiffon, whispering when she moved. But it wasn't the crystalline beast nor the gown's perfection that held her frozen—it was the circlet now adorning her hair.

Emeralds and seashells twined in an intricate design, cradling a luminous pearl at its heart—a tiara in everything but name. For the first time, Aurelia truly felt like a princess.

The joy was tempered by a hollow ache. The only thing missing was Exie and Septima. Her sister's laughter would have echoed through the chamber, bright and brash, while Exie's irreverent antics would have charmed even the most stoic Diapolisians. No celebration would be complete without them. Aurelia imagined Exie commandeering the band, belting out bawdy tavern tunes until even the king's consort joined in. The thought brought a soft smile to her painted lips.

Together, the three women swept into the corridor. Kason and Cristos waited at the far end. Kason's eyes widened the instant Holera emerged, her cobalt gown shimmering with a cinched waist that emphasized her impossible curves. Aurelia hardly caught a glimpse of his suit before he strode forward in two steps and kissed Holera breathless. She quickly turned away, heat rising in her cheeks, and found Calista at her side, radiant in her cherry-red gown, crowned with white blossoms. Surely, the healer would draw more than a few hungry stares when they joined the revelry.

But then—Cristos. Her breath caught. His obsidian suit was tailored to perfection, sharp as a blade, yet softened by the way it fit his broad frame. His leathery wings arched like black satin, making the blue of his eyes almost unearthly. He looked magnificent—terrifying and beautiful all at once. He crossed to her, his smile radiant, and his gaze roamed her body from jeweled crown to sandaled feet.

His hand cupped her face, warmth spilling through his palm. The world fell away as his lips pressed against hers, and she scarcely noticed when their companions disappeared down the hall.

"You look wonderful," he murmured.

She managed to return the compliment as they moved through the labyrinthine palace, her arm linked through his. His palm pressed into the small of her back—a gentlemanly gesture to any onlookers—but the heat of his hand against her bare skin told her the truth. He was teasing her deliberately, and her pulse quickened with each subtle caress.

When his hand slid lower to cup her bottom, she playfully smacked his stomach. He grunted obligingly, though she knew the blow hardly registered. She rolled her eyes and tightened her arm around his.

"Are Norithaean males not taught to behave like gentlemen?"

Cristos barked out a laugh before brushing his lips against her temple, careful not to disturb the seashell circlet. "Apologies, my lady. It is easy to forget oneself when in such ravishing company."

Her giggle caught in her throat as the ballroom doors swung open.

The opulence nearly blinded her. Crystal chandeliers blazed above, their light refracted through pendants until the entire hall shimmered like a starfield. Tall white candles in golden sconces lent a warm, romantic glow. King Ailani sat at the head of a vast dining table, Makoa beside him, their heads bent together in easy conversation. Holera, Kason, and Calista were already seated.

Cristos guided her forward, pulling out her chair with courtly grace before taking his place between her and the king. Servants glided in like shadows, setting flutes of champagne before them.

To her surprise, King Ailani raised his glass in salute, clinking gently against his consort's. His turquoise eyes gleamed with an unreadable expression. Aurelia's chest swelled at the sight of their shared adoration. In her own world, kings did not marry men and could not rule beside their chosen loves. Ekotoria was different—freer—and the thought filled her with quiet hope. If a ruler could love whom he pleased, then perhaps her sister Septima, too, could live without fear.

Dinner was served almost immediately, an intoxicating feast spread across crystalline platters: grilled fish brushed with citrus, jewel-bright fruits, vegetables roasted to a caramelized perfection, and shellfish glistening with butter and herbs. Aurelia's mouth watered as the scents mingled, so rich and strange that she almost forgot her unease.

They waited as the king served himself first, then filled their own plates. Minutes later, Cristos cleared his throat, drawing every eye.

"Since you are well aware of the reason behind our visit, we should discuss it."

The king dabbed delicately at his mouth, a golden brow arching. "Are we discussing my potential support in the war against Warbotach?"

Cristos inclined his head. "You have a history of remaining neutral, which I have always found admirable. However, Warbotach's invasions and their desire to cross into human lands affect us all."

King Ailani's expression remained serene, but his words were as sharp as glass. "It affects all of you, yes—but it has no impact on us. If Uldon wanted my territory, he would have come here instead of heading north, but he did not. He bypassed Diapolis in his hunger for the portal and the crown that controls it."

Cristos leaned forward, his voice tight but steady. "Just because he has not set his sights on you yet does not mean he will not. If he fails to breach the arch, who can predict what chaos he will unleash here? His land is dying, and he will not stop until he has claimed every inch of prosperity left in Ekotoria. With the aid of your warriors—and your dragons—he does not stand a chance. Please, help us defeat him once and for all."

The king's gaze flicked toward Aurelia, then back to Cristos. His expression was calm, but the coldness beneath it pierced her like a blade. "If I prematurely thrust this war upon my people, what is to stop you from requesting my aid in future conflicts? Neutrality keeps us safe. If I change my stance now, it will be expected again in the future. That, I cannot commit to."

Cristos dragged a hand down his face, fury simmering beneath his restraint. "Hundreds, perhaps thousands, are already dead. Norithae and Aegricia are lost. If Uldon breaches the human world, millions more will fall. He already controls more than two-thirds of this continent. Do you truly believe he will leave you in peace if trapped here? If you watch and do nothing, then the blood of countless fae and humans will stain your hands—or your own blood will flow in these 'neutral' streets."

A sharp crack split the silence. It was only the king's fist tightening around his goblet, but the anger blazing in his eyes was unmistakable. Aurelia's pulse raced as she grasped Cristos's hand beneath the table, silently begging him not to push further.

Makoa's calm touch on the king's hand smoothed the tension like water over fire. Ailani took a deep breath, the mask of charm slipping back into place. His smile returned, though it was thin as a blade. "I will give it thought. I may not reach a decision before you leave tomorrow, but I will consider it. You have my word. For now, enjoy the party. The path you travel is long, and who knows when you may have such pleasures again?"

Conversation died like a candle snuffed out. Servants moved with mechanical grace, clearing the feast away. Aurelia's heart ached as she looked at Cristos—his shoulders rigid, his gaze fixed on his plate, and his hand clenching hers so tightly it almost hurt. The weight of grief, of a kingdom lost and a father slain, seemed carved into every line of his face. Guilt gnawed at her; she had only deepened that burden with her anger the night before.

Then the music began.

The chandeliers dimmed, and a five-piece band filled the air with bright, lilting melodies she had never heard before, songs flavored by the sea and sun of Diapolis. The rhythms were infectious, drawing smiles even from strangers.

Cristos rose and offered his hand. She blinked, startled that he would dance after such a fraught exchange, but her heart leapt all the same. Dancing was something she had always loved, a secret indulgence she once shared with Septima in their Vaekrosan chambers. She slipped her hand into his, and he swept her into motion with surprising grace.

He led her in a flawless waltz, spinning her effortlessly beneath the golden glow. The strength in his arms and the way he looked at her, as if she were the only soul in the room, made her heart tremble.

Holera and Kason joined them, gliding past. Kason leaned toward Cristos with a wolfish grin. "Blood flowing through his neutral streets, eh? That line will echo in his head all night. Good one."

Cristos' mouth twitched into the shadow of a smile, though the couple had already drifted away. Aurelia flushed as she observed the way they moved together, sensual even in their innocence.

Nearby, Calista floated across the floor in Kimo's arms, the captain of the guard gazing at her as if she were the only flame in the room. Aurelia grinned at the sight and then lifted her eyes back to Cristos. For one night, she decided she would forget diplomacy and politics. There was nothing more to be done; the king would decide in his own time.

So, she danced.

They all danced, twirling for hours, laughter and champagne sparkling in the air until Aurelia's feet ached and her head spun. By the time Cristos carried her from the ballroom—after she nearly stumbled into a blazing sconce—the palace halls had emptied.

He tried to help her undress, but she twirled away from him, still humming the melody as though the music clung to her bones.

"Aurelia, hold still. Let me help you into your nightdress and wash your face."

"No," she declared, spinning again, her skirt flaring and the jeweled brooch glinting in the candlelight.

He groaned, reaching for her. "We leave tomorrow. You need rest. Please, just let me—"

She stopped short, unfastening the brooch at her shoulder. The bodice peeled away, baring her flushed skin beneath, and pooled at her waist. She cocked her head, a wicked smile curling her berry-stained lips.

"Satisfied?"

Cristos' eyes darkened, his wings twitching as hunger swept across his face.

"Very," he rasped, reaching for her again. Even in her wine-softened haze, Aurelia knew that sleep was no longer the night's priority.

CHAPTER THIRTY-NINE

DIAPOLIS

AURELIA

Aurelia's head throbbed painfully as her traveling party prepared to take to the sky the next morning. The sun had just begun to rise, its meager light forcing her to squint. She deeply regretted her overindulgence; the champagne had been delightful, but the hangover was excruciating. Her stomach churned dangerously as Cristos lifted her and cradled her in his arms. While she dreaded the flight, she was relieved that they were leaving their horses in Diapolis. The uneven road and the bumpy ride would have been unbearable for her.

The mood was somber as Holera's mighty wings cut through the air, leading the way with Kason riding on her back. King Ailani had promised to consider their request, but both he and his consort were absent as they departed. Aurelia found his lack of farewell to be a foreboding sign. She gazed over Cristos's shoulder, watching as the palace shrank into the distance. Her hope diminished as the structure disappeared. Despite his reputation, she thought he would help them in their desperate plight, if only to protect the future of his kingdom. If Cristos's passionate speech at dinner hadn't swayed Ailani's stance, she didn't believe anything could.

They traveled hard throughout the day, stopping only briefly to relieve themselves. They reached Claywind just as the sun set over the distant hills. If they maintained their grueling pace, they would arrive at their camp the following day. She felt guilty for Cristos and Holera; at least Calista could fly without hindrance, but Aurelia and Kason were helpless in the air. She wondered if it bothered the Aegrician male as much as it upset her.

They stopped at the same inn they had visited on their way to the capital, and Kason purchased three rooms for the night. They dined in the tavern before retreating to their chambers. The optimism that had filled them during their first visit had been replaced by a sense of defeat, and no one seemed to have the energy for drinks or lighthearted conversation as they had last time.

The gloomy atmosphere followed Aurelia and Cristos to their room. He prepared her bath in silence as soon as they entered, sitting on the floor of the bathing chamber while she washed up. The heavy sense of dread stole away the joy that soaking in hot water usually brought her. She finished quickly and climbed out.

Cristos bathed while she pulled on her nightdress and braided her hair. The pair climbed into bed shortly after and held each other in the dimly lit room. They avoided discussing King Ailani and the war, leaving little else to talk about. Diapolis' indecision heightened the likelihood of their failure, and it was hard to dwell on anything else.

A small, wistful part of her hoped that a raven would beat them back to camp carrying a promise of aid, but she knew that was unrealistic. Still, the thought of informing Blaedia that they had not secured additional forces was far from appealing.

Her disheartened spirit drained the life from her body, and exhaustion consumed her. She stared at the dark ceiling for hours, listening to Cristos' steady breathing, before unconsciousness eventually pulled her under, relieving her of the burden of failure.

A piercing scream ripped Aurelia from her dreamless sleep. She shot up in bed, her heart pounding, and whipped her head from side to side in an attempt to identify the source of the noise. The extinguished candles and a small strip of moonlight peeking through the curtained window did little to illuminate their room.

Cristos was already out of bed, fastening his trousers, before she realized that the shouts continuing to shatter the silence of the night were coming from the streets below.

"Something's wrong. Get dressed. Quickly." The urgency in his tone spurred her into action. Her hands trembled as she pulled on her fighting leathers. He had already strapped on all his weapons by the time she laced her boots.

Frantic thumps sounded at their door as Holera yelled over the chaos below, "Warbotach soldiers are attacking! Get outside now!"

Aurelia's blood ran cold at her words. She froze, eyes wide, as she watched Cristos grab her bow and quiver.

"Hurry!" he shouted, yanking the door open and dashing into the hall. She rushed after him, but stuttered to a stop when she caught sight of the expressions on her friends' faces as they waited in the hall—grim, sharp with purpose, their faces carved by firelight. They hastened down the stairs, shoving past patrons who darted about, trying to gather their belongings and flee the establishment while they still could. A woman clutched a crying child, another dragged a drunken husband half-awake by his arm, and a boy screamed for a lost dog. The inn had become a funnel of panic, and Aurelia nearly lost her footing as she pressed forward with her companions.

When they finally pushed their way through the tavern exit, they saw a dozen Warbotach soldiers mounted on scarlet horses. They galloped toward the inn, fire spewing from the crimson beasts' mouths, setting the town ablaze in their wake. Men, women, and children stumbled through the streets as the raging inferno forced them from the safety of their homes. Some civilians wielded weapons to defend their city, while others fled across the open fields bordering the town, desperately attempting to vanish within the tree line of Spectre Forest.

"Their horses breathe fire!" Aurelia gasped. The terrified faces and pain-filled screams of those falling victim to the Warbotach overwhelmed her senses. She focused on her heartbeats, willing herself not to cry amid the devastation surrounding her. The peaceful town of Claywind was unrecognizable as flames and chaos reigned.

Cristos thrust her bow and quiver into her hands. "Kill as many as you can and keep your distance. Stay safe, love." He kissed her hard and quick, disappearing before she could reply. The endearment felt far too much like a goodbye. She watched as he drew his long sword and charged the nearest Warbotach beast.

Fear like she'd never known consumed her when the horse reared back and unleashed flames the moment Cristos tried to dismount its master. She held her breath as he leaped into the air to avoid the blast, his sword catching the firelight like lightning.

Kason's expression hardened as he began barking commands. "Calista, warn King Ailani. Go!"

Without a word, Calista erupted into flames and shifted into her Phoenix form. Her massive wings kicked up dust and debris as she took off toward Embershell.

"Aurelia, Holera! Get to a higher place with a better vantage point."

Holera darted around the back of the tavern at his command. Aurelia ran after her, glancing back to see Kason, sword in hand, join Cristos, who was single-handedly battling three Warbotach soldiers.

She felt more at ease letting him out of her sight, knowing he had backup now. Holera had already climbed onto the roof using a cart parked alongside the inn. She reached down to help Aurelia up, knowing her shorter frame made the ascent impossible alone.

They ran along the rooftop until they reached the edge. Both notched arrows as they stared at the horror unfolding below. The blazing buildings illuminated the street, and Aurelia scanned the chaos for a target. Her heart stopped as she saw an enemy sword arching through the air toward Cristos' neck.

Afraid to distract him from the incoming threat, Aurelia bit back a scream and froze in horrified silence as time seemed to slow. The wicked blade gleamed in the firelight as she focused on her lover. Cristos ducked the swing at the last second and thrust his long sword upward. She watched as the weapon pierced the abdomen of the Warbotach soldier. The beast-like man collapsed against Cristos as the blade exited his back. Cristos pulled his sword free and threw the corpse to the ground just as another enemy bellowed in the distance and charged at him.

Holera elbowed Aurelia roughly to get her attention. "Focus, Aurelia. Aim for the ones still atop their horses, and then take down the fire-breathing beasts. Our men can handle those already on foot. Be careful not to hit anyone on our side; there are a lot of Diapolisians down there."

Aurelia nodded and took a breath to steady herself. She pulled back the string on her bow and exhaled as she launched an arrow at one of the mounted soldiers in the distance. Her trembling hands threw off her aim, and she missed.

"Damn it," she hissed, notching another arrow. Holera shot next and hit the same soldier in the eye. "Got him."

Aurelia had only ever shot animals, which had always filled her with guilt. How was she supposed to kill a person? She warred with herself internally as she tried to steel her nerves. Pulling the bowstring taut again, she scanned for another target.

All doubt about harming someone vanished when she saw a Warbotach soldier galloping toward a lone child in the street with his sword raised high. She released her arrow, not daring to breathe as it whistled through the air. It hit home, burying deep into the man's back. He fell from his steed but managed to climb to his feet. Aurelia notched another arrow, but just then, a Diapolisian woman ran him through with a spear before she could fire.

Aurelia watched the woman usher the child toward safety before setting her sights on another enemy. "Good job," Holera shouted as she downed another soldier with ease. The warrior's accuracy was impressive, and Aurelia felt a pang of envy. Would she have failed to save that small child if the townsman hadn't intervened?

She shelved her doubts and continued to rain arrows down on the barbarians below. The violent bloodshed lasted for several long minutes before they finally defeated all the Warbotach attackers, but it felt like a lifetime.

Aurelia and Holera watched as Cristos and Kason tied up the lone survivor and dragged him back to the inn. The soldier had attempted to escape when their defeat became apparent, but Cristos had pursued him. He threw a dagger at the deserter, impaling his thigh to prevent his escape, but Aurelia wondered why he hadn't killed the coward.

"Let's go," Holera said, grabbing Aurelia by the arm and leading her to the edge of the roof.

They climbed down and ran over to where Kason and Cristos stood, the injured Warbotach soldier firmly bound at their feet. The townspeople didn't waste time celebrating their victory; they gathered buckets of water and formed an assembly line to combat the raging fires threatening to destroy their town. The acrid smell of smoke and charred wood clawed at Aurelia's throat, while the cries of the wounded mingled with the sounds of the night.

Cristos held the injured man's lead, so Aurelia kept her distance as she scanned his body for injuries. She breathed a sigh of relief when she found none. Aside from a soot smudge on his cheek, he looked the same as he had the night before.

She turned to Kason and noticed that his arm had been sliced, though the cut didn't appear deep. He seemed unfazed by the pain as he tore a strip from the hem of his tunic and tied it around the wound. After he finished, he knelt down and began wrapping the Warbotach soldier's leg with another strip of fabric from his tunic.

"Why are you treating his wounds? Just end his miserable existence. He doesn't deserve to live." Holera's voice was harsh, and her eyes shot daggers at the bound man. Kason glanced up at her but continued his work.

"Because he's coming with us. It's only fair that we return the treatment Warbotach showed you."

The firmness in Kason's voice left no room for argument. His fierce expression conveyed the struggles he had endured while Holera was captured and imprisoned with her companions in Norithae.

CHAPTER FORTY

SPECTRE FOREST

AURELIA

Aurelia felt deep pity for the Diapolisians who fought desperately to save their home as flames consumed their small town, but her party could not stay to help. There was no time to waste; they couldn't even wait for Calista to return.

Holera and Aurelia hurried to gather their belongings and left a message for the healer with the innkeeper while Kason finished binding the enemy soldier's wounds. As soon as the women rejoined the others, Holera transformed. The flames that surged with her change drew the attention of those battling the relentless blaze, but once they realized it was not a fire they needed to fight, they returned to their task.

Kason threw the restrained soldier over Holera's back and climbed up behind him. He said nothing as he exerted his strength to keep the Warbotach man still, who struggled to break free. Aurelia wrapped her arms around Cristos' neck and buried her face in the crook, seeking comfort as he cradled her. He kicked off the ground, following Holera into the night sky.

They traveled at a brutally fast pace on their way back to the encampment. Violent winds lashed against their bodies, making the flight bumpy and unstable, but they didn't slow down. Aurelia was too afraid to speak, with the rushing air threatening to steal the breath from her lungs. All she could do was cling to her lover, inhaling his sandalwood-and-spice scent for comfort.

The sun rose as they soared over Spectre Forest, the now-illuminated trees a blur of green below them. She couldn't help but wonder if Calista had reached King Ailani yet. She fervently hoped the weight of the kingdom would come to the townspeople's aid.

Aurelia couldn't stop replaying the horrifying events in her mind. She could still hear the terrified screams and smell the singed flesh and burning homes. The faces of those fearing for their lives haunted her, and even worse, she could still see the lifeless eyes of the Diapolisians who hadn't been lucky enough to survive. The images of the soldiers she had felled with her arrows began to flit around her mind, mingling with the atrocities they had committed. They were barbaric, and there was little doubt the world would be a better place without them, yet she struggled with the fact that she had killed someone.

Cristos held her tighter as he followed Holera's rapid descent into the forest. She wasn't sure if he sensed her shame and heartbreak or if he was merely securing his hold as they prepared to land, but either way, she appreciated his comforting touch.

They landed just outside the protective barrier surrounding the camp. Though Aurelia could not see the barrier, she could feel its power buzzing through the air. They joined hands, Kason holding onto their Warbotach prisoner, and passed through the wards. The sensation of traversing the magic was far less uncomfortable than the mass of staring eyes that greeted them. The camp buzzed with warriors heading to breakfast, but they all halted as the group made their appearance.

Silence descended upon the lively clearing, and it unsettled her. She shifted her weight awkwardly before the general came to her rescue. Blaedia ran toward them, with Taryn just behind her and several other guards trailing along. As the watching warriors focused on their leader, Aurelia anxiously scanned their faces. A glimpse of ebony braids rushing through the air was her only warning before a body collided with hers, knocking the breath from her lungs.

"Lia!" Septima shrieked as she tackled her. Aurelia embraced her sister tightly, half-laughing and half-sobbing into her shoulder. They had only been apart for a few days, but it felt like a lifetime.

"I missed you so much." Her voice cracked as she murmured to her younger sister. Septima rolled off her, and they both sat up, dusting off their clothes. "How's Kano?" She was genuinely curious about her pet but not quite ready to share the recent events. It was always best to steer Septima away from starting an interrogation; otherwise, she knew she would never escape from the questioning.

Exie crouched beside them. "That cat is a big old baby," she said, waving her hand. "He is spoiled absolutely rotten."

Aurelia smiled softly at her words, aching to see her furry friend.

"Ready to get something to eat?" Cristos asked as he approached them. She glanced around him, watching the general order a few men to haul the prisoner away for safekeeping. Blaedia patted Holera on the back and followed behind the prison transport.

She nodded. "What are they going to do with him?"

Cristos helped her to her feet and wiped the tear tracks from her face before answering. "Blaedia is going to find out why they were in Diapolis and then use him to send a message to Uldon."

Septima and Exie joined the four returnees as they headed to the dining tent. They hadn't eaten since the night before and had severely overexerted themselves afterward—especially Holera and Cristos. They grabbed their plates and claimed a nearby table, devouring their meals. Aurelia was so ravenous that she didn't even taste the food before swallowing.

She habitually glanced around the tent as they ate, waiting for the healer to arrive, but Calista had not returned to the camp yet. Aurelia worried about both her safety and King Ailani's decision. If the events in Claywind weren't enough to convince the king to aid them against Warbotach, nothing would sway him. Just as Cristos had said, their neutral blood ran in the streets of Diapolis, and they were left waiting to see how he would react to the attack. They had no way of knowing until Calista returned.

Holera and Kason finished first and left the tent, likely to interrogate the prisoner or possibly take a shower. They were all covered in grime and blood, so showering seemed like a reasonable option. However, the look in Kason's eyes when he mentioned taking the prisoner with them led her to believe they were heading for the former. Cristos filled Exie and Septima in on the details of their disastrous trip during the meal. Aurelia remained silent, not wanting to discuss her experiences.

After they emptied their plates, Aurelia and Cristos quickly showered and set off in search of the prisoner. He was not hard to find. A newly erected tent stood beside the sparring ring, with two guards posted outside its entrance. Blaedia strolled out, wiping her hands as they approached.

"Oh, hey. Did the two of you get something to eat?"

Aurelia nodded.

"We did," Cristos replied, motioning toward the tent. "Did you find out anything from him yet?"

The general's face twisted into a fierce grimace. "They were sent to Claywind to deliver a message."

"What message?" Cristos moved in closer to Blaedia.

"That nowhere is safe. Uldon wanted to ensure King Ailani knew Diapolis was next. Apparently, he wants the entire continent under his thumb before he crosses the portal."

Aurelia gasped, her heart stuttering as she listened. "What if other towns were attacked?"

Cristos spoke at the same time. "Has word been sent to the king?"

Blaedia nodded. "A raven is being sent now. I wouldn't doubt that they targeted other towns. Hopefully, they can respond to the attacks quickly with the aid of their dragons."

"What's the plan moving forward?" Aurelia heard Cristos ask the general, but it was hard for her to concentrate on the conversation. All she could imagine was the scene that had unfolded in Claywind spreading throughout the rest of the peaceful, tropical kingdom.

"We march on Norithae next and unseat Uldon's general. I hope your people are ready to fight, as you mentioned, because we can't take back Aegricia on our own."

"They will fight. I will send word to my spies. They will ensure my people are prepared for our arrival."

Blaedia gave a curt nod and headed for her tent. Cristos pulled Aurelia into his arms as soon as they were alone, crushing her to his chest. He had undoubtedly sensed her crippling anxiety, and his firm hold helped ground her as the world spun beneath her feet. He waited until she calmed down before pulling away. The absence of his warmth felt almost painful, and she fought the urge to cry. Cristos leaned his forehead against hers. "I must go send a message to my people. You should visit Kano, and I'll meet you there as soon as I finish."

She nodded hesitantly; her frazzled nerves made her reluctant to part from him. Still, Aurelia stiffened her spine and started toward Kano's enclosure while Cristos went in the opposite direction. The air hummed around her, sending bumps along her arms. She shivered as she glanced around the camp, but no one else seemed to hear the vibrations that set her teeth on edge. She knew it had to be her own anxiety playing tricks on her, but she struggled to breathe as trepidation overwhelmed her. Her brisk walk turned into a mad dash across the camp. Seeing Kano would hopefully calm her.

The magnificent tiger sat at the edge of his enclosure and stared in her direction as if waiting for her to arrive. As soon as he spotted her, he stood on his hind legs, and the fence groaned under the weight of his massive paws. She pulled her medallion out and rushed to greet him. She barely stepped inside before Kano leaped on her. They tumbled to the ground, and he nuzzled her forcefully, pulling a giggle from her throat. His rough tongue left a slimy trail up her face as she pushed his giant head away from licking distance.

"Calm down, boy!"

Kano growled low in his throat, his version of pouting, and flopped onto his back for a belly rub. Aurelia chuckled as she caressed him. She was more grateful for the opportunity to do so than she had ever been before. She probably appreciated petting him more than he enjoyed receiving the affection. Just hours earlier, she hadn't been sure she would ever see her precious cat again, and she reveled in their time together.

The uncertainties of the future and the endless possibilities bombarded her thoughts. How would the war affect the gentle giant, Kano? His impressive size and ferocious bite would be beneficial in battle, but she didn't want him to get hurt. While Kano was loving, he was also protective. She had little doubt he would tear apart anyone who tried to harm her, but how could she take advantage of his unwavering loyalty and put him in harm's way? If the entire camp was to march on Norithae and then Aegricia, did the phoenixes expect him to join the attack? They needed all the help they could get, but as his guardian, it was her responsibility to ensure his safety.

Aurelia continued to argue with herself, her thoughts going in vicious circles. Both sides of her dilemma seemed valid, and she couldn't decide what to do. She leaned back against the trunk of a massive tree and closed her eyes, taking deep breaths of the fresh forest air to steady herself. Kano plopped his head in her lap, and she stroked behind his ears as she struggled with her indecision.

Warm lips pressed against her cheek, startling her awake. She hadn't even realized she had fallen asleep, but when she opened her eyes, the sun was lower in the sky. Cristos smiled as he leaned over her. She wondered how he had managed to get inside Kano's fenced-in home, but before she could ask, her sister Exie sat on the ground by her feet. Cristos took a spot beside her and wrapped his arm around her shoulders, pulling her close. "I saw you were asleep, so I went to talk to Blaedia."

Her eyebrows furrowed in confusion as she rubbed the sleep from her eyes. Hadn't they already gathered all the information they needed from her earlier? "About what?"

"I thought it was time to tell her who I am. Then I ran into Septima and Exie, and I told them as well."

Her eyes grew wide. "What did she say?"

Cristos chuckled. "Apparently, the general had already received Kason's message and knew. Septima, on the other hand, smacked me." Septima smirked at him. "But we've since made up," her sister added, rolling her eyes and chuckling.

Aurelia tilted her head as curiosity stirred inside her, but she decided to let it go for now. She would hound her little sister for the details later; it wasn't like the youngest Vesta sibling to be so forgiving. "Well, I'm glad. I think your secret is safe with them."

He nodded and kissed her temple. "I think so too."

They remained in the enclosure for another hour before the lunch bell rang. They all said their goodbyes to Kano and headed for the dining tent. A line was already forming when they arrived, but the camp was still bustling with activity. It was an unusual sight. Usually, as soon as mealtime was signaled, all activities halted as everyone rushed to eat. But that wasn't the case today. Dozens of warriors, both male and female, were paired up inside and outside the training rings. The sparring matches were intense and unrelenting, with clanging weapons echoing throughout the clearing. Blaedia must have informed them of the impending battle. As Aurelia watched them hone their impressive skills, she never felt more unprepared.

Aurelia and Cristos retired early that night. Now that the adrenaline of the attack had completely worn off, their long day had caught up to them, and sleep was imperative. Even as exhaustion tugged at her consciousness, Aurelia could not stop thinking about Uldon's plan to conquer the continent. Blaedia and Taryn had been so certain that he would stop at nothing to cross the portal and make the human realm his domain.

No matter how she looked at the situation, it just didn't make sense. Why did he suddenly decide to attack Diapolis? If anything, it just ensured that the tropical kingdom would join up in arms against him and add dragons to his enemies' ranks. His course of action baffled her. She curled up into Cristos' arms, tucking her head beneath his chin.

"Do you think Uldon is working with someone else? I mean, could someone be backing him in his bid to conquer Ekotoria? I just don't understand why he circled back to Diapolis if the human world is his end goal."

Cristos shrugged. "It's possible that he allied with someone from off the continent." He released a breath. "That's a scary prospect. Uldon is unstable, at best. If he has the power of another nation behind him... I sincerely hope that is not the case."

She agreed. Just dwelling over the possibility made her chest tighten uncomfortably. "It is quite terrifying. Did Blaedia tell you when we will head for Norithae?"

"They're still handling the logistics, but it sounds like we'll set out in a week or less if they can iron out all the details. We are going to move closer first. Once we're in position, scouts will advance ahead and release the prisoner to deliver a message."

She tilted her face up to stare at him with a furrowed brow. "What's the message?"

His blue eyes sparkled in the dim candlelight as he looked down at her. "Surrender or die."

The words sent a shiver of foreboding rippling through her body. Once the prisoner delivered that message, there was no turning back. Not that they could turn back, anyway. Ekotoria could not carry on as it was. War needed to be waged before peace could reign—if they won, that is.

Her sense of dread continued to grow as she fixated on the danger looming in their near future. Cristos lifted her chin and leaned down to kiss her gently.

"Don't worry, love. I won't let anything happen to you."

She smiled softly at the endearment, but his words did not assuage her fears. She had far more to lose in this war than just her own life.

CHAPTER FORTY-ONE

SPECTRE FOREST

AURELIA

The next morning came and went, but Calista still had not returned from Diapolis. They had received no word from her, and the entire camp was worried about her absence. Aurelia hoped that Calista's delay meant she was returning with members of the Diapolis military. The southerners would have little hope of finding the encampment without her, but that was probably just wishful thinking. There had also been no messenger ravens from King Ailani, and the silence grew heavier with every passing hour.

The atmosphere in the camp changed completely as they prepared to march on Norithae the following morning. People tended not to linger as much. The training rings were always occupied, and socializing after dinner decreased considerably. Before they had been captured in the forest, it had been common to end the night with drinks and card games in Exie's tent, but now all their spare time was consumed by war preparations. Aurelia imagined the same was true for the rest of the camp. With the promise of battle on the horizon, fun and entertainment were replaced by sparring and sharpening weapons. The once lively campfires grew quiet, replaced by the steady rasp of whetstones against steel.

Aurelia and Cristos spent hours outside their tent with Septima and Exie, honing their skills. While Aurelia pushed herself, sweat soaking her tunic, she couldn't match the intensity with which the phoenix trained. Exie seemed to have suffered no lasting damage from her injuries, and the ferocity with which she swung her blade was intimidating. Her strikes came fast and sure, the air whistling as her weapon cut through it. Aurelia almost felt sorry for her sister, being on the receiving end of those blows.

Septima and the blond warrior had gone public with their relationship while Aurelia and the others were in Diapolis. They continued to share Exie's tent and seemed incredibly happy together, but that affection vanished as they circled each other with swords raised high. Their faces were masks of concentration, and the clash of metal rang like thunderclaps across the training ground. As Aurelia watched them spin and slash in a violent dance, she couldn't help but think about their future. One day, Septima would age, while Exie would maintain her magical youth. The worry about their future mirrored one of Aurelia's greatest fears regarding her own relationship. At least she had some hope of an extended lifespan thanks to her mother's fae blood. Still, there was no guarantee she'd live longer, and she honestly wasn't sure what scared her more: losing Septima by not aging or losing Cristos by growing old.

When the dinner bell rang that evening, Aurelia's exhaustion was bone-deep. Her fatigued muscles screamed as she forced herself to lift each spoonful of stew. The meal tent was filled with the same seriousness that enveloped the rest of the camp. The usual chatter was gone; only the scrape of spoons against bowls and the occasional murmur punctuated the silence. There was no light-hearted conversation as they devoured their food.

When the couples went their separate ways afterward, a firm knot took root in Aurelia's stomach and refused to dissipate. With each passing moment, the move grew closer, tightening the pit in her stomach. She tried not to dwell on what the morning would bring as she and Cristos headed for their tent hand in hand, focusing instead on the promise of washing away the day's stench.

As Aurelia opened the tent flap to fetch a set of clean clothes before heading to the shower tent, she stumbled to a halt when she saw Cristos lighting a candle. The soft glow danced across the surface of a large metal basin, enough for her to soak in. Steam curled upward in ghostly ribbons, perfuming the tent with warmth and promise. Her eyes darted to Cristos in shock, and he smiled at her.

"What?" It wasn't even the question she wanted to ask, but her brain refused to function correctly as he cupped her face tenderly and kissed her.

"Surprise. I thought a bath would help ease some of your stress."

Her heart swelled at the gesture. How could she not fall for such a thoughtful man?

"How did you get this in here? When?" she asked as he grinned and kissed her again. They'd been training outside their tent's entrance all day, and she couldn't figure out how he had managed it.

"I begged Kason to help me. He snuck it in while we were at dinner."

She looked from him to the massive basin once again. The steam rose from the water in swirling ribbons that beckoned her. She felt tension begin to lessen in her sore limbs as she pulled off her shoes and unbuttoned her tunic. She slid the top off and let it fall in a heap at her feet as she began to unfasten her trousers. Cristos' hungry gaze followed her every move, but he didn't touch her as she stripped bare.

"I can't believe you did this. I hadn't even dared to wish for a bath since we returned." She was sure he could sense the overwhelming love she felt for him in that moment, but she still wasn't brave enough to say the words. "You're too good to me."

His eyes flashed with an unreadable emotion before he walked over to the soaking basin and offered his hand. Aurelia took it and stepped in, slowly sinking into the hot water. She let out a pleasure-filled moan as she fully submerged her aching body. The basin was too small for both of them to fit, but Cristos didn't seem to mind as he pulled a wooden stool over and sat behind her.

He used a glass to pour the gloriously heated liquid over her. "How's the temperature?"

She hummed, sinking further into the water. "Delicious."

"Do you want me to wash your hair?"

She nodded, stifling a yawn and feeling incredibly lucky to call such a man hers.

His strong fingers massaged her scalp, and the smell of lavender filled her nose, creating a relaxing yet sensual experience. The rhythmic movements sent a shiver of comfort down her spine.

"You look like you're about to fall asleep." His voice was like velvet, low and smooth, and the deep cadence lulled her heavy eyelids shut as he rinsed the shampoo.

"I just might. Thank you for taking such great care of me."

"Anything for you." He kissed her temple and set the glass aside before lathering up a cloth and beginning to wash her body tenderly. He rinsed the parts that weren't submerged as she sighed happily. There was nowhere in the world she would rather be than right there. "Are you ready to get out?"

She frowned as the pampering came to an end, but agreed. They were setting out for Norithae at first light, and they needed to rest. She expected Cristos to bathe after her, but after he helped her out, he grabbed a towel and began to dry her off. As he thoroughly rubbed the plush fabric over her body, her eyes fluttered shut once more. When his lips followed the path of the towel, she had never felt more cherished.

Kneeling at her feet, he spread her legs, tossing the damp fabric aside once he wiped away the last of the water droplets. His mouth found her core, and her knees buckled, but his firm hands gripped her waist. He supported her frame as he gave her slit a slow lick. Her thighs twitched, and he smiled against her heated flesh. She gasped as he hooked one leg over his shoulder. Another torturous swipe of his tongue had her tangling her fingers in his hair and yanking roughly. Her calf brushed against his wings, and they fluttered in response as he buried his face between her thighs.

She arched her back in pleasure, moaning his name as he ravaged her. He sucked on the sensitive bundle of nerves at her center, and she almost climaxed right there.

"Bed. Please." Desire laced her voice, making it unrecognizable as she issued the command.

Cristos obliged, lifting her and carrying her across the room. He pulled away and lowered her onto the fur blankets that covered their mattress.

She sprawled on her back, the smooth fur caressing her bare skin as she held his gaze. He was still fully clothed, and she leaned up to unbutton his tunic, but he pressed her back down gently. "Tonight is about you, love."

He bent her legs and pushed them up until her knees were even with her shoulders, then he spread them apart and lowered his head. Stars exploded in her vision as he worshiped her with his tongue. The pleasure he gave her was second to none, but she wanted more. There was no telling what the attack on Norithae's invaders would bring in the morning. Though she hated to focus on the adverse outcomes, it was entirely possible that this could be their last night together. She wanted to satisfy him as much as he satisfied her.

"Go wash up. I'll be waiting."

Cristos' ocean eyes darkened at her words, and he hastened to follow her directive. She'd never been sexually demanding before, but he had a way of filling her to the brim with confidence. She rolled over and watched him as he shed his clothes. He bathed in record time, but his hands lingered as he washed his hardened length and stared intently into her eyes.

Aurelia bit her lip as she enjoyed the view, squirming to relieve the tingling pressure that began to build between her legs once more. After rising from the tub, Cristos dried off quickly and returned to the bed, but it felt far too slow as the need coursed through her. His warm body slid along hers as he crawled onto the bed and claimed her lips in a deep and luxurious kiss.

The slow swipes of his tongue made her feel like they had all the time in the world. She ran her fingers through his silky black hair as his hands slid up her arms, gently pulling them above her head and holding them in place. She was left panting as his lips left hers and trailed down her neck, leaving sensual kisses in his wake. He shifted, adjusting his grip so that he held both of her wrists in one hand, pinning her to the bed as his other hand traced down the outline of her body until he reached her chest. Bowing his head, he cupped her breast, kneading it in his palm before gently easing it into his mouth.

She pulled at his hold, her hands aching to roam his muscular form, but he tightened his grasp and pressed her harder against the bed. He continued to suck and nip at her breast as his hand trailed downward, sliding over the plane of her stomach until he found that sensitive bundle of nerves at her center. His fingers circled it lightly, increasing in pressure until she panted. She undulated under him, her body on fire as it filled to the brim with lust. He slipped two fingers inside her, pumping and twisting vigorously as he wound her body up like a tightly coiled spring.

Her body craved the feel of him deep inside her, and she couldn't handle any more of his teasing. She begged him to impale her with his stiff cock, and her dirty words did the trick. He pressed her hands so hard against the mattress that it almost hurt as he slammed inside her. His pace was brutal and punishing. Electricity surged through her body, and her torso bowed off the bed with the force of her climax as he pinned the rest of her body down. Aurelia screamed herself hoarse, his name on her lips, as she rode the intense waves of her pleasure.

When she came back down from the high, he released his grip and hovered above her. His pace slowed dramatically, their bodies sliding against each other like smooth silk as he made love to her. The frantic energy was replaced with emotion as he languidly kissed her.

When he pulled away and rested his forehead against hers, his eyes shone bright in the dim candlelight as he murmured quietly.

"I love you."

"I love you, too."

The dangers they would face the next day fueled the passion that ignited between them. If this was their last night together, she wanted to savor every moment. They took their time, enjoying each other's bodies until they were exhausted and sated. When Aurelia finally fell asleep, it was in the arms of the man she loved.

CHAPTER FORTY-TWO

SPECTRE FOREST

AURELIA

Fog crept between the trees, swirling ominously throughout the camp as if Spectre Forest mourned the violence that awaited them on their journey north. The mist slithered low, curling around ankles like cold, ghostly fingers, while the muted hush of the forest created the illusion that even the trees were holding their breath. Warriors energetically flitted about, packing their tents and preparing to leave. They seemed to vibrate with anticipation, and the air buzzed with their pent-up energy. But Aurelia felt somber as she headed to breakfast. She understood their excitement; this was the first significant step toward reclaiming their home and rescuing their queen. Yet, she was not eager for the war to come and did not feel prepared enough to fight. Even Septima seemed hesitant as she assisted Exie with her lanista duties, her usual spark dimmed beneath the looming promise of battle.

After they ate, Aurelia and Cristos grabbed their weapons and satchels from their tent. A warrior approached, using her magic to shrink the tent down to a traveling size. The canvas rippled, folding impossibly small until it fit neatly into the warrior's palm. Aurelia was curious about how that particular magic worked—how entire shelters could be collapsed and hidden inside charms or pockets. However, she hesitated to ask as the warrior moved on to the following canvas structure, repeating the process effortlessly.

The moon had begun its slow descent beyond the horizon, but not a hint of daylight was found. A heavy gloom clung to the forest, and Aurelia couldn't shake the sense of foreboding that seemed to follow her as the eerie mist licked at her ankles. Each step felt as if it carried her closer to an unknown fate.

According to Blaedia, most of their forces would travel on foot through the forest to avoid detection. The element of surprise was imperative to achieve rapid success with minimal damage. Even the most confident warriors spoke in hushed tones, unwilling to shatter the fragile secrecy of their mission.

The general had sent a few phoenixes ahead to Aegricia to assess the state of their territory and civilians. As soon as they ousted Warbotach from Norithae, they would reclaim their home. The scouts were tasked not only with gathering information but also with quietly spreading the word among their people. When the time came, Aegricia needed all able-bodied citizens, even those who were not warriors, to take up arms. Most importantly, the people subjugated by Uldon needed to know there was still hope and that their army had not abandoned them. The weight of that expectation pressed heavily on Aurelia's chest.

While most warriors were to march on Norithae, Blaedia staggered their departures to minimize the risk of mass casualties if Warbotach attacked them during travel.

There would also be a flying squadron that would reach Norithae first to monitor the positioning of Warbotach's soldiers and set up camp to the northwest as they awaited their attack. They planned to send one of the more unassuming females into the city undercover as a merchant to covertly notify the citizens of their approach. Cristos had sent a raven to one of his most trusted spies the night before, but it was impossible to know if the message had been received. That uncertainty was yet another shadow trailing Aurelia.

As the first of the phoenixes set out beyond the wards, Cristos and Aurelia went to fetch Kano. The great cat would join their trek through the forest on a leash. His stripes gleamed faintly in the pale moonlight, his massive frame sleek and powerful, and Aurelia's heart clenched with worry. She feared that her beloved pet would get hurt during their travels, but he would be an invaluable source of protection. There was no way Warbotach's soldiers and their fiery mounts could ambush them with Kano present. He would sense any signs of danger and alert her. Still, her greatest fear was that the animal she had sworn to love and protect would be hurt more than her own safety.

Exie and Septima finished fastening the leather leash and harness onto Kano as they arrived. The harness wasn't necessary since Kano would never break the leash and run, but many warriors remained wary of his massive size and powerful canines. He was certainly strong enough to free himself from the tether, but he would never do so unless it was to defend Aurelia or her sister. It was a small concession to provide her traveling companions with peace of mind.

Aurelia wrapped the leather lead around her hand as the group of four made their way to the sparring rings with the tiger in tow. Most of the remaining warriors had already gathered and were conversing amongst themselves by the time they arrived. Travel packs and personal belongings littered the ground at their feet, waiting for the journey to begin. The subdued murmur of voices mixed with the hiss of fog, creating the impression of an army moving through a dream.

As Blaedia raised her fist in the air, the grim skies began to lighten. Dozens of warriors transformed into colorful flames, shifting into their firebird forms. They launched from the forest floor in unison, soaring high above the canopy of leaves that sheltered the camp. Aurelia watched in awe as a kaleidoscope of vibrant phoenixes took flight toward Norithae, their wings leaving trails of fire that briefly illuminated the shrouded dawn.

Taryn approached the invisible barrier surrounding them, accompanied by a few other females. The air in the clearing hummed as they removed the wards, the thick fog stirring as their magic swirled around. Aurelia felt the moment the shield dispersed, a strange weight pressing down on her chest, causing her anxiety to surge as they were left exposed to both enemies and the elements.

The temperature was frigid, but she was thankful there was no snow as they began their long march. They had to tread carefully through the dense trees and foliage at the start of their journey, avoiding gnarled roots that threatened to slow their progress. The thick canopy blocked most of the sunlight, allowing only narrow slivers to shine through like dying spotlights on the forest floor. The crunch of boots and the occasional creak of leather straps were the only sounds, quickly swallowed by the oppressive forest.

Despite the harsh weather and minimal illumination, the lush trees seemed to follow their own natural laws. In the Howling Forest of Vaekros, winter left branches barren while leaves decayed into the soil that once nourished them. But in Ekotoria, the trees clung tightly to their vibrant greenery as if they were prized possessions they could not bear to part with.

The absence of natural debris helped keep their footsteps stealthy as they trekked through the forest. Blaedia planned to march north until nightfall. Once the meager rays of sunlight were replaced by the moon's gentle glow, they would erect their protective wards once more and set up a temporary camp for the night. At daybreak, they would continue their journey toward a location just outside Norithae's borders, where they would establish a more permanent camp while waiting for news of the undercover warrior's success in alerting the citizens. Aurelia doubted she could breathe easily until they were once again surrounded by protective magic.

The general had carefully planned the positioning of both their camp and the northern camp of the flying squadron. When the time came, they would strike the invaders swiftly and decisively. With the Elder Sea along the eastern coast, Aegrician warriors approaching from the northwest and southwest, and Norithaean civilians gathering their forces in the center, Warbotach would have no avenue for retreat or the ability to request reinforcements. Blaedia left nothing to chance now that they were finally preparing to move against the barbarians who had captured her queen and forced her warriors to flee to the human world.

The large group maintained its steady march without wavering. For the first time, Aurelia didn't worry about being attacked by hellhounds or any of the other dangerous creatures that inhabited the Spectre Forest. Hundreds of phoenixes moved purposefully toward their destination, with numerous males mixed into their ranks. Even with their safety found in their vast numbers, they held their weapons aloft, ready to strike down any threat foolish enough to challenge them. This display of strength provided Aurelia with a small sense of comfort. They may well be marching toward death, but she was unlikely to meet her end before the battle began—hopefully.

Cristos's expression mirrored the steely resolve of their companions as he held Aurelia's hand firmly. Her other hand gripped Kano's leash so tightly that her knuckles turned white. They traveled in silence to avoid attracting unwanted attention. While it was unlikely they would encounter a force strong enough to intimidate their warriors, they did not want to risk losing the element of surprise by alerting Warbotach to their approach. Cristos would occasionally squeeze Aurelia's hand gently or lean over to kiss her temple. His small gestures assured her, providing comfort in place of the words he usually offered.

She kept stealing glances at Septima and Exie, who brought up the rear on a large black mare. The warriors didn't have many animals among them, aside from Kano, but the few they had remained under the lanistas' care as they traveled.

After Aurelia turned back from staring at her sister, she noticed a wide grin on Cristos' lips. He watched her intently as they trailed behind the phoenixes that led their party. It was hard not to blush with his gaze fixed on her.

"What are you looking at?" she whispered.

His broad smile only grew wider. "You."

She nudged him with her shoulder, careful not to stumble as they zigzagged between thick trunks and lush greenery. "I can see that, but why?"

Cristos leaned in and whispered in her ear, "Because you are so beautiful." His breath caressed the shell of her ear, sending tingles through her. She bit her lip to hide her smile as warmth spread throughout her body.

They continued their trek in silence. As the sun set, the group began to set up camp in a large clearing that was only a day's hike from the kingdom of Norithae. Though the open space was vast, it was minuscule compared to the one they had previously occupied. They had to erect fewer tents and double up to provide shelter for everyone.

Exie, Septima, Aurelia, and Cristos had to bunk together. Although Aurelia and Cristos had no chance to spend time alone, she was happy to spend time with her sister and friend.

After they placed their satchels inside their tent and secured Kano in his temporary enclosure, the couples headed for the shower tent. The original setup featured dozens of curtained stalls, but the makeshift bathing area consisted only of small basins and cloths for washing up. It was cold and uncomfortable after their journey through the freezing forest, but at least they had access to fresh water. Aurelia was grateful for that luxury now that war loomed just beyond the horizon.

The smell of roasting meat wafted through the air as they exited, clean but shivering as the cool night air rushed against their skin. The delicious aroma would have attracted every carnivore within a few miles if not for the wards, and Aurelia was thankful to be safely behind the magical barrier once more. The four made their way to the center of camp, where a giant, freshly built fire roared. Aurelia hadn't noticed the hunters gathering game as they marched on, but when she caught sight of deer and rabbit roasting over the large flames, she felt grateful they had.

She rushed to stand near the blaze, desperate for its warmth as she wrapped her cloak tighter around herself. Cristos came up behind her and pulled her into a tight embrace. His natural warmth enveloped her, and she snuggled against him as his wings curled around them, blocking the chilling breeze.

Aurelia scanned the clearing and saw warriors gathered around smaller bonfires scattered among the tents. The only times she saw the camp's occupants en masse were when they gathered to move locations. Their numbers were as intimidating as the controlled strength with which they moved, but she couldn't help but wonder if it would be enough to defeat Warbotach and their malicious king. Suppose everything went according to Blaedia's plan and they managed to take Norithae. Would there be enough survivors to reclaim Aegricia? Her fears were relentless and all-consuming as she returned her vacant stare to their roasting meal.

Aurelia watched the flames dance against the darkness, a small light struggling to conquer the night. Was that what they were? Cristos leaned forward and pressed his cheek against hers.

"What are you thinking about?" he asked.

She shrugged, and her eyes fluttered shut as she let his warmth permeate her, hoping it would thaw her icy trepidation. "A bit of everything, but mostly about the war and who will survive in the next few days."

He pulled away, and she instantly missed his heat until he spun her around. His gaze was fierce, shining with determination. "I've told you that I will let nothing happen to you, and I mean it." Cristos cupped her face gently and gave her a soft kiss. The gentleness of his lips reached the depths of her heart.

When he pulled away, she stared at him for a long moment, trying to commit every detail to memory. The way his blue eyes sparkled as brilliantly as the Elder Sea when he was happy. The way his thick, dark hair always stuck up in odd directions when he woke up. The way his chiseled bone structure softened when he smiled. The way he had looked at her when he told her he loved her. The sound of his voice as he said her name. His laugh. She wanted to lock every single thing about him in a war-proof box inside her mind.

"Even fighting side by side, you won't be able to watch me every second," she said, her voice trembling slightly. "I know you'll do your best to keep me safe, but there's no guarantee that I will remain so. If something happens to me, I don't want you to blame yourself. I would be sad if I were the reason you stopped smiling."

The passionate fire in his eyes softened as he stared at her. "What would there be to make me smile if I didn't have you?"

Aurelia brushed her fingertips along his cheekbone. She didn't have an answer to his question because if he were to die, her happiness would die along with him. He hugged her tightly, making it hard for her to breathe as he whispered in her ear, "Please don't fight. Stay in the camp."

She smiled at his words, but it didn't reach her eyes. Aurelia knew she wasn't the best warrior, but she couldn't stay safely tucked away while the two people she loved most in the world risked their lives. It wasn't just Septima and Cristos she worried about. The faces of her friends flashed through her mind: Exie, Taryn, Holera, Kason, even Blaedia. No, she couldn't let them put their heart and soul into the coming battle while she hid like a coward. "I can't do that. This war only has one outcome I can live with, and to achieve it, we will need every weapon raised against Warbotach. I may have left my father and brother behind, but I must do my part to protect them from magical subjugation."

Cristos cupped her face as he gazed into her eyes, his expression falling at whatever he saw looking back at him. Though she knew he wanted to keep his promise, there was no guarantee, and she was determined to join their ranks in battle. "Then please keep Kano by your side. I trust he will protect you if I fail."

Aurelia's heart sank at the thought of bringing her beloved tiger into the fight. She was supposed to protect him, not put him in danger. She remained silent, unable to agree with his suggestion. The rational part of her knew that Kano would rather die protecting her than live without her. Still, the emotional part was not ready to accept that.

Dinner being served brought their conversation to an abrupt halt, and Aurelia was glad for the reprieve. She needed time to think before making her decision. On one hand, the tiger would have no one if she and Septima both perished in battle. On the other hand, she had cared for him since he was a cub and loved him like a family member. For the first time, she regretted the day her father brought him home. Kano should have happily lived out his days as King of the Jungle, far away from a war that wasn't his to fight.

They ate in silence before heading to bed with Exie and Septima. With an early morning ahead of them, the four of them blew out their candles and crawled into their beds.

With Cristos' arm draped over her and his warm body pressed against her back, Aurelia tried to quiet her racing mind enough to fall asleep. Her old life had been safer, but it also felt empty. Even as she prepared to confront death, she had no regrets. Still, she longed for the day when her new life would become just as safe and predictable as the old one.

CHAPTER FORTY-THREE

SPECTRE FOREST

AURELIA

The chill of the isolated stone cell seeped into Otera's bones as she curled up on the damp floor in a futile attempt to warm herself. The heavy, moist air clung to her skin, infused with the scents of mildew and iron, and every breath puffed visibly in the cold. The wind whipped harshly through the tiny window overhead, carrying the hollow moan of the mountains beyond, while the moon's soft beams taunted her. Its gentle glow reminded her of her dreary situation. The night was free to come and go, while she remained trapped in time, never leaving her confining cell.

The wounds Uldon had inflicted the last time they met had healed, though faint scars remained as reminders of his cruelty. However, she had yet to see the Warbotach leader again. Bremusa was also absent, and with her went Otera's last vestige of hope. She spent her monotonous days wondering where her army was and if they were safe. Would they come for her and free their people? Or would she remain forgotten in that dreadful dungeon until she turned to dust?

Uldon's men had once captured her commander. Could he hunt her down again? And what if her general fell? Without Blaedia and Taryn, their forces were bound to crumble.

Doubt and fear intertwined into a toxic cocktail that plagued Otera. She wanted to cling to hope, but she had been trapped for so long. The endless days and nights blurred together until she could no longer track the passage of time. The very air felt stagnant, as though hope itself had withered and died in her cell. She closed her eyes, trying to muster the will to carry on when all seemed lost.

Suddenly, faint breathing reached her ears, startling her upright. She snapped her eyes open and whipped her head around, searching for the source. She heard it—a soft cadence of inhaling and exhaling. Or was her solitude beginning to warp her mind?

"Hello? Who is there?" The door hadn't opened, but she couldn't shake the feeling that another presence lurked somewhere in her lonely cage.

"Hello?" Otera climbed to her feet, her atrophying muscles trembling violently from disuse as she scanned the poorly lit room. The foreign breaths quickened, ragged and uneven, causing her own breaths to match their pace, chilling her blood. Yet the room remained empty.

Aurelia jolted upright, her chest heaving violently as she scanned the dark tent. Cristos slept beside her, not stirring at her sudden motion. Exie and Septima occupied the other bedroll, remaining blissfully unconscious while she tried to stifle her anxiety.

Her dream haunted her, and the shadowy surroundings took on the desolate chill of Otera's cell. It had felt so real, as if her spectral form had truly stood beside the imprisoned queen. The first time she had dreamed of the Aegrician ruler, the illusions were foggier, shrouded in uncertainty. But this time, Otera had known she was there. Aurelia understood it was just a dream, yet she couldn't shake the ominous feeling that had taken root deep in her chest.

Although Aurelia had never actually seen the woman before, she could tell that Otera had visibly changed between the two unconscious sightings. Her frame was more sunken now, with skin pulled tight over her bones as starvation and inactivity took their toll. Could her subconscious really be powerful enough to fabricate those minute details? Still, there was no way she had actually visited the dungeon while she slept.

Aurelia continued her internal debate as she tried to steady her frantic breathing. She wondered if this was what Variel had warned her about. Perhaps her mother's fae blood was manifesting within her veins. Was this magic? Were those encounters actually visions?

No. It was only a dream. It had to be a dream, because if it wasn't, she would have to accept harsher truths—that she might outlive Septima, witnessing her sister wither and die while her own youth remained. Fate was so cruel. She did not want to be a helpless spectator to loss, nor did she want Cristos to see her fading away.

The impossibility of their future weighed on her heart as she settled back down in bed. It was just a dream. The words became a mantra she repeated as she willed herself to fall back asleep. Cristos pulled her close, snuggling into her while a soft snore escaped his parted lips. She closed her eyes and firmly set her mind in denial as she drifted off into a blissful, dreamless slumber.

The following morning, a raven arrived as the camp hurried through breakfast in preparation for another long hike through Spectre Forest. Blaedia received the message and promptly shared its contents with their forces. The prisoner had reached Windreach, the capital city of Norithae, and delivered a warning to Warbotach. Their enemies were now aware that a battle was imminent, although they did not know when the Aegrician forces would strike.

Despite sending the prisoner back, which gave away an element of surprise, the usurpers were unaware that Norithae would be ready to raise their weapons alongside the Aegrician forces. Blaedia hoped that the taunting news would draw Warbotach soldiers out from under the palace walls. She wanted to ensure that innocent civilians still residing in the territory would be protected. She was determined not to sacrifice those who were too young or unable to fight.

However, they still had not seen any sign of Calista. As time passed, Aurelia grew increasingly worried. There was a chance that King Ailani would send his dragons and men to support them, but there was also the possibility that he might blame their presence in his kingdom for the attack.

Aurelia tried not to dwell on that negative possibility, as they would need his help to reclaim Aegricia. Norithae was lightly guarded compared to the phoenixes' northern territory. Aegricia held the crown, the queen who wielded it, and the portal. Uldon and the bulk of his forces guarded the kingdom and the power they so desperately desired with an intensity that would make reclaiming it nearly impossible without Diapolis' assistance.

After Blaedia shared the message with the camp, the warriors packed up with renewed energy, continuing their journey to Norithae with their weapons held high and fierce determination in their eyes. Aurelia's heart pounded nervously; this was it—the foretold war was about to begin, and time seemed to be moving far too quickly.

This leg of the trip was shorter than the previous one, as they planned to stop several miles away from the city to avoid detection by Warbotach. Blaedia was confident that patrols would scour the forest for any signs of their approach. To avoid being spotted, the most powerful phoenixes would create a protection barrier that moved with them as they neared the border of Norithae.

Aurelia was astonished to learn that a mobile ward was possible and asked Cristos why they hadn't marched under a shield the day before. He explained that it required an excessive amount of energy to perform and maintain the magic, so it was only used when absolutely necessary.

The warriors moved silently through the underbrush, prepared to exact their revenge, aware that the likelihood of encountering Warbotach soldiers was high as they approached their destination. They advanced with such stealth that even fallen twigs did not snap beneath their feet.

Even Kano padded carefully beside Aurelia. His warm flank pressed against her leg protectively, and his ears twitched as he focused on the natural sounds of Spectre Forest. Although the tiger may not have fully understood what was happening, he was always sensitive to the emotions of those around him. The way he walked lightly and remained close to her side was his usual response to her anxiety. She reached down to stroke his head, an action meant to soothe him, but it also helped relieve the weight on her own heart.

It was impossible for Aurelia not to recall her conversation with Cristos the night before, as her feline protector prowled beside her. He would despise being left behind while she charged headfirst into danger, but she would hate the thought of allowing him to accompany her into harm's way.

Aurelia stifled a sigh, afraid to make a sound as Cristos gripped her free hand. He held the pommel of his sword high in his other hand, ready to defend or attack at a moment's notice. Aurelia had her bow and quiver strapped to her back. While she held onto Kano's lead, it made it impossible to prepare her weapon, but it was still easy to reach if needed.

Spectre Forest underwent a drastic transformation as they progressed. The terrain grew increasingly rugged with every step. Aegricia, the northernmost kingdom in Ekotoria, rested high in the Aegrician mountains, with Norithae surrounded by rocky ranges. Windreach, Norithae's capital city, lay nestled in a deep valley accessible only by boat or through a relatively narrow pass that cut through the mountainside.

As they pushed onward, the air thinned and grew colder, with the fragrant scents of the forest's plant life being overpowered by the salty aroma of the Elder Sea. Their hike turned treacherous as the flat forest floor morphed into a steep incline littered with rubble that had cascaded down from the rugged peaks above. Aurelia focused on her feet, anxious about stumbling and drawing attention to their group. When she glanced up from the loose stones that threatened to trip her, she saw warriors methodically spaced around their perimeter, arms outstretched.

Although she couldn't see the wards they had created, she could feel the continuous hum of their magic in the surrounding air. The barrier muffled the sounds of the forest, making the frigid chill of the mountain air bearable once more. The knot of anxiety that had twisted in her gut since morning began to loosen. Her breaths became easier now that they were cloaked from their enemies. While she still felt a sense of dread about the upcoming battle, the temporary sense of security provided some calm.

They arrived at the site designated for their permanent camp just as the sun reached its zenith. A host of warriors cast lasting wards around the perimeter before the ones maintaining the temporary barrier released their magic.

Unlike their other camps, this site was not a large clearing. In fact, it could hardly be called a clearing at all. The small open glade had just enough space for the downsized bathing and dining tents.

The rest of the tents had to be staggered within the trees, but they managed to pitch more than in previous locations.

Aurelia and Cristos were given their own tent again. Kano still had his own enclosure, though it was far smaller than the one he occupied upon their arrival in Ekotoria. She was grateful it was sizable enough for him to be comfortable.

A solemn mood settled over the camp after the initial setup was finished. The warriors remained quiet, not conversing, and few lingered around the fires. Some trained, while others sharpened their weapons in the open, but most retreated to their tents.

Aurelia and Cristos quickly ate their lunch before spending time with Kano in his new home. Kano lounged with his head in Aurelia's lap, while Cristos sat a few feet away, sharpening his blades with a rough stone. Septima and Exie joined them shortly afterward. Her sister approached Aurelia while Exie pulled out her sword and joined Cristos in his task.

"How are you feeling?" Septima asked as she sat cross-legged on Kano's other side, stroking his fur as she gazed at Aurelia.

"Honestly," Aurelia replied, "I'm a bit scared."

"Same." Septima's face was more serious than usual, her beautiful features crinkling in a frown, worry shadowing her expression. Aurelia studied her younger sister's face as she had done many times before, searching for any sign of doubt. Although her fear was evident, there was no hint of regret in her expression. "But I think that's normal."

Aurelia considered her words and nodded. Exie had said the same thing weeks earlier. The sisters glanced toward the blond warrior, who was deep in conversation with Cristos. If Septima was not distressed over their decision to flee Vaekros and rush headlong into a foreign, magical conflict, then Aurelia resigned herself to whatever their future held.

She sighed heavily before responding. "Blaedia said we will march on Norithae tomorrow."

"Exie told me. War is inevitable—I know that—but I wish we had more time." Septima took Aurelia's hand and squeezed it. "We need to look out for each other. I cannot handle life without you, Lia."

The backs of Aurelia's eyes burned as she fought against the tears that threatened to fall. She squeezed her sister's hand back and cleared her throat, attempting to hide the overwhelming fear and love she felt as she glanced around their enclosure at the only family she had in Ekotoria. "I feel the same. That's what makes tomorrow so scary. I am more afraid of losing any of you than I am of dying."

Exie and Cristos joined them before Septima could respond. Cristos sheathed his sword and sat beside Aurelia, placing the weapon on the ground next to him. He pulled Aurelia into his lap and nuzzled her neck in a way that reminded her of the great cat now sleeping at her feet. She giggled and playfully swatted him as he planted a kiss on her cheek.

"What were you two talking about?" Exie asked, interlacing her fingers with Septima's.

"Tomorrow." Septima's usually chipper—and sometimes snarky—tone sounded glum as she answered her girlfriend.

Cristos wrapped his arms around Aurelia's waist and rested his chin on her shoulder as he addressed the group. "I think the war is on everyone's minds. It's hard not to think about it, but let's take it one step at a time. Focus on tonight; tomorrow, we focus on the battle. If you dwell on the enormity of war, it will swallow up the happiness for which we are fighting in the future."

Exie nodded. "We should probably grab dinner and wash up. We have a long day ahead of us. The more sleep we get, the better off we will be."

Aurelia couldn't argue with his logic, so she stood and said a long goodbye to Kano. She still wasn't sure if she would let him join the warriors' ranks tomorrow. If she didn't, this would likely be the last time she saw him until after the battle—if she even returned.

The others rose to their feet. Exie pulled Septima into a hug, and Aurelia tried to give them some semblance of privacy as the phoenix whispered in her sister's ear.

Cristos led the way out of the enclosure to the camp's epicenter. The familiar scent of stew met Aurelia's nose as her stomach grumbled impatiently. She wasn't sure if she would be able to quiet her anxious mind long enough to sleep, but at least she was hungry.

The Warriors had already formed lines when they reached the dining tent. The meal bell hadn't even rung, but she assumed they had the same idea of wanting an early dinner and an early bedtime. Aurelia hoped the bathing line wouldn't be as long. Although if the tiny basins were replaced with their usual stalls, a magically warmed shower would be worth the wait.

Holera and Kason occupied a large table inside the dining tent as Aurelia's small group entered. After everything that had rapidly transpired upon their return from Claywind, they had hardly seen the pair and hadn't spoken to them in days. Exie walked straight to their table and sat down without hesitation. The other three trailed behind her and claimed seats of their own. Aurelia looked forward to chatting with them; after spending so much time traveling together, she had genuinely grown to like and respect the Aegrician couple.

"Has anyone heard from Calista today?" Aurelia asked as she sat across from Holera. Cristos settled into the chair beside her as Holera glanced at Kason. He shook his head, his jaw clenched.

"Not unless Blaedia is keeping the message quiet," Kason said, sighing. His stiff posture relaxed, and his furrowed brow revealed the worry he didn't voice. "I'm hoping she is traveling with a Diapolisian fleet and will meet us in Norithae."

Aurelia held onto the same hope, but unless the healer showed up in the middle of the night, they wouldn't know until the last hour was upon them. Even if Calista searched for their new camp, alone or with Diapolis' dragons and warriors, there was no guarantee she could find them behind the strengthened wards.

Even though Aurelia was hungry, she ate slowly. She knew that sustenance was crucial, especially since she would have to fight for her life come morning, but the typically savory meal tasted like sawdust in her mouth. Her mind continued to reel, conjuring terrifying visions of possible outcomes. She looked up at the faces she loved so much and forced herself to finish her stew; she needed to be strong for them.

After dinner, Aurelia hugged her sister goodnight. It was a long, tight embrace that she had a hard time breaking free from. Once their extended farewell concluded, she and Cristos headed to the bathing tent. She felt close to tears when she entered and saw the divided shower stalls. She lingered under the hot spray longer than necessary, letting it wash away some of her nerves. She didn't know when she would have the chance to shower again, so she made sure to savor the moment.

When they climbed into bed that night, Aurelia hoped they would have more nights together. The fact that she could not count on that particular fate made her chest ache so much that breathing felt like a struggle. Cristos pulled her close and pressed his lips to hers, and suddenly, sleep was the last thing she desired. This could be their last night together, and she intended to make it count.

His tongue slid across her lips as he asked for permission, and Aurelia threaded her fingers in his damp hair, tilting her head to deepen the kiss.

Their kisses became feverish. His hands were everywhere. They slid across her back and caressed her breast. His light touches made her moan as his calloused palms glided along her bare skin, igniting her body with the same electricity he always invoked. His hard length rubbed against her sensitive bud as he ground against her. The thin cloth of their sleepwear was a maddening barrier between them. She slid her hand beneath his waistband and wrapped her hand around his stiff cock. She stroked him, running her thumb along the tip as she tightened her grip.

He groaned deep in his throat, and the sound sent delicious tingles up her spine as it empowered her movements. She bit his bottom lip and sucked it into her mouth before he pulled away with another groan, more frustrated than aroused.

"If you keep doing that, I'm going to bury myself inside you."

She released his hard length and playfully pulled at the fabric of his sleep trousers. "I was counting on that, so take these off."

Cristos shrugged a single shoulder as he grinned. "If that is what you want, I aim to please."

He made quick work of his pants, tossing them on the floor, before he pulled her nightdress off. His hands ran along her flesh as he slid the thin fabric over her head, and she hadn't realized removing clothing could be so sensual.

He leaned in to kiss her again, and she felt the tip of his cock at her entrance. She opened her thighs to give him better access, but he did not enter her. Instead, he reached between them and gripped his length and rubbed the tip in her wetness. Once. Twice. Three times.

She was ready to scream in frustration, but before she could, he began to slip slowly inside her, one delicious inch at a time.

Aurelia appreciated his gentleness, but it wasn't what she wanted. She wanted him undone. She wanted all of him, raw and uncensored. She slid her arms around him and began to stroke the wings that were folded against his back. That was all it took for him to throw caution to the wind and slam into her.

His hard thrusts and firm grip on her waist made her shriek in pleasure. The sound was somewhere between a scream and a gasp as he pounded into her with reckless abandon. The entire camp probably heard her, but in that blissful moment, she did not care.

Chapter Forty-Four

Spectre Forest

Aurelia

Time stopped for no one, and morning arrived far too quickly. A warning bell tolled through their hidden camp, jolting Aurelia from her blissfully dreamless sleep. The melodic gong had a deep, somber sound that sent a wave of dread washing over her as she rolled out of bed. Cristos followed her from the comfort of their warm fur blankets, and they donned their fighting leathers in silence. This was it. Their fragile peace was about to shatter before high noon, and they were being thrust into the chaos of war.

The still air seemed to vibrate with unspoken tension as Aurelia moved. Every buckle she fastened felt heavier, and every strap she pulled tighter, as if she were being prepared for execution rather than protection. She could not shake the trepidation compressing her chest. Battle was messy, and lives would surely be lost, even if they succeeded in reclaiming Norithae.

As she exited the tent with Cristos in tow, she glanced around the already bustling camp. Fires burned low, smoke curling skyward like prayer offerings. The familiar chatter of morning routines was replaced with clipped orders and grim resolve. She focused on the determined expressions surrounding her and wondered who might be living their final day. Would it be one of the cooks hurrying to finish preparing breakfast? One of the lanistas tending to the horses? Would it be one of her friends or family? Was it her last day?

They ate as soon as the food was ready, but Aurelia didn't taste a single bite of the porridge she forced down her throat. Each bite threatened to resurface as her knotted stomach protested against the meal. Her dark thoughts amplified with every passing second, cycling viciously as her anxiety reached new heights. The clang of spoons, the scrape of bowls—mundane sounds became unbearable, sharp enough to fray her nerves.

After finishing their meal, Aurelia and Cristos joined the warriors congregated at the heart of the camp. They were all strapping on armor over their fighting leathers, and Aurelia stared in surprise. She had assumed the Aegricians would take to the sky first and press their advantage, but it appeared they were planning to attack on foot instead. Hopefully, Warbotach held the same expectations and would prepare for an aerial assault. If there were more long-range fighters than swordsmen, perhaps their chances of survival and success would increase.

Holera waved the couple over once she finished donning her protective gear. The silver-haired phoenix looked fierce and deadly in the ebony Aegrician armor. It appeared to be composed of feathers, but it did not so much as ruffle in the stiff wind that tore through the open glade they occupied. Aurelia inspected the impressive design as she greeted the warrior. The breastplate was made of the thickest leather she had ever seen. It flared out at the shoulders and featured long panels that draped just past the groin, protecting both sides of the body. Even standing still, Holera radiated lethal beauty, like a goddess of war poised to strike.

Exie, Septima, and Kason joined them almost immediately. Kason handed Cristos a set of armor while Holera and Exie fitted Aurelia and Septima with undersized replicas of the Aegrician war garb. Their human forms were much smaller than the fae warriors, and the petite armor looked almost doll-like in comparison. As Aurelia adjusted the straps, she felt like a child playing dress-up rather than a soldier preparing for battle. Her fingers trembled as the armor whispered against her skin, as if passing cold judgment.

Once their armor was secured correctly, the Vesta sisters were handed a variety of weapons. Aurelia was not the worst with a sword, but she excelled as an archer. She received a filled quiver and bow, which she strapped to her back, along with a short sword and two daggers to ensure she wasn't left defenseless once her arrows were depleted. The thought of piercing an enemy from a distance weighed heavily on her conscience, but the very idea of running a sword through another living being—of having their blood coat her hands—made her stomach churn.

She looked down at herself, surprised by her appearance. Though she was neither mentally nor physically prepared for war, she certainly looked the part. Septima stood beside her, her grim expression mirroring Aurelia's as she was outfitted with multiple blades of her own. Cristos had already fastened his longsword vertically down his spine. He wore his shortsword at his hip, a dagger sheathed on each thigh, and three more small blades attached to a belt resting atop his armor.

Aurelia's heart thundered in her ears as she took in the sight of her battle-ready friends and family. Tears filled her eyes as she grappled with the possibility that not all of them might return to camp after the battle. The metallic clink of armor being tightened around them sounded all too much like a death knell.

Blaedia approached the gathered warriors with long, confident strides. Dressed in formidable armor and armed with an array of deadly weapons, she appeared invincible as she stood before them. Her powerful voice boomed throughout the camp, and Aurelia felt the telltale tingles of magic in the air as her amplified words resonated around her.

"Today, we fight to reclaim what is ours. Saving our queen and restoring our continent starts here. First, we will free Norithae from the Warbotach scum. With the aid of their people, we will advance north and rescue our homeland."

The general scanned the crowd, making eye contact with nearly everyone as she raised her hand and placed it against her heart. The passion and determination in her tone sent shivers down Aurelia's spine. "It is normal to feel afraid, but do not allow fear to still your hand. We must overcome our hesitations, for we fight for what is just. We fight for freedom. Defending the future of our people is the most noble cause. Whether you fall in battle or live to tell the tale, you are a hero, and your kingdom will forever be indebted to you. Fight hard and fight smart, and together we will conquer the enemy."

Blaedia paused, her gaze sweeping over her warriors once more. She raised her fist in the air and let out an impassioned bellow. "TODAY, WE WILL BE VICTORIOUS!"

Cheers erupted throughout their ranks, and the crowd began to chant her words fervently. Fists shot into the air as the warriors roared. Blaedia normalized fear and encouraged conquering it rather than condemning such an uncontrollable emotion, and her speech inspired Aurelia just as much as the spirited warriors surrounding her. She thrust her arm up and raised her voice to join the emboldened chorus.

Cristos stared at her as she shouted, a smile lighting up her face. His eyes sparkled as he grabbed her waist and pulled her close, kissing her deeply. For a moment, she forgot about the impending battle as their surroundings faded away, his passionate embrace drawing all her attention. He pulled away far too soon, and the cacophony of the camp filled her ears once more. His ocean-blue gaze held hers as he pressed his forehead against hers.

"I love you so much. Be careful and stay safe. I cannot live this life without you," he said, his words heavy with emotion.

Her heart seized at his declaration, and she kissed him once more, feeling the weight of their situation. Aurelia broke the kiss and cupped his cheek as she responded, "I love you too. Life without you isn't an option, so you are not allowed to fall in battle."

He gave her a crooked grin, though it didn't quite reach his eyes. She wanted—needed—to see happiness fill his features before they faced the danger ahead. Keeping her tone light, she shot him a playful wink. "Let's go get your throne back, Your Majesty."

He laughed, and his heartwarming smile returned, the one she craved. "What am I going to do with you?"

With a smirk, she shrugged. "You should have thought of that before. Now you're stuck with me."

"I have no complaints," he replied.

But their easy banter was short-lived. The Aegrician warriors began to form lines along the invisible wall of the camp. Aurelia glanced toward Kano's enclosure, still torn with indecision. Septima, having pulled away from a passionate embrace with Exie, turned to her.

"Go get him. He would want to be with us, no matter the outcome. Don't deny him the chance to protect the ones he loves," her sister urged.

Septima's words resonated deep within Aurelia. She realized her sister was right. If she stayed in the camp as Cristos had asked, she would regret not being able to fight alongside her family and friends. Survival be damned. She raced over to the enclosure and released the great cat, deciding against leashing him. She wanted Kano to roam free for two reasons: to gain the trust of the Aegrician warriors during battle and, more importantly, to allow him to choose whether to fight or flee. She wanted him to have some semblance of power over his role in Ekotoria.

With Kano and Cristos flanking her, Aurelia hurried to catch up with Septima and Exie as rows of warriors marched through the charged air of the wards and out into the Spectre Forest. They advanced toward Windreach in silence, determined to free Norithae and move north to liberate Aegricia, their strides fueled by purpose. Every single person held a weapon at the ready, scanning the woodlands they traversed. The forest itself seemed to hold its breath, ancient boughs shivering faintly as if even the trees understood what was at stake.

Kano let out a low warning growl as a small Warbotach patrol approached. The sound rumbled through the ground beneath Aurelia's boots, primal and commanding. Before she even processed the enemy's sudden appearance, several phoenixes broke away, their bodies bursting into flame as they shifted and dispatched the patrol before the soldiers had a chance to sound an alarm. The acrid scent of scorched flesh mingled with the smell of pine sap and damp earth, thickening the air.

Their forces pressed on, leading the group toward the treacherous mountain pass that would take them straight into the heart of the capital city.

Aurelia stretched up on the tips of her toes, straining to see if any of their people had been hurt. Her inferior height made it impossible to see over the mass of lanky warriors that marched in front of her, but she spotted the vibrant flames of a phoenix shifting through the throng of bodies. A firebird took to the sky, teal and crimson feathers clashing beautifully in the pale morning light.

The intense coloring looked like water and fire fighting for dominance over the impressive creature, but Aurelia's awestruck gaze turned horrified as it landed on the massive talons. Two bloodied bodies hung limp in the phoenix's grasp. She couldn't see well enough to identify them, but the dark Aegrician armor held her attention captive like an ominous omen. Mighty wings carried them overhead in the direction of their camp, and Aurelia's stomach clenched painfully as she silently hoped the injured would survive.

The warriors did not dally as their comrades raced toward their base in search of medical attention. They continued on, weapons never faltering from their readied position. The steady rhythm of boots crunching against earth and stone became a grim, drumlike beat. As their forces funneled into the narrow passage, Aurelia drew nearer to the point of conflict.

She passed six scarred bodies left to rot on the forest floor, their sightless eyes fixated on the thick greenery above. The bright sunlight that streamed through the canopy served as a morbid spotlight, illuminating the wounds that ended their lives. A stomach-churning gash split one soldier's throat, the crimson wound exposing interior tissue and pale glints of bone. Aurelia's insides lurched, and she fought to hold down her breakfast.

Cristos reached over and covered her eyes, turning her head to face forward as they continued to traipse through the forest. When they moved past the grisly sight, he removed his hand and intertwined their fingers. He gripped her hand so hard it throbbed, but she did not ask him to loosen his hold.

The dull ache, the feel of his strength, and the warmth radiating from him all served to reassure her. The prickles of pain reminded her she was still alive. Cristos was still alive. Kano. Septima. Exie. Taryn. Blaedia. Kason. Holera. Her eyes flitted around their ranks, focusing on each of their faces. At least for now, all the people she cared for in this world still soldiered on, and that would have to be enough.

A vicious snarl tore from Kano's throat. The unexpected ferocity made her heart slam into her chest as she jumped and whipped her head around in search of the threat. Several of the nearby warriors stepped away in fear of the tiger, but Aurelia knew better. He would not react so viscerally unless they were in imminent danger. His ears were flat against his head, and his lips were pulled back, exposing his sharp canines. The growl deepened, vibrating through her bones.

She slowed to match his deliberate steps as she forced herself to stop staring at the great cat and scan their surroundings. He was behaving far too fiercely, and she was certain he sensed something they could not.

Nothing seemed out of place as they continued forward, but once half of their forces had entered the mountainous pass, she spotted the first Warbotach soldier astride his fire-breathing steed. Before the Aegricians could react, dozens more appeared out of thin air and descended on them from all sides.

Her thundering heart and gasping breaths were at odds with her oddly calm mind. As her body screamed for her to flee, her mind cataloged the violence that erupted around her with unnerving clarity. The enemy had to have been hidden by wards, but they were not enough to fool Kano. They attacked almost as soon as he reacted to their presence. They'd effectively cut the phoenixes' forces in half as they blocked the rocky path that led to Windreach.

Sounds of battle echoed from the mountain's narrow pathway as chaos reigned inside Spectre Forest. Aurelia raised her bow, not allowing herself time to hesitate as she fired at the throng of invaders that tried to break through the wall of warriors. She did not know what would happen if they managed to infiltrate their ranks and fragment their formations, but she could feel the need to prevent that from happening deep in her soul.

Her arrows whistled through the air, accompanied by the other archers among their forces who shot at the enemy. The sounds of swords clashing, the roar of fire, and pain-filled screams overwhelmed the dense woods, turning it into a hellscape of sound.

She notched her last arrow and let it fly. It buried itself into the eye of a Warbotach soldier who was swinging his sword at Kason's turned back. Kason disposed of his opponent and turned to see the man she'd pierced with her shot. He nodded his thanks as she pulled her sword and turned her attention elsewhere.

Aurelia felt strangely empty as the fighting raged on. After it was over, she would have time to process the carnage her hands dealt, but for now, she needed to survive. Most of the Aegrician archers traveled at the front of their procession and were trapped by the soldiers that attacked the pass. When the few that remained ran out of arrows, the battle began in earnest.

Warbotach reinforcements continued to appear without warning to join the fray. Her allies were divided, their tight grouping destroyed. Cristos slashed at a swordsman who advanced on him as she raised her blade to deflect an attack. Kano sprang from her left, knocking her assailant to the ground before their blades could meet. He tore the man's throat out in an instant and returned to Aurelia's side, blood darkening his striped muzzle.

They were surrounded by enemies, but her furry friend never left her side. He only attacked the ones who advanced on her. When another soldier advanced on horseback, the tiger pounced. The man was thrown from his mount, the creature dead before it could expel the flame that had started to form in its mouth.

The rider hit the ground hard, rolling from the impact. His confused expression hardened into a rage-filled mask as he set his sight on her beloved pet. Aurelia lashed out with her sword, tearing open his gut with the strike. Hot blood sprayed across her knuckles, slick and shocking. She pivoted as an angry roar sounded behind her. Pain exploded in her left arm as a blade bit into it, white-hot fire racing through her veins.

Still, she felt detached from herself, as if she was merely an observer in her own body. Her instincts ruled as she lifted her sword with her right to engage with her attacker, but she never got the chance. She dove to the side to avoid being impaled by the man's broadsword as Kano tackled him from behind, the tiger's massive jaws snapping shut with a wet crack.

She and her tiger dealt unyielding carnage as the enemy continued to press them from all sides. She tried to catch sight of Cristos and Septima, but everyone was a mass of bodies. The Aegrician armor made them all look the same at a quick glance, and she could not offer more than that as she continued to fight against the seemingly endless stream of attackers. It was impossible to make sense of what was going on around her.

Kano unleashed a vicious growl behind her as he coiled his hind legs, poised to pounce. Aurelia reacted to his ferocity and ducked as he launched himself over her head. She turned in time to see the tiger topple another Warbotach soldier who had tried to sneak up on her. He tore at the man's face, shredding it to ribbons as they hit the ground.

"Thanks, boy." She turned to search for her next opponent as she said the words, but there were none. The attacks had ceased.

She wasn't sure if they had killed them all or if Warbotach had retreated, but she didn't care. There were more pressing matters. She strained her eyes, searching for Cristos, Septima, Exie, any of her loved ones, really.

Now that the danger had abated, she took in the horrifying scene before her. Dead bodies littered the ground. Aegrician, Warbotach, and fiery horses alike in their stilled chests and blank stares. Injured cries filled the forest as dozens of phoenixes took to the skies, undoubtedly scanning for more threats. Aegrician warriors walked among the bodies, searching for their survivors. If any Warbotach soldiers survived, they retreated because not a single scarred face scattered on the forest floor held any life.

A familiar face appeared in the tree line, and Aurelia felt like she could breathe again. Cristos was saturated in blood, but stood tall. From a distance, he did not appear wounded, and she sighed in relief as she rushed to his side. He smiled brilliantly as he ran to meet her and reached out to pull her into a hug before his smile faltered.

"Your arm!"

Aurelia glanced down. Her eyes widened as she stared at her blood-soaked fighting leathers and the long gash on her forearm.

"Are you hurt anywhere else?" Cristos' panicked voice was unnatural as he scanned the rest of her body.

"I am okay. It was not my sword arm, and Kano protected me. He took care of the attacker before I even laid eyes on him."

"Not your sword arm," he scoffed. "How in the realms did you go from being terrified of war to reassuring me that your sword arm is fine?"

His voice was frantic as he worried over her, and she couldn't help but grin. Cristos was usually so calm and collected during times of crisis, so seeing his unmistakable concern and love for her warmed her heart. She placed the palm of her uninjured arm over his heart and stretched to kiss him gently.

"I'm okay, I promise. Have you seen Septima? Exie? Holera? Anyone?"

Her smile faded as he shook his head grimly. "I will look for them as soon as we get you to a healer."

"I. Am. Fine." Her tone left no room for argument as she pushed through the sea of bodies in search of her sister and friends.

"Aurelia! Cristos!" She turned at the sound of Exie's shout, but the joy that had surged within her vanished instantly upon seeing the warrior. Exie was covered in blood and what looked suspiciously like organ tissue. She limped slightly as she hurried toward them, but it wasn't the unsteady gait or excessive gore that stopped Aurelia's heart. It was the panic and sheer terror evident in Exie's expression that made it impossible to breathe.

Exie sobbed as they rushed to her side. She managed to pull herself together long enough to speak, shattering Aurelia's world. "Septima is gone! I can't find her anywhere! We have to find her."

"What do you mean 'gone'? Where did you get separated?" Cristos asked, his calm demeanor contrasting with Aurelia's frozen state, consumed by desolate horror.

Another cry escaped Exie as she tried to explain. "No, she is gone. I saw one of those barbarians hit her over the head and carry her away on his fire beast. I tried to stop them, to get to her, but I couldn't. I was fighting too many at once and—" Her words turned into an anguished wail. "I couldn't save her. We have to find her."

The world spun violently as Aurelia struggled to grasp the meaning behind Exie's words. There was no way. It couldn't be true. Septima couldn't be gone, but...

Septima was gone.

The forest seemed to implode around her, its ancient silence pressing down like a tomb. The smoke from the battle still lingered in the air, mingling with the metallic scent of blood. Warriors shouted, searched, and bled around her, but all Aurelia could hear was the echo of Exie's despair and the thunder of her own heart.

Her legs trembled as if the ground beneath her had been stripped away, leaving her suspended between fury and despair. Cristos' hand closed over hers, steadying her, but even his warmth could not penetrate the icy void that hollowed her chest.

Somewhere, Septima still breathed—or so Aurelia told herself, clinging to the fragile ember of hope before grief consumed her entirely. She would find her sister. She would tear through kingdoms, scorch armies, and rend the world apart if she had to.

Because losing Septima was not an option.

To be continued...

CROWN OF THE PHOENIX SERIES 2

CROWN
OF THE
EXILED

C.A. VARIAN

Chapter One

Aurelia

The last words Aurelia Vesta wanted to hear when the chaos of battle settled and the enemy retreated into the forest was that her sister, Septima, the person she'd left her world for, was gone.

She knew there was a chance they all wouldn't make it back alive when they'd left the safety of their camp and traveled into Warbotach-controlled Norithae that morning. It was what had caused near constant fear in Aurelia's chest ever since Blaedia had planned the siege days earlier, but she never expected the enemy to take her sister.

Their decision to leave the human world only months prior had been the biggest decision of their lives, and albeit ill-planned, had been the right decision. They had been through so much already, both good and bad. They'd spent time in a dungeon and been attacked by hellhounds, but they'd also found love. Even traveling into a fae realm on the brink of war, and even after their father, Proteus, had ignored the fact that Septima was not attracted to males and had arranged their marriages anyway, they'd still found love.

Aurelia and Septima had run away from home, deciding any destiny was better than the one their father had made for them, but they'd never anticipated running into fae warriors in the forest of the human realm. They'd never even known another realm existed. The portal was so close to their home, but they could've never traversed it on their own. The Aegrician phoenix warriors were the only beings in either world with the ability to fly through the Marella Arch and travel between the worlds, although leaders of both realms decided long ago that the portal should remain unused to prevent exactly what threatened the two realms now—war.

Barbarians from the magical realm had been attempting to take over the human world for months, wanting to move to the fertile land on the other side since their own was dying with the spread of the desert on the southern part of the continent. No one knew why the Warbotach ruler hadn't stopped after his conquest of the northern kingdoms of Norithae and Aegrician but was instead desperate to continue his invasion beyond the realm, and no one knew who was backing him. The possibilities of those on other continents backing the king, and the powers they could potentially have, were endless, and they were terrifying.

Having conquered their way across the continent, the Warbotach king held the Aegrician queen, Otera, locked away in her own dungeon. Aurelia had only just discovered her own relation to the Aegrician queen weeks earlier. Otera was her aunt, her mother's sister, and she may never have the chance to meet her. Uldon, the barbarian king, intended to keep Otera locked away until she agreed to give her power to cross the portal, the power of her crown, to him and Aurelia didn't even know if it was possible for the queen to force the crown's power on another. The Crown of the Phoenix had always chosen the queen and who would control the portal between realms, but Uldon clearly believed there was a way for him to take that power. Otera had been held in the dungeon beneath her castle for the past several months as he tried to force her hand.

In the meantime, the Aegrician military, which consisted of phoenix-shifting females and the non-shifting members who worked with them, spent those months away from their kingdom, building up strength and trying to secure allies. If they had not fled, their enemies would have exterminated them. To keep the military and the kingdom's civilians safe, the queen and her leadership agreed on a plan to look for allies and bide their time until they understood what they were up against and were strong enough to win.

Until the previous morning, when they'd left their camp in the Spectre Forest and marched toward Norithae, Aurelia and Septima had been to Norithae only once before. Having been captured by Warbotach soldiers while on a hunt, they'd spent time in the dungeon there until the Norithae king, Cristos, had helped them escape. At the time, no one knew Cristos' identity. After the Warbotach cavalry had killed his father, leaving him the new king, Cristos had hidden who he was until he could do the same thing the Aegricians were trying to do---build up allies to take his kingdom back.

In the time since he'd helped them escape the dungeon, he and Aurelia had fallen in love. They had been through so much together, and now they stood in the forest, among the dead and the injured. Their own bodies were bruised and bleeding, but all that mattered in that moment was the devastating words coming from Exie. *Septima is gone.*

Aurelia's heart pounded in her chest, her own bleeding arm no match for her emotions. She had to find her sister.

Exie stood in front of her and Cristos, the blond warrior leaning to one side as her leg gushed blood from a wound in her thigh.

"We have to go after her," she said, her voice full of desperation.

Aurelia tried to focus her attention on her friend, but the adrenaline surging through her body made it difficult. Her eyes scanned the surrounding forest, searching the faces of the warriors who'd shifted back into their fae forms and were now trying to assess who needed a healer and who couldn't be saved. Septima's beautiful tawny face and long obsidian braids were not among them.

"We're going to find her, Exie," she said as she pulled the injured female into her arms. "We're going to find her, but you need to see a healer. You can't fight any more like this."

The warrior's head was shaking before Aurelia had even finished getting the words out. Exie had been injured in battle countless times before, but she'd never let it stop her, and she surely didn't intend to let it keep her from finding the woman she loved.

Just as Exie was about to respond, the tall silver-haired warrior, Holera, and her muscular male lover, Kason, darted out through the trees, bloody but not showing any obvious wounds.

"What's going on?"

Having been Exie's friend since they were young, Holera approached her friend first and looked her over, trying to assess the wound on her leg.

Face appearing grim, Cristos' eyebrows furrowed as he held onto Aurelia's hand. His touch grounded her. "Warbotach must have taken Septima. We can't find her anywhere. She's not among the injured." Exie crumbled, dropping to her knees and sobbing in her hands, completely ignoring her own injury.

"We have to find her,"

Exie said again, the words muffled through her fingers.

"You're wasting time! Go after her now or I'll go myself!"

Lowering herself to the ground, Holera tried to slow the bleeding.

"We're going to find her but you're not going anywhere but to a healer, Exie."

Holera turned to a passing healer, one whose name Aurelia did not know, and called out to her.

"You there, take Exie to the infirmary tent. Advise Blaedia that Septima has been taken and we're going after her. Look after Exie with your life. I want a full report on her when I return."

Cristos pulled Aurelia into his arms, his leathery black wings beating with a panicked urgency as he lifted them through the trees of Spectre Forest and into the sky. She ignored the injury to her arm, the sting of it barely noticeable against the painful wrenching of her chest. Being able to sense her emotions, Cristos kissed her on the cheek as they moved below the setting sun.

"Don't worry, Aurelia. We're going to find her."

Holding her bow at the ready and scanning the forest, Aurelia wasn't so sure. Holera and Kason flew beside them, Holera in her phoenix form while Kason sat astride her back, his own bow ready to strike.

The Warbotach cavalry had snuck up on their ranks as they'd moved toward Norithae to retake the kingdom. They'd been able to sneak up on such trained fighters by using wards that made them invisible, the same type the Aegricians used to camouflage their camps. If Septima was under those wards now, they wouldn't be able to find her. As they searched from the sky, Aurelia was worried that was the case. She could have been right under their nose and they wouldn't have seen her. They wouldn't even have been able to hear her.

They flew for hours, doing low sweeps over the forest and into the mountain pass, but Septima and the Warbotach warriors were gone, or they were hiding behind wards that cloaked their location. Either way, they would not find her on this night.

Aurelia sobbed against Cristos' chest as they made their way back to the location of their camp. They couldn't have gone any further, not without the full might of the military. Aegricia was a Warbotach stronghold. If her sister had been taken there, they would be powerless to get her back, not unless the Diapolisian king decided to provide aid, not unless there was a plan.

Just as they crossed into their own warded space, the temporary camp that had been set up only the night before, Aurelia saw the injured Exie sitting on a bench near the perimeter, her thigh wrapped in bandages. Returning to the camp without Septima in tow was soul-shattering enough, but the look on the blond warrior's face threatened to fracture Aurelia's heart completely. There was no doubt Exie would have gone after Septima if she could have. The fierce warrior had never backed down from a fight, but the injury to her thigh had rendered her nearly immobile.

"I'm going to find Blaedia and update her," Holera said before walking off, Kason following closely behind.

Aurelia had not seen the general since before they'd left for the battle that morning, not since Blaedia made the powerful speech that had every one of the warriors willing to die in battle. With the battle in Norithae being over, it would only be a matter of time before their camp was packed up again and moved into the capital city of Windreach, where Cristos would take his place on the Norithaean throne.

The betrayal still stung, but Aurelia understood why Cristos had not revealed his true identity as heir to the slain king. She may have understood, but she still didn't know how she felt about who he truly was, no matter how much she loved him. He wanted her to be his queen, but the thought of being the human queen of a fae kingdom (technically half-human after what she'd learned from the healer, Variel) was more than she could process, especially with her sister being missing. For the time being, she and Cristos loved each other, and they were together, but the future was still unknown. Being queen, the cryptic Aegrician prophecy, her mother's true identity... It was all too much to process, so Aurelia pushed the heavy thoughts to the back of her mind and turned her attention to Exie, who was still sitting on the bench.

"What happened?" The warrior shifted uncomfortably, her eyes squeezing shut before opening wide. "Was there no trace of her?"

Rubbing a hand over his inky black hair, Cristos shook his head as Aurelia lowered herself onto the bench next to her friend, taking Exie by the hand. With her hands already trembling, she realized she was holding Exie's hand just as much to console herself.

"There was no trace of her or of Warbotach."

Exie blew out a deep breath, her face crumpling.

"I should have gone after her."

"There's nothing you could have done, Exie."

Crouching in front of them, Cristos' features were soft.

"They must have hidden themselves behind wards, just like they did before they attacked us. I don't know how they are summoning the power to keep the wards up, but there's no other explanation."

"We have to find her. She's strong, but we can't leave her in Warbotach hands. If they realized who you are, Aurelia, if they realize her sister is Queen Otera's niece…"

She hesitated, her head moving in a slow shake.

"There's no limit to what they would do to Septima to get to you or to get to the queen."

Aurelia's stomach tightened into a knot, bile burning the back of her throat. She hadn't had time yet to realize what it would mean for Septima if Warbotach found out her connection to the queen who was locked away in her own dungeon. When she stood onto shaky legs, the burden on Aurelia's shoulders made them almost too heavy to carry. She swayed, Cristos swooping in and wrapping an arm around her waist before turning her toward their tent.

"We all need to get some sleep," he said as he held onto her. "There's nothing we can do right now, but we will find her. I promise you. We will find her."

When they walked away, Aurelia hesitant to leave her friend at all, Exie was still sitting on the bench with her face in her hands.

Chapter Two

Septima

Septima's silken braids swung wildly below her as she lay unconscious astride the saddle of a Warbotach warrior's horse. The monstrous rider dug his heels into his crimson mount, traveling swiftly under the cover of Spectre Forest, taking Aurelia's sister toward the kingdom of Aegricia and further from the only family she had in the fae realm.

The turbulence of the ride jolted her awake, but only for a moment, not long enough for her to realize what was happening to her. When she awoke again, untold hours later, the crackling of a fire warmed her skin, but the bindings that bit into her wrists burned more than the flames. She struggled, twisting in her spot on the leaf-littered forest floor, but it was no use. Her vision was still blurry as she opened her eyes, trying to make sense of the darkness, of the chaotic surroundings where nothing looked familiar. There was no Aurelia, no Exie, not even the colorful flap of fiery wings. She tried to stand, but ropes held her ankles tight, so she only fell to the ground again.

"Stop struggling."

The unfamiliar voice came from somewhere behind her. It was deep and gravelly. *Not a friend.*

Twisting to face him, the sight of the scar faced Warbotach male pulled a scream from her gagged mouth. She scurried back on the ground, coming to a halt only feet away from the stones surrounding the fire.

"You're not getting away, female. So, stop struggling."

With only flickers of memory, she didn't even know how she'd gotten there. Her head pounded, sending her vision spinning as she scanned her surroundings again. From what she could tell, she was still in Spectre Forest. Realizing she was alone in the forest with a lone Warbotach soldier, Septima's skin prickled, fear blooming from her chest and spreading across her body. She didn't know why he'd stolen her, or what he planned to do with her, but she'd never been so unsure of her safety. Not even when she and her sister had been locked away in the Norithaean dungeon had she been so afraid.

Thinking about her time in captivity brought back an ache in her heart, just thinking about Exie being tortured, just thinking about how out of her mind with worry her lover must be with her disappearance. And her sister—she couldn't even think about how worried Aurelia probably was. They were undoubtedly searching the forest for her, if they were even alive. With the violence of the battle she'd been taken from, she didn't even know if they'd survived. It was tearing her apart. She needed to get away from her captor and find her family and friends.

Even though she was a human in a magical world, and had only been there for mere months, she and her sister had found a new family, a new group of friends who would do anything to keep them safe. She'd found love, a love like she could have never had back in her home world where women were not allowed to marry other women. Exie was everything she'd ever wanted in a partner, and she knew her lover felt the same way. She knew Exie would tear down the world to find her, because she was strong and courageous, and the passion and love they felt for each other was real.

The male's dark eyes watched her as though she were an insect he needed to swat, but she broke the stare, scooting on the ground until she faced the fire, leaving her back to him. It wasn't until she turned around, and gazed across the fire, that she saw them. *All of them.*

Chapter Three

The days seemed to drag on since the last time Uldon had visited Otera's cell in the dungeon. She wasn't complaining. He was the last person she wanted to see. The face she really wanted to see, although it wasn't her true face at all, was Bremusa. Her friend, the elemental hiding in plain sight, had not been to her cell since she'd cleaned the queen's wounds. Otera wasn't sure how long it had been since she'd enraged the Warbotach king enough for him to strike her, but she didn't regret a thing.

He was getting desperate. After everything he'd already tried to bend her crown to his will so he could get through the portal and into the human world, he'd been unsuccessful. All it did was show how unhinged Uldon really was. The queen smirked as she traced her fingers along the new scar beneath her eye, the wound having healed quickly due to her fae blood.

With only the sliver of a window to let in a view of the sun and moon, she'd lost track of the days as they passed, each one blending into the next. She wasn't sure how long she'd been in the dungeon, and with no visits from Uldon to brag about his attempts to steal her power, she truly had no concept of time at all. So Otera sat in silence, a small flame dancing in the palm of her hand and waited for the sun to rise again and mark another day she would lose track of as she served her sentence as a prisoner in her own palace.

The silence was maddening, giving her too much time to think. Until she'd been told about the capture of her commander and several of her warriors, Otera had been strong. She'd done her best to steal her mind and not think about those she loved more than anything, but as time went on with nothing to fill her days, no kingdom to rule, the grief became overwhelming. The feeling of a pit growing in her stomach made it difficult to eat the meager meals they left for her on the dungeon floor. She knew she'd lost weight, knew her ribs had never been as pronounced as they now were. The urge to eat slowed just like the updates on her people.

At the beginning of her imprisonment, the ravens came regularly, their messages passed on through Bremusa. It didn't take long for the ravens to stop coming though, or at least the messages to stop coming to her. Bremusa no longer brought her daily meals. Instead, Uldon's sniveling, cowardly advisor brought them. He was too afraid of Otera to come alone, so he never entered the dungeon without at least one of the beastly, scarred warriors that filled the Warbotach ranks, which filled her with a delirious giddiness. In her shredded dress and filthy skin, she was certainly not as fierce as she'd been before being pulled from her bed in the middle of the night, so being able to intimidate at least one person felt like a victory. In her pathetic existence, it was the small victories that counted.

Chapter Four

Aurelia

There was a somber mood in the Aegrician war camp as Aurelia and Cristos made their way toward Kano's enclosure. The great tiger was always situated beside their tent, something Aurelia was grateful for. After the battle, she knew the lanistas had taken him back to camp while she'd looked for Septima. It warmed her to know he was unharmed after he'd ferociously defended her in battle. With her sister being gone, she needed to see him, if only to cuddle him for a few moments.

Cristos' muscular arm was still wrapped around Aurelia's waist as she walked, if only to hold her upright when all her legs wanted to do was collapse. She was exhausted and overwhelmed. With the disappearance of Septima, she'd almost forgotten about the battle that morning, about how she'd killed people that day. Even knowing she had no other choice, it wasn't something she could just brush off with ease. Their faces would haunt her sleep. A tinge of pain shot through her arm as they walked, the injury she had completely forgotten about had clotted but still needed to be cleaned and bandaged. The realization barely had a chance to brush past her mind before the commanding presence of the general approached from outside her tent.

Blaedia walked with a purpose, stopping in front of Aurelia and pulling her into an embrace. Aurelia froze in place, the sudden show of emotion unexpected. Nothing about the general spoke of her being one who would do such a thing.

"We'll find her, Aurelia."

Loosening a breath, Aurelia leaned into Blaedia as the female passed a hand along her back. Her tears had dried up, but the backs of her eyes still burned, the general's embrace only tugging at her frazzled emotions that much more.

"I have no doubt they're bringing her to Aegricia. If so, she'll be with Queen Otera. Our queen won't let anything happen to her. This I can promise you."

When Blaedia pulled away to look into her eyes, the general's face was visibly pained in a way Aurelia had never seen. She didn't know how many warriors they'd lost in the day's battle, but she couldn't imagine how it affected Blaedia when she'd led warriors to their deaths, no matter the reason.

Aurelia nodded, unsure how to respond. No one could make any guarantees about her sister, not even such a powerful warrior.

"Will we be heading to Norithae soon?"

Knowing taking back the city would bring with it another set of complications, she had to bite back her hesitation to ask. Complicated or not, they needed to move closer to Aegricia, closer to where the enemy would be taking her sister. If they couldn't reclaim Norithae, they would never be able to take back Aegricia, and that was their reason for doing everything. All of it was for Aegricia.

Blaedia glanced toward Cristos, the new king of Norithae, her face expectant as though she were waiting for him to speak. It still caught Aurelia by surprise to think about the male, who'd been her lover for months, being a king. She swallowed back her conflicted emotions while looking at his handsome face, tan skin, and bright cerulean eyes. His black hair was a bit longer than it had been when he'd broken her out of the dungeon, making him look even sexier. The massive leathery wings that framed his back still blew her away. He looked like a god, even with his torn, blood-covered fighting leathers. Glancing down at her own clothing, she realized they both needed a shower and something clean to wear.

Cristos ran his fingers through his hair before he looked up at Blaedia, his brow furrowed.

"We didn't fly over the capital. I didn't want to alert Warbotach if they were still there, but the pass was clear. Well, unless they were under wards, which is possible."

Blaedia nodded but let him continue.

"Still, we need to take back the city, if only to get us closer to Aegricia. We don't have time to waste."

"I agree," Blaedia responded, her face grim but determined. "I'll send one of my warriors into Norithae before us, someone who can put up wards, but we need to make a move soon, before Warbotach has a chance to recuperate. Norithae was just a stepping stone for them anyway. They never intended to hold onto it."

Still leaning her weight on her lover, Aurelia listened to their conversation as though she wasn't really there, but hoping they'd start walking again soon. She was beyond antsy, the need for a shower, time with Kano, and rest, making her limbs tingle with the desperation to do something, *anything*, beside standing there. Thankfully, able to sense her emotions, Cristos wrapped up his conversation with Blaedia, pulling Aurelia closer into his side as they began walking forward again.

"What do you want to do first, love? Kano or shower? Well, after we get your arm looked at."

It was honestly a question she didn't know how to answer. She didn't have the energy for either and didn't have the mental capacity to decide.

"I'm fine. *Really*. It's not that bad. Let's just shower first so we can try to get some sleep after I visit with Kano. If I fall asleep with him, just leave me there."

Cristos chuckled and the sound of it warmed her deep within.

"There's no way I would leave you on the cold ground if you fell asleep, but you are welcome to fall asleep there."

Leaning over, he kissed her on the temple.

"I'll just have to carry you back into the tent after."

She grinned, the gesture instantly filling her with guilt.

"You know how much I love carrying you. We are going to the healer's tent first though. I don't want your arm to get infected."

After going to the healer's tent and getting her arm cleaned, stitched, and bandaged, Aurelia and Cristos showered quickly. With the aid of fae magic, the water was thankfully warm. Normally, she would have luxuriated in the warm water, would've wrapped her arms around her lover and kissed him until she was dizzy, but they were too drained, and she had to be careful not to get her fresh bandages wet. They barely shared words as they soaped their bodies and rinsed off, pulling on clean tunics and trousers. By the time they'd gotten to Kano's enclosure, the great cat wasted no time darting to the fence to greet them.

Having a clean body and clean clothes made Aurelia feel a tiny bit better, but even that filled her with guilt. She didn't even want to think about the condition her sister was in, how much Septima probably wanted a hot bath and clean clothes. The air squeezing out of her lungs, she loosened a breath as she laid the magical medallion against Kano's enclosure and entered through the opening, Cristos following behind her.

A burst of endorphins surged through Aurelia at the first touch of Kano's silky fur against her hand and the tiger nuzzled the leg of her trousers. He'd been covered in blood when she'd last seen him, so she was relieved the lanistas had bathed him, or at least given him the means to bathe himself. She checked him for wounds, passing her eyes and hands on each of his limbs, his back, and belly, but there were none. As viciously as he'd fought in the battle, as many Warbotach soldiers and horses as he'd killed, she felt foolish having been so hesitant to allow him to fight in the first place. He'd saved her life more than once that morning, and many other lives as well.

"He looks well," Cristos commented as he patted the tiger on the head, Kano leaving Aurelia momentarily to lean into his touch. They both sat on the ground, Kano laying between them with his head on Aurelia's lap.

"He does. It's a relief." She hesitated, leaning her head over Kano and kissing him on the head. "I was so worried."

Scooting closer to her on the ground, Cristos wrapped his arm around her shoulder and kissed her on the cheek. Her eyes closed as she leaned into him, his warm breath skittering across her body and igniting something deep inside her.

"I know you were, love, but he's fine. We are all going to be okay. Septima will be okay, too."

Tucking further into his side, Cristos' arm around her a solid weight to ground her, she closed her eyes, his words giving her body permission to relax. She needed sleep so badly. They both did. Somewhere in that moment, with Kano's head in her lap, snoring softly, and Cristos' arm around her shoulders, her head against his chest as his intoxicating spice filled her senses, Aurelia fell asleep.

When Aurelia awoke, at what had to have been hours later, she was tucked beneath fur blankets, Cristos' warm skin smelling of sandalwood and spice flush against her back. He'd carried her there after she'd fallen asleep in Kano's enclosure just like he'd said he would.

In the windowless tent, it was impossible to see the sky outside, but Aurelia knew it was the middle of the night by the silence of the camp around them. There was nothing to do but go back to sleep, but anxiety filled her mind. How could she sleep in a warm bed when her sister was out there in the hands of their enemy? If she couldn't do anything, she could at least feel guilty.

Kicking off her blankets, she tried to get out of bed, maybe go back to Kano's enclosure and think, but warm, muscular arms wrapped around her waist and pulled her back down.

"Where are you running off to in the middle of the night?"

The gravel of his voice when fresh from sleep sent shivers into Aurelia's bones she couldn't ignore, no matter how much worry was on her shoulders. She didn't fight his affections, nuzzling into his chest as he ran his hand up her back.

"I know it's hard to do nothing, but there's nothing you *can* do right now. The best thing you can do is keep up your strength so you can fight when you need to."

Nodding against his chest, she took in his breath-taking scent. Being away from her sister was like having a missing limb but having Cristos by her side meant the world to her. They hadn't known each other for long, but it truly was as though fate had pulled them together. He was the other part of her family now, another limb she couldn't imagine losing. Her heart would truly wrench in two.

Hollowness built in Aurelia's chest, the sheer powerlessness making her limbs heavy. She knew he was right, but it was impossible to live life as usual when her sister was missing. It just felt *wrong*.

"We need to be doing something."

The backs of her eyes burned but her tears were all cried out.

"I feel like part of me is missing without her. I'm her older sister. I'm supposed to be able to protect her."

"Don't blame yourself, love. This is war. You couldn't have prevented what happened."

There were no words that could have eased her guilt, but she knew he was trying, and he meant what he said. No one blamed her for Septima's capture, but they didn't have to. At fault or not, guilt would plague her until Septima was rescued. Rolling her onto her back, Cristos leaned over her, kissing her gently.

"Blaedia has a plan, a good plan. We need her support in any move we make. She knows that kingdom better than anyone. If we barged into Aegricia now, we would die. You know it's true."

She did, but when she closed her eyes, steadying her breaths while in his arms and trying to fall back asleep, the ache in her chest remained.

CHAPTER FIVE

AURELIA

The sound of voices fluttered through the darkness like spirits. Sliding her hand along the wall, Aurelia stepped forward, the need to get closer to them leading her movements. It was always night when she came here. There was never even a beam of sunlight to light her way, no light aside from the single flame she'd seen once or twice, lighting the face of who she knew to be the queen. Even after so many visits as a specter, Aurelia still didn't know how she could enter these moments in the night, nor did she know if they were anything more than a mind plagued with anxiety.

No light burned this night as she moved forward, careful not to stumble although she knew she wasn't really there. It wasn't possible. The voices grew louder as she crossed the room, but the words came less frequently the closer she got. A familiar flicker of fire came to life in the back of the room, halting her steps as the brilliant blue eyes of Otera reflected its light, and the dark-haired figure across from the queen came into view. Before Aurelia could reach out her hand and tell her sister they were coming for her, the darkness returned, taking her sister with it.

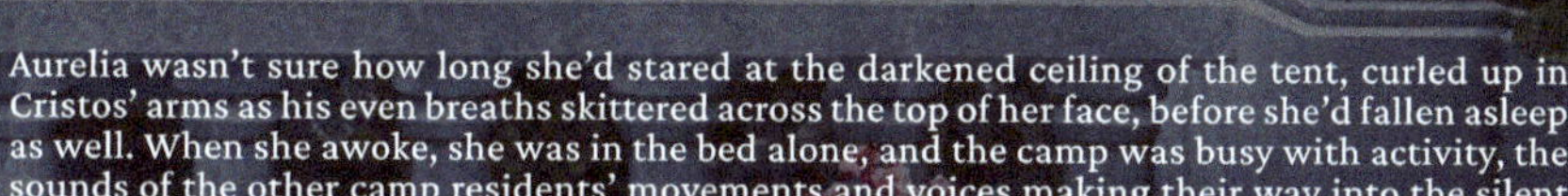

Aurelia wasn't sure how long she'd stared at the darkened ceiling of the tent, curled up in Cristos' arms as his even breaths skittered across the top of her face, before she'd fallen asleep as well. When she awoke, she was in the bed alone, and the camp was busy with activity, the sounds of the other camp residents' movements and voices making their way into the silent tent.

Her dream remained on her mind, the significance of it not lost on her, but she had no way to know if it had been real, and not simply her mind wishing for her sister to be with Otera. With Blaedia having mentioned that possibility before she'd gone to bed, it had likely been no more than her subconscious mind seeing what it desperately wanted to see: *her sister still alive.*

Although Cristos' warm skin was no longer against hers, she realized she wasn't alone by the prickle of awareness peppering her skin. Ever since they'd met, she'd always known when he was near. It didn't take long to see the electric blue eyes of her lover gazing back at her from near the water basin, a gentle smile on his handsome face bringing a smile to her own.

"Good morning."

Hanging the towel on a shelf, Cristos abandoned what he was doing and crossed the space in a few long strides, sitting beside her on the bed and leaning over to place a kiss on her lips. She closed her eyes at the touch of his mouth against hers, as though, if only in that moment, she could forget everything else.

"I hope I didn't wake you."

Aurelia shook her head and pulled him into another kiss before responding. Time stopped for a moment as his pillow-soft lips lingered.

"You didn't."

Glancing toward the entrance flap and seeing a sliver of sunshine stealing its way in, Aurelia pulled herself up on her elbows.

"Have they rung the breakfast bell yet?"

Seeming to want to keep her in bed a little longer, Cristos slid his legs beneath the blankets, forcing her to scoot over and let him lie next to her. She grinned, the temptation of a moment of pleasure too much for her to turn away with him so close, with his bare, muscular chest warming the side of her body. His skin felt like deliciously heated silk as he pulled her on top of him.

Pushing her obligations and worries aside, she submitted to him as his tongue tasted her lips and his hardness pressed against her center as she straddled him. There had always been something about him that was irresistible, like a gravitational pull from his body to hers, and she was powerless to stop it, not that she wanted to. In that moment, as he gripped her hips and pulled her against him, sliding her body along his cock and sending her nerve endings into a frenzy, she would have done anything for him.

Sliding his hands between their bodies, Cristos made quick work of the ties on Aurelia's tunic, dropping it to the floor beside their bed and wasting no time pulling her forward and sucking the peak of her breast into the hot well of his mouth. She gasped, the ecstasy of the moment such a contrast from what she'd been feeling for the past twenty-four hours. For this moment, she would allow herself to feel something other than the guilt. The feeling of his mouth on her skin, and how he trailed his tongue up the side of her neck, sent parts of her throbbing, begging for more.

"I love you," he said, the words sweet in her ear.

Expressing their love was a new thing, but it was real. She knew it was. She pulled his mouth to hers again as he fumbled with her undergarments, sliding the thin material down her thighs and tossing it over his shoulder.

They watched each other for a moment, their eyes locking as they panted. Naked on the bed, Aurelia leaned back on her elbows, and Cristos was on his knees between her legs, trousers still on but his cock straining against the inseam.

Biting her lip, she looked him over, at what pressed there.

"I want you. *Now*," she said as she reached forward and unlaced his trousers.

He watched, still breathing heavily but with an amused look on his face.

After a few moments of her struggling, he chuckled, leaning in to kiss her as he took over. He wasted no time between when he crawled over her, fitting himself between her thighs, and when he sheathed himself inside her. After the anxiety, fear, and pain of the past day, she didn't want to go slow. Not this day. She wanted him hot and hard, wanted her body so full of sensations, so full of pleasure and passion, that the hurt had no room to remain.

The tension in her belly coiled with every stroke of his hard length inside her, the slide of their bodies creating friction in all the right places. He held onto her ankles, lifting them over his shoulders as he drove into her from on his knees, his beautiful black wings spread open behind him, framing him like a god and keeping him balanced. The sight of him was all it took for Aurelia's climax to burst out of her, the ripple of pleasure making her legs stiffen against his shoulders as she screamed his name. Her body spasmed around him, squeezed the pulsing cock inside her until his body tensed and trembled, Cristos groaning with his own orgasm before falling over her, his wings tucking back in tight against his back.

There were no words, not for several moments, only the aftershocks of the intense love making—heavy breathing and soft moans, the rustling of blankets as Cristos pulled her beside him. When she slid into the crook of his shoulder, tracing her fingers along the sweat on his abdomen, her body felt boneless, like she could lay there all day. Maybe she would.

His cerulean eyes were on her when she glanced up to look at him, joyful and sated. Even after all they'd done together, she still blushed.

"I want you to be my queen, Aurelia."

Aurelia hadn't completely avoided his question, but she hadn't agreed either. The question of whether she wanted to be his queen didn't have a simple answer. She'd told him she loved him, told him they'd discuss long term plans once Septima had been found. Thankfully, the breakfast bell had interrupted the conversation she wasn't ready to have. There was no question whether she wanted to be with him. It was a resounding yes. But to rule Norithae, a kingdom she knew nothing about, to rule a kingdom at all... That gave her pause.

There was so much more to consider, including the prophecy handed down to them only weeks prior by Variel, the reclusive healer and wolf-shifter who lived in a warded cabin in Spectre Forest. The healer had known Aurelia's mother, had even been an advisor to Cristos' mother before she'd been killed, and knew more about their world than most. According to Variel, the Elemental of Spectre Forest and a powerful oracle, had prophesied: *Raging fires will fade to gentle embers, and a new day will make a new dawn. When the throne-less queen falls, the phoenix will be reborn from the ashes and rise again, bringing with it unity and peace once more.*

With the prophecy being so cryptic, there were a lot of questions as to who the throne-less queen was. Variel believed it was the exiled queen, Joneira, who'd murdered Aurelia's great-grandmother, the previous Aegrician queen. Aurelia's grandmother had been murdered as well. It had all been a coup to steal the Aegrician throne, but Joneira had been ousted years later and then the crown had chosen Aurelia's aunt, Otera, to rule.

Everyone had always suspected Joneira to be dead, but if the female who'd brought about Aurelia's mother's death was alive and was planning to come back and finish what she'd started... Aurelia didn't even want to think about that. The Warbotach barbarians were enough to contend with without adding in the possibility of an exiled queen and her unknown supporters.

They dressed quickly, leaving their tent and heading to the dining structure where dozens of warriors had already begun to line up. Aurelia caught Exie in the corner of her eye leaning against a tree, the warrior's eyes missing their usual zest for life. It was disheartening but not surprising. Aurelia was going through a similar stage of grief and hopelessness. Her sister and Exie had gotten very close since they'd left their father's home, first friends and then lovers. All her sister had ever wanted was to be a badass warrior and for the freedom to be with whoever she wanted to be with and not have someone else choose for her. Leaving their home had been the only way to make that happen.

With her injured leg still wrapped in bandages, Exie didn't run forward to greet them, but instead limped into the dining tent as they approached, taking her place in line behind the others.

"How did you sleep?"

Aurelia didn't expect Exie to have much of a response, at least not a positive one, but she didn't know how to initiate small talk with the situation they were in, so she chose the first question that came to her head.

Exie shrugged as she reached for her tray of porridge and roasted meat.

"I'm not sure. If it wasn't the pain in my thigh keeping me from sleep, it was the nightmares forcing me awake."

Reaching around Aurelia, Cristos took a tray for her and for himself, dipping his chin in the direction of the tables, signaling for her to lead the way. His thoughtfulness didn't go unnoticed. Her insides warmed as visions of their passion-filled morning flashed through her head, a moment of ecstasy when she was so filled with pain.

Exie aimed for their usual table near the sidewall of the dining tent where Holera and Kason were already seated, the couple eating their breakfast as they carried on a conversation. No matter how many times the camp had been moved, their table seemed to always be in roughly the same spot, and the same people always sat there. Septima's absence at breakfast was just another stab at the fresh wound.

Leaving Septima's chair empty, Exie sat across from Holera. Kason and his mate paused their conversation to look up and smile at her, but their own worried exhaustion lined their faces.

"I don't know if you've heard," Holera said, setting her spoon down in her bowl, "but we move to Norithae tomorrow to reclaim the city."

Chapter Six

Septima

Septima awoke to the squeal of an iron door hinge. The fact that she'd been taken by at least a dozen Warbotach soldiers, and not just one, had foiled her escape plan before it had even gotten off the ground. At some point, as she'd sat by that fire surrounded, someone had knocked her out.

Her head spun as she tried to sit up, her wrists and ankles no longer bound, and she blinked several times to clear her vision. She heard footsteps before she could see who was walking toward her, but when the figure passed in front of the sliver of light coming in through the window, her breath caught in her throat.

"Are you okay? I'll get you some water."

Even with her filthy, tattered dress and body that was showing signs of how long she'd been in a dungeon, Septima couldn't mistake the female for anyone other than Queen Otera. A tear trailed down Septima's cheek as she watched Aurelia's aunt cross the darkened room and then return with a small cup of water. The queen looked so much like her sister.

Taking the cup and draining it quickly, Septima was still thirsty, and very hungry. She wasn't even sure how long it had been since she'd eaten.

"Yes. I—uh."

She quickly assessed her wrists and ankles that were scraped and bruised but nothing that wouldn't heal.

"Yes. I think so. Are you Q-Queen Otera?"

The female's eyes grew wide at the question and she searched Septima's face for a moment. Otera was beautiful. Although knotted and dirty, her hair was crimson just like Aurelia's, and hung in loose waves down her back. Even her eyes, as blue as the sea, were the eyes of her sister's. It wrenched Septima's heart open, but in another way, it soothed her.

"I am."

Otera's mouth opened to say more, but something caught her attention and she reached toward Septima, tucking her long braids behind her ear.

"You're human."

Her voice was full of wonder, disbelief, yet curiosity as well. Scooting back ever so slightly, a flicker of flame bloomed in the queen's hand as they stared at each other for several awkward moments.

"How? I don't understand."

Until that moment, Septima had not even considered that Otera wouldn't expect to see a human. Her kind hadn't been allowed in Ekromos for longer than Septima even knew, if ever. The queen may have looked human, aside from her pointed ears and the brilliant swirl of fire that danced in her palm, but she wasn't. She was fae. Septima's own sister, who she'd grown up with since she'd been taken in as an infant, was half fae, although neither of them had ever known about that part of her heritage.

"I am. My name is Septima."

"But the portal... Humans aren't allowed to cross. How did you get into our realm?"

Confusion was clear on Otera's face as she waited for her cell mate's response, which didn't come quickly.

There was so much Septima needed to tell the Aegrician queen, but didn't know where to start, and also didn't know if they were truly alone. If there were any Warbotach spies within hearing distance, she didn't want to share any information that could put her friends and loved ones in danger. Otera must have noticed her hesitation, because she motioned for Septima to follow her toward the back wall of the space where there was another set of benches.

"As long as you speak quietly, you can speak freely here. There's a guard posted outside, but he's probably at the end of the corridor smoking his pipe or pleasuring himself. He's not exactly worried I'll escape."

Septima couldn't help but to huff a laugh, although thinking about the scar faced Warbotach beasts in any sexual manner was disgusting.

"My sister and I—."

Now it was Septima's turn to hesitate.

A dozen scenarios flitted through her mind as she debated which details to share and which to keep to herself. After a few considerations, she decided to withhold that her sister was Otera's niece, at least for the time being. If Warbotach realized Otera had family on the continent, they would surely track Aurelia down to use as leverage. It was best to keep that part a secret until she knew they wouldn't be able to use Aurelia against the queen.

"My sister and I came into this realm with your military—with Exie and Taryn, and Blaedia."

If she hadn't been able to see the queen's face with the flame still dancing in her hand, Septima may have missed how the queen's eyes lit up at the sound of Blaedia's name, at how her breath faltered.

"Blaedia? You know Blaedia?"

The reaction was unexpected, and it made Septima wonder if there was more about them she didn't know, which was likely. There was a lot she didn't know.

"Yes. I know her. Her war camp took my sister and I in when we ran away from home. She let us stay with them. Then had us trained and protected. They took care of us."

Nostalgia seemed to play in the smile that spread across Otera's lips, as though she was remembering her own time with her military, or maybe someone special.

"It sounds like something they would do. They have always been an honorable representation of their kingdom."

Memory vanishing from her eyes, the queen returned her gaze to Septima.

"How did Warbotach get to you?"

Leaning back against the cold stone wall, Septima readjusted herself on one of the benches that lined the space.

"Your warriors are coming for you. We began moving toward Aegricia days ago, but a Warbotach legion caught us where Spectre Forest meets Norithae."

The clang of a rusty bolt startled Septima, effectively ending their conversation as the door creaked open. Framed by light from the sconces in the corridor, the Warbotach male in the doorway was the thing of nightmares. The scar across his face, stretching from his forehead, disappearing beneath his eyepatch, and ending at his chin, was grisly. It was almost as though he had purposely gotten it infected so it wouldn't heal well.

Septima swallowed back her grimace, along with the fear burning the back of her throat, as Otera stood in front of her. Even with the conditions she'd been living under, there was still a presence about her that told others she was a born leader and she would always rise from the ashes.

The male chuckled as he took a step into the cell, the sound guttural and almost animalistic.

"What are you gonna do, queen? Stop me from getting to the human behind you?"

Septima stiffened, her arms wrapped tightly around herself but Otera didn't back down, still blocking his view as her hands clenched into fists at her sides.

"I can certainly try."

AURELIA

The army arrived at the gates of Norithae by midday. Since Blaedia had sent warriors to scout the city beforehand, they knew what to expect: a city that had been fled in a hurry. From the unburned buildings and fields, it was clear Warbotach hadn't expected the attack, at least not on the day when it happened. If they had, the city would have been left in ruins.

Instead, the citizens of Norithae crowded at the gates, lined the streets, and dropped to their knees to receive their king. His own military, weary but loyal, stood proudly, what was left of them anyway. Aurelia wasn't sure how many of Norithae's soldiers had been killed, or how many may have been taken prisoner by the barbarians, but what remained couldn't have been the entirety of what Cristos' father had built before his death.

Aurelia had never thought about the fact that Cristos' kingdom had watched him grow up, had known who he was all along, even though Warbotach hadn't. He'd hidden his identity, had walked among the barbarians as a Norithaean soldier and nothing more. She wasn't sure how he'd done it and had never asked, but the barbarians had seemed none the wiser when she'd seen him in their ranks.

Making their way through the city, she walked by his side, Kano leashed and following at her heels, with the full might of the Aegrician military behind them on foot, horseback, and as a beautiful array of phoenixes in the sky.

Exie, still injured from the gash to her leg, had begrudgingly agreed to ride on horseback. There had been some arm folding and pouting like a toddler, and not like the fierce warrior she was, but Blaedia had ultimately won the argument and the blond warrior had been hefted onto the back of a glorious black steed. Aurelia hadn't seen her since they'd left, since the animals held up the rear of the procession, but she intended to check in with her friend once they were settled in the city.

Cristos reached for Aurelia's hand as they neared the palace. It was a surreal moment. The last time she'd been there, it had been when he'd freed her and her companions from the dungeon after they'd been captured by Warbotach. She remembered their last walk through the city, when she and the others had been brought into Norithae in a cage that was pulled on a cart by a Warbotach horse.

Something about the look that had been in Cristos' eyes when she'd begged him for help told her he was good, even if she hadn't known who he was yet, or whose side he'd been on.

After only a few days, however, after Exie had been tortured, Cristos had killed the guard at the dungeon entrance and snuck them out of the city, taking them to Variel's cottage in the forest. That was where their romance had begun, and they'd been on the move ever since. Now, walking at his side toward his home, was the closing of a chapter in a way. The one thing that was missing was her sister.

"Are you okay, love?"

Squeezing Aurelia's hand gently, Cristos got her attention as they moved through the droves of people lining the streets. It wasn't a question she knew how to answer, so she simply squeezed his hand back and smiled before turning to look at the crowd again.

What truly warmed Aurelia's heart were the children, dozens of them, who stood near their parents. In their dresses and tunics, tiny leather wings flaring out at their backs, children held onto the skirts of their mothers or sat on the shoulders of their fathers. It told her the city was now safe.

Just like in Aegricia, Warbotach did not seem interested in attacking civilians, and they didn't seem interested in the kingdom of Norithae. She knew they intended to take the human lands, but she still wondered what they'd planned for the future of Ekotoria. Was Warbotach conquering Ekotoria with the help of an ally who intended to take it while they moved on to the human lands? It was a possibility that left a tinge of unease in the pit of Aurelia's stomach where everything else had gone to fester.

"They love you."

As they'd left the public spaces and entered the palace gates, it was the first thing that came to her mind. Silver lined Cristos' eyes when he turned to look at her, and she realized she'd been so caught up in her own thoughts as they'd moved through the city, that she hadn't realized how emotional it must have been for him. She stopped walking and turned to face him, pulling him into an embrace.

"They're happy to have you back, Your Highness."

Huffing a chuckle, he kissed her on the forehead.

"I just hope I don't let them down. I'm nowhere near the male my father was."

Blaedia interrupted the moment before Aurelia could respond. The military had moved in behind them in the palace courtyard, filling out nearly all the available space.

"Everyone's exhausted and needs to eat," she said, sheathing her sword. "We need to stable the horses as well."

He nodded, dipping his head to one of the Norithaean soldiers standing nearby.

The male was tall, taller even than Exie, but with silver hair like Holera's. His hazel eyes were bright in the midday sun as he approached, his hand resting on the hilt of his sword. When he stepped in front of them in full armor, his heels clicked to attention and he dipped in a bow.

"Sire."

Cristos stiffened slightly, the title clearly something he would have to get used to.

"It's still Cristos to you, Faidon."

The male dipped his head but smirked. It was clear they were friends.

"Show the Aegrician warriors to where they can house their animals and their people. We'll meet in the war room in two hours. We need to secure the city."

Faidon turned on his heel and led Blaedia and the others away, a lanista taking Kano with them. Part of Aurelia wanted to take him into the palace, but it had been a long journey and he would need to be fed. Plus, he had already become so used to living outdoors, and seemed to enjoy it. She was assured she'd be able to see him afterwards, so she patted his head and let the animal handler take him away.

Instead of following the alley which would have taken them to the dungeon, the way she'd been led the last time she had entered the city at Cristos' side, Aurelia walked into the large front doors of the palace and into the grand foyer.

Servants flitted about the space, cleaning everything within sight. They'd probably been doing just that since Warbotach had abandoned the city days before. All work ceased when Cristos walked in, every eye and smile turning in his direction.

Aurelia stepped aside as the palace staff flooded around their king, each one shaking his hand or hugging him, everyone speaking at the same time. Even with everything that had happened, she couldn't help but to giggle.

By the time they'd left the foyer of the palace, Cristos took the lead as they moved up the stairs and down a gold-paneled corridor. Aurelia could tell where artwork had been pulled from the walls, and could see the tears in the wallpaper, but the space was still beautiful.

"Warbotach inflicted a lot of damage," she said.

Cristos stopped walking to examine one of the statues that rested on a pedestal next to a set of double doors.

"They did," he responded, leaning over to kiss her on the lips, "but we'll rebuild."

It was something to look forward to—rebuilding the two kingdoms, reinstating Otera to the throne, and getting Septima back. She smiled, nodding against his chest as he pulled her close. Reaching forward, he opened one of the double doors and they stepped inside a massive bedchamber.

Unlike most of the palace, where there was evidence of the Warbotach warriors' presence, the room they entered was immaculate, fit for a royal.

"Is this your bedchamber?"

Aurelia hesitated, stepping around Cristos as he dropped their satchel and his sword on the nearest chair.

"I mean...was it your bedchamber before everything happened?"

When he turned to look at her, as he unbuttoned his cloak and dropped it with their other belongings, he was grinning. Stepping forward, he reached for her cloak, unfastening the button.

"It was."

He lifted his eyes from hers, scanning the room.

"Although it's cleaner than when I left it."

When he dropped her cloak to the chair and ran his hands up her back, she closed her eyes, leaning into him as shivers raced through her body. The day had already been long, the march from the last camp taking several hours. There was so much more to do—Aurelia knew that—but she was exhausted. Even her exhaustion was tinged in guilt, however, and sadness, for her sister who wasn't there. She had to believe Septima was still alive, but she couldn't have known for sure. She couldn't go find her, not yet, and that left her chest in a permanent state of brokenness.

Streaming in through the window, the sun created shimmering rays of light across the center of the room, highlighting the midnight blue settee and chaise lounge that took up the center of the suite. The enormous four poster bed against one wall was large enough for her and Cristos, even considering his wings. As she scanned the room again, she realized all the furniture had been outfitted for those with wings. She guessed in a kingdom of winged people, it was to be expected.

"It is quite clean. I'm surprised it's not more damaged."

Cristos pulled away to open the balcony doors, a crisp sea breeze fluttering the curtains and filling Aurelia's nose with a mixture of brine and fresh linens.

"I suppose they didn't want to destroy the place while they were living in it. Although, the servants said only a few of the higher ranking Warbotach warriors stayed in the palace itself. The rest slept in the barracks."

Aurelia wondered how many of the Warbotach ranks stayed in Norithae, whether it had been a large proportion of their military, or if they'd simply taken the city, killed the king, and moved on. Not wanting to upset Cristos, she didn't mention it. The slain king had been his father, and Warbotach was gone, anyway.

Cristos lit the fireplace before pouring two glasses of deep red liquid from a decanter and handing one to her.

"This wine is made right here in my kingdom."

Notes of berries and a hint of apple met her nose when she lifted the glass to take a sip. It smelled remarkably like the wine she'd had in her homeland of Vaekros.

They stepped out onto the balcony, the city a flurry of activity.

"It's pleasant, reminds me a bit of home."

He watched her face for a moment, his hand settling on the small of her back, and she realized he was reading her. "Is that a good thing?"

"There are some things about home I miss." Turning her attention to the sea, she watched the ships sway in the harbor. "I miss my brother more than anything, but nostalgia is a good thing. I left for Septima, though, and I don't regret that. Now, I just have to find her."

Chapter Eight

Aurelia

By the time they made it down to the barracks, after grabbing a bit of bread and roasted meat from the kitchens, Blaedia and a few other Aegrician warriors were already assembled in one of the larger rooms, Taryn included. Ever since they'd been rescued from the Norithae dungeon weeks prior, the Aegrician Commander had been scarce, remaining in the background while she planned moves with Blaedia.

Aurelia smiled at her, touching her on the arm as they passed through the open doorway and around the large table in the center. She squeezed Cristos' hand before walking toward Exie who was seated on a bench on the far side of the room.

The warrior smiled as Aurelia approached, even if it had been half-hearted. Her thigh was still in bandages, the white of them a sharp contrast against the black of her fighting leathers. Aurelia lowered herself onto the bench next to Exie.

"I'd ask you if you wanted to take a walk, but—"

Not letting her finish the statement, Exie rose from the bench, reaching down a hand.

"But nothing. It's too stuffy here, anyway. Let's go."

Taking one final look at Cristos, who was standing over a large map on the table as he spoke with Blaedia, Taryn, and some of the winged Norithaean warriors, Aurelia followed Exie out the door and into the chilling evening air.

"How's the leg, Exie?"

With Exie's longer limbs, it was difficult for Aurelia to keep up with her, even with her limp. She had to walk faster to keep up.

"I hope you're taking time to rest."

Not stopping until she reached the courtyard, Exie sat down on a stone bench. Aurelia sat beside her.

"I've rested enough."

Exie couldn't seem to hide the frustration in her voice as she stretched her long legs out in front of her.

"We all have. We need to go after her."

"I understand how desperate you feel."

Reaching for Exie's hand, Aurelia squeezed it in her own.

"Finding Septima is my priority, too, but we have to be smart. They're meeting right now and I one hundred percent believe they'll figure out a way."

Exie blew out a breath, squeezing Aurelia's hand back.

"I know. I know they will make the best decision for the kingdom, but if I could just go after her alone...Maybe I could get her back without endangering anyone else."

Aurelia started shaking her head before Exie had even finished, but the injured warrior didn't seem to notice.

"Exie...Otera has been in the dungeon for how long? If she hasn't been able to escape yet, then you aren't going to be able to break Septima out either. I don't want to put either of them in danger in a botched escape attempt."

When Exie let go of Aurelia's hand and dropped her face into her palms, Aurelia knew she recognized her words as the truth, even if she didn't like them. Aurelia rubbed her friend's back, watching as two Norithaean soldiers walked past and toward the gates. Exie blew out a breath, smoothing her hair out of her face.

"If they don't come up with a plan soon, I'm going to go after her. I can't just sit by and do nothing."

There was nothing Exie said that Aurelia didn't feel deep within her own heart, but she was no warrior and she knew that. Where Exie may have been successful in finding a way into Aegricia and freeing her sister, Aurelia had no chance. She didn't even know how to get to the northernmost kingdom.

"I am fully on your side, Exie. We're in this together."

Smoothing her hands down her trousers, Aurelia stood before reaching down a hand.

"Come. Show me where the lanistas are keeping my tiger."

Exie rose, no argument on her tongue as she led the way around the palace and onto the grounds in the back of the enormous structure. The sun had already begun to make its descent into the horizon as they used the enchanted medallion to open Kano's enclosure. The great cat wasted no time darting forward and nuzzling Aurelia's trousers, nearly knocking her off her feet. She giggled, dropping to sit on the ground, Exie right beside her.

Aurelia and Exie stayed in Kano's enclosure until a familiar silhouette appeared from around the palace, broad shoulders framed in magnificent black wings. The grounds were dark, the sun replaced by the moon, but the torches scattered throughout set his features in firelight. Stretching, Aurelia and Exie stood. Giving Kano one more kiss on the head, Aurelia stepped out the enclosure and took Cristos by the hand, Exie following closely behind. Exie returned to the barracks, insisting on staying with the other warriors, while Cristos and Aurelia returned to his bedchambers.

There was so much on Aurelia's mind when the door clicked shut behind them. She'd missed the entire meeting between Cristos and the leaders of both kingdoms' militaries. There was undoubtedly a lot of information he would share with her, and she wanted him to, but not yet. The exhaustion of the day was weighing on her, and all she wanted to do was take a bath, and curl into her lover's arms as they fell asleep.

She hadn't even considered no longer sleeping in a tent, but it brought a smile to her face as she walked past the enormous piece of furniture and into the bathing room. Adding more wood to the fire, Cristos followed behind her, dropping his cloak on a chair as he walked by.

The sunken tub in Cristos' private bathing room was the largest she'd ever seen, even larger than what they'd bathed in when in the Diapolisian palace. Stepping around her, his hand grazing around her waist, he turned on the tap before pulling her to him. After the long day, the embrace felt amazing, his scent calming her senses.

"Was it a good meeting?" she asked, her own curiosity getting the better of her.

He grazed his nose against her cheek, nodding as he went.

"It was. The kingdom is being secured by both ground warriors and those in the sky. Blaedia is also sending scouts north toward Aegricia so they can get a better idea of how the city is being guarded."

Some of the tension in her body relaxed at his words and she leaned into him, wrapping her arms around his waist.

"So, Warbotach is truly gone from this kingdom?"

He nodded again, wrapping the laces of her tunic around his fingers as he untied them one-by-one.

"From what we can see, they are gone."

Tugging on the final tie, Cristos slid her tunic down her shoulders, dropping it to the floor.

"I have one more piece of good news."

Heart leaping in her chest, she looked into his eyes, hoping it was news about her sister but knowing deep down it wasn't.

"Yes?"

Smoothing her crimson hair off her shoulders, he slid his fingers beneath her breast band, unclasping it.

"Blaedia received word from Calista."

The pounding in her chest sped up, hope filling her while she waited for his next words.

"King Ailani is assembling his forces. There's yet to be any formal alliance, but it sounds promising."

She loosened a breath, leaning against him again.

"That's great news."

"It is something to give us hope, for sure."

Cristos pulled his tunic over his head, tossing it on top of hers.

"Would you like to bathe? I know you must be tired."

As though his words had given her body permission to rest, Aurelia yawned as she reached to unbuckle her trousers. Cristos removed his own before guiding her into the tub and stepping in behind her. Scooping up water in a copper mug, he poured it over her shoulder, the warm water relaxing her as it spread across her chest. He'd always enjoyed washing her hair, doting over her. She still didn't think she deserved a male like him, but she wasn't complaining. Methodically, Cristos wet her hair, massaging lavender shampoo into it, and she closed her eyes and savored the moment.

"Did you enjoy your time with Exie?"

The bass of his voice hit her low in her body. It always seemed to deepen at night.

Nodding, she opened her eyes to the flickering candlelight.

"She's hurting, wants to go after Septima alone."

"Hmm."

Trickles of warm water ran down Aurelia's back as Cristos rinsed her hair.

"I hope Blaedia speaks to her tonight then. It wouldn't be wise to act on impulse right now, no matter how badly she wants to."

"She knows that, and I don't think she would leave now, especially not injured."

For the remainder of their bath, Aurelia hoped she was right. If Exie did leave on her own, it could possibly put all the plans made by Cristos and the military leaders at risk. By the time they'd gotten out of the tub and climbed into bed, she'd pushed that worry to the back of her mind. It was impossible not to when her lover's scent was filling her senses.

Cristos' fingers trailed up Aurelia's stomach as they laid on the bed together, both still nude from their bath.

"One day," he said, his hand flattening on her belly.

"I hope we can have a family—you and I."

He hesitated, his fingers moving to her chin and lifting her face to look at him.

"If that's something you want, of course."

The sincerity in his eyes nearly brought her to tears. It was a beautiful thought, a future she'd never imagined. Reaching up, she took his hand in hers, kissing his palm.

"I think I would like children someday...when it's safe enough to have them."

"I'll make the world safe again, my love."

Wrapping his arms around her, he rolled her on top of him, her legs falling at his sides.

"We'll make it safer together."

When she looked into his eyes again, instead of responding, she kissed him. The touch of Cristos' body against hers consumed her as their lips pressed together, their tongues coming together in a sensual caress. His hands gripped her backside, pulling her against his hardness that was pressing in between her thighs.

"I feel like you're trying to distract me, Cristos."

Her words were merely a series of pants as she buried her face in his neck.

Pulling her against his hardness again, he chuckled.

"Is it working?"

A jolt of pleasure filled her at the friction of his skin against the most sensitive part of her and she hissed into his ear. Seeming to energize him, Cristos pulled her neck to his mouth, kissing and sucking the sensitive flesh while she ground against him. Exhaustion was replaced by urgency with every slide of him against her wetness until they were no longer able to resist, and he plunged into her.

There would be more nights where they could take their time, but after such a long and emotional day, they made love hard and fast, the sounds of their pleasure filling the entire wing of the palace. After all the time they'd spent in a camp full of tents, Aurelia didn't care.

Chapter Nine

Otera

After all the time Otera had been in the dungeon below her castle, she'd never expected another person to be brought into the cell with her, and certainly never expected to see a human face staring back at her when she first heard the guard drop someone on the other side of the room. Standing in front of the injured female, a purple knot already growing on the side of her head, Otera hoped her presence alone was enough to send the guard back out the dungeon without taking the new prisoner with him. Already injured, the human girl wouldn't stand a chance against Uldon. He'd already been losing his touch with sanity, or at least his grip on his temper.

"She needs a healer," the queen demanded, her voice resolute. "You can speak to her *after* she sees a healer."

The human female's breathing was ragged behind her, only giving the queen more of a desire to protect her. Otera knew her words didn't stand for much anymore, but she had to at least *try* to buy the girl some time. If Uldon sent in Bremusa, maybe she could get a message to her warriors. Maybe she could tell them she had Septima, let her sister know she was safe.

The guard grunted, sparing them no words before turning on his heel and leaving the cell, the heavy door slamming shut behind him. Otera pitched forward with relief, her hands bracing her on shaky knees as she sucked in breath. Reaching for Otera, Septima placed her hands on the queen's arm and guided her back onto the bench. She may have put on a brave face, but after so much time in the dungeon, Otera knew she was weaker than what she portrayed.

"Thank you."

Otera nodded, leaning against the cold stone wall as she took Septima's hand. It had been easier to live in the dungeon when she didn't have to look at the faces of her people, but having someone in the cell with her, someone to look after, that would make her life considerably more difficult. She needed to keep the young female safe, but she didn't know if she had the power to make that happen.

"You're welcome. Although I don't know how long he'll stay gone. His king isn't known for his patience."

As the guard's heavy steps retreated down the hallway, Otera loosened a breath and Septima slouched against her shoulder.

"If they send in Bremusa, we'll try to send a message to my military. I want them to know you're okay."

"Do you think that will work?"

Hope blooming in her eyes, Septima sat up a little straighter.

"Getting a message out, I mean?"

It wasn't often in Otera's long life that she'd responded to a question with a shrug, but it was all the guarantee she could give her new confidant.

"There's no guarantee. When I was first brought down here, the ravens found their way to Bremusa, which kept me more up to date on the movements of my military and my enemy's. After a while, they became fewer and fewer, until they stopped coming altogether. Whether Warbotach was shooting them down, or Blaedia stopped sending them, I'm not sure."

Something flickered in Septima's eyes, some sort of realization, something she needed to share but didn't know if she should. She remained silent a moment, before turning her deep brown eyes to Otera.

"I remember Blaedia speaking to Taryn about the ravens when my sister and I first arrived. At that time, they thought the ravens were being shot down. I overheard Blaedia saying her thoughts about it."

Hope crushing slightly in her chest, Otera slid further down on the bench and laid on her side.

"If they are being shot down, then our message may not make it through, but I'd still be willing to try—if we get the chance."

Septima nodded, laying down on the bench as well, her head nearly touching the top of Otera's. The queen cleared her throat.

"The guard may come back, or he may send a healer, but at least for now, it would be best if we tried to get some rest."

There was no response as Septima's breaths turned even, lulling Otera's own exhausted mind to sleep as well.

CHAPTER TEN

AURELIA

"I want them to know you're okay."

Queen Otera leaned against the stone wall of the dungeon, her fingers interlaced with the woman at her side. Aurelia watched from the shadows of her mind, which were also the shadows of the room. She was still unsure whether what she was experiencing was real or a dream. If what she saw in her mind was real, Septima was safe, but there was no guarantee she would remain that way. Although Aurelia didn't know what Warbotach knew, they had an interest in speaking to her sister, and it was only a matter of time before the guard who'd only just left would return. All she could do was hope Otera could keep Septima safe until they could free them both.

Aurelia watched them for a while. She listened as Septima told the queen what she knew about the ravens, and as they laid on the bench beside each other like the oldest of friends. She remained there until her sister fell asleep, cherishing every moment she got to glimpse her sister's beautiful face, even if it was only a dream.

When Aurelia awoke the next morning, it took a moment to realize where she was. With silk sheets against her bare flesh and the scent of fresh linens, the only thing familiar was the warm body of Cristos next to her. It almost felt wrong, waking up in such comfort when she knew her sister was in a dungeon, but there was nothing she could do to change Septima's circumstances. At least not yet. She had to trust in the process, trust that Cristos and the generals were in control of the situation, and that their plans would get her sister back safely. It was the only way she could continue her day without Septima by her side.

The fire had nearly burned down to the grate when Cristos' eyes opened. Aurelia had been watching him sleep for a while, unable to resist when he looked so peaceful. With all their recent travel, his ebony hair had grown long, nearly falling into his eyes as his brilliant blue gaze met her own.

"Good morning."

His voice was still rough from sleep and the ruggedness of it sent a shiver through her, as it always did.

"Good morning."

Tucking her hair behind her ear, he leaned forward and kissed her.

"What's the plan for today? More meetings?"

As if on cue, a knock sounded on the suite's door. Cristos' eyes flicked up, mild annoyance on his face as he rose from the bed, pulling on a pair of trousers and answering the door. Still undressed, Aurelia wrapped the sheet around her body and ran behind the dressing screen, pulling on a tunic and trousers quickly before returning to Cristos' side. If they were discussing going into Aegricia, she wanted to be there when they did.

The same soldier she'd seen only briefly when they'd arrived, Faidon, stood there in full uniform, his hand on the pommel of his sword.

"The Aegrician flyers have returned, Cristos. General Ryze requests a meeting."

Having never heard Blaedia's full name, it took Aurelia a moment to realize who he was speaking of. Come to think of it, she didn't know any of her newfound family's surnames, aside from the true surname of her mother, the anticipated queen of Aegricia before she'd been chased out of her kingdom and murdered: *Lumino*. Aurelia swallowed back the thought as Cristos turned to her, the warrior pivoting on his heel and walking away.

His boyish early morning appearance replaced by that of a king, Cristos braced his hands on her shoulders.

"I guess my trial as a ruler truly begins today. Ready or not."

Even if he doubted his capability as a king, Aurelia didn't. The passion he held for his kingdom would have never allowed him to act in any way that wasn't in its best interest. She smiled, rising to his toes and kissing him.

"You are ready, and you won't be ruling alone. Like it or not, you have two kingdoms at your side...and you have me."

It wasn't a promise to be his queen, but they both understood that. Married or not, they were in this fight together. The rest would have to come later. He took her hand, squeezing it gently.

"And that's how we will win this war—all of us—together."

Taking only enough time to eat eggs and toast, Aurelia and Cristos left the palace for the barracks, arriving just as Blaedia and the Norithaean generals gathered around the map on the table in the center of the room. Having not taken part in the meeting the night before, Aurelia didn't know the names of the leaders from Cristos' kingdom, but she knew she'd get to know them in time.

Instead of standing around the table, where the bodies with wings already took up so much space, she moved to the other side of the room where the familiar head of blond hair leaned against the wall. Holera sat beside Exie, the two of them deep in conversation as Kason held his own conversation with one of the Norithaean warriors. Taking a seat next to the two females, Aurelia listened as the Aegricians and Norithaeans readied to discuss their next course of action.

"The city of Flamecliff is completely surrounded, but the city itself is warded," Blaedia said, Cristos' expression visibly tense. "My warriors were turned around at the gates. The wards go into the clouds and beyond."

Heart sinking into her stomach, Aurelia reached for Exie's hand. Septima was unreachable without war. She knew it, and Exie knew it too.

Cristos paced as Blaedia and Taryn looked over the map, a dark haired Norithaean officer doing the same.

"Is there any way to take the wards down?"

The Aegrician general listened as one of her warriors spoke something into her ear before turning back to Cristos.

"There may be a way to take them down if there are enough of us, but we may have bigger problems to contend with."

Blood chilled in Aurelia's veins as Exie tightened the grip on her hand. Cristos stiffened as he turned to the general, her words putting an end to his pacing.

"What could be a bigger problem than Warbotach?"

Her face resembling something Aurelia had only ever seen on the general before their last battle, it was clear Blaedia didn't want to say out loud whatever she'd been told.

"There have been sightings across the sea, mutterings of armies from the other continents encroaching on Ekotoria."

Swearing, Cristos combed his hands through his hair. Aurelia's breath faltered. She didn't know anything about the other continents in the fae realm, aside from what Exie and Cristos had discussed briefly one night when they'd sat in Kano's enclosure. There were other continents with other rulers, but even Cristos had admitted to knowing little about them.

"We'll send out flyers today, and ravens. We need to know what we're up against, and how much time we have."

He turned toward Faidon, the weight of his decisions lining his handsome face.

"We'll need to notify King Ailani. We cannot wait any longer for his decision, not if we're going to prevent this continent from falling from the armies that may be heading toward our shores. I think we will know soon who Uldon is receiving support from, or who he's running from."

Before Cristos finished speaking, Exie stood and stormed out of the room without a word. Holera, who had been silent during the meeting, followed behind her. Aurelia hesitated a moment before following her friend. She wanted to remain in the meeting and continue listening to what Cristos and the leaders of the two kingdoms would plan, but Exie needed her more. Aside from herself, she knew Exie had her sister's best interest at heart above all others.

Once outside, it didn't take Aurelia long to find her friend. Sitting on the same bench in the courtyard where they'd spoken the day before, Exie's golden hair glowed in the sunlight as she spoke with Holera. Aurelia didn't have to talk to Exie to know why silver lined her friend's honey-colored eyes. Enemies flooding onto Ekotoria's shores would only make rescuing Septima that much more impossible, even without the wards. It had remained unsaid in Blaedia and Cristos' discussions, along with freeing the queen, but everyone knew turning their sights to the shores and away from Aegricia was a tradeoff they would have to make, at least until they knew more about the possible threat the rumors posed.

Blowing out a breath, Aurelia took the last few steps toward her friends and lowered herself onto the bench next to them. Exie glanced up at her, the corner of her mouth lifting in a forced smile.

"She's still safe, Exie. I saw it."

She'd never mentioned her dreams to Exie before, but her friend needed hope.

Exie searched her face for a moment before responding.

"What do you mean you saw it? How?"

It was a question Aurelia didn't know how to answer but she couldn't just leave it in the air.

"I don't know how it happens, or if it's even real, but the more I see Otera in my dreams, the more I wonder if I'm seeing her, the real her. If it is real, then Septima is with her, and she's protecting her."

Holera leaned forward, resting her elbows on her knees. Exie exhaled before speaking.

"What have you seen, Aurelia? Specifically."

Taking Exie by the hand, Aurelia told her friends everything she could recall. She began with the very first vision she had of her aunt when she'd first entered their camp after fleeing her father's home. The more she spoke, the larger their eyes grew.

"Variel spoke of this happening, when she told us about your mother."

It had seemed like a lifetime ago, and Aurelia tried to replay the conversation Exie spoke of in her head, but to no avail. That entire day had been too much for her to comprehend, and their lives hadn't slowed down since then so she could have time to reflect. She shook her head, and Exie took that as permission to continue.

"She and Cristos said you may come into powers over time. Maybe that's what this is, powers from your mother's blood revealing themselves as you begin to transition."

Aurelia swallowed around the growing lump in her throat as Cristos and Variel's words found their way into her memory. There was no question of the truth about her mother, not after seeing her mother's reflection in Otera's face, but to acknowledge her own body was anything other than human...It wasn't something Aurelia had ever considered, no matter how true she knew it to be.

"So, do you think what I'm seeing is real?"

Although she already knew the answer, she still asked. When she lifted her eyes to her friends, her answer was confirmed.

"How will I know when my transformation is complete?"

Exie shrugged, but Holera answered.

"With no other humans in our realm, there's no way to know what level of powers you'll develop, or if you'll see any physical changes."

"There's one person who may be able to answer your questions, though," Exie added, Aurelia turning a curious glance to her.

"Who?"

"Variel."

CHAPTER ELEVEN

Aurelia

Exie's words weighed heavily on Aurelia as she and Cristos returned to their suite that night. Twelve warriors had been sent out that afternoon, some from each kingdom. Ten of the warriors had been given orders to search the seas to try to find out more about the alleged armies heading to Ekotoria. Kason and Holera had been sent straight to Diapolis to demand an audience with King Ailani, and to hopefully return with his army, and his dragons, at their backs. After their recent trip to the southern kingdom, Cristos realized the couple were the best people to send to seek that meeting.

The idea of returning to Variel's cottage in the woods with everything that was happening, if she could even find it, was unthinkable. She wouldn't have been able to pull Cristos away from his kingdom in the middle of a war, but if learning about her powers could somehow aid them in winning the war... There was no guarantee that would be the case, but if it was at all possible, it needed to be explored. Still, she wasn't ready to leave just yet, not after merely a day, and not after having been captured from Spectre Forest only weeks earlier. She'd been thrown into the dungeon in the very palace where she now slept. If Warbotach had warriors hiding in the forest, she did not want to become their prisoner again. Her sister needed to be her number one priority, and being thrown into a dungeon, even if it was the same dungeon as Septima, would only make rescue more impossible.

After talking with Exie and Holera, Aurelia had gone to Kano's enclosure, putting the large tiger on a leash and taking him for a walk around the palace grounds. With everything she and her friends had talked about, she really needed to clear her head. Although Kano received more than just a few passing glances from the staff and soldiers, he seemed to enjoy his time out of the confines of his enclosure. He tested the limits of his leash more than once, chasing after small creatures as they traversed the forested area at the back of the property and climbing over boulders scattered along the cliff that overlooked the sea.

She'd returned him to his enclosure just before dark and returned to the palace and Cristos' side.

Sitting next to her on the settee, Cristos passed Aurelia a glass of wine, the red liquid tart on her tongue. She was tired. They both were, but the palace staff had been asked to bring their dinner up to their room that night, so they couldn't go to sleep just yet.

A fire flickered in the grate, warming her chilled limbs from spending so much time in the cool Norithaean breeze. They were quiet for a while, Aurelia's feet in Cristos' lap as they waited for their dinner to be brought up.

"What happened with Exie today…when she ran out?"

Cristos' voice broke the silence, and Aurelia's endless thoughts.

"I know these new developments can't be easy for either of you, not with Septima being stuck behind those wards."

Aurelia shrugged before responding, her mind needing a moment to gather her thoughts.

"I think she just feels hopeless. We both do. With the wards, she knows she can't go after Septima. It took away that option."

Nodding, he rubbed her feet.

"We will get her back, Aurelia. This I promise you. With this new threat, King Ailani will help us. I have to believe that."

Even if she wasn't confident in the future of the continent, she knew he truly believed what he said.

"She's just never seemed further away, more unattainable."

A knock sounded on the door before he responded and Cristos rose to answer. He returned a moment later with a platter holding their dinner and placed it on the table. At least for the moment, Aurelia dropped the conversation. There was nothing they could do to get Septima back yet. She was hungry and she was tired, so that conversation would have to wait until another time, along with the conversation about revisiting Variel.

"How do you feel about stew?" he asked as he opened the lid on the pot, the savory scent of the meat and vegetable stew wafting through the air. It reminded her of the meals they'd eaten back at the Aegrician war camp for all the time they'd lived there.

Cristos pulled out Aurelia's chair and she lowered into it before he slid her closer to the table. Her mouth watered and she realized it had been hours since she'd had anything to eat.

"Stew sounds great. I don't think we've had any since we were in the forest camp. Actually—"

Hesitating, she took in a deep whiff of the scent.

"It smells a lot like Aegrician stew."

He chuckled as he lowered himself into his chair and filled two bowls, sliding one in front of her.

"That's because it *is* Aegrician stew. The cooks from the camp cooked for us tonight and brought it in. They thought you would like that, and I agreed."

The grin on his face told her he knew he'd done something good. The camp had begun to feel like home, but the palace was not home yet, so he'd brought something from home to her. Cristos was such a thoughtful male, one who always found a way to take care of her, even when she couldn't think about herself.

She smiled back at him, taking a bite of the steaming meal, the bits of meat and vegetables tender and flavorful.

"Thank you for thinking of this. It makes me miss my sister a little more, but that camp was home to us for a while. It was where we felt safe."

The corner of his mouth tugging up, Cristos reached across the table and took her hand, kissing her on the knuckles.

"It was the first place we'd ever been together, *made love*. The Aegrician camp was the first place I realized I loved you, realized you were meant to be my bonded mate."

Aurelia froze, the words *bonded mate* hitting her by surprise. They were lovers, yes, and even hoped to get married one day, but mates, as seen by the fae, were something so much more. She stumbled over her words for a moment, the right response failing her.

"Mate? Bonded mate?"

The change in his expression sent a dull pain in her heart. He looked almost...rejected.

"I know it's not a human tradition, and it's not something that humans feel, but it is something that happens for the fae."

Lifting her hand to his face, he rubbed it along his cheek, his eyes falling closed as her skin caressed through his stubble.

"When the fates decide that two people are bonded mates, their bodies tell them it is true. It's a draw to that person that you can't deny. As a half-human, maybe you hadn't felt it, maybe you won't unless you transition into more of your fae blood, but I have felt it."

His words confused her. If he'd felt they were mates, why hadn't he told her? Maybe he had and she hadn't understood. There was still so much about their world she didn't know. She squeezed her eyes shut, her mind trying to remember his words, trying to see the signs she may have not noticed.

"When did you feel this?"

Smiling, he kissed her knuckles again, but she could see the sadness in his eyes, the rejection he felt that she didn't want him to feel at all. It broke her heart that she'd made him feel that way, even if she hadn't intended to.

"In Variel's cabin when I was fixing your bathwater and you touched me."

He hesitated, his blue eyes darkening.

"When you passed by me, your shoulder brushed against my wing, and I felt the surge of the bond. When I laid down on the bedroll to sleep, I knew you were my bonded mate, even if you didn't, and it was all I could think about."

She shook her head, not to deny him but to make her head remember. Although he hadn't said anything to her, she'd noticed how he stiffened when she'd brushed into his wing right before he'd laid down on the bedroll and appeared to go to sleep. Even then, she'd known something had changed between them after that moment. She'd noticed a temporary change in his demeanor.

"Why didn't you tell me?"

"There were many reasons why I didn't tell you. We'd only just met, and you were human. I knew humans didn't have bonded mates, so I didn't think you would understand, and I didn't want to scare you off. Also, since you were human, I knew you probably wouldn't have felt the bond, so I may have been bonded to you, but I didn't know if you'd ever acknowledge being bonded to me."

Standing from the table, he moved his chair closer until their knees were touching, taking both her hands in his.

"After that night, Variel told you about your mom and I didn't want to add to the overwhelming amount of information that had already been dumped on you. Once we left Variel's, we'd gotten attacked, had gone to Diapolis, and then everything that had happened there, then the attack on the way back from Diapolis before immediately going into war… It had never been a good time. Not until now."

The entire time he'd known they were fated for each other but hadn't told her. It was another truth he'd kept from her, but she understood why. She had been overwhelmed at Variel's cottage, and they had gone through so much in so little time. It would have been too much to process, but had she known they were mates, she would have never had to wonder what their future would be. She thought about all the times she'd told herself she would never work as his queen because she was human, but it had never even been an option to say no, not if they were bonded mates. If they were bonded mates, then they belonged to each other and they would be together forever. It wasn't such a bad thought.

Cristos watched her, his eyes expectant. He loved her so much. There was no question.

"I understand why you didn't tell me," she said, leaning forward to kiss him, her lips lingering for a moment longer. "But now that I know, I suppose you expect me to marry you and be your queen."

Smirking, he pulled her onto his lap.

"I was going to marry you and make you my queen regardless."

He kissed her deeply, dragging his fingers through her long crimson waves.

"I'm going to make you my wife, and then I'm going to put babies in your belly. We're going to build a family and a future here…a safe one."

After everything they'd gone through, the words were pure sugar in her ears. The promise of a safe future filled with love and family was all she'd ever wanted. She couldn't have asked for anything more. All they needed to do was get her sister back and win the war. If they could do those things, she would gladly marry Cristos and rule at his side.

Ever since she'd been a child, she'd never known what kind of future she had to look forward to, not with the lack of rights for women in Vaekros, including in their choice of a spouse, if they even married. Now, knowing Cristos was her mate, she finally had a future to look forward to, had something to fight for, and she was ready.

Chapter Twelve

Septima

The cell was cold when Septima awoke on the bench against the dungeon wall, Otera's crimson mane draped over her arm. They'd fallen asleep like that, merely inches apart, and hadn't stirred until rays of sun shone through the slender window on the wall, cutting through the darkness. The cell door squealed as Septima rubbed the sleep from her eyes. An elderly female shuffled in, followed by a Warbotach guard dragging a large barrel of water. Jolting awake, Otera's legs swung around as she sat up.

"Bremusa."

The hunched-back female watched Septima's face with a curious stare as she moved toward the queen, a bundle of fabric beneath one of her arms. Sitting up to face her, Septima could barely breathe, her mind trying to interpret her expression. To her relief, the Warbotach male closed the door, leaving without trying to take her with him. After the standoff between the guard and Otera the night before, she had been dreading the Warbotach guard's return.

"I'm here to look over her wounds," Bremusa said, motioning to Septima. "I have fresh clothes for both of you, and water for a bath."

Otera huffed as she leaned forward to take what Bremusa was carrying and set it on the bench beside her. "What's the occasion for fresh clothes and a bath? That's not Uldon's style."

"He doesn't tell me his reasons, Your Majesty. They just give me the orders." Moving toward Septima, Bremusa lowered herself onto the bench beside her. "Can I check your head?"

Nodding, Septima slid her braids to the side to show Bremusa the spot on her head that was still sore from where she'd been hit. "It's not as bad as it was," she said through clenched teeth as the healer touched a tender spot. "My head is clearer this morning. I'm not as dizzy."

Otera stood, reaching into the barrel and dampening a rag before handing it to Bremusa. The elderly female took it and proceeded to clean Septima's scalp gently, taking her time as she wiped around the root of each braid. Behind her, the queen had unbuttoned her dress and begun wiping herself down with another rag. Septima tried to not look at how Otera's ribs protruded so blatantly, but it was hard to look away. The queen needed to get out of the dungeon. They both did.

"What's your name?" So lost in her thoughts, Septima hadn't even noticed that Bremusa had stopped cleaning her hair.

She cleared her throat, eyes shifting away from the queen who had pulled on one of the simple white dresses they'd been given. "Septima. My name is Septima."

Bremusa leaned forward, the cloth moving to wipe the dirt from her face. "And you came from the human realm, Septima?" The question churned in her gut, but she nodded. "And you have family on this continent, or did you come alone?"

Telling anyone else about Aurelia would put her at risk, so Septima hesitated. Otera noticed the turn of the conversation and sat next to her, the queen finished dressing and finger combing her long crimson locks. "Let's get Septima cleaned up and changed before the beasts return for you and the water," she said, reaching for Septima's hand. "We can talk more when we are no longer at risk of being overheard."

The guard returned a short time later, removing the barrel and Bremusa, but leaving Septima and Otera where they were. Septima exhaled a breath of relief as the heavy door squealed shut and the bolt on the outside clanged into place. She didn't know why the guard hadn't demanded to take her with him as he had done the night before, but she wasn't going to get her hopes up that he wouldn't return for her that night, or even the next day. All she could do was hope. A meager breakfast had been left for them, plates with bread and cheese, along with glasses of water, had been laid on the bench near the window. They sat beside each other, nibbling on the little food they had as the sliver of sunlight warmed the chilly cellar.

"Bremusa is a very old friend of mine," Otera said, her voice just over a whisper in case the guard was listening outside the door. "My sister…" She hesitated, the queen's eyes going distance for a moment. "My sister, Messalina, and I have known Bremusa since we were children."

Hearing her mother's name, Aurelia's mother's name, threatened to rip Septima's heart in two. Messalina hadn't been Septima's mother by birth, and she'd died before Septima was only a toddler, but she still loved her, and mourned the life she could have had with her. She knew Aurelia missed her mother every day. For a moment, Septima thought about telling Otera that Messalina was her mother, but she couldn't, not yet, not if it would put Aurelia at risk.

"How long have you been here? In the dungeon, I mean."

The queen hesitated for a minute, glancing toward something at the back of the stone room that Septima couldn't see. "A few months, although I admittedly lost count. Time seems to stand still in this room."

"Do you ever get to leave?" Septima couldn't imagine being stuck in that dungeon for months. Just the thought of that happening, of them not being rescued soon, caused her stomach to churn.

"Uldon has summoned me on a few occasions, mostly so he can brag, or rave like a lunatic. He's becoming quite unhinged, so we really are safer here until we get free."

It made sense. If the Warbotach king really was losing control of his sanity, or simply his temper, then stone walls separating him from them was a deterrent, even if it would only give them a false sense of security. Uldon had a key to their cell, after all. All he'd have to do is use the key and then they would no longer be safer from him than if they'd been standing in his chambers.

"So, what is our plan? I know you were unable to talk to Bremusa about contacting Blaedia and the rest of the military, since we were worried about being overheard-"

"Bremusa," Otera cut her off. "Knows things most people don't. I didn't need to tell her for her to already know exactly what I needed her to do. If she can find a way to send that message, she will. I have total confidence in her."

Otera's words settled Septima's stomach, if only a little. "How well do you know Blaedia and Taryn—oh, and Exie?"

A smile lifting on the queen's lips, Otera pulled her legs onto the bench beneath her and crossed them as though she were sitting on the grass outside. Septima leaned against the wall, pulling her knees to her chest.

"I know all three of them *very* well. Blaedia is my mate, and I miss her terribly, more than anyone." The admission took Septima by surprise, but she didn't interrupt. "Taryn has been in my military for as long as Blaedia has, for as long as I've been queen. Exie came from a class behind them. She and Holera trained in the same group, but under Blaedia as my general."

Hearing the queen speak so openly about her love life encouraged Septima to share with her as well, if only about that. She still wasn't ready to disclose her sister's identity yet. "Exie and I are together," she admitted, feeling her cheeks heat as soon as the words left her mouth. "I love her very much and I hate how much she must be worrying."

Taking Septima by the hand, Otera's blue eyes softened even more. "Exie is a good female—a bit wild and unruly sometimes—but as loyal as they come. I promise Exie is probably trying her best to find a way to rescue you. After everything she's been through, she wouldn't be one who'd be able to just sit by and wait."

Septima didn't want to outright ask what Otera was referring to, but the queen seemed to notice her confusion. "Her lover, a female she thought was her mate, died many years ago. It hit Exie very hard and I worried she'd never be the same again, but she's resilient, and has grown through her grief."

The tear in Septima's heart throbbed at learning the woman she loved had not only loved before but had lost in such a horrible way. Losing someone by choice would have been so much easier than losing someone because of death. Exie had never disclosed anything about her lover dying, but Septima realized it was probably because it had been too painful to bring it up. When Exie was ready to talk about her loss, Septima knew she would be there for her.

CHAPTER THIRTEEN

KASON

Kason and Holera, along with eight other warriors from the combined kingdoms, had left Norithae only hours after the meeting where they'd learned about the added potential threat to their borders. Since they'd recently returned from an envoy to the seaside kingdom, Blaedia and Cristos had agreed that sending the mated pair back to speak to King Ailani was the best choice. After decades together, Kason and Holera did nearly everything together, and Kason had a way about him that tended to get things done. If anyone could give the hesitant king the nudge he needed, Kason was that person.

Aside from meeting with King Ailani, their other task was to bring their missing healer, Calista, back to Norithae. Calista had been sent to notify King Ailani of the Warbotach attack on his border town weeks prior, when they had been involved in the attack on their returning trip from his kingdom, and she'd yet to return to the Aegrician camp. They had received a communication from Calista, but Blaedia was concerned she was being held by the king for some sort of insurance, and if that was the case, she needed to be retrieved.

There was no way to know if that was the case until they spoke to Calista, but if King Ailani was holding one of their healers against her will, Aegricia would have bigger problems to deal with than just Warbotach and the enemy ships closing in on them from other continents.

The trip from Norithae to Diapolis was extensive, especially since they were unable to fly all the way into the capital city of Embershell. Although Holera could physically fly the whole route, with breaks in between, King Ailani held the last of the continent's dragons, and the beasts patrolled his kingdom extensively. Even with sending prior notice to the king about their impending arrival, there was no way to know if the dragons would see the approaching phoenix as a friend instead of an enemy, so they were always instructed to handle the final leg of the journey on horseback. It made the trip longer, but it was safer.

Riding on the back of his mate in her phoenix form, as Kason had done for the past nearly three decades, he stroked Holera's silver feathers as her mighty wings worked against the chilled wind over the Elder Sea. As they'd done on their last trip to Diapolis, they hoped to make it to the southernmost part of Spectre Forest before stopping to camp for the night. Leaving from Norithae, which was on the northern part of the continent, was a farther journey on the first day than what they'd achieved last time, but they'd certainly faced larger feats than that, so he and his mate were hopeful they could handle the extensive hours in the air.

Kason watched the water as they traveled, admiring the beauty of his continent while hoping it wouldn't be destroyed in the coming days or weeks. Ever since the exiled queen, Joneira, had stolen the Aegrician throne more than twenty years ago, there had been few years of relative peace on their continent.

Otera's rule had been prosperous, once Joneira had been ousted, but there had always been the threat of Warbotach from the dead region of Ekotoria, and there had always been the fear that Joneira would return. Kason had never believed any of the speculation that she was dead. She was simply biding her time until she could return and take it all.

Huffing out a breath and shifting his weight, he watched the edge of Spectre Forest come into view as the sun began to set over the edges of his world. The further south they flew, the warmer the air became.

Holera's wings leveled out as they turned back toward the land, sailing across the breeze along the coast, the wind nearly pulling Kason's long hair from the band holding it at his nape. He rubbed at Holera's silver feathers on her neck again, wishing it was the warmth of her ivory skin against his palm instead. Just thinking about it made his cock begin to stiffen in his leathers. He truly was the luckiest of males to have her in his life.

"We're almost there, my fierce beauty."

She couldn't speak to him in her phoenix form, but her chest rumbled below his hand telling him she'd heard him. Grinning to himself, he continued to stroke her neck, the need to touch her one he'd never gotten over, and never would.

"I look forward to staying at the inn tomorrow. You deserve a soft bed for the night."

He meant every word and she knew it. The thick tree canopy of Spectre Forest thinned as they reached the edges of the forest, giving Holera the perfect opportunity to land. They touched down in a clearing with the grace of a songbird, Kason jumping down from his mate so she could stretch her massive body and shift into one with much more seductive curves.

Dropping their bags on the dirt at his feet, he approached her as she shifted, sliding his strong hands up her back.

"You must be tired. I'll set up camp."

Holera grinned, pulling him by the front of his shirt to kiss him. He groaned against her lips.

"You relax."

"You know I've never been a fair maiden needing coddling," she said as she reached for branches, tossing them into a pile for a fire. "You can set up the tent, but I can collect firewood. I'm tired, but I'll rest after."

Watching for a moment, Kason smirked at her as she reached for another fallen branch and stuck out her tongue at him. She truly was the most stubborn of females. He'd been trying to take care of her from the start, but she always insisted on taking care of herself. One day, he told himself as he pulled their tent from a bag and placed it on the ground. One day, when their continent was at peace, he would fill her with his child and she would let him place her on the pedestal she deserved, if only for a little while.

Although Holera had claimed to have more energy to spare after their long flight from Norithae to the edges of Spectre Forest, she had fallen asleep against Kason's chest as they'd sat before the fire eating some of the dried meat and bread they'd brought. Carrying her into the tent and covering her had filled him with pride, and he'd watched her slumber for a while, caressing her hair as her chest rose and fell with the gentle breaths of sleep.

When they woke the next morning, after taking a moment to eat and pack their belongings, they set off for the second part of their journey by air. Although they'd taken the entire kingdom of Diapolis on foot when they'd journeyed south with Cristos, Calista, and Aurelia, Kason and Holera opted to travel to the border town of Claywind by air since they were traveling alone. Once there, they would have to buy horses for the rest of their trip. In Claywind, they planned to rent a room at the inn for the night, something Kason was looking forward to. With as uncertain as Ekotoria's future was, a warm bed to make love to his mate, good food, and strong whiskey, would be a welcomed release.

Although the town of Claywind was part of the Diapolisian kingdom, it couldn't have been more different from the capital city on the coast. Made up merely of a strip of structures at the town's center, and farms or ranches along the lone road that passed through, they would have flown over it without noticing had they not known it was there. The one thing that had changed since their last visit was that many of the buildings had been left as nothing more than charred remains after the attack by Warbotach weeks earlier.

By the time they landed on the road in front of the tavern, which had not been destroyed, the sun was already beginning to set, painting the sky in a beautiful array of pastels. Kason tossed his and Holera's weapons, as well as their packs, over his shoulder, leaving his lover to walk unencumbered. She never complained, but he knew carrying his weight couldn't have been easy, even if she was massive as a phoenix.

Grinning at her as she walked next to him, he gave her a single wink before scooping her up in his arms. She swatted at him, but only haphazardly, before giving up and going limp against his chest.

"I told you I didn't need coddling, you big brute."

Kason chuckled as he kissed her on the forehead.

"Just because you don't need coddling, my beautiful warrior, doesn't mean you won't get it."

Leaning forward, Holera grasped the handle of the tavern door and pulled it open as Kason carried her inside. The smell of roasting meat and the sound of live music greeted them as they entered, and Kason set his lover down near a small table in the corner before pulling out her chair.

"I'll go speak to the bartender about a room," he said, dropping the packs on the floor by the table. "I'll be right back."

Holera didn't argue as Kason walked away, sitting in one of the chairs and propping her feet up on the other. Even if she didn't complain, Kason knew she was tired. Over the past few weeks, they'd done nothing but train, fight, and travel. She may have been a warrior, but it was a lot for anyone to handle in such a short period of time.

Chapter Fourteen

Kason

After filling up on roasted meat and vegetables, and enjoying a stout glass of whiskey, Kason and Holera ascended the stairs to the second level and retired to their room for the night. Knowing they would be requesting an audience with the Diapolisian king the next day placed a heavy weight on Kason's shoulders, a weight the whiskey had been unable to ease. He tried not to let his own stress show as he ran Holera's bath, but he worried they would not leave Diapolis with the king's support, or that they would not leave Diapolis at all.

"You're distracted." Watching the warm water fill the tub and lost in his own thoughts, Holera's voice caught Kason by surprise. When he turned to look at her, her brilliant violet eyes searched his face. She pulled the first lace of her leathers loose, the top sliding open to reveal her perfect ivory skin.

Abandoning everything he'd been dwelling on, he rose and pulled her to him. "I *was* distracted. I'm not anymore."

His mate was always so reserved around others, but the mischievous grin she saved for only him pulled a rumble from his chest. Leaning forward, he kissed the skin peeking through the opening in her leathers before untying the rest of the laces until her top slid down her shoulders.

Gentle fingers cupping his chin, she forced him to look at her. "What's on your mind?"

He chuckled, nuzzling into her neck. "At the moment, all I'm thinking about is your skin on my tongue."

Although he knew his refusal to tell her what was really on his mind frustrated her, it only took a few moments of his kisses against her neck and she'd abandoned all demands of talking. After three decades together, he knew exactly what he needed to do to distract her as well, so he lifted her, carrying her into the bedchamber and placing her on the bed. Crawling over his mate's body like a hungry predator was one of Kason's favorite things to do, and he didn't care if she'd bathed yet or not. She would get her bath, but he couldn't wait any longer to touch her.

Holera groaned, rubbing her fingers up his back as he kissed her neck. "I thought I was going to take a bath." The way her warm breath fanned across his ear nearly made him come undone. Sliding his hand around her ankle, he wrapped her leg around his hip before grinding his hardened length against her center. She hissed, digging her nails into his backside and pulling him closer.

"You can bathe after. I like you a little dirty."

A breathy hum came out of Holera as she leaned up and took Kason's bottom lip into her mouth, sucking gently until he opened for her and kissed her deeply, hungrily. His hands caressed the curves of her breasts, tracing down her flat stomach before gripping her hips and holding her in place as he slid his cock against her again.

Wrapping her other long leg around his waist, she flipped them over, straddling him as he laid on his back, her hands going to the buckle of his pants. "If you want me dirty," she said, her voice husky and full of need as she undid the buckle on his pants, the clasp falling open to reveal the dark hair below his belly button, "Then I want you naked."

He chuckled, wasting no time to flip her back over and slide his pants down his hips, kicking them to the floor before helping his mate remove the remainder of her clothes. Never hesitant to demand what she wanted from him, Holera reached between them, fitting his hardness at her entrance before wrapping her legs around his hips, pulling him into her warmth.

Kason groaned, sliding his fingers into his mate's silver hair and pulling her lips to his, his tongue caressing hers in a sensual dance, only building their need for each other. They moved together, Holera's body squeezing his cock exquisitely, driving him nearly over the edge but he clenched his teeth, giving his body no choice but to delay his climax until his mate had gotten hers. No matter how little time they had, he always insisted she get her pleasure first. It meant way more to him than his own needs.

Draping her beautifully long legs over his shoulder, Kason rose onto his knees, gripping her hips and lifting them so he could drive his cock into her at just the right angle to make her orgasm shatter through her at a level that would have her still feeling the effects the next day. He wanted her to scream his name so loud the patrons would hear it downstairs in the tavern.

Holera's natural scent, mixed with the sweet scent of her arousal, had him drunk and he growled, leaning back over her and taking her hands in his own. She didn't argue as Kason guided her arms over her head and had her grip the headboard. "Hold on, my fierce mate."

Her violet eyes flared with lust as she did as he asked, gripping the headboard with both hands while Kason lifted her legs and drove into her, *hard*. Holera screamed his name, her orgasm hitting her quickly, her cunt squeezing him inside her and sending him over the edge. When they were spent, Kason collapsed over his mate's body, sweat drenching them both.

Chapter Fifteen

Taryn

Flapping her great crimson wings, Taryn led a group of ten warriors over the Spectre Forest toward the western side of the continent. They'd been flying for hours but didn't intend to stop and sleep until nightfall. Five Norithae warriors flanked her own in the sky, three males and two females, all flying toward the setting sun. Letting out a keening sound, the only way she could communicate in her phoenix form, she leveled out her wings, allowing herself to coast down toward an opening in the tree canopy. The rest of the group followed her lead.

Setting down as the light faded from the sky, a few of the warriors gathered firewood while others put up the tents. Taryn and Silia, one of her lieutenants, walked the perimeter, putting up cloaking wards around the space they would call home for the night. With time being of the essence, they couldn't stop for long, but they needed to at least get a few hours of rest before continuing to the coast.

"What do you think we'll find once we get across the continent?" The last of the wards erected around the camp, strong enough to last until daylight, Silia turned to Taryn, her eyes heavy with exhaustion.

It was the same question Taryn had been asking herself since they'd gotten the news about the armada heading to their shores, but she feared the answer, not for herself but for her people. If Ekotoria was invaded again, she didn't think they would be able to survive it, even if Diapolis sent in troops to help them. Their chances were far worse than she wanted to admit.

"Aside from the Inferno Territories, I don't know what else is out there. I'm not sure if any of us do." Letting out a deep breath, Taryn opened the flap to their tent, Silia following her inside. "Hopefully we find nothing at the coast. Hopefully the messages were wrong."

The next morning came too quickly for Taryn's sleep-deprived body. After the long march from their camp in Spectre Forest to the kingdom of Norithae, and the battle they'd found when they'd gotten there, she hadn't had much time to rest before being sent on the mission to the western edge of the continent. She stretched her long limbs and pulled her dark hair into a braid.

Leaving the tent after pulling a pair of leathers back on, she stepped out into the predawn morning to find most of the group already awake and eating around the fire. One of the Norithae warriors,

Lars, smiled at her, handing her a piece of bread and dried meat. Taking it gladly, she lowered herself onto the log next to him, enjoying the warmth of the fire.

"Everyone is almost ready to fly out," he said, passing a mug of water to her as well. She glanced around, noticing most of the tents were put away and she regretted sleeping for so long.

"That's good. We should be able to make it to the edge of the forest today. We can camp under the cover of the trees again before heading out over the sea."

"Unless they've beat us there."

Although it was something Taryn didn't want to think about, she knew there was a possibility the invaders would already be on land by the time they made it to the coast. She just hoped that wouldn't be the case.

Having left the campsite shortly after breakfast, the group of ten warriors, following Taryn's lead, flew several more hours toward the western coast of Ekotoria. The sky was clear, giving them an unobstructed view of the ground, but giving anyone on the ground an unobstructed view of them as well. With the thick tree cover of Spectre Forest, she hadn't seen anyone, but that didn't mean no one was there. As they got closer to the edge of the landmass, the lush forest thinned, giving way to a more chaparral landscape. From their height in the air, she could just barely make out the sea and the sails of ships on the horizon.

Chapter Sixteen

Aurelia

It had been two days since the warriors left Diapolis, Kason and Holera heading to Diapolis to meet with the king and the others scouting out the alleged ships sailing for their shores. Cristos had spent most of the past few days in council with the leaders from both militaries, while Aurelia spent a lot of her time training with Exie. If the war was coming, she needed to be prepared, and she knew Exie needed a distraction.

The air was warmer on the third day of waiting for news, Aurelia's tunic damp with sweat as she aimed her bow and fired an arrow at the target. Exie whooped, firing her own arrow and burying it in the target just beside Aurelia's. Aurelia sucked in a deep breath, the brine from the sea so like the air in Vaekros, the thought of her home filling her with a tinge of sadness. Until their recent battle with Warbotach, she'd had a piece of home with her. She and Septima had been there together, but now Septima was gone, and her absence was sometimes like a living weight on her shoulders. Kano was still with her, and she'd spent time with him every day, but he wasn't her sister.

"What are you thinking about?" Exie asked as she held Aurelia's arrow in front of her. Aurelia hadn't even noticed her retrieve it.

Lowering herself to the ground, she set her bow and quiver by her side. Her friend sat beside her. "I'm just thinking about home. Until Septima was taken, I hadn't missed home that much." She shrugged, letting out a breath. "Well, aside from our brother, but now that she's gone...it just makes me miss home a little bit more."

Exie nodded, patting Aurelia on the leg. "I miss her too. Did you see any new visions of her last night?"

Reluctantly shaking her head, Aurelia dug into the ground with her arrow, making random shapes in the dirt. "I haven't had any visions in a couple of days. I wish I knew how to make the visions happen instead of them just coming out of nowhere."

"Well, you know what I think you should do. You need to talk to Variel. She seemed to know a lot about your heritage. Plus, she's an oracle. If anyone can help you hone your abilities, it would probably be her."

"I know, but even if I wanted to go to her, it's not safe. Cristos would never be okay with me leaving the protection of the city."

Exie shrugged, pulling out her water canteen and taking a sip. "If you can't go to Variel, why can't Cristos bring her here?"

The thought had never occurred to Aurelia. All she knew Variel left the city when Cristos' mother had been murdered and had remained in the forest behind protective wards ever since. "I think it's more likely Variel wouldn't want to come back to the city, but I could bring it up to Cristos...see what he thinks."

Aurelia and Exie spent a little more time on the grounds, practicing archery and sparring, before Cristos found them later that day, after his meetings with the military leaders. Although Aurelia intended to speak to him about Variel, as Exie had suggested, she decided to wait until they'd settled down for the night. She was already drenched in sweat by the time he approached and Exie wandered off.

"Did you save any energy for me?" he asked as he pulled his sword from its sheath between his wings. "Or did Exie wear you out?"

Smirking, Aurelia scooped up her sword from where she'd laid it on the ground. "I've always got energy for you."

Cristos swung before she was expecting it, but she met his blade with her own, the sound of metal against metal ringing out in the evening air. Letting out a chuckle, he stepped to the side to avoid her swing. "Woah! You just keep getting better, my love. You almost took my leg off."

"I wasn't aiming for your leg."

Aurelia's response surprised even her, and she couldn't help but to snicker as Cristos' face fell in mock offense. "You would've made our nights very quiet." Tossing his sword to the ground, he rounded on her, scooping her into his arms, her blade clattering to the ground. "And that would've been too bad. I'm rather fond of our nights."

Just as they were about to kiss, Exie ran back up to them, a look of urgency on her face. "Blaedia needs to talk to both of you *now*. We just got a raven from Aegricia."

Aurelia's heart stilled in her chest and she pulled away from Cristos' arms without another word, following Exie as she ran toward the barracks. He didn't hesitate to follow behind. By the time they got into the barracks, several members of both militaries were already waiting around the table to hear the message.

The general tipped her head at them as they entered the room, her expression revealing nothing about what was held in the piece of paper in her hand. Slipping his arm around her waist, Cristos pulled Aurelia close as Blaedia handed him the message. "A raven just found its way to us a little while ago...the first we've seen in a while."

Aurelia's chest tightened uncomfortably as she waited for him to unroll the letter and read it, hope and fear about news of her sister warring inside her. Sensing her anxiety, he squeezed her gently and opened the letter, holding it out so she could see it. The message was brief, but it was enough.

Septima is with Otera in the dungeon. They're safe for now.

Cristos read the letter out loud, the room silent as everyone hung on each word. Beside them, Exie slumped into a chair, breathing out an audible breath. Aurelia placed a hand on her shoulder.

Taking the letter back, Blaedia's eyes went distant for a moment before she seemed to snap back into the present. "This is good. This is what we hoped for. They're together and Otera will protect her."

"So, what now?" Aurelia asked as she lowered herself into the chair next to her friend.

Moving behind her, Cristos placed a hand on her shoulder. "We just have to wait until our warriors get back, so we know what we're up against. Until then, we need to focus on discovering how to get through Warbotach's protective shield around the city."

Blaedia nodded, slipping the note into her cloak pocket. "I'll speak to my warriors with the warding gift and make a plan for a siege on the walls once we have backup. They'll have to start preserving their power now if there's any chance of us getting through."

Chapter Seventeen

Kason

Waking the next morning, Kason and Holera ate breakfast in the tavern before setting off on foot for the ranch where they would get a horse for the remainder of their journey to Diapolis. The process had been quick, and the pair had set off on the back of an ebony steed named Moondancer before the sun made it to the highest point in the sky. After a half of a day riding on horseback, the giant gates, framed by magnificent statues, came into view as they arrived at the capital city of Embershell.

As had been the case on their first trip into Diapolis, the palace guards met them at the gate. Kason recognized one of them, the golden-haired Captain of the Guard, Kimo, who led the group, but it was the female on the horse with him that caught Kason by surprise.

"Calista?"

Holera's voice had been low, just loud enough for Kason to hear her. Grunting his acknowledgement, he urged their horse forward. The Aegrician healer lifted her hand in greeting as they moved through the massive city gates.

"His Majesty is expecting you at breakfast tomorrow," Kimo said, turning his horse to walk alongside them. "He knew you would need to rest from your travels."

Although Kason nodded, his jaw stiffened with annoyance. It was not unlike King Ailani to put off a meeting when it entailed discussions of an alliance.

"Time is of the essence, so if we could meet with—."

"That will not be possible," Kimo interrupted Kason before he'd even finished getting the words out. "King Ailani is not in the capital this evening. He will be back in the morning."

With the king not in the capital, there had been nothing Kason could have said to make the meeting happen any sooner. He was more than a little frustrated, but with nothing else to do, he and Holera retired to their guest room, cleaned up, and tried to rest from their long journey. Before leaving the foyer, they'd asked Calista to come to their room later that night so they could speak with her. They still didn't know why she'd never returned to the war camp with her people. There had been speculation that she was being held against her will, but she had not appeared distressed as she rode on Kimo's horse. If anything, she appeared content.

Thoughts of where King Ailani could possibly be plagued Kason as he ran Holera's bath, something he enjoyed doing for her when they had a tub to take advantage of. Having stayed in the war camp for the past many months, they'd been forced to use the showering tent for their nightly cleaning, aside from the times when Kason filled a copper trough with warm water, and had it brought into their tent.

Holera came into the bathing room as Kason turned off the tap wearing nothing more than a silk robe and Kason's mouth went dry. It didn't matter how many times he'd seen the curves of her breasts or the toned muscles of her stomach, she always brought him to his knees.

"Thank you for getting it ready for me," she said, fatigue clear in her voice. "You truly spoil me."

He grinned, getting to his feet and pulling her to his chest. "As I always will."

Just as Kason was getting out of the tub, his hair still dripping onto his shoulders, a knock sounded on the door to their suite. As Holera answered, Kason could see Calista's crimson hair from over her shoulder. His mate moved aside, allowing the Aegrician healer to pass.

Taking a few steps into the room, Calista closed the door behind herself, her face unreadable. Holera led her friend to the seating area where the two females sat on the luxurious emerald settee.

"I'm glad to see you're well, Calista. We were all worried about why you hadn't returned."

Pulling out three glasses from the hutch, Kason poured whiskey in each before setting two on the table in front of them.

The healer nodded, taking a sip from her glass.

"I was asked to stay here as an emissary as well as a guide if King Ailani chose to sail his military northward. I know messages were sent, but I admit I wasn't privy to what was contained in them."

Pulling out a chair, Kason sat beside his mate, who cleared her throat before speaking.

"And does the king plan to send his military northward?"

Calista glanced over her shoulder, looking at the closed door, before turning back to them.

"I haven't been privy to King Ailani's private meetings to discuss plans either, so I don't know much."

"Well, then, tell us what you do know."

Leaning back in her chair, Calista seemed to be thinking about Kason's request, but she didn't speak quickly, making him wonder what kind of secrets she'd been asked to keep. She may have been telling the truth about not knowing anything, but Kason wasn't so sure.

After a few silent minutes, Calista drained the rest of her whiskey and turned her eyes on Kason.

"I don't know if King Ailani plans to take his ships and dragons north, but I do know he's gone to the dragon's keep. That's where he is now. He left as soon as he received Blaedia's message about the ships heading toward our continent. If I had to guess, I'd suspect he's there to prepare his men and dragons for war."

Chapter Eighteen

Otera

The sound of the metal hinges squealing pulled Otera from a deep sleep as she laid on one of the benches against the dungeon wall. Scrambling to her feet, she stood tall by the time the Warbotach guard sauntered in, the sneer on his face making him look even more menacing.

"Why are you here?" Although Otera tried to fill her voice with authority, she realized she held none. The clenching inside her chest told her so. "I see no food or water you've been sent to deliver."

Huffing something under his breath, he stepped forward, pulling manacles from around his back just as Septima opened her eyes, causing her to jolt upright. "I didn't come here for a delivery errand, *queen bitch*," he said, his voice more a growl than actual speech. "I came to get you and bring you to the king. He has need of you."

Otera's body stiffened, her heart beating in a panic. The last time she'd seen Uldon, he'd struck her, so she wasn't looking forward to seeing him again, not unless she could kill him. "If the king needs to speak to me, then he should come here."

Closing the distance between them, the guard yanked Otera's arms forward, trapping them in the manacles. She struggled against them, but it was no use. Turning to look at Septima, the fear in the human's eyes turned Otera's stomach. If Uldon took her away, Septima would be alone. She'd promised to protect the human and she couldn't do that if she was gone.

Struggling against the manacles again as the guard held onto them, trying to drag her from the dungeon, flames burst from Otera's hands, sending the guard screaming as his flesh melted away in the heat. Using the temporary distraction, she slammed the iron manacles hard against the guard's head, knocking him unconscious.

"Hurry, Septima, get the key!"

With no hesitation, Septima rose from the bench, scurrying across the floor and grabbing the tiny copper key before placing it in the manacles. Otera sighed as the chains clanked to the floor and she immediately grabbed the guard's sword.

"If we're going to try to get away, we only have a few minutes to do so." Eyes wide, Septima didn't speak for a moment and Otera had to shake her shoulders gently. "Septima, do you want to try to escape?"

A hesitant nod was all she saw before pulling the shocked human toward the door.

"Then we need to go now!"

The injured guard had come to the cell alone, leaving the dungeon door wide open and the corridor empty. Otera held her finger up to her lips, telling Septima to remain silent as they snuck down the corridor. The sun had yet to shine through the slender windows of the palace's lower level, telling

Otera it may have still been night. As they got to the end of the corridor leading into the servants' area, they stopped, Otera listening for voices through the door.

"If we can get through the servants' kitchen and out the back door, we can hide in the mountains and make our way around the city under the cover of darkness."

Otera's voice had been nothing more than a whisper but Septima nodded. Blowing out a deep breath, the queen nudged the door to the kitchen open just a few inches and peeked inside. To her surprise, a familiar set of silver eyes stared back at her from the sink. *Bremusa.*

The elemental's eyes went wide as she saw the queen and the human peering through the doorway of the kitchen and she abandoned what she was doing to dart across the room to them, pulling them inside.

"Your Highness, you're going to get caught. How did you get out?"

By the way Bremusa was scolding her at the same time as hugging her, she didn't know if her friend was angrier that she'd endangered herself or relieved she'd gotten out of the dungeon.

"Let's save that story for when we're somewhere safe. Is there a way to get us out of here?"

After a few moments of thinking, Bremusa pulled Otera across the room and into a closet where several uniforms and cloaks hung from hooks on the wall.

"Here. Change into these and tie your hair back."

"Do you have it, Bremusa?" Otera knew she needed to flee while she could, but she couldn't do it without her crown, or at least without knowing it was safe and out of the hands of Uldon. Bremusa nodded, her lips falling into a fine line.

"It's with the Shadow Glass, Your Grace. He can't get to it."

Relieved, Otera dropped her dress to the floor and pulled on a servant's uniform. Septima did the same.

"Good. We need to get out of here before the guard wakes and realizes we're gone."

Bremusa grinned, and in a matter of moments, a beautiful onyx-haired woman stood where the elderly female had been only moments before.

Having never seen Bremusa shift before, Septima's jaw fell open and she sputtered for words.

"Bremusa's an elemental," Otera said as she fastened the guard's sword at her waist. "She can shift forms."

Seeming to snap out of her shock, Septima pulled the hood of her gray cloak over her head just as Bremusa nudged open the door, her own head covered by the hood of her black cloak.

"Traders are here to replenish the storage. If we can get into one of their wagons, they may be able to get us to port, or into the pass."

Sneaking out of the closet and back into the empty kitchen, the three women crept across the room to a door that led out into an alley behind the palace where deliveries were made.

Otera held the hilt of the sword in one hand and Septima's trembling hand in the other. Her heart beat like a war drum in her ears, the danger of their situation not lost on her. Still, she knew they had to take the opportunity while they had it.

Pressing her shoulder to the door, Bremusa nudged it open, the chill of the night air fluttering Otera's cloak. As Bremusa suggested, there were four carts parked in front of the storage buildings at the back of the palace, their owners busy unloading goods and not looking in the direction of the back door.

Bremusa dipped her head before pushing the door open enough for them to walk through and out into the alley.

After so long in a dungeon, the scent of the briny water and the feel of the breeze against her face, made the backs of Otera's eyes burn, but she ignored the sensation, instead focusing on maintaining her newfound freedom.

Creeping forward through the shadows, they hid behind the wheel of the front-most cart, waiting for the owner to unload the last of his product before slipping inside, the leather cover falling back in place as though they'd never been there.

CHAPTER NINETEEN

KASON

Calista left shortly after telling them where the king had gone, but Kason was unable to get what she'd said out of his head. If what she suspected was true, and King Ailani was readying his troops, they would at least have a fighting chance of taking their kingdom back. He didn't want to get his hopes up, however. Until they'd spoken to the king himself, there was no way to know what his plans were.

When he and Holera woke the next morning in crisp sheets on a four-poster bed, his mind went directly to the looming war and the king's decision. Even the scent of his mate's skin couldn't stray his attention from the meeting they were to have that day. Their entire world rested on what King Ailani decided to do. Before they'd even had a chance to talk about what they would say to the king when they saw him, a servant knocked on the door to escort them to breakfast.

Taking a few minutes to get dressed, Kason and Holera left their guest quarters, following behind the servant down the corridor and into the dining room. After having visited the Diapolisian palace only weeks before, they could have found the room themselves, but didn't complain as she led the way.

By the time they'd stepped into the dining room, King Ailani and his consort, Makoa, were already seated at the table, cups of tea in their hands, carrying on a hushed conversation.

Their heads lifted as Kason and Holera entered, both of their faces spreading into smiles. The king may have been smiling with his mouth, but it didn't quite meet his eyes. A guard closed the door behind them as they took their seats at the table, Kason taking the chair closest to King Ailani.

"Welcome back, Kason. Holera," the king said, raising his mug as the servant set tea in front of each of them. "I hope your accommodations have been comfortable."

Raising his mug, Kason took a sip just as three servants returned, setting multiple dishes down in the center of the table.

"Your palace is beautiful, truly," Holera responded before Kason had a chance.

He grinned at her, taking her hand in his and kissing her knuckles. "It's just as my mate said. I hope we can one day return to Embershell under better circumstances and have a chance to explore the city."

A more personable host than his husband, Makoa nodded, his smile genuine. "We will have a great feast when the continent is no longer at risk."

Kason didn't want to read too much into Makoa's statement, but it had been hard not to.

"Although I appreciate your hospitality, Your Highness, my mate and I really should be getting back to Norithae. With the threat of invaders coming from another continent, no sword can be spared."

Setting his fork down on his plate, the king wiped his lips with a napkin.

"That is actually why I could not meet with you last night. I received a message from your general only hours before your arrival, speaking of ships being spotted off the coast of our continent. I felt it vital to send my own people to verify the claims."

Kason swallowed the lump in his throat.

"And have you made your decision?"

Taking a single glance at his consort, King Ailani returned his eyes to his guests across the table.

"I've realized that if I want the whole of the continent to remain free, and not be destroyed, I have no choice but to get involved."

Chapter Twenty

Aurelia

Although she'd seen it in her visions, having proof her sister was with the queen calmed some of Aurelia's worry. Septima was still in a dungeon, but she was alive, and she wasn't alone. Considering all the other possibilities, she realized Septima being in the Aegrician dungeon with Otera was the best-case scenario.

When she and Cristos retired to their suite that night, after sharing a dinner with the leaders of both militaries, it was with a lighter heart. They knew where Septima was, and they were going to rescue her.

Pulling off her boots, she let out a groan. Sparring with Exie, and then with Cristos, had her muscles tight and achy. If she was going to fight in another war, she knew she would have to work up her resistance.

Cristos grinned, handing her a glass of wine.

"Do you need me to rub those for you?"

Shaking her head, she pulled off her socks.

"I appreciate the offer, but I think what I really need right now is a bath and sleep. Today has been...a lot."

Kissing her on the top of the head, Cristos sauntered into the bathing room, the sound of water running meeting Aurelia's ears only a moment later. She smiled to herself, their conversation from the night before returning to her mind. He'd told her she was his bonded mate, a connection she'd suspected from the start, but having been raised in the human world, hadn't known for sure.

Standing and stretching out her limbs, she followed him.

Walking into the room and seeing Cristos leaning over the tub, running her bath, reminded Aurelia of when they'd first met and had escaped Norithae together, spending time at Variel's cottage while Exie healed. Even then, having only just met her, he'd warmed her water and run her baths.

It was just one of the things he'd always done for her without her ever having to ask.

He turned to look at her as she approached, a playful grin on his face as he rose to his full height and pulled her into a hug.

"We're going to get her back," he said as he kissed her, his lips lingering for a moment. "Soon."

Nodding against his chest, Aurelia listened to the steady beating of his heart.

"I know we will. I can feel it."

Squeezing her one more time, Cristos helped her remove her clothes before helping her into the tub and climbing in behind her. Sliding back between his legs, she leaned against his chest as he poured the warm water over her hair and shoulders. The sensation of the water cascading down her body relaxed her and soothed her aching muscles.

They laid there for a while, Cristos washing her hair and then her washing his, engaged in small talk that had nothing to do with a looming war. When they climbed into bed, wrapped in each other's arms as the fireplace flickered, it was with hope for the future.

The palace was relatively quiet when they woke the next morning. Aurelia and Cristos made their way down to the kitchen, taking a seat at the workbench just as the cook, Paulus, pulled a pan of rolls from the oven. The scent made Aurelia's mouth water.

The gray-haired male smiled at them as he turned around and saw them sitting in his kitchen, waiting to be fed.

"I could have sent your meal up to your rooms, Your Grace."

Setting the hot pan down on the wooden countertop, Paulus pulled the kettle off the fire and set it, along with two mugs and tea bags, down on the table in front of them.

Cristos grabbed the tea kettle, filling both their mugs.

"After all the time I've spent away, Paulus, it's just good to be back here with my people."

The cook dipped his chin before turning back to the stove and cracking eggs into a pan.

"We are glad to have you back, Your Grace. Breakfast will be ready in ten minutes if you and the lady are hungry."

Setting his mug down in front of him, Cristos cleared his throat.

"Paulus, when Warbotach was here, did you have a chance to interact with them much? Overhear their conversations?"

Aurelia stilled her breaths as they waited for a response. She wasn't sure what information Cristos was looking for with his inquiry, but she saw the disappointment on his face when Paulus shook his head.

"Most of the staff were allowed to remain in the palace and continue their chores, but the Warbotach invaders were careful to keep conversations of a sensitive kind away from the ears of their enemies. Aside from being instructed on what to cook, and where I could and could not venture, they didn't speak to me."

Clearing the disappointment from his expression, Cristos took a sip of his tea.

"And were you treated well, Paulus? You and the other servants?"

Paulus turned his back to them as he buttered the rolls and plated the rest of their breakfast.

"Warbotach may be a bunch of unsophisticated brutes, but they had no interest in angering the people tasked to cater to them. Plus," he said as he placed their plates down in front of them, filled with eggs, fried potatoes, and fresh buttered bread. "I don't think any of them wanted poison to end up in their porridge."

Aurelia snickered, her hand covering her mouth, so she didn't accidentally spit out her food. When Cristos turned to look at her, his eyes flickered with amusement.

"No, I guess they wouldn't have wanted that, although I do wish you would have done it anyway. Then we would've had a few less brutes to contend with moving forward."

"Aye," the older male said as he sat at the table across from them with his own plate of food. "I may not have rid the world of any Warbotach scum, but other citizens certainly did. They didn't all leave this city on the back of a horse, Your Grace." Chuckling, Paulus took a sip of his tea. "I believe Madame Sidonia at the Fearless Whisper Club down by the harbor rid the world of at least three."

Just thinking about a fierce brothel madam doing the work of a warrior and taking out their enemies sent Aurelia into a fit of giggles.

"I need to meet this female! What did she do to them?"

Cristos took a bite of his eggs, tipping his head for Paulus to answer the question.

"Madame Sidonia has very strict rules in her brothel, and if her workers feel threatened, they are allowed to defend themselves. The workers may not be trained warriors, but there are many potions kept on the premises that would knock a male out with one sip. Word has it that several Warbotach males found more in their glasses than whiskey."

"If her potion is that effective, we should get some batches of it made in case we need to use it for the war. Maybe we can find a way to get it into the Warbotach camps."

The words left Cristos' mouth just as she'd had the same thought.

"Exie and I could go and talk to her today, while you meet with Blaedia and the others."

Taking the last bite of his breakfast, Cristos nodded.

"I think that's a great idea. It'll give you a chance to meet your people, and for them to meet you, since you will be their queen before too long."

CHAPTER TWENTY-ONE

Taryn

The armada sailing toward the Ekotorian coast chilled Taryn's fiery phoenix blood. There were more than just ships coming for them. There were dragons. Three of them. With less than a dozen warriors with her, there was nothing they could do to stop the invaders from coming ashore. At that moment, they were utterly helpless.

Letting out a signal call, the commander circled back over the forest, landing in a clearing before they could be sighted. She shifted quickly, leaning over with her hands on her knees as she tried to catch her breath. Her heart pounded painfully against her ribcage, fear that only came with the threat of war filling her.

The other warriors landed one-by-one at her side, Lars immediately starting to pace as the phoenixes shifted into their fae forms.

"We are so fucked," he said, his wings tucking in tightly against his back. "We have to get back to Norithae and warn everyone. Maybe evacuate the cities."

Taryn's mind went straight to Kason and Holera, wondering if they'd met with the king of Diapolis yet. She wondered if his military was gearing up to join their fight in the north at that very moment. Even if he did send his warriors and dragons, the cities would still have not been safe for their civilian population. If there was a risk of the cities burning to ashes, they needed to get the children and those incapable of fighting somewhere safe.

Straightening her back, Taryn scanned the troubled faces of the warriors around her. No matter how brave they were, none of them were a match for a full-grown fire-breathing dragon. It would take many warriors to fight even one, and their invaders had three. She didn't know how many dragons King Ailani had, but she hoped it was more.

"Lars is right. Even if King Ailani is sending his dragons and ships full of warriors along our eastern shore right now, the cities are no place for our civilians. We need to go back and evacuate. We need to bring those who can't fight into the mountains and away from the coast. They will need camps set up and wards to shield them."

"Who could be leading this?" one of the Norithaean warriors asked, a yellow-haired male that Taryn had yet to get to know. "Who would have something to gain by supporting Warbotach?"

Taryn stiffened, the words leaving her mouth before she'd even finished processing the thought.

"Can you think of no one?"

The sound of Lars' steps halted as he turned to face her.

"The exiled queen. *Joneira.*"

Chapter Twenty-Two

Septima

The wheels of the produce cart squealed as the driver edged the horses to take it forward. Septima's nails dug into Otera's hand but the queen didn't seem to mind. Not knowing where the driver was headed, all they could do was hope he took them out of Warbotach-held Aegricia before the guards realized they were gone. They maintained their silence, the three of them huddled together, the bumpy road putting Septima to sleep.

Rubbing the sleep from her eyes, Septima awoke just as the sound of the horses' steps slowed, the cart rolling to a stop as they sat quietly inside. Septima held her breath, hoping the merchant intended to head to bed and not to reload his cart. She didn't know where they were, but it was clear they hadn't simply traveled to the Aegrician harbor to board a ship. They'd been traveling for long enough to have been out of the city completely, however. That, in itself, was a relief.

A sliver of sunlight beamed in through a slit in the cart's cover as they listened to the driver disconnect his horses, his steps fading into the distance.

"We should go now," Bremusa said, pulling the cover aside to peer outside. "It's a farm. We're somewhere in the valley between Aegricia and Norithae."

A flutter of excitement filled Septima's chest. "My sister is in Norithae with the Aegrician military. We need to get there."

Bremusa nodded, peering outside again. "Once we get out of here, I can shift, and we can get to Norithae before nightfall."

A few moments later, the dark-haired elemental slid through the opening in the cover, her boots silent as they hit the ground.

Sucking in a breath, Septima scooted to the edge of the cart, dropping to her feet and then stepping out of the way so Otera could climb out behind her.

Rocky cliffs ran along the back of the property, but the farm was extensive, fields of crops stretching as far as she could see. The merchant was nowhere in sight, having left the cart parked on the side of a large wooden barn to stable his horses. Chickens searched the grounds for bugs, scurrying away as the three females stepped toward them.

Septima wasn't familiar with the landscape of the northern part of the continent, but the view took her breath away. The mountains were massive, snow still dusting their peaks although the winter would give way to spring before long.

Motioning for them to follow her, Bremusa crept behind the barn, shifting with a flair of fire, leaving a large golden phoenix where the female had been only moments before.

With no time to spare, Septima climbed onto the large phoenix's back, Otera saddling in behind her, and Bremusa's great golden wings flapped, lifting them off the ground and into the sky.

Chapter Twenty-Three

Kason

With the alliance they'd gone to Diapolis to achieve secured, Kason and Holera set off toward Norithae by air with a fleet of ships at their backs. The envoy King Ailani had sent to the western coast had yet to return, but the accounts were undeniable. The continent was under attack, and from more than just Warbotach.

Kason and Holera had met with Calista briefly before leaving Embershell, discovering there was more to her remaining in the southern kingdom than just as assurance. She and the Captain of the Guard, Kimo, had become mated. Once the war was over, she intended to make Embershell her home.

Knowing people were still finding joy in their lives and planning for their futures filled Kason with hope for his own life with Holera. Maybe, once their kingdom was free, they could return to the cabin in the mountains and have a family.

Unable to make the entire journey from Diapolis to Norithae in one stretch, the couple returned to the tavern in the town of Claywind. Taking a table in the back of the room, Kason ordered whiskey and dinner, as well as a room for the night. Instead of sitting across the table from his mate, Kason pulled his chair right next to her, wrapping his arm around her shoulder and pulling her close. The need to be close to her, to touch her, was palpable.

"I'm tired," Holera said as she snuggled into his side. "I'm so ready to crawl into bed after we eat."

Kissing her on the forehead, Kason nodded.

"I think we will both pass out the moment our heads hit the pillow."

The server returned with their meal a moment later, and they ate quickly, ready to retire for the night. The morning would come early and bring with it another long journey. Once they returned to Norithae, war would follow, and rest would be difficult to come by.

Without the worry of whether King Ailani would assist in the war or not, there was much less weight on Kason and Holera's shoulders to keep them up that night. Holding his mate in his arms, Kason caressed Holera's back until she fell asleep.

Sparing only enough time to eat breakfast the next morning, Kason and Holera left the town of Claywind by air, flying north for Norithae. Once over the Elder Sea, they could see King Ailani's fleet in the distance, sailing northward on the water, as they soared through the clouds. With his dragons escorting his ships, Holera circled around, choosing to fly over the forest instead. Although they were King Ailani's allies, they didn't want to take the chance of getting in the way of an angry dragon.

They landed in Norithae at least a day ahead of when Diapolis' ships would make port, giving them time to catch everyone up on what was to come. As late as it was, there were not many people still awake on the palace grounds, aside from the guards who were on duty. Kason and Holera aimed directly for the barracks, knowing the general would want them to meet with her as soon as possible, but a call sounded just as they crossed the grounds. A phoenix was approaching them from the north, from the direction of Aegricia.

CHAPTER TWENTY-FOUR

SEPTIMA

Bremusa's golden wings carried the two escaped prisoners further from the dungeon that had held them with every beat. Holding firmly onto the reins, Septima watched as the kingdom of Aegricia passed in the distance, the sun moving across the sky and finally going into its slumber by the time they'd reached the kingdom of Norithae.

Flying over Norithae had been a surreal experience after having been carted into the kingdom as a prisoner and marching into the kingdom as a soldier. She'd never seen it from the air, never seen the majestic view of the palace, with its towers and dark granite walls, or how the sea crashed against the cliffs. The moonlight reflected off the water and hundreds of fires burned in the windows of the palace and across its grounds, making the scene appear magical.

Although she didn't know what kinds of wards were protecting the capital city, excitement still filled her. She and Otera were free at least, and she would be reunited with her sister and her mate soon.

Over the past few days, she'd been trying not to think about Exie so she wouldn't have to let in the pain of missing her, and the worry of never seeing her again. Missing Aurelia had been hard enough. Now that they were about to be reunited, the emotions that filled her were powerful and burned at the backs of her eyes.

Touching down on the street outside the palace gates, Septima and Otera climbed off Bremusa's back, the elemental shifting back into her fae form quickly. It only took a moment for the gates to open, and for no less than a dozen guards to come running out, swords in their hands. Otera lowered her cloak, stepping forward into the flickering light of the guards' torches, a collective gasp echoing through the space as they recognized the Aegrician queen. She was clearly the last person they'd expected to see in their streets.

The guards parted as two figures moved past, barreling to the front of the group. Blaedia broke through the crowd first, freezing in place as Exie fell to her knees beside them. With a burst of emotion, Septima darted past and dropped beside her lover, pulling Exie in her arms.

Exie's shoulders shook as she sobbed, running her hands up Septima's back and down her arms. "Are you okay? Did they hurt you?" Pulling away just enough to study her face, Exie cupped Septima's cheeks with her hands, her eyes welling with emotion as she leaned forward and kissed her. "I was so worried about you. I was so worried."

Exie pulled Septima to her chest again, burying her face in Septima's neck. Stroking Exie's hair, Septima leaned back and looked into her lover's honey-colored eyes again.

"I'm here, and I'm not hurt. It's going to be okay."

As Exie and Septima held each other outside the palace gates, Otera and Blaedia were in each other's arms as well. So wrapped up in her own reunion, Septima had nearly forgotten how long Otera had been away from her mate, but seeing them hold each other, she knew their love for each other was strong. There was no doubt Blaedia would see Otera through her recovery from captivity.

The sound of boots caught Septima's attention and she turned toward the group of guards to see Kason and Holera running out through the palace gates. Holera's hands went over her mouth as her steps slowed, shock on her face as she took in the sight of her queen and then turned to look at Septima.

Taking his mate by the hand, Kason approached Blaedia and the queen, bowing from the waist. "King Ailani's fleet will be here by morning and the invaders are nearing the continent's western shores. We will need to evacuate the cities and prepare for an attack."

Blaedia stiffened, tucking Otera further into her side.

"Then we must get Septima and Otera inside so they can eat and rest, and we must wake Cristos."

CHAPTER TWENTY-FIVE

AURELIA

The sound of someone pounding on the bedchamber startled Aurelia out of a deep sleep. Cristos mumbled something before rolling out of bed and shuffling to the door. Sliding out of bed, Aurelia slipped her cloak over her nightdress, heading to the door just as a few excited words met her ear when the servant spoke to her mate.

"The queen is here."

Forgetting about her shoes altogether, she rushed past Cristos and the servant, her heart pounding as she followed the sound of voices. Cristos chased after her, his heavy footsteps echoing through the corridor, but she didn't slow down for him to catch up. Just as she turned the corner into the palace foyer, her steps faltered as her knees threatened to collapse from beneath her. Standing in the entrance, safe and holding onto Exie, was her sister.

"Sissy!" her sister cried out when their eyes met, Septima leaving Exie's side and closing the space between them, wrapping her arms around Aurelia. Aurelia's body sagged against her little sister, disbelief and joy warring inside her.

Pulling away to look into her sister's face, the first of Aurelia's tears fell.

"I don't understand. How did you escape? How did you get here?"

The smile that spread across Septima's face expanded Aurelia's heart. Septima's eyes flicked over Aurelia's shoulder before looking back at her.

"I'm here thanks to your aunt."

Words stuttering out of her, Aurelia turned in the direction Septima was looking, her mouth falling open as she gazed at the face that looked so much like her mother.

To Aurelia's surprise, the queen was wrapped in Blaedia's arms. She hadn't even known that Blaedia had a lover or a mate, much less that she'd been in a relationship with the queen. The general had always kept her personal life private, at least in the conversations they'd had. Suddenly, the emotion Aurelia had glimpsed in the general's eyes as they'd discussed Otera previously made sense.

Catching her stare, a flash of recognition showed in the queen's eyes and she took a hesitant step toward her niece. Aurelia turned to her sister, who still stood by her side, their fingers interlaced.

"Does she know who I am?"

Septima shook her head, but the side of her mouth lifted in a smile.

"No. I didn't want to say anything where Warbotach could overhear, but you look just like her, so I think she just figured it out."

When Aurelia turned back around, her aunt had moved several steps closer. Aurelia shrugged, unsure what to say. Before she could utter a word, a female with onyx hair and quicksilver eyes approached her, her expression in complete awe.

The female reached out, cupping Aurelia's cheek with her hand.

"You look so much like your mother. Messalina and I were close friends."

Turning to Otera, the dark-haired female motioned the queen forward.

"Come, Your Majesty. Meet your niece: the queen who was promised all those years ago."

A loving hand settled on the small of Aurelia's back as Cristos moved closer to her, showing support if she needed it. With everything going on, she'd nearly forgotten he was there.

Septima's hand grounding her, Aurelia watched as the queen approached with a look of confusion on her face. Just like Aurelia, Otera's hair hung in long crimson locks, but the color had dulled with the many months she'd spent in the dungeon.

"Are you Messalina's daughter?" Although her expression was cautious, Otera's tone sounded hopeful. "It can't be true. How? How is this possible?"

Before Aurelia could respond, the palace doors swung open and Kason and Holera walked in, followed by Taryn and the group of warriors that had been sent across the continent a few days earlier. The look on Taryn's face twisted Aurelia's stomach. It was clear whatever news she had to share wasn't good.

Cristos, recognizing the importance of whatever they needed to discuss, waved the group toward the dining room.

"Come, let's all go sit down so we can talk. I think everyone could use a glass of whiskey."

By the time they'd all piled into the large palace dining room, every available chair had been taken. Two servants passed around glasses of whiskey while another two headed to the kitchens to prepare food. With the queen, Bremusa, and Septima having just escaped from the dungeon, and the warriors having flown from across the continent, there were many hungry mouths to feed. Aurelia sat between Cristos and her sister, the queen and general on his other side.

Taking a sip of her whiskey, Taryn cleared her throat, drawing their attention.

"We need to evacuate the city. There are more than just ships heading toward our shores. There are dragons."

Heart dropping into her stomach, Aurelia set her glass down on the table, unsure how to process what she'd just heard.

"I thought the only dragons left were in Diapolis."

"On the continent, yes, but I'm not sure if any of us know what lives outside of Ekotoria," Cristos said, tapping his finger on the side of his glass. "Do we know where they're coming from, Taryn? Any indication from what you saw?"

The commander shook her head, turning her eyes to one of the Norithae warriors who sat near her. Their eyes shared unspoken words as the servants set plates of meat, cheese, and fruit along the center of the table. Once the servants left the room, Taryn returned her attention to Cristos.

"We didn't get close enough to see the flags on the ships," she said, "but they're sailing with three full-grown dragons. We flew back straight away so we could evacuate the city before they got here. We need to get the civilians away from the coast."

Tension in Cristos' face was undeniable, his eyebrows furrowed as he scratched the stubble on his chin.

"We will need to send out warriors tonight to set up a camp in the valley and ward it."

The warrior beside Taryn stood.

"I'll go to the barracks now and pull together a group to start gathering supplies."

Cristos nodded and turned to Kason as the warrior left the room, Taryn following him.

"What happened in Diapolis? Did King Ailani agree to assist us?"

With everything that had transpired since she'd been awoken in the middle of the night by banging on their bedchamber door, she'd forgotten all about how Kason and Holera had just returned from the southern kingdom.

"King Ailani's fleet is on the way here as we speak," Kason said as he set his whiskey on the table. "He'd heard about the threat to our western coast, not only from Blaedia's letter but from his own people too. He did not say which way he'd been leaning before he learned of the foreign threat, but he did admit it was the deciding factor in his decision to send aid."

Aurelia's chest squeezed uncomfortably as Kason spoke, not from fear, but from what it meant that the Diapolisian fleet would be arriving on their shores the following day. War was upon them and there was nothing they could do to stop it. They'd known it was an eventuality for months, had even fought in a battle when entering Norithae, but a full-scale war had been avoided up until that point. Once the Diapolisian warriors and dragons arrived on their shores, war would follow shortly thereafter, and Aurelia knew she wasn't ready. If she was being honest with herself, she didn't think she could fight at all.

Some of the tension in Cristos' face seemed to relax a little, but just as he was about to respond to Kason, Otera leaned forward in her chair, fire blazing in her eyes. "I don't know whose armada she's commanding, but there is no doubt who is leading the charge toward our shores." Shifting in her chair, Otera's hands dug into the armrests. "Joneira means to take Aegricia again."

"Joneira?" Cristos' voice was laced with incredulity. "The exiled queen? You think *she's* behind this? That she's supporting Warbotach's bid to take over the human lands?"

Otera nodded, draining the rest of her whiskey.

"I think they made a deal. I think Warbotach agreed to help her take back Aegricia and that she would bring allies to help them take over the human lands."

Dread burning in her throat, Aurelia tried to swallow it back.

"Do you think they would try to bring their dragons through the portal? Humans have no way to fight something so destructive."

Septima's hand slid into Aurelia's, the touch providing some comfort. The queen's mouth fell into a thin line as she turned her eyes to Bremusa, the female dipping her head in the smallest of nods. When Otera turned back to look at her niece, something flashed behind her eyes that Aurelia couldn't decipher.

"We won't let that happen, even if we have to destroy the portal itself."

"Destroy the portal," Cristos said, the words sounding more like a question. "Is that even possible? It's been there as long as the kingdoms themselves."

The thought had never occurred to Aurelia. She squeezed her sister's hand, waiting for the queen to explain but it was her dark-haired friend who spoke.

"The portal is connected to the Aegrician crown. If I destroy the crown, the portal will be destroyed as well."

"But if the portal is destroyed, that means I could never return to the human lands. Septima and I would never be able to see our father or brother again."

When they'd first been taken in by the Aegrician warriors, Exie had warned them that they'd never be able to return to Vaekros once they'd left, but Aurelia had never considered the finality of it. She always knew in the back of her mind that the portal was there just in case she needed to go home.

"If Bremusa destroys my crown," Otera said, glancing toward her friend again, as though she were looking for confirmation. "The Ekotorian portal will be destroyed, but there are undoubtedly other portals in our world. I'm not sure where they are, but there are stories of them existing in faraway places."

Resting his elbows on the table, Cristos tapped his finger on his glass, his eyes scanning the faces in the room.

"If we destroy this portal, it's safe to say Warbotach would just go looking for another way into the human lands."

Otera nodded, lifting her glass for the servant to fill it.

"That's why we need to destroy them once and for all."

Chapter Twenty-Six

Otera

Once the plans for evacuating the city were in place, Otera was set up in a bedchamber in the palace. Although Blaedia was hesitant to stay apart from her warriors, she returned to the barracks to get her belongings before returning to the suite with her mate.

Otera sat for a moment on the chair in front of the fire, taking in the beauty of the room and breathing deeply. She was free after months of living in a dungeon, and she didn't know how exactly to process it.

Exhaustion pulled her to the bathing room, along with the fact that she hadn't had a good bath in longer than she could remember.

Turning on the tap, she watched as the steam rose from the water. The door to the bedchamber clicked open and Otera recognized Blaedia's footsteps right away, the sound of them filling her heart with warmth.

She'd missed her mate more than she wanted to admit, and now that they'd been reunited, she didn't even know what to do. It had been so long since they'd touched, since she'd been touched by anyone aside from being manhandled by the Warbotach beasts.

Dropping her bag on the ground, a grin spread across Blaedia's face as she saw Otera sitting by the tub, and she crossed the room quickly before scooping the queen up in her arms.

"I've missed you," Blaedia said as she nuzzled into Otera's neck. "Let's get you into the tub. I know you must be looking forward to it after all you've been through."

Pulling back enough to look into Blaedia's silver eyes, Otera grinned before pulling her mate's mouth to hers, kissing her deeply. The taste of her and the feel of Blaedia's tongue caressing hers, pulled a groan from the queen's throat.

"It's not the only thing I've been looking forward to."

"Is that so?"

Blaedia spoke against Otera's neck before kissing the flesh there.

"There are many things I missed, so let's get you in the tub, and I can show you. We have a lot of time to make up for."

With no more convincing, Otera unlaced her tunic, tossing it to the ground before reaching forward, pulling on the clasps of Blaedia's leathers.

"Will you join me?"

Leaning forward, Blaedia kissed her again, nibbling on Otera's lower lip as she unbuckled Otera's trousers. When they dropped like a puddle at her feet, she wrapped her arms around her lover, backing her toward the tub and guiding her inside.

Blaedia slid into the tub behind her mate, pulling her between her thighs. Otera leaned back against her lover's chest, trailing her fingers up and down Blaedia's thigh. Warm water cascaded over her body as Blaedia poured water over her with a glass.

"Would you like me to wash your hair, my fires?"

The feeling of the warm water sliding down her body, and Blaedia's soft skin against hers, brought back feelings Otera hadn't allowed in since she'd been forced into the dungeon. She was incredibly aroused and would have allowed Blaedia to do anything to her at that moment.

"I would love for you to wash my hair, and then I want to get out of the tub so I can thank you properly."

Blaedia leaned forward, kissing Otera on her neck as she slid her hand up Otera's stomach and squeezed her breast gently.

"Then let me get you clean so I can take you to bed. It's been a long time and I don't think I can handle waiting much longer."

Sliding into bed with Blaedia for the first time since before she'd been thrown in the dungeon, Otera crawled on top of her mate, straddling Blaedia's waist. The candlelight flickered, illuminating her mate's exotic beauty, her up tilted eyes the color of melted silver, her skin that always looked sun kissed, and the deep onyx of her silky hair.

"You're so beautiful like this," she said as she caressed her hands down Blaedia's perfect breasts.

Her lover's eyes swirled with desire as she looked at her, stroking her hand through Otera's long crimson waves before moving her attention down to Otera's breast, taking her hardened nipple into her mouth.

"You're just as beautiful as the day I met you, my fires."

Leaning forward, Otera pulled Blaedia's mouth to hers, grinding against her mate's body between her thighs. The friction was delicious, but she needed more. After so long without release, she needed this.

Always perceptive to her needs, Blaedia flipped them over, settling between Otera's thighs as she laid on her back. The first swipe of her mate's tongue through her folds sent a stroke of lightning through Otera's body. It had been so long since she'd been touched in such a way, so every sensation was magnified.

As Otera thrusted her fingers into her lover's hair, Blaedia licked her cunt again, closing her mouth around the sensitive bundle of nerves and sucking as she slid two fingers inside.

Desperate for release, Otera moaned, writhing beneath Blaedia and stroking her back with her foot. Every thrust of Blaedia's fingers inside her had her body winding tighter and tighter, the sounds coming from Otera's mouth loud and raw, although she tried to muffle them with a pillow.

When the intensity of her mate's mouth on her cunt increased, Otera's release crashed into her, Blaedia's name on her lips as her thighs squeezed around her head.

Otera collapsed on the bed, satiated and spent, with her mate in her arms. She only took a moment to recover before rolling her mate over again, intending to give to Blaedia just as much pleasure as her mate had just given to her. She may have been tired, but they had a lot of lost time to recapture.

CHAPTER TWENTY-SEVEN

AURELIA

Although she wanted to spend time with her sister, having just gotten her back, Septima had Exie now, and Aurelia knew she was exhausted. So, while Septima and Exie followed the servant to the guest chambers set up for them, Aurelia went with Cristos to the barracks as the warriors readied to leave for the mountains. With the Diapolis fleet arriving within the next day, the city needed to be evacuated of those citizens who were unable to fight. They hoped the city would survive the war, but there was no guarantee it would not be turned to cinders with dragons fighting on both sides.

By the time they got into the barracks meeting room, Lars had already gathered a group of warriors from both sides, as well as supplies to take to the location of the camp. Aurelia didn't know much about the landscape of the northern part of the continent, but Cristos instructed them to find a place within the valley to set up camp, somewhere safely away from any large settlements that may be targeted by their foreign invaders.

Although Taryn and Lars had intended to join the flyers in looking for a location for the camp, Cristos chose Faidon to lead the group since Taryn and Lars had just returned from the journey across the continent. With war looming, it was clear Cristos wanted the soldiers to have a chance to rest before they'd be needed to fight. Aurelia admired his consideration for his soldiers. He'd doubted his ability to be king from the start, but she didn't think there was even one other person who didn't respect and believe in him.

Once the group of warriors left, loaded with supplies, she and Cristos returned to their bedchamber to get a few more hours of sleep.

As soon as the door shut behind them, Cristos turned to her and pulled her into his arms.

"I promised we would get her back, but I hadn't expected her to free herself."

Smiling against his chest, Aurelia nodded. She closed her eyes, indulging for a moment in the feeling of his heart beating against her chest.

"I still can't believe it's real. I can't believe she's back and safe."

Caressing her back, Cristos kissed her on the forehead.

"Hopefully knowing she's safely tucked into bed in the palace will help you to sleep better tonight. Although I know what's ahead is enough to keep you awake."

Pulling away, she looked into his brilliant blue eyes. Even with several days' worth of stubble on his face and hair that needed a trim, he was the most handsome man she'd ever seen.

"I'm certainly not ready for a war, but I don't think any of us are."

Cristos nodded, kissing her deeply. Eyes falling closed, she wrapped her arms around his back, caressing the base of his wings. He groaned as his tongue caressed hers, lifting her into his arms and carrying her to the bed. Laying her gently on the silken sheets, he crawled over her, settling between her thighs.

"You can never truly be ready for war, but I'm not going to let anything happen to you. I told you that when we sat on Variel's roof, and nothing has changed since then."

Aurelia knew they needed sleep, but at that moment she didn't care. Her sister being safe gave her the permission she needed to enjoy herself without the sting of guilt. She didn't know what the next several days would bring, which was a feeling she was experiencing more and more, but her relationship with Cristos was something she could always depend on.

When Aurelia awoke the next morning, the bed beside her was empty, but the sheets were still warm. Her mate had woken, but he hadn't been gone long. Stretching her limbs and yawning, she tossed the blankets off and climbed out of bed. If he wasn't in their suite, then she expected to find him in the kitchens or in the barracks. Going into the bathing room, she cleaned her face and her teeth and pulled on a tunic and trousers, lacing up her boots before leaving their chambers. Before she even made it to the door of the kitchen, voices met her ears.

Opening the kitchen door, pure joy hit Aurelia when she saw her family sitting at the large prep table, talking as they sipped tea. Cristos, Septima, and Exie all turned to face her as she walked in, her sister jumping up from the table and running forward to embrace her. The many braids Septima had worn for years had been replaced by a single plait down her back. Aurelia pulled away to look into her sister's face. Septima looked vibrant and happy, beautiful as always.

"We didn't want to wake you, sissy. Are you hungry? Paulus is making a big breakfast for us."

Aurelia smiled so wide it nearly hurt as she followed her sister to the table. Choosing a chair between Septima and Cristos, her mate leaned over to kiss her as soon as she sat.

"Warriors flew down the coast this morning and reported that King Ailani's fleet will be here in a few hours," he said, pouring her a mug of tea. "We've sent another group toward the western side of the continent to get a better idea of the location of the invaders."

"You've certainly been busy this morning."

She hadn't thought Cristos had been awake for long, but by the list of things he'd already accomplished that morning, she realized he must have left their bed hours before she woke.

"Has the evacuation started?"

Cristos nodded.

"Those who couldn't fly themselves were either carried, traveled on horseback, or by wagon. The camp is set up in the valley to the west. It's many miles away from both kingdoms and the coast so the area should be safe from attack. Wards have been set up just in case, and enough supplies were brought to sustain the people for weeks. We've ordered a small regiment of soldiers to remain there, as well as a healer. They should be safe in the camp until this is over."

Just hearing about all the preparations that were in place, especially those to keep the civilians safe, settled some of the anxiety that had been plaguing Aurelia ever since they'd first marched toward Norithae.

The door to the kitchen opened and Blaedia and Otera walked in just as Paulus started to set plates of food down on the table in front of them. There was evidence of Otera's months in the dungeon, her body still showing signs of having been underfed, but the queen looked clean and well-rested. It would take time for her to return to the female she once was but being back with her mate would allow her to recover.

Walking hand in hand, Blaedia led Otera to the table, pulling out the chair for her to sit, before sitting beside her. The smile on her aunt's face warmed Aurelia's heart. She'd never known that Otera had a mate waiting for her when she escaped the dungeon, so knowing she had someone who loved her and would take care of her meant a lot to Aurelia.

Once everyone had a plate in front of them, Paulus left the room, leaving the six of them to eat and talk in private.

Septima had not exaggerated when she'd said the cook had created a big breakfast for them and the smells wafting in the air in front of her made her mouth water. Not only did the plate have eggs and toast, but he'd also fried pieces of ham for them and sliced fresh apples. Stomach growling as she took her first bite, Aurelia closed her eyes when the flavors hit her tongue, smiling as her family, both blood and found, talked with one another as they enjoyed their meal.

Chapter Twenty-Eight

Taryn

Although Cristos asked Taryn, Lars, and the rest of the group who'd traveled to the western coast to stay behind when the first fighters sought out a site to set up camp for the evacuees, she and Lars chose to fly out the next morning to transport those who couldn't fly themselves.

Setting out at first light, Taryn flew with a mother and child on her back toward the western part of the valley. Lars flew at her side, carrying the mother's other child.

In her phoenix form, she couldn't converse with the winged male at her side, or those riding on her back. She kept her eyes facing forward, flapping her great crimson and black wings in a steady rhythm, taking them just below the clouds. The journey was only supposed to take them a few hours, if the threatening storm didn't delay them. Cristos expected them to return to Windreach that evening, so she hoped the storm would hold off.

By the time they got to the camp, however, the thought of returning to the city was dashed. Although winter was coming to an end, it seemed to want to hold on as long as it could, and the freezing rain that pelted Taryn as she shifted back into her fae form was proof of that.

Securing her hood over her head, she led the mother and children into the dinner tent, Lars entering behind them.

"Is there anyone here who can reinforce the wards? Hold off the weather a bit longer?"

Lars shook his head, moving toward an empty table and sitting down. One of the cooks approached them, dropping off mugs of hot tea and plates of meaty stew. The scent made Taryn's mouth water, so she wasted no time taking a bite while waiting for Lars to respond.

"Most of the warriors who can ward have returned to Windreach toward the city. Since they intended to hold the wards steady in case of attack, they had to go back."

Although Taryn understood the reason why they'd left, the camp would be incredibly uncomfortable without a way to block out the storm. Everyone would need to stay in their shelters.

"Is there enough firewood?"

If there wasn't, she knew it would be difficult to find dry firewood since the rain had already started.

"We should have enough. A group went to Spectre Forest early in the day to get more. They have a shelter to keep it dry and I believe all the tents are stocked. Once these people finish eating, we just need to get them into tents for the night and hope the storm doesn't get any worse."

Frigid wind blew through the space as another Norithaean warrior escorted an elderly couple into the dining tent. They sat at a table near the fire, the cook immediately bringing them mugs of hot tea and plates of dinner. She watched them for a moment, grateful they'd been brought somewhere out of harm's way before the city was attacked.

Thoughts of her mate flooded into her mind, squeezing the ache that had been in her chest since the day she and the warriors had been forced to flee their kingdom. It had been months since she'd seen Cassius, and with no ability to contact him, she had no way to know if he was okay, or if he was even still alive. Not knowing ate away at her, pushed her to focus solely on her training and the war. Being captured by Warbotach weeks earlier and forced into the dungeon had nearly broken her, but the hope of seeing him again had pulled her out of the dark place she'd fallen into. She couldn't lie to herself, however. Going so long without the touch of a male and being around such handsome warriors in Norithae had been more than tempting.

When she turned her attention back to Lars, she pulled the image of Cassius' handsome face back to the forefront of her mind, hoping her willpower would not break. Her survival in the war was not guaranteed, and if she would die in the days to come, she didn't want to spend the rest of her time alone.

Finishing the last of her stew, Taryn stood, turning a glance toward the exit.

"If we aren't going back to the capital until after the storm, I guess I should turn in and try to get a few hours of sleep. I'd imagine there are tents for us?"

Lars nodded, standing as well.

"There are. Come. We can ask the cooks which ones are available."

Chapter Twenty-Nine

Septima

The storm hit just as the Diapolisian fleet entered the Norithaean harbor. Warriors were sent down to help secure the ships, but the dragons, six in all, had continued into the mountains, undoubtedly, to look for shelter. Septima followed Exie into the palace meeting room, taking a seat around the perimeter of the room as the military leaders of the three kingdoms filed into the room, followed by both kings and the queen.

After everything they'd shared in the dungeon and on their escape, Septima wondered how the queen was feeling now that she was back in the arms of her mate, free at last. From the brightness in Otera's eyes and the flush of her cheeks, Septima believed the queen would truly recover from her ordeal. The war was weighing on all of them, but they also all had reasons to be hopeful. With the arrival of King Ailani from Diapolis, they had a chance to win the war.

Dressed in a gold-embroidered violet tunic with well-fitted black trousers, the king of Diapolis did not look like what Septima had imagined. His hair was the same golden color as Exie's and hung in loose curls past his shoulders and his turquoise-colored eyes didn't show the same sleep deprivation that the rest of them did. He entered the room hand-in-hand with his consort, a handsome male dressed to sail into battle, and sat near the head of the table, just to the right of Cristos and directly across from Otera and Blaedia. Servants entered quickly, pouring glasses of whiskey for everyone in the room. Septima took hers gladly, enjoying the burn of the liquid as it hit her throat.

Reaching across the table, Cristos shook King Ailani's hand, dipping his head to the king's husband. "I can't tell you how much we appreciate you being here to aid in this fight. I understand why you were hesitant."

King Ailani nodded, taking a sip of his whiskey. "My spies came back from the western sea speaking of ships and dragons from the Inferno Territories. If Uldon is bringing in allies from off the continent, those with many ships and dragons, there is more he wants than to simply cross the portal."

"He's conquering the continent for Joneira," Bremusa interrupted. "When she was forced out of Aegricia after she'd taken the throne by force, she'd threatened to return."

"But why after all these years?" King Ailani asked. Cristos remained quiet, sipping his whiskey as he listened to the others.

Although Septima had expected Otera to respond, Bremusa spoke again. "She is returning to prevent the prophecy of the Shadow Glass from coming to pass, the prophecy that got Otera's grandmother, mother, and sister murdered."

Seeing how her sister stiffened, Septima reached out and held Aurelia's hand. They'd both lost their mother to Joneira's henchmen, and not to a plague as they'd always been told. Aurelia leaned forward in her chair. "What prophecy? Is it the same one that Variel told us?"

Bremusa leaned forward in her chair, the silver of her eyes like swirling melted silver. "When I spoke to the Shadow Glass more than two decades ago, the it predicted Messalina would have a daughter with a human mate, and that daughter would be chosen by the crown to serve over a combined northern kingdom. Messalina left her home as barely an adult, left her realm to find her human mate and do her part to fulfill the prophecy, to save her kingdom. She died to keep that future queen safe. Now Aurelia is of age, and Joneira aims to stop her from fulfilling the prophecy she tried to prevent years ago."

Chapter Thirty

Aurelia

Blood turned to ice in Aurelia's veins, and her breath caught in her throat, her chest tightening at Bremusa's words. Bremusa was the legendary elemental she'd only heard about before, the one who'd spoken the prophecy she'd learned about while at Variel's cottage months prior. She knew about the prophecy, and she knew her mother had been killed by one of Joneira's supporters after she'd stolen the Aegrician throne. What Aurelia never knew was that her father had been part of that prophecy, or that she herself had been the entire basis for the prophecy that had sent her mother out of her kingdom in the first place. Holding her sister's hand tightly, her heart threatened to break in two. Her mother had died to protect her and her ascension to the throne, a throne in a world she had never even known existed.

"Why would the throne choose me to rule? I don't even have any magic." There was so much more Aurelia needed to know, but she started there. She was nowhere near qualified to be a queen. She'd been pushing back against marrying Cristos to avoid being queen up until only recently.

Bremusa turned to her, the swirling of her eyes making it impossible for Aurelia to look away. "You do have magic, Aurelia. Your ability to see through the eyes of others, to walk like a spirit in their lives, will only get stronger the longer you are in your ancestral land."

Remembering her conversation with Exie only days ago, Aurelia turned to look at her friend, who was sitting next to Septima. Exie nodded at her, the side of her mouth tipping up in a smile. "Would you be able to show me how to use my abilities, Bremusa? Or do you know of someone else who could do so?"

With a genuine smile on her face, Bremusa nodded. "Your mother was my best friend. I would be honored to help you learn to use your powers."

Cristos' hand slid to her thigh, squeezing gently to offer support as he turned to face the other monarchs. "We need to talk about what's coming and how best to protect the city while we take Aegricia. Has there been any word about how far out the invaders are?"

King Ailani nodded, chewing a bite of the meat the servants had just placed on platters on the table. "My flyers say the ships should be docking at any moment, so my guess would be that they will be upon Norithae within three days, four at the most."

"Then we should get rest tonight and march on Aegricia as soon as the weather clears," Cristos said to the room at large. "We need to try to retake the kingdom before the invaders arrive. If we have fewer enemies to fight at once, maybe we'll have a better shot at taking back Aegricia before we must face whatever is coming. We will need a way into the city, though. We need the wards taken down."

Finishing off the rest of her whiskey, Bremusa leaned forward in her chair, placing her hands flat against the table. "I can take them down."

They spent a bit more time discussing the march into Aegricia and plans for Bremusa to take down the wards before retrieving the crown where it was hidden in the caves of the Shadow Glass, a magical mirror that gave her prophecies. If all else failed, Bremusa intended to destroy the crown, which would in turn destroy the portal, making it impossible for Warbotach, or anyone else, to cross into the human lands.

After plans were set in place for the days to come, Cristos and Aurelia left for their suite, as everyone else went to rest as well. There were still warriors and guards watching the perimeter of the palace grounds, however, and others reinforcing masking wards regularly to make the palace and surrounding lands invisible. Guards and warriors were set on a rotating duty schedule, allowing everyone time to get adequate rest when they were not needed for protection.

Watching the icy rain falling across the palace grounds from the balcony window, Aurelia sipped on a glass of water as Cristos stood behind her with his arms around her waist. The feel of his muscular body against hers always grounded her, made her feel so much safer.

"Hopefully the rain clears up soon, so it'll be safe to march north tomorrow."

There was a confidence in Cristos' words that Aurelia did not feel. They would march into battle again, and there was no guarantee any of them would walk out of it alive. Her stomach was in knots and her chest threatened to squeeze the breath from her lungs. She knew she couldn't survive in a world where Cristos or Septima didn't exist, and that terrified her.

There was more than just the war filling her with trepidation, however. Her monthly bleeding was late, and she was too afraid to tell him. If Cristosknew she was potentially pregnant, he would insist she go to the camp with the rest of those who couldn't fight, and she wasn't willing to do that. If he and her sister were going to fight, then she needed to be there with them, even if only to work with the healers.

Sensing her emotions, he set their glasses down on a side table, pulling her around to face him and cupping her cheeks with his hands.

"Something is on your mind, and don't tell me it's just the war, because I can sense that it's not. What's wrong?"

His finger stroked her jaw, the gentle touch luring her eyes to close. She hesitated to respond for a moment, not ready to tell him the truth but knowing she couldn't keep it from him either. When she reopened her eyes, his face was only inches away as he leaned in and gave her a gentle kiss on the lips.

"You know you can tell me anything, my love. There is *nothing* you can't tell me."

Searching his face, she knew he meant every word. Blowing out a deep breath to calm her fears, she decided to tell him the truth.

"I don't know how to say this so I'm just going to say it plainly. My monthly bleeding is a few weeks late. I think I'm pregnant."

For a moment, Cristos did not respond. He only looked at her, each second of silence only tightening her chest more. Just when she'd nearly pulled away from him to walk away and busy herself, a smile spread across his face and he swooped her up into his arms.

"This is wonderful news, my love. The best news."

Setting her back down on her feet, he scanned her face again.

"Unless this isn't something you wanted…"

In better circumstances, circumstances in which she wouldn't have to worry about losing those closest to her, she would have probably been overjoyed, but she didn't want to tell Cristos that. She didn't want to ruin his happiness.

"I just wish it was better timing. I wish this baby would be coming when war wasn't looming over us like a dark cloud and I didn't have to worry about what our future held. When I bring a baby into the world, I want the world to be safe."

He kissed her again, slow and cherishing.

"This baby only gives us more to fight for. We need to make Ekotoria safe again, not just for our baby, but for all the children on this continent."

Cristos wrapped his arms around her, lifting her and carrying her to the bed before pulling her on top of him.

"You know."

She smirked, trailing her finger down his chest.

"This is the kind of thing that got us into this mess."

Lips spreading into a devilish grin, Cristos pulled her forward and nuzzled into her neck, his tongue and mouth kissing up her neck before finding their way back to her lips. "And I don't regret a thing."

Even with the war on her mind, and a pregnancy she knew she wasn't ready for, his skilled tongue teased her until her body craved more, making the thoughts of the next day flee her mind, at least for the moment. When he pulled away to catch his breath, she yanked him back to her, all her passion pouring into the kiss.

With her legs straddling him, his cock lined up perfectly with her sex, the press of it against the sensitive bud at her center sending shudders of pleasure through her. Her hips rolled against him, the cloth of his trousers between them maddening as his cock dragged along her cunt. Even with his trousers between them, the sensation was ecstasy, her back arching with the pleasure of it as she moaned against his mouth.

Sitting upright, Aurelia tugged off her tunic and tossed it to the floor, Cristos pulling her back to him and taking the peak of her breast into his mouth. He kissed and sucked as he lifted his hips to meet hers, the sensation against her most sensitive spot nearly bringing her to climax.

"I love you," he said as his mouth left her breast and he pulled her into another kiss, his tongue caressing hers in a sensual dance as he rubbed his shaft against her folds.

"If you love me, you'll help me take these off."

Desperate to feel his skin against hers, Aurelia fumbled with the buckle of her trousers, sliding to the side so she could remove them, Cristos using the moment to take his off as well.

She gazed at his body for a moment, at the rippling muscles beneath sun kissed skin, at the impressive cock that jutted in the air as he laid on the bed, watching her. Even his massive wings, that were just as black as his hair, turned her on.

When she climbed back on top of him, Cristos snaked his arm around her and flipped her onto her back before crawling on top of her. Sliding his hand between their bodies, he grasped his cock and traced her folds in teasing circles using the tip that already glistened with precum. She groaned, her hips bucking as she grinded against him.

Sensing her need, he slid his cock toward her entrance, dipping it in her wetness. Before she could complain about not wanting to wait anymore, Cristos thrust inside her, slamming all the way to the hilt. Pulling her legs over his shoulders, he lifted her hips with his hands, angling her body where he hit the most sensitive spot inside of her. Her moans turned to screams as he filled her completely, every stroke bringing her closer to fracturing.

"You feel so damn perfect, my mate."

Her body begged for release, her belly clenching tighter as he thrusted inside her. Sliding one hand from her hip to her folds, Cristos' thumb stroked her sensitive clit, his ministrations pulling her closer and closer toward climax. When her orgasm finally hit her with the intensity of a lightning storm, she bit into the pillow trying to quiet her screams. Cristos leaned forward and kissed her, the kiss absorbing her moans as his own release hit him a moment later. They collapsed against each other, satisfied and in love as Aurelia fell asleep with no thought of war in her mind.

Chapter Thirty-One

Aurelia

When Aurelia woke the next morning, it was not Cristos at her side, but her sister. Lying next to her on the bed, Septima stroked her hair, the touch reminding her of times before they'd left their home in Vaekros. Aurelia stretched, taking in Septima's beautiful features.

"I like your hair like this," she said, as she smoothed her sister's long braid over her shoulder. "Where is everybody?"

Flopping onto her back, Septima interlaced their fingers. "The rain stopped sometime during the night, so Cristos and the military leaders are trying to get everything ready for those who will be marching toward Aegricia."

Although Aurelia had not intended to tell anyone else, she believed she was pregnant, she knew she had to tell her sister or face Septima's wrath when she did find out. Rolling over on her side, she loosened a breath, trying to steady her nerves. Even if they had not been facing a war, becoming a mother was something she hadn't seen for herself at that point in her life.

"There's something I need to tell you, sissy."

The side of her mouth lifting into a smirk, Septima's face was full of mischief. "You're pregnant."

For a moment, Aurelia lost her ability to speak, but it passed quickly. "How did you know?"

Her sister's smirk spread into a toothy grin, and she threw her arms around her, squeezing Aurelia tight enough to force the air from her lungs.

"I knew something was different about you the moment I saw you in the foyer when I got back. You're not hiding it as well as you think you are, sissy."

"I'm not hiding it at all!"

Aurelia threw herself onto her back, staring at the ceiling as she wondered whether she was lying to Septima and to herself. Although she didn't know for sure, because she hadn't yet seen a healer, she'd wondered about this for at least a week before telling Cristos. "I only told Cristos last night. I haven't even seen a healer to confirm."

Placing her hand on Aurelia's stomach, Septima let out a deep sigh. "Well, you should see a healer right away, especially with the war coming in the next few days, but I have little doubt that you're with child. Actually, Exie called it before I did. She said she's been smelling it on you for weeks but had been too preoccupied with my capture to mention it."

Aurelia groaned, placing her hand on her sister's. "Great! If Exie could smell it on me, then I wonder who else can as well."

Rolling off the side of the bed, Septima reached out her hands to help her sister up. "Well, come on. We should get you to the palace healer so she can check everything before you go trying to march into battle."

Dressing quickly in a tunic and trousers, Aurelia washed her face and cleaned her teeth before pulling on her boots and following her sister out of the bedchamber and toward the healer's rooms.

Although she'd never been to the palace infirmary, Aurelia knew exactly where it was after having been given directions by Cristos before they'd gone to bed. She hadn't said anything to Septima, but her mate had already insisted she see the healer in the morning to be examined. He didn't want her to take any chances if she was carrying their child.

He'd taken the news much better than she'd expected him to, and his joy at learning he would be a father had allowed her to sleep peacefully after they'd made love.

As she walked to the healer, however, Aurelia found herself thinking about her mother and everything she'd learned in the meeting the night before. She thought about how frightened her mother must've been to leave her realm all by herself, and how much pressure the prophecy had placed on her shoulders. She couldn't imagine being told that she had to find a mate in a different world to create a daughter who would save her kingdom someday.

The whole thing sounded so fanciful, and it would have been unbelievable if it were not for the fact that Aurelia knew the prophecy was true. Variel had said as much when they'd stayed at her cabin and she had learned the truth about her lineage. She'd learned she was not the human girl she always thought she was.

If only Aurelia could speak to her mother and tell her how brave she thought she was, and how much she loved her and appreciated what she'd done to bring her into the world. Messalina may have died when her children were small, but she'd been an amazing mother in the time she was alive. She had given her children all of her, and had sacrificed herself to save them, to protect them from someone who would commit unspeakable acts to steal the throne from her family.

Joneira knew she could never fully be queen if the crown did not choose her, so she would have never been given the power over the portal, but it didn't seem like she cared about that. All she'd cared about was sitting on the throne and wielding power she didn't truly have, which was why they had been able to get rid of her and put Otera on the throne after less than a decade.

Aurelia didn't know every detail about what had happened back then. She knew Joneira had her mother murdered, but she hadn't known Joneira had killed her great grandmother, the female having been queen for nearly a century, nor that she'd killed her grandmother as well.

She wanted to talk to Otera and learn more about her mother and about how Otera had survived those years when Joneira had been in power. Her aunt must have gone through such devastation, losing her mother and grandmother, her sister, and her kingdom, all within a handful of years. Even though Aurelia had never known the elderly women, the knowledge of the tragedy of her family hurt her heart.

As they approached the entrance to the infirmary, Aurelia promised herself that, when she left, she would find her aunt and talk to her. There was so much she needed to know. She hoped that wherever she found Otera, Bremusa would be there as well. The elemental had told her that her mother had been her best friend and promised to help her with her magic. With the war coming at any moment, and Aurelia's powers still being new and untested, there was no time to waste before learning how to wield them, just in case she could be useful in the war.

Although most of the palace had painted walls, the corridor leading to the healer's rooms were stone, similar to the corridor in the dungeon. Since both spaces were on the lower levels of the palace, Aurelia assumed that was why.

When they walked into the room, the first thing she saw, aside from the many shelves and cabinets filled with bottles of potions and dried herbs, was an elderly Norithaean female leaning over a counter with her large black wings tucked in against her back. When the healer turned around to face them, still wiping her hands on a rag, her eyes went wide.

"I've been wondering when you were going to come to me, milady."

Taking a few steps toward Aurelia, the female's head tipped to the side. "You are with child, are you not?"

Aurelia nodded as she entered the room with Septima by her side. "And you could tell that by just looking at me?'

The fae truly were more skilled at detecting things about a person, which made Aurelia wonder what else they could tell about a person just by smelling them. Suddenly she felt quite uncomfortable.

The healer chuckled and moved around the space, waving Aurelia over and indicating for her to sit on top of an examination table. With only a moment of hesitation, she did as she was asked.

"We fae can tell a lot about a person by their scent. Before you were with child, your scent was that of a half-human, half-Aegrician female. Once you became pregnant with your mate, our king's child, a new scent mixed with yours, the scent of a Norithaean. Now that the king's scent has become part of yours, it will be hard to hide your pregnancy from others."

Although Aurelia did not think the healer was trying to scare her, her words did fill her with fear, fear for her child, fear for herself, and most of all, fear for her mate. If their enemies could detect that she was carrying the Norithaean king's child, they could use her as leverage against him. If she was taken hostage, with or without his child in her belly, Cristos would do anything to get her back, and their enemies would know that.

She could not march into battle, not if it put her child's life at risk, and not if it put Cristos' life at risk. Just thinking about him marching to Aegricia without her made the backs of her eyes burn and her stomach twist into knots. If something happened to him, she wanted to be there, she wanted to protect him, but with a life growing inside her, she couldn't, because the baby needed her protection more.

"Lie back right here so I can check the baby."

So lost in her own head, the healer's words took Aurelia by surprise. With Septima's help, she laid back on the table, Septima tucking a pillow behind her head as the healer moved in close to her and covered her with a sheet.

"I'm gonna need to check everything to make sure everything is in good working order. Would that be okay, milady?"

Aurelia nodded although she didn't know what kind of medical equipment was used for pregnancy in the fae realm, which made her admittedly nervous. She'd never been around anyone pregnant while living in the war camp in the forest.

"Can you help me remove your trousers, so I can check your belly?"

Aurelia nodded and reached to her buckle, but her sister moved in to help, unbuttoning her trousers and sliding them off her feet before returning to her side.

"Are the fae able to find out the sex of the baby before it's born?"

Septima asked, taking over the conversation because she knew her sister was distressed.

The healer nodded but lifted her arm in a slight shrug.

"We are sometimes able to tell the scent of the baby when it is big enough, but not always. We say that the strongest babies put off the strongest scent."

She chuckled, but the sound was warm.

"I would think our King Cristos would make a strong child, and that we will know sooner than later if it is a son or a daughter."

Aurelia remained still as the healer touched her belly, placing a glass against it to listen to the heartbeat. She wished she would be able to hear it herself, because that would make it more real to her. With her belly still flat, and no other signs of pregnancy showing, she didn't see a pregnant woman when she looked in the looking glass, but she knew that would change as her belly grew and the baby started to move inside her.

"From what I can tell, milady, the baby is strong and healthy. You are doing a wonderful job taking care of it in your belly. I will want you to check back with me at least once every two weeks, more if you have any trouble. Don't ever feel like you're being silly if you have a worry. I know as a first-time mother, it can be scary, so don't hesitate to come to me if you're worried about something, even if you're worried it's nothing."

Aurelia nodded, pulling herself up on her elbows as the healer walked away to allow Septima to help her back into her trousers.

It wasn't necessarily sad tears when a flutter of emotion hit Aurelia and she started to cry. She was overwhelmed but she knew they were happy tears. She and Cristos would have a baby together and they would be a family. They would create the world they said they would, and that was something to look forward to.

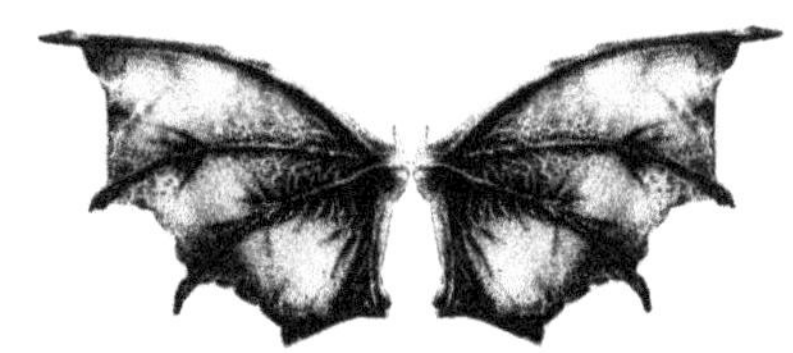

CHAPTER THIRTY-TWO

Aurelia

Once they left the healer's rooms, Septima and Aurelia headed toward the barracks where they expected to find Cristos, Exie, and the rest of the military, who were planning the attack on Warbotach. She wanted to talk to Cristos, but she also wanted to speak to Otera. She hoped to be able to talk to both before the armies left, because then it would be too late.

The air outside was still frigid from the icy rain the night before. Aurelia pulled her cloak closer to her body to protect her from the wind as a shadow flew overhead. She lifted her eyes to the sky to see one of the dragons from Diapolis flying over the palace before turning toward the sea. Seeing them always took her breath away. They were such majestic yet terrifying creatures.

Entering the barracks, there was a flurry of activity as warriors from all three kingdoms moved around the space, going in and out of different rooms and talking amongst themselves. She could hear the clatter of swords as warriors trained in the rooms suited for that. Usually, when the weather was nice, the warriors would train out on the grounds, but with the icy rain that had left the grounds wet and the air still too cold, it appeared many of the warriors chose the more comfortable option to train before they were forced out into the elements to either march or fly to the northern kingdom.

In the barracks meeting room, she found Cristos and Otera, along with Blaedia, King Ailani, and several other military leaders. Taryn and Lars had also returned from the civilian camp in the valley and were sitting side-by-side against the wall, with mugs of hot tea in their hands. As soon as Cristos saw her, a bright smile crossed his lips, and he crossed the room to her, pulling her into his arms and kissing her deeply. "Good morning, beautiful."

Lifting her off the ground, he kissed her again. "I take it you went to the healer this morning."

She nodded, not yet ready to talk about it in front of everyone else. When he pulled away, the giant smile still graced his face and his blue eyes were the brightest she'd ever seen them. "We'll be finished up here soon and then you and I can get some lunch and talk about what she said."

With one more kiss, Cristos set her down on the ground and turned back toward King Ailani, continuing a conversation she must have interrupted when she'd walked in.

Catching Queen Otera's eye, Aurelia approached her and asked if they could talk privately. Nodding, her aunt followed her out of the room and into another that was usually used for training but was currently vacant. Blaedia had watched them leave the room, but merely touched her lover on the hand and remained behind.

When they were in the private space and the door was closed, Otera pulled her niece into her arms, squeezing her tight and caressing her back with her hand. Guiding Aurelia to one of the benches along the wall, Otera and her niece sat down, still arm-in-arm.

"I was hoping you would find me this morning," Otera said, her face a picture of joy. "You look so much like your mother."

Aurelia studied her aunt's face for a moment before responding. "So, do you."

Although Otera smiled, Aurelia could see the pain behind her eyes. "My mother is why I wanted to speak to you. So much was said last night that I didn't know, and I need to know more. I hoped you could tell me more about my mother and about what she went through to have me."

Otera nodded, taking Aurelia by the hand. "Let me first say that your mother, Messalina, never wanted to be queen. Although we do not have power over who the crown chooses, Messalina always hoped it would not choose her. When Bremusa consulted the Shadow Glass, as our grandmother's time on the throne was coming to an end, the Shadow Glass told Bremusa, who is a powerful oracle, that Messalina's daughter would be queen, and that the child would come from a union between her and a human mate. The Shadow Glass predicted that Messalina's daughter would combine the kingdoms of the north as queen and would bring peace to the continent at last."

"On the night Joneira and her henchman raided the palace and killed my grandmother, Messalina and I were not at the party. We'd left not long before to go find Bremusa, who had gone that morning into the caves to consult the Shadow Glass again and had not returned. We were concerned something had happened to her and so we took Blaedia and a few other warriors and had them carry us to the caves so we could look for her."

Going silent for a moment, Otera blew out a breath. "By the time we got to the caves, it was clear something was wrong. Bremusa had been held in place by chains made of dragon bone. They were enchanted to harm her if she tried to escape, and it took powerful magic to get her free. We discovered that Joneira and her supporters had gone to the caves when Bremusa was there and had tortured her to get her to reveal the secrets of the Shadow Glass. Joneira wanted to know if she would be able to take power. She wanted to know how to take it by force. After Bremusa gave her little information, she was chained and left in the caves. A ward over the cave entrance prevented anyone from entering, and her from exiting, so just to get into the cave itself took time. The Shadow Glass told Joneira that in order to take the throne, she would have to kill the queen and the queen's descendants, because although the crown is not passed on in families, the crown intended to pass to the queen's granddaughter...*Me*. Messalina never went back to the palace after that night. With Joneira knowing about the prophecy and knowing it would be Messalina's child who took the throne and combined the kingdoms, it was not safe for her to return to the palace. We knew that Joneira was already on her way back to the palace to kill our grandmother. With a bag Bremusa had packed weeks before and hidden in the cave, Messalina was sent through the portal on the back of one of the warriors and forced to go to the human realm to look for her mate. I was sent into hiding while the warriors went back to the palace to try to stop the inevitable."

When Aurelia turned to look at her aunt, Otera's cheeks were damp from her tears.

"I never saw my sister again after that night. I never spoke to my sister again after she left the caves on the back of that phoenix. We exchanged ravens for years, but the ravens stopped when she lost her life."

A sob broke from Otera with that last admission and Aurelia wrapped her arms around her aunt, her own tears sliding down her cheeks.

"We'd always intended, when she'd left that night, that she would return when it was safe, but she died before that ever happened. We knew about you and your brother, but it was safest for you to remain with your father. Drawing any attention to you with Joneira still alive would have put your life at risk so we didn't take any chances."

Aurelia sniffed and wiped the moisture from her cheek.

"Dd my father know what my mother was?"

Otera nodded, giving Aurelia's hand a gentle squeeze.

"From the messages we received from your mother, your father knew everything. They were very much in love. If there was any good in my sister having to leave, it's that she knew love, true love, and she had you and your brother. Those things make her life worthwhile."

The emotions that warred inside Aurelia made her chest ache. Pain and confusion, love and hope, all battled inside her. Turning to face her aunt, Aurelia tucked the hair behind her ear.

"There's something I need to tell you, Aunt Otera." She hesitated, debating if she wanted to tell anyone else her secret. "I'm pregnant."

The grin returning to Otera's face, she pulled Aurelia into a hug, kissing her on the cheek. "That's wonderful news, Aurelia. Your mother would be so proud of you. This gives us so much more to fight for, and when we win against Warbotach, we will win for your baby, the heir to the combined kingdoms of northern Ekotoria, because I will be stepping down when you become queen of Norithae. The prophecy must come to pass."

CHAPTER THIRTY-THREE

KASON

Packing their belongings for the journey north, Kason and Holera prepared to leave Norithae with a group of warriors that would head closer to Aegricia and begin the process of trying to remove the wards around the city. They intended to set up camp in the caves nearby and use the combined powers of the warriors who had warding abilities to begin chipping away at those protections put in place by Warbotach. Bremusa, being a powerful elemental, would be joining them on their journey because she claimed to be able to take down the wards on her own.

Leaving just before sunset, Kason slung their bags over his shoulder and holstered his sword and bow, following Holera into the palace courtyard, where the other warriors were already ready to go. She shifted in a flash of fire and Kason climbed onto her back, settling himself in as he always did. In a flap of her beautiful silver wings, she launched them into the sky aiming toward the mountains that separated Norithae from Aegricia.

The night air was cold, the storms from the night before having left the air still feeling like winter when spring should have been setting in. Kason pulled his cloak tighter around his body, fastening the fur hood over his head and pulling a scarf in front of his face. The cold wind didn't seem to bother his mate when in her phoenix form, but the higher they went into the clouds, the more uncomfortable it was for him.

Not wanting Warbotach to know their intentions, the group of Phoenix and Norithae Warriors flew high over the mountains, only swooping down low once they had bypassed the city all together and could land safely near the caves without being seen.

Landing in a small valley between the mountain peaks, Kason was glad the mountains blocked the wind. Finding firewood to keep them warm would be difficult, however, since the area that far into the mountains did not have many trees. Thankfully, most of the warriors had packed some just in case.

The other warriors landing nearby, the Phoenixes shifted back into their fae forms with a flare of fire, and the group set out in search of a comfortable cave where they could spend their time without being seen by their enemies.

Already knowing the area because of her time having to go to the caves where the Shadow Glass was, the place where she received many of her prophecies, Bremusa showed them to a location where they could be safe and warm while trying to work on the wards.

Setting up camp several hours before sunrise, Kason and Holera escorted the elemental to the boundary of the wards around the city, standing guard as she assessed the protections the Warbotach mages had put into place.

Kason held his hand on the hilt of his sword, keeping his senses alert as he scanned the darkness around them. Although the Warbotach leaders would not have expected them to set up camp in the mountains behind the city, it did not mean they didn't have patrols in that area.

Bremusa walked the perimeter of the area, not in the form of a female, but in the form of a large black wolf. A predator hunting for its prey was all the barbarian warriors would have seen if they'd come across her. Being an elemental, Bremusa could shift into nearly any creature, giving herself the ability to mask who she was altogether so her power would not be used against the Aegrician people.

Holera patrolled near Kason's side. Although she was a warrior and could protect herself, he didn't want his mate too far away from him where he could not protect her if someone did show up to attack. There were more dangers in those mountains than just their enemies. Many vicious creatures hunted through the mountains and caves, as well as the forest land beyond, creatures they didn't yet know existed but could tear her to shreds before she had the chance to shift and fly away. As long as he was alive, he would always protect her just as he loved her, with his last breath.

Camouflaged in the darkness of the night, the elemental female had moved out of sight shortly after they began their watch in the area. All had been silent for at least an hour or two, until the sound of pounding footsteps approached Kason and Holera from the darkness.

Reaching for his mate, he pulled Holera against his chest, backing up toward the caves and holding his sword aloft to strike whatever was coming to attack. His heart pounded wildly, expecting a hellhound or another bloodthirsty beast to burst out of the darkness when it was too late for him to see it and strike. Relief washed over him when it wasn't a bloodthirsty beast that approached them from the shadows, but Bremusa in her wolf form, running straight toward them and into the caves behind them. It only took a moment for him to see what she was running from - a mountain wendigo. Before he could think, Kason lifted Holera, tossing her over his shoulder and bolting toward the cave. Wendigos were flesh-eating monsters, vicious creatures who had strength, speed, and sharp claws. They did not need weapons as he did.

The creature gained on him, swiping just out of its reach as he ran, the creature's claws grazing the side of his arm. He hissed, but didn't stop, running faster than he had in a long time to get his mate to safety.

A blast of icy air hit him from the front as Bremusa stood in the opening of the cave, arms in the air, shooting power like he had never seen toward the creature.

"Get behind me! NOW!" She screamed over the sound of the wind erupting from her fingertips. It was not easy to rush through the bursts of icy wind that swirled like a tornado around him but he clenched his jaw and held Holera tightly against his chest and forged ahead, making it into the cave just as the animal screamed, swept up and unable to fight the cyclone of wind coming from the elemental.

Once inside the cave, Kason set his mate down on the ground and she immediately reached towards his arm to assess his wound.

"Kason, come in the tent with me so I can dress this wound right away. You're bleeding pretty heavily."

He wanted to go back to the cave's entrance and help the others fight the beast in case it got past Bremusa's powers, but before he had a chance to argue, his mate pulled him by his non-injured arm. She would not have taken no for an answer. So, instead of twisting out of her grip, he followed her into their tent to let her take care of him.

By the time Kason and Holera made it back out of the tent, his arm cleaned with a fresh bandage, the activity at the cave's entrance had mostly died down. A few warriors guarded just inside the cave, but the beast was gone.

Bremusa sat near the fire in her fae form, leaning over one of the Norithae warriors who had joined them, the male bleeding heavily from a gash in his leg. They darted forward to see if they could help, although neither of them was a healer.

"What happened? What can we do?" Holera asked as she kneeled down next to Bremusa, reaching to put pressure on the wound.

Moving away as Holera covered the wound, Bremusa dug through her satchel.

"A few of the warriors ran forward to try to kill the beast while I used magic to hold it in place, but it lashed out and got his leg before the other warrior sliced its head off. All we can do now is try to stop the bleeding."

Lowering himself to his knees, Kason leaned forward to help his mate, pressing his hands against the male's leg as the warrior laid unconscious.

"How will you work on the wards if there are wendigos in this area? If there's one, then there are more."

Approaching the injured male again, Bremusa leaned over him, Holera moving her hands away as the other female applied a balm to the wound, the substance slowing the flow of blood to merely a trickle. Seeming to be happy with the progress, she reached for a roll of bandages and wrapped them around the male's leg, covering the wound.

"I'm going to go back out tomorrow, but I will go in my true form, and no one is to follow me."

Chapter Thirty-Four

Aurelia

By the time Aurelia finished talking to Otera and they'd left the training room to return to the others, the military leaders and monarchs were already filing out of the meeting room, everyone dispersing in different directions. Catching her eye, Cristos smiled and walked toward her, wrapping his arm around her waist and kissing her on the forehead.

"Are you hungry, my love? We could probably go to the kitchen and see what they're cooking, or if you'd like, we can take food back to our rooms."

The way he always tried to take care of her made Aurelia grin against his chest as she walked nestled below his shoulder.

"Do you know if Septima will be going into the kitchen?"

Although she and Christos needed to talk, she would've liked to sit down and eat with her sister if possible, especially since they would be leaving for war within a day.

"I believe Septima and Exie have flown out over the forest so Septima can practice her archery."

Although she really wanted to spend more time with her sister, Aurelia understood Septima's need to train. With them going into battle, she realized training may have been more important at that moment than lunch. Still, she promised herself that she would at least try to have dinner with Septima that night, maybe even eat with everyone. It may have been the last opportunity they would be able to spend together, which was a painful thought. Even now, with Kason and Holera having already left for the Aegrician mountains along with Bremusa and a few other warriors, it was already too late for everyone to dine together.

"Since they're not available, let's get food brought to our rooms so we can talk in private and then maybe we will be able to have dinner with everyone tonight."

Christos nodded, his chin against the side of her head.

"I think everyone would like that very much."

Continuing through the palace, arm-in-arm, Cristos asked a servant to bring their meal to the suite and they headed up the stairs.

Turning to face her as soon as the door to their suite closed, Cristos pulled Aurelia into his arms, lifting her up and kissing her, his lips lingering for a moment. When he pulled away, she could see by the look on his face that he was more interested in talking about what she'd learned at the healer than what plans he'd made in the war room.

"What did the healer say to you about the baby? Is everything going to be okay? Are you and the baby healthy?"

Aurelia giggled at how rapidly the questions came out of him. He was indeed excited to be a father, and it warmed her heart to see him with so much hope and joy. Taking him by the hand, she led him to the sitting area in front of the fireplace, lowering herself onto the sofa as Cristos added a few logs to the stack, lighting a fire quickly.

"I wanted to talk to you about something else as well, my love," he said.

Approaching the sofa, Cristos sat next to her, taking her hands in his.

"The warriors are leaving tomorrow to go north, but before I go, I wanted to know if you would marry me. I love you more than life. If something happens to me, I need to know you and our child will be taken care of."

"Cristos... I..."

She hesitated, shaking her head slowly as she squeezed his hands tighter.

"You know I'll marry you, but please don't talk like that. Nothing is going to happen to you and you're not leaving without me. I've been thinking about it a lot, and I know I can't fight in the war with our baby inside me, but I'm still going with you. I can work in the healer's tents. I can help in some way, but I'm not staying behind. I just can't."

Warm tears slid down her cheeks and Cristos swiped them away with his thumb.

"I don't want you or our baby anywhere near Warbotach. I don't know what I would do if something happened to you—to either of you."

Dropping his hand from her face, he placed it on her belly that was still flat, no sign of her pregnancy showing yet.

"I know I just found out he or she is growing inside you, but it's all I've been able to think about. This child is a promise of a better future for our kingdom. It's something good when there's so much bad, a new life when there will be so much death. After what happened to Septima at the battle when we took back my kingdom, I can't take a chance of the same thing happening to you. While you're here, you're safe. The palace is warded, so even if the invaders to the continent passed through Norithae to get to Aegricia, they wouldn't be able to get into the palace grounds. They won't be able to get to you. I can't protect you like that if you come with me."

"I understand your point, but it doesn't change my mind. There's no way you and my sister are leaving this kingdom without me, pregnant or not."

His face tensing, Cristos remained quiet for an agonizing moment, the moment only interrupted by a knock on the door. Rising before she could, he crossed the room and answered the door, taking their meal from the servant and setting it on the table. She followed him to the table and sat down, her stomach already growling.

"And you will stay with the healers?" Cristos asked, his eyes searching her face. "If you come north with us, you'll remain in the warded camps?"

Knowing she couldn't promise what he was asking, it took Aurelia a heartbeat to nod. She intended to stay in the camps and help the healers, but she knew she would leave the camp in an instant if she received word that he or her sister was injured.

"I will stay in the camps, but I have conditions."

When he turned up to look at her as he placed their food into plates, there was a curious look on his face, one eyebrow arched in that way she loved.

"Conditions?"

Taking a bite of the delicious casserole the servant had brought to them, she had to chew her food before she could answer.

"Yes. I don't know if it's possible, but I want to find Variel and take her with us. She's a powerful healer. That's what you told me when we met, when she healed Exie from both physical and magical wounds. Between her being a healer and an oracle, and her ability to shift, she would be really helpful in this war. We need her."

The look on Cristos' face was contemplative as he took a sip of his whiskey.

"She may be difficult to find, but we can certainly try. Although..."

He hesitated, his eyes going distant before he turned them back to her.

"Variel left this palace when my mother was murdered and has chosen to live away from society ever since. We may find her only to discover she doesn't want to join us in this war at all."

"I do understand that, but we have to at least try. We have to go to her and give her that option. Plus, she seemed to know so much about what changes I would go through when I came into my fae body, and into my powers. I feel like I need to learn more from her. Maybe I can find a way to help in this war if I can learn more about my powers."

"If I say yes, that we will look for Variel tomorrow, then will you marry me tonight?"

Nearly choking on her food at the urgency of his question, Aurelia took a sip of her tea.

"You really want to get married tonight?"

Cristos smiled, his blue eyes bright.

"The armies are leaving tomorrow. Septima, Exie, and Otera intend to join them, as do I. It may not be the wedding you'd hoped for, at least not until the war is over, but Septima and your aunt will be there if we do it tonight, as will some of our friends. When the armies march north tomorrow, you and I will go south to Variel. With or without her, we can find our way back to the armies before nightfall tomorrow night. I know where they plan to camp."

The rest of the afternoon went by quickly once they'd decided. Cristos left their suite to plan for the event while Aurelia spent time with her sister, needing to do some planning of her own.

With the little time they had, and everything else that needed to be done, there was no time to look for a dress or plan the kind of party she would've had in Vaekros, but as Cristos said, they would plan a grander wedding ceremony once they returned from war, once they *won* the war. Along with the baby growing inside her, the wedding would be one more thing to look forward to.

By the time Aurelia found her sister in the kitchens, she and Exie having only recently returned from training in the forest, it was clear the entire palace knew there would be a wedding that night. The underlying mood was tense, but the wedding lifted spirits, if only a little.

"A lot of changes going on in your life right now, sissy."

Taking a seat next to Septima and Exie, her sister's brilliant grin was infectious.

"You're growing up all of a sudden."

Aurelia snorted, reaching for the fresh bread on the table in front of her.

"I may be doing grown up things, but I don't feel like I'm ready for any of it."

Kissing Exie on the cheek, Septima stood from the table.

"Let's go find something for you to wear."

"Where? We can't leave the palace grounds to go into town, not now. I doubt anything is even open."

Her grin only spreading wider, Septima reached down her hand for Aurelia's.

"We may not be able to go into town, but one of the servants let slip that Cristos' mother's gowns are still in the palace. His father never parted with them. I was asked to bring you to find her when you came down, so we can choose a dress for you to wear tonight."

CHAPTER THIRTY-FIVE

AURELIA

The rooms where Cristos' father had resided were opulent, but it was clear one of the barbarians had used the space for his own needs when they'd taken the city. There were damages to some of the furniture and slashes in a few of the walls from a blade, but the servants had done their best to fix up what they could.

Aurelia and Septima followed the elderly servant, a female named Maelia, through the gilded space and into a large dressing room, the walls lined with wooden floor to ceiling cabinets.

"King Marcellus was a loving husband to Queen Cordia. Her death nearly broke him, as it did her son."

Heart breaking for her mate, Aurelia watched as Maelia opened one of the cabinets, the space filled with the most beautiful gowns she'd ever seen.

"He never gave his heart to another female and kept all her things safely tucked away. If the king was here today, he would be filled with joy for his son, but since he's not," she said, holding her hand up in an invitation for Aurelia to look at the dresses, "I know he would be happy that his beloved's dresses are being given to his son's new wife."

With a sweet smile on her face, Maelia stepped aside to allow Aurelia access to the opened cabinet. Not knowing what to look at first, her hand moved across the dresses, allowing the exquisite fabrics to slide through her fingers. Although she didn't recognize some of the fabrics, many felt like satin and others were dripping with lace or trimmed with jewels. She didn't know how she would've been able to choose one of them when they were all so beautiful, but her sister didn't seem to share the same difficulty.

"This one."

Slipping past her, Septima dug her hands into the closet, pulling out a gold embroidered ivory dress with long skirts that flared away from a fitted waist. Holding it in front of herself in the looking glass, Aurelia admired the intricate designs expertly sewn across the bodice.

"I think it might already be your size, sissy."

As she held the dress against her body, she agreed. "Should I try it on?"

If she were being honest, she was a little uncomfortable wearing Cristos' mother's clothing, not because his mother had worn it before, but because she didn't want to ruin it. Also, she didn't know how Cristos would respond to seeing her in something his father had held onto for so long because it was important to him and their family. The servant, however, truly believed it would be acceptable for her to wear the queen's clothing, and she trusted her judgment, only hoping it didn't upset anybody to have the queen's clothes be given away.

Taking the dress from her hand, Septima worked to remove it from the hanger as Aurelia and the servant untied her tunic and trousers, her clothing dropping to the floor. When she was left in only her underclothes, Septima helped her to pull the dress on, going behind her to lace up the back.

Although she'd spent most of her life in the human lands in dresses and gowns, she'd only worn one since entering Ekotoria. The emerald dress she'd worn in Diapolis to attend King Ailani's party had been beautiful, breathtaking even, but it had been nothing compared to the ivory and gold dress that had once belonged to the queen of Norithae.

"This is the one," Septima said, and Aurelia couldn't have agreed more. In that dress, with her crimson hair and bright blue eyes, she knew she looked stunning.

"Yes, this is the one."

After leaving the royal chambers with her dress, Septima, Aurelia, and the servant went back to her and Cristos' quarters so they could help her get ready. As Maelia started her bath, Septima went to her own quarters to find Exie and Cristos. She also intended to find out more about the ceremony, what time it would take place and where it would be located. She also, Aurelia knew, was going to forbid Cristos from going back to their suite and seeing her before the wedding. Although her sister had not said so much, Aurelia knew she would be giving Cristos those orders.

By the time Aurelia got out of the bath, Septima was back and wearing a mischievous grin, Exie at her side. Drying off her hair as she sat in front of the vanity in her robe, she watched them approach from behind her through the looking glass.

"What are you grinning about, Septima? I can always tell whenever you've been up to something."

"Nothing at all," her sister responded, but Aurelia didn't believe her. Narrowing her eyes at Septima, her sister raised her hands in mock surrender. "All I did was tell Cristo he has to refrain from coming in here until after the ceremony. Nothing else—I promise."

Aurelia turned back around to face the looking glass, squeezing the towel into her long crimson waves as she tried to dry her hair enough to fix it before the ceremony. "Did anyone tell you where we're going to be during the wedding?"

"I spoke to Cristos as he had just come into the dining room to get something to eat, and he said they would be setting up the main balcony overlooking the sea. The servants have already been lighting candles and preparing the seating, food, and drinks for tonight."

Although they had a balcony off their suite, Aurelia had never seen the balcony Exie was talking about and she was excited to see the view that must've been beautiful enough for him to want to do it there above any other place on the grounds.

"I would've thought they'd want to do it in the courtyard, but I'd imagine with all of the rain and the cold temperatures, that wasn't an option."

Exie nodded. "That's correct. He said they'd thought about the courtyards first, because they are beautiful, but the ground is still wet and it's a bit too windy to be comfortable. Plus, Septima made it clear your hair would get messed up with all the wind and humidity and she knew you wanted to look your best."

Her sister knew her well, and Aurelia couldn't argue with her reasoning.

"Not to mention," Septima said, "I wouldn't want you to get that beautiful gown all dirty or stained going outside in the mud."

Before Aurelia could verbalize her agreement, a knock came at the door, and Exie walked away to answer it. Although she couldn't see him from where she was sitting, she couldn't mistake her mate's voice as he and Exie spoke in the doorway.

"I just need to get my clothes, Exie," Cristos said with more amusement than agitation in his tone. Septima darted toward the door a moment later, responding "no" loudly enough for Aurelia to hear. She snickered but didn't get up from where she was sitting.

"You are not coming in this room and seeing my sister before the wedding and giving your marriage bad luck, Cristos. Just tell me what you want, and I will go get it for you."

Cristos groaned but agreed, explaining to Septima where to find the uniform he wanted to wear for the wedding. Only a moment later, her sister walked past her, going into the large wardrobe and pulling out a few pieces of clothing to give to Cristos at the door. They exchanged goodbyes, Cristos explaining where they would need to meet him and at what time, before he walked away, closing the door behind him.

Staring at herself one final time in the looking glass, Aurelia was taken aback by how stunning the gown was on her. What she would be getting married in was a dress that was made for a queen. It only took her a moment before the realization hit her that she was about to become a queen, something she never saw for herself.

The irony hit her a moment later at the words Otera had spoken to her only that morning. Her mother had never wanted to be queen either, but it was her daughter who'd been destined to be queen. It was almost as though the prophecy was coming to pass even before the war. By the end of the night she would be queen of Norithae, and when Otero stepped down after the war and allowed the crown to pick the prophesied queen, Aurelia would become queen of both kingdoms.

Just the thought of it squeezed at her chest, threatening to take the breath from her lungs. Life was moving too fast, the drastic changes too much for one person in such a short span of time. She knew she would adapt and overcome everything in her life that was happening, but it was still overwhelming at that moment. Taking in a deep breath, Aurelia exhaled slowly before sliding on the golden shoes that had also belonged to Cristos' mother and walked toward the door.

Following Septima, who had also changed into a beautiful gown, and Exie, who wore an immaculate warrior's uniform, Aurelia left her suite and headed through the palace to the place where she would become Cristos' wife.

Entering the main ballroom, she was blown away by the beauty of the space. Candelabras and sconces lit the room, highlighting the beautiful artwork and sculptures that lined the walls. The glass doors in the back of the room were opened to a large balcony and the pastel sky beyond, as the sun set over the water. Light music fluttered down on the breeze, although Aurelia was unsure of what type of instrument was being played. Septima and Exie led her toward the balcony, stopping just outside as a servant scurried through the doorway to tell whoever was inside that she was ready. Only a moment later, the servant returned and ushered them inside.

Holding her sister's hand, just as she had when they'd entered the Aegrician war camp all those months ago when they'd left their home, Aurelia walked through the threshold and onto the balcony, her heart pounding wildly as she glanced around at her friends, and even those she'd never become acquainted with, all seated and waiting to witness the union.

Turning toward the sound of the music and seeing her mate standing in front of the balcony railing with the sunset at his winged back took Aurelia's breath away. He truly was the most gorgeous male, a perfect mate, and she couldn't believe he was hers and she was his.

The moment their eyes met, Cristos smiled, his eyes sparkling with joy at the sight of her. Smoothing out the front of his crisp, black tunic, he walked forward to take her hand.

"I believe I've seen that gown before," he said, as he pulled her to him and kissed her deeply. For a moment, the world around them disappeared as his lips caressed hers. "But I didn't realize it was still here. It looks beautiful on you. I'm so glad the servants kept my mother's clothing safe all this time and thought about showing this to you."

Some of the tension that had been building in her chest loosened at his words, relief flooding through her that he wasn't upset about her wearing his mother's dress.

"I have to admit, I wasn't sure if you would be unhappy with me for wearing something of your mother's."

Pulling away to scan her face, Cristos slid his hand down her cheek, the feeling sending shivers through her body, even with everyone watching.

"I would never be upset with you, and certainly not for that. I can't wait another moment to marry you, Aurelia. I know it's not the way that we wanted it to be, but once the war is over, we will have so much to celebrate, and another wedding will be just the way to do it. We'll have a big party with all our friends. We'll dine and dance, and then we will enjoy lots of time together before the baby comes."

The plans for their future sent the warmth of hope spreading through her chest. Kissing him again, she leaned her cheek against his chest, glancing back toward the railing where he had been standing. Her mouth dropped when she noticed the familiar face who stood there waiting for them. *Variel.*

Chapter Thirty-Six

Aurelia

"You found her,' Aurelia said, her tone incredulous. "How?"

"I didn't want us to not be able to leave with the army in the morning, so I went to look for her on my own while you spent time with Septima today."

Mouth opening and closing, she was speechless for a moment.

"Why didn't you tell me?"

Cristos smiled and kissed her on the head before wrapping his arm around her waist and leading her toward the shifter.

"I didn't want to worry you and I believed I would be able to find her quickly. Plus, I knew you would want to spend our final day here with your sister and I didn't want to take that away from you."

As soon as she approached Variel, Aurelia darted forward, wrapping the older female in her arms. It had only been a few months since she'd seen her, but in that moment, the shifter felt like family and family was what she needed. When Variel pulled away, a wide grin spread across her face.

"I told Cristos I wouldn't be leaving the forest to come into the city again, but he insisted I needed to come and marry you two, and *that* was an event I couldn't miss. Since I'm already here, I guess I might as well help in the war. It'll take all of us to win our kingdom back."

The backs of Aurelia's eyes burned with Variel's words. They meant more to her than Variel probably knew. Ever since she'd realized she was likely coming into her fae powers, she knew she needed to meet with Variel. She knew the woman who had been like a mother to Cristos ever since his own mother had been murdered would be able to teach her to use her powers for something good.

"I can't thank you enough for leaving your home to come here, Variel," Aurelia said, meaning the words so much more than she could even express. "I know it wasn't easy for you to leave your home, and I know you didn't intend to come to the city again, but it means so much to all of us that you're here."

The shifter nodded, patting Aurelia on the arm. "I know there's a lot that we need to talk about, and we will. But let's get the two of you married first, and then you and I will talk later."

Aurelia glanced at Cristos before turning her eyes back to Variel. "Wait a minute, you are going to marry us?"

She really didn't know anything about how marriages were conducted in the fae world, or who was responsible for conducting the ceremonies, but she had no idea Variel was able to do it. The healer nodded, a grin on her face. "I am."

Otera and Septima walked up behind them, taking a place near Aurelia's side as Cristos reached out and held her hands. The moment felt surreal as Aurelia watched Variel murmur words to herself, and a momentary sense of panic hit her when the healer pulled a dagger from a sheath at her side, continuing to speak just under her breath.

"Give me your hands."

Although Cristos gave his hand right away, setting it facing up in Variel's right hand, Aurelia was hesitant after seeing the dagger, but blew out breath and turned her hand over, sliding it on top of Variel's left hand.

"In our world, unlike in the human world, it is the mating bond that determines when two people have chosen each other to be their partner in life. Marriage is a second choosing, a way for you to tell the world that you belong to each other."

Placing Aurelia's hand on top of Cristos,' Variel lifted the dagger and sliced it across Aurelia's palm, a hiss bursting through her teeth. She'd nearly pulled her hand away, but the intensity in Cristos' eyes told her not to, told her it would be okay, and for her to trust him.

Blood slid from the wound, pooling in her hand as Variel made an exact slice on Cristos' palm as well. A moment later their hands were joined, their blood mixing together as Variel wrapped their hands in a strip of cloth.

"As bonded mates, your bodies already knew your hearts beat for each other, but now your blood flows together, making you one. Wherever you go from here, and no matter what happens from here, you will always be connected. Your blood will always flow in each other's veins."

Placing her hands on either side of theirs, Variel murmured a few more words before warmth radiated from her hands, soothing the pain from the wounds she'd inflicted.

When Variel moved away, Cristos leaned forward, his lips finding Aurelia's, the kiss filled with enough emotion to bring tears to Aurelia's eyes. As soon as they pulled apart, cheers erupted from their family and friends, sending Aurelia back into Cristos' arms as she broke into a fit of giggles, the stress leading up to that moment dissolving away into joy. She knew it would fade by the next day when they marched toward war. For that moment, however, she had just married the love of her life, and for that night she wasn't going to let the thought of war ruin her joy.

After the wedding ceremony concluded, they'd spent the next few hours eating, drinking, and spending time with their friends as a few warriors played upbeat music. Aurelia had gotten to speak to Variel briefly, but with all the revelry, it had been too distracting to have such an important discussion. With the trip in front of them the next day, they agreed to talk then, or at least when they made camp on their way.

Aurelia and Cristos made it back up to their suite as everyone else turned in for the night. Although they would have liked to enjoy the festivities longer, the long journey ahead made it a smarter decision to go to bed early while they still had a soft bed to sleep in.

When they got back to their suite, Aurelia was completely exhausted, but she stifled back a yawn as her husband led her to the bathing room and turned on the tap over the tub. They took a bath quickly, both of them realizing how badly they needed sleep.

Once out of the bath, they crawled into bed, Aurelia already mourning the comfort of a real mattress and linens and dreading the nights she would be sleeping in a tent again. It was the least of all her worries however, since war brought many unthinkable outcomes, but she chose to put those as far from her mind as she could until she couldn't anymore. Sliding up against her husband's side, she breathed deeply, his sandalwood and spice scent always managing to calm her.

"How's your hand?" Cristos asked, flipping over her palm to check the wound that was barely visible. He grinned, kissing her palm. "It seems Variel is a good healer, indeed."

Aurelia yawned, her hand covering her mouth.

"She is, although I wish someone had warned me. That hurt."

Chuckling, Cristos rolled onto his side and pulled her against his chest.

"I'm sorry about that, but it feels better now?"

She nodded, rolling him onto his back and leaning over to kiss his chest.

"It does."

Rising to her knees, Aurelia pressed kisses down her husband's chest and stomach. Cristos groaned as she moved her mouth lower, his fingers threading through her hair.

Although she was exhausted, she didn't want to go to sleep on her wedding night without showing her husband pleasure.

Scooting lower on the bed, she took his cock into her hand, swirling her tongue around the crown of it. Although his thickness stretched her mouth to the limit, she still craved the taste of his skin against her tongue. She squeezed him in her hands, his length as hard as steel, and stroked him, taking him into her mouth, the salty taste hitting her tongue and making her moan. His hips bucked, trying to encourage her movements.

Working his length with her hand and her mouth, she savored him, wanting nothing more than to bring him to orgasm.

His breath sharp as he got close to climaxing, Cristos dragged her up by her shoulders until she straddled him, her own need driving her as she sunk down onto his cock. Leaning forward as their hips moved together, she gripped the back of his head, pulling him to her and kissing him, the movement of his tongue as owning as his length inside her.

When her release hit her, the shockwave of it sent tremors throughout her, the clinching of her body sending them into ecstasy together.

CHAPTER THIRTY-SEVEN

KASON

Kason and Holera awoke the next morning at first light, the fire in their tent burned down to embers, leaving it uncomfortably cold. By the time they dressed and made it out to the main fire in the cave, Bremusa was already there, tending to the injured warrior. He'd made it through the night since her treatment had stopped his bleeding, however his leg was still too injured to walk, leaving him temporarily handicapped.

Before they'd gone to bed the night before, Bremusa had told them she would go out into the valley in her true form, however neither of them knew what her true form was. They knew she was an elemental, but her kind was very rare, at least from what Kason knew. He didn't know much about elementals, aside from the fact that they held immense magic, allowing them not only to shift into any creature they wanted, but to do things others in his world could not.

Although there were protective wards over the entrance to their cave, one of the warriors still stood guard, because if Warbotach happened upon them, there was no guarantee their wards would not be broken by others with the power to do so.

One of the things that unsettled Kason was that although elementals were rare, Warbotach had someone at their disposal that was strong enough to create a standing ward around the city of Flamecliff and keep it steady, which he knew was a task not many could accomplish. Even the people in his own ranks, warriors like Taryn with the ability to establish masking words, could not hold them in place for very long without the help of others with the same power. After talking with his general, he realized Uldon may not have been able to change the will of the crown with whoever's magic supported him, but he certainly had more power in his ranks than they realized.

"If the two of you can watch over him, I'm going to go out and try to test the boundaries and strength of these wards."

Setting the canteen aside she had been using to give the injured warrior water, Bremusa blew out of breath.

"Although I spent months in the same palace as the Warbotach king and his men in a disguise, I was not privy to the inner workings of his court, nor did I know all the magic he tried to use in order to bend the will of the crown. I cannot reveal everything Otera and I did in order to protect the crown. All I can say is he will not be able to accomplish what he's trying to accomplish with the crown at this point. I do know he's been looking for me, but he never knew the elemental he sought was right under his nose. What I am afraid of, from what I've seen with these wards so far, is that he may have not needed me at all. It appears as though he's found someone or something very powerful to exploit. These are the reasons why I didn't use my true form last night and I'm hesitant to use it even today."

Hanging on each of Bremusa's words, Kason leaned forward, placing his elbows on his knees as he sat on the ground near the fire.

"My true form can get me through the valley without being seen by the fae, but if he has another elemental in his grasp, or some other creature with similar powers, there's a chance they will sense me in my true from, when they couldn't have in this form, or in the animal form I took last night."

Standing, she walked around the fire, kneeling in front of Kason and Holera. Kason's breath caught in his lungs because he didn't know what she was going to do next.

Reaching out her hand, Bremusa placed her palm against his forehead.

"Whatever you do, do not come after me if I don't return. If I am captured, I need you to know where to find the most powerful object in our world."

Before Kason had a moment to object or to ask questions, magic pulsed from the elemental's palm into his head, sending images through his consciousness.

As though he were drifting on the wind, Kason watched as his near invisible form traveled through the valley, passing cave after cave, until he stopped in front of one. Although this cave didn't look any more important than all the others, the force calling him into it was undeniable. Moving forward without steps, he watched as his translucent hand rose to his neck, pulling an amulet away from his skin and placing it against the stone wall.

For a moment, all he could hear was buzzing. The sound filled his ears, creating a disorienting sensation. When the buzzing stopped, his body drifted into the cave, the darkness pulling him further through each cavern, the labyrinth confusing and overwhelming. When his body finished its journey, his arm reached forward into what looked like an empty burrow in the rock and pulled out a sparkling crown.

When the female pulled her hand away from Kason's forehead, he swayed where he sat, the release of magic making him dizzier.

"What—is it not—?"

Although he tried to speak, the words wouldn't come, at least not words that made any sense.

Reaching into her satchel, Bremusa pulled out the same amulet he'd seen around his neck in the vision and placed it in his palm.

"Do not share what you've seen, because if you do, the information could get into the wrong hands and the world as we know it could end. I'm only sharing this with you so someone other than me knows where to find it if something happens to me, and I can't get to it when I need to. With that item, the portal can be destroyed. If all else fails, it's what we will have to do to keep the barbarians out of the human world."

Placing the amulet around his neck, Kason turned to his mate, reaching out to touch her, knowing it would calm his racing heart. The information he'd been given was so much bigger than him and he didn't believe he was the right person for such a task. It wasn't that he wasn't strong or loyal, but because he didn't have the powers some of the other Ekotorians had. If it came time for the crown to be retrieved and destroyed, he knew he wouldn't be able to do it, because he didn't have the magic in his own body.

Still, he understood why Bremusa shared her secret with him. Although Holera would've been just as trustworthy for such a task, she was a target simply because she was a phoenix warrior. Bremusa needed someone who seemed, at least to the barbarians, to not be a magical threat. He may have been a good fighter, but he was certainly not anything special, at least to no one but his mate.

Still tied up in his thoughts, motion in Kason's peripheral vision caught his attention and he turned to see Bremusa shift into what she called her true form. For a moment, he couldn't look away. Where the dark-haired fae female had stood only moments before, nothing remained but a translucent swirling mass. In a matter of seconds, the entity drifted out of the cave and disappeared from sight.

Chapter Thirty-Eight

Aurelia

Waking the next morning at first light, Aurelia and Cristos gathered their packed bags and left their suite to eat breakfast in the kitchen. The servers had already gathered food for their journey, which had been split up among the warriors for transport. Most of the warriors would travel on foot to maintain stealth behind moving wards, however there were approximately four dozen winged warriors, both Aegrician and Norithaean, who would travel in the sky to join Kason's group in the mountains behind the city of Flamecliff. They did not know if Bremusa had managed to take down the wards, but the hope was that she had managed to weaken them enough so the others with warding powers would be able to work together to destroy the rest of the protective barrier around the city.

Pulling her cloak on and securing her bow and quiver over her back, Aurelia followed Cristos to the barracks, where they were to meet everyone else who was leaving for the journey that day. Soldiers would remain in Norithae to protect the city from invaders, but Bremusa and other warriors with powers to establish wards had put as many protections on the city as they could. Although, with Bremusa having left with Kason's group, they were not sure how long the wards would last. Because of that, several of the warriors who had warding abilities were forced to stay behind to protect the city.

By the time they made it into the war room, Septima and Exie were already there, as was Otera, Blaedia, and many other military leaders from all three kingdoms. The Diapolisian fleet had left the morning before, most of their fighters traveling north by ship, the king and his consort part of that group. The dragons under his control left as well, flying overhead to protect their ships.

Although Aurelia had fought with herself about bringing Kano to Aegricia, she ultimately decided not to leave him behind. The great tiger had been a vital part of their victory in the battle of Norithae and she couldn't deny how important it seemed for him to protect her. After spending so much of their lives together, she couldn't deny him that.

Cristos had been very vocal about the decision to bring the tiger along, arguing that Kano could provide security in the healers' camps, where Aurelia intended to remain during the duration of the war. Unlike their journey toward Norithae, however, Aurelia would not be able to walk beside Kano. With her being pregnant, Cristos and the healers insisted she travel by horseback for the extensive journey north.

Approaching Septima as everybody left the war room for the courtyard, Aurelia slipped her hand into her sister's.

"Are you ready for this? After what happened last time?"

Even if Septima was ready to go back into war, Aurelia was not, not after almost losing her sister forever.

Septima shrugged as she rubbed her thumb along Aurelia's hand.

"You know Blaedia told us from the beginning that you can never truly be ready for war. You can never truly be ready to face the possibility of your death, but we go into war anyway, because we're fighting for something worth fighting for. I know we didn't look at it that way when we first got here, not exactly. But now we both have mates. Well, you have a husband and a child on the way. I have Exie. We have a life and a family here that are everything to us. So, I guess the answer is complicated, but no, I'm not ready to die, but I am ready to die for all the things that are worth dying for here in Ekotoria."

The backs of Aurelia's eyes burned from Septima's words, the subtle reminder of everything they had to lose and everything they were fighting for. Septima may have been her younger sister, but she was wise beyond her years. Hearing Septima refer to Exie as her mate brought joy into Aurelia's heart. It was, after all, the reason they'd fled their home in the first place.

Once they arrived in the courtyard, Aurelia saw Cristos saddling her horse, and Exie standing with Kano on his leash at her side. With as large of a tiger as Kano was, a leash made of leather would not prevent him from running off if he truly wanted to, so it was more of a reminder to him of which way they wanted him to go, and it helped the others to feel safer in his presence. Although he'd grown up domesticated and would not attack someone unless he or someone he loved was being threatened, he was still a huge tiger, and could be very intimidating, so they put a leash on him, which at least offered the façade of him being in control.

Approaching Cristos and her mount, Aurelia slid her hands up her husband's back, slipping in front of him and sneaking a kiss. He grinned as he looked at her face and then hefted her up, placing her on the saddle before she even had a chance to tell him that she could've gotten on the horse herself.

"Are you going to ride up here with me?"

As soon as she asked the question, her face heated with the memory of the other times she's ridden on a horse with him. When they'd taken their trip to Diapolis and back, he'd rubbed her between her thighs relentlessly while she rode on the horse in front of him, nearly bringing her to climax many times only to tease her and let it go. She didn't know if it would've been such a good idea to have such intimate touches when surrounded by the military of three kingdoms, but it did sound like a good time.

Cristos cocked an eyebrow, his grin mischievous.

"Why, my wife, would you like me to ride on the horse with you? Would you like me to wrap my arms around you and keep you safe?"

His grin only became more wicked the warmer her cheeks got. He knew exactly what he was doing.

She shrugged, sliding her hand against the horse's silky black fur.

"I don't know. Maybe it's you who wants to ride with me because you can't handle being so far away."

He chuckled, taking a step closer to the horse until he was right against her leg and sliding his hand up the inside of her thigh.

"I do love touching you, and I don't like being too far away from you, but I will only be walking at your side. If you feel unsafe, however, I would be happy to sit behind you and wrap you in my arms to keep you safe."

When the convoy set off within the hour, Cristos sat astride the horse right behind Aurelia and she couldn't stop grinning. Although she knew he wanted to ride with her, she had little doubt that when he climbed on the horse, he said he was doing it to keep her safe. She didn't argue, and was happy he wanted to be close to her. Although, if he did try to make her orgasm in front of everyone, she intended to push him right off the horse and onto the ground.

Since they were merely marching toward where they would make camp for the night, and not into war that day, there were no high energy speeches given to the group like Blaedia had done the morning they'd left for the battle in Norithae. The queen, however, did give some words of encouragement in the courtyard before everyone set off.

Otera spoke about the kingdom, its future, and everything that had happened and its past. She talked about the people, how important they were, and how vital it was for their kingdom to be free of barbarian rule again.

Shortly after Otera's speech, the winged warriors who were assigned to meet up with Kason and Holera's group left. Although they set off in the morning, the group would not be meeting up with Kason at the caves until nightfall. Since there was a risk of them being spotted by Warbotach if they flew too close to the coast, they had to detour further to the west.

Once they'd arrived at the caves, magically gifted warriors like Taryn, intended to join Bremusa in trying to bring the wards down. There were other warriors with the abilities to create and hold wards that traveled with the group on foot as well, so they could place wards around them when they stopped to camp at night. They would also place traveling wards around them periodically when they were in areas that didn't provide enough cover.

With the kingdom of Aegricia's capital city being warded so well, they didn't expect to see many Warbotach fighters out and about in the mountains, aside from the few that would have been patrolling their border. The situation would have been different had the Aegricians not taken back the kingdom of Norithae, but that victory had pushed Warbotach further north into the mountainous kingdom of Aegricia. So, until they got into the northern kingdom, Blaedia and Cristos didn't feel there would be a great risk to them as they traveled.

Although the leadership believed they were safe as long as they traveled through Norithae, Aurelia wasn't wholly convinced that would be the case. Just as when they'd traveled north the first time, there was a tightness in her chest, an uneasiness that made her feel as though danger was lurking. She didn't place all her trust in that sensation, however, because she didn't want to confuse anxiety for intuition, and the ominous feeling plaguing her could've been either of those two things.

Instead of traveling in her fae form, Variel moved through the pass as an enormous black wolf, prowling in and out through their ranks like a predator hunting for its next meal. She was incredibly intimidating in that form, which was exactly why she'd chosen it. Blaedia and Queen Otera led the group, Otera riding a black stallion in the front of the procession with Blaedia at her side. After all she'd suffered in the dungeon, the queen needed to rest while she could.

Traveling on much higher alert than they had when they'd gone south to Diapolis, Cristos spent much of the time watching the landscape around them for movement or attackers, instead of caressing and teasing his mate's thigh. Aurelia didn't mind because she was also distracted. After they'd been caught off guard before, she wanted to give all her attention to making sure nothing snuck up on them. Since they were unsure whether there were any enemies around, they chose to travel in relative silence, not wanting their voices to reach their enemies' ears and bring unnecessary danger to them.

By the time they got to their intended campsite in the mountain pass, most of the light was already drained from the sky, leaving them in moonlit darkness. Instead of following the pass straight north, the procession of soldiers had detoured west into the mountain valley, where they would be able to find caves to set up camp. Also, since they'd set up camp far to the west, they were not close enough to the city for Warbotach to sense them or see them, unless they'd been looking for them.

Once the perimeter of the campsite had been established, several warriors with the ability to create wards, as well as Variel, who'd been successful at warding her own property within Spectre Forest, established several layers of protection around the camp.

As soon as the cooks set up the dining tent and started roasting meat, Aurelia's stomach growled. They'd packed dried meat, bread, and cheese, as well as a little bit of fruit for the trip, but she'd eaten very little. The nausea from the pregnancy had only just started to set in, making it difficult for her to eat until later in the day. With her husband and sister marching into battle the following day, she realized the nausea had probably been from stress as much as from the pregnancy.

With exhaustion weighing on both of them, Aurelia and Cristos set up their tent and then headed to the dining area. The sooner they ate, the sooner they could shower and get to sleep. Although Aurelia knew what the morning would bring, as well as the agreement she'd made with Cristos, she still had no idea how she would handle her loved ones walking away from the camp, knowing they may never return. Part of her knew she wouldn't be able to stop herself from going after them, hence, putting herself and her baby in danger. Whether she would break her promise was the only thing on her mind as they moved across the camp in search of dinner.

CHAPTER THIRTY-NINE

TARYN

Taking a wide detour around the city of Flamecliff, it took Taryn and the other winged warriors most of the day to arrive in the mountain location where Kason and his group were supposed to be. They flew low through the valley, Taryn warding them as they traveled, hoping the ward worked well enough to prevent them from being seen by their enemies. Although they didn't expect any of Uldon's warriors to be in that area, it didn't mean there were none, and she didn't want to take that chance.

After an extensive low-flying search, Taryn spotted a Norithae warrior outside a cave, emptying his bladder against the rock. She swooped down, landing just beside the male, scaring him enough that he jolted back, urinating all over his pants. He didn't speak however, since they needed to keep their voices at a minimum until they were inside the warded space of the cave. Instead of shrieking or yelling out obscenities, he dipped his chin at her and showed her into the caves that had been warded by Bremusa, making them invisible at first glance.

Walking in followed by the other warriors, Taryn saw Holera and Kason standing in front of the fire, an injured warrior asleep on a bedroll at their feet.

"How many do you have with you?" Kason asked, looking over her shoulder at the other warriors that were filing into the cave.

Taryn turned around as well, catching Lars' eye as he walked inside with a few of his men.

"There are nearly fifty of us, so we're going to need a large place to set up camp. We did bring food. If you need more."

Leaving Kason's side, Holera approached Taryn and pulled her into a hug. She'd never been a very affectionate female, aside from her relationship with her mate, but with everything they'd gone through over the past several months, Taryn appreciated the show of affection. They'd been comrades in the Aegrician military for a long time, so they certainly cared about each other.

"Where is Bremusa?" Taryn asked, glancing around the cave, yet not seeing the elemental. "Has she been able to get through the wards yet?"

Holera shrugged.

"She left this morning in her true form to get a better look at them and see if she'd be able to weaken them, but she hasn't returned. She made us promise her that we wouldn't go looking for her, so we've just been waiting."

"That reminds me," Kason interrupted. "Keep the warriors in the cave at night. If they have to go out into the valley, tell them to only go for short periods, and not to go any further than just outside the cave entrance." Tilting his head at the injured warrior on the ground, Kason scratched his cheek and grimaced. "We got attacked by a wendigo last night. The beast who attacked us nearly killed him before it was put down, but there are more out there, so we don't want any of our people to be out in the valley at night if we can help it."

"And we can try to help her from here," Taryn added. "There are several warriors with me who have warding abilities. Maybe, if we all put our power together, then we can at least punch holes in the wards large enough to let warriors through and civilians out."

Kason nodded his agreement and led the way toward the back of the cave, showing the other warriors where there were more chambers, so they could set up their tents and fires. After traveling all day, everyone was exhausted and needed to get at least a few hours of sleep before they tried to work on the wards. Removing wards took a lot of energy, and it was energy Taryn didn't have at that moment.

Knowing that within a day, the armies of four kingdoms, plus an unknown enemy, would be converging in her home for war, and that many wouldn't make it out alive, Taryn glanced at the faces of the warriors in the caverns, looking for the one who made her feel something she hadn't felt in a long time. If she was going to die in the coming days, then she wanted to feel something good first, she wanted to feel the touch of a male, wanted to feel desired. So, when she looked up at Lars again, before climbing into her tent that had been purposely set up away from everyone else's, he didn't hesitate to follow her inside.

When Lars entered Taryn's tent and saw her unlacing her tunic, his nostrils flared, and he stepped forward, pulling her against him and kissing her. They'd never spoken about taking each other to bed, had never kissed or touched, but Taryn knew they felt something for each other. They were at least sexually attracted to each other, and at that moment, that was all she needed.

Angling her head to the side, she slid her fingers into his hair, pulling him closer to her as she deepened the kiss, her tongue sliding against his to taste him. He groaned, the kiss becoming more ravenous as she tugged at the laces on his fighting leathers, trying desperately to undress him without her lips ever leaving his. His wings flared out behind him as he reached around, his top ripping as he yanked it off and tossed it to the floor. Gripping Taryn around her hips, he lifted her, her legs wrapping around his waist as he carried her across the space.

For a moment, they were only lips and tongues and limbs twisted in each other as they touched and tried to take off the remainder of each other's clothes. She may have been desperate to be touched, but it was clear he was as well.

When Lars laid her back on the bed and climbed over her, she finally pulled out of the kiss, realizing she needed to tell him the truth, even if it cost her their night together. Her conscience wouldn't have been able to rest if she'd kept her mate a secret.

"I need to tell you something."

Her voice was nothing more than a desperate pant as she searched his face in the firelight. Leaning over her, he nuzzled into her neck—kissing, licking, and sucking the sensitive flesh there, and she gasped as the hardened bulge in his pants rubbed between her thighs.

"I have a mate at home. I haven't seen him in a long time, and I don't know if I'll ever see him again, but I just wanted you to know that."

Pulling away until he could look at her eyes, Lars traced his finger down her cheek. "Are you sure you want this?"

It only took Taryn a moment to nod. He kissed her again, his tongue finding hers and caressing it, the touch making her molten.

"If you're sure you want to be with me, even if it's only tonight, then you don't owe me an explanation."

His response surprised her, but if she were being honest, it was exactly what she'd wanted to hear. There would be no strings attached between them, and if they survived the war and something grew between them that was more than that, then they would assess their relationship then.

Confident in her decision, at least in what she needed at that moment, Taryn reached between them and gripped his hardened cock that was still straining against the inside of his leathers. Lars groaned, the sound guttural, as he ground himself against her hand.

"Take them off," she said, more of a demand than a request. Nodding as their lips found each other again in a punishing kiss, he reached down, untying his leathers as she gripped him through the fabric and shoved them down his hips. Taryn's own trousers made their way to the floor a moment later.

When the warrior crawled over her again, settling himself between her thighs, he sunk his stiff cock into her all the way to the hilt as though he'd been waiting his whole life to do it and could wait no longer.

Lars' thrusts were punishing, bringing her to climax repeatedly as she stifled her screams with a blanket. When he finally met his release, they collapsed against each other, panting but still kissing each other, unable to get enough. Taryn knew they needed to sleep, but she also realized, as his cock hardened again against her leg, that it was going to be a long night, and she would regret nothing.

Chapter Forty

Aurelia

Finding their way to the dining tent, there was already a line of warriors waiting to get their meal before they found rest for the night. With there being Norithaean warriors, as well as Aegrician warriors, there were many more mouths to feed than what there had been in the war camp before. By the time they made it through the line and inside the tent to get their meal tray, the space had been completely full. Looking toward where they'd always sat before, Aurelia was glad to see Septima and Exie seated at one of the tables against the tent wall, Otera and Blaedia beside them. Aurelia and Cristos aimed directly toward them, sliding into two of the empty chairs.

"How was your ride here?" Septima asked Aurelia before taking a bite of her stew.

"To be honest, after what happened on our march into Norithae, how there were warriors hiding behind wards to attack us, I was basically nervous the entire time. I'm just relieved we made it here."

Aurelia surprised herself by admitting all she had at the table in front of everyone, but after all they'd gone through together, they were her family even if they weren't blood. Septima nodded, stretching her arm across the table to touch Aurelia's hand.

"I would be lying if I said I hadn't been afraid of the same thing, especially after what happened to me last time."

All Aurelia could think as they sat at the dinner table was that her sister could be facing a much worse fate when she left to go to Aegricia and there was nothing either of them could do about it. She remained silent for the rest of the dinner, her loved ones talking around her as she dwelled on whether or not it was the last time, she would be able to sit with them. All she wanted was more time, but it was the one thing they didn't have.

When Aurelia awoke the next morning to the sound of Cristos sheathing his sword, her chest was heavy, and her stomach was in knots. The night before, when they'd sat at dinner with the others, and then she'd returned to the tent with her husband, her heart had gone numb, too many emotions choking her for her to process. Waking and knowing that everyone was leaving her behind filled her with a panicked urgency, the promise she made to Cristos no longer her priority.

Noticing she was awake, Cristos crawled back into bed with her and pulled her into his arms. She closed her eyes as he caressed her back, the warmth of tears trickling down her cheek.

"This is not goodbye, my love. The pain from worry will consume you if you let it and I don't want you to feel that way. The future we have planned is too good for fate to take it away from us."

Although she knew he believed everything he said, she couldn't bring her own mind to accept it as truth.

"Please don't leave me behind."

With all the words tumbling through her head, those seemed like the ones that needed to come out the most.

Cristos ran his fingers through her hair, a touch to soothe her but it only broke her heart more.

"I told you when we met that I wouldn't let anything happen to you and I can't break that promise now. If I know you're safe here, that you and our child won't come to harm, my mind will be able to focus on the war. I can't protect myself if my sole focus is protecting you."

Out of everything he'd said, those words rang true. She knew if she were with him in Aegricia, that he would worry about her and the baby, that he would sacrifice himself to protect her. It was the last thing she wanted, but every piece of intuition inside her told her that she needed to be there. No matter how desperate the drive was for her to follow him, however, she knew she couldn't tell him, not without running the risk of him focusing on her instead of staying alive. So, even though she believed it was a lie, she nodded.

There were so many things she wanted to say, but before she could utter another word, the bell rang, signaling it was time for him to leave.

Just as they'd done before she'd left for Diapolis, she and Septima had agreed, when they'd embraced the night before, that she would not see her off. Neither of them wanted to feel as though it was a goodbye. So, although Aurelia wanted to spend every last second looking at her sister's face, she couldn't bring herself to leave the tent. She didn't want to say goodbye to her sister, or her friends, or her husband, so she remained in bed as Cristos kissed her one more time and left her alone with her thoughts.

The moment the flap closed behind him, the barely contained grasp on her emotions shattered, sobs pouring out of her as the strings holding her heart together finally ripped apart.

At some point, as Aurelia grieved for what could happen to those she loved, she had fallen asleep. When she woke up hours later to the sound of a throat clearing, it took her a moment to realize where she was, to realize why her body felt like it couldn't go anymore. Rubbing her eyes and trying to make sense of the shadows around her, Variel stepped into view.

"I thought you'd never wake up."

Pulling herself up onto her elbows, it took Aurelia a moment to respond. As filled with agony as she was, she couldn't imagine why Variel was waiting for her to wake up. If it had been up to her, she would've preferred to sleep until the warriors returned.

"Variel... What's going on?"

Taking a few steps forward, the older female sat at the edge of the bed, her face more solemn than Aurelia had ever seen her.

"I know Cristos wants you to stay here where you and his heir are safe, but you and I need to be in Aegricia. You may not have a hold on your powers yet, but I know they cannot win the war without you."

Blinking rapidly, Aurelia couldn't immediately process Variel's words. Her mind was a confused mess.

"What do you mean they can't win the war without me? If I do have powers, then I don't even know how they work. I don't have enough power to make a difference in this war, so I don't understand why the war can't be won without me."

Whatever Variel thought Aurelia could do, she didn't agree.

"Aside from the power to see other people's experiences while I dream, I don't have any other special powers like some of the other warriors. I don't know how to create fire like Otera or build wards like so many others."

The side of Variel's mouth tipped up in a half smile.

"You have more power than you realize, and I will show you how to use it in time, but if we're going to catch up with the warriors before it's too late, then we need to go now. Dress warm and bring as many weapons as you can carry. I'll meet you in the breakfast tent when you're ready."

Chapter Forty-One

Septima

Leaving the camp had been one of the most difficult things Septima had ever done in her life. She knew her sister wanted to join them, but she understood why Aurelia couldn't, and she didn't disagree with the reasoning. With Aurelia being pregnant, the best place for her was in the camp where she'd be safe. Still, Septima knew her sister, and she couldn't help but think about the agony Aurelia had probably been going through since they'd left the camp.

Walking between Exie and Cristos, Septima held the hilt of her sword tight. With her capture merely a week before, she knew the two warriors would not allow her out of their sight, and she couldn't help but to be relieved. She knew she could fight and be a benefit to the military in the war, but she was nowhere as capable as they were. Her self-doubt only grew as dozens of Warbotach warriors poured out from between the trees, sneaking up on them from behind masking wards just as they had done in the battle of Norithae.

Although Septima drew her weapon, Exie stepped in front of her, slashing her sword across a Warbotach warriors' chest who was just about to strike her. Blood gushed from the wound, landing on Septima's leathers as the body hit the ground.

"Thank you," Septima yelled before spinning around, nearly missing the low swipe of an enemy's blade as he rode right past her on horseback, the horse breathing fire and nearly missing one of the Norithae warriors nearby.

Running past her, Cristos' wings flapped, launching him into the air as he flew over a group of Warbotach soldiers, slicing one of the warrior's necks from his shoulders as he flew past.

The sound of buzzing filled Septima's ears, drowning out the screams and wails of war. The world spun as another Warbotach warrior darted toward her, his crimson horse lying bleeding on the ground. Septima's sword met her attacker's blade in the air, the sound of metal against metal echoing throughout the mountain pass. The skirmish lasted for what seemed like only minutes before the group of their enemies had either died or fled.

Not yet to the boundary of the wards around Flamecliff, they still had much more area to cover before they could've expected to see the bulk of Warbotach's army. Still, they couldn't move forward yet, because the dead, and those who were injured, needed to be flown back to the camp west of their location.

Turning back towards the collection of warriors who were looking over the injured and dead on the ground, Septima saw her mate running toward her, her leathers covered in blood. Septima darted forward, wrapping her arms around Exie and kissing her face repeatedly.

"I'm so glad you're okay! Have you seen Cristos?"

Nodding, Exie looked over Septima's shoulder and pointed. Septima turned to look as well. Once she spun around, she saw Cristos kneeling on the ground over one of his warriors, his head lowered in his hands.

Taking Exie by the hand, Septima approached her brother-in-law, only to see that the male lying in front of him was no longer alive, but she recognized him immediately as Faidon, one of Cristos' most trusted advisors and warriors.

Putting her hand on Cristos' shoulder, she wanted him to know she was there for him. He looked over his fallen warrior for a moment, his face twisted with pain and guilt, but after a few minutes, he shook his head and stood.

"We need to get him back home so he can have a proper burial," he said to another one of his other warriors whose name Septima did not know. "Take his body back to Norithae."

The male nodded, lifting his fallen comrade, before taking to the skies on his wings. As soon as he'd flown away, Cristos turned to face them.

"We need to find Blaedia and the queen to discuss our plans moving forward. If any of those Warbotach warriors managed to slip away and go back in and inform their king where we are, then we'll lose any element of surprise we had."

CHAPTER FORTY-TWO

AURELIA

Variel and Aurelia left the camp hours after the rest of the military, so they wouldn't have been able to catch up unless the others got stopped for some reason. In order to speed up their trip, they'd taken horses from the camp, but even that wouldn't have allowed them to catch up with their people before they'd arrived at their destination. As they rode along the pass toward the north, Variel held a masking ward around their location to keep them safe from unwanted attacks. Because Variel's wards were as secure as a stone wall, they were able to talk as they traveled without worrying about being overheard.

"What did you mean by saying they wouldn't be able to win the war without me? What powers do you think I have because I haven't seen any, aside from those I told you about?"

Variel nodded, guiding her chestnut colored horse closer to Aurelia. "Since you were prophesied to be chosen by the crown and become the queen over both kingdoms, if there is no other choice but to destroy that crown, you would have the power to do it."

"How would I destroy it if it's so powerful? I don't even know how to use my power."

"The crown will know your desires. Once it becomes yours, you'll be its master so if you choose for it to destroy itself, it will."

The uneasy feeling in Aurelia's chest grew, her intuition telling her there was more than what Variel was saying.

"If the crown chooses the queen, how can I become its choice, its *master*, if Otera is still alive? Has it not already chosen her? Is she not its master?"

Turning her eyes to Aurelia's, Variel shook her head. "You are right in that the crown has chosen Otera to be queen, but come morning, Otera will no longer be queen and the crown will have to choose another. The crown will choose you and you need to be there to receive it, so you can destroy it."

Aurelia's heart dropped into her stomach, nausea making her breakfast rise to the back of her throat. "Are you saying that Otera will die? That she **has** to die?"

Disbelief, followed by horror, rushed through Aurelia's body, leaving her with a feeling of dread, a feeling of something amiss inside her chest. Variel cleared her throat, leaning forward to pet her horse. "Yes. Otera will have to sacrifice herself, but she knows this. She has for a long time."

After Variel told Aurelia that the aunt she'd only just met, who had just gotten out of a dungeon, had to die to protect the portal into the human world, Aurelia tunneled into herself, going quiet for many miles as they traveled. It broke her heart to know, not only that she would lose her aunt and her aunt would lose her life, but that her aunt knew she would have to be sacrificed and had been living with that knowledge the entire time. Aurelia I couldn't imagine living with such knowledge.

As they rounded a bend in the mountain pass, the air got cooler, forcing Aurelia to pull her cloak and hood tighter around her body. The dread tightened in her chest as they moved forward and saw blood on the ground, where an attack must have happened, however, all the warriors had already left, either on their own, or in the arms of a warrior who would fly them to either see a healer, or to be buried. Bile rose in Aurelia's throat as their horses stepped through the evidence of such violence, hoping none of the blood spilled had been from someone she loved.

Chapter Forty-Three

Otera

Otera's heart pounded like a war drum as they traveled the last few miles into Aegricia under protective wards. She had little doubt Warbotach was watching the path, however none of their warriors showed themselves. Walking on the side of her horse, Blaedia held her sword aloft, her head on a swivel as they closed in on the location where the wards were said to have been but when they approached the boundary into the city of Flamecliff, there was barely a barrier keeping them out. Wherever Bremusa and the others were and whatever they'd done to damage the wards, it had helped. From the look on Blaedia's beautiful face, she'd been surprised by the lack of wards as well.

Making their way down the main streets of Flamecliff, it was like a ghost town. There were no businesses open and no people on the streets, not even a Warbotach soldier was in view. A shudder ran through Otera's body, the sight of her beloved city without signs of life chilling her blood.

"Where is everyone?" She asked her mate, her voice made louder by the silence around them.

Reaching up and touching her on the leg, Blaedia shook her head. "Uldon wouldn't have evacuated the city, not when he could use the innocents as bargaining chips."

Otera clenched her teeth. Concern for her people was palpable as she imagined where they could have been, or what the barbarian king could have done to them. There was no question he was ruthless, but she couldn't imagine he'd killed them all. At least she hoped he hadn't.

The keening call of a dragon pierced the silent sky, the beast swooping low over the palace towers before flying back over the sea. Otera sat taller on her saddle as the harbor came into view, a dozen Diapolis ships moving toward the coast as her warriors approached from the opposite side of the city. Still, there had been no sounds or movement at the palace, at least not from what Otera could see with the protective walls that encased it.

A whistle sounded only moments after the dragon disappeared in the distance and Blaedia stopped walking, holding her finger up to her mouth as she listened. The warriors behind them halted, everyone silent as Blaedia planned their next move.

"We're surrounded," she said, the words no more than a whisper.

Otera stiffed, her horse shifting on its feet. She'd barely had a moment to turn to look at her mate before the first of Warbotach's soldiers busted out of a masking ward, appearing as though they'd been there the entire time. As Otera pulled her sword from its sheath, Blaedia spun around, slashing her weapon at the enemy closest to her, missing as his horse stormed past and into their ranks.

Having spent so much time in the dungeon, her basic needs neglected at the barbarian king's amusement, Otera knew she wasn't physically capable of fighting as she had been before. Still, as Aegricia's queen, she couldn't expect her warriors to risk their lives if she wasn't willing to risk her own. The queen already knew what she had to sacrifice in the end for her kingdom, and as she nudged her horse to go forward, it was for Aegricia that her blade swung.

Dressed in dark, fur-trimmed leathers, the scarred-face barbarians were easy to pick out in the crowd. Otera's horse bolted forward, the queen slashing her blade down on the neck of an enemy soldier who had one of her warriors cornered. As soon as the queen galloped away, the warrior shifted in a flash of fire and launched herself into the air, notching an arrow and firing it at the Warbotach warriors who had finally appeared on the palace walls.

Having lost sight of her lover, Otero's chest squeezed painfully, the worst-case scenario plaguing her mind as she turned her horse around and headed back in the other direction. Still too far away, the Diapolis fleet had yet to make landfall, the lack of breeze barely pushing the sails.

Screams and the clanging of swords littered the once silent air, but Otera didn't think twice about charging back into the chaos. If she would have to sacrifice herself for her kingdom, she intended to take Uldon's soldiers with her.

CHAPTER FORTY-FOUR

KASON

Although Bremusa had told the rest of them not to follow her after she left, by the time the morning came and she had still not returned, the entire group knew they could no longer stay behind. They needed to find out if the wards had been taken down and they needed to know if the rest of their warriors had made it to Flamecliff. If they had, then they needed to fight.

Leaving their camp set up in case it would have been needed later, the warriors left the cave for the valley. It only took a moment of conversation before the Aegrician warriors shifted and the entire group launched into the air, headed for the northern side of Flamecliff. With the Aegrician army attacking from the southwest, and Diapolis attacking from the east, flying in from the north would allow them to surround Warbotach on all sides.

Leaning forward on Holera's back as she flew, Kason stroked her silver feathers, hating that he was flying her into battle again.

"When this is all over, you and I are going to the cabin for a very long time." Although his mate couldn't speak in her phoenix form, she leaned her head back, rubbing it against his leg. With the near constant need to defend their kingdom since Joneira had invaded it more than two decades prior, they had spent very little time in his cabin in the mountains and it was long overdue.

As they crossed the last mountain peak before Flamecliff and the palace came into view, Kason realized right away that whatever the elemental had done, or whatever the others who had ward powers had done, it had been successful. There was still a bit of interference as Holera swooped below the clouds, a slight film in the air, but the ward had not prevented them from entering through the boundary as Kason had expected.

Securing his bow in his hand and pulling an arrow from his quiver, Kason cycled a breath, trying to steal his nerves as he planned his shot carefully. Not expecting an attack from the north, every single Warbotach warrior was facing the opposite direction, firing their own arrows at the warriors below. The rest were on the road heading out the city, the fight happening from the walls of the palace all the way to the mountain pass.

Taryn and the other phoenix warriors cut over the palace toward the southwest, flying out of sight but undoubtedly landing on the street below so they could shift and fight. The Norithae warriors, however, those who could fly and notch an arrow, remained in the air, Kason joining them in firing on the unsuspecting enemy.

It only took a few arrows meeting their marks before the Warbotach warriors on the battlements realized their true threat was behind them. Kason patted Holera on the side as she pitched hard to the right, narrowly avoiding an enemy arrow.

Seeing that the Norithae warriors had the battlement and inner courtyard under control, Holera soared back toward the west, landing in an alley between two buildings. Jumping off her back quickly, Kason slung his bow back over his shoulder and unsheathed his sword as his mate shifted back into her fae form.

Kason wrapped his arms around her and pulled her into a lingering kiss. "If something happens to me—."

"Don't," she said, placing her finger in front of his mouth. "Don't you say goodbye to me right now." The sound of fighting drew both their attention as Holera kissed him again. "You promised we would go back to the cabin when this is over and I'm going to hold you to that."

This side of Kason's mouth lifted in a grin as he laced his fingers in hers, leading her toward the chaotic scene on the streets of their beloved city. "In that case, be careful. I love you."

Chapter Forty-Five

Aurelia

Climbing down from her horse, Variel kneeled on the ground, touching the crimson stain in the dirt. "They can't be far now. I would say they were here within the past hour." The healer climbed back onto her mount, urging the horse forward.

After less than an hour of walking, the clanging of swords, grunts, and screams echoed throughout the mountain pass, telling them they'd found their warriors at last, but the enemy had found them first. Aurelia leaned forward, preparing to send her horse into a gallop, but Variel moved toward her, grabbing her arm.

"We can't rush forward, Aurelia. You're not supposed to be here. We can't distract them, or get you killed. Just like how you move in your dreams, we will need to be not seen and not heard. We will walk amongst them under wards for as long as we can while we try to inflict damage on the enemy without them knowing we're there."

A part of Aurelia still wanted to rush forward and see her mate and sister to make sure they were okay, but she knew Variel was right. If Cristos or Septima saw her, it would be just as Cristos had said before he'd left the tent. They're sole focus would turn to her and to getting her safe. It would put them in danger, which was the last thing she wanted. Although finding those she loved was a need Aurelia didn't think she could fight, she reluctantly nodded her head and sat back up in the saddle.

"So, what do we do?"

Turning to Aurelia, Variel pulled her bow off her shoulder. "Do you know how to fight? If so, that's what you do. Pull out your bow and aim those arrows high, killing the warriors on horses first. But whatever you do, stay near me. It's the only way to keep you in my wards and safe from being seen."

Aurelia nodded and followed Variel as the horse bolted forward, stopping just outside the cluster of fighting warriors as the city of Flamecliff came into view. Pulling her bow off her shoulder, she notched an arrow as she looked for a target. Variel moved at her side, firing an arrow that hit a Warbotach warrior, sending him tumbling off his horse before he ever saw her coming, not that he could see her at all.

In the chaotic scene of bodies, it had been impossible for Aurelia to make out who was friend and who was foe. They moved closer to the palace where the Diapolis ships loomed in the distance, the southern warriors not yet on land. There were no signs of their dragons, but Aurelia doubted they were far. Warbotach warriors lined the battlements, firing arrows at the warriors below. Guiding their horses around the field of warriors, Variel and Aurelia fired arrow after arrow at the barbarians on horseback, downing many and leaving their opponent speechless.

Screeching through the sky, another dragon approached the city from the west, setting fire to the ground below. Aurelia watched in horror as warriors on both sides fled its attack.

"Those aren't the dragons of Diapolis," she said as Variel's eyes followed the beast's movement in the sky.

The older female shook her head as she turned back to Aurelia, her eyes growing wide as she looked over Aurelia's shoulder. "What? What do y—?"

Aurelia spun around in the saddle, her eyes falling on the rows of soldiers rounding the bend in the pass, warriors in colors she hadn't yet seen. The invaders from off the continent had finally arrived.

"Joneira's returned to take this kingdom back," Variel said, the words chilling Aurelia's blood. "And I'm not going to let her do it." Before Aurelia could process that her mother's killer was in Aegricia, Variel's horse darted forward, leaving Aurelia with no choice but to follow. She knew she couldn't fight Joneira, not in her condition, but she could kill some of the exiled queen's soldiers while under the cloak of Variel's wards.

An ear-shattering roar sounded behind them and Aurelia looked behind herself just in time to see one of the Diapolis dragons launch itself at the invading one, jaw clenching down on its massive black tail as they fought. Although there were warriors fighting on both sides of her, Aurelia forced her eyes forward, not wanting to get distracted by looking for her loved ones and falling out of Variel's protection.

A horn blew behind them as the Diapolis fleet finally made landfall, their warriors a collective roar as they entered the fray. Aurelia's insides churned as her horse bolted toward the invading army. She followed behind Variel without question, but she had no idea what the healer's plan was once they got there.

The approaching army was extensive, but the numbers were not as great as the combined militaries of Norithae, Aegricia, and Diapolis. As they approached the group of invaders, their uniforms as red as a phoenix's fire, Variel unsheathed her sword, slashing it at the enemy as her horse bolted past. Variel's wolf form had always intimidated her, but she'd never suspected the female was a warrior. For a moment, Aurelia watched in disbelief at the ferociousness of the elderly female who'd taken care of them at her cottage as though she was a doting grandmother.

Afraid to lose the protection of the wards, Aurelia urged her horse forward, pulling her sword from its sheath and attacking the enemy soldiers along the outside of the lines, the others' eyes growing wide as their comrades fell at their feet due to an unseen force.

A scream pierced the air behind her as two dragons sailed through the air in her direction, the dark green beast in front shooting the center of the enemy forces with fire as its pursuer snapped at its tail. The heat of the flames blasted against Aurelia, sending her horse into a panicked frenzy as she tried to hold on. Although she knew she needed to follow Variel to stay under the cover of the ward making her invisible, Aurelia was forced to turn her mount around and flee away from the threats in the sky as another line of fire shot down on the enemy warriors like a lightning bolt. Variel had disappeared into a confusing scene in her search for Joneira, as had the wards that had protected Aurelia since they'd left the camp.

Riding back toward the palace, the scene filled Aurelia with horror, causing her to retch over the side of her mount. Holding on to the saddle with everything she had, she leaned over the horse as it fled the fire, wiping her mouth on her sleeve as she heaved.

Doing her best to pull herself back upright, Aurelia scanned the sea of bodies on the ground and warriors left standing. The remaining Warbotach soldiers had fled toward the harbor as the Diapolis fleet and four of their dragons overwhelmed them. One of the beasts lay dead on the ground near the palace gates, although she wasn't sure if they'd been from their ally or from their enemy.

Although the barbarians fled toward the harbor, dozens of Norithae and Diapolis warriors ran past her, aiming for the invaders in the mountain pass. Aurelia moved out of their way as they passed, only a few of them noticing her as they headed toward their new enemy.

A guttural cry met Aurelia's ears as she looked for her family in the survivors. Turning toward the sound, it only took her a moment to notice the collection of warriors toward the walls of the palace, Exie among them. Her heart leaped erratically as she nudged her boot into the horse's side and pulled on the reins, forcing it to move in the direction of her friend but before the animal traveled more than a few feet, a strong hand grabbed her ankle.

Chapter Forty-Six

Aurelia

Startled by the feeling of someone's hand on her ankle, Aurelia twisted to the side, yanking her foot away only to see Cristos standing beside her. Blood and dirt covered him, but she was relieved not to see any visible wounds.

"You cannot be here," he said, his features tense, a muscle flicking in his jaw. "We have to go. Now."

His words sent her heart plummeting into her stomach, the realization something was gravely wrong hitting her instantly. "No. Cristos, what aren't you telling me? Where's my sister?"

Her head twisting side to side, Aurelia looked for Septima in the devastating scene before Cristos climbed onto the horse behind her and twisting her face to him. "My love, look at me. Septima is fine. I promise you, but I have got to get you out of here."

Shaking her head as tears trailed warmth down her face, she pulled her face away from him and tried to climb off the horse only for him to stop her. Letting out a frustrated grunt she struggled against him. "Cristos, stop! Tell me what's wrong! What are you trying to hide from me?"

He closed his eyes for a moment as though to gather his patience. When he opened them again, his features fell, his eyes softening. "Aurelia. Septima is fine but Otera—."

Aurelia's heart lurched, her body collapsing against his as she cried into his chest. She knew what he was about to say but she still needed to hear it out loud.

"Where's Otera? Where's my aunt?" Her words tumbled out of her mouth as broken sobs. "Please take me to her."

Hesitating, Cristos looked away and it was clear he wasn't sure if he should say anything more. Blowing out a deep breath, he turned back to look at her, his eyes turning glassy. "My love, she didn't make it. She was fighting one of Uldon's warrior's and she didn't survive." He pulled her against his chest, massaging her back as she cried, the rest of the war around them fading into the distance. "I'm so sorry, my love. I'm so sorry."

Sniffling and wiping her eyes on her sleeve, Aurelia straightened her back and looked into the eyes of her husband. "Take me to see her."

With a nod, Cristos wrapped his arm around her and led the horse toward the gathered group, stopping a few feet away and dismounting before grabbing Aurelia by the waist and lifting her off the horse. Although she'd asked him to show her to her aunt, as they walked toward the growing gathering of Aegrician warriors, Aurelia tucked her face against his chest, too afraid of what she would see in the middle of the circle.

Looking toward the ground, she didn't see her sister approach until Septima's hand slid into hers. "It's going to be okay, sissy."

The sound of crying, so many warriors crying, squeezed Aurelia's chest painfully, nearly bringing her to her knees as her own sobs overtook her. Her feet became leaden as she got close enough to the circle to see the locks of crimson hair spread out on the blood-soaked ground. Cristos held her tightly against his side, giving her the support she desperately needed. Without him and Septima, she knew she would have fallen. With her aunt lying dead on the ground, the chosen queen of Aegricia, the exiled queen's fate no longer held a place in Aurelia's mind. If Variel hadn't managed to kill her, then the other warriors would.

Another screaming sob met Aurelia's ears, the sound of someone's heart breaking in two pulling Aurelia out of her own grief as she stumbled forward, falling to her knees next to Blaedia who was draped over Otera's body.

"Warbotach are heading to the portal. They've taken some of our warriors hostage on the Diapolis ships. We have to stop them from trying to cross," said Kason as he darted toward them, the male dropping to his knees when he recognized his queen's body on the ground.

Exie turned to face him, sheathing her sword before she shifted. "If we let them get away, then all this was for nothing. Otera, our beloved queen's death was for nothing. Taryn as well. So many were lost today. We have to stop them." With her proclamation finished, Exie shifted, and before Aurelia could stop her, Septima climbed on Exie's back with her weapons in hand and they launched into the sky. Warriors from Norithae joined the Aegrician phoenixes into the sky as well as several Diapolisian dragons with riders all in pursuit of the Warbotach warriors.

As Aurelia kneeled at her aunt's lifeless form, brushing her hair out of her beautiful face, a translucent swirling mass floating over Otera's body and quivered before moving to the side and shifting into a beautiful onyx haired female with swirling quicksilver eyes. *Bremusa.*

For a moment, even Aurelia's tears stopped falling as she stared at the female, shock from seeing her elemental form rendering Aurelia speechless. Bremusa darted toward her, startling Aurelia back. "We have to go now, Aurelia. I need you to come with me."

Aurelia fell on her bottom as Cristos moved in to catch her. "Take her where, Bremusa? What's going on?"

"Otera and I had a plan for when this happened. We need to carry out that plan and we need to do it now. Please. We don't have time to discuss this right now. I need you to come with me."

Although she didn't know what the plan entailed, she'd heard of a plan from both Variel, and Otera, so she trusted Bremusa was telling the truth, even though she didn't know the female all that well. She had been her mother's best friend after all. Nodding, Aurelia rose onto shaky legs, Cristos wrapping his arm back around her waist for support.

"Okay, where do we need to go?"

Bremusa stepped forward, her raven-black hair billowing in the wind as she closed her eyes and began to transform. In a flash of fire, she took on the form of a majestic phoenix, her golden feathers shimmering in the fading sunlight. She let out a piercing cry as she soared into the sky, leading the way deeper into the mountains.

Lifting Aurelia into his arms, Cristos thrust his powerful wings and they too took to the air as well. Leaving the wreckage behind on the ground, Aurelia's thoughts were a whirlwind of memories, fears, and determination. She would not let Otera's death be in vain. No matter what it took, she would protect the portal and their people.

Chapter Forty-Seven

Aurelia

Flying over the palace and into the mountains beyond, Aurelia watched as the warriors in the sky attacked the Warbotach barbarians below as they tried to get to the portal aboard the stolen Diapolisian ships. The sun began to set as they turned toward the valley between two of the mountain ranges, the peaks impossibly high to travel to on foot. The rocky terrain was still covered in ice in some places. In other areas there were ravines waiting to swallow a person who would never be seen again.

The golden phoenix in front of them, Bremusa, let out a keening call before leveling her wings and swooping low. The dark-haired female landed on the ground below, seemingly searching for something. Cristos landed a moment later by her side, Aurelia still in his arms. He kissed her on the cheek and caressed her back. "I love you. I was so worried."

Her tears had dried as they'd flown, curiosity at what Bremusa had in store for her stealing all her attention at that moment, distracting her momentarily from her inevitable grief. "What are we looking for here?" she asked Bremusa as Cristos finally set her down on shaky legs. "Can we help you look?"

Shaking her head, Bremusa ran her hand across the rock mountain face until her hand disappeared as though the mountain had swallowed it. "Ah, here it is. Follow me," she said as she stepped through what had at first appeared to be a rock wall. It had been warded.

Cristos passed her a curious glance but still guided her forward with his hand against the small of her back, unsheathing his sword, just in case.

As they ventured deeper into the hidden passage in the rock, the rugged mountains that loomed overhead seemed to cast their imposing presence even within the cavernous depths.

"Since Otera sacrificed herself, the crown must choose another. We already know who it will choose, because you are prophesied to become queen of both northern kingdoms, but..." she trailed off as she slid her hand into a small space between the rock and pulled out a sparkling crown.

Crafted from pure gold and adorned with radiant gemstones that shimmered like flames of a phoenix's feathers, the crown exuded an aura of majestic power that made Aurelia's breath catch in her throat.

"The crown Warbotach has is a fake?" she interrupted, her tone shocked.

Bremusa nodded, holding the crown toward its future master. "The crown Uldon has been trying to force his will upon is indeed a fake. When worn upon the chosen queen's head, the crown bestows upon her the abilities of the phoenix, granting her strength, resilience, and the power to rise from the ashes of defeat. When I place this crown on your head, it will accept you as its master, and then you will tell it to destroy itself. Destroying the crown will destroy the portal, which is the only way to prevent Warbotach from crossing into the human lands, at least from here, and prevent this from hopefully ever happening again."

Sucking in a breath, Aurelia glanced toward her husband and he dipped his chin, the subtle gesture of support she needed before turning back to Bremusa and nodding. Without another word, the elemental placed the crown delicately onto Aurelia's head.

A flash of fire erupted from Aurelia's fingers, startling her. She tried to blow them out before they burned her, but the truth was, the flames hadn't hurt her at all.

"As a phoenix queen, Aurelia, the fire will not harm you," Bremusa said, taking the crown from Aurelia's head and placing it in her hands as Bremusa still held the other side. "Now close your eyes and command the crown to destroy itself. You are its master so it has to listen. We need to do this now."

Closing her eyes, Aurelia was unsure if it would work, but she did as Bremusa requested, repeating the command in her mind, visualizing the crown in her hand. After only moments, sounds of breaking glass echoed through the cavern as the crown fractured along its center and then spiderwebbed out, the pieces getting smaller and smaller until it crumbled and slipped through her fingers like sand. Before Aurelia had a chance to register what had just happened, the ground shook at their feet, sending her to her knees as parts of the cave began to crumble as well.

"We have to get out of here!" Cristos yelled as he lifted Aurelia in his arms and ran through the maze of caverns, searching for the exit as Bremusa followed in his footsteps, pieces of the cave breaking off as they passed. The quaking grew in intensity as they ran, fear of being crushed inside the cave sending Aurelia's heart into a panic. When they made it back into the valley, Cristos held her tightly against him as an explosion vibrated the entire world, forcing them to their knees.

The last thing Aurelia remembered was the flaming red wings that flared out her back—a symbol of her new role as queen, her newfound powers, and the unbreakable bond she shared with the people of Aegricia. Then everything went black.

To be continued...

EPILOGUE

VARIEL

There was an eerie orange glow over the battlefield as the sun dipped below the horizon. Variel parried a blow from Joneira, her breaths coming in ragged gasps as their blades clashed with the sound of ringing steel. Sweat and blood mixed in the dirt beneath their feet, the air around them thick with the heat of battle.

"Is this all you've got, oracle?" Joneira sneered, her eyes flashing with malice. "I expected more from the *great* Variel."

"Save your taunts." Variel's muscles strained as she pushed back against Joneira's blade. "We're not finished yet."

Around them warriors clashed in a whirlwind of violence, blood flowing like rivers into the forest. The fierce cries of Variel's allies intertwined with the guttural war cries of the barbarians and Joneira's supporters, creating a cacophony that echoed across the land.

Dragons soared above the conflict, casting shadows on the ground with their massive wings as they battled midair. As their claws tore at scales and flesh, their roars shook the ground beneath Variel's feet. Their maws were filled with fire, scorching the ground and igniting the trees in a blaze of destruction.

The weight of Variel's people's hopes and fears rested on her shoulders as she fought. She must kill Joneira—If only to prevent Aurelia from having to do the job herself.. It was time for the exiled queen to pay the ultimate price for what she had done.

With each swing of her sword she channeled her anger into her attacks, determined to bring an end to the senseless conflict, but Joneira was a formidable foe. Her strikes, swift and relentless, drove Variel back, step by step.

"Your cause is lost!" A feral grin spread across Joneira's face as she pressed her advantage. "You can't win!"

Variel summoned the last of her strength as she surged forward, slashing low. "I will fight to my last breath to protect the chosen queen!"

The chaos and violence of the battle seemed to close in on them, the press of bodies and the clash of steel threatening to overwhelm Variel's senses. The scent of blood and fire filled the air, the heat of the flames licking at her skin. It was a desperate, terrifying struggle, and she knew that one wrong move could mean the end for her and her allies.

In the midst of the raging battle, the ground beneath Variel and Joneira shuddered, a blast from the sea tossing them to their feet. The sudden appearance of a tear near the treeline behind Joneira caught both warriors off guard, their eyes widening as they watched the air shimmer and swirl.

All around them, the cacophony of battle continued unabated, but for a moment, they were both transfixed by the pulsating energy that threatened to consume them.

"Impossible!" Joneira gasped, her sword faltering in its relentless assault.

As Variel watched the portal, the swirling air held her transfixed. The vortex grew larger, engulfing both combatants in its swirling depths. Their swords clattered to the ground, forgotten as the warriors were ripped away from the battlefield and into the unknown.

Together, Variel and Joneira hurtled through the void, the fabric of reality bending and twisting around them. The sensation of being sucked through the portal was unlike anything Variel had ever experienced, as if every muscle in her body was being stretched and compressed at once, like a piece of taffy pulled apart by invisible hands. The swirling colors surrounding her seemed to bleed together, forming a kaleidoscope of chaos that overwhelmed her senses.

As suddenly as it had begun, the disorienting journey came to an abrupt end. With a final violent wrench, Variel and Joneira were ejected from the portal and sent hurtling through the air. They landed hard on the ground, dozens of warriors hitting the ground beside them, all gasping for breath as they struggled to make sense of their surroundings. Variel didn't know where she was, but one thing was for sure—she was no longer in Ekotoria.

CROWN OF THE PHOENIX SERIES 3
CROWN
OF THE
PROPHECY
C.A. VARIAN

Prologue

Variel

There was an eerie orange glow over the battlefield as the sun dipped below the horizon. It was the kind of light that spoke not of endings but of things yet to come. Variel parried a blow from Joneira, her breath coming in ragged gasps as their blades clashed with the sound of ringing steel. Sweat and blood mixed in the dirt beneath their feet, the air around them thick with the heat of battle.

"Is this all you've got, oracle?" Joneira sneered, her eyes flashing with malice. "I expected more from the great Variel."

"Save your taunts." Variel's muscles strained as she pushed back against Joneira's blade. "We're not finished yet."

Around them, warriors clashed in a whirlwind of violence, blood flowing like rivers into the forest. The fierce cries of Variel's allies intertwined with the guttural war cries of the barbarians and Joneira's supporters, creating a cacophony that echoed across the land.

Dragons soared above the conflict, casting shadows on the ground with their massive wings as they battled midair. As their claws tore at scales and flesh, their roars shook the ground beneath Variel's feet. Their maws were filled with fire, scorching the ground and igniting trees in a blaze of destruction. Ash rained from the sky, coating armor and skin alike and turning the air into something almost too thick to breathe.

The weight of Variel's people's hopes and fears rested on her shoulders as she fought. She had to kill Joneira—if only to prevent Aurelia from having to do the job herself. This was the battle destiny had saved for her, a clash not just of blades but of futures.

With each swing of her sword, she channeled her anger into her attacks, determined to bring an end to the senseless conflict. But Joneira was a formidable foe. Her strikes, swift and relentless, drove Variel back, step by step.

"Your cause is lost!" A feral grin spread across Joneira's face as she pressed her advantage. "You can't win!"

Variel summoned the last of her strength as she surged forward, slashing low. "I will fight to my last breath to protect the chosen queen!"

The chaos and violence of the battle seemed to close in on them, the press of bodies and the clash of steel threatening to overwhelm Variel's senses. The scent of blood and fire filled the air, the heat of the flames licking at her skin. It was a desperate, terrifying struggle, and she knew that one wrong move could mean the end for her and her allies. The sheer intensity of the battle was palpable, a relentless force that threatened to consume them all.

In the midst of the raging battle, the ground beneath Variel and Joneira shuddered, a blast from the sea tossing them to their feet. The sudden appearance of a tear near the treeline behind Joneira caught both warriors off guard, their eyes widening as they watched the air shimmer and swirl. The earth itself seemed to recoil as if it knew what had been unleashed. All around them, the cacophony of battle continued unabated, but for a moment, they were both transfixed by the pulsating energy that threatened to consume them.

"Impossible!" Joneira gasped, her sword faltering in its relentless assault.

As Variel watched the portal, the swirling air held her transfixed. The vortex grew larger, engulfing both combatants in its depths. Their swords clattered to the ground, forgotten, as they were ripped away from the battlefield and into the unknown.

Together, Variel and Joneira hurtled through the void, the fabric of reality bending and twisting around them. The sensation of being pulled through the portal was unlike anything Variel had ever experienced, as if every muscle in her body was being stretched and compressed at once, like a piece of taffy pulled apart by invisible hands. It was like falling through a storm of shattered glass and molten stars, each fragment cutting and burning as it rushed past.

As suddenly as it had begun, the disorienting journey came to an abrupt end. With a final violent wrench, Variel and Joneira were ejected from the portal and sent hurtling through the air. They landed hard on the ground, dozens of warriors hitting the earth beside them, all gasping for breath as they struggled to make sense of their surroundings.

When she rose to her knees, the world around her was foreign, the air sharp and metallic, the sky the wrong shade of night. And she knew, with bone-deep certainty, that Ekotoria had been left behind.

CHAPTER ONE

Aurelia

With the stones tumbling from the mountains around them, Aurelia, Cristos, and Bremusa took to the sky and returned to the battlefield, Aurelia held tightly in Cristos' arms. The first sight of Flamecliff sent a chill down her spine. Ash drifted like gray snow through the broken streets, settling on toppled beams and shattered glass, a mockery of winter's peace. Much of the once-beautiful city was now a charred, smoldering ruin. The smoke billowed into the sky like the last breath of a dying world, while the moans of the wounded reverberated throughout the air, punctuated by the cries of wounded warriors searching for survivors.

Aurelia's heart ached as she surveyed the devastation. The sour scent of burnt flesh mixed with the acrid smell of scorched earth made her stomach turn. Buildings lay in shattered heaps, their once proud façades crumbled under the weight of destruction. As they ventured deeper into the chaos, the ground beneath their feet was slick with blood, staining the soles of their boots. She clenched her fists, trying not to lose her composure. Every muscle in her arms trembled with the effort, her grief clawing to escape as surely as the smoke clawed toward the heavens. It was her duty as queen to be strong for her people, but grief threatened to overwhelm her.

"By the gods," Cristos muttered, his voice catching in his throat as he surveyed the devastation around them, his wings twitching involuntarily.

With her crimson hair whipping about her face, Aurelia's blue eyes searched desperately for any signs of life among the carnage. As she stared at the scene, she wasn't sure where to begin.

"Flamecliff has suffered greatly," Bremusa began, her silver eyes somber as she gazed at the wreckage, "but we will rebuild."

As they continued their search, Aurelia's gaze fell upon the crumpled form of Taryn, the warrior's sword still clutched in her hand. A choked sob escaped Aurelia's lips as she knelt beside her fallen comrade, brushing the long brown hair from Taryn's lifeless face.

"She deserved better than this." Unable to hold back any longer, a sob burst from Aurelia's throat. "They all did."

Cristos placed a hand on her shoulder, his touch grounding her. "She was a brave warrior, my love. She fought valiantly until the end."

"We've lost too much," Aurelia choked out, her vision blurred by the tears that finally spilled over. She glanced around the city as groups of warriors searched for survivors among the fallen. She knew her sister and Septima were out there somewhere, perhaps with— The reality of losing her aunt hit her hard, stopping her in her tracks and wrenching her heart wide open. "First Otera and now Taryn... How many more must die before this war is over?" The thought settled like ice in her chest—war did not care for queens, sisters, or lovers. It would take until nothing remained.

"Let their sacrifices not be in vain," Bremusa said, her voice steady despite the emotion that sparked in her eyes. "We will continue our fight in their honor."

With a nod of her head, Aurelia wiped her tears away with the back of her hand. She straightened her spine, her resolve hardening as she turned to face Bremusa. "You're right, Bremusa. Our people are counting on us."

With Cristos' arm wrapped around her waist, they followed Bremusa further into the ravaged battlefield, their boots crunching over the charred earth and their eyes scanning the destruction around them.

"Aurelia!" a familiar voice called out, cutting through the thick air that lay over the battlefield. Aurelia turned to see her sister rushing toward them, her dark eyes red-rimmed with tears. Exie followed, her golden hair matted with dirt and sweat.

"Thank the gods you're alive!" Aurelia cried, embracing her sister as tightly as she could. Septima clung to her, her body shaking with sobs. When Aurelia pulled away, her hands slid up to touch her sister's face. "When the two of you flew toward the portal, I feared the worst."

As Aurelia embraced her sister, tears trailed down her dusty cheeks, but she couldn't help but feel relief. A lot of people had perished in the war, but Septima and Cristos were okay, and that was something to be happy about. Still, her heart broke for all the lost—Taryn, her aunt—who she never had a chance to know.

Looking over Septima's shoulder as her sister rubbed her back, Aurelia gazed at the destroyed portal, at the crumbling stone façade that had once encircled it like the frame of an antique mirror.

Just as she was about to pull away and tell Septima about what had transpired in the mountains—about the crimson wings that were now hiding away inside her—a violent explosion rattled through the city, and the remaining portal crumbled into the sea.

Screams erupted around them as Aurelia and Septima were forced apart and thrown several feet back. With a crash, Aurelia collided with the stone exterior of the building, sending pain exploding through her bones.

Ears ringing, she scanned her surroundings for her sister and her husband, but in the cloud of dust and ash, it was impossible to see anything.

"Cristos! Septima!"

With ash forcing her to cough and sputter, Aurelia forced herself onto her feet and did her best to assess her body for injuries. Her back ached, but her hand went instinctively to her stomach, hoping her child was unharmed inside her.

"Aurelia!" Cristos' voice cut through the ringing in her ears, drawing her toward the direction of the sea.

"Cristos! Where are you?"

The sound of heavy boots stomping met her ears a second before strong arms wrapped around her, holding her close.

"Are you hurt, love?" he asked, pulling away just enough to look into her eyes. Aside from a cut above his eyebrow, Aurelia was relieved that Cristos seemed to be unharmed.

Nodding, she rose onto her tiptoes and kissed him. "I'm okay, but where are the others?"

Before he could answer, Septima's voice sent Aurelia darting through the dusty air, Cristos on her heels. As she ran, her breath sat heavy in her chest, not knowing what she would find when she laid eyes on her friends again. But as the ash cleared, Aurelia's feet stumbled. What she saw, who she saw standing in the ashes like the phoenix she was, sent Aurelia to her knees. Otera was alive.

Scattered among the destruction, figures rose from where their lifeless bodies had lain only moments before. The air itself seemed to hum, heavy with the raw pulse of scattered magic, as if life had been borrowed from the very bones of the earth.

Tears clouded Aurelia's vision, so she closed her eyes, hoping, but not expecting, the risen to still be before her. But when she reopened them, she realized they were not figments of her imagination. The once dead Aegrician warriors were now alive.

"Otera..." With shaky legs beneath her, Aurelia stood, taking two steps closer to her aunt with Cristos' arm around her waist. "Otera... I—I don't understand."

Beside the resurrected queen, Bremusa stood with a hand on her friend. "The destruction of the portal caused its magic to disperse, bringing life to its protectors as its final act."

Trying to absorb the words, Aurelia remained silent, even as Septima and Exie moved closer to her side. Even Blaedia, whose hands searched her mate for injuries, remained silent.

Bremusa tipped her head toward the largest group of warriors, who, like Otera, had risen. "My powers tell me the portal has moved; history proves it, but with its magic diminished, it will be nearly impossible to find. Still, we must find it. The fate of the human realm depends on its protection."

The portal had been the very lifeline connecting the human realm and the fae realm for as long as the worlds existed. It allowed Aurelia and Septima, if they ever chose to, the possibility of returning home. Now, with its destruction, an unnerving cloud of scattered magic hung in the air, as if waiting to be claimed by forces unknown.

"What does this mean for our realms?" Cristos asked, his hand tightening around Aurelia's back.

Bremusa turned her eyes to Cristos, the quicksilver in them drawing Aurelia into their depths. "Both worlds are now isolated from each other. With the magic scattered, there's no telling what consequences we may face."

The words settled over Aurelia heavier than ash, a prophecy unspoken but felt—that their war had only just begun.

CHAPTER TWO

AURELIA

Bremusa's words echoed in Aurelia's mind, their implications rattling her already fragile nerves. The weight of isolation clung to her like a vice, whispering that even the most delicate joys might shatter under the burden of fate. There had been too many changes in too short a time, but at least Otera, Taryn, and many others had risen from the ashes when the portal crumbled. That was one positive amid a sea of devastation.

As the injured were brought into infirmary tents for healing, Aurelia, Cristos, and their closest family and friends—including Otera and Blaedia—made their way to the palace near the harbor. For years, it had been Otera's home, but with her sacrifice, she was no longer the queen of Aegricia. Still, Aurelia hoped her aunt would choose to continue living there. They had only just met, and Aurelia looked forward to getting to know her mother's sister and learning from Otera how to be a ruler. Growing up in a royal family, Otera understood the responsibilities of monarchy better than anyone. Once the dust settled and the bodies were laid to rest, they needed to find a way to unite Aegricia and Norithae, just as the prophecy foretold.

"Once we get settled," Cristos said, sliding his arm around Aurelia's waist as they stepped through the massive wooden doors, "we'll send for a healer to check on you and the baby. I know you feel fine, but I would feel better knowing that everything is as it should be."

Aurelia nodded, her eyes absorbing the palace for the first time. For months, she had seen the dungeon in her dreams, witnessing Otera's neglect and abuse at the hands of the Warbotach ruler, but she had never set foot in the palace herself.

It was clear from the outside that Aegricia was a wealthy kingdom, one that had stood for centuries. The palace, constructed from a light-colored stone that looked nearly silver in the sunlight, held a majestic splendor that rivaled Diapolis in the South. Norithae's palace was beautiful, but there was something truly magical about seeing the place where her mother had been raised. Each polished arch and gleaming stair seemed to breathe with history. Yet, grief stained the grandeur, reminding Aurelia that walls alone could not keep out ruin. Although the barbarians had controlled the city of Flamecliff for months, living in the palace as if it were their own, the lack of destruction inside indicated that Uldon—or whoever he had claimed the city for—intended to stay there for a long time.

"I'm surprised there isn't more damage," Aurelia remarked, scanning the entrance as servants moved about the space, attending to their tasks as if their lives depended on it. However, the moment the doors closed behind them, every set of eyes in the room turned to face them.

"Your Majesty," an older woman said, dropping her broom and crossing the room to greet them. Otera stepped around their group, her leather garments nearly torn to shreds, and her waist-length crimson hair matted with blood and ash. The servant bowed deeply, reaching out to take Otera's hands. "I cannot tell you how relieved we are to see you."

Two more servants entered the room: a younger woman with golden hair carrying a tray of water glasses and an older man with several cloths draped over his arm.

Otera smiled, gently squeezing the servant's hand. "It's good to be home, Muriel, but there is much to do. First, I should introduce you to the new queen of Aegricia."

Aurelia's heart fluttered at Otera's words, but she remained silent. "My niece, Aurelia, has come to fulfill the prophecy. My time as queen is over."

The word "prophecy," spoken aloud in the echoing hall, seemed to ripple through the servants like a gust of wind, their eyes widening as if they, too, could feel destiny stir. With wide eyes, Muriel reached for Aurelia's hand, catching her by surprise. Although she knew it was true, acknowledging her new position was something she wasn't entirely ready for. "You'll always be queen, Otera, no matter what the crown says."

A knowing smile spread across Otera's battered face as she took one of the cloths and wiped the blood from her arms. "I'll be here to support you and Cristos, Aurelia, in whatever capacity you both need."

As exhausted as everyone was, the conversation in the foyer of the palace didn't last long. With so much left unsaid, the servants escorted Aurelia and Cristos to one of the suites in the east wing of the castle, overlooking the sea. Blaedia and Otera, along with Septima and Exie, were led to other areas within the massive structure. The group planned to reunite that evening for the funeral pyre of those who had fallen, but with the early morning sun streaming through the balcony doors of their bedroom, all Aurelia could think about was sleep.

Similar to their rooms in the Norithae palace, the suite they were brought to was vast, featuring a large four-poster bed with bright white, fluffy linens. Several pieces of gold-upholstered furniture filled the space in front of the fireplace. It was pristine and cozy, a stark contrast to the carnage outside.

Guilt swam through Aurelia's mind as she sat in such a place while so many suffered, but she knew there was only so much she could do in that moment. Her reflection in the gilded mirror by the hearth seemed almost foreign—illuminated by the firelight while others lay in shadow. Most of the civilians in Flamecliff had left the city, and the healers, who had remained at their camp during the violence, were now attending to the injured. She was just one person, and without rest, she would be no good to anyone.

"I'll prepare your bath, my love," Cristos said, kissing her on the cheek before disappearing into the bathing room.

Aurelia didn't follow; she was entranced by the view through the window and the way the sunlight made the sea sparkle like diamonds. Just as the sound of water reached her ears, a knock on the door echoed through the room, pulling her attention away from the view.

Crossing the room, she opened the door and felt relieved to see a servant standing beside a cart topped with bowls of steaming porridge, holding a stack of clean clothes in her hands. "I know it's not much, Your Majesty, but with all those who need attention, we managed to gather some clean clothes and a warm meal for the two of you. I hope this can sustain you for a little while."

Aurelia smiled and reached out to take the clothes from the young woman's hands. "This is perfect, Miss…"

"Kassandra," the girl said, dipping into a curtsy. Although it was difficult to tell with fae, Aurelia guessed she couldn't be much older than a teenager.

"It's nice to meet you, Kassandra."

Cristos called her name, drawing Aurelia's attention briefly. "My husband and I will be getting cleaned up and trying to rest, but if you could see to it that a healer finds me at dinner time, I would appreciate it."

Kassandra replied with a nod and another smile before bringing their food into the room and then disappearing down the corridor.

Closing the door, Aurelia set the clothes down on the bed and walked into the bathing room, her heavy heart fluttering at the sight of her husband removing his leathers, his massive wings stretching at his sides. He was magnificent.

"A servant, Kassandra, brought a warm meal and clean clothes for us," she said.

Cristos turned to face her, licking his lips as she unbuckled her leathers and let them drop to the floor. "And the healer? Are they sending someone?"

Kicking his soiled clothes to the side, he closed the distance between them and slid his hand against her still-flat stomach, as if he could already feel their child kicking. Given everything they had been through, their unborn child was a beacon of hope for the future.

As Cristos leaned down to kiss her stomach, she threaded her fingers into his thick black hair. "I asked her to send someone this evening. We both need rest, and there are so many who need a healer more than I do right now."

With a nod, he wrapped his arm around her waist, guiding her to the steaming bathtub. "Then let's get you cleaned up and into bed."

Pounding on the door reverberated through the chamber, jolting Aurelia from a deep sleep. Cristos, her steadfast companion, slipped out of bed with a swiftness that revealed his readiness, answering the intrusion before she could fully process the disturbance. Muffled voices and purposeful footsteps followed, weaving an unspoken narrative of urgency. A moment later, Cristos returned to her side, accompanied by an elderly Aegrician woman with long, elegantly braided silver hair.

With a warm smile that accentuated the crinkles around her eyes, the elder introduced herself. "Good morning, Your Majesty. My name is Cordelia. Would it be alright if I check on you and your baby?"

Aurelia, still grappling with the abrupt awakening, nodded with a hint of confusion. "Yes, but I feel fine."

Cordelia approached, placing her bag on the bedside table, and withdrew a device to listen to Aurelia's heartbeat. The air hung heavy with unspoken concern as Cordelia began her examination. "Your husband explained the transformation you went through when the portal fell."

A surge of memories cascaded through Aurelia's mind—the chaos in the mountains and the searing sensation of wings bursting forth from her back. She shuddered, seeking reassurance. "Do you think it caused harm to our child?" Her gaze flicked to Cristos, noting the worry etched on his face.

The silence that followed was laden with anticipation. After feeling Aurelia's stomach and prompting her to turn onto her side, Cordelia ran her ice-cold hands up Aurelia's back, shifting her tunic aside for a more thorough examination. "Your skin looks as it should, Your Majesty—just like any of our warriors. And your child is showing no signs of distress." Still, Cordelia's eyes lingered on Aurelia's back for a moment too long, as though some secret lay beneath the skin that even she could not identify.

Letting out a breath that Aurelia felt in her own chest, Cristos drew closer, taking Aurelia's hand and kissing her knuckles. "Well, that's good news, love."

Cordelia hummed her agreement from her position at Aurelia's back. "Indeed, it is. However, I want to see you rest for a few days—just to be sure."

An immediate protest formed on Aurelia's lips, a testament to her resilience and sense of duty. Before she could voice her objections, Cristos shook his head, offering gentle reassurance. "I know we all have a lot to do right now, love, but everyone is here to help. It's not worth risking harm to you or our child if you overdo it."

While Cristos's words made sense, an internal struggle began to brew within Aurelia. As queen, she felt an intrinsic responsibility to be at the forefront, actively participating in the challenges facing their kingdom. The idea of lying in bed while her people toiled and suffered seemed inconceivable. Though she yearned to argue, the weight of Cristos's gaze and the healer's advice compelled her compliance. She reclined on the bed and turned her attention to Cordelia. "For how long? Is there anything I should be aware of? Any warning signs?"

Cordelia's lips curled into a small smile as she tidied up her tools. "Well... I've never seen a transformation like this before. Even in the lore, this doesn't happen—not the way it happened to you—so I can't provide an exact answer. Still, I think if you rest through tomorrow and don't experience any bleeding or pain, you should be fine—both you and the baby."

Bidding Aurelia and Cristos farewell, Cordelia left their quarters with a promise to return the following day. Aurelia huffed out a breath, frustration making her nerves antsy at the thought of not leaving their rooms for two days. Part of her wanted to escape, at least to go down to the kitchens and get to know the people working in her palace. Just as she was about to climb out of bed, another knock sounded at the door. Only a moment later, her sister walked in.

Relief and dread mingled in Aurelia's chest—her sister's presence was a balm, yet every knock on the door seemed to carry the weight of fate demanding to be heard.

Chapter Three

Kason

Although the fight had destroyed much of Flamecliff, leaving rubble along the mountain pass that separated Aegricia and Norithae, the Singing Lantern tavern emerged virtually unscathed. Amid the devastation, it remained a refuge, offering hot meals and warm beds to those who had nowhere else to go. The walls were infused with the scents of smoke and old whiskey, a cocoon of familiarity standing defiantly against the encroaching ruin outside.

Bruised and battered from the battle, Kason and Holera slid into a booth at the back of the room and ordered a decanter of whiskey. The atmosphere in the city was tense, yet their people were resilient, just as phoenixes were meant to be.

Sitting next to him, Holera's silver hair was caked with soot, and the smudges across her face blended with the battle paint she often applied before a fight.

"Do you want to head upstairs?" he asked, wrapping his fingers around her slender hand. He could sense how frayed her nerves were after the day's extremes. The thought of potentially losing her made him want to hold her tighter—to protect her from all harm. The memory of her wings faltering in battle had nearly torn him apart, leaving him with a fear he dared not express.

They still had too many dreams waiting to manifest—dreams of retiring from the fight and starting a family. However, their kingdom had faced near-constant threats since they had met, and the timing had never felt right. Soon, he promised himself. They would retire to their cottage tucked away in the mountains, and he would keep her in bed for days, worshiping her as she deserved. He envisioned a hearth fire instead of battle flames, imagining her laughter echoing through rooms untouched by war—a dream so fragile it almost hurt to contemplate.

Exhaustion weighed down Holera's lashes, and she nodded. "Yes. I feel if I don't get these leathers off soon, they may become permanently affixed to my skin." Even her usual spark was dimmed; the fire in her violet eyes was shuttered beneath a fatigue carved by years of relentless battle.

Kason chuckled, standing up and positioning himself to lift her from the chair. If she were too weak to walk, he fully intended to carry her. "Well, we can't have that, my stunning warrior. I won't tolerate anything blocking me from tasting every inch of your skin."

Even in her half-asleep state, she grinned, not protesting as he lifted her into his arms. With his other hand, he grabbed the decanter of whiskey and carried them both up the stairs.

For as long as they had been together, there was one room at the tavern that was Kason's whenever he needed it. He hadn't used it much over the past year. As an emissary for Aegricia, he had traveled for the queen. He hadn't spent enough time in Flamecliff to warrant buying a home there. He could have taken a room in the palace, but a life as an upper-class male was not in his blood. He had been born and raised in the Aegrician outlands, deep within the mountains, while Holera had grown up in the rural plains of Western Aegricia. Neither of them relished the thought of living in the city or being under constant scrutiny. Staying in the palace would mean being watched by hundreds of staff and guards, which was why they had never chosen to stay at the Aegrician palace; instead, they had opted for the Diapolisian palace when there was no other easy option.

Climbing up the wooden stairs to the second level, Kason set the decanter down on the small table in the corridor and fished the key from his pocket. Holera was already asleep in his arms, so once they were inside the room, he gently laid her on the settee. With tender hands, he removed her boots and leathers, careful not to wake her. He knew she would want to clean up before bed, so he had no issue tending to her while she slumbered. The battle had drained both of them, but as a phoenix shifter, her body underwent a metamorphosis he could never experience.

Once his beautiful mate was stripped bare, he filled a wash basin with warm water and used a cloth to clean the worst of the grime from her before tucking her into bed.

After washing himself as best as he could, he climbed into bed beside her, pulling her smaller body against his chest where she fit perfectly—like a missing piece of him that made him whole again. Outside the windows, destruction lay everywhere, but for the moment, their enemies were gone, and the healers were tending to the sick and injured. All that remained for him and his warrior mate was to rest so they could face another day. They knew their kingdom would soon need them again, so they needed to take advantage of this moment of peace.

Waking the next morning, Kason pulled Holera close, wishing they could stay in bed all day. But he knew they couldn't. Duty called to them, even if they couldn't hear it with their ears. "Just a little longer, and we can hide away," he repeated to himself as they dressed and left the inn to head back to the palace.

Tents lined the treeline on both sides of the main road leading toward the harbor, not only infirmary tents but also temporary shelters for those whose homes had been affected by the war. It was a temporary solution, but it was necessary.

Taking Holera by the hand, Kason nodded at the guards by the front gates as they swung open. "We're going to have to talk about finding the missing portal," Holera said, her violet eyes shining in the rising sun. "And who's going out to look for it."

Kason nodded, pulling her to his side so he could kiss the top of her head. "Is that something you want us to do? Do you want to be part of that team?"

Although he asked the question, he already knew the answer. As long as they went together, he didn't care. They were always a team, no matter where they went.

She shot him a side-eye, her feisty attitude making him chuckle. "Point taken."

As they opened the palace's front doors, they were met with a chaotic scene. Servants and guards bustled around the main entrance and corridor. "You're the best diplomat for this kingdom I know, my love," Holera said, squeezing his hand. "If anyone can get to the bottom of where the portal's magic went, it's you."

Kason grinned at his mate's compliment, fully aware that she meant it, but he also knew she had her own agenda. "You're just saying that because you want to go."

The smirk that lifted the corner of Holera's full lips made his desire stir, but he pushed it aside as they turned down the corridor into the eastern wing, heading toward the war room. This was the meeting space where Queen Otera had spent a lot of her time. She was no longer queen, but Kason didn't doubt that Aurelia would continue this tradition. That was why he was surprised when they entered the large room and found Otera, Blaedia, Bremusa, and Cristos there, but no Aurelia.

When Kason and Holera stepped into the room, every head turned to look at them. "Oh, Kason and Holera," Blaedia said, dipping her head in greeting. It was the friendliest expression the usually severe general ever displayed. Blaedia may have been stunning, but she rarely smiled. Her mate, Otera, beamed as Kason and Holera approached her, with Holera pulling her into a hug. Even his mate tended to be serious and didn't often show her emotions, but after witnessing their queen's death and the rise from the ashes, all their foundations had been shaken to the core.

"Where's Aurelia?" Holera asked, clearly wondering the same thing as Kason.

Cristos smiled and stepped around the table to hug Holera. "My stubborn mate is begrudgingly on bed rest for a few days. She's okay, but the healer wants to ensure that our child in her womb suffers no ill effects after everything Aurelia went through yesterday."

Kason gripped Cristos' forearm, dipping his chin and smiling. "I'm sure they're both fine, but it's good that the healer is forcing her to rest. The kingdom will still be here, as will the work."

Nodding, Cristos turned to look down at the map spread out on the table. "There will be a lot to do for a very long time." The weight of his words pressed upon them like the map itself—lines and borders that signified responsibility, not rest.

Chapter Four

Aurelia

The walls seemed to close in around Aurelia as she lay in bed, staring at the flickering flames in the fireplace while the rest of her kingdom dealt with the aftermath of the war. The thought of everyone else managing the decisions—the work, the grief—while she remained warm in her bed filled her with guilt. Each muffled voice from the corridor pressed against her conscience, reminding her that rest was a luxury others could not afford. She understood why the healer wanted her to rest for a few days; her child was worth it, but that didn't ease her mind.

Around midday, the door to her chambers opened, rousing her from her nap. She expected to see a servant bringing in a tray of food or perhaps the healer checking in on her, but it was Cristos who walked in, carrying a tray of food. For a moment, memories of their first meeting flooded her mind—not when he walked alongside the cart carrying her after the barbarians had captured her and her friends, but when he entered the dungeon to bring her and the others food. It felt like years since they'd met, even though it had only been months. The handsome winged stranger who had rescued her from the barbarians had become everything to her, bringing a smile to her face as he entered the room. The memory of chains still lingered in her dreams, but the weight of his arms around her now was proof that captivity had given way to love.

"Did I wake you, my love?" he asked, setting the tray down on the table and crossing the room to kiss her, the scent of roasted meat and vegetables making her stomach rumble.

As the kiss lingered, the aroma of their lunch was replaced by Cristos' sandalwood and spice scent, drawing a groan from her chest. It was one more thing about him that comforted her, even in her most tumultuous moments.

When he pulled away, she shook her head, a smile lifting the corners of her lips. "I was just dozing. You didn't wake me."

Cristos smiled back, cupping her cheek in his palm. "I hope you've been getting lots of rest...and that you're hungry. Otera had the cook, Ellisar, prepare a lunch with plenty of fresh vegetables for you."

Taking her hand, Cristos helped Aurelia out of bed. Her body ached from her ordeal, but it was nothing she couldn't manage. "You'll have to thank her for me. Will you be meeting again this afternoon? How did it go this morning? Did you see my sister?"

Pulling out a chair for her, Cristos chuckled at how quickly the questions left her mouth, unable to answer one before she asked another. "We met this morning and discussed what needs to be done in this first stage and delegated tasks so we won't need to meet again tonight. I understand that Exie and Septima have been in town since early this morning helping with cleanup, so I haven't seen them yet today."

Taking a bite of her food, Aurelia closed her eyes, willing the nausea building in her chest to dissipate. When she opened her eyes, she gazed out the window at the sea, amazed at how the sun made the surface sparkle like diamonds. The portal, once a massive archway of jagged stones eroded by the sea, was no longer there; its remains had sunk to the depths, where they would never be seen again. But the essence of the portal itself, the magic that had allowed Aurelia and her sister to enter Aegricia all those months ago, was gone. Its absence left a silence more haunting than battle cries—a gap in the world that seemed to echo inside her chest.

Her expression turning pensive, she returned her gaze to her husband, finding him watching her. "And the portal...when will the search for it begin?"

Before Cristos could respond, a knock sounded at the door, drawing their attention. Cristos stood from the table and crossed the room, and Aurelia's heart leaped when he opened the door to reveal her sister and Exie standing there. She hadn't realized how much she needed to see Septima until she was standing in front of her, dirty clothes and exhaustion evident, but safe.

"Sissy!" Aurelia exclaimed, a smile spreading across her face that mirrored the expression on Septima's face. She moved to stand, but Septima was at her side in an instant, the speed of her movement catching Aurelia by surprise. Still at the door, Exie and Cristos chatted.

Septima lowered herself into Cristos' chair, leaned forward, and pulled Aurelia into a hug. "It seems the portal's collapse changed more than just you," she said, raising an eyebrow. It didn't take long for Aurelia to notice that Septima's once perfectly rounded ears had begun to taper at the top. Aurelia's mouth fell open, her hands bracing on Septima's shoulders as she searched her sister's face. The faint point of Septima's ears glimmered like a newly unveiled secret, marking a change that bound them even closer to this realm.

"The magic... it turned you fae?" Aurelia asked, her eyes wide with surprise.

Septima's smile widened. "I saw a healer this morning. They aren't sure how much it will affect me—like if it will lengthen my lifespan—but I've definitely started developing some fae traits! I'm faster, and my wounds have already healed."

For a moment, Aurelia didn't respond, relief flooding through her even as questions lingered. She hadn't even had time to consider whether the new magic in her veins would affect her own lifespan. "That's amazing, Septima."

"That's not all," Septima said, gazing out the window before returning her deep brown eyes to Aurelia. "Bremusa said if we can find the portal, we may be able to cross it. We could see Amadeus again...and Father."

The thought had never seemed possible to Aurelia. To prevent Septima from being forced to marry a man, she had agreed to never see her father and brother again. At the time, it felt like the right decision, but it didn't numb the aching hole in her chest created by the loss of those she loved. Even with everything she had been going through over the past few months—new husband, a child on the way, and a found family—she still missed them. "But the treaty—"

Septima shook her head, but it was Exie who spoke as she and Cristos approached the table. "The treaty was with Aegricia and the portal off its coast. The new portal, wherever it is, will require a new treaty. Diplomats from our realm will have to venture into the human realm and work with their kingdoms to create a new agreement."

The thought unsettled Aurelia—her homeland had been a cage. Yet, the idea of strangers negotiating its fate without her present made her blood run cold. The prospect should have relieved some of the tension in her chest, but it only tightened it further. "But I won't be able to go." Aurelia's gaze flicked up toward Cristos, as if seeking permission, even though she knew he would never stand in her way, especially not when there was a chance to see her family. He held her gaze but remained silent. "The baby... the kingdom. I'm needed here."

With the weight of her decisions dragging her down, Aurelia turned her gaze back to the endless blue outside the window, a tear trailing down her cheek as disappointment sliced through her heart. "You must tell my father and brother how much I love them when you see them, Sissy. Tell them how sorry I am for abandoning them."

Lowering himself onto one knee, Cristos slid his fingers along her cheek, wiping away her tears as he nudged her to look at him. "Otera can run the kingdom while you're away, my love. Many people are capable of taking care of Aegricia while we're gone. I won't let you miss this opportunity for closure, and I won't let anything happen to you or our child."

After they ate lunch, Septima and Exie left to return to the cleanup effort outside the palace. Cristos had another meeting scheduled with Otera and some others, but he sent a message asking them to meet in his and Aurelia's chambers instead of the war room. Aurelia, although on bedrest, was determined to be involved in the decision-making regarding the post-war world. As the new Aegrician queen—one who didn't feel qualified at all—she wanted to learn from her aunt, whom she had thought she'd lost just a day earlier. Important decisions needed to be made, and she didn't want to miss the opportunity to contribute.

While Cristos prepared their private dining area for the meeting, Aurelia slipped into the bathing room to freshen up and put on a tunic and trousers. When she walked back out, Otera, Blaedia, and Bremusa were already there, looking over a large map spread out on the table.

"Otera!" Seeing her aunt, who looked so much like her mother, tore at Aurelia's heart. The former queen truly was a phoenix. Otera smiled and wrapped her arms around her niece.

"Aren't you supposed to be resting?" Otera asked.

Looking up at them, Cristos smirked. "Your niece doesn't know the meaning of the word."

Aurelia scoffed, pulling away from Otera and sitting at the table. "I can rest and still be part of the discussions. Spending more time alone when so much needs to be done may drive me insane."

It wasn't until after the words left her mouth that she realized how insensitive it was to complain about such things after Otera had spent months in the dungeon below her own palace. However, Otera seemed unfazed. She rubbed Aurelia's shoulder, then moved to stand beside Cristos, leaving a space for Aurelia to see the map between them.

"We're sending scouts to the south and west," Cristos said, tracing a path toward Diapolis and the forested area north of Warbotach. "If there's a portal there, the scouts should be able to sense it."

Bremusa nodded, her long black hair pulled back in a braid slipping over her shoulder as she twisted her head to look at him. After having seen her as an elderly woman with a hunched back in many visions, it was strange for Aurelia to see Bremusa in her true form. Her shifting ability was astounding. As a full-blooded elemental centuries old, Bremusa looked no older than twenty-five. However, her quicksilver eyes spoke of an ancient wisdom that Aurelia could only dream of.

"I will consult the shadow glass," Bremusa said, pulling a second map from underneath the first and placing it on top. "My intuition tells me it may not be on the continent at all—that someone may have seen our hand before we played it and could take the magic that dispersed to them. I must admit, even I wasn't prepared for what would happen when we destroyed the crown. I believe the portal has moved. I sense its power remains in our world, but never before have I lived in a world without it. If a portal to the human world is truly gone, how would any of us ever know?"

Her words seemed to carry the weight of prophecy, each syllable falling like ash—truths that even time itself seemed reluctant to reveal.

Aurelia felt her mouth go dry, her heart sinking as her sister's hope had just lifted it from despair. "So, you're saying we may search for it forever and never find it?" Aurelia asked, the possibility of having no way back to the other half of her family making her stomach turn. "It may no longer exist?"

When Cristos' eyes met hers, Aurelia knew he understood the unspoken fear behind her words. As long as there was a portal, the option to see her father and brother remained. But if the portal were gone, she would never see them again. The thought hollowed her chest, filling her with grief not of losses past, but of futures stolen before they could be lived.

Chapter Five

Variel

Variel's eyes fluttered open, her chest heaving with labored breaths. The cold dampness of the forest floor seeped through her clothes, sending shivers down her spine. Panic set in as the unfamiliar forest seemed to close in around her. The air was heavy and suffocating, as though the trees themselves leaned closer to listen to her fear.

"Where are we?" she muttered under her breath, struggling to sit up. Her keen wolf senses picked up the distant groans and moans of injured warriors, both friends and foes, scattered throughout the trees. The stench of blood and sweat filled the air, but there was no sign of Joneira, although Variel instinctively knew they had ended up in the same place. The mixed scents clung to her like ghosts, as if the earth itself mourned the bodies it could not yet bury.

The forest was dense and mountainous, with towering ancient trees casting shadows upon the moss-covered ground. Although the branches swayed gently, thickets of brambles grew abundantly, their thorns gleaming with malice. Even though Variel knew they weren't in Spectre Forest, her instincts warned her of dangers lurking in the shadows.

"Thalius, wake up," Variel whispered urgently as she shook the shoulder of the Norithaean warrior beside her. There were both Norithaean and Aegrician warriors in the chaotic scene around them, but there were nearly twice as many enemy soldiers. Variel knew she needed to get her allies hidden away before the enemies woke and launched another attack. There would be time to fight each other later, but first, they needed to figure out where they were and create a camp for shelter. Once everyone was rested and healed, they could locate the portal and return to their world.

Jolting awake, Thalius' eyes flickered open, confusion etched across his face. A wound on his forearm had already begun to stitch closed, indicating it had been there for at least a day. Even with the fae resilience knitting his flesh, the pallor of his skin told her that time was running thin.

"Where are we?" He scanned their surroundings, uncertainty clouding his handsome features.

Variel shrugged, helping him to his feet. "I'm not sure, but we're no longer in Ekotoria. We need to wake our allies and get away from this site before our enemies awaken. Many people need healing before they can fight again."

The sun dipped below the horizon as Variel and the other warriors found a clearing in the lush forest, the cool mountain air indicating that the night would only get colder. They had been hiking for hours, narrowly escaping their enemies before realizing they had been transported to another place.

Only Variel and one other member of her group could create invisibility wards, so they set to work erecting a barrier around the campsite while the others pitched the few tents they had and built a fire. There was not nearly enough shelter for everyone to have their own tent, as not everyone had brought camping gear while they fought. However, they intended to share and make the best of what they had. A few warriors had ventured out to hunt just before darkness fell over the camp, but the unknown terrain and lurking enemies made that a risky endeavor.

As the wards enveloped them in a protective bubble, the air inside warmed, and the sounds of the forest diminished. With the protective ward in place, their enemies could pass by their camp without seeing them. Still, Variel felt the air pressing against her like glass—thin, fragile, just a tremor away from collapse.

The hunters returned to the camp just as Variel finished bandaging the last of the injured warriors. Their wounds were healing quickly thanks to their fae blood, but she wanted to ensure they wouldn't get an infection while out in the wilderness.

Morwen, an Aegrician warrior, walked across the camp with a deer slung over her shoulder and dropped her kill on the ground by the fire. Pulling her blade from a sheath at her thigh, she crouched down to begin breaking down the animal.

"Do you need some help?" Variel asked, taking her own dagger and slicing into the deer's stomach to clean out its bowels as Morwen skinned and filleted the animal.

Working together, they quickly prepared the meat for the fire, filling the campsite with an aroma that made Variel's stomach growl. Her wolf senses urged her to devour the flesh while it was still raw. If she had been in wolf form, she would have done just that. The beast inside her stirred, restless and hungry, reminding her that survival often came at the cost of teeth and blood.

While the deer cooked over the open fire, Variel slipped back inside the tent she would share with four other warriors. She removed her clothing and washed it in a basin of water they had filled from a nearby stream. After hanging her damp clothes on a hook, she slipped out the back of the tent, shifting into a massive black wolf and slipping into the shadows.

In her wolf form, Variel was able to blend into the darkness and explore her surroundings in relative safety. She longed to bathe in the stream and wash away the remnants of battle from her skin. No matter what dangers lurked in the forest, she felt confident she was one of the most formidable creatures there.

The distant murmur of the campfire faded behind her as the forest enveloped Variel in a symphony of nocturnal sounds—the hooting of owls, the chirping of crickets, and the distant howling of other creatures echoing through the trees. Under the veil of the moonlit night, her black fur glistened as she moved silently through the dense forest, her senses heightened in her lupine form. A cool breeze rustled through the leaves, carrying the scent of pine and earth, guiding her through the darkness. In her wolf form, navigating the rugged terrain was no challenge at all.

As she padded along the narrow trails, her keen eyes caught subtle movements in the underbrush where creatures stirred in the shadows. Heading back toward the direction they had traveled earlier that day, the stream beckoned to her with its gentle flow, a soothing melody that would help cleanse the traces of conflict from her fur.

Upon reaching the water's edge, Variel dipped her snout into the cool liquid, reveling in the refreshing sensation that washed away the signs of battle from her face. Moonlight danced on the rippling water, casting a silver glow on her sleek, obsidian form.

As Variel lingered by the stream, her lupine senses attuned to her surroundings, an unsettling realization began to form. The usual magical aura she had come to expect—the presence of mythical creatures, portals, even the faint echoes of sprites—was conspicuously absent. Her large ears twitched as she strained to catch the distant whispers of magical wings, but the night remained still, devoid of any enchantment.

Confusion furrowed her brow, and unease settled in her stomach as the realization she had been trying to deny pressed upon her: this was not a magical continent. Though there were other realms in the magical world of Ekotoria—many of which Variel had never visited—this place was not magical at all. Wherever the portal had dropped them, they had been left to fend for themselves in the human realm. The weight of this revelation pounded through her like a second heartbeat. It was clear now that this land was silent because it lacked the magic that once sang. The thought that there might be no way for them to return home filled Variel with a sense of dread.

CHAPTER SIX

BREMUSA

Moonlight glittered off the Elder Sea as Bremusa, in her golden phoenix form, soared low over the remnants of the portal. She searched for any trace of it, but it was simply gone. The portal was missing, along with the magic that had once surrounded it. The ships that had raced toward the portal in a last-ditch effort during the final hour of the war were also lost; they either lay at the bottom of the icy blue waters or drifted somewhere in the realm, poised to cause chaos another day. However, Bremusa was not focused on those lost enemies at that moment. Her priority was to locate the missing portal and return it to its rightful home in Aegricia, restoring balance between the worlds. There was no telling how the absence of the portal could affect their realm, and Bremusa wasn't eager to find out.

Below her, the sea churned like a wounded beast, its dark waves swallowing every trace of what had once connected their realms. Though her feathers bristled in the wind and she inhaled deeply, seeking the pull of the magic, it was of no use. The portal, wherever it was, remained out of her reach.

Circling around a bottomless whirlpool, she summoned the power of the water deep within herself, forcing it out with a thunderous beat of her massive wings. At her command, the waters stilled, revealing remnants of a ship—broken planks and torn strips of a sail—rising to the surface. The wreckage bobbed like corpses in a graveyard of water, silent testimony to the futility of greed. The Warbotach, who had raced for the portal, were gone, swallowed by the very power they had bled so many to control.

Leaving the wreckage behind, Bremusa flew against the wind over the snow-covered peaks of the Aegrician mountains. For centuries, she had made this journey, gaining knowledge from the Shadow Glass—an enchanted mirror passed down from her mother, a powerful elemental even stronger than she. The Shadow Glass enhanced her ability to foresee what others could not and to provide prophecies that could shape their world. The last prophecy she had received spoke of Aurelia, Messalina's daughter, who was predicted to return to Aegricia, take the crown, and unite northern Ekotoria, bringing peace to their continent once more.

Just the thought of Messalina sent a sharp pain through Bremusa's chest. Her laughter still echoed in her memory, haunting Bremusa more deeply than any battlefield cry ever had. Messalina had been her best friend, Otera's sister, and Aurelia's mother. She had been chased out of her kingdom and slaughtered by the exiled queen, Joneira, who had stolen the throne during Messalina's grandmother's reign. It was Bremusa's prophecy that had sent Messalina into the human realm to find her mate, and not a day had gone by without Bremusa doubting her decision. Messalina had found her mate and given birth to two children, but she was murdered before her children reached adulthood. Messalina's life had ended tragically, just like that of her mother and grandmother, leaving Otera to rule alone from the throne while grieving for her entire family.

The entrance of the cave where the Shadow Glass lay hidden came into view as Bremusa dove past the tallest ridge. The magic protecting the entrance rippled as she landed just inside, shifting back into her fae form. The moment she took a step into the cavern, unease prickled her skin like a thousand tiny spiders, the air stinging with sour magic. It was the kind of wrongness that made the heart falter, as though even the stone remembered what had been stolen.

Slowing her steps, Bremusa slid her dagger out of its sheath at her thigh, the blade gleaming in the ethereal moonlight. The air in the cave was frigid, sending her breath into dancing plumes in front of her. She listened for footsteps, but the mountains were silent, aside from the distant taps of a waterfall that had thawed in the cold. Bremusa's instincts told her that no one was there. Still, when she peeled back the final ward and stepped into the interior chamber where the Shadow Glass was kept, she realized someone had been there, and they had taken something incredibly valuable.

The metal clattered against the stone floor as Bremusa's dagger slipped from her trembling hand, her breath catching at the sight of the empty cave wall. For as long as she could remember, a large mirror had leaned against the jagged stone surface. Its intricately carved frame was covered with vines that had somehow thrived in the darkness. They wove through every crack and crevice, as though the mirror's power gave them life in a place where the sun could not reach. Now, with the Shadow Glass ripped away, the vines hung broken and dying. The once palpable thrum of power that filled the air was gone, and silence enveloped the chamber like a tomb, stripping it of breath and leaving her adrift in a void where prophecy once flourished. Even Bremusa's mind, usually brimming with the knowledge the mirror wished to share, was now unbearably quiet.

Her heart echoed a slow, thunderous beat, rattling her bones and threatening to drop her to her knees. As her emotions warred within her, she felt uncertain about what to do first, where to look, or whom to tell. All she could do was step forward and trace the stone that had once been hidden by the mirror, its color bleached from years of protection. It felt cold, lifeless, and ordinary, unworthy of the greatness that had once stood before it.

Shaking her head, she backed away, scanning the empty chamber. She inhaled deeply, hoping to catch a hint of who had been there before her, but the intruder had covered their tracks well. There was no trace of their scent, only remnants of an unrecognizable magic, alongside the brine of the sea and the fragrant pine of the distant Spectre Forest.

Several moments passed as Bremusa stared at the vacant wall until a bat flitted by, breaking her trance and prompting her into action. She slid her dagger back into its sheath, crouched down, and pressed her hands to the ground, closing her eyes. She focused her mind on the energy around her—the particles in the air—willing her senses to reveal any trace left by the thief. A swirling vision formed in her mind.

Wood creaked, rocking and swaying in the churning sea as boots hurried overhead, creating a kind of cadence. The craft groaned, as though it might burst at any moment under nature's fury. Her mind cleared. Although the vision was brief, it imparted one essential piece of information: wherever the Shadow Glass was, it wouldn't be easy to find. The rhythm of the boots on the groaning deck lingered in her mind, a promise of storms yet to come.

With her stomach churning from the realization and acid burning in her throat, Bremusa stood up on shaky legs and glanced back at the spot where the enchanted artifact had once been, its absence a stark reminder of all they had to lose.

The return flight to the palace reminded Bremusa of the night she had sent Messalina Lumino away more than two decades earlier. That night, the Shadow Glass was still in its rightful place, but someone had broken into the cave, abused its power to uncover its secrets, and forced their way into the palace to kill the queen. Now, the stakes were just as high, even though the queen was asleep and relatively safe in her bed. With the Shadow Glass potentially in enemy hands, everyone was at risk.

As she circled around the highest peak and descended into the mountain pass, Bremusa landed just inside the terrace of her north-facing tower. She wasted no time leaving her rooms and made her way down several floors of stairs across the palace to the wing where she would find Aurelia and Cristos.

"You," she called, raising her hand to signal one of the guards standing at attention near the end of the corridor by Otera and Blaedia's rooms. The young male guard, Lukas, turned his head and nodded in acknowledgment. "Summon the former queen and the general to your new queen's rooms. It's urgent."

Her voice trembled under the weight of centuries, for she knew all too well that when prophecies went missing, entire realms could unravel.

Chapter Seven

Aurelia

A chaotic pounding at the door jolted Aurelia from a fitful sleep, the door swinging open before she had even rolled out of bed. Each blow echoed like thunder in her chest, pulling her from uneasy dreams into a waking storm. Beside her, Cristos jumped out of bed and grabbed his sword from against the wall. Muffled voices reached her ears just moments before Bremusa appeared around the corner, her dark hair a mess and her eyes wild.

"Your Majesties—I—" the guard who had been stationed at their door gasped, running up behind Bremusa, his face flushed, likely from arguing with the elemental before she burst in.

Cristos raised his hand. "It's okay, Pelius. If Otera or the others arrive, please let them through."

With a quick nod, the young guard turned and left the room.

Once he was gone, Aurelia and Cristos turned their attention back to Bremusa, who looked as if she hadn't blinked. "What's wrong, Bremusa? Did something happen?" Aurelia asked, pushing the blanket off as she swung her legs over the side of the bed.

"Otera," Bremusa replied.

"No," she added quickly, stepping forward to place her hand on Aurelia's forearm, halting her movements. "Otera is fine. I've summoned her and Blaedia."

As though their names had been called upon the wind, the former queen and the general entered the room, Otera still fastening the laces on her tunic. "What's happened?" she asked, concern etched on her face.

Every eye in the room turned to Bremusa, who clearly had something urgent to share. Aurelia's heartbeat slowed, but not to a calming rhythm; it was an uncertain pace, as if unsure whether it was safe to make a sound.

Bremusa glanced over her shoulder to ensure the door to the suite was closed before fixing her gaze on her new queen. "We face more than mere uncertainty. The Shadow Glass—our compass through chaos—has vanished."

The words hung heavily in the room, a thick silence spreading as if even the flames in the hearth dared not crackle.

After a pregnant pause, Otera finally spoke. "Missing?"

"Without it, the balance we fight for remains a dream caught in morning's light," Bremusa explained, her spine straightening with resolve. "If it falls into hands that crave not restoration but ruin, our kingdom will bleed shadows until none remember the sun."

Her voice was solemn, each syllable pressing on Aurelia's shoulders like unseen chains.

"Then we must find it," Otera declared, her words slicing through the tension. "For Aegricia, and for the realms that share its fate."

Bremusa's eyes went distant, as if she were seeing something beyond the present. "Through a veil of mist and time, the gateway beckons. It is not just a path, but a promise—to heal the fractures splintering our lands."

"But where, Bremusa? Where do we search?" Even with her royal poise, Otera's face grew flustered.

Instead of responding verbally, Bremusa reached out, placing her hand gently on Otera's cheek. Closing her eyes, Otera settled into the touch. Aurelia quickly realized what was happening: Bremusa was sharing a vision with her aunt.

The vision was brief, lasting only a minute. When it was over, Otera opened her blue eyes, confusion creasing her brow. "A ship? To where?"

"Inferno Territories?" Cristos interjected as he carried two chairs from near the table and placed them closer to the bed for the others to sit. Otera lowered herself into one chair, while Blaedia opted to stand by her side, resting a hand on her mate's shoulder.

Otera and Bremusa nodded in agreement. "There are only so many continents in the fae world that require a ship to reach... well, known continents, anyway," Bremusa clarified.

"I don't understand how anyone could have gotten past the wards protecting it. They should have been impenetrable," Otera remarked, pulling her long crimson hair over her shoulder to braid it.

Bremusa nodded. "They should have been. I reinforced them myself." It was clear to Aurelia that, although she didn't know Bremusa well, the elemental was flustered, almost speechless about the turn of events. "All I can conclude is that the destruction of the portal affected them in some way, allowing someone to slip past them in the chaos and manage to smuggle it out."

Though Aurelia had been thrust into the position of queen in the fae realm, she felt like a newborn, learning from those around her. She didn't know what questions to ask or what dangers could befall them, nor did she understand what powers the Shadow Glass held. This realization stung—how could she be queen when she still felt like a child, peering at the world through someone else's eyes? "I would like to see your vision," she said, breaking the silence.

Flashbacks of the vision still lingered in Aurelia's mind as she nibbled on her breakfast a short time later, still unsure of what they were searching for. For all they knew, the ship in the vision Bremusa had shared with her might have gone straight to the bottom of the Elder Sea when the portal exploded, rather than sailing west toward the Inferno Territories. There was even a chance that the Shadow Glass had made it onto a ship headed for Diapolis, prompting the unsettling thought that King Ailani might have betrayed them. However, no one wanted to entertain that possibility. Still, it was something Holera and Kason would have to explore.

With the sea now silent beneath Bremusa's powerful influence, Aurelia didn't believe the artifact had gone down with any of the doomed ships. Yet she wasn't prepared to completely rule it out. If she were honest with herself, the artifact could be anywhere. With their departure within the hour, they had no clear target to pursue, which was her greatest fear. The last thing she wanted was to fly aimlessly through the elements on an endless search for something that might never be found, but she understood the stakes. She was acutely aware of her responsibilities.

The thought turned her bread to ash in her mouth, and fear coiled tighter with every imagined betrayal.

"I've packed your bags, Your Majesty," Kassandra said, her lips curving into a smile. "I've included some ginger root and other herbs for your nausea, as well as vitamins to keep you and the baby healthy on your journey. I truly hope you will be back home soon."

Aurelia nodded, glancing over Kassandra's shoulder as Cristos walked back into the room. "I hope so, too, Kassandra. Thank you for being so thoughtful. I'm sure you've packed everything I'll need."

With a dip of her chin and a small smile at Cristos, Kassandra slipped out of their chambers, leaving them alone. Aurelia pushed her plate of eggs and toast away, offering the remnants to her husband, who leaned over to kiss her.

"Exie and Septima are already heading down to the courtyard, along with Bremusa and the healer," he said, lowering himself into the chair beside her and taking a bite of her food. "Otera is sending a raven to the coast ahead of us to prepare a ship for our voyage to the west. We could fly over the Irriboia Sea, but storms are common, and we don't want to be caught over water during a storm."

A shiver ran down Aurelia's spine, a reminder of the significant risks they were taking. "I wouldn't want to be caught in a storm on a ship either," she replied.

Reaching out, Cristos wrapped his hand around hers, lifting it to kiss her knuckles. "We will have scouts with us who will fly ahead to keep an eye on the weather. If something is ahead, we'll do our best to navigate around it. I won't let anything happen to you, your sister, or Exie, and I won't let anything happen to our child. This, I can promise you."

Aurelia knew he meant what he said, and she trusted Cristos with her life, but they'd been through so much in such a short time, so although she trusted him, it was fate she did not trust. She didn't say that aloud. Instead, she leaned forward, sliding her hand around to cup the back of his head, the silky strands of his black hair threading through her fingers. "Do you think anyone would miss us if we took a little longer to get downstairs? I mean... It'll be a while before we find time alone together again, right?"

The curl of Cristos' lips against hers sent a shiver through Aurelia's body for a whole different reason than fear, temporarily sending their obligations to the back of her mind.

Sliding his arm around her back and another beneath her knees, Cristos lifted her from the chair, carrying her across the room to their bed, his lips never leaving hers as he walked. They didn't have a lot of time, but he was unhurried in the way he unlaced her tunic and slipped it down her shoulders, kissing her across her collarbone.

"We'll always find time to be alone, my queen, no matter where we are."

Pulling away from his lips, Aurelia grinned as she scooted back on the bed, wiggling free of her trousers and kicking them onto the floor. He did the same. "Even when we're in the air, my king? Will we find a way to be alone even then?"

The mischievous glint in his bright blue eyes always set her blood on fire. With the last of his clothing dropping to the ground, leaving his gorgeous, muscled body on full display beside the bed, he climbed over her, settling between her thighs. He dragged his length against her center, where she was already drenched for him. "I'll perch in a tree with you somewhere if I have to, but I'll get you alone somehow."

Before Aurelia could say anything more about his plans to make love to her in a tree, he thrust himself inside her, forcing a gasping breath from her lungs. Her fingernails dug into his shoulders below his outstretched wings, grasping for purchase as he hooked her leg around his hip, pressing in deeper.

Sex between them had always been intense, a genuine bond between mates, but it had only grown more intense since they'd married, and even more so since she'd begun to transform to full-fae, since being mates had become part of her being as much as it was of his.

"You know I can't go too long without being inside you, my love," he whispered against her ear before kissing his way from her neck back to her lips, caressing her tongue with his. Inside her core, her climax built, the coil tightening with every roll of his hips against hers, his cock hitting that sensitive spot inside her that always drove her wild.

"I don't want to go without being with you either."

Their lips fused once more as his touch sent a ripple of heat down her spine. He knew how to make her feel alive in a way that no one else ever had. She loved Cristos with all her heart. They were a family, and they were continuing to build one together.

Cristos' hand skimmed along her back, kneading her skin in a way that made her shiver as his hips drove into her. He knew her body too well, knew how to wind her tight until every nerve strained for release, holding her on the brink until she was desperate for more.

When he finally gave it to her, Aurelia toppled over the edge with a cry against his mouth. The chamber, the world beyond their bed, ceased to exist—there was only the heat of his body, the thunder of his heart, and the relentless drive of his hips as he followed her into ecstasy. His kiss swallowed her moans, his muscles tightening as his own release surged through him, their pleasure crashing together until she was trembling beneath him.

With a final thrust, he let out a guttural groan, his release warming her insides as their breaths mingled between them. For a moment, all they could do was rest in bed together in each other's arms, hoping it was a moment they would be able to return to again soon.

The morning sun had just risen above the horizon when Aurelia and Cristos stepped out of Kano's enclosure and into the courtyard, leaving the relative safety of the palace behind. Aurelia gazed out over the Elder Sea, where the arched portal once stood—a haunting reminder of the father and brother she had just left behind. When she and Septima had agreed to give up their lives as humans and never look back, she had never thought of it as a decision that she couldn't one day reverse. She had never imagined that she would lose the possibility of returning to the human realm to see her family. But now...

Turning her head away from the sparkling water, Aurelia reached for Cristos' hand, interlacing her fingers with his as they walked toward Septima and the others, who were lingering near the barracks. She forced a smile when her sister glanced her way, despite the turmoil churning inside her.

With her sword strapped to her back, Septima stepped forward, her long ebony hair braided in her signature style, and pulled Aurelia into a hug. "How are you feeling this morning, Lia? Sick again?"

Aurelia shook her head, releasing Cristos' hand so he could continue toward the rest of their group and plot their course. There was so much to plan. "We were just trying to steal a few more moments alone before we can't for a while. None of us knows what we're heading into."

Septima's features softened as she rested her hand on Aurelia's forearm. "We'll find it, sissy. We have to. And when we do, we'll bring Amadeus—and maybe even Father—back to Ekotoria with us."

A snicker escaped Aurelia. "Could you imagine our father ever leaving Vaekros for any reason?"

Septima's smile faltered slightly as she pulled Aurelia closer, tucking her against her chest. "Maybe his priorities have changed since losing us."

There was no need to say that both of them hoped that was the case. They wished with all their hearts to reunite their family and get back the father they had once known before the loss of their mother had changed him and hardened his heart. But they both knew it was a fantasy. No matter how badly they wanted their father back, that man had died with the love of his life.

"Are you two ready?" Exie asked, moving to stand beside Septima, who reached forward to take the large pack from Exie's hands. Since Exie would have to shift into a phoenix, Septima would need to hook the bags onto the saddle. Several yards away, Cristos stood speaking to Kason and Holera, who were preparing to leave for their own mission to the southern part of the continent—back to Diapolis. Aurelia hoped that King Ailani had not betrayed them by taking the Shadow Glass; if he had, they would be walking into a trap. All they could do was have faith in Kason, Holera, and the shaky alliance with the isolationist king.

Forcing her eyes away from her husband, Aurelia turned back to look at Exie, who was still waiting for her answer, and nodded. "Do we know how long it will take to get to the coast?"

Exie glanced toward the west, as if she could see the other side of the continent beyond the tree canopy of the Spectre Forest. "If the weather holds, probably no longer than two days. If it doesn't... Let's just hope we can find a tavern along the coast with an inn."

The air grew thick with expectancy as they stepped out into the open courtyard of Flamecliff. A tapestry of faces lined the ramparts and courtyards, subjects and allies whose hopes clung to the bravery of those who dared to venture beyond the safety of stone walls.

"May the winds be a gentle caress at your backs," a veteran warrior called out, her voice carrying the weight of experience and unspoken fears.

"And the stars guide you through the darkest nights," a young acolyte added, her eyes bright with unshed tears.

A swell of emotion filled Aurelia's chest as she looked upon her people, their faces etched with a mix of admiration and anxiety. Their hope clung to her like a mantle—heavy yet fragile—and she knew that one misstep could shatter it. She raised a hand, not just in farewell, but as a silent vow that she would return, bringing with her the light of balance.

"Keep the hearths burning," she called back, her voice steady even as her heart raced against her ribs. "We shall return with the dawn."

The promise felt like iron on her tongue, a mix of vow and prayer.

Chapter Eight

Kason

Leaving Flamecliff toward Diapolis was a journey Kason and his mate had taken many times before, but this time felt different. The sky seemed wider than ever, yet each wingbeat carried the weight of suspicion and the unsettling thought of betrayal. They were uncertain about what awaited them. While they believed King Ailani had been their ally in the war against Joneira and Warbotach, they questioned whether he might use this opportunity to seize the Shadow Glass and betray them. The possibility that he was leading his mate into a trap tightened Kason's chest as he climbed onto her magnificent phoenix form. They launched into the air from the courtyard of the Aegrician palace. Every instinct urged him to turn back, yet duty bound him as if he were in chains. He was aware that they had obligations to their kingdom, so despite the risks, they had no choice but to fly south.

Settling on Holera's back, Kason rubbed her silky silver feathers, a gesture he always made when riding her. He watched the sparkling water below them. Even after so many years together, he would have preferred for her to ride on his back, but since she was the only one capable of becoming a phoenix, the only time she rode him was in their private moments. Just the thought of it sent blood rushing to his cock, making him wish they could stop and camp for a few hours, just so she could indulge him.

"We can camp in the same place we stopped last time, my fierce warrior—if you would like," Holera said, lifting her head and opening her beak, her chest rumbling with agreement. Chuckling, he shifted his weight, ensuring their bags and weapons were secure on the saddle before massaging her neck again. It was a long flight, but that didn't mean he couldn't make it enjoyable for her by talking and touching her. Touching her was his favorite thing in the world, whether she had beautiful skin or silky feathers. As long as it was her, he would shower her with affection no matter the form she took.

Storm clouds gathered over the sea in the distance as the sun began its descent toward the horizon. However, it held off just long enough for Kason and Holera to reach the edge of Spectre Forest. Each flash of distant lightning seemed to serve as a warning from the gods that no journey could remain unchallenged.

Finding a clearing safe enough to set up camp, Holera landed, and Kason quickly dismounted, grabbing their supplies so she could shift back into her fae form. They barely had time to establish wards around their campsite, create a fire, and set up their tent before the rain began to fall. A canopy stretched from the front of their tent to a small grouping of trees a few feet away, allowing them to stay dry while they sat by the fire and ate a simple dinner of meat and fruit.

"After this trip south," Holera began, leaning her head on Kason's shoulder as he wrapped his arm around her smaller frame and pulled her closer, "I hope we can return to our cottage and maybe visit my mother."

Kason nodded, kissing the top of her head. "I would like that, as would she." He exhaled slowly, hesitating to choose his next words. He wondered if it was the wrong moment to speak, but he dared to express his thoughts anyway. "Maybe we can stay home for a while... start a family."

The words felt fragile in his mouth, like spun glass— a dream so delicate it might shatter under the weight of war. Silence stretched between them, the hooting of an owl in the distance making Kason think that perhaps mentioning children had been a mistake. Just as his mind began to chastise him for pressuring her, Holera lifted her face, her violet eyes meeting his. What he saw within them told him she was not opposed to the idea at all. "You would be an amazing father."

Unable to contain himself, Kason leaned over and kissed her. "And you would make a fierce, stunning, wonderful mother." He raised an eyebrow, sliding his hand up Holera's thigh, skimming over the heated fabric between her legs, and resting on the lower part of her flat stomach. "And just the thought of seeing you pregnant with my child has me ready to burst through my trousers. So how about we go to bed?"

Although fatigue weighed down Holera's features, the corners of her lips curled into a grin. "I suppose we should practice for when that time comes."

Chuckling, Kason stood and reached down to help her to her feet. "We can practice as often as you would like to, my mate."

With the pot of water they'd heated over the fire in hand, Kason followed his sleepy mate into their tent, sealing the entrance behind them.

"Would you like a bath, my flame? We don't have a tub, but we've got hot water and my hands. There's probably a little soap in my satchel."

A cascade of Holera's silky platinum hair slid over her shoulder as she turned her head to look at him, the side of her mouth tipping up as her trousers dropped to the floor, pooling at her feet.

"Are you offering to bathe me, my love?" Twisting around to face him, her slender fingers threaded into the laces of her tunic, Kason's eyes tracking the movement as she pulled them loose achingly slowly. Even after decades together, she was the most exquisite creature he'd ever seen. The years had not dulled her fire, though the exhaustion etched into her eyes reminded him how fiercely she had carried their people through endless battles. He craved her on a carnal level that only mates could understand. It was a hunger that could never be sated, and he didn't want it to. Every second he got to spend with her made him the happiest male in the world.

Kason nodded, dragging his tongue across his lips. "It would be my pleasure."

Holera took a step forward, her tunic slipping down her shoulders, her pink nipples pebbled against the chill.

"You can't bathe me if you're just going to stand there with the pot of water in your hands, my love."

His cock throbbing painfully against his zipper, Kason set the pot down beside their bedding and then reached for her, wrapping his lips around her nipple.

Holera's back arched as he sucked on the tender flesh, her fingers threading into his long hair and pulling out the cord tying it back. The bucket of water beside his feet was forgotten as he wrapped his arm beneath her legs and scooped her up, carrying her to the bedroll. "I don't mind it if you're a little bit dirty, my warrior."

"This I kn—ow—" Words turning into a moan, Holera's head fell back as Kason's hand trailed up her thigh, leaving a trickle of warm water across her skin. His hands caressed her leg from her hip to her toes, caressing her skin with just enough warm water to soothe and clean her.

The fire outside their tent still flickered, illuminating the side of her stunning face as her mouth fell open, a gasp escaping on a breath when his tongue slid between her folds to taste her. "You taste delicious to me, my mate."

Everything about her was perfection. No matter where they were—what they'd gone through together—his fierce warrior was perfection. How her body welcomed him inside, warm and wet, how her sharp nails scraped along his back until he growled her name against her lips. There was no female in their world, or in any, who could have set his world on fire like she did.

When they fell asleep that night, with the crackle of the fire and the distant sounds of the forest to lull them to sleep, all Kason could think of was returning home to a peaceful kingdom with his mate, so he could take her back to their cottage and fill her with his child. In that vision of hearth and home, he saw not just survival, but the promise of a future worth every wound he carried.

AURELIA

The first leg of their trip toward the western coast of Ekotoria had been relatively uneventful, giving Aurelia and Cristos plenty of time to talk as he held her against his chest—the same way he'd held her whenever they traveled together. Exie and Septima flew alongside them, Exie in her phoenix form and Septima astride her back. There were several other people in their party, including Bremusa, who flew as a brilliant golden phoenix, competing with the rays of the sun at high noon. The space beneath Aurelia's shoulder blades tingled with the need to release her wings and fly, but having only just received them, she was not confident in her ability to fly safely. There was so much she needed to learn about the changes to her body first. Plus, she loved being in her mate's arms—strong and incredibly warm—as he spoke just inside her ear. "You've gone quiet, my wife. What's going on in that pretty head of yours?"

Cristos nuzzled into her neck, his lips pressing against her skin as his powerful wings flew them over Spectre Forest. Shivers raced down Aurelia's spine, her body coming alive under his affections even as her mind had indeed drifted. "I was just thinking about my mother... How frightening it must have been to be pregnant while knowing people wanted to kill her, knowing they wanted to kill *me*."

As though he wasn't holding her tightly enough, Cristos pulled her closer, his muscles tightening. "Is that when your parents moved to the city—in hopes that being within the kingdom's walls would keep her protected?"

Aurelia nodded. "My parents moved back to the mainland of Vaekros when my mother was pregnant with Amadeus, although I know she preferred to remain in Breqan. We were never told about my mother's fae heritage, so I never knew about her thoughts or fears growing up, but looking back..."

For a moment, she fell silent, pain making the backs of her eyes burn. In her periphery, she glanced at her sister, Septima's long braids whipping in the wind as she leaned over and held onto the reins of Exie's saddle. As though she could feel her sister's stare, Septima turned her deep brown eyes to Aurelia's, a question in them. Her lips mouthed the words: "Are you okay?"

Even though Aurelia knew her eyes were glassy, she nodded and smiled. When they stopped for the night, they could talk, and judging by the position of the sun, it wouldn't be long before they did so.

"You never knew your lives were in danger?"

So caught up in her own head, Cristos' question caught Aurelia by surprise. She shook her head, leaning into his warmth. The lower the sun sunk toward the horizon, the cooler the temperature became. "I never knew any of it. As far as I knew, we were ordinary humans. The most danger we were ever in was the risk of war when our kingdom became too power-hungry. When my mother got sick... When they told us—"

Her throat constricted with the words, knowing they had always been a lie but remembering how it felt to be so young and know her mother was dying on the other side of the wooden door and to be not allowed to go inside and save her, to be unable to turn the knob and tell her mother goodbye and that she loved her. No matter how much time had passed, the pain of losing her mother never eased. She only wished she had a painting of her mother's face, but Otera looked so much like her. Even her own face, her red hair and blue eyes were her mother's, but it wasn't the same. There had been something so special about Messalina Lumino, the kindness in her heart and the beauty in her smile, that could never be replaced.

Shaking her head, she tried to force the vision from her mind. "Even when they told us my mother was sick, they kept us away. We weren't allowed to go near her at risk of catching her illness—weren't allowed to say goodbye. Now I know it was because she wasn't sick at all. It was all a lie."

As the sun set below the horizon and stars lit up the moonless sky, Aurelia and the rest of their group descended into Spectre Forest to find a place to camp for the night. After such a long day, Aurelia would have loved to spend the night in a tavern where she could sleep on a real mattress, but there were no cities in the center of the continent, so it wasn't an option. When they reached the coast, she hoped that would change.

Setting down in a clearing near a small stream, Bremusa immediately began erecting wards around their perimeter to protect them from any passersby, while a few of the others gathered wood for a fire. As Exie and Cristos erected tents, Aurelia joined her sister near the stream, filling pots with water to cook a stew with the dried meats and vegetables they'd packed for their journey. Everyone had a part to play, a role to keep things running smoothly and safely. As queen, some would have expected Aurelia to retire to her tent and prop her feet up, especially with her being pregnant, but that wasn't who she was, and she had no intention of hiding away while everyone else did the work. So, while she couldn't do the most labor-intensive jobs at their camp, she could cook, so that was what she chose to do.

"What was wrong earlier?" Septima asked, hanging the pot over the already blazing fire, her expression not hiding her concern. "It was clear across your face, even though I know you tried to hide it behind a smile."

With the last of the meat sinking into the stew broth, Aurelia fell back on her heels, warming her hands by the fire.

"Do you ever think we're just chasing ghosts?"

For the next several minutes, as they watched the food boil over an open flame, Septima and Aurelia shared their thoughts about the mission they were on. They'd left the capital so quickly—the embers from battle barely turned into ash in the wind—so there had barely been time to discuss the journey they were going on and what they would do if they found nothing. The last thing Aurelia wanted was to be a pessimist, but she was queen of a kingdom that she'd only just laid her eyes on, and was expected to somehow merge the northern half of the continent based on a prophecy spoken before she had even been born.

With the king of Norithae already her husband, part of her work was already done for her, but they had cities to rebuild and people to rally. Although Cristos had been raised in the monarchy, neither of them had ever ruled before. They had so much to do and so much to lead Luckily they had one valuable resource willing to be there for them every step of the way: *Otera*. The list of what they had to do continued to get longer with every day that passed, but with Otera as their mentor, Aurelia only hoped they didn't let their people down.

While the small group ate around the fire, they discussed the next leg of their journey, which would take them to the western coast of Ekotoria—a place Aurelia had yet to see. If it were for any other reason, she would have been excited to explore her world. Still, it sounded, at least from the plans their group was making, as though they would be exploring parts of their world that even Cristos had yet to see. The idea was exciting, but they didn't know what they might encounter, and that made it scary as well.

Chapter Ten

Taryn

A crimson sun crept over the jagged mountains, casting a warm glow on Taryn's face as she lay in bed. She blinked away the sleepiness and stretched, her heart heavy with the loss of her mate and the guilt of finding solace in Lars' embrace. She knew she couldn't wallow in self-pity forever; there was work to be done.

Blowing out a breath, she swung her legs out of bed and quickly dressed in a tunic and trousers. As soon as she stepped out of her tent and strode through the camp, joining the throng of workers, she caught sight of Otera and Blaedia standing amidst the chaos. The former queen and her mate were surveying the damage and directing the rebuilding efforts after the devastation caused by not only the war, but also by the portal's destruction.

"Good morning, Taryn," Otera said, her voice gentle as the morning breeze.

"Morning." Taryn attempted to smile, knowing it didn't meet her eyes. "What can I do to help?"

"Help us tend to the injured warriors," Blaedia suggested, gesturing to a makeshift infirmary nearby. "They need our strength now more than ever."

Nodding, Taryn followed them toward the rows of wounded males and females. As they worked together, cleaning wounds and applying healing poultices, Taryn couldn't help but feel a gnawing ache in the pit of her stomach. She looked around, taking in the pain etched on the faces of those who had survived while others perished. Her own life had been spared when she'd been brought back from the brink of death, but so many others hadn't been so fortunate.

"Otera," Taryn murmured, swallowing hard as she glanced at her friend. "How do you deal with it? The guilt, I mean."

"Ah." With a sigh, Otera paused her work to meet Taryn's gaze. "There's no easy answer, my friend. We all carry our burdens, but we must also remember that our lives have been given back to us for a reason."

"Exactly," Blaedia chimed in, her voice firm yet kind. "We are phoenix warriors, Taryn. We rise from the ashes of defeat and continue to fight for those who can't."

Taking a deep breath, Taryn allowed their words to wash over her like a soothing balm. Her survivor's guilt still weighed on her heart, and the loss of her mate made her heart feel torn in two and bleeding, but she knew to wallow in it would do no good. Instead, she needed to channel her energy into helping rebuild Flamecliff and healing those who needed her.

"Thank you," she whispered, her eyes glistening with unshed tears. "I'll try my best to make every moment count."

"Always, Taryn." Otera smiled, placing a reassuring hand on her shoulder. "Together, we will rise again."

The night descended upon Flamcliff like a velvet shroud, draping the realm in hues of deep purples and somber blues. Taryn's heart, a tempest of sorrow and remorse, sought shelter from its relentless squall. The day's labor had dulled the edge of her anguish, but now, as the night sky whispered secrets to the stars, her soul yearned for solace that stone and mortar could not provide.

The water of the Elder Sea sparkled beneath the moon and stars as Taryn's phoenix form perched high on the Aegrician cliffs, watching schools of fish swim happily below the surface, not realizing a predator was in their midst. To their luck, she wasn't hungry. She hadn't eaten in days, but still she had no appetite. Blaedia would say she was torturing herself, punishing herself for what happened to her mate, but it didn't matter.

While she'd been taking another male to her tent on the night before they went into battle, her mate had been struck down in a rebel movement in the city streets outside the palace. While she was with another male, the male she was supposed to be with for the rest of her life was taking his last breath, and she hated herself for it. So, if she was punishing herself by not eating, then just as well. She deserved it, at least in her own mind. The destruction of the portal had brought her back from the ashes—it had forced life back into her when so many others had not been so lucky. Out of all the people who'd died in that war, she did not feel deserving of a second life.

Letting out a call of mourning that echoed over the silent sea like the souls drifting on the phantom breeze that ruffled her feathers, she launched herself off the cliff, soaring over the sea and toward the Norithaean camp they'd set up just outside the city, using the talisman around her neck to allow her to pass through their wards. Once she was inside the camp that was so much like their own, she didn't mingle, instead heading straight for the row of tents against the back side of the camp, slipping in through the tent flap.

"Taryn," Lars murmured, rising from his makeshift bed to embrace her, his muscular arms enfolding her like a protective cocoon, shielding her from the harsh realities outside. "I've been really worried about you."

Ever since the night they'd spent together in the mountain valley in her tent, she'd been using him as a distraction, or at least that was what she'd been telling herself. The truth was, Lars was incredibly handsome, with long, chestnut hair, golden eyes, and majestic leathery wings, and she was spiraling more into self-loathing every day. She found herself once more within the canvas confines of Lars' tent, trembling hands reaching for the male whose very touch ignited a firestorm of forbidden pleasure. She wanted to feel something—anything—aside from that guilt and pain. Lars never failed to make her feel.

"Have you?" Suppressed emotion made her voice tremble and she buried her face in the crook of his neck, inhaling his scent—earth and fire, mingling with the faintest hint of sea spray.

"Of course," he replied, his breath warm against her ear. When he pulled back a little, his golden eyes searched her face as if attempting to read her thoughts. "You've been carrying so much weight on your shoulders lately."

She nodded, unable to deny the truth in his words as she unbuttoned her cloak, hanging it on an empty chair. "It's too quiet everywhere but inside my head. I can't stop thinking about what we all lost—about those who deserved so much better."

Tucking a lock of her dark hair behind her ear, Lars dipped his chin, understanding without needing more explanation from her. He hadn't yet found his mate, and she didn't feel deserving of ever having one, so they found something in each other. Cassius had only been dead for a few days, but she'd spent every night since in Lars' bed—every night since she'd come back from across the veil, or wherever she'd gone when she'd taken a sword to her heart.

Threading his fingers into her hair, he tipped her head back, forcing her to look at him. He knew she didn't want to meet his eyes, but he wasn't giving her the option. "Let me help you forget, even if it's just for a little while?"

Everything inside of her said no, torn between her loyalty to her lost mate and her need for physical connection. But in the end, her desire for an escape won out, so she nodded, rising on the tips of her toes and pressing her lips to his. Lars was slow to respond, sending her already broken heart plummeting into her stomach, but as though he could sense it, he wrapped his arms around her, deepening the kiss.

Taryn met his tongue stroke for stroke, needing to forget the loss she'd suffered and how the dark pit inside of her seemed to grow and fester with each breath. Slipping her hands between their bodies, she reached for the clasp on his trousers, never leaving their kiss as she released his hardness from its confines. To her relief, he didn't stop her, and he wasn't gentle with her. Instead, he unbuckled her trousers, shoving them down her thighs while his mouth kissed and sucked hers, the touch desperate.

"Turn around," he said, his deep voice raspy with lust. "Hold on to the table. I want to see your pretty cunt in the air."

She didn't hesitate to obey, to turn around and brace herself against the table as his powerful thrusts forced so much pleasure into her body that the hurt had no choice but to hide away in the shadows for a while. A fierce blaze consumed them, their bodies entwined in desperate abandon. As she pulled in shaky breaths, Taryn held onto the table with Lars' muscular form draped over her, his seed trailing down her thigh. For a moment, she tried not to think, allowing her eyes to close and the afterglow of her orgasm to flow through her body, to bring in the light, but there were some places it couldn't go.

"Thank you." Although she hadn't intended the words, and wasn't sure what she'd meant by them, they'd found their way through her lips, and she hadn't missed the way Lars' body flinched.

"Thank me, for what?" Straightening, he backed up a few steps, grabbing a rag to wipe them clean. The absence of him inside of her was agony, and all she wanted, at that moment, was for him to slide back inside her, but the confusion on his face told her the moment had shifted. "This isn't a business transaction, Taryn, and I'm not doing it just to do you a favor. You don't have to thank me."

His response to her gratitude was jarring, raising an alarm inside her chest. "I wasn't trying to upset you, Lars. It's just that..." Guilt and grief, heavy and throbbing, took root in her chest, forcing the air from her lungs.

Reaching for her tunic, she pulled it over her head quickly before tugging her trousers up her legs, barely turning to look at him as she headed toward the tent flap. Before she stepped out into the chilly night air, with her hand wrapped around the tent flap, she spoke without looking back. "I'm just really sorry, Lars. I'm sorry for all of it. I'm sorry for using you so I wouldn't have to dwell in my grief—so I wouldn't have to accept my role in everything my people have lost. I'm just...sorry."

Clad in nothing but regret, Taryn slipped from Lars' tent, the cool air caressing her skin as she shifted into her phoenix form, her fiery wings like banners of defiance against the starry sky. Her heart still raced with the echoes of their passionate encounter, but she needed to clear her mind, to find some semblance of balance amidst the turmoil that threatened to engulf her.

As she soared above Flamecliff, the sea stretched out below her like a vast, unending expanse of midnight silk. Her keen senses picked up on a strange undercurrent—a deep, unsettling rumbling that seemed to resonate from the very heart of the sea itself.

Suddenly, the ground beneath her shook violently, as if the world itself was convulsing in pain. The powerful earthquake sent shockwaves through the land, causing buildings to tremble and people to cry out in fear and confusion.

Landing back near the palace, Taryn watched from the parapet as the sea roiled and churned before her eyes, transforming into a monstrous wave that seemed to defy nature itself. It towered over the harbor of Flamecliff, casting a massive shadow that stretched far across the land. In an instant, the tidal wave crashed down with an earth-shattering roar, obliterating everything in its path.

CHAPTER ELEVEN

AURELIA

As Aurelia slept beside Cristos in their tent in Spectre Forest, time's relentless march slowed, momentarily retracing its steps under the influence of a memory. It broke through her dreams, which were little more than fantasies. Much like the forest surrounding her, she found herself in the lush embrace of another place—the Howling Forest. The dream unfolded with a clarity so sharp it stung, as if memory itself had been lying in wait. Sunlight played hide and seek among the leaves, dappling the forest floor with patches of warmth. In this dream, the air whispered secrets that only the trees could understand, and the only struggle was between one's imperfections and the pursuit of mastery.

"Focus, little bird," said the mellifluous voice of her mother, its tone resonating with an ancient wisdom that filled Aurelia with boundless respect and affection. "Let your breath guide the arrow—let your spirit calm the storm within you."

Her mother's presence was a soothing balm, her guidance the compass by which Aurelia navigated her young life. With wide eyes, filled with the innocence of youth and the determination to make her mother proud, she drew the bowstring with hesitant strength.

"See how the bow becomes an extension of your being," Messalina continued, gently correcting Aurelia's stance. "You are not separate from it, nor is it from you. Together, you create harmony in tension, potential waiting to be released."

"Like the wind cradles the hawk aloft?" Even at her young age, the metaphor flowed from her lips with newfound understanding.

With a brilliant smile that radiated pure love, Messalina nodded. "That's right, my sweet. Now, release." Messalina's words glowed in Aurelia's chest, imprinting a lesson that would endure even beyond her mother's breath.

Aurelia's eyes snapped open as the earth subtly shuddered beneath her, a sinister whisper against the forest floor underneath their tent. Her heart quickened, an erratic drumbeat echoing the unease that slithered through her veins. It felt as if the land itself breathed uneasily beneath them, restless in its grief. Beside her, Cristos shot up on the bedroll, reaching for her to ensure she was okay.

Without taking a moment to process the disruption in their slumber, they dressed quickly. By the time they stepped outside the tent, they found the others already gathered, their faces etched with concern in the dawn's half-light filtering through the tree canopy. In the center stood Bremusa, her silver eyes cradling the secrets of the cosmos within their depths.

"The very sinews of Ekotoria tremble with longing for what has been stolen from its grasp—the portal. Its absence is a gaping wound in the fabric of our realm," she declared.

Nausea twisted in Aurelia's stomach at the elemental's words, sending bile rising in her throat. "Could it be creating such a drastic effect on the land already?" she asked.

Bremusa nodded, gazing up at the sky while her obsidian hair slid over her shoulder. "Time weaves an intricate and obscure tapestry. Yet, each thread quivers with purpose. These circumstances are unprecedented, but if my senses are correct, the balance of our continent teeters on the edge of ruin without the portal's power to anchor it."

Her words fell like stones into Aurelia's gut, each one a reminder that destiny has no patience for the unprepared.

With the earth trembling beneath them, the small band of warriors, including Aurelia, sprang into action. Tents were dismantled, and bedrolls were tightly bound, every item of their hasty encampment quickly swallowed by packs as if it had never existed.

As they returned to the clearing with their supplies packed, Aurelia secured her bow and quiver to her shoulder and took her husband's hand.

"Ready, my love?" he asked, unfurling his mighty wings, a dark canvas against the lightening sky.

The tremors had stopped. There had only been one, but Aurelia still scanned the forest, wondering how far the epicenter had been and hoping it wasn't in Aegricia.

As the rest of their group began to launch into the air, heading toward the coast, Aurelia allowed herself to be lifted into Cristos' embrace. Beside them, Septima stood next to Exie as her mate shifted—Exie's golden hair catching the newborn sun's rays, igniting like the flames from which they were born. With a cry that split the dawn's stillness, Exie leaped skyward, her colorful wings lifting them above the forest in moments.

Once Septima and Exie disappeared from view, Cristos' wings made a powerful downbeat, and they ascended, soaring above the treetops, leaving only the ghost of their presence lingering in the air.

The western coast of Ekotoria unveiled itself like a forgotten verse from an ancient tome, its rugged cliffs and sapphire waters taking Aurelia's breath away. Yet, the beauty could not soften the edge of her unease; even the waves seemed to whisper warnings in their endless rhythm. They had been flying for most of the day, and while the flight had been quiet, peaceful even, they were all exhausted when the sea came into view. Aurelia's gaze swept across the quaint hamlet as they descended, the brine of the sea infiltrating her senses and reminding her of home.

"Looks like a good place to lay low for the night," Cristos murmured into Aurelia's ear, the warmth of his breath sending shivers down her spine.

Leaning into his muscular frame, Aurelia nodded. "It'll be nice to get a bath and sleep in a real bed."

Cristos chuckled, angling his wings to land. "That it will, and maybe there will be whispers of what we're searching for—something that can lead us in the right direction."

Aurelia shrugged and glanced at her sister, who was already unsheathing her sword. She surveyed the haphazard collection of wooden buildings that made up the town. It looked humble enough, but in the land of the fae, appearances could be deceiving. "As long as they're friendly."

As soon as his boots touched the ground, Cristos set Aurelia down beside him but reached for her hand. "Stay close. We don't know what we'll find here."

The group wove through the narrow streets, taking in the sights and sounds of the bustling harbor town. Locals exchanged gossip as they tended to their chores or bartered over goods, seemingly unaware of the king and queen's presence among them, which was exactly how Aurelia wanted it. She pulled her hood over her head to draw less attention to herself. The locals may not have known her, but they certainly recognized her aunt, who looked very much like her.

"Over there." Exie pointed to a worn-looking tavern with a crooked sign that read "The Salty Serpent." "It may not be the finest establishment, but it should suffice for our needs."

Inside, the air was thick with the smell of ale and roasting meat. The patrons eyed the newcomers warily but didn't let their curiosity interrupt their conversations. Exie and Septima approached the barkeep, a grizzled man with a patch over one eye, and inquired about renting a room. Aurelia and Cristos stood off to the side, studying the room.

"Only got three left," he grunted, handing her three tarnished keys. "Upstairs, second door on the right. Payment will be due in the morning."

"Thank you," Septima replied, slipping a few coins onto the counter. "We'll be sure to settle our debt before we leave."

"See that you do," the barkeep said, eyeing the coins with an expression Aurelia couldn't quite place.

As her companions settled around a large table near the back of the room, Aurelia couldn't shake the nagging feeling that they were being watched. She glanced around the dimly lit tavern, trying to discern any signs of danger or deceit. Every shadow seemed to lean closer, and every whisper was laced with secrets meant to pierce.

"Keep your ears open," Cristos whispered across the table. "We need to learn what we can about this place, its people, and any information regarding the missing portal or the rebel groups operating nearby."

"Of course," Exie replied, reaching for a tankard of ale and taking a slow sip. "Let's see what we can overhear."

For the next few hours, while they ate their dinner—everyone but Aurelia enjoying a pint of ale—the group listened intently to the other patrons. Their eyes darted between various tables as they tried to glean helpful information from the snippets of conversation drifting through the air. But by the time Aurelia was yawning and the group was ready for bed, they were no wiser than when they had entered.

Aurelia's reflection shimmered in the moonlit window, her gaze drawn to the silver curve of the crescent moon against the distant horizon. Beside her, Cristos' muscular frame filled the doorway, his leathery wings folded tightly against his back as he stepped into their rented room at the tavern.

"Did you find anything?" she asked, her voice soft and tentative.

Closing the door behind him, he crossed the room toward her. "Nothing concrete, but we won't give up, my love. We will find the portal, I promise."

As he reached her side, Aurelia leaned into him, seeking solace in the warmth of his embrace. The weight of their quest bore down on her, but in Cristos' arms, she found a reprieve from her worries. She turned to face him, locking her eyes with his, filled with love and understanding.

"Thank you," she whispered, lifting her hands to cup his face. "It can be so overwhelming at times."

Leaning forward, he pressed a gentle kiss to her forehead. "Let me help shoulder that burden, my queen. Together, we can face anything."

With no more words to express her doubts, their lips met in a passionate embrace, hearts pounding in unison as they lost themselves in one another. In that moment, their connection transcended words, the depth of their love shining like a beacon in the darkness that surrounded them.

Wrapping his arms around her, Cristos lifted Aurelia and carried her to the bed, laying her down on the blankets and crawling on top of her.

"Remember," he breathed into her ear, his voice deep and husky, "we are bound by more than love. We are bound by fate, and destiny has chosen us to restore balance to Aegricia."

Lowering his lips to hers once more, Cristos kissed her thoroughly, slowly, and deeply. Their bodies entwined, every touch conveying the intensity of their love and desire for one another.

In the midst of their intimate moment, a sudden explosion shook the tavern's foundations, and the sound of screams and clashing weapons filled the air. Aurelia and Cristos sprang apart, their hearts pounding for an entirely different reason.

"An attack," Cristos growled, his eyes flashing with rage. "If the rebels recognized us, they'll try to assassinate us."

Pulling on her clothing without a second thought, Aurelia reached for her weapons, securing them in place. "Quickly, we must help the others."

The resounding clang of steel on steel echoed through the smoke-filled streets, its harsh staccato punctuated by cries of pain and fury from both friend and foe alike. Aurelia's heart pounded against her chest like a wild bird seeking escape, the heat of battle and her fierce love for her people fueling every move. She danced through the chaos, her bow singing death as it unleashed arrow after arrow into the bodies of the rebels in red robes—those who killed indiscriminately as they advanced down the streets.

"Stay together!" she shouted to her companions, her eyes scanning the scene. Cristos fought by her side, his sword flashing like lightning as he cut down anyone who dared approach them. The others had spread out, each engaging in their own skirmishes amidst the destruction.

"Quickly, to the harbor!" Bremusa urged, her silver eyes alight with the intensity of her elemental powers. "We must reach our ship before they overwhelm us!"

Aurelia nodded, and the group began to fight their way toward the harbor, their movements swift and purposeful. They encountered enemy after enemy; the rebels' crimson capes, like apparitions of blood, were everywhere they looked, but their determination never wavered. Septima and Exie moved in perfect harmony, their swords a blur of lethal precision. At the same time, Bremusa unleashed torrents of fire upon their foes.

"Almost there!" Aurelia called, her voice strained but hopeful as they neared the water's edge.

As the group approached the harbor, they were met with a horrifying sight: two of their warriors, Rockie and Nikoleta, lay sprawled upon the ground, bloodied and unconscious. Aurelia's heart clenched at the sight, but she knew they had no time to grieve or tend to their wounds. They needed to escape, and they needed to do it immediately.

"Help me with them!" Aurelia cried, her voice breaking as she struggled to lift Rockie's limp form. Cristos moved in to assist, his strong arms easily hoisting the warrior onto his shoulder, while Septima and Exie helped with Nikoleta.

"Leave us," a weak voice whispered, and Aurelia looked down in shock to see Rockie's eyes flutter open. "You must go. We will only slow you down."

Closing her eyes for only a moment, she shook her head. "Let's go!" she shouted, and the group made their final push to the ship, cutting down any adversaries that stood in their way. They scrambled aboard and set sail just as a fresh wave of enemies surged toward them. The wind caught their sails, carrying them away from the burning town of Shadewater and toward the uncertain future that awaited them in the Inferno Territories. Behind them, smoke clawed at the heavens, a dark hand reaching to drag them back, but the sea pulled them forward into fate's uncharted waters.

Chapter Twelve

Kason

Emerging from the shadows, Kason and Holera entered Embershell, the capital city of Diapolis, through the massive city gates. Disguising themselves as weary travelers, Kason's piercing green eyes swept over the bustling urban district, the hood of his cloak pulled over his head to hide the intricate tattoos snaking up his neck. He and his mate had been to Embershell before, so remaining undercover would not be easy. Beside him, Holera's silver hair had been dyed black, allowing her to better blend into the shadows.

"Keep close, love," Kason murmured, his voice a low rumble only Holera could discern amid the cacophony of haggling merchants and boisterous street performers. His hand, discreet beneath his cloak, found hers, his thumb tracing the archer's calluses born from a thousand released arrows.

"If we're going to manage to not draw attention to ourselves," she said, glancing up at him with a smirk. "You'll have to manage not to get into any bar fights."

Kason chuckled, lifting her hand to kiss her knuckles. They were a formidable team, both in love and in battle, taking on everything together. "I'll do my best."

As they strolled through the lively streets of Embershell, they came upon a tavern named The Dragon's Roost. Its facade was a tapestry of timeworn stones, its sign creaking gently in the sea breeze, depicting a dragon curled around a chalice with scales glistening under the flicker of torchlight. As they stood outside, one of the winged beasts flew overhead, its roar echoing through the night.

Sliding his arm around Holera's back, Kason pulled the door open, ushering her inside.

Inside the raucous establishment, the scent of spiced meat mingled with the tang of sea salt from the nearby docks. Kason led the way to a table nestled in the seclusion of a shadowy nook.

"Perfect for an evening of espionage," he said, the hint of a smile playing on his lips. Once Holera slid into the booth, he slid in beside her, wrapping his arm around her waist and lifting his hand to the server. They'd been traveling for two days, so he was more than ready to get his mate into bed and start fresh in the morning. After he ordered two ales and a room for the night, Kason leaned back against the wall, stretching his long legs out beneath the table. Holera pulled her bow and quiver from her back, leaning it against the table within arm's reach—a habit born from necessity. Her gaze flitted across the room, sharp and observant, missing nothing. Laughter erupted from a group of sailors across the room, their tales of monstrous sea creatures louder than the rest.

Their ale arrived shortly thereafter, served by a grizzled bartender with a face weathered by years of hard living. Kason took a long sip, relishing the bitter taste as it slid down his throat. Beside him, Holera tore into her meal as though she hadn't eaten all day. When Kason gave it some thought, he realized they hadn't eaten much that day since they'd spent so many hours on horseback.

"Is it tasty, my fierce warrior? Or are you preparing to eat for two?" Even as he chuckled, she shot him a scowl—one that was meant to appear vicious—but it only made her look sexier.

Sliding his hand up her toned thigh, he leaned over to whisper in her ear. "I bet it's not as tasty as you are."

With the piece of fish still in her mouth as she tried to chew, she rolled her hips against his hand beneath the table, seemingly unworried if someone was watching them.

With the number of patrons in the tavern, listening in to any one conversation was nearly impossible. Holera's gaze flitted across the room, taking in the patrons who were as varied as the many realms they hailed from—merchants, sailors, adventurers, all with stories etched on their faces. For the first hour, they listened to the conversations going on around them, hoping to catch any whispers of intrigue or betrayal. But the talk was of mundane matters—local gossip, tales of adventure, the boasts of prowess in battle. Sipping on ale and dining on grilled fish and vegetables, Holera and Kason listened to mindless chatter and the tunes of a half-drunken bard. Kason's frustration grew with each passing minute, his patience wearing thin as the night went on.

Their mission weighed heavily on Kason's mind, a shadow that lurked in the corners of his thoughts, waiting to be brought into the light. They were there to uncover the truth, to discover if the King of Diapolis had betrayed them, and if he'd stolen the legendary Shadow Glass while everyone else had been too distracted by the war to notice. As they sat at the table in the back of the tavern, Kason couldn't shake the feeling of unease that gnawed at him. The war had left scars on all the kingdoms involved, wounds that still festered beneath the surface, and it was well-known that King Alani was an isolationist. If the Shadow Glass had fallen into the wrong hands, it could tip the delicate balance of power on Ekotoria, plunging the realm into chaos once more.

When the hourglass of patience had all but drained, a young barmaid with a coquettish smile stopped by their table, refilling their ale. "Anything else I can get you two lovebirds?" she purred, her eyes lingering on Kason's tattooed bicep.

Holera's violet eyes narrowed playfully, her possessive hand resting on Kason's. "We're fine for now, thank you," she said, the steel in her voice unmistakable. The barmaid retreated, casting a pouting glance over her shoulder.

"Jealous?" Kason teased, draping an arm around her shoulders.

Leaning into his side, she nibbled his earlobe. "Not if I can help it, but if she comes back—"

With a chuckle, he slid his hand up to cradle the back of her head, pulling her into a kiss. For a moment, as his tongue slipped inside to taste the female who was his in every way, the world around them disappeared, but like a spark igniting tinder, the atmosphere shifted. Two merchants entered the tavern, their voices low and conspiratorial as they took a seat nearby. Kason leaned forward, his senses alert as he strained to catch their conversation.

"They say the caves off the coast are filled with treasures beyond imagining," one of the merchants said, his voice a low murmur that still made it to Kason's ears. "Objects of magic, they say, more precious than the golden statues of Lyrandar."

"Aye, but they're guarded by powerful wards," the other replied, his tone cautious. "Only those with the right connections can gain access."

Kason exchanged a glance with Holera, a silent understanding passing between them.

"They speak of high-valued objects," Holera murmured, her voice barely audible above the din of the tavern. "If the king is hiding the Shadow Glass, it could be hidden in those caves."

"Another shipment is due to arrive in three days' time," one of the merchants said as he took a deep sip of his drink. "If we can secure it, we'll be set for life."

The mention of a shipment sent Kason's heart into a quickened beat. Three days' time... If the shipment contained the Shadow Glass, they had a deadline, a window of opportunity to uncover the truth before it slipped through their fingers.

The flickering glow of candlelight danced upon the walls of their modest room above the tavern, casting gentle shadows that lent an air of intimacy to the space. Holera stood by the window, her hair cascading down her back like a silken waterfall as she gazed out at the moonlit landscape. Kason watched her for a moment, admiring the serene beauty she exuded even in moments of quiet contemplation.

"Let me run you a bath, love" he said as he stepped up behind her and kissed her neck, breaking the silence that had enveloped them. Holera turned her face up to smile at him, her violet eyes reflecting how tired she was after such a long two days of travel.

"That sounds lovely, thank you."

When Kason was finished filling the copper tub with steaming water, Holera slipped out of her clothing in the bedchamber, hardening him with more desire than should have been physically possible, but he pushed it back. After spending the night before in a tent, he knew how badly she wanted a bath, and taking care of her needs was always his priority.

Once the tub was full, he gestured for her to step into the bath, his strong arms steadying her as she lowered herself into the inviting embrace of the water. She sighed contentedly, a sleepy smile tipping up the sides of her lips.

"Lean back, so I can wash your hair." Giving him a grateful nod, Holera tilted her head back and closed her eyes as Kason's skilled hands began to work the fragrant soap through her temporarily black tresses. She was beautiful with any color of hair, but he couldn't wait to remove the darkness and bring the platinum of her natural hair back out.

"What do you think we'll find in those caves?" she asked, her voice barely audible above the trickle of water as he rinsed her hair with a mug of water. "What do you think of the merchants' tale? The magic they spoke of could be potent enough to turn tides."

"Who knows? Stories are like the sea—both hold secrets beneath their surfaces." Leaning forward, he lathered his hands with soap and smoothed them along her curves, needing to touch her more than he needed his next breath. "But one thing is certain, my fierce warrior: investigating this further, especially under the nose of the king, could pose great danger. We must be cautious. Although I know it's necessary, I don't like putting you into these perilous situations."

Holera hummed in agreement, her eyes opening to meet his gaze. "Promise me, Kason," she whispered, holding his hand on her stomach with her own. "Promise me that we'll make it back home after this. Settle down and live our lives for ourselves for a while."

The vulnerability in her eyes was something Holera rarely showed, not to anyone but him. His heart swelled with emotion, his hands cradling her face as he pressed a tender kiss to her lips. "I promise you this and so much more, my mate. I told you, I'm putting a child in you after this—if that's something you want as well."

She reached up, her hand clasping his on her cheek. "It's a future we can both dream about until we can make it come true."

As Holera emerged from the bath, her skin glistening like moonlight on waves, Kason prepared his own. He sank into the tub, muscles easing as the heat seeped into his bones. Holera, perched on a stool beside him, traced patterns in the condensation on the stone walls, her thoughts seemingly as fluid as the ripples she drew.

"Tomorrow we should blend in with the market crowds, listen to the gossip. If the caves hide treasures, someone's tongue will be loose enough to guide us," she mused, her gaze flitting to Kason's inked skin, where a massive phoenix coiled around his arm and onto his chest—an image he'd had made permanent on his skin the moment she'd accepted him as her mate. Holera was a stunning female, the most breathtaking in all of Ekotoria, but her phoenix form was absolutely majestic—a true work of art that could never be duplicated.

"Agreed," he affirmed, submerging deeper, letting the water rise to his shoulders. "But when night falls, we'll take to the cliffs."

Skin still flushed and slightly damp from the bath, Kason guided Holera to the bed with tender reverence, his hands tracing the contours of her shoulders before easing her down onto the soft expanse of the quilt. They were both tired, but he'd waited all day to touch her, and it had been a day too long.

Starting at her forehead, Kason's lips pressed a trail of fervent devotion on Holera's body, stopping at her lips as he dragged his cock against her center. Their kisses were deep, hungry, as if each moment might be their last. His hands explored every inch of her, memorizing the curves he knew so well, as if they had been carved into his very soul. As her fingers raked down his back, his mouth wandered down, lingering at the hollow of her throat where her pulse beat a rhythm akin to his own. When he reached the valley between her breasts and lavished attention to her nipples, she arched off the bed, a gasp leaving her lips. With her fingers threading into his hair, she rolled her hips, only encouraging his descent further.

Submitting to her unspoken demands, he kissed and licked his way down her stomach, drawing closer to the apex of her thighs, where her essence beckoned him like a siren song. With his hand on her knee, he spread her legs open for him, taking her in for a few slow heartbeats that only made his cock grow painfully harder. His tongue danced over her clitoris, a flicker one moment, a slow, sensual drag the next, that had her grinding against his face. The taste of her brought a rumble from his chest, stoking flames inside his core that he knew reflected what burned inside hers.

Slipping his finger inside her, he rubbed the sensitive spot on her inner wall, knowing exactly what it took to make his mate shatter into pieces. And shatter she did.

Climax hitting her like the waves crashing outside their window, Holera's body tensed around him, a moan leaving her lips as the taste coated his tongue. He kissed and licked her through her orgasm, savoring every drop of her arousal until she was limp on the bed—pliable and ready to take all of him.

"You are so beautiful," he said as he pulled her close to his chest, her legs wrapping around his waist as he flipped them over. "I could look at you like this all the days of my life and never desire another view."

Eyes glazed by lust, Holera guided her hand to his throbbing cock, positioning it at her entrance. Her touch was almost too much to bear, but he held on, his restraint hanging on by the thinnest of threads. "You're not so bad yourself."

They both groaned as she slid down onto him, the wet warmth of her body welcoming him like it was made for him, because it was. The scent of their arousal mingled with the sea air, crashing waves outside echoing the pounding of their hearts. Every kiss and breath they shared deepened the love between them, filling Kason's heart until it felt like it may burst.

With his hands gripping her perfect backside, Kason's thrusts became more urgent, more demanding, as he claimed her completely, every inch of him belonging to her and only her. He was lost in her, drowning in the perfection of her body, the way she felt wrapped around him like a second skin. Her nails clawed at his flesh, the sting of pain only spurring him on, heightening the pleasure beyond anything he'd ever known before her. Time didn't exist before her.

Their climaxes hit like a tempest, a maelstrom of sensation that ripped through them like a force of nature. Wave after wave of ecstasy crashed over them, the pleasure so intense it left them both gasping for breath, their bodies intertwined in a tangled mass of limbs and sheets.

As the tremors subsided and Holera lay there panting heavily on top of him, her heart hammering against his own, Kason couldn't help but marvel at the depth of his love for this female. She was his compass star, his guiding light in the darkest of times. And in that moment, he knew that as long as they were together, they could face any storm and emerge stronger for it.

Chapter Thirteen

Aurelia

The sun dipped low on the horizon, casting a brilliant spectrum of colors over the sapphire waters of the Irriboia Sea as the ship cut through the waves. The vessel groaned beneath them, its timbers creaking like old bones, as if the sea itself was listening for secrets carried on the wind. They had been aboard for less than a day, having just barely escaped the port town after being attacked by rebels.

In the candlelit quarters of the healer, Alteria, Rockie, and Nikoleta lay side by side on narrow cots—Rockie with a severe gash on her left arm, and Nikoleta with a broken collarbone and an arrow wound in her thigh. The scent of healing herbs filled the air, mingling with the salty sea breeze that filtered through the open porthole.

"Try to relax," murmured Alteria, her skilled hands weaving magical threads that danced around Rockie's wounded arm. Although fae healed quickly, magic in Ekotoria had become unpredictable since the portal's destruction, preventing many from using their powers as they once had. Each spark of Alteria's weaving flickered like a candle threatened by a draft, proof that even the most reliable powers had grown uncertain.

"Thank you," Rockie whispered through gritted teeth, sweat beading on her brow. Nikoleta, ever the stoic Aegrician warrior, simply nodded, her jaw clenched as Alteria rewrapped her shoulder.

From the shadowed corridor, Aurelia and Cristos entered through the narrow doorway. Cristos leaned against the frame while Aurelia stepped closer, concern etched on her face. "Is there anything we can do to help?"

"Your presence is already a comfort, my queen," Alteria replied with a hint of a smile. "They will recover soon enough. For now, they just need rest."

"Thank you for taking such good care of our friends," Cristos said, resting a hand on Aurelia's shoulder.

"Of course, my king. It is my duty and honor." With a respectful dip of her chin, Alteria turned back to her patients, lifting a glass of water to Rockie's lips.

With one last look at the injured warriors, Aurelia and Cristos made their way back above deck, where Bremusa, Septima, Exie, and Vasilis were waiting for them.

Back above deck, where the sky stretched vast and endless, Aurelia and her council gathered near the ship's railing, the setting sun casting a golden glow over the horizon. Surrounded by loyalty, Aurelia felt the weight of responsibility settle upon her like iron upon her skull. If only Otera, Blaedia, and Taryn had been there as well, but she trusted them to look after Aegricia while she was gone. She only hoped the earthquake they had felt in Spectre Forest hadn't originated from Flamecliff.

"Tell us about the Inferno Territories," Aurelia said, directing her question to Bremusa, the eldest member of their group. "What should we expect when we arrive?"

Bremusa gazed out at the horizon as if she could see the territories in the distance, the sunset reflecting in her silver eyes. "The Inferno Territories consist of many islands and three kingdoms on the main continent. However, we must tread carefully, distinguishing allies from those who would seek to harm us. Monarchs can be fickle, and many have powerful mages at their sides. The power of the portal pulls me in this direction, but that doesn't mean we aren't sailing into a trap."

Her words were as steady as the sea, yet an undertow of dread pulled Aurelia into cold depths.

Amidst the many pressing priorities on her mind, she couldn't ignore her worsening morning sickness, which had transformed into nearly all-day discomfort since boarding the Siren Song. Thankfully, Kassandra had packed herbs in her satchel, and she had already had to ask the ship's cook, Cisseus, to prepare tea multiple times.

"Do you think the Shadow Glass was used to divert the portal away from us?" Cristos asked, wrapping his arm around Aurelia to steady her as the ship rocked. "Is that even possible—that someone could have had the foresight to do that?"

Without hesitation, Bremusa nodded. "We would be foolish to think otherwise. If I can sense its power, others can as well. I do not know of any of my kind still existing in this world, but whispers on the wind hint that they are out there."

Raised in the human realm, Aurelia knew little about creatures like Bremusa—*elementals*—but the warning in Bremusa's tone made her skin crawl. There was so much she needed to learn about her new world and its inhabitants if she was to lead them successfully.

"Can you tell us more about the specific kingdoms?" she asked, leaning back against Cristos' chest. He wrapped his arm around her waist, his warmth soothing the anxious knot within her.

"We can consult the most recent map," Vasilis suggested, speaking up for the first time. Being from Norithae, he wasn't someone Aurelia knew well. Still, Cristos had grown up with him, making the winged male a valuable member of their group. "The map we have is from a recent diplomatic mission. It should be accurate, although it doesn't include all the smaller islands."

In the dim glow of oil lamps swaying with the gentle motion of the ship, Aurelia, Cristos, and the others huddled over the expansive map spread across the oaken table in their quarters. The Inferno Territories sprawled before them—a tapestry of potential alliances and lurking dangers, each kingdom a piece of the puzzle they needed to solve.

Bremusa leaned in, her silver eyes catching the lamplight as she traced the borders with a slender finger. "Here," she said, pointing to one of the larger outlines on the main continent. "Cineris, with its ash-veiled mountains, is probably as far north as we can go by land. King Damianos has supported our monarchy for centuries, but we must beware of the shadow creatures that haunt Cineris' mountain passes, along with the stories of powerful mages who control them. They can be dangerous—soul-sucking."

Aurelia pictured faceless wraiths clinging to the mountains, feeding on every fragile dream.

"Shadow creatures?" Septima repeated, stepping closer to Exie. Her deep brown gaze flickered to the dark corners of the room as if expecting ethereal foes to emerge from the shadows.

"More myth than menace," Vasilis interjected, his fingers dancing across the charted waters just beyond the territories, where serpentine lines marked treacherous currents. "Yet myths often bear truth, especially here, where the veil between worlds is thin."

"Thin enough for a portal, perhaps?" Cristos asked, gently squeezing Aurelia's shoulder.

"Indeed," Bremusa responded, her smile as enigmatic as ever. "But not necessarily the portal we're looking for. There are false portals—those that reflect our deepest desires and darkest fears—portals we would hope to never stumble into."

Just the thought of such a portal sent a shiver down Aurelia's spine and turned her stomach. "And this kingdom?" Aurelia asked, pointing to the northernmost tip of the continent, which was colored nearly all in black.

"The Scorched Realm," Bremusa said, her tone revealing far more than her words. "It's as fierce as its name suggests. Fire mages rule there, their power drawn from the volcanoes that scar the land. There is no monarch, but a sorceress—Zervia. I knew her once—long before I found my way to Aegricia and became the closest friend of your mother."

The comment took Aurelia by surprise, her heart flipping. "My mother?"

Bremusa nodded, her sharp features softening. "Messalina and I were the closest of friends before she fled Aegricia, and I became the advisor and confidant of her sister." She huffed out a laugh, her silver eyes growing distant. "She and I were like sisters—always getting into one thing or another—while Otera was forced by your great-grandmother to entertain the court. Both sisters hated it, but Messalina always found a way to escape her grandmother's near-constant parading."

The memory softened Bremusa's silver eyes, and Aurelia caught a glimpse not of the elemental but of the girl her mother had once laughed beside.

Even as a smile spread across her lips, longing filled Aurelia's heart. Bremusa's admission made her want to know her even more—not as an elemental, but as the keeper of her mother's memory. After so many years without her, Aurelia craved every scrap of Messalina she could find.

Stepping around the table, Septima moved closer to Aurelia and reached for her hand. "Our mother had a rebellious spirit."

Aurelia's old friend dipped her chin, a smile spreading across her lips. "Indeed, she did."

Pushing the memories aside, Aurelia cleared her throat. "What about the other kingdoms? Where will we first make land in the Inferno Territories?"

Vasilis leaned over the table and traced a line southward to where the sea met the shores, the land depicted in a brilliant shade of green. "We are likely to touch land at the Emerald Enclave in a few days. It's shrouded in perpetual mist and is said to be home to elusive nature spirits."

All eyes turned to Bremusa, who could be considered a nature spirit herself. "Queen Thesipha is a dryad—a forest nymph. If the portal has appeared on her lands, she will undoubtedly want to see it gone. The last thing she desires is war there. Bloodshed would tarnish her land and destroy everything she and her people cherish. We already know the lengths some would go to in order to control access to the human world. No matter where this portal manifests, it will draw conflict."

Aurelia's gaze drifted to the map's green expanse, wondering if the misty forests would welcome them or swallow them whole.

CHAPTER FOURTEEN

TARYN

The once bustling harbor of Flamecliff lay in ruins, its splendor snuffed out like a candle in a tempest. Taryn's heart thundered in her chest, a relentless drumbeat as she wove through the chaos with the grace of the mythical phoenix she harbored within. Broken statues lay shattered in the streets, scattered like discarded toys. The harbor, usually teeming with activity, now resembled a graveyard of splintered wood and twisted metal, the carcasses of mighty ships beached like so many whales. The sea's retreat had left scars in the earth itself, as though the waves had clawed away the city's soul before abandoning it. Her eyes, reflecting the fiery hues of the sun that had risen after the tsunami washed away the bloodstains of war, yet left destruction in its wake, scanned the wreckage, seeking signs of life amidst the desolation.

"Otera! Blaedia!" she called out, her voice slicing through the cries of the injured.

"Over here!" From the other side of the washed-out street, Otera's red hair appeared, Blaedia beside her with a young female in her arms. As Blaedia rushed past her, heading for the infirmary tent further down the street, Otera pulled Taryn into a hug.

"I'm so glad you're okay!" the former queen said, relief filling her voice. "We are so lucky this area wasn't busy when the water came in, but keep looking for anyone who may be hurt."

Taryn nodded, rubbing Otera's back before pulling away to look amongst the rubble.

"Taryn!" The desperate call pierced through the destruction, seizing Taryn's soul. Heart leaping in her throat, she spun around.

Through the haze emerged a winged figure, Lars' strides as frantic as a storm-chased sailor. In his eyes burned a desperation that mirrored her own, an unspoken prayer that neither had lost the other to water or ruin. Their eyes met across the distance, twin oceans of emotion crashing into one another. With every step he took, the weight of worry lifted from her shoulders until he was close enough for her to see the glistening tracks of tears on his worried face.

"Taryn!" he cried again, his voice ragged with relief, and she flew into his arms, the force of their embrace a testament to the affection that had blossomed between them in the shadow of loss. She sank into his arms as they encircled her, allowing him to pull her in.

"By all the stars, I thought I'd lost you," he whispered into her hair, his breath hot against her scalp. "When I felt the ground shake... saw the water rise..."

"Never that easy to get rid of me." She smiled, the lightheartedness of her words belying the tremor that shook her frame. But it was true—after everything that had happened in recent days, it seemed as though the veil wasn't ready to take her yet.

They pulled back just enough to look into each other's eyes, finding comfort when the world seemed intent on rending itself apart.

"Come," Taryn said, reaching out to take his hand. "We have work to do."

Her voice carried not just urgency but defiance, a vow that grief would not be the only thing to define her.

For the next several hours, Taryn and Lars joined those who were uninjured as they looked for survivors and helped those who needed it. Otera had been right when she'd said they were lucky with the timing. Since the war had only just ended, many of Aegricia's citizens were still outside the city in camps, leaving a tiny percentage of the populace in the area near the harbor. There were still many injured, but so many fewer than there could have been.

Once the injured had been tended to, Taryn and Lars went to the palace to help with meal preparation and distribution. As the sun set over the Elder Sea, draping the broken harbor in a blanket of darkness, they were both exhausted. For a moment, once everything had gone quiet, Taryn glanced down the street where she knew her home still stood, debating if she should attempt to spend the night there. But after only that moment, she decided against it, realizing she would probably never be able to return there again—not with the ghost of Cassius still there. Just the thought of his scent lingering on the sheets sent tears that burned the backs of her eyes. The memory of him clung like smoke, impossible to banish, choking even in the quiet. She turned away, blowing out a breath as she willed the emotion to return to the shadowed corners of her heart, where she could put up walls to keep them right where she wanted them.

"Are you okay?" Lars' smooth voice cut through the misery of her thoughts, pulling her attention. "Can I do something to help you, Taryn? If there's anything I can do, ju—"

Before he could finish, she wrapped her arms around his neck, pulling her lips to his in a desperate kiss. "If you want to make me feel better," she whispered against his lips, her voice trembling, "I need your cock inside me."

Lars' eyes widened, and he chuckled, mischief twisting his lips. Without another word, he scooped Taryn up into his arms, his massive bat wings unfurling behind him. They took off into the sky, leaving the city far behind as they soared over the sea.

With her legs wrapped around his waist, Taryn clung to Lars as they flew higher and faster, the cool wind whipping through her long hair. Even with the brine of the water beneath them, all she could smell was Lars' scent, woodsy and fresh, intoxicating. Threading her fingers into his long brown hair, she pulled his face to hers, tracing his lips with her tongue. "This is fun and all, but I asked for your cock to be inside me."

He grinned, the look purely wicked as he flipped her around in the air in front of him, pulling her until her back was against his chest, his massive wings sending them higher into the clouds.

"Then take off your trousers." The way his breath coasted against her neck as he gave the order sent warm wetness between her thighs.

Taking not even a moment to think, she unclasped her trousers as his arms held her in front of him. The air from his wingbeats fluttered against her naked flesh, only turning her on more. When her trousers were tucked safely into the satchel over her shoulder, she reached between them, finding his stiff cock already freed from his clothing, the tip dripping with precum as she gripped it.

"Are you ready for me to put that inside your pretty cunt?"

Taryn looked around, the sky dark aside from the crescent moon and a million stars, but she could tell they were very high up, which made her a little uneasy without her wings. She'd never been so high without her own phoenix form to keep her safe. "You—uh—want to do this here?"

Without saying a word, Lars lifted her slightly, wrapping his hands around her waist and thrusting into her from behind, all the way to the hilt. A moment later, they were soaring through the air as Lars held onto her hips, thrusting into her without restraint.

"Scream to the stars, Taryn. Tell them how good it feels to have me so deep inside you while your life is in my hands."

And when she did, her cry scattered into the night sky like sparks, as though the heavens themselves bore witness to their joining. The thrill of their lovemaking in the air was intoxicating, each thrust driving away the darkness that lingered in her heart.

"Harder," Taryn gasped, her body arching against his, urging him to take her with all he had.

"Are you sure?" Lars panted, clearly holding back.

"Please," she insisted, her nails digging into his muscular thighs as she sought release from the turmoil within her.

Lars obliged, his wings beating powerfully as he took them higher still, their bodies moving together in a passionate dance that defied gravity. When their climaxes hit, the world fell away as they screamed their orgasms to the stars and moon.

Something at that moment clicked into place that she'd thought had clicked for her a long time ago—something that only happened once in someone's lifetime: a mating bond. It was not chosen, not sought, yet it was rooted in her bones with a certainty that terrified her as much as it steadied her.

In the heart of the palace's grand hall, rays of sunlight filtered through the stained-glass windows, casting a kaleidoscope of colors upon Taryn's face as she studied the map spread out before her. Lars stood beside her, with Otera and Blaedia across the table. The weight of the decisions they had to make bore down on her like a dragon perched on her shoulders.

"Moving people inland is our best bet," Blaedia said, her fingers tracing the path southward from Flamecliff to Spectre Forest.

"Agreed," Otera replied, her voice decisive, like the queen she'd been for decades. "I cannot bear the thought of more suffering because we failed to act." For a moment, the former queen went silent, sadness darkening her features. "We've already lost so much."

Taryn dipped her chin, knowing precisely what had crossed the queen's mind when the shadows moved across her eyes. Not only had they lost people, but she and the former queen had also lost their lives. If the portal hadn't been destroyed, dispersing its magic across their world, they would both still be dead. "There is a large clearing not far from the Norithae camp in Spectre Forest. That would be a good location. It is a few miles away from the coast."

"Then it's settled," Otera said, tapping her finger on the map. "We will begin the relocation immediately. Gather volunteers, supplies—anything necessary to create a sanctuary for our people in Spectre Forest."

With their meeting over, Taryn and Lars wasted no time organizing the relocation efforts, utilizing those who were able-bodied to pack up horse-drawn carts with all the supplies they needed. She didn't know how long their people would need to stay away from the city—disrupting their daily lives—but their safety was of the utmost importance. Some would need to spend their days in the city to help with rebuilding and cleanup efforts, but those who were not required in the city, like the elderly and children, could remain in the camp until their capital was safe once again.

As night fell, the once-empty clearing boomed into a thriving camp, filled with the sounds of laughter and camaraderie. Taryn watched as children played among the tents, their imaginations transforming them into phoenixes soaring above the sea. In that moment, she allowed herself to hope that they were forging a brighter future for all. "We're making progress, but there's still so much to do."

"Take it one day at a time," Lars said, wrapping his arm around Taryn's waist and pulling her against his body. "Even the mightiest statues begin as mere lumps of clay. Just like the phoenixes they are, your people will rise from the ashes. We will rebuild, and we will be stronger for it."

"Thank you," she whispered, leaning into his touch, her mind still reeling from the undeniable sensation she'd experienced the night before—the mating bond that had fallen into place between them. They hadn't talked about it afterward, both too exhausted when they arrived back at the Norithae camp, but she had no doubt Lars had felt it too. Even though she knew fate controlled the bond shared by true mates, and that it wasn't a decision she'd made herself, it still filled her with more guilt for the male she'd only just lost—the male she'd spent so many years of her life with. Her heart mourned him, and probably would for the rest of her life, but everything else in her life was too confusing to grieve, at least for now. One day, when the world grew quiet, the loss of Cassius would hit her like a tsunami that had wreaked havoc on her beloved city, and when that time came, she would have no choice but to open the floodgates.

But for now, she clung to the fragile present, knowing storms could be postponed but never denied.

CHAPTER FIFTEEN

KASON

Sunlight filtered through the curtains, causing Holera's silver hair to shimmer as she lay draped across Kason's larger frame. The morning air was filled with the tantalizing scent of freshly baked bread and the distant hum of the market, gently pulling them from their slumber. Kason opened his eyes to find Holera gazing back at him, her expression filled with love and warmth.

"Good morning, my phoenix," he murmured, brushing a strand of hair from her face and kissing her forehead. "Are you ready for today's adventure?"

With a lazy stretch that made her silver waves ripple across the pillow, Holera let out a contented sigh. "Always."

As they climbed out of bed, they dressed for the day ahead in outfits that would help them blend in with the townsfolk. Kason chose a tunic that matched the sea's azure, while Holera opted for a simple dress that fluttered with each movement. Though she grumbled the entire time about wearing a dress, Kason couldn't take his eyes off her. The violet dress accentuated every one of her curves, and he looked forward to removing it from her body that night.

Leaving the tavern shortly after breakfast, they ventured into the bustling market, the vibrant colors and enticing scents enveloping them like a warm embrace. Hand-in-hand, they meandered through the stalls, eavesdropping on conversations between merchants and shoppers, hoping to glean further information on the coastal caves. The market's noise was a cloak and a curse—its chatter thick enough to conceal their presence, yet thin enough to hide whispers worth dying for.

For several hours, they wandered around the market, sampling the local delicacies and inhaling the scents of exotic spices and fresh fruits. Their keen ears picked up snippets of conversations, but most were about mundane things.

They sauntered down the pier, pretending to be a mated couple merely on a stroll. With the day's catch being unloaded and merchants preparing ships, there were many lingering near the harbor. Kason knew how much sailors loved to share tall tales, so he hoped they could overhear something of use near the water.

"Did these come from the caves?" one merchant asked another as they haggled over the price of a magical trinket. Waiting for the response, Kason and Holera stopped walking. Hoping not to appear like eavesdroppers, Kason wrapped his arms around his mate, pulling her into a kiss. She didn't resist, sliding her fingers into his hair as she slid her tongue into his mouth.

"Rumors, mostly," the other merchant replied, his voice skeptical. Unable to help himself, Kason kissed Holera deeper, the taste of her stiffening his cock in his trousers and making it difficult to pay attention. "But if they hold even a fraction of the treasures people claim, it would be worth the risk."

"Are you going to go and take care of your woman, or does someone else need to do it?" a gruff voice said from behind them. Kason's head snapped to the side, his arms pulling Holera even closer.

Behind them, one of the merchants was watching, his hand palming his cock through his trousers. The lewd gesture was as dangerous as a blade, for it tempted Kason to break their cover with blood.

Kason snarled, reaching for his blade, but Holera wrapped her hand around his, stopping him. With a sneer at the merchant, whose greasy hair hung in knotted clumps around his face, Holera slid her arm around Kason's back, pulling his attention back to her. "Let's go back to the room, killer, so instead of beating him down, you can take all that rage out on my cunt."

Stepping away from the pier, Holera led Kason back toward the tavern, his blood still boiling from the merchant's behavior. He wanted nothing more than to beat the male's face in, but his mate came first.

The moment they reached their room above the tavern, Kason lifted Holera, her legs wrapping around his waist as he pressed her against the wall.

"You should have let me hit him," he growled, unclasping his trousers.

Holera kissed him wildly, her words broken between kisses. "We can't afford to draw attention to ourselves."

Harder than it had ever been, Kason's cock sprang free. Not bothering to remove her undergarments, he hooked his finger into them, nudging them aside as he thrusted up into her.

A groan tore from them both when he drove in to the hilt, the warmth of her body consuming him like an inferno. "Your beauty already draws attention, my fierce warrior," he said, thrusting into her with a brutal cadence. "And your scent—gods, you smell delicious."

The obscene, wet sounds of their coupling echoed through the hall. Gripping her hips to angle her just the way he wanted, Kason surged into her with unrestrained passion. Every stroke was a promise of possession, a proclamation of love, and an oath of protection. Her nails dug into his back, her body pulsating in rhythm with his.

For a moment, Kason forgot about the vile merchant by the docks and about their mission altogether. It was just the two of them, as it always would be. But after he brought his mate to the clouds and they sank to the floor sweaty, boneless, and sated, their obligations were still waiting.

Clad in the darkness of night, Kason and Holera emerged from the back door of the inn, their black cloaks billowing like the sails of phantom ships setting a course for uncharted waters. Every shadow felt alive, stretching long fingers toward them as if to warn them back. The moon hung overhead, a silent sentinel casting its pale glow upon the towers of the palace that loomed in the distance.

"Ready?" Kason asked, his voice barely audible over the sounds of music and revelry still drifting from the tavern.

With a gleam in her dark eyes that reflected the stars, Holera nodded. "Always."

Taking to the back alleys, they walked hand-in-hand, their weapons hidden beneath their cloaks as they made their way toward the sea. Being a coastal city, Embershell was bordered by the sea on two sides, with only one road leading in and out. To avoid drawing attention, they headed for the cliffs.

Reaching the far end of the silent beach, Kason pulled her close. "If we see even a hint of a dragon, we halt our mission for the night. Nothing is worth putting you in danger."

Holera kissed his neck softly. "That's something I can agree with."

With one more kiss, Holera shifted, her silhouette transforming into a majestic phoenix. Her feathers shimmered like quicksilver in the moonlight. Sliding onto her back, Kason felt a surge of power as they launched into the sky.

The southern coast of the continent was framed by jagged cliffs and rock formations—countless hiding places carved by the sea. Kason scanned the cliffs, searching for openings large enough to conceal the trade of priceless artifacts.

Then he saw it—a massive shadow heading straight for them. Holera veered sharply toward the cliffs, plunging into the gaping mouth of a cave.

The cave's entrance yawned wide, a dark maw ready to swallow them whole. The air inside was damp and metallic, with a faint, lingering taste of secrets too long buried. Holera touched down on the jagged terrain with grace, shifting back into her fae form as Kason kept a watchful eye on the skies.

Satisfied that they were alone, Kason lit a torch, the flame flickering as shadows receded. Stalagmites rose like guardians around them, protecting secrets older than the merfolk who called Diapolis home.

Kason and Holera walked for what felt like hours, their hope dimming like the flickering light of a torch against the oppressive darkness. Just as doubt began to seep into Kason's resolve, they entered a grotto aglow with coral that hummed with magic, its luminescence a tapestry of aqua and emerald hues. The light pulsed as if the cavern itself were drawing breath, a living witness to their presence.

Kason reached for Holera's hand, the sight stealing his breath away.

"How?" Holera whispered, awe evident in her voice.

Equally entranced, Kason kissed her hair. "I don't know, but experiencing this with you makes it even more special."

"Do you think anyone knows this is here?"

Kason shrugged, rubbing her knuckles. "If they do, I hope they forget about it—at least for tonight."

The air was thick with enchantment, and it didn't take long before the grotto ensnared them. It was as if the grotto demanded tribute, weaving their bodies closer until love itself became an offering. They discarded their garments and stepped into the water, its warmth feeling like a lover's touch. With skin as smooth as satin beneath his hands, Kason pulled Holera close, her violet eyes shimmering in the ethereal light. His lips found hers, and passion rose like the tide.

"Kason," Holera gasped, her voice a plea. "I need you. Now."

"I need you, my fierce warrior. Forever."

Their union sparked the cavern alive. The luminescent coral flickered like stars, as if responding to their joining. No words could capture the flood of devotion coursing through Kason as he met her movements thrust for thrust, their beings intertwining until climax tore through them, the soul of the grotto joining in a release that transcended flesh.

As their shared rapture ebbed into tenderness, they remained locked together, knowing they had created something more wondrous than any artifact could be. In that moment, Kason wondered if they had uncovered not just treasure, but a prophecy written in flesh and light.

Chapter Sixteen

Variel

The scent of earth was strong beneath Variel's paws, a rich blend of pine needles and damp soil invading her heightened senses. She moved silently through the dense underbrush of the human realm, the sleek black fur of her wolf form blending with the darkness of the forest under the crescent moon. Muscles rippled beneath her coat, every fiber of her being attuned to the faintest sign of Joneira or the elusive portal they both sought as she navigated the rugged terrain. Each step pressed into ground that felt more like a battlefield than soil.

The oracle's intuition guided her movements, a gift of foresight flickering in her mind as if an invisible thread connected her to her fate. They had already been trapped in the human realm for three days, and there was still no sign of a way back home or of their enemies since leaving the site of their awakening.

Her dark eyes glowed in the moonlight, scanning the surroundings for any disturbance—a broken branch, a scrap of fabric caught in thorns—anything that might reveal where her enemies had gone. Her lupine ears twitched at every sound, sorting through the hoots of owls and the scurrying of rodents, searching for presences that didn't belong.

Moving like a specter, she slipped past the outskirts of a small human settlement, where laughter and firelight spilled into the night. Variel knew well the dangers of crossing paths with humans, who would kill her the moment they spotted her, so she did her best to stay out of their way. Instead, the shadows became her allies, and she their willing accomplice, gliding through the night unseen and unheard, yet ever present. The laughter of humans echoed behind her like a foreign song, reminding her that she was a ghost in their world—just one misstep away from peril.

A mile deeper into the forest, where the unstable portal had left them behind, the scent of charred earth and the tang of blood still hung heavily in the air. Trees stood like wounded sentinels, their bark bearing witness to the events that had transpired there, but there was no sign of the others—no sign of Joneira—no sign of a way back home. The portal, along with her enemies, was gone.

With near-silent footsteps, her senses pulled her along the winding path toward a large river that cut through the landscape. For a while, she walked beside it, but as the river broadened, the scent she pursued became fainter, diluted by the fresh water in the breeze until it vanished altogether. The current sang a siren's song, tempting her to slip beneath its surface, but Variel knew better than to enter. With the strength of its current, the river could wash away more than just a scent. Not finding what she sought should have deterred her, but determination coiled within her like a spring, compelling her to veer away from the water's edge, her eyes scanning the wilderness for any other signs she may have missed.

The human realm she found herself in was a cacophony of new sights and sounds, an orchestra created by the rustling leaves and the distant calls of unfamiliar creatures. A family of deer emerged from the underbrush, their movements tentative and watchful. In the fae realm, such creatures bore the spirits of the ancients, whispering the secrets of the forest. Here, however, they were merely prey, caught in the relentless cycle of life and death—a harsh reminder of the human realm's raw simplicity.

A rabbit dashed across her path, its heartbeat a frantic drumbeat against the stillness of the night. Recognizing the panic in its eyes, she allowed it to continue on its way, at least for the moment.

As she wove through the endless foliage of the untamed forest, Variel's steps slowed when an anomaly in the landscape caught her attention. A tangle of vines and moss cloaked a jagged opening in the hillside—an entrance to a hidden world below.

Watching the opening for a moment, she shifted her weight, the pads of her paws pressing into the soft soil as the dark cave beckoned her closer. She knew that entering it was risky, but her desperate need to find a way back home pushed her forward. With a cautious step and heightened senses, she stepped into the opening.

Inside, the darkness felt alive, waiting and watching. Variel shrugged off the unsettling sensation. The air clung damp against her fur, thick with secrets that hadn't seen daylight in centuries. Still in her wolf form, her eyes adjusted to the lack of light, revealing a tapestry of symbols etched into the rocky walls.

The markings were both foreign and familiar, like a song from a half-remembered dream. Although she couldn't read them, she could feel their significance, or at least she believed so. Tracing a claw across one of the glyphs, a surge of ancient energy reverberated through her, sending a shiver down her spine. It was as if she were touching the heartbeat of the earth itself, a rhythm older than the divide between realms. Each symbol seemed to be part of a larger puzzle, a map leading to the secrets that could either bridge realms or destroy them.

Staring at the walls before her, Variel's mind raced. Could these markings be remnants of a time long ago when humans and fae walked side by side? Or perhaps they were a key left by the creators of the universe to unlock the path home? Or were they merely the carvings of a primitive society that knew nothing of the world?

As Variel stood inside the main chamber, the fur on the back of her neck rose, a tickling sensation that sent a clear signal of approaching danger. Pressing herself against the cool stone wall, she felt the shadows wrap around her like a cloak. The damp, earthy scent of wet stone filled her nostrils as she squeezed her eyes shut, concentrating on the sounds that pricked at her ears.

Footsteps—measured and deliberate—approached the mouth of the cave, the unmistakable sound of multiple boots drawing closer. Variel's heart quickened, the rhythm becoming an erratic drumbeat against the silence. Her instincts screamed at her to flee. She was a lone wolf, and there were several of them, yet she stood frozen, her form melting into the darkness of the cave's recesses. The cave seemed to tighten around her, as if the stone were conspiring with her fear.

Through the narrow slits of her eyes, she watched as four of Joneira's soldiers entered—her enemies, unaware of her presence. Although their faces were hidden in shadow, the scent of them and the gleam of their weapons were unmistakable. They were not human; they were warriors from the Inferno Territories.

"Spread out," one commanded in a low growl. "The queen said the portal's magic may linger somewhere in these mountains. We need to search everywhere."

"She will reward us handsomely if we find it first," another replied, greed dripping from his words.

Variel's pulse thudded in her ears, loud enough that she feared they might hear it. They were not just soldiers; they were hunters like her, seeking a prize that could tilt the balance of power. Her muscles tensed, ready to spring into action. Still, her mind held her back—she could not risk revealing herself and endangering her people.

As the warriors dispersed, their boots scraping against the stone floor, she inhaled deeply, memorizing their scents and voices. Holding her breath in the hope that they would not detect her, she crept along the cave's edge, silent as a serpent. Her thoughts raced, each heartbeat bringing her closer to a decision—whether to attack if they saw her or to flee.

"Imagine the chaos we could create with such power at our command," one warrior mused, malice twisting Variel's stomach.

"Power to bend the realms to our will," another added. His words slithered through the chamber like venom, poisoning the very air she breathed. Wondering if they planned to tell Joneira about their findings or if they aimed to harness the power for themselves, Variel realized that although they might lack the ability to control it, desperation rarely deterred ambitious seekers.

Their words struck a chord within Variel, igniting a fire that seared through her veins. She was engaged in more than just a quest for balance—it was a battle for the very soul of her world. If her enemies claimed the portal's power, everything she loved would be plunged into shadow and ruin.

Swallowing her trepidation, she slipped from one hiding spot to another, remaining in the shadows. The warriors' conversation faded into the background; their plans etched into her mind—a map of treachery she was determined to thwart. No matter what it took, she would find the portal first, protecting her world in the process. There was no other option. Failure was not an option—it meant extinction, and she would not allow her people to fade into myth.

Chapter Seventeen

Exie

Thunder cracked like a whip, tearing Exie from her dreams of sunnier days. She jolted awake, her heart pounding against her ribs as another violent shudder rocked the ship. Beside her on the small bed, Septima groaned, sitting up with wide, alarmed eyes.

"What happened? What was that?" Septima asked, panic clear in her voice.

Exie slid out of bed and shoved her feet into her boots. "The sea is angry. Look for your sister—" She hesitated, leaning toward Septima as she dressed in her tunic. "Please stay below deck where it's safe."

Before Septima could argue, Exie dashed out of the room, heading above deck. She didn't look back to see if her stubborn mate had listened; she was sure she wouldn't.

Above deck, the scene was chaotic. In the darkness of night, rain lashed the timbers, and waves surged like sea monsters rising from the depths. Lightning stitched the sky from horizon to horizon, each bolt piercing open the sea's roar and turning the deck into a stage of fury.

Amid the tumultuous storm, Bremusa stood firm at the bow, her hands outstretched as if she could control the water. Exie wasn't sure of the limits of the ancient elemental's power, but she knew that a powerful warding spell could help—at least a little. Her mind raced, mapping the ship in an instant—mast, lines, crew, Septima—triage wrapped in strategy, because panic helped no one.

"Exie!" Cristos yelled from the mast, where he was helping the crew with the sails. "We need all hands!"

Darting across the deck, Exie grabbed the rope, her muscles straining as she fought to stabilize the mast. It sent her heart into her stomach when Septima rushed up behind her, reaching for the ropes as well.

"Keep her steady!" Vasilis roared above the noise, aiding the captain in steering the wheel with the tenacity of a seasoned mariner, his eyes fixed on an unseen horizon beyond the storm's veil.

"Exie!" a voice called from somewhere behind her. "I need your help to create a shield!"

It only took Exie a moment to realize it was Bremusa summoning her.

As the vessel heaved beneath them, Exie and Bremusa stood shoulder to shoulder, sheets of rain soaking through their clothing. With her heart thundering in time with the celestial clash above, Bremusa extended her hands, palms facing the tempest's wrath. Exie's blonde hair, pulled back into a long braid, whipped in the violent wind as she mirrored the gesture. Together, they summoned the essence of Exie's phoenix lineage and Bremusa's elemental power—a swirling vortex of flames that danced at their command. Their magics intertwined like braided fire, neither overtaking the other, stronger for the union.

"By the fire reborn," Exie cried out, invoking the ancestral mantra. Heat surged within her at the words, an inferno waiting to be unleashed.

"Let our protection be as the eternal sun," Bremusa added, her voice strong against the howling wind.

A burst of fire erupted from their joined hands, spiraling upwards. It unfurled like the wings of a mighty phoenix, enveloping the ship in a cocoon of protection that miraculously did not burn it. Heat licked their cheeks without burning, a living veil that turned rain to steam and force into harmless mist. The fiery shield, undulating with each roll of the ship, held back the torrential fury, diverting the vengeful spears of water that sought to claim them for the depths.

The crew watched in awe as the sea's chill was replaced by the warmth of the phoenix's fire. In the glow of the fiery dome, faces etched with exhaustion were briefly illuminated with hope, their fears reduced to mere embers flickering in the night.

Yet, as the maelstrom raged on, a cold shiver ran through Exie's veins, extinguishing her momentary triumph. The ghosts of her past flooded into her mind, threatening to overcome her with memories. She saw it again—the harbor of Flamecliff, the destruction, the day she lost her mate. The scalding memory seared her heart anew as her new mate stood braced against the mast of a violently rocking ship in the middle of a stormy sea. She knew she wouldn't survive losing this love. She tasted iron at the back of her throat as the sorrow bubbled up, forcing it down with the stubbornness that had kept her alive.

The tempest howled its ancient fury, transforming the ship into a mere plaything in the grasp of an enraged sea. Exie's heart beat a frantic rhythm against her rib cage, each thump echoing the thunder outside. Amidst the chaos, a singular thought sliced through her fear: Septima. Her beloved, her mate, her heart's compass in this world.

"Exie!" Bremusa's sharp, urgent call pierced through the haunting visions, her hand squeezing Exie's tightly. "Stay with me! Hold the flame!"

Struggling against the swell of grief, Exie tightened her grasp on the present. She couldn't allow the specters of her memories to extinguish the fire that safeguarded those she loved.

As abruptly as it had begun, the storm's intensity faded. The waves, though still formidable, no longer sought to dominate the sky and the ship. The winds softened their mournful howl into a weary sigh, and the protective fire shield flickered, allowing Bremusa and Exie to let the magic fizzle out.

"Exie!"

Septima's voice cut through the lingering echoes of the storm, a siren's call sweeter than any melody. Exie's feet barely touched the deck as she sprinted toward her mate. The distance between them vanished in an instant, and they collided, both of their clothes soaked from the storm. Exie buried her face in the crook of Septima's neck, inhaling the salt that lingered on her skin. Her fingers traced an unspoken question along Septima's ribs, and the answer came in the form of a nod and a sigh that steadied Exie's pulse.

"Are you hurt?" she murmured, her hands roaming over Septima's back, searching for any injury.

Septima shook her head, rising onto her toes to give Exie a kiss. "I'm fine. We're both fine."

Around them, the ship groaned in relief, its timbers settling as if in gratitude to the warriors who had defended it. The sea's rage subsided to a begrudging calm, the last of the waves caressing the hull like a remorseful lover. High above, the clouds parted, allowing the stars to witness those who dared to weather the storm.

With the storm passing as quickly as it had set in, Exie wrapped her arm around her mate's waist and led her back below deck. After everything they'd just experienced and how much of her power had been drained, her hands still trembled, no matter how strong she was trying to be. She'd always been the warrior—the brave one—but at that moment, Septima stood taller. The sight did not unmake her; it remade her—two pillars sharing the same roof.

Back above deck, the crew was still getting the ship back into working order, but Cristos had already returned below deck as well, heading toward the healer's quarters, which was where Aurelia had remained during the storm. There was no doubt the new Aegrician queen would have been above deck with the rest of them if not for the future of their kingdom in her womb. Aurelia was more stubborn than her sister.

Arriving back at their small private quarters, Exie opened the door, closing it behind them. The moment they were alone, she pulled Septima against her body, their wet clothing dripping onto the wooden floorboards.

"I thought I was going to lose you." The words created physical pain inside Exie's chest, but they had to be said. The loss of Theoni was still a fresh wound on her heart—barely held together by roughly laid stitches—no matter how long it had been since her lover had died, and no matter how much she loved Septima.

"Wherever I go," Septima said, the candlelight reflecting in her dark gaze as she leaned closer and gave Exie a soft kiss on the mouth with those delectably full lips, "we're going together."

Exie nodded, kissing Septima again. "Well, the only place I want to take you for a long time is happy places... places where you won't have to wear drenched clothes."

Lifting a brow, Septima reached for the ties on Exie's tunic, pulling the knot loose. "We don't have to wear drenched clothes now."

Exie didn't resist as Septima lifted her tunic over her head, dropping the wet fabric to the ground. Her nipples pebbled in the cool air, her mate immediately wrapping her lips around one and sucking.

Heat flooded into Exie's core as Septima kissed her breast, her mate's other hand giving attention to the rest of her too-sensitive body. The storm's roll still moved through Exie's legs, a slow sway that met Septima's mouth and made the small room feel infinite.

Even as her body buzzed with fire from her mate's touch, Exie pulled away a moment later, hooking her fingers in the hem of Septima's tunic and lifting it over her head before tossing it to the side. "You shouldn't stay in wet clothes either, my flame. You'll catch a chill."

Rich brown skin shone in the candlelight, water from Septima's wet clothes leaving a sheen on her skin. Exie took her in for a moment, blown away by the beauty of her mate's body, before reaching forward to unlace Septima's trousers, letting them slide to the floor. Once her mate was bare before her, the scent of her arousal made it difficult for Exie to think about anything else. She kicked off her boots, dropping her soaking trousers to the floor.

"I don't think I can catch a chill with you, Exie." Septima's voice was no more than a purr as she crawled onto the small bed, her curvy backside in the air as she looked at Exie from over her shoulder. Exie stepped forward, climbing onto the bed beside her.

"Why is that, my flame?"

When Septima rolled over onto her back, pulling Exie on top of her, the mischievous grin on her face could have sent any male or female to their knees. "Because you're so hot, of course."

The side of Exie's lips lifted in a smile. "Is that so?"

Before Septima could respond, Exie leaned down, retaking her lips.

Their tongues met, tangling together and igniting a fierce fire within Exie's core. Their mutual desire was ready to explode like a dragon's fiery breath.

As the flames of passion raged in her heart, Exie's hands roamed, caressing the familiar curves of her mate's body. Septima's skin was warm beneath her fingers, the heat radiating from her like the sun on a summer's day. Exie shed her fear and grief, allowing herself to be consumed by the love that blazed between them.

With one hand still exploring Septima's curves, Exie trailed her other hand down her mate's body, leaving a trail of goosebumps in her wake. She traced the delicate lines of Septima's breasts, her fingers brushing over the tight peak of her nipple, causing her mate to arch her back, her hips shifting restlessly beneath her.

"You're so beautiful," Exie whispered, her voice hoarse with desire.

Kissing her way down Septima's neck, her lips found Septima's swollen peak, her teeth grazing lightly before her mouth enveloped the taut nub.

Septima's breath hitched, her fingers tangling in Exie's long hair, a gaspy moan leaving her lips. The sound made Exie smile against Septima's skin, her tongue flicking at the sensitive nipple again before she moved to the other breast, giving it the same attention.

Her lips traveled lower, her hands guiding her way as she traced a path down Septima's body, her fingers teasing the smooth skin of Septima's stomach until they brushed against the soft curls between her legs.

The sight of her mate's arousal, damp and swollen, sent a wave of desire coursing through Exie, and she couldn't hold out anymore, slipping two fingers inside Septima, feeling the heat and wetness surrounding her digits. For so long, she had wanted nothing more than pleasure from the females she'd brought to her bed, having lost someone she loved so dearly, but Septima was different—a human female still so young, decades younger than Exie. She had taken her body, heart, and soul so completely.

Septima's moans were like a siren's song, only filling Exie with more fire, with a deeper need to please her. Each slow creak of the ship matched the rhythm of her hand, drawing out exactly the response she sought from her mate. Using her mate's body language as a cue, she quickened her pace, fingers sliding in and out with a rhythm that matched the rhythm of her heart, massaging the sensitive spot inside that drove her mate wild. Septima's hips moved in time, her breath coming in short pants. Exie continued to explore, her fingers slick with Septima's arousal as she traced a path from her entrance to her clit, her touch feather-light. Septima's moans filled the small cabin, her body begging for more.

The scent of sex filled the air as Exie lowered her head between Septima's thighs, eager to please her mate. She licked her lips, savoring the taste of her mate's nectar, before diving in with abandon.

Her tongue danced over Septima's swollen folds, tracing the curves and dips.

"Oh," Septima whimpered, her hips undulating against Exie's face. "Please."

Knowing what her mate needed, Exie slipped her finger back inside, the tight heat of Septima's core clenching her fingers. Her mouth continued its work, sucking and licking the bundle of nerves at Septima's apex, the taste of her mate nearly sending her eyes back in her head.

As Septima's breaths became shorter, her moans more frantic, Exie doubled down, her fingers increasing their rhythm. Watching her mate's pleasure-addled face from under her lashes, Exie hummed softly, the vibrations causing Septima to shudder violently, her hips thrusting harder against Exie's mouth.

When the spiral burst, Septima cried out, her muscles clamping tightly around Exie's fingers, her body shaking with the force of her climax.

With one final lick, Exie pulled her fingers away, her own desire surging through her body at the taste of her mate. She slowly moved up Septima's body, their eyes locked, the passion between them like lightning.

Hand finding Exie's face, Septima's fingers brushed through Exie's wavy hair, her thumb tracing the edge of Exie's mouth.

"You are the love of my life, Exie," Septima whispered, emotion pouring through her dark eyes. "I can't imagine a world without you."

Exie smiled, love warming her chest. "And I can't imagine a world without you, my flame. You're my everything."

Wrapping her legs around Exie's waist, Septima flipped them over until she was straddling her. As Exie watched her mate's stunning body in the candlelight, Septima reached into the satchel beside the bed, taking out the flexible phallic-shaped rod they often used in their lovemaking and sliding it through her release where it still glistened between her folds. Exie couldn't turn away; every move Septima made filled her with desire even more.

Exie gasped as Septima pressed the rod inside her before lowering herself onto the other end, connecting their bodies as one. Their eyes met, and Septima's gaze deepened, keeping Exie spellbound. Her body trembled with the intensity of the connection, the desire building between them like the tempestuous sea they had just fought.

With a cry, Exie thrust her hips upward, meeting Septima's every move as their bodies melded together, both their juices slickening the object connecting them, allowing it to go deep enough to allow their bodies to touch—to rub together and increase the pleasure.

Moans growing louder, Septima's breath came in short gasps as she rode Exie. The object between them stretched Exie's tight walls, sending shockwaves of pleasure through her body with each thrust, her gasps mingling with her mate's.

Exie's fingertips dug into the soft flesh of Septima's hips, her nails leaving crescent shapes in Septima's smooth brown skin. The sight of Septima's pleasure only fueled her own desire, and she arched her back, meeting each of Septima's thrusts with equal passion. The desire coursed through her like a wildfire, igniting her body and soul.

Their bodies moved in perfect sync, the rhythm of their lovemaking echoing throughout the small room. The air was thick with the scent of their arousal mingling with the smell of the sea and salt in the air.

As their passion reached its peak, Exie and Septima cried out, their arms gripping each other tightly as their hips rolled through their orgasms.

In the aftermath, they lay together, gasping for breath, their bodies entwined in a tangle of limbs and sweat. Exie's gaze was locked on Septima's, her love and devotion evident in every ounce of her heart.

"I love you," Septima whispered, pressing a lingering kiss to Exie's lips. "You are my world."

Exie smiled, tracing the lines of Septima's face with her fingers. "And you're mine, my flame. Forever and always."

Outside, the sea exhaled; inside, Exie traced a slow circle over Septima's sternum, sealing a vow she would spend her life keeping.

Chapter Eighteen

Aurelia

Creaking timber and the gentle sway of the ship woke Aurelia from dreams filled with visions of phoenixes soaring over tempestuous seas. She blinked away the remnants of sleep, her eyes adjusting to the modest light that peeked through the porthole. With a stretch, she rose from her bed, the ship's rhythms now a familiar dance beneath her feet, although they still turned her stomach slightly. The lull of calm seas felt almost indecent after the violence of the storm, as though the ocean itself was catching its breath.

Cristos had already left their quarters, probably to go above deck and speak with the captain, so she pulled on her cloak and headed out in the same direction.

Upon stepping onto the deck, the warmth of the sun kissed her skin, a welcome contrast to the biting cold of the storm that had raged just the night before. The skies were a vibrant azure, and the calm sea stretched out endlessly before her, its surface shimmering like a sea of diamonds.

"Good morning, Your Majesty," called out Alteria, the healer, from across the deck where she tended to Rockie and Nikoleta, who were resting in lounging chairs in the early morning sun.

"Morning, Alteria." With a genuine smile, Aurelia made her way over to join the healer. "How are they doing this morning?"

"They're doing much better," Alteria replied, her voice warm as the gentle rays of the sun. "Their wounds are healing nicely." The scent of poultices mingled with salt and tar, the fragrance of survival carved from hardship.

Aurelia nodded, kneeling beside Rockie to inspect the warrior's bandages. "Rockie, how do you feel? Are you in any pain?"

"Better, Your Majesty," Rockie responded, wincing slightly as Aurelia adjusted her bandage.

"Please call me Aurelia, Rockie. I'm still the same person who stayed up drinking with you and Exie while you both tried to teach me how to play that game I could never figure out."

With a chuckle, Rockie nodded. "It was a fun night. We definitely need to have another night like that once we are more settled."

Nikoleta lay nearby, her eyes closed and breathing steadily as Alteria applied a fresh poultice to her bruises. Aurelia moved to her side, offering assistance where she could. As she did so, her thoughts drifted to the responsibility weighing on her young heart—the lives of those in Ekotoria and those in the human realm who depended on her success. Every bandage and every bruise she saw seemed to stitch itself into her conscience, a tally of what she owed to both the living and the dead.

With the injured warriors tended to, Aurelia stepped away, allowing them time to rest. As she made her way across the sunlit deck, the gentle sea breeze brushed against her fiery red hair, easing her troubled thoughts. A smile spread across her lips when she found Cristos, Exie, Septima, and Bremusa gathered near the ship's railing, their eyes focused on the distant horizon. A thin seam of cloud stitched the sky to the water, resembling destiny if one stared long enough.

"Only a few more days until we reach the Inferno Territories," Cristos said, reaching out for Aurelia's hand and pulling her against his chest as he pressed a gentle kiss on her lips. "Good morning, my love. How did you sleep? I didn't want to wake you."

She beamed up at him, always happy to see her handsome husband in the morning. "I slept pretty well. Is there anything we should prepare for when we arrive?"

Although she was in Cristos' arms, she directed her question to the group. Bremusa looked toward the horizon, always seeming to see what everyone else could not. "We should work on honing your new powers, my queen, as well as your ability to fly."

A numbing sensation washed over Aurelia at Bremusa's suggestion—fear, she realized—but she also understood that the fear was misplaced. Learning to use her new powers, along with her wings, was important. However, she hadn't seen her new crimson appendages since the war, and even acknowledging the power that now hummed through her veins was intimidating.

Aurelia lowered her chin. "Shall we take a walk and talk, Bremusa?"

After giving Cristos a kiss on the cheek, Aurelia stepped away from the group, following behind the female she knew held much wisdom, along with secrets about her mother that no one else knew.

The wind whispered through Aurelia's fiery red hair as she and Bremusa walked side by side along the deck, the sea stretching endlessly around them. The salty sea breeze filled her senses as she squinted against the bright morning sun. The ship rolled gently beneath her feet, a far cry from the violent tempest that had battered them the night before.

"Ever since I arrived at the Aegrician war camp, when my sister and I first ran away from home, I've had these... visions," Aurelia began, her words hesitant. "I've been able to see through Otera's eyes. I thought they were dreams at first, not knowing who Otera was or how I fit into this world. Somehow, I was able to witness what she saw when she was in the dungeon of the Aegrician palace before the war. Even in her most lonesome moments, I was somehow there with her, although I was nothing more than a specter."

Halting in her steps, Bremusa's silver eyes widened with surprise. "You've seen through Otera's eyes?" she asked, intrigue lacing her voice. "This is a rare ability, one I've only read about in ancient texts." Bremusa's gaze sharpened, not with doubt, but with the keen assessment of a strategist who had just learned of a new kind of blade.

Aurelia nodded, her mind racing. "What could it mean? And why Otera?"

Leaning over the railing, Bremusa went quiet for a moment, seemingly pondering the question. Aurelia rested her forearms on the railing beside her, watching as two dolphins swam in front of the ship. "Before you became queen, I told you that Otera needed to sacrifice herself for you to fulfill the prophecy and take her place. Although I don't know for sure, I believe there is a connection between the two of you that grants you this ability."

Even though Bremusa's words lacked concrete evidence, they made sense to Aurelia. The truth was, the recent events in their world were unprecedented, so no one had all the answers—not even Bremusa.

"You mentioned wanting to teach me how to use my powers..." Aurelia blew out a breath, glancing over her shoulder. "And my wings."

Seeming to sense her unease, Bremusa smiled. "I can't imagine how difficult it must be for you to go through so many changes in such a short amount of time. Your mother was always one to face challenges head-on, with an adventurous spirit. Gods..." Shaking her head, a smile crept up the side of her lips. "She was infinitely rebellious—never afraid to do what she wanted, even if it wasn't befitting someone of her status. It drove your great-grandmother mad. I remember the last day we spent together before she was forced to flee. We snuck out of the palace to go to the Dusty Lantern for a few drinks, leaving Otera to entertain her grandmother's court. Otera hated it, but Messalina hated it even more. All she wanted was adventure, not the life of a royal. She would have been so proud of the woman you've become, Aurelia. I promise you that."

The mention of Messalina washed over Aurelia like sunlight glimmering on waves—both dazzling and painful—illuminating the absence that influenced her every choice. Tears pricked at the corners of her eyes, and she blinked them back, swallowing against the lump in her throat.

It was both comforting and overwhelming to learn more about the woman who had given her life—a woman she missed more than words could express, a woman whose legacy continued through her. "Thank you, Bremusa. Your guidance means more to me than you can imagine."

"Remember," Bremusa began, turning to face Aurelia fully and placing a hand on her forearm, "that I am here for you, just as I was for your mother. Together, we will face whatever challenges the Inferno Territories hold and find the missing portal. Then we will return home so you can lead your people into the future and raise your child in peace."

Aurelia gazed at the moonlit sea, its surface shimmering like a thousand tiny stars. The sea breeze ruffled her hair, bringing with it the scent of salt and some unknown floral aroma.

"Thank you," she said, turning to the dark-haired elemental beside her. "Your help means more to me than I can express."

Bremusa smiled, an unusual sight on such an intense face. "Of course, my queen. I was the one who told your mother that her future daughter would be queen, so I consider it an honor to mentor you on this journey."

For the next two days, as the ship made its way toward the Emerald Enclave on the southernmost tip of the Inferno Territories, Aurelia and Bremusa dedicated every spare moment to honing Aurelia's new powers. Although they also worked on meditation, they began by attempting to summon Aurelia's wings, which she found incredibly challenging. She hadn't seen her wings since the end of the war, but she believed they were still there.

"Remember to focus on your core," Bremusa instructed as Aurelia closed her eyes, the energy within her body swirling and shifting.

With a deep breath, Aurelia visualized her wings emerging, the same as she had been doing for the past two days. This time, however, she felt a sensation of feathers sprouting from her back. A rush of adrenaline coursed through her, and she exhaled. Suddenly, her wings burst forth—vibrant and bristling with magic. The weight pulled at her back, but the surge of freedom overshadowed the strain. Her new form was a promise written in feathers and fire. Achieving this lifted a weight from her shoulders, just as the approval on her mentor's face did.

"Beautiful," Bremusa said, smiling as her own stunning golden wings erupted from her back in a burst of fire. "Now let's work on controlling them."

For hours, Aurelia practiced extending, retracting, and manipulating her wings under Bremusa's watchful eye. Even Cristos joined in a few times, offering a more detailed explanation of how his wings worked, although his were quite different and did not retract. There was still so much about flying that her husband could teach her. Each day brought progress but also challenges. Her muscles ached from the effort, and her mind grew weary from the strain.

On the third day, they turned their attention to Aurelia's newfound ability to create fire. She had used it during the war and to destroy the crown, but she had been unable to summon it since then.

Aurelia sat cross-legged on the quarterdeck near the stern, staring at her hands and focusing her energy on generating a small flame. The first few attempts yielded nothing more than a few sparks, but with Bremusa's guidance and persistent encouragement, Aurelia eventually managed to produce a flickering flame in the palm of her hand. Its light trembled, fragile as a newborn star, yet it carried the same gravity: potential vast enough to burn or to save. It wasn't enough to melt a crown or set fire to a pyre, but it was a start.

As the sun dipped below the horizon, its final blaze made the edge of the world appear ablaze. Aurelia closed her eyes, her breathing steady.

"Allow your mind to drift," Bremusa said, kneeling just inches in front of her on the deck. "Visualize the connection with Otera as a thread woven between you. Once you find the thread, follow it…"

Although Aurelia didn't know what she was looking for, she concentrated on Bremusa's words, reaching out for the ethereal connection she shared with her aunt. The distant sound of laughter from somewhere below deck reminded her of the others, but she pushed those thoughts aside, focusing intently on the task. However, no matter how hard she tried, she couldn't feel Otera, and all she saw was the darkness behind her eyelids. "I can't force them to come to me. Maybe she's too far away."

Shoulders slouching, Aurelia opened her eyes to find Bremusa just inches from her own. The look of disappointment on her mentor's face made her stomach sink. "It's okay to fail," Bremusa said gently. "What's not okay is giving up and never trying again. Eventually, you'll not only be able to reach into Otera's mind, but you'll also be able to connect with others, which can be a power beyond measure. However, it can also be dangerous." Bremusa's eyes held no jest; some doors, once opened, could never be shut, and Aurelia felt the weight of that warning burrow beneath her skin.

Leaning forward, Bremusa placed her slender hands on either side of Aurelia's face, her elemental power sending warmth through Aurelia's skin. "Now, envision extending that thread, branching out to others whose mental walls cannot keep you out. Perhaps one of the crew, someone who wouldn't know how to protect their mind from such an invasion."

Aurelia furrowed her brow in concentration, her heartbeat slowing as she immersed herself in meditation. She could almost feel the threads stretching, connecting her to unseen minds. The sensation was both exhilarating and frightening. It felt like progress, and as they worked over the next few hours, Aurelia found it easier to locate the thread and pull on it.

As they finished their meditation session, the tantalizing aroma of roasted vegetables and freshly baked bread wafted through the air, signaling that dinner was ready.

Opening her eyes, Aurelia blinked against the twilight and smiled at Bremusa as she stood and brushed off her tunic. "Thank you. I'll keep practicing."

Together, they joined Cristos and the rest of their group on the upper deck, settling around the rough wooden table laden with food that had been stocked when they arrived at the harbor. Outside, a shimmering fog enveloped the ship, casting an eerie glow over the wooden planks and swaying sails as it drifted closer to the Emerald Enclave. The mist swirled like a living thing, curling tendrils over the ship as if testing whether they were intruders or guests. Aurelia gazed out at the misty horizon, anticipation and trepidation battling within her.

"Tell me more about Queen Thesipha," she asked Bremusa, her voice barely audible above the gentle lapping of the waves against the ship's hull.

"As I mentioned before, Queen Thesipha is a dryad, a forest nymph with a deep connection to nature." Although they couldn't see through the haze that surrounded them, Bremusa looked ahead, her silver eyes reflecting the eerie light of the fog. "She rules over the forest spirits that dwell in her palace, which is situated within the oldest of trees. Its bark bears centuries of petitions, with each leaf rumored to remember the hands that pleaded beneath it."

"Will she be willing to help us?" Exie asked, looking up from her plate of roasted vegetables.

Bremusa nodded. "I believe so. Queen Thesipha has always been an ally to those who seek peace and harmony, but just because she believes in your cause doesn't mean she will fight for it. If we can convince her that our quest for the missing portal will prevent war from reaching her shores, she will hopefully grant us her aid."

As the moon rose, the group slowly dispersed, leaving Aurelia and Cristos alone. They wasted no time heading to their quarters, exhaustion making Aurelia's limbs feel heavy. The moment Cristos closed the door behind them, she went directly to the copper tub in the corner of the room, which was filled with steaming hot water poured by one of the ship's crew.

"Do you want some company?" Cristos asked, pulling off his boots and placing them beside the door.

Aurelia nodded, untying her tunic and draping it over the back of a chair. Over the past few weeks, her flat stomach had begun to swell—not by much, but enough to reveal that she was expecting. Cristos' eyes roamed over her figure, the cerulean blue of his gaze deepening with heat.

"I'm not sure how well we'll both fit," she said playfully.

Undeterred, Cristos smirked as he crossed the small room, sliding his arm around her waist and pulling her close. With the weight of the world on her shoulders, Aurelia sank into him, closing her eyes in relief.

"One more day, my love. One more day and we'll be off this ship, at least for a little while," he reassured her.

Nuzzling against his chest, she wrapped her arms around him and rubbed her hands up his back to the base of his wings. "Hopefully, we can find what we're looking for and return home—for good this time."

Aurelia didn't need to hear Cristos agree; she could already sense that he felt the same way. They all did.

Leaving the hope for a quick resolution hanging in the air, Cristos undressed and climbed into the copper tub behind Aurelia, his magnificent wings draping over the back. The ship wasn't nearly as comfortable as the palace, but it was certainly better than living in a tent camp—aside from the seasickness. They were fortunate to have a tub at all; there were only a few on the ship, and they had been inviting their friends to enjoy theirs since the first day. Everyone was ready for the luxury of private amenities once again.

"Can you believe we'll soon be parents?" Cristos asked, enveloping Aurelia in his strong arms and pulling her against him. The question lingered in the steam, fragrant with hope and fragile as glass.

Closing her eyes, Aurelia shook her head, a smile forming on her lips. "Sometimes it feels like a dream."

Cristos nodded and gently tapped her shoulder, signaling for her to lean forward. After so many shared baths, she knew he intended to wash her hair, and she felt grateful. Her eyes remained closed as he poured warm water over her, fingers massaging lavender soap into her hair. "Have you thought about names?" he asked.

The question made Aurelia smile wider, warmth blooming in her chest. With everything else happening, she'd spent very little time thinking about the life growing inside her, and that needed to change. "For a girl, I think I would like to name her Lina, after my mother. If it's a boy, perhaps Faidon, after the friend you lost. Unless you have another name in mind?"

Cristos shook his head, squeezing some of the water from her hair. "Both are very special names. No matter what, our child will be cherished—the most loved in all the continent." Saying the names aloud filled the quiet with hope, soft as the sunrise on still water.

With their skin still damp from the bath, Aurelia and Cristos slipped into bed, their bodies still bare. Aurelia traced her fingers along the smooth, damp skin of Cristos' chest, feeling the steady rhythm of his heartbeat beneath her touch. Their eyes locked, the fire between them burning brighter than the candles that surrounded them.

"You've been working so hard with Bremusa over the past few days," Cristos said, leaning forward to brush his lips against hers. "I'm proud of you."

The pride in his eyes told her he meant what he said. "Thank you for believing in me."

Brushing his lips across hers again, Cristos' fingertips traveled along her collarbone, down the curve of her breast, and further still to the swell of her belly where their child grew within her. His touch was gentle yet possessive, as if he sought to claim every inch of her as his own, although he already had, both inside and out.

"Your beauty takes my breath away. It has since I first laid eyes on you," he murmured against her neck, nipping at the sensitive skin there before moving lower to capture one of her nipples between his lips.

Aurelia gasped, arching into him as pleasure rippled through her body. Her hands tangled in his dark hair, urging him to keep kissing her, keep touching her. It had been days since they'd made love, and her body needed him. He kissed and sucked, the sensation sending lightning straight to her core.

"Cristos."

With no clothes between them, the hard bar of his cock slid against her entrance, teasing her with the promise of bliss if only he shifted his hips a little. "What are you asking for, my queen?"

The moment the words left his mouth, he rolled against her, his erection sliding through her juices until the tip of him breached the surface. Before he could pull back, she wrapped her legs around him, pulling him inside.

A groan rumbled out of Cristos' chest as he thrusted deep, filling her in the way she'd craved to be filled, the tension in her body melting away as he moved inside of her. If fate was to be believed, they had an entire lifetime to go slow, but this wasn't the time.

They made love hard and fast, Aurelia's whimpers undoubtedly heard across the entire ship, but she didn't care. She loved her husband, and her body sang for him, so when their climaxes washed over them, neither one of them stifled their moans.

Spent and tangled, Aurelia whispered a silent vow into Cristos' shoulder—that no matter the storm ahead, their child would know a world worth living in.

Chapter Nineteen

Aurelia

The sun rose over the awakening sea, shedding light on a sight that was almost too breathtaking to be real—a mirage—an oasis in the endless blue that would surely disappear before they could touch it. The breeze fluttered Aurelia's hair, the brine of the sea mingling with a floral scent she couldn't place. The fragrance seemed to drift from the land ahead, as if the forest was already reaching across the waves to greet or warn them.

"Land ho!" Exie called out from her precarious perch on one of the masts. Aurelia marveled at how she could hold on without falling; the phoenix warrior had proven to be capable of circus-level aerobatics. The two sisters looked up at her and snickered.

Beside Aurelia, Septima stretched and rubbed her eyes. "Finally! I've never been so ready to set foot on solid ground."

Aurelia mirrored the sentiment, but trepidation still weighed down her feet on the wooden planks below. They had no idea what awaited them in the unruly forest ahead, nor how the queen of that land would respond to their unannounced intrusion, and that filled Aurelia with unease. She instinctively brushed her hand against her stomach, feeling the weight of both crown and child pressing heavier than armor.

Squeaky hinges pierced the silent air as the crew lowered the anchor and dropped the sails, ensuring they didn't get too close to the land. Not only was there no harbor, which made it difficult to approach the coast safely, but if they needed to make a fast getaway, they wanted the ship to be able to set sail without navigating shallow waters.

"Are you ready?" Cristos asked, stepping up from behind her, his voice catching Aurelia by surprise and sending her heart leaping. She nodded, allowing him to lift her into his arms. A downward flap of his wings sent them launching into the air. Behind them, Exie and Bremusa transformed into their phoenix forms, while Septima climbed onto Exie's back. Vasilis brought up the rear of their group, but Rockie and Nikoleta were forced to stay behind with the healer, as they were still recovering from their injuries.

The lush canopy of the Emerald Enclave spread across the southern end of the continent as far as Aurelia could see from the air. The sight was magnificent, but she knew danger lurked somewhere within the shadows. The treetops moved in a single hush, as though the forest spoke a warning she had not yet learned.

Landing on the grassy coastline, Cristos set Aurelia down beside him, reaching over his shoulder to unsheathe his sword before dipping his chin to Bremusa. She was the only member of their group without a weapon in her hands. Even Aurelia notched an arrow into her bow, scanning the treeline for any movement.

"Do you think they know we're here?" Exie asked, taking a step forward to shield Septima from view. Bremusa tilted her head as if in thought, but before she could answer, a rustling came from the forest ahead. Two dryads stepped out of the brush—forest nymphs, creatures Aurelia had only ever heard of in fairy tales.

A few inches shorter than Aurelia, the two female dryads blended nearly perfectly with their environment. Aurelia rubbed her eyes to ensure she wasn't imagining them. When she reopened her eyes, the two dryads were still there. The air around them smelled of rain on leaves and crushed mint, a living signature of the grove they guarded.

Dressed in flowing robes the color of clovers, with intricate braids twisted throughout their long hair, adorned with dozens of multicolored flowers, the two ethereal creatures took hesitant steps forward. In the early morning sun, their skin shone like leaves kissed by dawn's light. Their wide eyes glinted with the wariness of deer in twilight, narrowing with distrust as they observed the newcomers.

Beside Aurelia, Bremusa reached into her satchel, making one of the nymphs jolt in surprise. The nymph's fear faded when Bremusa held out a single golden acorn. The small object caught everyone by surprise. Aurelia had never seen an acorn in such a color; it gleamed like a sun trapped in seed form, pulsing faintly as though alive.

Lifting the golden acorn before her, Bremusa dipped her chin, a gesture that silently conveyed to the dryads that she meant them no harm.

"A gift," Bremusa said, her tone soft, her eyes even softer. "A gift for your queen if she would honor us with her presence and listen to our plight. We mean no harm to your people or your land. We come in search of aid, not conquest."

After a moment of silence, the two nymphs exchanged glances, sharing an unspoken thought before they nodded in unison and turned their fixed stares back to Bremusa. Although they may not have fully trusted her or the rest of the group, they seemed at least willing to bring them to their queen.

Suddenly, the dryad on the right, whose hair was nearly as brilliant a crimson as Aurelia's, sprang forward and took the acorn from Bremusa's palm. With a gesture that seemed to summon the morning breeze, she nodded. "Follow."

At that singular command, the nymphs remained silent as they turned their backs on Aurelia and the rest of her group, darting back into the forest. Although Aurelia felt uncertain, it appeared that Bremusa understood their silence, giving a single nod to Aurelia before following the nymphs deeper into the woods.

Navigating through trees and brush, Aurelia and the others followed the two tree nymphs for what felt like hours, moving further away from the relative safety of their ship. Aurelia walked beside Cristos, their hands brushing against each other occasionally, a subtle reminder that he was there. Roots like ancient ribs rose from the earth, and the light grew dimmer, creating a quiet green hush that made their breathing sound unnaturally loud.

"Are we doing the right thing by trusting them?" she whispered to him, hoping only he could hear.

Cristos met her gaze, his blue eyes steady. He squeezed her fingers gently. "I don't think we have any other choice."

As the group continued to follow their guides, Aurelia's thoughts swirled like a tempest, grappling with the dangers that lay ahead. The forest grew denser, making the path nearly impassable. Soon, the landscape shifted, leading them away from the ground altogether.

Ascending the spiraled roots that twisted skyward, the group approached Queen Thesipha's court—a palace not built, but grown within the arboreal citadel. The living architecture of interwoven branches and blossoms resembled something out of pure fantasy. The path itself seemed to breathe, roots shifting minutely underfoot, reminding Aurelia that this was no dead stone hall but a living body of wood and leaf.

They were led through two massive double doors made from the thick branches of an oak tree into a windowless chamber guarded by two satyrs. The room was dimly lit, casting eerie shadows against the gnarled roots snaking around its walls. A chill ran down Aurelia's spine as she studied the satyrs—creatures she had only encountered in fairy tales, never imagining they were real. Although humanoid, their muscular bodies were covered in coarse fur, with tails and twisted horns sprouting from their foreheads. They leaned against their spears, their golden pupils glinting in the half-light, their feral stares unblinking, making Aurelia feel as though prey had willingly wandered into a den.

The tension in the room was palpable, tightening Aurelia's chest. Cristos' jaw became rigid, revealing that he felt the same unease. No one seemed willing to speak, especially not with the satyrs watching them as if they were plotting to take over the kingdom.

Finally, after what felt like at least an hour of waiting, another set of doors creaked open—doors Aurelia had not even noticed before. They revealed a grand walkway lined with towering trees, sparkling lights hanging from their branches. Aurelia couldn't help but gasp at the sight. Branches interwoven with vines formed a canopy high above, dappling the floor with golden sunlight. The air was thick with the scent of blooming flowers and damp earth. A hush fell from the leaves, as if the forest's attention was turning to the throne.

As they entered the throne room, Aurelia's gaze locked onto Queen Thesipha, who sat perched upon a living throne woven from the roots of a colossal tree. Her eyes were sharp as emeralds, and her expression was guarded and unreadable. Although the queen of the Emerald Enclave dryads was no taller than any of the females in their group and bore no visible weapons, Queen Thesipha radiated power. It was palpable in the air around her, as though the entire forest was holding its breath, waiting for her command. Flowers unfurled at her feet in slow motion, responding to her presence as if she were spring incarnate. Aurelia swallowed her insecurity and hung her bow back over her shoulder in a gesture of peace. They were outnumbered anyway.

The two satyrs who had watched them like hawks in the waiting room now stood by her side. A blond-haired female pixie perched on her shoulder, her tiny wings tucked tightly against her back. Aurelia forced her spine to straighten, even though she felt tired and was nowhere near confident enough to represent the fae world—a world she had only just begun to be a part of, even if it flowed through her blood.

"Speak," the queen commanded, her voice melodic but her tone stern. "Tell me why you dare intrude upon my realm."

"Your Majesty," Bremusa began, bowing from the waist. "We come seeking your aid in our quest to find a portal that has disappeared from our land—a portal my people are fated to protect, which may be hidden on this continent. The portal is missing, and one of the most powerful artifacts in our world has been stolen. We mean no offense or harm to you or your people, but if we don't find these items, we are all in danger."

"Many have sought my help only to betray me in the end," the queen replied coolly, narrowing her eyes. "Why should I trust you?"

Aurelia clenched her fists at her sides, the weight of their mission heavy on her shoulders. Taking a deep breath, she attempted to summon every ounce of courage before speaking. "Your Majesty," she began, her voice steady and strong, "my name is Aurelia Vesta, descendant of the great queen Faenia Lumino and niece of Otera Lumino, the queen of Aegricia, until she sacrificed her life to protect the portal that separates our realm from that of the humans. She sacrificed herself to fulfill the prophecy that placed me on the throne."

"Is Otera Lumino dead, then?" Queen Thesipha asked, her eyes widening.

Grief tugged at Aurelia's stomach, even though she knew her aunt was very much alive. She shook her head. "When the framework for the portal was destroyed, sending its magic to become lost in our realm, Queen Otera and many others rose from the ashes. She was dead, but she is now alive."

Curiosity flashed across the dryad queen's face as she leaned forward in her throne, but it cleared quickly. "That's impossible."

Everything Aurelia knew about the world told her that the queen was right, but Otera was dead, and she was now alive. There was no question about that, no matter how improbable it seemed.

As Aurelia struggled to prepare an explanation that could convince the queen, Bremusa touched her arm, searching her face for permission to speak on her behalf. Aurelia nodded.

"I understand your disbelief and hesitation, but we did not come this far to deceive you. The fate of our world depends on finding this portal and keeping it out of the hands of those who would exploit it for nefarious purposes. I know you have doubts, but please understand that our intentions are pure. We aim only to locate the portal and return it to its rightful place."

The queen fell silent for a few moments, her fingers drumming against the armrests of her throne. The tension in the room made Aurelia's skin crawl as they waited for a response; each second felt like an eternity. Finally, the queen sighed and nodded, acknowledging the gravity of the situation. "Very well," she said, reluctance still evident in her voice. "You will need to stay here as my guests until at least tomorrow while I speak with my people and make arrangements. I will send two of my most powerful trackers with you, along with a few guards, to assist in your search and to protect our interests. Our land must be safeguarded at all costs; it is our lifeblood."

Bremusa dipped her chin and took a step back. For a moment, Aurelia thought the queen was dismissing them, but when she scanned their faces, it was clear the queen had more to say. Aurelia swallowed, eager to hear the queen's following words.

"Be wary, outsiders," Queen Thesipha warned, her voice regaining its edge. "My Enclave is ancient and full of secrets. Tread carefully, lest you unleash something that cannot be contained." The branches overhead rustled, though no wind stirred, as if the Enclave itself agreed with her warning.

Chapter Twenty

Kason

Kason and Holera slept in the day after their excursion into the caves off the coast of Embershell, neither of them discussing the sensation that had overcome them inside the grotto—how the magic of the the coral seemed to lure them into the water, how something after they'd left just felt *different*. After they'd come down from the high they'd given to each other when they made love, they'd made it safely back to the tavern and had gone to sleep. They were both drained, as though the cave had taken just as much as it had given.

Waking the next day, Kason's head spun as though he'd drowned in several mugs of whiskey, and it took him a moment to get his bearings and remember where he was. But beside him was the most important person in the world to him, so he got caught up in her before he thought too hard about it.

Holera rolled over onto her back, her eyes still sleepy as she looked up at him. "I haven't felt this drained after a full night of sleep in a long time, if ever."

Sliding his hand up to cup her cheek, Kason leaned forward and kissed her gently on her lips, savoring the spark he felt every time he touched her. "You must have needed sleep, my fierce warrior."

The night wrapped Embershell in its velvety embrace as Kason and Holera, shrouded in shadows, made their way back to the clandestine caves. The moon was a crescent, barely more than a silver eyelash against the dark canvas of the sky. The damp sand muffled their steps as they walked down the dark beach, Kason's eyes fixed on the yawning maw of the cavern ahead—a different cave from the one they'd found themselves in the night before.

"Look," Kason whispered, his gaze fixated on the faint lights up ahead—a boat disappearing around the curve of the continent. "Something's happening up there. They were definitely anchored somewhere up ahead."

Holera nodded, her silver hair catching the scant moonlight from beneath the hood of her cloak, every strand that was no longer dyed black. Their footsteps echoed softly off the damp walls as they entered the opening of the largest cave, Kason's hand on the hilt of his blade as he walked a step ahead of his mate.

On near-silent feet, they ventured deeper into the darkness, where the sound of the sea faded to a ghostly murmur. Faint echoes of movement reached them—the clink of metal, the muffled thud of heavy objects being set down. Intrigue quickened Kason's pulse, drawing him onward like a moth to a flame, although they were undoubtedly stepping into a potentially dangerous situation.

Rounding a corner, they found themselves in a larger cavern, illuminated by flickering torchlight dancing across the walls. At least six figures, draped in darkness, caught Kason's eyes, their silhouettes hunched over crates that seemed to swallow the light. They appeared to be organizing whatever was inside the crates, but Kason and Holera were too far away, and it was too dark to see what was inside.

"Who are they?" Holera whispered, her voice barely audible over the dripping of water from the stalactites.

Kason shook his head. "I don't know." Turning back toward the figures, his eyes narrowed, trying to make out more details in the dim light.

With one more glance at Holera, he brushed his hand against hers for a brief moment before edging closer toward the crates, keeping to the shadows. He strained his ears, attempting to catch snippets of conversation among the figures, but the air in the space shifted, the hair on the back of his neck standing on end. His instincts screamed danger, but before they could move, the sound of footsteps approached them from behind. They were trapped. *Cornered.*

"Who are you?" A gruff voice sent Kason's heart into the ground beneath his feet. He whirled around, his protectiveness over Holera surging within him. Fear gripped him like a vice, but he refused to let it show. He was by no means a weak male, and his mate was as fierce a warrior as any Aegrician warrior, but they were outnumbered.

"Speak!" another voice barked, and Kason opened his mouth to respond when suddenly a sack was thrust over his head. Panic bubbling inside him, he reached for Holera's hand, but she was quickly pulled away from him.

"Let us go!" she screamed, the desperation in her voice like a sword to his soul. "We can explain!"

A low chuckle was the only response she received.

"Please don't harm her." It took everything inside Kason to remain calm as hands pulled his arms behind his back and bound them together, the cold blade of a dagger poised at his throat. "Let her go. Just take me."

There was no response, but he could hear the rustling of them doing the same to Holera beside him.

The rough hands gripping Kason's arms sent shivers down his spine; the scent of body odor and whiskey assaulted his senses. Multiple people dragged them toward the shoreline, the sound of crashing waves growing closer with each step. The sack over his head made it difficult to breathe, as did the panic seizing his lungs.

"Where are you taking us?" Kason demanded, his voice muffled by the fabric of the sack. There was a brief silence before a gruff voice replied.

"Shut your mouth before I gag both of you."

Despite the threat, Kason leaned to the side, his shoulder brushing against hers before he was pulled away.

They walked for several minutes across the sand before the ground beneath their feet became more solid—a ramp, Kason realized. A sudden lurch beneath his feet signaled that they had been led onto a small boat, the gentle rocking making it even more challenging to maintain his balance when someone else was forcing him to move without him being able to see.

Led to the rear of the vessel, they were both forced to sit down on a wooden bench, Kason's body instinctively scooting closer to his mate the moment she dropped down beside him. Their captors' hands were no longer on them, but they weren't far away.

The journey felt like an eternity as the boat slid through the calm waters of the Elder Sea, anxiety mounting with every stroke of the oars. When the boat finally came to a halt, Kason's heart pounded in his chest, the uncertainty of where he and his mate were being taken tightening his chest.

"Get up!" one of the captors growled, yanking Kason roughly to his feet. Unable to help himself, he growled right back, but forced his temper back when Holera's fear changed her scent, turning it bitter. If something happened to him, he knew she would be left alone to fend for herself, and he couldn't let that happen.

For the length of several blocks, they were escorted side-by-side, Kason stumbling when the wooden docks met the stone ground of the mainland.

Hinges squealed as two heavy wooden doors were pulled open and they were forced inside a building and down a long hall. When they were pulled to a stop, Kason's breath stilled.

"Remove the sacks," a smooth, authoritative voice commanded, one Kason knew well. A shiver of dread ran down his spine.

When the sack was pulled off Kason's head, he blinked furiously against the sudden brightness, but when his eyes adjusted, he recognized the opulent throne room and the male sitting on the throne. At the heart of the room sat King Ailani, ruler of Diapolis, his piercing turquoise eyes fixed on Kason and Holera with a mix of curiosity and displeasure.

"Care to explain why you're spying in my capital, friends?"

Chapter Twenty-One

Aurelia

Night fell over the lush landscape of the Emerald Enclave, with the palace blending seamlessly into the surrounding nature, illuminated by the moonlight. The air was thick with tension as Aurelia and her companions gathered around a table draped in gossamer silks. Aurelia's mind was restless as she considered what lay ahead.

After meeting with the dryad queen, they had been shown to their guest rooms within the palace and treated as honored guests. If the queen still harbored doubts about their intentions, Aurelia couldn't tell. However, the queen had immediately gone to meet with her advisors upon bringing Aurelia and the others to their private chambers. The knowledge that their fate was being discussed without their input only deepened Aurelia's anxiety. Every bite of food felt like consuming borrowed time, and every glance at her companions reminded her that they were already facing judgment without a defense.

"Queen Thesipha was not making an idle threat," Bremusa observed, her silver eyes reflecting the flickering candlelight as she sipped her wine. "Having her people accompany us as we travel inland will certainly help, but there are dangers on this continent that even I cannot confront. We will have to rely on their guidance, even if it's clear they still do not trust us."

The ever-stoic Vasilis nodded, pouring more wine into his goblet. "Trust isn't easily earned, but I believe that once they get to know us better, they'll see that we are genuine. If we don't restore balance, it could also negatively impact their land. I believe the queen understands that."

Exie leaned back in her chair, stretching her long legs beneath the table. "Let's just hope her people are as powerful as she claims. I'm a damn good tracker, but I know nothing about this continent except what I've read."

Sensing the weight of their shared unease, Aurelia cleared her throat, attempting to exude the confidence that the queen had just shown. "I realize this alliance is fragile, but we must trust that the dryads will honor the queen's commitment to our cause. We cannot let doubt weaken our resolve. This is too important."

The lush canopy of the Emerald Enclave arched over them like a protective cloak, but Aurelia could not shake the weight on her shoulders as they departed from the sanctuary of the dryad palace. The air was fragrant with the scent of damp earth and wildflowers, but it did little to soothe her simmering nerves. Cristos' shadow loomed beside her, his hand brushing against hers as a reminder that he was there for her. He always had been.

Walking alongside the two dryad trackers, Solitaria and Gillia, Bremusa's silver eyes scanned the forest, clearly following a trail that Aurelia couldn't sense. She enjoyed working with Bremusa on the ship, but since making landfall, she had found it challenging to work with the elemental again. The two dryad trackers moved with innate grace, their forms blending seamlessly with their surroundings, while the satyr guards, Joc and Strov, flanked their group, their cloven hooves treading lightly on the mossy ground, weapons at the ready. Their presence was a constant reminder that hospitality was conditional; the Enclave's eyes walked beside them in flesh and horn.

The tree canopy was too thick for them to keep track of time, but Aurelia knew hours had passed by the burning in her leg muscles and her intense desire to collapse. Still, they kept hiking, each footfall taking them deeper into the heart of the forest where sunlight merely dappled through the leaves in fleeting golden kisses upon the forest floor. Shadows pooled like ink between the roots, and Aurelia could not tell if the hush belonged to reverence or ambush. The air itself seemed to thrum to life, vibrating with the unseen current that Bremusa navigated, her connection to the land serving as their compass through this realm of towering trees and hidden dangers.

"Are you sure this is the right path?" asked Gillia, one of the dryads. They were supposed to be the group's guides, but instead, they had allowed Bremusa to take the lead—not that anyone could have stopped her.

"Trust me," Bremusa replied, not even turning to glance at the dryad who had asked the question. "My connection to the Shadow Glass will lead us to the portal. If they are together, I will find both."

"Right," said Solitaria, her voice tinged with doubt as she exchanged a glance with Gillia before falling silent.

As they moved deeper into the forest, Aurelia couldn't help but marvel at the beauty surrounding them—towering trees adorned with leaves of every hue, crystal-clear streams cutting through emerald moss. A fragrant breeze rustled the leaves, carrying the songs of birds and the distant murmur of a babbling brook. It should have been a scene of perfect serenity, but Aurelia's heart was heavy with unease.

Cristos' hand hovered near her elbow as they navigated the uneven forest floor, never straying more than a few inches away from her side. "Watch your step, my love."

Nodding, she smiled faintly and reached out to take his hand. Her eyes darted nervously between the shadows of the trees, haunted by Queen Thesipha's warnings about the dangers lurking in the enchanted realm. Despite their strong party, she couldn't shake the feeling that unseen eyes were watching their every move. After being ambushed by hellhounds and Warbotach barbarians in Spectre Forest, Aurelia was no stranger to surprise attacks. With those she loved by her side and a child growing inside her, she didn't want to take any chances.

"Are you alright, Aurelia?" Cristos asked in a low voice, ensuring he wouldn't be overheard by their companions. He rarely addressed her by her first name, so his concern was apparent. Since they had left the palace, he had been vigilant in caring for her, making sure she had enough water and food, even offering to carry her so she could rest her legs—something she had already accepted.

Running her fingers through her fiery hair, Aurelia shrugged. She knew she couldn't hide her feelings from her mate, her husband. "I'm just... uneasy. I'm not sure if it's the feeling of being watched or if it's just the power of suggestion making me believe there are eyes on me when there aren't."

He lowered his chin and wrapped his arm and wing around her, pulling her close. "Her concerns were meant to keep us alert, not to paralyze us with fear. We are well-prepared for whatever may come our way. I won't let anything happen to you or those we love."

His confidence felt like a lifeline, but Aurelia's instincts coiled tightly, whispering that love alone might not be enough to keep the shadows at bay.

As the sun sank low, casting its fading golden rays through the foliage, the group emerged from a thick grove to find themselves on the banks of a breathtaking river. The water shimmered like liquid silver, reflecting the vibrant colors of the surrounding landscape. Despite the beauty of the scene, tension prickled at the edges of Aurelia's consciousness.

"Look at this," Septima exclaimed, her awe temporarily eclipsing the worry that had plagued Aurelia all day. Turning her gaze to the water, Aurelia tried to allow the soothing sounds of its flow to relax her. Their journey had already been emotionally and physically draining, and all Aurelia really wanted was to stop and rest. However, as they approached the water's edge, a guttural growl echoed through the trees, followed by the sound of snapping branches. The silver water lost its serene shimmer; it seemed to recoil, warning them of the predator breaking through the wood.

Feeling her heart drop into her stomach, Aurelia reached for her bow, notching an arrow as the rest of her group drew their weapons. Cristos stepped in front of her, but she maneuvered to the side, aiming toward the treeline.

From the shadows of the forest, a monstrous beast lunged at them—its teeth bared and eyes filled with malice. It was a hellhound. Its fur appeared to smoke, as if fire smoldered beneath its hide, and its breath reeked of iron and rot, the stench of nightmares made flesh.

"Take cover!" Septima shouted, pulling one of the dryads behind her just as the creature swiped its massive paw, barely missing Septima's arm.

Vasilis spun around and slashed at the beast, slicing across its front leg. As it shrieked in pain, he scooped up Gillia and soared into the sky, taking her safely across the river.

"Exie, Bremusa! Get them across the river!" Cristos commanded, his wings unfurling as he reached for Aurelia.

"We can't leave them!" she protested as Cristos lifted her and launched into the air, leaving the two dryads behind. Aurelia watched, breath caught in her throat, as Exie and Bremusa shifted into their majestic phoenix forms to carry the others to safety. But the beast, furious, surged toward Septima before they could help.

"No! Exie!" Panic seized Aurelia's lungs as she watched from above—the beast snarling and snapping while the others struggled to hold it at bay. "Cristos, we have to help them! Just let me take the shot!"

Not waiting for his permission, she reached into her quiver for another arrow, aiming it at the creature, even though she knew she was too far away. She was about to scream at him, about to wiggle loose, but Cristos flew them a little closer, allowing Aurelia to get the creature in her sights.

The taller of the satyrs, Joc, jabbed his spear at the creature, black blood splattering on the ground as a hole was torn into its side. But it did not stop; it swung around, wrapping its jaws around Joc's wrist. The satyr screamed, trying to free his arm while the other satyr, Strov, provoked the creature to lure it away.

Frustration boiled through Aurelia as she tried to get a clear shot, aiming for the creature without hitting the two satyrs. They were moving too much, making it far too risky to shoot, but she had no choice. The satyr was losing too much blood, and the beast wouldn't let go. Taking a deep breath to steady her nerves, Aurelia lifted her bow, took aim, and fired. Time slowed; the string bit into her fingertips, her heartbeat syncing with the arrow as if her entire world balanced on its flight.

CHAPTER TWENTY-TWO

VARIEL

Raindrops clung to the edges of Variel's fur cloak, each one shimmering like a tiny crystal as they rolled off into the muddy streets. The scent of damp earth filled the air, mingling with the familiar tang of iron and wood—the lifeblood of any human settlement. The oracle wolf shifted her weight from foot to foot, trying to keep warm in her humanoid form. Something tugged at Variel's instincts like a thread caught in her claws—subtle but insistent—a nudge that the day had changed direction.

"Good day to you," she called out, her voice barely audible above the din of the rain as she approached the store owner. "I'm looking for supplies, clothing, bandages, and such."

"Ah, of course!" the man replied, his eyes darting between Variel's obsidian gaze and the pouch of gold she offered. "Right this way."

As they walked through the cluttered aisles, Variel's fingers brushed against the rough-hewn surfaces of wooden shields and cold iron blades. Each item carried its own story, the whispered memories of battles fought and lives lost. Her thoughts wandered back to her comrades in the camp. They needed supplies, and more importantly, they needed to find the portal and get back home.

A flash of fiery red hair across the market caused her heart to skip a beat, nearly sending her crashing into a rack of tunics.

"Excuse me," she said, her voice sharp, her eyes darting from the woman across the street to the human man before her. "Who is that woman?"

"Something wrong?" the store owner asked, concern creeping into his voice as he followed her gaze.

"Who is she?"

Looking from the woman with flowing red hair back to Variel, the man nodded. "Ah, that's Lina, the dressmaker. She's been in town for years now. A fine craftswoman, I must say. Keeps to herself, mostly, but she's very kind."

The moment the name Lina left his lips, Variel's heart flopped like a fish out of water in her chest, but she did her best to hide her disbelief. Names carried power, and this one struck like a key turning in an old lock.

"Thank you," she murmured, her mind still racing. The woman bore a striking resemblance to Aurelia—Cristos' Aurelia—the queen of Aegricia. Every feature of her face and every curl of her crimson hair mirrored that of the queen. It couldn't be a coincidence. The only problem was that Aurelia had no biological sisters, and Aurelia's mother, Messalina Lumino, was supposed to be dead. She had been killed by Joneira's assassins more than a decade prior. Yet, here she was, in the flesh, a radiant smile spread across her stunning face as she spoke with an elderly customer about a dress that needed mending.

"Will this be all?" The shopkeeper's voice brought Variel back to the present abruptly.

"Yes, thank you," she replied, her eyes never leaving the very-much-alive Messalina Lumino as she passed the gold coins into the man's hand. Her thoughts churned like the stormy skies above, weighing the risks and rewards of approaching this woman and wondering if she was simply imagining things. Every fiber of her being screamed that it was too dangerous to trust anyone in such uncertain times, but the lure of such a powerful ally, so closely connected to Aurelia, was too strong to resist.

The only question was: what could she possibly say to a woman who had faked her death to protect her realm and her family? How could she tell her that the foe who had once wanted her dead could be anywhere, ready to finish what she had started all those years ago? The moment Variel approached Messalina Lumino—the moment she said her name out loud—she knew she could be signing Messalina's death warrant.

A soft gust of wind tousled Variel's obsidian hair as she stood in the shadow of a towering oak, watching the red-haired dressmaker from a distance. The woman's nimble fingers expertly worked on a silky fabric draped over her arm, making her appear glamorous, with the tips of her ears appearing rounded. She seemed human, but Variel could scent the fae on her. Glamour softened the lines of her ears, but scent could not be deceived; the truth hung in the air, bright as iron. There was no doubt about which world she came from. Variel's heart raced as she steeled her nerves, trying to formulate the words to bridge the chasm between them.

Blowing out a breath and forcing a smile across her aged face, she stepped into the sunlight, approaching the dressmaker's booth. "Excuse me."

The dressmaker looked up, cerulean eyes meeting Variel's gaze. "Can I help you?"

After just one glance into the woman's eyes, Variel had no doubt about who she was in the presence of. It took her a moment to find her words and catch her breath.

"Is everything okay, ma'am?" Messalina asked again, her blue eyes softening with concern.

A hush fell over the marketplace as a sudden gust of wind whipped through the stalls, carrying with it the scent of impending rain and the promise of a storm to come. Variel scanned the area around them, ensuring no one was in earshot before she spoke.

"Please know that I come to you with the most honorable intentions," she said, reaching out to touch Messalina's hand. The moment their skin met, Variel forced a surge of her power through their connection, relief flooding her heart when Messalina's eyes widened. In that instant, Variel knew she would be believed.

"Please understand, I did not come here to seek you out, Lina. I didn't know you were alive—no one in my world knows you're alive, but you are in danger, and your daughter needs our help in our world. We need to speak in private. Soon."

Even in this moment, the wrong word could unmask a life carefully stitched together. Variel kept Messalina's true name hidden behind her teeth.

Messalina's eyes widened, shock coloring her features. "My d-daughter?" she stammered, quickly composing herself. She glanced around nervously, as if fearing that someone might be listening in on their conversation. "Meet me at dusk in the forest, beyond the eastern edge of town. There is a small cottage there, hidden amongst the trees. We can speak privately there."

The sun dipped below the horizon, casting deep shadows across the forest as Variel strode toward the eastern edge of town. Her heart pounded in her chest, echoing the rhythm of the raindrops that began to fall from the darkening sky. Every one of her lupine senses was attuned to the world around her, ensuring she wasn't being followed until the cottage came into view, at which point she shifted back into her humanoid form.

Through the windows of the small wooden structure, candlelight flickered, creating silhouettes of the figures inside. Variel hesitated for a moment, taking a deep breath before knocking.

"Variel," Messalina said, stepping aside to allow her in. "This is my husband, Proteus," she continued, resting her delicate hand on the forearm of the dark-haired man standing behind her, "and my son, Amadeus."

As Variel entered, she dipped her chin, taking in the appearances of both males. It only took her a moment to notice how much Amadeus resembled Aurelia. However, his hair was a dark brown like his father's. "Nice to meet you both," she said.

Messalina allowed her husband to wrap his arm around her waist. "Do you bring news of our daughter? Of our daughters?"

"Indeed." The gravity of the situation tightened Variel's chest, forcing her to swallow. "Aurelia and Septima are in our realm—Ekotoria. Dozens of warriors and I are trapped here, searching for a way back. The last time I saw Aurelia was during the Battle of Flamecliff. Messalina... Joneira is trapped here with me."

Proteus's stance had the economy of a seasoned soldier; Amadeus's gaze flashed a protective heat, quick as flint. Amadeus's eyes widened in shock as Messalina's hand flew to her mouth, tears welling in her eyes. Proteus's hands clenched into fists at his sides.

"Tell us more," Messalina urged, her voice trembling with emotion.

Variel took a deep breath, but her gaze turned toward the decanter of whiskey on the counter. "Shall we sit and have a drink then? This may require something strong."

The whiskey rose warm as a hearth, passing a small measure of courage hand to hand.

Once they were all seated in the small area in front of the fire, mugs of whiskey in hand, Variel took a deep sip, savoring the burn on the way down before daring to discuss something so dire. "A war rages in the fae realm," she began, her voice growing steadier as she recounted the unfolding events within Ekotoria. "Warbotach invaded Norithae and then Aegricia before attempting to overtake the entire continent." She blew out a breath, locking eyes with each of her listeners, who hung on her every word. "At first, we didn't realize there was anyone behind Warbotach's invasions, not until the War of Flamecliff, when Joneira invaded Aegricia with dragon-wielding armies from the Inferno Territories. During that conflict, the portal controlled by the Aegrician crown was destroyed, its magic dispersed, and we—and Joneira—were dropped into the human realm with no obvious way to return home."

"Joneira?" Proteus growled, his anger a palpable force within the cramped space. "What does she want? What role does she play in this?"

Taking another sip of her whiskey, Variel turned her eyes to the fire. "Her motivations are unclear, but we know she poses an imminent threat to all we hold dear." When she looked back at those sitting across from her, she made eye contact with each family member in turn. "We cannot afford to underestimate her."

If Joneira found a foothold here, she would not only finish old work—she would plant the seeds for new wars.

"Then what do you propose?" Proteus asked, his voice calm despite the storm raging both outside the cottage and inside his deep blue eyes.

Variel did not need to ponder her answer. "We must unite. We must gather our allies and face Joneira head-on, for the sake of our families, our people, and our realm."

"At first light, we move," Proteus declared. "No rumors left behind, no names spoken in the open."

The mountains loomed like slumbering giants, their silhouettes etched against the starlit sky. The air was cool, and Variel's breath created wispy clouds in front of her as she walked. Owls punctuated the darkness with low calls, while the underbrush seemed to hold its breath, as if even the smallest creatures knew to remain silent. With their decisions made, Variel and her companions left the cottage under the cover of darkness. They headed toward the camp they had set up further up the mountain.

Messalina had spent years in Breqan, building a life there, but nothing was more important to her than returning to her homeland to reunite with her daughters. After Variel shared her truth about the war and what had brought her to the human realm, Messalina recounted her struggles to keep her family safe. She detailed how her husband had helped her fake her own death and hide her away in another land, allowing the threat against her to diminish. Until that point, Messalina and her family had lived under constant threat, facing several assassination attempts from Joneira against Messalina and even her children. Removing herself from her home was the only option that Messalina believed she had, and it seemed to have been the right choice. Under the protection of their father and the care of servants, Aurelia had grown into a wonderful young woman.

From what Variel learned during their dinner together, Messalina's husband, Proteus, had left his position with the Vaekrosaean government after Aurelia and Septima ran away. He and Amadeus had traveled to Breqan to reunite with Messalina, and they had been together ever since. Before that, Proteus had only seen his wife while on military campaigns; it was where they had first lived as a married couple. However, Messalina had not seen her son since she left home, disguised as a dead woman. Variel could see the depth of Messalina's love and longing for her children in her eyes. She had lost so much of her life and family because of Joneira, and now that Joneira was back, Variel wondered who would want to kill whom more.

As they hiked higher up the mountain, the forest grew denser, casting shadows that melded together into an impenetrable wall. With three more souls beside her—two humans—the weight of the darkness pressed down on Variel like a leaden cloak. She palmed a charm at her belt, anchoring a quiet ward behind them so their trail would fade like mist. She knew their enemies could be lurking anywhere, and bringing Messalina into her group only heightened the risk. Yet there was no turning back, nor would Messalina have wanted to. Now that Messalina knew her daughters were in Ekotoria and needed her help, nothing could have prevented her from finding a way back to them.

"Stay close," Variel murmured, her voice barely audible over the rustling leaves. "The path is treacherous, and the night holds more than shadows."

Messalina nodded silently, determination etched on her features like armor. Even in the dim moonlight, her eyes sparkled with a fire kindled by years of hiding, now burning with the need to act and fight for the future of her bloodline. Proteus, steady beside her, surveyed the forest with the practiced gaze of a trained soldier, his officer's wisdom providing unspoken comfort. Amadeus appeared as a fierce protector, ready to spring into battle to safeguard his sisters.

They ascended higher, where the chill bit deeper and the stars seemed to draw closer, curious observers of their clandestine journey.

As they approached the camp, apprehension coursed through Variel's veins; she was uncertain how her people would respond to Messalina's reappearance. With a gesture, she parted the veil of their protective wards, stepping into the secure perimeter of the camp, with Messalina and her family following closely behind. The air cooled upon her skin, and a familiar pressure eased as the camp's quiet magic accepted them.

Variel caught Thalius' scent before she saw him. The Norithaean warrior stood guard not far from the camp's perimeter. The slide of his sword and the rustle of his wings told her he was aware of their approach.

"Stand down, Thalius," she called softly enough for him to hear. "It's just me."

For a moment, everything fell silent; only the sound of their gentle footsteps against the leaf-littered ground broke the stillness. But as they stepped into the clearing, a deep gasp shattered the quiet.

"It can't be," gasped Kalliopi Icarus, an Aegrician warrior standing beside Thalius, her mouth agape and golden eyes wide. "Messalina?"

The name rippled through the clearing—shock followed by a dawning relief that felt like rain after a drought.

Variel's gaze shifted from the fiery-haired princess at her side to the dark-haired warrior, then back again. By the time she turned her eyes back to Messalina, the princess was already running, throwing her arms around Kalliopi. It was clear in that moment that Messalina would be received with open arms by her people, no matter how long she had been gone. Around them, lanterns brightened one by one, as if the camp itself had decided to welcome her home.

CHAPTER TWENTY-THREE

AURELIA

The fading sun created deep shadows between the ancient trees of the Emerald Enclave's wild forest as Aurelia's group gathered around the injured satyr. His breathing was labored, and blood oozed from a deep gash in his arm where the beast's teeth had dug in. The bite had ragged edges where the teeth had torn through skin; heat throbbed under Aurelia's palm, even through the cloth. Aurelia's heart clenched with worry as she watched Bremusa cover the wound with her hands, a silver glow emanating from her pale skin. Although Bremusa wasn't a healer, she possessed healing abilities among her many powers.

"Will he be alright?" Aurelia asked, stepping closer to Cristos, who pulled her even closer to him. Even though she knew it wasn't her fault they were in this situation, she couldn't shake the feeling of responsibility for the satyr's injury. That thought felt like iron—useless guilt, yet stubborn as blood.

Bremusa didn't look away from her patient. "His injury is severe, but there is deep magic in this land and magic in his blood. My powers can do the rest, but we must set up camp here tonight so he can rest."

Cristos nodded, his strong arms wrapping protectively around Aurelia. "We'll set up camp. Take all the time you need."

For the next hour, wards were created around the small camp as tents were erected and a fire was lit. The wards settled with a soft pressure in the air, a hush that felt like a hand over the camp's mouth. The queen had graciously provided them with food for their journey, so the dryads prepared a meal of root stew. The injured satyr was set up inside a tent beside his comrade, resting peacefully under a concoction harvested from the surrounding forest that aided in pain relief.

"Tell us more about the Emerald Enclave," Septima prompted, stirring the stew with a wooden spoon as it hung over the fire. "What dangers lie ahead?"

Solitaria sighed, her green eyes gazing into the distance, where the forest was illuminated by thousands of luminescent bugs. It was breathtaking, and Aurelia could tell that the dryad agreed, even though she had lived there her entire life. "This land is filled with enchantments and ancient magic. It's wondrous."

"You must be careful, however," Gillia chimed in. "Creatures roam these forests—dangerous ones like the hellhound that attacked us, and the terrain itself can change without warning to protect itself. It's a beautiful place, but it is not safe. Don't let its beauty fool you."

"Paths have been known to fold back on themselves, and clearings can vanish like a breath on glass."

As the fire's embers crackled and glowed, Aurelia snuggled into Cristos' side, watching the flames. Bremusa approached her. "May I speak with you privately?" she asked, her silver eyes gleaming in the moonlight.

After a brief glance at Cristos, Aurelia nodded. "Of course."

She gave her husband a quick kiss on the lips and followed Bremusa toward the edge of the campsite, where a gentle stream babbled. The grass soaked her ankles, and the stream's breeze carried the faint scents of resin and crushed mint, a clean contrast to the campfire's smoke. Aurelia looked across the water, where fire sprites had just begun their nightly dance among the foliage. "What's on your mind, Bremusa?" she asked.

Bremusa lifted her hand, a spiral of silver light swirling at her fingertips. "Earlier tonight, I was thinking about whether you and I can combine our powers to locate the portal," she began, her voice hushed. "I believe we might amplify each other's abilities. Our connection could be strong enough for us to sense the portal's presence or for your visions to reveal its location."

"But we must be careful," Aurelia replied. "Shared sight can blur the self. If I pull too hard, I could drag you deeper than you intend."

After days of working together on the ship, the idea didn't surprise Aurelia. Still, she also lacked confidence in her ability to summon useful visions. Still, for her people, she would try anything. So, although she was unsure, not that she could have been sure of anything, she sat down on the grass-covered ground beside Bremusa and reached out her hands. "Let us try."

Beneath the shadowy canopy of an ancient oak tree, Aurelia and Bremusa intertwined their fingers, palms pressing against one another as their eyes fell closed. The energy between them pulsed and hummed like the gentle rhythm of a heartbeat, causing Aurelia's own heart to slow. Her hearing narrowed; each heartbeat became a distant drum in fog, and soon the camp, the fire, and even Cristos faded to the far side of a pane of glass. She didn't think about anything in particular, simply allowing the surge of power from her friend's hands to fill her, while the bubbling of the stream soothed her.

For what seemed like hours, but was probably only minutes, their bodies swayed gently in unison, as if drawn together by an unseen force. Time lost all meaning, and the world around them faded until only their shared consciousness remained.

Suddenly, Aurelia gasped as a surge of energy unlike anything she had ever experienced coursed through her veins. She gripped Bremusa's hands tighter, trembling with the force of the energy within her.

"Something's happening," she whispered, her voice barely audible. "Can you feel it?"

As if a door had opened, allowing a flood of power to wash over them, darkness enveloped Aurelia before she could hear Bremusa's response.

Aurelia's body went limp, her consciousness slipping from the physical world and plunging her into a dreamlike state. She could no longer sense Bremusa's presence or hear the gentle trickle of the stream nearby. Instead, she found herself adrift in an ethereal realm that existed parallel to the one she had been in, guided by a faint yet persistent pull that beckoned her forward, leading her through the forest by a golden thread.

A shimmering golden thread glowed before her, brightening as she wrapped her fingers around it. It hummed a note she felt more than heard—one she recognized from Otera's steady courage and her mother's voice in memory. She followed its winding path, the silken strand urging her onward through the lush landscape that shifted and blurred with every step. Whispers of a phantom wind rustled the leaves above, but they didn't flutter her hair.

"Where are you leading me?" she wondered aloud, her voice barely more than a breath, mingling with the sounds of nature. There was no response, only the unyielding pull of the thread that tugged her onward.

Fear and anticipation warred within Aurelia's chest, sending her heart pounding and her breath loud enough for her to hear. The realm felt both real and foreign, as if it were a product of her own memories twisted by some unseen force. It was overwhelming—*otherworldly*—and she was utterly alone.

Days seemed to pass as the landscape changed from dense forests to expansive plains. The golden thread never wavered in its course, even as the ethereal sun rose and set and then rose again. Aurelia's feet grew sore, her muscles ached from the constant trek, but she didn't feel hungry or thirsty, so she pressed on, driven by something innate within herself and the draw of the luminous golden string.

When day turned to night on the second day, mountains appeared before her, a deep cave nestled within, its jagged peaks piercing the sky.

"Is this where you want me to go?" Her voice trembled as she twisted the golden strand in her fingers, the entrance beckoning her where the strand disappeared within. A sense of foreboding settled in her stomach. She felt that if she entered the cave, she might never step back out. The air cooled and thinned, as if the mountain had lungs and was holding its breath. No one responded to her question, only the steady tug guiding her into the darkness.

With a deep breath and a quick glance around her, she stepped inside the cavern, the golden thread illuminating her path. Usually, she would have been scared, but at that moment, in a world that didn't quite feel real, she wasn't afraid—not in the sense that she would turn and run away. There was nowhere to run, not if she wanted to return to Cristos and Septima. If she were asleep, she would wake once the vision had finished with her. Until then, she needed to follow Bremusa's instructions and pay attention to what the vision was trying to show her.

As she ventured deeper into the main corridor, she noticed droplets of water trailing down the stone walls. An ethereal light began to pulse in the distance, casting an eerie glow across the cave's interior. The closer she got to the source of the light, the harder her heart beat, the racing of her pulse making her feel lightheaded, but she didn't stop walking. She couldn't.

It wasn't until she arrived at the back of the cave that she saw the figure standing before her and the object that person was guarding. There, in front of a swirling vortex of energy inside a large mirror with an intricately carved frame—a portal—stood a fae female. Her hair was as white as fresh snow and cascaded down to her hips. Symbols ran along the frame like ivy—some familiar from temple mosaics and others older than any script she'd ever seen. Though the female's face was stunningly beautiful, Aurelia sensed something was amiss—a hidden truth lay just beneath the surface. As she peered closer, the illusion fell away, revealing the woman's true visage, or rather the face the woman wanted her to see: a terrifying old crone, with pale eyes swirling with power that were fixed on the portal before her. The wrinkles of her face were deep against her sharp cheekbones. The shift wasn't a blink, but rather a peel, as beauty sloughed off like wet paint, revealing the bone-honest face beneath.

A gasp escaped Aurelia's mouth without her permission, and she instinctively took a step back, reaching for the dagger at her thigh. "Who are you? What is this place?"

Although Aurelia could see the female standing no more than a few feet away, the female did not respond, her attention focused solely on the pulsating energy before her. It was then that Aurelia realized the gravity of her discovery—the reason the vision had brought her to that very cave, where a portal's power resided, guarded by a being whose intentions remained a mystery. Aurelia didn't know where she was or how to get back, but she understood why she was there. The crone before her had somehow trapped the portal there, although she didn't know how or why.

Invisible and ghostly, Aurelia hovered over the crone's shoulder. Her heart raced, and her stomach turned as she gazed upon the swirling glass of the powerful mirror—the Shadow Glass. This was the object that had foretold her birth more than two decades earlier. The very thought sent a twinge of pain straight into Aurelia's soul, making her wonder how, or if, she could find her way back to the human realm through that portal and reunite with her father and brother, since her mother was gone. She missed her mother every day—a loss she would never overcome, no matter how many years passed. The energy emanating from the mirror's surface was unlike anything she had ever encountered—a storm of raw power that seemed to call to her very soul. Yet it was not just the portal's energy that held her transfixed. There was something about the Shadow Glass itself, a dark allure that drew her closer, like a moth to a flame.

"Is this all I've been searching for?" Aurelia whispered, her words lost in the maelstrom of magic surrounding her. Deep down, she knew this was the key to everything: the salvation of her kingdom, her beloved family, and perhaps even herself. Even as she moved closer, studying the crone with a cautious eye and pondering the ancient sorceress's role in the grand tapestry of fate, the crone did not react. Her eyes remained swirling, as though her body was present but her spirit was somewhere else—just as Aurelia found herself in her own plane. The thought sent a shiver through her body as she wondered if, back at the bank of the stream, her own body—her eyes—looked the same.

It was then that the unthinkable happened. After countless minutes—or perhaps hours—Aurelia had lost count. The crone seemed to sense Aurelia's presence in the room. The golden thread twanged in her fist—heard but not seen—like a warning shot through her nerves. Coming out of her trance, the crone's pale eyes snapped into focus, narrowing as they scanned the cave before finally locking onto Aurelia's ethereal form, still shimmering beside the golden thread. Blood turned to ice as fear rooted Aurelia's feet to the spot, as though her boots were made of lead.

"Who dares intrude upon my sanctuary?" the crone snarled, her voice bone-chilling and filled with rage. "I know you're here. Show yourself!" Before Aurelia could react, the sorceress raised her arms. She cast a spell that made Aurelia's spectral body flicker and waver, sending a shudder through her very being.

"Wait!" Aurelia cried out, desperation clawing at her throat. "I didn't mean to intrude. I...I need your help." She didn't know what else to say. For the first time in her vision, she was genuinely terrified. Although Otera had sensed her presence before, she had never been seen while in a vision. This time was different; her circumstances suddenly felt very serious and very dangerous.

"Help?" The crone sneered, her eyes alight with malicious amusement. It took Aurelia a moment to realize that the crone could hear her, which made her heart race. She glanced down at her hand, which was wrapped around her dagger. Her fingers were no longer spectral but transitioning before her eyes to flesh and blood. A flutter low in her belly answered the change—a protective ache that sharpened her focus. Nausea twisted in her stomach, and her thoughts automatically drifted to the child in her womb as bile crawled up her throat. "You seek help from one such as me? Foolish child, you know not what you ask."

Swallowing hard, Aurelia fought to maintain her composure, not wanting to reveal the fear that paralyzed her. "*Please*. My kingdom is in danger, and I believe the power within this glass can save us."

The crone's gaze drifted back to the swirling vortex of energy within the Shadow Glass, her hand pulling out a jagged dagger from her cloak. Aurelia froze, realizing the crone was blocking her path to the exit, and her form was nearly solid. "The portal's power calls to you, does it not? It sings a siren's song that few can resist." With her eyes never leaving Aurelia's, she took a step forward. "But beware, young queen, for its power is not easily wielded or controlled."

Taking one last look at the Shadow Glass, Aurelia bolted, skirting along the side of the cavern. The crone's blade skimmed the side of her cloak as she brushed past.

Faster than she should have been able to run, the crone chased after her, throwing a bolt of energy that crumbled part of the wall. The shock rolled through the stone; grit rained from the ceiling, and the golden thread snapped taut, yanking at her toward the mouth of the tunnel. Aurelia's spectral form flickered and wavered as she attempted to escape the crone's magic, her heart pounding like a thousand drums in her ears, matching the rhythm of their footfalls. The cavern seemed to close in around her, the air itself feeling menacing.

Cristos' voice, edged with panic, pierced through the haze of Aurelia's subconscious mind, or perhaps it was part of her dream. His words vibrated along an unseen thread, as if he had found it in her and was pulling her home.

"Come back to me, love," he pleaded. The mantra became louder and more desperate with each repetition. "Please, Aurelia. Come back to me."

Although she knew the way out of the cave, the corridor seemed to stretch longer as she ran, the end always just out of reach. The weight of the crone's presence bore down on her, threatening to trap her within the nightmare forever.

"Aurelia, please. Please. Please, come back." Cristos' cry tore through the chaos, becoming a lifeline for Aurelia to cling to. It felt as though she could sense him touching her skin, a surge of electricity affirming that he was her mate. She focused on his voice with all her might, willing herself to wake up and escape.

Stumbling over a rock, Aurelia fell to the ground, her dagger clattering as it skittered away.

For a moment, time stood still. Her body was unable to move as the crone closed the distance between them and swung her blade. Aurelia screamed and scrambled away, but just as the gust of wind from the crone's movement rustled her hair, her eyes snapped open to find herself lying on the ground, shivering uncontrollably, with strong arms wrapped around her, holding her upper body in Cristos' lap. His blue eyes were wide with concern as he pulled her against his chest.

"Thank the gods you're awake," he said, tucking her head beneath his chin. "I was so worried."

Taking a few deep breaths, Aurelia tried to shake off the lingering terror from her encounter and to understand what had made this dream feel so much more real than all the others. Though her body was drained and there was still much she didn't understand, one thing became clear as a newfound certainty settled over her mind like the first rays of sunlight piercing through a stormy sky.

"I know where it is." Her voice trembled, but the certainty within her had weight; it settled in her bones like a compass pointing true. Cristos' voice, edged with panic, pierced through the haze of Aurelia's subconscious mind, or perhaps it was part of her dream. His words vibrated along an unseen thread, as if he had found it in her and was pulling her home.

"Come back to me, love," he pleaded. The mantra became louder and more desperate with each repetition. "Please, Aurelia. Come back to me."

Although she knew the way out of the cave, the corridor seemed to stretch longer as she ran, the end always just out of reach. The weight of the crone's presence bore down on her, threatening to trap her within the nightmare forever.

"Aurelia, please. Please. Please, come back." Cristos' cry tore through the chaos, becoming a lifeline for Aurelia to cling to. It felt as though she could sense him touching her skin, a surge of electricity affirming that he was her mate. She focused on his voice with all her might, willing herself to wake up and escape.

Stumbling over a rock, Aurelia fell to the ground, her dagger clattering as it skittered away.

For a moment, time stood still. Her body was unable to move as the crone closed the distance between them and swung her blade. Aurelia screamed and scrambled away, but just as the gust of wind from the crone's movement rustled her hair, her eyes snapped open to find herself lying on the ground, shivering uncontrollably, with strong arms wrapped around her, holding her upper body in Cristos' lap. His blue eyes were wide with concern as he pulled her against his chest.

"Thank the gods you're awake," he said, tucking her head beneath his chin. "I was so worried."

Taking a few deep breaths, Aurelia tried to shake off the lingering terror from her encounter and to understand what had made this dream feel so much more real than all the others. Though her body was drained and there was still much she didn't understand, one thing became clear as a newfound certainty settled over her mind like the first rays of sunlight piercing through a stormy sky.

"I know where it is." Her voice trembled, but the certainty within her had weight; it settled in her bones like a compass pointing true.

Chapter Twenty-Four

Kason

For the first time since their arrival in Embershell, trepidation flooded through Kason. He had never been the kind of man to become easily frightened, but having his mate kneeling on the floor in front of King Ailani was not a safe situation. The air was thick with tension, nearly suffocating him, even though the sack had been removed from his head. He fought to maintain his composure. Beside him, Holera was silent, and her scent indicated that she was just as uneasy as he was. The magnificent marble floors and gold-encrusted walls seemed to mock their current predicament. The glittering chamber, intended to awe guests, only deepened his unease—beauty draped over suspicion like a mask that threatened to crack at any moment.

"Your Majesty," Kason managed, his voice strained from the pain in his shoulders caused by being tightly bound. "We came to Diapolis on a diplomatic mission. We meant no harm. You've known us for years. My mate and I are not spies."

King Ailani narrowed his eyes at the couple before him, leaning forward in his gilded throne, his finger tracing the carvings on the armrest. His consort, Makoa, stood by his side, as stoic as ever. "And yet, here you kneel, accused of spying in my kingdom. Do you take me for a fool?"

"Of course not, Your Majesty," Holera replied, drawing the king's turquoise eyes to her. "We have always been friendly with you and your kingdom, as has our former queen, Otera, and our new queen, Aurelia. Our sole purpose in Diapolis was to gather information that could benefit us all."

"Information?" King Ailani scoffed, his voice dripping with skepticism. "Or secrets to use against us?"

Turning to glance at Holera, Kason's chest tightened. "King Ailani, our past visits as your guests should prove our allegiance. We have fought alongside your soldiers and shared in your victories. We would never betray you or your people."

"Then explain your presence in areas of Diapolis where outsiders are forbidden," the king demanded, his tone icy and unyielding.

Hesitating for a moment, Kason exchanged a worried glance with Holera. He knew their intentions were just, and neither of them had realized the caves were forbidden. However, convincing King Ailani of that fact was proving more difficult than he had anticipated. The king of Diapolis had always been an isolationist, so forming an alliance with another kingdom was never something he seemed comfortable with. Kason straightened his spine. "After the ashes settled and friends and enemies alike departed our lands, a powerful artifact, held in our kingdom for centuries, was found to have been stolen. We don't know who took it, but we do know that if it falls into the wrong hands..." He shook his head and blew out a breath. "If this artifact, which can control the portal between worlds and can tell prophecies that can build or break kingdoms, ended up in the wrong hands, it could destroy us all. We hoped to discover the truth and bring it to your attention so we might stand united against any danger. This is far bigger than just the north or south of the continent. This affects us all."

His voice wavered despite his resolve—the plea not only for their lives but also for the fragile hope that even an isolationist king might set aside caution for the sake of their shared realm.

A flicker of something akin to fear passed across the king's eyes, but it quickly vanished. When he turned his gaze back to Kason, however, there was more kindness in his eyes than before. "Words are easily spoken, Kason. Actions speak much louder."

Taking a deep breath, Kason dipped his chin and then glanced back at his mate before looking at the king once more. "Allow us this chance to act on behalf of our shared interests, and you will see that our loyalty is unwavering. We need to work together against this threat."

King Ailani's gaze lingered on Kason and Holera, his eyes flicking between them as if he were searching for any sign of deception. After a slow heartbeat, Makoa placed his hand on the king's shoulder, a silent exchange between them that clearly carried significance. "Very well," the king finally said, his tone still more clipped than Kason would have liked. "I will grant you this opportunity to prove your allegiance. But be warned, should I discover that your loyalty has wavered, there will be no mercy."

Relief washed over Kason, easing not only his chest but also his shoulders and back as the guard unfastened his bonds. He stood behind Holera, stretching his arms before reaching for her hand. "Thank you, Your Majesty. We will not disappoint you."

The king nodded once, his long, golden curls spilling over the embroidered lapel of his sapphire jacket. "Rise and go freshen up." Behind them, the double doors of the throne room opened as two guards stepped into the entrance. "I will meet with my scouts and advisors to discuss this matter. We shall reconvene once you have had time to rest."

As Kason and Holera entered the guest room in the west wing of the palace, which overlooked the sea, he let out a breath and shut the door behind them. They both sighed, the stress of their capture and audience with King Ailani slowly dissipating now that they were alone.

"I think we convinced him," Holera murmured, a grin tugging at the side of her full lips. "But I'm still not sure if we're safe here."

Kason nodded and pulled her against his chest, kissing her deeply. "I know, fierce warrior. For now, let us take advantage of this moment of respite. I'm sure you're ready for a bath."

Her smile growing wider, Holera nodded, running her hands over her disheveled platinum hair that had become messy beneath the sack. "I'm always ready for a bath."

A large copper bathtub stood in the corner of the bathing room, steam rising from the hot water within. The Diapolisian palace was luxurious, a stark contrast to the tavern they'd been staying at for the past few days. Approaching it, Kason discarded his clothes as he went, his cock already hard from having his arms around his mate. Holera followed suit, stripping her dark clothes off and dropping them to the floor.

Holera stepped into the tub, a sigh escaping her lips. For a moment, all Kason could do was watch her. Her beauty took his breath away.

The warm water lapped at Kason's skin, soothing his aching muscles as he slid into the tub behind Holera. Taking a bath together was one of their rituals—one they both seemed to enjoy. If they could both fit in a tub, then they almost always used that time to relax together.

"I wasn't sure we were going to make it out of today," he admitted, cupping his hands and filling them with water to wet Holera's hair. Her eyes fell closed. "If something had happened to you—"

Violet eyes opened to meet his, her hand reaching for his wrist. "Don't. Don't do that. Nothing happened, and we are both okay."

He knew she was right, and he hated dwelling on the what-ifs, but seeing her bound beside him was a sight that would haunt his dreams. Still, he smiled and nodded. "I know, but I'm taking you home after this. Back to our cottage."

The words steadied him, a lifeline he clung to amid the storm of politics and war. That promise of hearth and family was the only future that mattered.

And he meant it. He was going to take her home and raise a family.

Lifting herself up in the tub, Holera spun around and slid her leg over him. "I already told you that I'm ready for that, too. I'm ready to make you a father."

The feel of her warmth enveloping him as she straddled him and took him deep sent his eyes rolling back in his head. Candlelight flickered from the sconces on the wall, casting a reflection in her dark eyes. His lips met hers in a hungry kiss the moment she was fully seated. With his arms around her, he lifted his hips to meet the roll of hers, every deep stroke stoking the fire inside his core. He marveled at the feel of her skin beneath his hands, so soft and yet so powerful.

"Maybe we can start now," he whispered, his voice gravelly with lust. He leaned in, capturing her lips with his, his tongue slipping in to taste her. Every swipe of her tongue against his spun the spiral low in his stomach tighter, until holding back his climax was nearly impossible.

Holera's head tilted back when her orgasm hit, her cunt squeezing him so tight it made his eyes water. Bracing his hands on her hips, he drove up into her harder, swallowing every moan against his lips until his own release barreled through him, leaving him breathless and more in love than he had ever been.

Yet even as bliss warmed his veins, a shadow lingered in the back of his mind—peace was fleeting, and every stolen moment with her might be their last.

Dressed in the garments provided by servants earlier that day, Kason and Holera entered the grand dining hall, where King Ailani and his consort awaited them. The tension in the room loomed like a storm cloud over the table, creating a stark contrast to the brilliant morning sun streaming through the stained glass windows. As they approached the ornate table laden with mouthwatering dishes, the king's piercing turquoise gaze remained fixed on them.

The air felt charged, as if the very light from the stained glass was struggling to reach them, bending under the weight of grim tidings.

"Please, sit," King Ailani said, his tone light despite his serious expression. Kason could sense that something was troubling the monarch, and it created a pit in his stomach. He realized that something had changed overnight, and they were about to learn what that was.

"Good morning, Your Highness." Kason pulled out a chair for Holera and then took a seat directly across from King Ailani. A servant followed closely behind, pouring hot water into their mugs of tea. "Have you found out anything new?"

King Ailani leaned forward, tapping his fingers on the table. "I met with my scouts and advisors last night. They discovered information about an elemental sorceress in the Inferno Territories. Rumors suggest she is incredibly powerful—capable of feats that belong in legends. It's said that she wishes to access the portal to create a rift between the worlds, allowing the fae to enter the realm of humans and even opening the rift that separates the veil, which would allow the dead to roam free."

The thought of an entire world bent and broken under unnatural rule made Kason's skin prickle, as if the sorceress's influence already extended across the sea.

As he processed the king's words, a cold knot formed in Kason's stomach where the pit had once been. The stakes had just risen, and the weight of responsibility bore down on him. He reached beneath the table and took Holera's hand, feeling her palm grow clammy.

"Do they have any idea where she is?" Kason asked. The Inferno Territories were a massive continent across the Irriboia Sea, along with the surrounding islands. He had only visited a few times on diplomatic missions.

Genuine concern creased the king's brow. "She's elusive, but my advisors believe she is moving north with an ancient force capable of bending nature itself to her will. If she succeeds, she could reshape our world in her twisted image, plunging us into darkness. A group of my most powerful trackers and magic wielders left for the continent aboard dragon-escorted ships this morning."

Kason exchanged a brief glance with Holera, trepidation evident in her violet eyes. They both knew their friends, and the new queen had already departed for the Inferno Territories. If something happened to those people, it was a frightening possibility that left him struggling to breathe.

"We must return to Aegricia at once and warn our people."

CHAPTER TWENTY-FIVE

VARIEL

The morning rays of the sun shone over the forest in the human territory of Breqan, cutting through the mist that clung to the trees like a lover's embrace. Variel stood at the edge of the camp, her keen eyes scanning the terrain ahead as she contemplated the steep ascent toward the caves where she had encountered Joneira's warriors before. The morning mist clung stubbornly to the treetops, veiling the path like a warning, as if the forest itself wished to hide what lay above. There was so much at stake if she was going to lead her people into the viper's den without knowing whether the portal was even there. Still, they dismantled their makeshift camp because they couldn't return home if they didn't search for the portal.

After she had arrived back at camp the night before with the long-lost Aegrician princess, Messalina Lumino, along with Proteus and Amadeus, the entire group sat around the fire for hours. Everyone was shocked to see Messalina and had a million questions for her about how she had managed to hide away for so long. By the time Variel curled up in her corner of one of the tents, she was exhausted.

"Variel," Messalina said, checking the straps on her bow and quiver. "We're ready to go."

With a slight nod of her lupine head, Variel set off along the trail, more than a dozen of her people following behind. The wind whispered through the trees overhead, and the scent of damp earth filled her nostrils. Moss and lichen clung to the rocks beneath her feet. She could hear the quiet conversations of the others behind her, but she didn't focus on them. Even without listening, she could feel their nerves pressing against her own—each heartbeat quick, each step too loud for a group hoping to remain unseen. Instead, she paid attention to the sounds of the forest around them. If an enemy were to happen upon them, her heightened senses would serve as their first line of defense. Despite the uncertainty in the air, Variel pressed onward.

As they climbed higher, the temperature dropped, sending shivers through Variel's fur. Icy tendrils of mist curled around her legs, obscuring the path and making each step more treacherous than the last—especially for the others. She glanced back at them, relieved to see determination still etched on their faces despite the biting cold.

After hours of hiking northward toward the place she had been just days earlier, Variel shifted back into her humanoid form and pointed to a clearing they had reached in the forest, not far from the river. "We can set up camp here."

Even as she spoke and they began to erect tents and set up wards around the campsite, a sense of threat lingered in the shadows of the darkening woods, something lurking just beyond their reach. They were within an hour's walk from the caves, and it was close enough for the power within them to call to her.

As night fell and the moon illuminated the world below, Variel shifted back into her wolf form, her senses instantly sharpening. Leaving the protection of the campsite, she led Messalina, Proteus, Amadeus, and several other warriors toward the caves, her muzzle to the ground as she searched for any trace of their enemies.

The group moved silently through the darkness, each step weighed down by the burden of their mission. Variel's ears flipped back and forth, straining to catch the faintest whisper of sound. Her nostrils flared as she caught a whiff of something—a male scent with hints of embers and freshly roasted meat. She closed her eyes, summoning the power that flowed just beneath her skin. The rest of her friends stood behind her, remaining hidden by the thick brush as she forced her power away from her body, and the wards around the enemy camp fell away. The flicker of a bonfire and approximately ten enemy warriors came into view, their laughter and conversation telling her they didn't sense the threat.

A low snarl rumbled through her chest, her lips lifting to reveal a maw filled with deadly pointed teeth. Her group moved around her, Messalina pulling her sword from its sheath. Every guard sitting around the fire looked up as her obsidian wolf form stepped out of the shadows, leaping forward with a fierce growl.

The sound of clanging steel and screaming filled the silent mountain air as Joneira's soldiers jumped up from their seats, drew their weapons, and attacked.

Messalina roared, her sword slicing through the air as it found its mark, tearing a gash into a male's ribcage. Blood immediately covered his white tunic, and he crumpled to the ground—not dead, but there was a very good chance the wound would prove to be fatal. The copper tang thickened in the air, iron and smoke mingling until every breath tasted of death itself. Although Variel's group outnumbered their enemies, several members of both sides had already sustained injuries, making them evenly matched.

Variel's teeth sank into the arm of an enemy who came after her with a dagger. She reveled in the taste of blood, but her satisfaction was short-lived. While one male struggled against her bite, more desperate to get her unattached than to get his sword that lay on the ground only feet away, another enemy blade slashed for her. Searing pain raced up her foreleg when a short sword slashed across the limb. Her vision spotted at the edges, a howl clawing at her throat. Still, she bit it back, refusing to give her enemies the satisfaction of hearing her scream.

Releasing the enemy's arm, she yelped and launched herself into the air on her hind legs, tearing his throat out before turning on the warrior who attacked her. The moment both enemies lay at her feet, she stumbled toward the treeline, her breath growing ragged. Her form shifted without her permission, but it gave her the fingers she needed to rip off part of her enemy's cloak and wrap it around her arm to stop the bleeding.

"Variel!" Messalina cried, concern lacing her voice as she dispatched another foe.

"I'm okay. Look for Joneira!" With a wince, she pulled herself back to her feet. The pain was intense, but she refused to let it hinder her.

"Amadeus, behind you!" Proteus darted toward his son, his warning arriving just in time for Amadeus to deflect the dagger aimed at his heart. Though he managed to avoid a fatal blow, the weapon grazed his shoulder, leaving a bloody gash in its wake.

"Thanks," Amadeus grunted, his face twisted in pain as he turned to fight another enemy who had pinned one of the Aegrician warriors to the ground.

As the last of the enemy warriors fell, Variel searched for Messalina and found her rummaging through the tents. The shadows swallowed them whole as they slipped between the clusters of erected structures, keeping them out of sight if any enemies lay in wait. The scent of sweat and blood hung heavily in the air, mingling with the aroma of pine. Despite her injured arm, she kept her focus sharp, her senses attuned to every whisper and rustle around them.

"Can you sense her?" Messalina asked quietly, her eyes darting from side to side, her grip tight on her sword.

Lifting her nose to the air, Variel breathed in deeply. The scent of the exiled queen was undeniably nearby. "Her presence is here, but it's faint. She can't be far."

They stepped through the forest on near-silent feet, leaving the camp behind. It didn't take long for them to realize where Joneira's scent was leading them: to the cave.

The dark granite surrounding the cave's entrance reflected the moonlight like a beacon, guiding them to what they were searching for. A cold air seeped from within, carrying the metallic scent of blood and the ancient whisper of power gone awry. Variel stopped and turned to look at the Aegrician princess beside her. Even in the moonlight, Messalina resembled her daughter so closely that, given the slow aging of the fae, she appeared more like Aurelia's sister than her mother.

"She's inside. The portal is as well—or at least I believe it is. The power is somehow warped or not in its full form, so I don't think it can be used to cross back to our world in its current state."

Worry flashed across Messalina's eyes as she undoubtedly thought of her daughters, who were still in the fae realm fighting their own battles. However, she nodded firmly. "We end this now. Once she's dead, we can figure out how to get back across. I will find a way to reunite my family."

With her dominant arm still burning in pain, Variel held her dagger in her other hand, knowing she wouldn't be able to wield it as effectively as she needed to. The two women stepped into the dark maw of the cave, their footsteps light but their breathing heavy.

"You," a female voice hissed. A flicker of fire in a palm illuminated the face of Messalina and Variel's mortal enemy. "You were supposed to be dead."

Messalina scoffed and took a step forward. "I guess you're not as good as you thought."

The laugh that escaped Joneira was pure malice as she circled Messalina, her eyes flicking to Variel. "And you... couldn't just mind your own business."

Her voice echoed like a hiss through the stone, sharp enough to cut, her eyes glinting with the fire of someone who had waited decades for vengeance.

Variel snarled, but before she could strike Joneira with her shortsword, a figure stepped out of the darkness. His face was scarred, and his eye was covered with a patch. Variel's heart sank the moment she recognized him. A walking dead man. "Uldon."

The Warbotach monarch smirked, his scarred lip lifting. "As an oracle, should you not have known I'd made it across on the back of an Aegrician before the portal crumbled?"

When the portal was destroyed, Variel had been engaged in battle with Joneira and hadn't seen what had happened to the Warbotach barbarians who invaded the northern part of the continent. She had seen them departing in ships and on the backs of hostage Aegrician warriors, so she had assumed they all perished in the blast.

Swallowing back her fear, knowing Uldon was brutal and she was injured, Variel raised her sword. His smile widened—he could undoubtedly scent her blood in the air. "It seems the rest of your warriors are gone, so you're not as scary as you used to be."

His grin fell as a snarl ripped from him. A moment later, he lunged. When Uldon swiped low with his sword, Variel met the strike, the force of it rattling her bones. Behind them, the other two women charged at one another.

"Your family will never be safe," Joneira taunted as she lunged, narrowly missing Messalina's side. "I'll hunt them down, just like I hunted you."

"Never!" Messalina roared, but Variel was too focused on fending off Uldon's strikes to assist her. Gritting her teeth, Variel caught Uldon's blade with her own and pushed back with all her strength, barely making him stumble. Her heart pounded with every strike as she charged forward again, her sword arcing toward Uldon's throat, but he quickly parried, countering with a blow aimed at her ribs.

Despite the stinging pain that burned through her injured arm, Variel managed to twist away, narrowly avoiding his lethal blade. Her breath came in ragged gasps, but her thoughts remained focused. Survival depended on it.

On the other side of the cavern, Joneira pressed forward with a flurry of blows that forced Messalina to retreat. She stumbled, her foot catching on a loose stone and sending her sprawling to the ground.

"Pathetic," he sneered, the slash of his sword barely missing her waist.

The sound of approaching boots sent hope rushing through Variel's chest. She kicked out, catching him off guard and knocking his sword to the floor. With a primal scream, Messalina rolled to the side, narrowly avoiding Joneira's blade. She then launched herself upward, her own sword finding its mark as it slid between Joneira's ribs and pierced her heart.

The others arrived from behind, with Proteus swiping at Uldon, momentarily diverting the barbarian king's attention from Variel. She fell to her knees, her chest pumping rapidly with exertion.

Only feet away, Joneira's eyes widened in shock, disbelief etched across her features as blood stained her lips. She tried to speak, but only a gurgle emerged along with the blood trickling from the corner of her mouth before she crumpled to the ground. Dead.

For a moment, Messalina stood over Joneira's lifeless body, a mixture of emotions clouding her stunning face. "This is for my mother and grandmother," she said, slashing her sword down and slicing across Joneira's neck. The exiled queen's head rolled forward, her lifeless golden eyes staring up at the ceiling.

Amid the sound of her own blood rushing in her ears, Variel heard the moment Uldon's large body hit the ground, but she didn't turn away from Messalina and the greatest enemy their kingdom had ever known. It was finally over. All they had to do was find a way back home. Yet even in victory, silence pressed down heavily; the cavern was thick with smoke and blood, and the knowledge that endings always give rise to new beginnings—some darker than the last.

CHAPTER TWENTY-SIX

AURELIA

After Aurelia had been saved from her vision, Cristos carried her into their tent, and she fell asleep in his arms. For the rest of the night, she slept soundly, free from thoughts of the crone invading her dreams.

The next morning, before she awoke, Vasilis had left with the injured satyr, Joc, taking him back to the palace. With two fewer people in their party, the group set off north toward the kingdom of Cineris, where the Voiceless Mountains cut across the center of the continent. Once they were within an hour's walk of the mountains' base, they set up camp for the night.

Later that night, with Cristos' arm draped over her waist, Aurelia's eyes fluttered open, revealing a sliver of moonlight filtering through the canvas of the tent. She lay on her side, listening to the whispers of the wind through the trees. The whispers gave way to a louder sound—or perhaps it wasn't a sound at all, but a deeper calling that burrowed into her mind, guiding her thoughts—what to hear, what to do. It beckoned her to follow. This soundless summons coiled through her mind like smoke, invasive and impossible to dispel.

Taking a deep breath, she slipped out from beneath Cristos' embrace. With the moonlight illuminating little within the tent, she did her best to find her weapons and then quietly stepped outside.

The fear gripping her heart threatened to consume her, but she steeled herself against it, or at least attempted to. Silently, she tiptoed past her friends' tents, hoping none of them would notice her absence. A pang of guilt pierced her heart, but she shook her head to clear her thoughts as she lit a torch from the fire and stepped beyond the camp's protective barrier.

"Forgive me," she whispered to everyone, her voice barely audible over the sounds of nighttime creatures. "I cannot risk your safety any longer. This burden is mine to bear." She hated the lie in those words, but if Cristos woke and followed her, he could get hurt because of her recklessness, and she could not let that happen.

Aurelia shivered as the chill of the mountainous forest landscape enveloped her; the shadows of the trees seemed to reach out and ensnare her as she moved through the underbrush. Even without the golden thread as her guide, the pull of the portal grew stronger with each step. Her heart pounded in her chest like the beat of a tribal drum, urging her forward as she approached the mouth of the cave where she believed the portal was hidden.

A cacophony of dripping stalactites and the distant rumble of an underground river filled the cave as Aurelia inched her way deeper into the darkness. The pull of the portal intensified, nearly dragging her forward as if she were being pulled by chains. She couldn't turn around; she couldn't break free. The darkness pressed closer with every step, thick as tar, as though the cave itself resented her trespass.

Suddenly, a gust of wind extinguished her torch, plunging her into complete darkness. Aurelia's breath caught in her throat, and her stomach sank as dread washed over her. Then, as if materializing from the shadows, the silver-haired elemental sorceress appeared before her. This time, she wore the face of a young woman, not that of an old crone.

"Ah, the little queen has finally arrived," the sorceress sneered, her eyes glinting like ice. "Did you truly think you could steal what I've worked so hard to find without consequence?"

"The portal doesn't belong to you," Aurelia shot back, discreetly pulling one of the daggers from her thigh sheath. "You stole it from my kingdom, where it's been for centuries."

"Such naivety." Before Aurelia could react, the sorceress raised her hand and launched a barrage of magical energy toward her. Instinctively, Aurelia dove out of the way, narrowly avoiding the deadly strike. A second later, she was running.

"Run all you want, little queen," Cyrena called after her. "But know that I will find you in the end. I'll put an end to the decades-long prophecy myself."

As Aurelia sprinted through the cave, shards of rock rained down around her, illustrating just how powerful the sorceress was. She knew she had to find a way to stop her, but she didn't know how.

When her foot caught on a jutting rock, she stumbled, losing her grip on the dagger just as she had in her vision. The dread in her stomach only grew. The dagger skittered across the uneven floor, disappearing into the shadows. Panic surged as she reached for another dagger, aware it wouldn't be effective against the elemental's power.

"Ah, there you are." With a snarl, Aurelia's attacker threw another magical strike at her. This time, it was aimed at her abdomen.

The pain that followed was like nothing she had ever experienced, a searing agony that threatened to consume her entirely. Fear rose in her chest, but something fiercer rose with it. She was more than a target; she was a mother defending a future.

"Your unborn child will never see the light of day," the sorceress hissed, her voice devoid of any trace of humanity. "And neither will you."

Clutching her stomach, tears streamed down Aurelia's face as she struggled to remain standing. She knew she couldn't give in—not just for her own sake, but for the life growing inside her. If she didn't find a way to stop the sorceress, everyone she loved would be in danger.

"Enough!" A powerful voice echoed through the cave, shattering the silence. Aurelia turned her head to see Bremusa stepping into the corridor, her silver eyes swirling with raw power. "You will not harm her, Cyrena... Sister." The revelation cleaved the air sharper than any blade, fracturing Aurelia's understanding of both allies and enemies.

The words hit Aurelia's stomach like stones, and the air suddenly felt thinner. She never even knew Bremusa had a sister.

Cyrena's icy laugh rang out, sending chills down Aurelia's spine. "So, you've finally come out of hiding, dear sister. How amusing. I thought you'd perished alongside our pathetic family."

Bremusa tightened her lips into a thin line and locked her jaw, a tendril of silver power swirling in her palm. "And you were supposed to be dead—killed for your crimes against our people. I survived your massacre, and I won't allow you to hurt Aurelia or her child. You may have faked your death before, dear sister, but you will die today."

As Aurelia cradled her arms around her middle to protect her unborn child, Bremusa launched herself at Cyrena. Their magical powers clashed in a dazzling display of light and shadows, both women vying for dominance. Silver energy clashed against ice, one power steady as a river's current, while the other was jagged like shards of a breaking glacier.

Although Aurelia wanted to help, she didn't know how. She was unsure if her power was strong enough to be of any use in the fight, but she felt it was her duty to protect the baby inside her womb, so she kept her distance.

The cave trembled under the force of their magic, rocks crashing down around them. Despite Bremusa's valiant efforts and extensive elemental powers, it quickly became evident that Cyrena was stronger than her sister.

"Is that all you've got, sister?" Cyrena taunted, her voice dripping with venom as she circled Bremusa. "You always were the weaker one—"

A sudden strike from Bremusa cut off Cyrena's taunts, but the sorceress only laughed harder, her wicked glee echoing throughout the cave.

Desperation clawed at Aurelia's insides as she watched Bremusa falter, exhaustion etched on her stunning face. She knew that if Cyrena won, it would mean certain death for both of them, for her child, and for countless others. Yet, she didn't know how to intervene without endangering her unborn child.

"Aurelia!" Cristos shouted, his wings tucking tightly against his back as he and the others surged into the cavern, racing toward them with their weapons ready.

"Too late for that." With a flick of her wrist, Cyrena directed a surge of dark magic toward the entrance, aiming at Aurelia's friends and family. Boulders tumbled down, sealing them away from one another and trapping Aurelia and Bremusa inside with their enemy.

"No!" Aurelia cried out, panic threatening to send her to her knees as she saw her friends disappear behind the rockslide. She turned swiftly to Bremusa, urgency flooding her blue eyes. "We have to do something!"

Bremusa nodded, her silver eyes unblinking. "The portal and the Shadow Glass... It's our only chance."

Together, they rushed forward, clasping their hands tightly as the hum of power from the portal flowed through them. The sensation was intoxicating yet frightening—raw energy coursing through Aurelia's veins, threatening to consume her if not harnessed correctly.

"Focus," Bremusa urged, her voice barely audible above the chaos. "Channel the power of the portal. We can do this."

As Cyrena snarled at them from only a few feet away, Bremusa threw out her arm, trapping Cyrena in an invisible web of magical energy. The sorceress's eyes widened as she struggled against her restraints, her hands held above her head.

"Your love for your people makes you weak!" Cyrena spat, attempting to break their concentration.

Aurelia did her best to focus, trying to ignore the venomous words coming from the sorceress's mouth. The light from the portal danced across Aurelia's face, reflecting in her eyes as she and Bremusa stood their ground. Cyrena's twisted visage was chilling, but Aurelia pushed those feelings aside.

"Your defiance will be your end!" Cyrena shouted, pulling one arm free. She hurled another barrage of dark energy at them, barely missing as Bremusa yanked Aurelia out of the way.

The air crackled with energy as their two forces collided—the dark energy pouring off of Cyrena and the glowing silver energy that coiled around Aurelia and Bremusa's joined hands, forming a protective shield against Cyrena's attacks. It created a symphony of destruction that echoed through the cavern, sending rocks tumbling to the ground around them.

"Impossible!" Cyrena snarled, her rage palpable. "You cannot defeat me!"

As she continued to struggle against her invisible binds, Cyrena managed to free her other arm. She thrust it forward, attempting to push the two of them back, but their shield of silver energy held firm. Aurelia had so much she wanted to say in response, but she couldn't afford to break her concentration.

As they maintained their grip on Cyrena, the portal behind her began to shift and change. Its once shimmering surface transformed into a solid black vortex.

A sense of dread trickled down Aurelia's spine, twisting her chest into a knot. "Is that—"

Aurelia's words were cut off by a scream from Cyrena, her eyes widening as she fought to escape.

Taking a step closer to her sister, Bremusa tightened her grip on Aurelia's hand. "The veil—a realm where the dead sleep in eternal slumber." Its pull felt wrong, like a tide that recedes forever without returning.

A shudder ran down Aurelia's spine at the thought of what lay behind the portal. She didn't understand why such a place would open in the Shadow Glass, but it was clear that Cyrena had stolen both for her own horrific purposes. Now, with the veil opening behind her and Cyrena at someone else's mercy, terror gripped her.

The cavern trembled, dust and debris raining down as Aurelia and Bremusa strained against Cyrena's overwhelming power. Even though Cyrena was held in place by their invisible web, her arms were free, allowing her to counterattack.

"When I count to three," Bremusa said, lifting their joined hands to raise their shield of power. Behind Cyrena, the portal roared, spinning like an oppressive vortex and whipping their hair around their faces. "We're going to push forward—give it everything we have. We're going to force her into the veil, where she should have been all along."

Gritting her teeth and wiping sweat from her brow with her free hand, Aurelia nodded.

With a shared glance, they poured every ounce of their strength into a final push. As if propelled by an unseen force, Cyrena was flung back through the air, her screams swallowed by the dark maw of the portal.

"No!" she shrieked, clawing at the air in a futile attempt to escape her fate. But the pull of the veil was too strong, and Cyrena vanished into the darkness with one last, desperate wail. For a heartbeat, the cave seemed to exhale. Yet, Aurelia knew the silence did not promise safety—only the next storm waiting to rise.

Heart pounding in her chest, Aurelia collapsed to her knees, gasping for breath. In the back of the chamber, the portal began to calm, its once terrifying presence reduced to a quiet hum.

"Is...is it over?" she whispered, her eyes fixed on the spot where Cyrena had been consumed by the veil.

Bremusa lowered herself to the ground beside Aurelia, her delicate hand reaching out to smooth across Aurelia's stomach, closing her eyes as if reading the fetus's thoughts. "Time will tell, but we have won this battle. We all have."

The sun dipped low in the sky, creating a golden crown over the horizon as the group approached the capital city of the Emerald Enclave. Aurelia could feel the gratitude from the dryads surrounding them, their presence a gentle brush against her senses. Queen Thesipha, the dryad queen, stood tall and regal, her golden hair rustling softly in the breeze.

"Your courage and strength have preserved our home," Queen Thesipha said, her voice akin to the wind through the trees. "We are forever in your debt."

With a genuine smile, Aurelia inclined her head respectfully. "Thank you, Thesipha, but we couldn't have succeeded without your help."

"Still, you've shown us the importance of unity and trust," Thesipha continued, her emerald eyes shimmering in the sunlight. "In truth, we should have been more welcoming to you when you first arrived."

Reaching out, Aurelia placed her hand on Thesipha's arm. "It's never too late to learn from our shared experiences and grow, my friend."

Thesipha nodded, her gaze full of gratitude. Even the tiny pixie on her shoulder grinned, her iridescent wings fluttering. "Farewell, Aurelia, Queen of Aegricia. Give my best to your aunt, and may our paths cross again under happier circumstances."

Aurelia wished she could believe that happiness awaited just beyond the horizon, but she had already learned how fragile peace could be.

Turning her gaze from Aurelia to Bremusa, Thesipha inclined her chin. "And to you, Elemental of Spectre Forest, Bremusa, thank you for healing Joc. His mate and children need him."

Bremusa bowed from the waist. "May the forest continue to thrive and flourish."

As they bid farewell to the dryads, the sound of waves crashing against the shore caught Aurelia's attention. The ship that would carry them back to Ekotoria awaited them, its sails flapping in the wind.

With no other work in the Inferno Territories, they boarded the craft, giving the Shadow Glass to Bremusa so she could ward it below deck. Once the Shadow Glass had gone silent, she and Aurelia locked the portal within its intricate frame, intending to return it to its home in Aegricia.

Standing on the bow as the ship began to pull away from the shore, Aurelia gazed out at the Emerald Enclave, its verdant canopy fading in the distance. The forest had taught her many lessons, but perhaps the most important was this: trust in those who stood beside her, for their strength was her strength. Together, they could rise again. Yet behind them, the forest's shadows lingered like watchful eyes, a reminder that no victory came without something left behind.

CHAPTER TWENTY-SEVEN

AURELIA

The Aegrician sun dipped low in the sky, casting long shadows across the palace courtyard as Aurelia and her companions returned home from their multi-week trip to the Inferno Territories. The air was thick with the scent of pine and snow, a sweet reminder of their victory, even as much of the city lay in ruins—some parts even worse than when they had left.

As they approached the back doors of the palace, familiar faces gathered to greet them, bringing a smile to Aurelia's lips. Yet, despite her smile, she and Cristos could not ignore the twisted wreckage and debris littering the harbor and coastal areas of Embershell. Something had happened while they were gone—something significant. The harbor's broken ribs jutted from the surf, and every splintered beam felt like a warning that victory would never come without a cost.

"Kason! Holera!" Exie cried, rushing into the arms of her friends, with Septima at her heels. Relief filled Aurelia's chest as she smiled at the couple as well. Her chosen family deserved the reunion, but after two weeks away, her best friend needed her more. Even though she was exhausted and hungry, she wanted to see Kano. So, with Cristos' hand in hers, they walked across the grounds toward the massive enclosure that provided a safe home for her pet tiger.

Upon reaching the enclosure, they found Kano pacing restlessly, his muscles rippling beneath his striped fur. He looked up as they approached, his eyes brightening with recognition. In an instant, he was on his hind legs, holding onto the top of the gate. Just seeing his excitement filled Aurelia with warmth, but also guilt for having left him behind. Back in Vaekros, they had always been together, but ever since arriving in Ekotoria, various upheavals had forced her to leave him where it was safe.

"Hey there, big boy!" Reaching into her tunic, she pulled out the medallion she wore around her neck and placed it against the gate, causing the enclosure to open with its magic. By the time she stepped through the gate, Kano was already at her feet, nuzzling his large striped head against her trousers until she sat down on the ground. His golden eyes locked onto hers, expressing what his voice could not.

"I missed you, too, Kano," she whispered into his soft fur, tears pricking at the back of her eyes. His purr rumbled through her palms, easing the ache behind her ribs, if only for a moment.

Closing the gate, Cristos lowered himself to the ground beside them, and Kano automatically rolled onto his back, exposing his belly in a clear invitation for them to rub it. And they did. For the next thirty minutes—perhaps an hour—Cristos and Aurelia stayed right there, showering affection on the massive cat, who was very much a part of their family.

Once the moon was high in the sky and Kano had been given his meal for the night, Cristos and Aurelia walked back to the palace, feeling famished, exhausted, and in need of a bath.

"Ah, there you are!" Otera called out as they entered the dining hall, her fiery hair catching the light of the flickering candles. The room was already filled with laughter and conversation, the air charged with relief at their reunion, though everyone knew there was much to discuss. Still, Aurelia couldn't help but smile at the sight of her closest friends gathered around the table: Kason, Holera, Breusa, Taryn, Otera, Blaedia, Septima, Exie, and several other high-ranking warriors and advisors, including a handsome Norithaean warrior named Lars, who sat beside Taryn, whispering in her ear as she smiled. Rockie and Nikoleta had healed nicely from their injuries before setting sail, but they, along with Vasilis and Alteria, had returned home to their families upon arriving back in the capital, so they were not seated at the table with the others. Laughter filled the hall, but a tightness lingered in the air, as if the stone itself remembered the waters that had risen where they should not have.

"Welcome back," Kason said, his boyish grin a comforting sight as they took their seats between Septima and Otera. "We only arrived back a few days ago from Diapolis."

Seated on the other side of Otera, Blaedia tilted her chin in greeting to her new queen and king, her expression serious. "Tell us everything." Aurelia interlaced her fingers with Cristos' under the table, bracing for truths that would not spare them.

"Let us not dwell on our recent hardships," Otera said, setting her whiskey glass on the table. "Instead, let's discuss what has transpired while we were apart so we can make decisions for our future."

Taryn leaned forward, pushing a loose strand of dark hair behind her ear. "An earthquake shook the city, quickly followed by a tsunami that tore through the harbor." Her eyes flicked toward the window, where the dark outlines of ruined structures could barely be seen in the moonlight. "Many buildings near the water were destroyed, but thankfully, the palace and most of our citizens were spared due to the evacuation efforts before and just after the war." Her words settled heavily in the silence, more suffocating than any stone, even as the fire crackled in the hearth.

Blaedia nodded. "There's still much damage to repair, but we've already begun the process. Our people are strong and resilient. We will rebuild, as we always have."

Beside Taryn, Lars took a sip of his whiskey, the plate of roasted meat and vegetables already empty before him. "And the Norithae camp is here to stay for as long as Aegricia needs us. If our king and queen see fit, we can send for more able-bodied citizens to come north and extend the camp. Our own seaside capital was spared."

Some of the tension in Cristos' jaw eased with Lars' words, his chin dipping in acknowledgment. Both Aegrica and Norithae had been under siege by Warbotach for months, and Cristos' own father had been murdered by the barbarians. Therefore, any good news was long overdue. Although Aurelia and Cristos were now married and ruled both kingdoms, there was no guarantee that their people would blend seamlessly or work together. Seeing that they were willing to do so, at least thus far, filled her with gratitude. It was reassuring to know that, even in her absence, her friends and family—her people—had been working tirelessly to protect and support their portion of the continent. Not that she ever doubted Otera's leadership. "Thank you all for everything you've done while we were gone," she said.

Cristos squeezed her hand and raised his glass. "Our people couldn't have asked for better guardians while we were away. A toast to all of you."

For a moment, glasses were raised in cheers, candlelight reflecting in the golden liquid in most of their glasses—most, that is, apart from Aurelia and Holera, a coincidence Aurelia had not missed.

As they sat around the table, Aurelia's heart clenched at the thought of the destruction her people had faced during her absence, but knowing most of the city had been evacuated just before the war gave her some relief. For the next hour, over dessert and tea, the group discussed their next steps, specifically how they would protect the Shadow Glass and the portal within it from falling into the wrong hands again. As the others spoke, Aurelia's eyes continued to glance out through the massive dining room windows at the remnants of the destroyed harbor, which loomed in the distance under the light of the full moon. Every time it caught her eye, it sent a shiver through her, a haunting reminder of the devastation nature had wrought upon Aegricia.

Although an earthquake and tsunami were natural occurrences, Bremusa had agreed with Otera's assessment that the release of the portal's power had caused the catastrophic event. Therefore, the sooner they returned the portal to the land, the less likely it was—hopefully—for such an event to happen again. Preventing the realm's land from unleashing punishment on them for destroying the portal had to be their top priority, even if they weren't sure it would work. Doubt had teeth, but delay had claws. They chose the path that bled the least.

The wind howled through the jagged peaks of the northern Aegrician mountains as Bremusa, Cristos, Aurelia, Septima, Exie, Otera, and Blaedia made their way along the treacherous path leading to the hidden caves after dinner. Leaning back against Cristos' chest as the horse walked forward, Aurelia pulled her hood tighter around her face to protect it from the biting cold. Due to the wind, they could not fly into the mountains as they had planned, as flying would have made the trip more hazardous.

"Are you sure this is the right place?" Exie shouted from the back of the horse in front of them, with Septima riding by her side. "All these caves look the same."

"Absolutely," Bremusa replied, her silver eyes scanning their surroundings. She didn't even have to think about it. "These caves have been protected by our ancestors for generations, and I've been coming here since before you were born. With the strength of the magic here, there is no place more secure under wards." Wind threaded through the rocks like a low voice, and Aurelia couldn't shake the feeling that the mountain listened back.

Aurelia tightened her grip on the pommel, feeling Cristos' arms tighten around her as they ascended another incline. Worry churned in her thoughts, not just for the Shadow Glass and the portal but also for her people and their kingdom. She understood the weight of responsibility resting on her shoulders, yet she couldn't shake the undercurrent of fear that she might fail if someone stole the Shadow Glass again, luring the portal away and causing the land to rebel against them.

As the group finally reached the entrance to the cave system that Bremusa had pointed out, Exie and Blaedia lit torches, the flames casting flickering shadows across the rock walls as they passed them to Septima and Aurelia. Cristos, Exie, and Blaedia lifted the Shadow Glass between them once the horse-drawn cart could no longer navigate the rocky terrain. The atmosphere grew tense as they ventured deeper into the darkness, with narrow passageways echoing their footsteps and the whispered conversations of those around them.

"Once we're inside the chamber and reinforce its wards, we'll transfer the portal's power to the new Aegrician crown. With the power that Aurelia and I summoned in the Voiceless Mountains, combined with that of Blaedia, Otera, and Exie, we should be able to create an impenetrable barrier around the cave," Bremusa said, her voice low as she took the lead. "The crown will be placed within a hidden cavity in the chamber, while a duplicate will remain in the palace for Aurelia to wear as she sees fit. With any luck, this will ensure its protection and deter any future attempts to steal it. If Uldon couldn't tell that the crown he had was a fake, then no one should be able to tell."

"Are you ready for this, love?" Otera asked, walking at Aurelia's side and searching her niece's blue eyes for any hint of doubt.

Aurelia hesitated for a moment, her heart pounding against her ribcage. The fear that threatened to consume her was just that—fear. The truth was, she wasn't alone, and that was what she needed to focus on. Pushing her hesitation aside, she nodded. "Yes. I'm ready."

As they entered the warded chamber, a wave of overwhelming energy washed over Aurelia—a powerful force that seemed to hum with ancient magic. After they leaned the massive mirror against the wall, she reached out to touch its gilded frame, her hand trembling noticeably.

"Let's do this together," Otera said, extending her hand to grasp Aurelia's. One by one, the others joined in, their hands forming a circle around the artifact and the crown. A tremor of energy gathered where their hands met, steady as a heartbeat and bright as drawn steel.

Bremusa dipped her head, closing her eyes as if grounding herself. When she reopened them, the atmosphere in the chamber shifted. "When I close my eyes at the end of the chant, you should do the same. When you feel the power shift inside you and we reopen our eyes, it will be done."

The air around them crackled with energy as the five females joined hands, their fingers intertwining tightly. The power they summoned pulsed through Aurelia's veins like a raging river, flowing from her right hand, which was held by Otera, to her left hand, held by Bremusa. Just like in the Voiceless Mountains, Aurelia didn't fully understand how to harness the magic within her veins and bend it to her will, but with her and the others serving as an energy source, Bremusa's silver eyes opened and focused on the objects before them.

"By the ancient bond that ties us, we channel this power into the heart of Aegricia," she said, her voice unwavering. A sudden gust of wind swept through the chamber, lifting Aurelia's hair and causing the torches to flicker wildly. "From one vessel to another, may it serve to guard our lands and our people. Let it be done." The chamber tightened around them, and then the pressure broke like a wave, leaving the air sharp and clean.

As Bremusa's voice fell silent, her silver eyes closed, signaling for everyone in the chamber to do the same. The wind inside picked up again, swirling around them as though they were at the center of a vortex. Aurelia straightened her back, her heart rate quickening with every moment that chaos reigned within the stone walls. For several seconds, panic built in her chest, making her feel as if the storm would never end. Just when she was ready to scream for it to stop, the wind stilled, and the chamber grew nearly silent.

A subtle pressure squeezed her left hand, indicating that it was safe to peek. However, Aurelia hesitated, scared of what she might see. When she finally opened her eyes, the portal came to life before them, swirling with colors and creating a vivid window into a world she recognized—one she had missed for so long.

Moving beside Aurelia and taking Bremusa's place, Septima's gaze fixed on the figures materializing within the portal. "Is that...?"

Aurelia gasped, her hand rising to cover her mouth as tears filled her eyes. "Mother." Joy cut as deep as grief. Aurelia felt an overwhelming urge to run, yet she couldn't move at all.

If only there had been one figure on the other side of the window—if there hadn't been so many others she knew in her heart to be alive—she might have thought she was looking at the veil. But unlike the swirling black vortex she and Bremusa had sent Cyrena into, she was staring at the vibrant colors of another world, a living world.

As Septima and Aurelia held hands, tears streaming down both their faces while they stared unblinking at Aurelia's reflection on the portal's surface, their mother—Aurelia's by blood and Septima's by choice—stepped forward through the shimmering gateway. Her fiery red hair framed her ageless face. Behind her followed their father, Proteus, their brother, Amadeus, Variel, and a dozen Norithaean and Aegrician warriors, all appearing weary but alive.

"Impossible," Otera whispered at Aurelia's side, placing a hand on her niece's shoulder.

The weight of the revelation was almost too much to bear, sending Aurelia's heart into a rapid beat that drowned out every other sound around her. Her legs faltered beneath her, and she collapsed to the cave floor, with Septima following suit. The world around her spun as she tried to make sense of the impossible sight before her: their mother, Messalina, the woman she had thought lost forever, was crossing the portal into Ekotoria with her father and brother, both of whom had lived in the human realm their entire lives, escorted by a cadre of Norithaean and Aegrician warriors. A giggle burst from Aurelia's throat as she locked eyes with Variel, not surprised at all that the oracle had managed to bring her family back to her.

"How?" Aurelia choked out, her voice trembling with emotion. The resemblance between her and her mother was striking. Yet, there was a strength in Messalina's eyes that Aurelia had only just begun to find within herself.

Stepping the rest of the way into the chamber, Messalina opened her arms and pulled both her daughters into a hug, with their father and brother enclosing them in their embrace. Proteus's callused hand trembled against Aurelia's back, and the small, human imperfection undid her.

"Later, my love. For now, let us just be grateful that fate has brought us together again." Gratitude filled the room, but fate seldom stopped at mercy; it always asked for something in return.

Chapter Twenty-Eight

Aurelia

Four Months Later

The soft glow of moonlight filtered through the delicate white curtains, and the open window allowed the gentle sea breeze to flutter the gauzy fabric. Aurelia and Cristos carefully unfolded soft linens and placed them in the corners of the exquisite crib that Otera had gifted them. It was specially made from pine, featuring phoenixes engraved along the sides and gold leaf flames adorning the posts—a stunning piece of Aegrician craftsmanship. The scent of pine mingled with the sea air, creating a fragrance that blessed the cradle with both the strength of the earth and the calm of the ocean. The symbols represented the rebirth and renewal that had come into their lives so many times since they met.

As Cristos leaned down to tuck in the edges of the blanket, his arm brushed against Aurelia's swollen belly, prompting the baby to kick from within, making her gasp. It was a reminder that life stirred inside her, even as the world outside their chamber bore scars of war. Over the past several weeks, their little bundle had become increasingly active.

"Are you alright, my love?" Cristos asked, turning to face her. His cerulean eyes were filled with concern, undoubtedly thinking that it might be time. The healer had said the baby could arrive at any moment, so they were doing their best to prepare. Although they had plenty of people in the palace who could assist in setting up the bed or organizing the baby's clothes, they often wanted to take care of those tasks themselves.

Rising on her toes to kiss him, Aurelia smiled. "Yes, I'm fine. Our little one is just restless tonight."

His lips curved into a smile as he placed his hand on her belly, the child responding with another kick.

For a moment, they stood there, gazing at the crib while Cristos held Aurelia close, one hand resting on her abdomen.

"It's perfect, and having my mother back... my father, brother, and sister here with us... It's just perfect. If only your family could be here as well." Even as her heart swelled with so much love, she thought it would burst, joy and grief intertwined; love often arrived with its shadows. Discovering that her mother was alive and spending the past four months with both her found and blood family had felt like a dream—a real dream that she was able to experience as a person, not a spirit. With her father and brother settling in Ekotoria for good, their family could focus on healing and building the relationships they all deserved. But Cristos' parents were gone, and she knew it pained him. "I can't believe we're going to be parents soon. It's surreal."

"My parents are with us in spirit." Cristos kissed the top of her head, his voice carrying a tender note of awe that resonated deep within her soul. "After everything, we will finally have our family together. We'll be able to raise our child in peace."

Peace. For so long, it seemed as though peace would never touch their shores, but with their enemies defeated and the portal restored, Ekotoria had become calm. Unshed tears blurred Aurelia's vision as she processed this thought.

"I couldn't have done any of this without you and our friends. Our kingdoms are stronger because we stand side by side."

***

Finished setting up the crib so it would be ready for when their child made its debut, Aurelia and Cristos headed back into their bedchamber. Candlelight flickered in the moonlit darkness, chasing away shadows and creating a peaceful ambiance in the room.

"Come, my love." With his hand on the small of her back, Cristos guided her to their spacious bed, helping her to climb up. "You deserve some rest." Rest had become rare and precious, a treasure as necessary as steel had once been.

Pushing herself up on the bed, she curled her finger at him in a come-hither motion. "Only if you join me."

She didn't have to ask twice. Without a moment of hesitation, he slid onto the bed beside and patted the mattress beside him. The back rubs had become their nightly ritual, one she would miss once the baby was born.

Sliding off her sleeping gown, she rolled onto her side next to him, his strong hands finding the tense knots in her shoulders. She sighed as her body melted into the mattress under his fingers, every muscle relaxing one by one. "Your touch is like magic."

"Anything for you, my queen," Cristos whispered, pressing a tender kiss to the nape of her neck.

Aurelia's breath caught in her chest, a shiver of desire cascading down her spine. Even though her body was swollen and tired, he still found a way to make her body sing, and desire made her feel more alive than fear ever had. The more he touched her, the more she wanted him.

Rolling over onto her back, she slid her hand around his back, pulling his mouth to hers, the passion of his kiss leaving her breathless. Their tongues entwined, teasing and tasting each other, igniting the fire within Aurelia. His hands cupped her cheek, tipping her head and deepening the kiss. Moaning softly, she arched into him, her body desperate for more of his touch.

Knowing how sensitive her body was, his fingers trailed down her neck, over her collarbone, and then lower, tracing the curve of her breasts that had become so much fuller over the past weeks. She gasped, her nipple hardening under his touch, which only encouraged him to wrap his lips around the tight bud. His fingers found the delicate fabric of her undergarments and, with a soft tug, slipped them off her body.

"You're so exquisite like this," he whispered against her skin, his voice husky with desire.

Every cell in her body was on fire, his words only heating her more. "Please, Cristos... I need you."

When her fingers threaded into his thick hair and gently guided his head to move down between her thighs, he didn't hesitate. Sliding down her body, his tongue trailed a teasing path along her inner thigh before reaching the source of her heat.

"What do you need, my queen?"

He knew the answer to the question, and she was beyond words, only gasps leaving her lips as the ghost of his warm breath skittered across her most sensitive parts.

With the first swipe of his tongue, Aurelia's mind went blank, every thought replaced by the intense pleasure coursing through her body. She gasped, her fingers tangling in his hair as he continued to explore her. Each flick of his tongue sent shivers up her spine, drawing her closer to the edge. Her breathing grew ragged, her chest heaving, and the world around her shattered as ecstasy overwhelmed her, wave after wave of pleasure crashing through her body until she was left trembling beneath him.

Wordlessly, he positioned himself above her, his throbbing cock poised at her entrance. "Is this what you want?"

All she managed was a nod before he guided himself inside her, stretching her body around him deliciously.

Hooking one leg over his shoulder, he began to move, his hips rocking with a steady rhythm as he buried himself deep within her. Aurelia wrapped one hand around his thigh, loving how his muscles flexed beneath her fingertips.

"Ah, gods...Aurelia." His pace quickened, the friction sending shockwaves of pleasure coursing through her.

"Harder, Cristos," she urged, her nails digging into his back. The pressure building inside her was unbearable.

Cristos obliged, his thrusts coming deeper and faster, his wings flaring out behind him as he seemed to lose himself in the intensity. The world around them seemed to melt away, leaving only the two of them. She gripped his thighs harder, pulling him deep into her core, wanting to feel every inch of him.

Finally, the dam broke, and Aurelia cried out, her body clenching around him as her climax sent her into pure ecstasy. With a deep moan, his body shuddered as he rode through his own orgasm.

Spent and breathless, he collapsed beside her, pulling her close as they tried to catch their breath. As they lay there, tangled in each other's arms, Aurelia knew it was only the beginning of their life together, and that brought a smile to her face as she drifted off to sleep, knowing her dreams that night would be happy ones. Outside, the sea kept its rhythm, steady as the breath of a kingdom finally at peace.

The sun rose above the horizon three days later, its rays reflecting the tension coiled within Aurelia's entire being. She lay on the bed, sweat pouring down her face as she panted through another contraction, each one more powerful than the last. The chamber felt smaller with every wave of pain, time itself bending around her struggle.

"Almost there, my love," Cristos murmured, his voice a soothing balm against the searing pain tearing through her body as he held her hand tightly.

"Can you... Can you see the baby yet?" Aurelia gasped between labored breaths, her heart thundering in her chest as fear and anticipation warred within her.

"Very soon," her mother reassured her, standing beside the healer, Cordelia, who was providing assistance. "You're doing so well, little bird."

"Remember, deep breaths," Cordelia advised, checking Aurelia's progress while bracing her hand on Aurelia's knee.

"If it's a girl, her name will be Calliope," Aurelia whispered, tears streaming down her cheeks as another contraction surged through her.

Leaning forward, Cristos kissed her on the forehead. "It's a beautiful name. I love it."

Her mother stepped closer, taking Aurelia's other hand. "It's after my mother, who was taken too soon." She smiled gently, brushing Aurelia's crimson hair off her sweaty forehead. "She would be very proud."

"Push, Aurelia!" Cordelia urged, reaching for the clean towel in Septima's hands. "Your baby is almost here." The command rang out like a battle cry, but this was the fiercest fight of her life.

With a guttural cry, Aurelia summoned every last ounce of strength from her exhausted body and pushed. The world around her blurred into nothingness as she focused on bringing their precious child into the world.

"Here they come!" Eyes glassy with emotion, Septima placed her hand on Aurelia's knee. "You're doing so well, sissy!"

In mere moments, the pressure in Aurelia's lower body turned into the worst pain she had ever experienced, but then it eased as their child entered the world.

"It's a girl!" Cordelia exclaimed, pulling the baby close in a towel and beginning to clean her.

Tiny wails filled the room as Aurelia collapsed back onto the bed, her body wracked with exhaustion but her heart overflowing with love. Beside her, Cristos still held her hand, his glassy eyes unable to look away from his daughter, especially as the healer placed the tiny bundle in his arms.

"Meet her, my love," he said, leaning down to place the child on Aurelia's chest. "Meet Calliope." Aurelia traced the tiny hand with her fingertip, wonder eclipsing every scar of the past.

Days later, the kingdom prepared to welcome its newest princess. As the sun rose, bathing the palace in golden light, Aurelia cradled Calliope in her arms, feeling a fierce protectiveness and love that she had never experienced before.

Together, she and Cristos stepped out onto their balcony, with their stunning blue-eyed baby in Cristos' arms. Calliope's tuft of crimson hair caught the sunlight beautifully. The crowd's roar rose like a tide, washing away every doubt Aurelia had ever known.

"Today, we introduce our daughter, Calliope, to her people," Cristos said, smiling down at Aurelia with a joy that only true love can bring.

Aurelia gently touched their baby's cheek before gazing around at the scene. Behind them on the balcony stood their family—both biological and chosen—including Aurelia's mother, father, sister, and brother. Three of them were people she never thought she would see again until that fateful night in the caves. Supported by their presence, she recalled the prophecy spoken to her mother before her own birth and made a promise to her kingdom: "She will be a symbol of hope, unity, and strength for our kingdom as we usher in a new age of peace." And although she knew that peace was as fragile as glass, she also understood that hope was the fire that reforged it.

Chapter Twenty-Nine

Kason

Five Months Later

Kason cradled their newborn son, Kyro, gazing at the tiny sleeping face nestled against his chest. The baby's soft tufts of silver hair caught the gentle light filtering through the cottage window, casting a warm glow on his smooth cheeks. Kason's heart beat slower, steadier, as if the world itself had paused to honor the small miracle in his arms. He marveled at the delicate perfection of his child, tracing the curve of the little one's lips with his thumb.

When he glanced back up at the bed, he met stunning violet eyes watching him, with Holera's silver hair shimmering in the dim glow of the fire. Having only given birth a few days earlier, she was still recovering. They had sent the healer back to Flamecliff. Still, his mate was nowhere near ready to resume her usual activities, no matter how stubborn she was. Even in her weakened state, she radiated strength, her spirit too wild to be confined by rest. If it were up to Holera, she would already be soaring through the skies or practicing her already expert-level skills with her bow.

Leaving the warmth of the fire at his back, Kason crossed the room to where she rested, sitting on the edge of the bed. "He's perfect, my fierce warrior. Just like you." The words were simple, but within them lived every vow he had ever made to her.

Holera smiled, her gaze softening as she reached out to gently stroke their baby's cheek. "I don't know about me being perfect, but he definitely is. I can't believe he's finally here, and that we created this beautiful child together." Her voice held both disbelief and reverence, as if motherhood were a gift she had stolen from the stars.

The warmth of love exploded in Kason's chest as his gaze shifted from the child in his arms, who was a perfect blend of both of them, to his mate. The sight of them together filled him with a fiercer devotion than any battle ever had. "Indeed, we did... even if magical coral made it happen."

The sun dipped just behind the Aegrician mountains as Holera shifted out of her phoenix form in front of her mother's cottage just outside Flamecliff. Kason stood by her side, holding their one-month-old son in his arms. Excitement bubbled in his chest at the thought of introducing their little bundle to their friends and to Holera's mother, Aura. They had traveled to Flamecliff for a special occasion, but they only had one night to spend in Aura's cottage before heading to the palace. The path smelled of pine and hearth smoke, each breath steeped in memory and homecoming.

"Ready?" Holera asked, adjusting her cloak, her silver hair brilliant against the dark fabric. Against Kason's chest, their baby slept soundly, wrapped in a blanket to keep him warm in the cool mountain air.

Nodding, Kason followed her to the front door, but before Holera had a chance to knock, the door creaked open. Aura's face lit up like the first rays of morning sun as she opened the door wider to welcome them inside.

"Holera! Kason!"

Kason's grin widened as he uncovered their child and held him up toward his grandmother. Aura's violet eyes sparkled even more. They hadn't seen the matriarch for months, so while she knew her daughter was pregnant, she hadn't yet met their child. "And this is Kyro... your grandson."

"A boy?" Aura reached out, brushing her fingers across the baby's soft cheek. "Hello, little one." Her words seemed to wrap the child in generations of love, binding the past to the future with nothing more than a whisper. Pure awe and love filled Aura's voice as she gazed down at the baby, whose tuft of silver hair matched her own. As Kyro opened his vibrant green eyes, he gripped his grandmother's finger, eliciting a laugh from her. "Oh, you're going to be a strong boy, just like your father."

The pride in Kason's chest burned even brighter at the compliment, but he couldn't take the credit. "He's going to be strong like his mother," he said, placing Kyro in Aura's outstretched arms. "Not even my strength can compare to her fire." His voice held quiet pride, not in himself, but in the fierce, unyielding woman he was blessed to call his mate.

CHAPTER THIRTY

OTERA

Under a canopy of intertwining branches in the palace gardens, Otera and Blaedia stood before Bremusa, a surge of unwavering love coursing through Otera's veins. Their loved ones encircled them, but it was Otera's sister, Messalina, who stood just to her left that brought tears to her eyes as she prepared to commit herself to Blaedia for eternity. Otera had believed Messalina to be dead for more than a decade. Her sister's silent support during this crucial moment meant the world to her. The garden's blossoms seemed to blur as if even the flowers wept at the sight of love reclaimed.

"Otera and Blaedia," Bremusa began, her silver eyes nearly white in the sunlight. "You have chosen to unite your lives, to merge your destinies, and face whatever challenges life may bring together."

As she spoke, Otera's heartbeat thrummed in her ears, yet her hand remained steady as she clasped Blaedia's—her mate for decades and the love of her life.

With a ceremonial dagger in hand, Bremusa extended it to them. "Give me your hands."

Having attended many Aegrician weddings in her life, Otera understood why Bremusa wanted their hands and happily placed hers into Bremusa's, feeling relief wash over her when Blaedia did the same.

"Blood is life," Bremusa said, making a shallow cut across each of their palms. "And from this moment on, you will be joined by the very essence of your beings."

Crimson beads welled up, yet neither flinched. Instead, they gazed into each other's eyes as Bremusa turned their palms together and wrapped their hands in a white cloth. The cloth absorbed their mingled blood, symbolizing a bond that would outlast crowns and kingdoms.

"Our kingdom has witnessed your fierce dedication to one another and how your love has grown since you chose each other as mates so long ago. By connecting yourselves through marriage, you demonstrate to each other—and your people—just how deeply you love one another. As your blood flows together, you become one. No matter where you go from here, you will always be a part of each other."

Tears burned in the back of Otera's eyes as she looked up at the woman she adored—the one who had never given up on finding her when she had been taken, and who had never left her side since her return.

With her free hand, Blaedia stroked Otera's cheek, wiping away her tears. "You are everything to me, my fires, and I cannot wait to see what fate has in store for us." Her words were as steady as steel yet warm as flame—a promise no storm could undo.

As the sun dipped toward the horizon, Otera and Blaedia's reception was in full swing in the palace gardens, with laughter and music filling the night air.

Otera scanned the crowd, her heart brimming with joy. Once, it had been a tomb of grief; now it beat like a drum of celebration. Surrounded by love and even new life among her friends, the scene stood in stark contrast to a year prior, when their entire continent had been brought to its knees by the barbarians from the south. Just a few feet away, Cristos and Kason held their babies, laughing about something Otera couldn't hear. The sound—simple and full of life—was more triumphant than any war cry. Even her commander, Taryn, who had died in the war and been brought back to life, had found true love; she rested a hand on her slightly swollen belly while Lars whispered sweetly in her ear.

In the middle of the dance floor, Septima danced with her father, while Aurelia twirled with her brother. Messalina looked on, her big blue eyes shining with pure happiness as she watched over her family. The circle of family, once shattered, felt whole again beneath the lantern glow.

"Look at them all," Otera whispered to her new wife, gesturing toward the crowd. "Have you ever seen such a happy sight?"

A grin spread across Blaedia's lips as she leaned in and kissed Otera softly, lingering just long enough to send a shiver down Otera's spine. "Love is powerful enough to overcome any evil, my fires."

Near the center of the dance floor, Exie, who had already enjoyed several glasses of whiskey, let out a whoop and transformed into her brilliantly colored phoenix form in a burst of fire, launching herself into the air. Moments later, Aurelia's crimson wings erupted from her back, and she followed Holera as they ascended. Blaedia placed another kiss on Otera's lips before stepping away, a mischievous glint in her eyes. Even in matrimony, she remained the fire Otera had fallen in love with—untamed, radiant, eternal. "I'll be right back!"

In flames that rivaled those of the garden's central fire, Blaedia's crimson and black phoenix form shot into the sky behind her friends.

The air crackled with energy as the phoenixes soared, their vibrant feathers shimmering in the sunset—each one unique yet beautiful. Otera stood among those she loved, watching as the phoenixes danced through the sky, their joyous calls echoing all around her. Her heart swelled with pride for all they had accomplished and hope for the future generations of Aegricia. It was a new chapter, filled with light and love, and she could hardly wait to see what wonders it would bring. As the phoenixes carved trails of fire into the twilight, Otera realized that the prophecy had not only been fulfilled; it had blossomed into something even greater: a legacy of love strong enough to light every dawn to come.

Epilogue

The crackle of fire filled the great hall of the palace, with flames dancing across the carved stone like golden feathers. Outside, the night was cold and silent, but within these walls, laughter warmed the air.

Aurelia sat with Calliope in her arms, the infant's crimson hair glinting in the firelight. Beside her, Cristos leaned close, his wing wrapped around them like a living shield. Across from them, Holera and Kason watched as Kyro's tiny fists clenched in the air, the babe safely nestled in Holera's embrace. Kason grinned, his eyes shining with a joy fiercer than any victory on the battlefield.

On the other side of the hearth, Otera rested her head against Blaedia's shoulder, their hands entwined, wedding bands glinting softly. For once, the queen-turned-matriarch felt no burden pressing down on her. Her blue eyes softened as she watched the younger generation—her niece, her family—experiencing the peace she had once feared they would never know.

Messalina sat nearby with Proteus at her side, their hands clasped tightly as if afraid to let go again after so many years apart. Amadeus lounged close by, teasing Septima as though no time had ever separated their family. For Aurelia, seeing them all together—both blood relatives and found family—felt more miraculous than any prophecy fulfilled.

Exie snorted into her whiskey, making Septima laugh from her seat nearby. Even Taryn, her hand resting protectively over her swelling belly, rolled her eyes fondly as Lars tucked a blanket around her shoulders.

The fire popped, sending sparks toward the high-vaulted ceiling. In the quiet that followed, Aurelia glanced around at everyone, her heart so full it ached. "The prophecy brought us here," she said softly, "but love... love is what will carry us forward."

No one argued, for no one needed to. The flames glowed brighter, reflected in every gaze, and in that moment, the future felt certain: whatever challenges lay ahead, they would face them together.

The End.

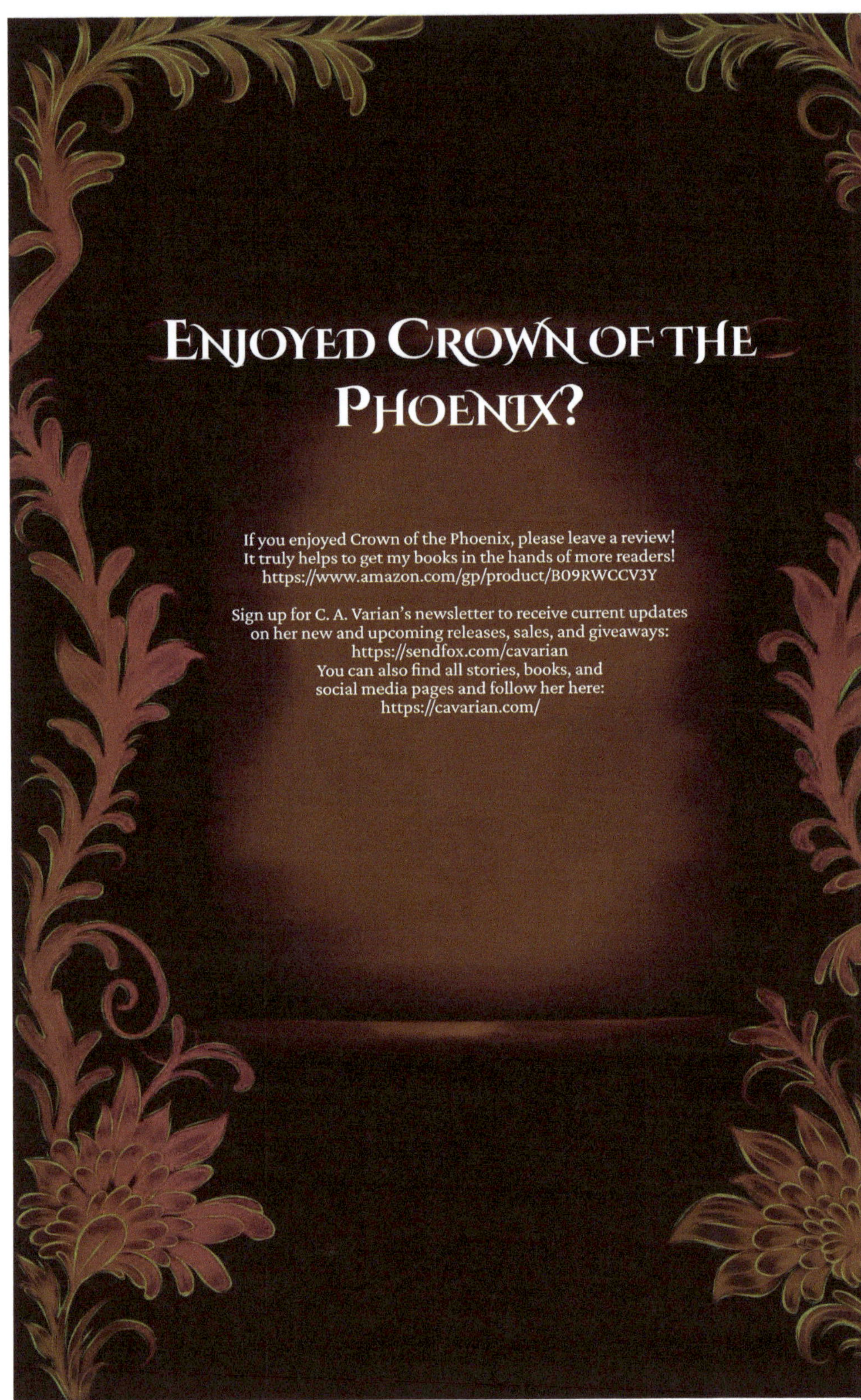

Enjoyed Crown of the Phoenix?

If you enjoyed Crown of the Phoenix, please leave a review!
It truly helps to get my books in the hands of more readers!
https://www.amazon.com/gp/product/B09RWCCV3Y

Sign up for C. A. Varian's newsletter to receive current updates
on her new and upcoming releases, sales, and giveaways:
https://sendfox.com/cavarian
You can also find all stories, books, and
social media pages and follow her here:
https://cavarian.com/

Also by C.A. Varian

Crown of the Phoenix Series
Crown of the Phoenix
Crown of the Exiled
Crown of the Prophecy
Mate of the Phoenix
Shadowed by Prophecy
Shadowed by the Veil (Coming Soon)

My Alien Mate Series
My Alien Protector
My Alien Rescuer (coming soon!)

Other World Series
The Other World
The Other Key
The Other Fate

Hazel Watson Mystery Series
Kindred Spirits: Prequel
The Sapphire Necklace
Justice for the Slain
Whispers from the Swamp
Crossroads of Darkness
The Spirit Collector
The Darkness that Follows (Coming Soon)

The Cursed Waters Duet
Song of Death
Goddess of Death

Survivor & Savior Duet
Saving Scarlett
Keeping Caroline

Standalones
Second Chance with Santa
When Everly Saved Emerald Hollow (Coming Soon with A.A. Weaver)
Spirit of the Dying Flower
The Gladiatrix & the Fallen Son (Coming Soon)
Wings of the Forgotten (Coming Soon with J. Paige)
The Moon-Cursed Crown (Coming soon)

Acknowledgements

This book would not exist without the people who carried me when I couldn't carry it alone.

To my amazing Executive Assistant, Jessica, thank you for helping me keep my head on straight. You make it possible for me to keep this thing going.

To my incredible PA, Aly Dust, thank you for being a creative force and a constant source of support.

To my awesome editor, Willow Oak Author Services, thank you for keeping up with my crazy schedule.

To my super supportive Street Team, your enthusiasm, love, and loyalty made all the difference. You were the wind at my back through every draft.

To my husband, children, and family, thank you for your patience, love, and for understanding that writing a book means sometimes living in another world.

To my readers, thank you for returning to the page, for believing in haunted girls and broken curses, and for holding space in your hearts for stories like this.

Thank you to my cover designers, Leigh Cover Designs, for the dust jacket design, Lune Aesthete, for the paperback design, as well as D'Arte Oriel, for the awesome hardcase design.

From the bottom of my heart, thank you.
XOXO, Cherie

About the Author

Born and raised in the heart of Louisiana's Cajun Country, I'm a passionate writer of dark, fantasy, paranormal, and even alien romances—if there's a romance involved, chances are I've written it. My stories are filled with mystery, magic, and intense emotional connections that keep readers on the edge of their seats.

When I'm not writing, you'll find me creating special editions of my books packed with all the bells and whistles—character art, exclusive swag, and more for my readers to treasure. I love connecting with fans, whether it's through my TikTok shop, my website, or in person at events where I can share the stories I pour my heart into.

As a proud mother and new grandmother, I've faced many challenges in life, including a battle with chronic Lyme disease, but I've never let it define me. Writing is my escape and my passion, and with the support of my amazing assistant Jessica, my husband Trevor, and my daughters, Arianna and Brianna, I'm living my dream of writing full-time. Even my two youngest sisters pitch in, helping me with various tasks for the business—it's truly a family affair!

At home in the coastal region of Mississippi, surrounded by love, laughter, and inspiration, I'm never without my two Shih Tzus, Charlie and Luna, along with my three mischievous cats—Ramses, Simba, and Cookie. Whether I'm doting on my furry companions, reading, or soaking up family time, every moment is a precious one. (As of October 2025, we lost Simba unexpectedly, but I cannot bear to remove his name yet.)

Join me as I continue to create worlds full of romance, adventure, and unforgettable characters that you won't want to put down!

D'ARTE ORIEL BOOK COVER DESIGN

D'Arte Oriel: High-Quality Book Cover Designs & More

At D'Arte Oriel, we specialize in crafting stunning book covers that capture the essence of your story. Our services include e-book and print cover designs, NSFW and Non-NSFW illustrations, and much more.

wallflowerdesigns.custom@gmail.com

CANGXXX GRAPHICS
B O O K   D E S I G N S

CXG SPECIALIZES IN MANIPULATED AND ILLUSTRATED BOOK COVERS SPECIALLY ROMANCE AND FANTASY. HOWEVER, WE ARE STILL FLEXIBLE WITH OTHER GENRES AND GRAPHICS, AND WE ENSURE EVERY ARTWORK THAT WE MADE IS VISUALLY CAPTIVATING, EYE-CATCHING AND A READER MAGNET. WE ARE EXCITED TO WORK WITH MORE OUTSTANDING AUTHORS IN THE FUTURE, IF YOU'RE INTERESTED IN US, SEND US A MESSAGE IN CANGXXXGRAPHICSOFFICIAL@GMAIL.COM AND LET'S MAKE THE BEST COVER FOR YOUR BOKS!

JM DESIGNS
CUSTOM & PREMADE
COVER DESIGNS
ILLUSTRATED COVERS
JOLLYMEEK MALABAD
ArtistryMeek
bijorntolentino226@gmail.com
THE SEVENTH LORD
F. G. SPARKS
THRONE FLAMES
AUTHOR NAME
Kingdom OF DECEIT And DESIRE
BOOK 1
MELINDA HAYDE
ILLUSTRATED ARTS

HI! I am Chan Art.

I've been editing for almost 3 years for international authors.

I offer lots of services like:

BOOKCOVERS

Character Art

Spread

Paperback

Hardback

Header and Breaker

I specialized in making Manipulation and I can't do illustration or drawing.

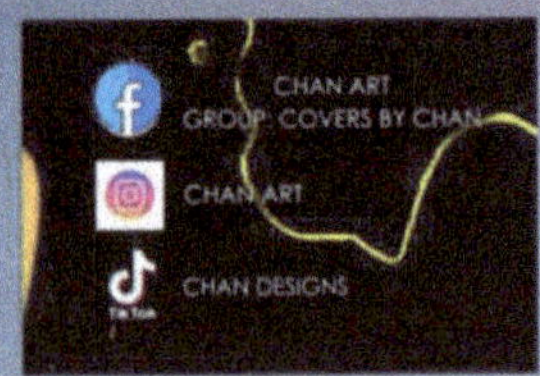

shaipremades@gmail.com
shaidesigns.carrd.co
shai.premades

SG
DESIGNS
BOOK COVER DESIGNER

SERVICES:
· BOOK COVERS
· CHARACTER ART
· INTERIOR DESIGN
· EDGES X H&B

SG Designs aka SHAI is a freelance graphic designer and book cover editor, currently balancing her studies with her creative career. With over six years of self-taught experience, Shai honed her skills in crafting visually captivating book covers that would leave long lasting impressions

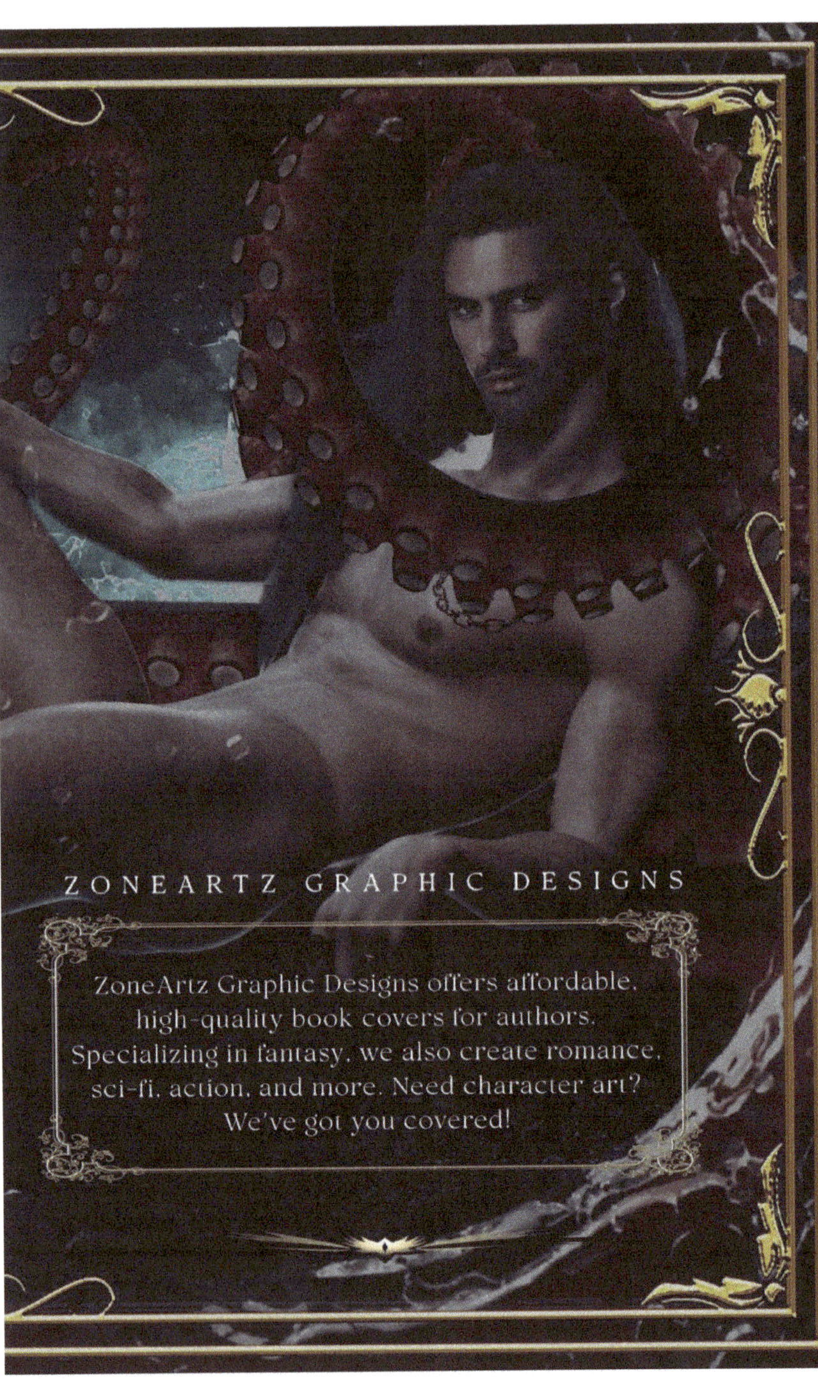
ZONEARTZ GRAPHIC DESIGNS

ZoneArtz Graphic Designs offers affordable,
high-quality book covers for authors.
Specializing in fantasy, we also create romance,
sci-fi, action, and more. Need character art?
We've got you covered!

I'm Sheri-Lynn Marean of SLM Creations, and I'm an author and artist.

I began drawing at 12 years old, mostly animals but really anything that caught my fancy. Over the years, I've sold original drawings, paintings, limited edition prints … I'm also a published paranormal and fantasy romance author and learned how to create in Photoshop in order to make my own book covers.

I quickly realized that I loved creating pretty digital art, and I wanted to do so for other authors.

I'm always learning and trying to improve my skills, and currently offer custom & pre-made book covers in the paranormal romance, fantasy, urban fantasy, dystopian, and sci-fi romance genres. I've recently branched out to include interior chapter art, painted edges, and character art via a mix of photo manipulation and over-painting.

Meet Athena Crest Arts!

Athena Crest Arts brings your stories to life with stunning and affordable book covers! Specializing in epic fantasy, young adult, and typographical designs, we craft visuals that captivate readers at first glance. Now expanding into illustrated book covers and character art, we're here to elevate your book's creative appeal.

Need a custom cover or artwork for your next masterpiece? Let's make magic together! ✨

Alijah Arts

Looking for a captivating budget friendly book covers, interior arts, and character arts? Contact us now!

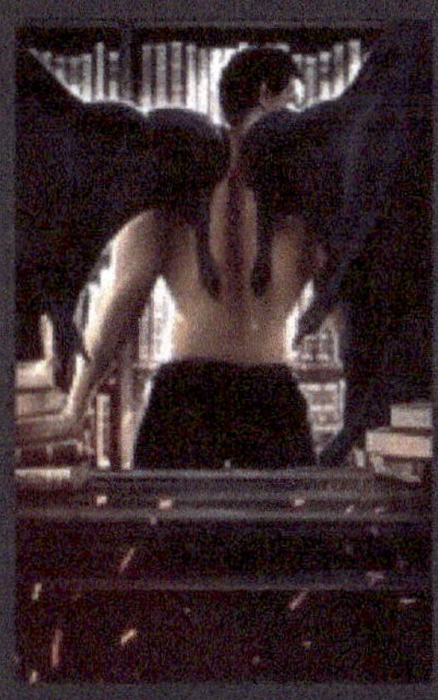

CONTACT US ON:

FACEBOOK PAGE: ARMAIN DESIGNS

INSATAGRAM: BOOKCOVERSBYALIJAH

TIKTOK: ARMAIN DESIGNS